READER'S DIGEST
CONDENSED BOOKS

www.readersdigest.co.uk

The Reader's Digest Association
Limited 11 Westferry Circus
Canary Wharf London E14 4HE

For information as to ownership of
copyright in the material of this
book, and acknowledgments, see
last page.

Printed in France
ISBN 0 276 42783 1

READER'S DIGEST
CONDENSED BOOKS

*Selected and edited
by Reader's Digest*

CONDENSED BOOKS DIVISION

THE READER'S DIGEST ASSOCIATION LIMITED, LONDON

CONTENTS

PUBLISHED BY MICHAEL JOSEPH

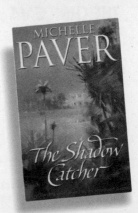

PUBLISHED BY CORGI

THE SUMMER THAT NEVER WAS

page 297

Peter Robinson

Summer, 1965. Fourteen-year-old Alan Banks is beset by guilt when his friend, Graham Marshall, disappears during a morning paper round, never to be seen again. The case is unsolved, the file closed. But when the middle-aged Alan, now a detective inspector, is asked to investigate the disappearance of another teenage boy, vivid memories of that summer return. An atmospheric and gripping crime novel by a master of the genre.

PUBLISHED BY MACMILLAN

THE CHRISTMAS TRAIN

page 445

David Baldacci

Journalist Tom Langdon's life is a mess. And, to make matters even worse, he's got to cross America by train to spend Christmas with a woman he's not sure he loves. But Tom has no inkling of just how eventful the three-day trip will be: friends, old and new, are among his fellow passengers and they're about to change his life for ever. A charming romantic comedy, packed with surprises, from a best-selling American writer.

PUBLISHED BY MACMILLAN

RAIN FALL

Barry Eisler

On the streets of Tokyo, John Rain is pursuing his latest target.

As usual, his task is to make the hit look like a death from natural causes. As usual, there is risk and danger at every turn.

The difference, this time, is that Rain's personal life is about to become entwined with the shady, dangerous world he inhabits.

PART ONE

Harry cut through the morning rush-hour crowd like a shark fin through water. I was following from twenty yards back on the opposite side of the street, sweating with everyone else in the unseasonable October Tokyo heat, and I couldn't help admiring how well the kid had learned what I'd taught him. He was like liquid the way he slipped through a space just before it closed, or drifted to the left to avoid an emerging bottleneck. The changes were accomplished so smoothly that no one would recognise he had altered his pace to narrow the gap on our target, who was now moving down Dogenzaka towards Shibuya Station.

The target was Yasuhiro Kawamura, a bureaucrat connected with the Liberal Democratic Party, or LDP, the political coalition that has been running Japan almost without a break since the war. His current position was vice minister of Land and Infrastructure at the Kokudokotsusho, the successor to the Construction Ministry, where he had obviously done something to seriously offend someone because serious offence is the only reason I ever get a call from a client.

I heard Harry's voice in my ear: 'He's going into the Higashimura fruit store. I'll set up ahead.' We were each sporting a microprocessor-controlled receiver small enough to nestle in the ear canal. A voice transmitter about the same size goes under the jacket lapel. The transmissions are burst ultrahigh frequency, which makes them hard to pick up if you don't know what you're looking for, and they're scrambled in case you do. The equipment freed us from having to maintain constant visual contact. So even though I was too far back to see it, I knew where Kawamura had exited. Solo surveillance is difficult, and I was glad I had Harry with me.

About twenty yards from the Higashimura, I turned off into a drugstore, one of the open-façade structures that line Dogenzaka. I wanted to give Kawamura about three minutes to get his fruit before I came out, so I examined a selection of bandages that gave me a view of the street. The way he had ducked into the store looked like a move calculated to flush surveillance, and I didn't like it. If we hadn't been hooked up, Harry would have had to stop abruptly to maintain his position behind the target. Instead, I knew he would continue past the fruit store, give me his location, and fall in behind when I told him the parade was moving again.

The fruit store was a good spot to turn off, all right, too good for someone who knew the route to have chosen it by accident. But Harry and I weren't going to be flushed out by amateur moves out of some government antiterrorist primer. I've had that training, so I know how useful it is.

I left the drugstore and continued down Dogenzaka, more slowly than before because I had to give Kawamura time to come out of the store. Shorthand thoughts shot through my mind: Are there enough people between us to obscure his vision when he comes out? What shops am I passing if I need to duck off? Is anyone helping Kawamura spot surveillance? If I had already drawn any countersurveillance attention, they might notice me now, because before I was hurrying to keep up with the target and now I was taking my time, and people on their way to work don't change their pace that way.

I heard Harry again: 'I'm at one-oh-nine.' Meaning he had turned into the landmark 109 Department Store.

'No good,' I told him. 'The ground floor is lingerie. You going to blend in with teenage girls picking out padded bras?'

'I was planning to wait outside,' he replied, and I could imagine him blushing.

'Just hang back and wait for my signal as we go past,' I said, suppressing the urge to smile.

The fruit store was only ten yards ahead, and still no sign of Kawamura. I could take a chance on just stopping, maybe to fiddle with a cellphone. Still, if he looked, he would spot me standing there, even though, with my father's Japanese features, I don't have a problem blending into the crowds. Harry, a pet name for Haruyoshi, being born of two Japanese parents, has never had to worry about sticking out.

When I returned to Tokyo in the early eighties, my brown hair, a legacy from my American mother, worked for me the way a fluorescent vest does for a hunter, and I had to dye it black. But in the last few years the country has gone mad for *chappatsu*, or tea-colour dyed hair, and I don't have to be so vigilant. I like to tell Harry he's going to have to go *chappatsu* if he wants to fit in, but Harry's too much of an *otaku*, a geek, to give much thought to issues like personal appearance. I guess he doesn't have that much to work with, anyway: an awkward smile, a tendency to blink rapidly when he's excited, a face that's never lost its baby fat. But the qualities that keep him off magazine covers confer the unobtrusiveness that makes for effective surveillance.

I had reached the point where I was sure I was going to have to stop when Kawamura popped out of the fruit store and re-entered the flow. I hung back, watching his head bobbing as he moved down the street. He was tall for a Japanese and that helped.

Just as I'd redeveloped the right distance, he stopped and turned to light a cigarette. I continued moving, my attention focused on the backs of the suits in front of me, just a bored morning commuter. After a moment he started moving again. I allowed myself the trace of a satisfied smile. Japanese don't stop to light cigarettes; if they did, they'd lose weeks over the course of their adult lives. Kawamura's obvious attempt at countersurveillance confirmed his guilt.

Guilt of what I don't know. I insist on only a few questions. Is the target a man? I don't work against women or children. Have you retained anyone else to solve this problem? I don't want my operation getting tripped up by someone's idea of a B-team, and if you retain me, it's an exclusive. Is the target a principal? I solve problems directly, like the soldier I once was, not by sending messages through uninvolved third parties like a terrorist. I like to see independent evidence of guilt. It confirms that the target is indeed the principal and not a clueless innocent.

Twice in eighteen years the absence of that evidence has stayed my hand. Once I was sent against the brother of a newspaper editor who was publishing stories on corruption in a certain politician's home district. The other time it was against the father of a bank reformer who showed excessive zeal in investigating his institution's bad debts. I would have been willing to act directly against the editor and the reformer but apparently the clients in question had reason to pursue a more circuitous route that involved misleading me. They are no longer clients, of course.

I'm not a mercenary, although I was nothing more than that once upon a time. And although I do in a sense live a life of service, I am no longer samurai, either. The essence of samurai is not just service, but loyalty to his master, to a cause greater than himself. There was a time when I burned with loyalty, a time when I was prepared to die in the service of my adopted liege lord, the United States. But loves as uncritical and unrequited as that never last. I am a realist now.

As I came to the 109 building I said, 'Passing.' Harry would know I was passing his position and would fall in after a moment. The popularity of cellphones with earpieces makes this kind of work easier than it once was. It used to be that someone walking alone and talking under his breath was either demented or an intelligence or security agent. Today you see this sort of behaviour all the time.

The light at the bottom of Dogenzaka was red, and the crowd congealed as we approached the five-street intersection in front of the train station. A diesel-powered truck slogged through the intersection, its loudhailers blaring right-wing patriotic songs drowning out the bells that commuters on bicycles were ringing to warn pedestrians out of the way.

The Dogenzaka intersection is like this night and day. At rush hour, when the light turns green, over 300 people step off the kerb at the same instant, with another 25,000 waiting in the crush. From here on, it was going to be shoulder to shoulder, chest to back. I would keep close to Kawamura now, no more than five yards, which would put about 200 people between us. I knew he had a commuter pass and wouldn't need to go to the ticket machine. Harry and I had purchased our tickets in advance so we would be able to follow him right through the barrier.

The light changed, and the crowds swept into one another like a battle scene from some medieval epic. I watched Kawamura as he cut diagonally across to the station, and manoeuvred in behind him as he passed. There were five people between us as we surged past the attendant's booth. I had to stay close now. It would be chaos when the train pulled in: 5,000 people pouring out, 5,000 people stacked fifteen deep waiting to get on, everyone jockeying for position. Foreigners who think of Japan as a polite society have never ridden the Yamonote at rush hour.

The river of people flowed up the stairs and onto the platform. We were swimming upstream against the people who had just got off the train, and as we reached the platform the doors were already closing. The next train would arrive in two minutes.

Kawamura shuffled down the platform. I stayed behind him. I felt the rumble of the next train as Harry walked past me, the slightest nod of his head indicating that the rest was with me. I had told him I only needed his help until Kawamura was on the train. Harry had done his usual good work in helping me get close to the target, and he was now exiting the scene. I would contact him later.

Harry thinks I'm a private investigator and that all I do is follow these people around collecting information. To avoid the suspicious appearance of a too-high mortality rate for the subjects we track, I often have him follow people in whom I have no interest, who of course then provide some measure of cover by continuing to live their happy and oblivious lives. Also, where possible, I avoid sharing the subject's name with Harry to minimise the chances that he'll come across too many coincidental obituaries. Still, some of our subjects do have a habit of dying, and I know Harry has a curious mind. So far he hasn't asked, which is good. I like Harry as an asset and wouldn't want him to become a liability.

I moved up close behind Kawamura. This was the most delicate part of the operation. If I botched it, he would see me and it would be difficult to get sufficiently close to him for a second try.

My hand dipped into my pocket and touched a microprocessor-controlled magnet, about the size of a quarter. On one side the magnet was covered with blue cloth, like that of the suit Kawamura was wearing. Had it been necessary, I could have stripped away the blue to expose a layer of grey—the other colour Kawamura favoured. On the opposite side of the magnet was an adhesive backing.

I withdrew the magnet from my pocket, protecting it from view. I would have to wait for the right moment, when Kawamura's attention was distracted. The train emerged at the end of the platform and hurtled towards us. Kawamura pulled a cellphone out of his breast pocket. Started to input a number.

OK, do it now. I brushed past him, placing the magnet on his suit jacket just below the left shoulder blade, and moved several paces down the platform.

Kawamura spoke into the phone for a few seconds, then slipped it back in his breast pocket. I wondered whom he had called. It didn't matter. Two stations ahead, three at the most, and it would be done.

The train stopped and its doors opened, releasing a gush of human effluent. When the outflow slowed to a trickle, the lines waiting on either side of the doors poured inside until we were all held firmly in place, with no need to grip the overhead handles because there was nowhere to fall. The doors shut and we moved off.

I exhaled slowly, feeling the remnants of nervousness drain away as we reached the final moments. Kawamura was standing in front of the door at one end of the car, about three feet from me, his right hand holding one of the overhead bars. I needed to stay close now.

This had to look natural: my speciality, and the reason my services are always in demand. Harry had obtained Kawamura's medical records from Jikei University Hospital, which showed that he owed his continuing existence to a pacemaker installed five years earlier.

I twisted so that my back was to the doors—I didn't want anyone who might speak English to see the prompts that were going to appear on the screen of the handheld PDA computer I was carrying. I had downloaded a cardiac interrogation program, the kind a doctor uses to adjust a patient's pacemaker. And I had rigged it so that the PDA fed infrared commands to the control magnet. The only difference between my set-up and a cardiologist's was that mine was miniaturised and wireless. That, and I hadn't taken the Hippocratic oath.

The PDA powered up instantly. I hit the ENTER key and selected 'threshold testing'. I was offered a range of parameters: rate, pulse width, amplitude. I quickly set the pacemaker at its lowest rate of forty beats per minute, decreased the pulse width as far as it would go, then changed to amplitude. The unit was preset at 8.5 volts, and I started dropping it a half-volt at a time.

When the train pulled into Yoyogi Station, Kawamura stepped off. *Damn, just a few more seconds*, I thought, bracing to follow him out. But he was only allowing the people behind him to leave the train. When the Yoyogi passengers had exited he got back on. The doors closed, and we moved off again.

At two volts, the screen warned me it would be dangerous to decrease output further. I overrode the warning and took the unit down another half-volt, glancing up at Kawamura as I did so. He hadn't changed his position.

When I reached a single volt and tried to go further, the screen flashed, 'You have programmed the unit to minimum output values. Please confirm.' I entered, 'Yes.' There was a one-second delay, then the screen started flashing bold-faced letters: **Unacceptable output values. Unacceptable output values.**

I closed the cover, but left the PDA on. There was always the chance that the sequence hadn't worked the first time around, and I wanted to be able to try again if I had to.

There wasn't any need. As the train pulled into Shinjuku Station and jerked to a stop, Kawamura stumbled against the woman next to him. The doors opened but Kawamura remained, gripping one of the upright bars next to the door and clutching his package of fruit, commuters shoving past him. I watched him rotate counterclockwise until his back hit the wall. His mouth was open; he looked slightly surprised. Then he slid slowly to the floor. I saw one of the passengers who had got on at Yoyogi stoop down to assist him. The man, a mid-forties Westerner, tall and thin, shook Kawamura's shoulders.

'*Daijoubu desu ka?*' I asked, my left hand moving to Kawamura's back, feeling for the magnet. Is he all right? I used Japanese because it was likely that the Westerner wouldn't understand and our interaction would be kept to a minimum.

'*Wakaranai,*' the stranger muttered. I don't know. He patted Kawamura's increasingly bluish cheeks and shook him. So he did speak some Japanese. It didn't matter. I pulled the magnet free. Kawamura was done.

I stepped past them onto the platform and the inflow immediately began surging onto the train behind me. Glancing through the window nearest the door as I walked past, I was stunned to see the stranger going through Kawamura's pockets. I had an urge to get back on, but that would have been stupid. Anyway, it was too late. The doors were already sliding shut. I saw them catch on something. They opened slightly and closed again. It was an apple, falling to the tracks as the train pulled away.

From Shinjuku I took the subway to Ogikubo, the extreme west of the city. I wanted to do a last SDR—surveillance detection run—before reporting to my client. Heading west against the incoming rush-hour traffic, made the job of watching my back easier.

An SDR is just what it sounds like: a route designed to force anyone who's following you to show himself. Harry and I had of course taken full precautions en route to Shibuya that morning, but I never assume that because I was clean earlier I must be clean now. In Shinjuku, the crowds are so thick that you could have ten people following you and you'd never see a single one of them. By contrast, following someone unobtrusively across a long, deserted train platform with multiple entrances and exits is nearly impossible, and the trip to Ogikubo offered the kind of peace of mind I've come to require.

It used to be that, when an intelligence agent wanted to communicate with an asset so sensitive that a meeting was impossible, they had to use a dead drop. The asset would drop microfiche in the hollow of a tree and, later, the spy would retrieve it. You never put the two people together in the same place at the same time.

It's easier with the Internet, and more secure. The client posts an encrypted message on a bulletin board, the electronic equivalent of a tree hollow. I download it from an anonymous payphone and decrypt it at my leisure. And vice versa.

The message traffic is pretty simple. A name, a photograph, contact information. A bank account number, transfer instructions. The phone is used only for the innocuous aftermath, which was the reason for my side trip to Ogikubo.

I used one of the payphones on the station platform to call my contact—a Liberal Democratic Party flunky I know only as Benny. Benny's English is fluent, so I know he's spent some time abroad. He fancies himself a hard guy. Probably he learned the lingo from a too-steady diet of Hollywood gangster movies.

After the usual exchange of pre-established codes to establish our bona fides, I told him, 'It's done.'

'Glad to hear it,' he said in his false tough-guy way. 'Any problems?'

'Nothing worth mentioning,' I responded after a pause, thinking of the guy on the train.

'Nothing? You sure?'

Better to say nothing, which I did.

'OK,' he said, breaking the silence. 'You know to reach out to me if you need anything. Anything at all, OK?'

'There's only one thing I need,' I said, reminding him of the money.

'By tomorrow, like always.'

'Good enough.' I hung up, automatically wiping down the receiver and keys on the remote possibility that they had traced the call and would send someone to try for prints. If they had access to Vietnam-era military records, and I assumed they did, they would get a match for John Rain, and I didn't want them to know that the same guy they had known over twenty years ago when I first came back to Japan was now their mystery freelancer.

I was working with the CIA at the time, a legacy of my Vietnam contacts, making sure the Agency's 'support funds' were reaching the right recipients in the governing party, which even back then was the LDP. The Agency was running a secret programme to support conservative political elements, part of the US government's anti-communist policies, and the LDP was happy to play the role in exchange for the cash.

I was just a bagman, but I had a nice rapport with one of the recipients of Uncle Sam's largesse, a fellow named Miyamoto. One of Miyamoto's associates threatened to blow the whistle if he didn't receive more money. Miyamoto asked me if I could do anything about this guy, for $50,000, 'no questions asked'. I told Miyamoto I couldn't do anything myself, but I could put him in touch with someone.

That someone became my alter ego, and over time, I took steps to erase the footprints of the real John Rain. I no longer use my birth name or anything connected with it, and I've had surgery to give my eyes a more complete Japanese appearance. I wear my hair longer and wire-rimmed glasses give me a bookish air. Today I look more like a Japanese academic than the half-breed warrior I once was. I haven't seen any of my contacts from my bagman days in over twenty years, and I steer scrupulously clear of the Agency.

Miyamoto had put me in touch with Benny. For a while I worked for both of them, but Miyamoto retired about ten years ago. Since then, Benny's been my best client. I do three or four jobs a year for him and whoever in the LDP he fronts for, charging the yen equivalent of about $100k per. Sounds like a lot, I know, but there's overhead: equipment, multiple residences, a real but perpetually money-losing consulting operation that provides me with tax records and other means of legitimacy.

Benny. I wondered whether he knew anything about what had happened on the train. The image of the stranger rifling through Kawamura's pockets was as distracting as a small seed caught in my teeth. Maybe the guy had been looking for identification. Or he could have been Kawamura's contact, on the train for some kind of exchange. Maybe that was their arrangement. Kawamura calls the contact from Shibuya just before boarding and the contact knows where to board as the train pulls into Yoyogi Station. Sure, maybe.

It felt like Benny knew something and that feeling made it hard to put this little coincidence aside. If he'd broken one of my three rules by putting a B-team on Kawamura, I'd find him and he would pay the price. But there was no obvious way to acquire that confirmation.

The money appeared the next day, as Benny had promised, and the next nine days were quiet. On the tenth, I got a call from Harry. He told me he was going to be at Galerie Coupe Chou in Shinjuku on Tuesday at eight with some friends, I should come by if I had time. I knew to count back five listings in the restaurants section of the Tokyo City Source Yellow Pages, making our meeting place Las Chicas, and to subtract five days from the date and five hours from the time.

I like Las Chicas for meetings. The place is surrounded by twisting alleys that snake off in a dozen different directions, offering no choke points where someone could set up and wait. I know those alleys well, as I make it my business to know the layout of any area where I spend a lot of time. I was confident that anyone unwanted would have a hard time getting close to me there. The food and the ambiance are good, too.

I got to the restaurant two hours early and waited, sipping one of the chai lattes for which the restaurant is celebrated. You never want to be the last one to arrive at a meeting. It's impolite. And it decreases your chances of being the one to leave.

At a little before three I spotted Harry coming up the street. He didn't see me until he was inside. 'Always sitting with your back to the wall,' he said.

'I like the view,' I answered, deadpan. Most people pay zero attention to these things, but I'd taught him that it's something to be aware of when you walk into a place. The people with their backs to the door are the civilians; the ones in the strategic seats could be people who deserve a little more attention.

I had met Harry about five years earlier in Roppongi, where he'd found himself in a jam with a few drunken off-duty American Marines in a bar. Harry can come off as a bit of an oddball: sometimes his clothes are so ill fitting you might wonder if he stole them from a random clothes line, and he has a habit of staring unselfconsciously at anything that interests him. The staring drew the attention of the jarheads, one of whom loudly threatened to stick those thick glasses up Harry's Jap ass if he didn't find somewhere else to look. Harry had complied, but this apparent sign of weakness served only to encourage the Marines. When they followed Harry out, and I realised he hadn't even noticed what was going to happen, I left too. I have a problem with bullies—a legacy from my childhood.

Anyway, the jarheads got to mess with me instead of with Harry, and it didn't turn out the way they had planned. Harry was grateful.

It turned out that he had some useful skills. He was born in the United States of Japanese parents and grew up bilingual, spending summers with his grandparents outside Tokyo. He went to graduate school in the States, earning a degree in applied mathematics and cryptography. He got in trouble for hacking into files that one of his cryptography professors had bragged he had hack-proofed. There was also some unpleasantness with the FBI, which had managed to trace probes of the nation's Savings & Loan Administration and other financial institutions back to Harry. Some of the honourable men from deep within America's National Security Agency learned of these high jinks and arranged for Harry to work at Fort Meade in exchange for purging his growing record of computer offences. Harry stayed with the NSA for a few years, learning the blackest of the NSA's computer black arts along the way. He came back to Japan in the mid-nineties, where he took a job as a computer security consultant with a big global consulting outfit. The magic of an NSA top-secret security clearance blinded Harry's new corporate sponsors to what was most fundamental about the shy thirtysomething they had hired. Which was that Harry was an inveterate hacker. He never did security work on a system without leaving a back door that he could use whenever the mood arose. He hacked his own firm's files to uncover the vulnerabilities of its clients, which he then exploited. Harry had the skills of a locksmith and the heart of a burglar.

Since we met I've been teaching him the relatively above-board aspects of my craft. He's in awe of the fact that I've befriended him, and has a bit of a crush on me. The resulting loyalty is useful.

'What's going on?' I asked him after he had sat down.

'Two things. First, it seems Kawamura had a fatal heart attack the same morning we were tailing him.'

I took a sip of my chai latte. 'I know. It happened right in front of me on the train. Hell of a thing.'

Was he watching my face more closely than usual? 'I saw the obituary in the *Daily Yomiuri*,' he said. 'A surviving daughter placed it. The funeral was yesterday.'

'Aren't you a little young to be reading the obituaries?'

He shrugged. 'I read everything, you know that. It's part of what you pay me for.'

That much was true. Harry kept his finger on the pulse.

'What's the second thing?'

'During the funeral, someone broke into his apartment.'

'How did you find out about that?' I asked.

He slid a folded piece of paper towards me. 'I hacked the Keisatsucho report.' The Keisatsucho is Japan's National Police Agency, the Japanese FBI.

I unfolded the paper and started to scan its contents. The first thing I noticed was the name of the person who had prepared the report: Ishikura Tatsuhiko. Tatsu. Somehow I wasn't surprised.

I had known Tatsu in Vietnam, where he was attached to Japan's Public Safety and Investigative Board, one of the precursors of the

Keisatsucho. The government sent Tatsu to Vietnam to make wiring diagrams of the routes of KGB assistance to the Vietcong. Because I spoke Japanese, I was assigned to help him learn his way around.

Tatsu was a short, stout man with a gentle face that masked intensity beneath. He was frustrated in postwar, neutered Japan, and admired the warrior's path I had taken. For my part, I was intrigued by a secret sorrow I saw in his eyes. He spoke little of his family, of two young daughters in Japan, but when he did his pride was evident. Years later I learned that there had also been a son who had died in circumstances of which Tatsu would never speak, and I understood where his sorrow came from.

When I came back to Japan we spent some time together, but I had distanced myself since getting involved with Miyamoto and then Benny. I hadn't seen Tatsu since changing my appearance and moving underground. Which was fortunate, because I knew from the reports I hacked that Tatsu had a pet theory: the LDP had an assassin on the payroll. In the late eighties Tatsu came to believe that too many key witnesses in corruption cases, too many financial reformers, too many young crusaders against the political status quo were dying of 'natural causes'. In his assessment there was a pattern here, and he profiled the shadowy shape at the centre of it as having skills very much like mine.

Tatsu's colleagues thought the shape he saw was a ghost in his imagination, and his dogged insistence on investigating a conspiracy had done nothing to advance his career. On the other hand, that doggedness did afford him some protection because no one wanted to lend credence to his theories by having him die suddenly of natural causes. I imagined that many of Tatsu's enemies hoped he would live a long life. I also knew this attitude would change if Tatsu ever got too close to the truth.

So far he hadn't. But I knew Tatsu. In Vietnam he had refused the usual attaché's cushy life of writing reports from a villa, insisting instead on operating in the field. His superiors had been horrified at his effectiveness, he once told me bitterly over substantial quantities of sake, and they had ignored the intelligence he had produced. In the end his persistence and courage had been wasted. I wish he could have learned from the experience.

But I supposed that was impossible. Tatsu was true samurai, and would continue serving the same master no matter how many times that master ignored or even abused him. Devoted service was the highest end he knew.

It was unusual for the Keisatsucho to be investigating a simple break-in. Something about Kawamura's death, and what he was doing before it, must have attracted Tatsu's attention. It wouldn't be the first time I had felt my old comrade in arms watching me as though through a one-way mirror. I was glad that I'd decided to drop off his radar so many years earlier.

'You don't have to tell me whether you knew about this,' Harry said, interrupting my musings. 'I know the rules.'

I considered how much I should reveal. If I wanted to learn more, his skills would be helpful. On the other hand, I didn't like the idea of his getting any closer to the true nature of my work.

'I didn't know about it,' I said after a moment. 'This is an unusual case.' I saw no harm in telling him about the stranger on the train.

'If we were in New York, I'd tell you it was a pickpocket,' he said when I was done.

'Pickpocket would be a poor career choice for a white boy in Tokyo. You have to blend.'

'Target of opportunity?'

I shook my head. 'Not too many people are that cold-blooded. I think he was a Kawamura contact, there for an exchange.'

'Why do you suppose the Keisatsucho is investigating a simple break-in?' he asked.

'I don't know,' I said. 'Maybe Kawamura's position in the government, his recent death. That's the theory I'd go on.'

He looked at me. 'Are you asking me to dig?'

I should have let it go. But I've been used before. Had Benny put a B-team on Kawamura? I might as well let Harry provide some clues. 'Let me know what you find. And watch your back, hotshot. Don't get sloppy.' The warning was for both of us.

TELLING HARRY to watch his back made me think of Jimmy Calhoun, my best friend in high school, of who Jimmy was before he became Crazy Jake. Jimmy and I joined the army together when we were barely seventeen. I remember the recruiter telling us we would need parental permission. 'See that woman outside?' he had asked us. 'Give her this twenty, ask her if she'll sign as your mother.' She did. Later, I realised this woman was making her living this way.

Jimmy and I had met through his younger sister, Deirdre. She was a beautiful, black-haired Irish rose, and one of the few people who was nice to the awkward, out-of-place kid I was in Dryden. Some idiot told Jimmy I liked her, and Jimmy decided he didn't like a guy with slanty eyes hitting on his sister. He was bigger than I was, but I fought him to a standstill. After that, he became my ally against the bullies, my first real friend. Deirdre and I started dating, and woe to anyone who gave Jimmy a hard time about it.

I told Deirdre before we left that I was going to marry her when I got back. She told me she'd be waiting. 'Watch out for Jimmy, OK?' she asked me. 'He's got too much to prove.'

Jimmy and I did Special Forces training together at Fort Bragg, then wound up in the same unit, in a joint military-CIA programme called the Studies and Observation Group, or SOG. SOG's mission was clandestine reconnaissance and sabotage missions into Cambodia and Laos, sometimes even into North Vietnam. The teams consisted of three Americans and nine Civilian Irregular Defense Group personnel, usually Khmer mercenaries recruited by the CIA, sometimes Montagnards. Three men would go into the bush for weeks at a time, living off the land.

We were the elite of the elite, small and mobile, slipping like silent ghosts through the jungle. All the moving parts on the weapons were taped down for noise suppression. We operated so much at night that we could see in the dark. We didn't even use bug repellent because the V.C. could smell it. We were that serious.

We were operating in Cambodia at the time Nixon was publicly pledging respect for Cambodia's neutrality. Our activities weren't just clandestine, they were outright denied, all the way to the top.

We started out all right. Before we went, we talked about what we would and wouldn't do. We'd heard the stories. Everyone knew about the massacre at My Lai. We were going to keep cool heads, stay professional. Keep our innocence, really. I can almost laugh, when I think about it now.

Jimmy became known as 'Crazy Jake' because he fell asleep in the middle of our first firefight. Tracer rounds were coming at us from beyond the tree line, everyone was hunkered down, firing back at people we couldn't even see, and it went on for hours. In the middle of things Jimmy took a nap. Everyone thought that was pretty cool. While they were saying, 'You're crazy, man, you're crazy,' Jimmy said, 'Well, I knew everything was jake.' So after that he was Crazy Jake. Outside the two of us, I don't think anyone ever knew his real name.

Jimmy didn't just act crazy; he looked it. A teenage motorcycle accident had almost cost him an eye. The doctors got it back in, but couldn't get it to focus in line with his good eye, so Jimmy always looked as though he was watching something off to the side while he was talking to you. 'Omnidirectional,' he liked to say.

Jimmy wasn't a big guy, but people were afraid of him. Once, a military policeman with a German shepherd confronted Jimmy about some unruly behaviour in a bar. Jimmy acted like he wasn't even there. Instead, he stared at the dog. Something passed between them, and the dog whimpered and backed away. The incident became part of the growing legend of Crazy Jake, that even guard dogs were afraid of him. But there was nobody better in the woods. When the sound of the insert helicopters receded into the distance, everyone wanted him there.

Memories, crowding me like a battalion of reanimated corpses.

Waste 'em means waste 'em. Num suyn!

There's no home for us, John. Not after what we've done.

Let that shit go, I told myself, the refrain white noise familiar. *What's done is done.*

I needed a break, and decided to take in a jazz performance—my haven from the world since I was sixteen. Club Alfie is a *raibu hausu*, or live house, catering to Tokyo's jazz aficionados. The place is always packed and you need a reservation, but I knew Alfie's mama-san, a roly-poly old woman. She was past the age of flirting but flirted with me anyway, and loved me for flirting back.

That night I took the subway to Roppongi, Alfie's home, running a medium-security SDR on the way. As always, I waited until the station platform had cleared before exiting. No one was following me, and I walked up the stairs into the Roppongi evening.

Roppongi is a cocktail composed of Tokyo's brashest foreign and domestic elements, with sex and money giving the concoction its punch. It's full of Western hostesses selling risqué conversation and often more to their *sarariman* customers; stunning Japanese girls on the make for rich boyfriends; foreigners selling controlled substances that might or might not be what they claim; everybody hungry and on the make, a universe of well-adorned predators and prey.

Predictably, there was a crowd of people outside Club Alfie and a young guy standing at the door, checking reservations. '*Onamae wa?*' he asked me, as I made my way forward. Your name? I told him I didn't have a reservation, and he looked pained. I told him I was an old friend of Mama's and needed to see her, could he just get her? He bowed and disappeared behind a curtain. Two seconds later Mama came out. Her posture was businesslike, but when she saw me her eyes crinkled up in a smile.

'*Jun-chan!*' she greeted me. Jun is Mama's pet name for Junichi, my

Japanese first name, bastardised to John in English. I bowed to her formally but returned her welcoming smile. I explained that I just happened to be in the neighbourhood and hadn't had a chance to make a reservation. I didn't want to be a bother—

'Tonde mo nai!' she interrupted me. Don't be ridiculous! She hustled me inside, dashed behind the bar, and whisked the bottle of Cao Lila I kept there off a shelf. Snatching a glass, she motioned me to a seat at a table in the corner of the room.

She poured me a drink, and asked me if I was with someone—I don't always come to Alfie alone. I told her it was just me, and she smiled. Seeing Mama made me feel good. I hadn't been there in months, but she knew exactly where my bottle was.

My table was close to the small stage. The room was shadowy, but a light hanging from the ceiling illuminated a piano. Not a great view of the entrance to the club, but you can't have everything.

'I've missed you, Mama,' I told her in Japanese, feeling myself unwind. 'Who's on tonight?'

She patted my hand. 'A young pianist. Kawamura Midori. She's going to be a star.'

Kawamura is a common Japanese name, and I didn't think anything of the coincidence. 'What's she like?'

'Wonderful—she plays like an angry Thelonious Monk. And completely professional. She lost her father only a week and a half ago, poor thing, but she kept her engagement tonight.'

'I'm sorry to hear that,' I said slowly. 'What happened?'

'Heart attack on Tuesday morning, right on the Yamanote. Kawamura-san told me it wasn't a complete surprise—her father had a heart condition. We have to be grateful for every moment we're given, *ne*?' She patted me on the hand again and slipped away.

I saw Midori and her trio walking briskly, expressionless, towards the stage. I shook my head, trying to take it all in. I had come to Alfie to get away from Kawamura and everything associated with him, and instead here was his ghost. I would have left, but that would have been conspicuous. And at the same time there was an element of curiosity, as though I was driving back past the results of a car accident I had caused, unable to avert my eyes.

I watched Midori's face as she took up her post at the piano. She looked to be in her mid-thirties and had straight, shoulder-length hair so black it seemed to glisten in the overhead light. I tried to see her eyes but could catch only a glimpse in the shadows. She had framed them in eyeliner, I saw, but other than that she was unadorned. Not that she needed to be. She looked good.

I could feel a tension in the audience. Midori raised her fingers over the keyboard. Her voice came, quiet: 'One, two, one two three four,' and then her hands descended and brought the room to life.

It was 'My Man's Gone', an old Bill Evans number. I liked the way she played it. She brought a vibrancy to it that made me want to watch as well as listen, but I found myself looking away.

I lost my own father just after I turned eight. He was killed by a rightist in the street demonstrations that rocked Tokyo when the Kishi administration ratified the 1960 US/Japan Security Pact. My mother didn't make it easy for me afterwards, although I believe she tried her best. She had been a State Department staff lawyer, part of the team MacArthur charged with drafting a new constitution to guide postwar Japan into the coming American Century. My father was part of Prime Minister Yoshida's staff, responsible for translating and negotiating the document on terms favourable to Japan.

Their romance, which became public shortly after the new constitution was signed in May 1947, scandalised both camps, each of which was convinced that its representative must have made concessions on the pillow that could never have been achieved at the negotiating table. My mother's future with the State Department was effectively ended, and she remained in Japan as my father's wife.

Her parents broke with her over the cross-cultural, cross-racial marriage, which she entered into against their wishes, and so my mother adopted Japan, learning Japanese well enough to speak it at home with my father and with me. When she lost him, she lost her moorings to the new life she had built.

Had Midori been close to her father? Perhaps not. Perhaps there had been fights over what to him might have seemed a frivolous career choice. And if there had been fights, had they had a chance to reconcile? *What the hell is with you?* I thought. *You've got nothing to do with her or her father. She's attractive, OK. But drop it.*

I looked around the room, and all the people seemed to be in pairs or larger groups. I wanted to get out, to find a place that held no memories. But where would that place be?

So I listened to the music. I felt the notes zigzagging playfully and I let them pull me from the mood that was rising around me like black waters. I hung on to the music, until Midori's hands seemed to blur, until the heads I saw around me in the semidarkness and cigarette haze were rocking and hands were tapping tables and glasses, until her hands blurred faster and then stopped, leaving a moment of perfect silence to be filled with a burst of applause.

A moment later Midori and her trio made their way to a small table and Mama joined them. I couldn't slip away without paying my respects to Mama, but didn't want to stop at Midori's table. Besides, an early departure would look odd. I was going to have to stay put.

Admit it, you want to hear the second set. It was true. Midori's music had settled my roiled emotions, as jazz always does. I would enjoy the second set, leave quietly, and remember this as a bizarre evening that somehow had turned out all right.

That's fine. Just no more about her father, OK?

Out of the corner of my eye I saw Mama walking in my direction. I looked up and smiled as she sat down next to me. 'Well? What do you think?' she asked.

'You're right, she's going to be a star.'

Her eyes twinkled. 'Would you like to meet her?'

'I don't think she'd like me, Mama.'

She leaned forward. 'She asked about you.'

Shit. 'What did you tell her?'

'I told her that you are a jazz enthusiast and a big fan of hers, and that you came here tonight especially to hear her.'

'That was good of you,' I said, realising that I was losing control of the situation, and not sure how to regain it.

She smiled. 'Well? Don't you think you should introduce yourself? She's expecting you—look.' She turned and waved to Midori, who waved back.

'Mama, don't do this,' I said, knowing that it was already over.

She leaned forward. 'Don't embarrass me. Say hello.'

The hell with it. I walked over to Midori's table. I sensed that she was aware of my approach, but she gave no sign until I was directly in front of her. Then she looked up and I was struck by her eyes. Unreadable, even looking right at me, but not distant, and not cold. They seemed to radiate a controlled heat.

I knew instantly that Midori didn't have a clue who I was.

'Thank you for your music,' I said to her, trying to think of something else to say. 'It rescued me from something.'

The bass player, supercool in his head-to-toe black threads, snorted audibly, and I wondered whether there was anything between them. Midori simply said, '*Domo arigato,*' the politeness of her thanks a form of dismissal.

'No,' I told her, 'I mean it. Your music is honest, it's the perfect antidote for lies.' I wondered what the hell I was saying.

The bass player shook his head. 'We don't play to rescue people. We play because it pleases us to play.'

Midori glanced at him, her eyes registering the slightest disappointment, and I knew that these two were dancing steps that never led to the bass player's satisfaction.

'But jazz is like sex, isn't it?' I said to him. 'It takes two to enjoy it.'

I saw his eyes flare open as Midori pursed her lips in what might have been a tightly suppressed smile.

'We're happy to go on rescuing you, if that's what we've been doing,' she said in a tone as even as a flat-lined ECG.

I held her gaze for a moment, trying unsuccessfully to read it, then excused myself. I ducked into Alfie's washroom, where I reflected that I had survived some of the most brutal fighting in Southeast Asia but still couldn't beat one of Mama's ambushes.

I emerged from the washroom, acknowledging Mama's satisfied grin as I did so, then returned to my seat. A moment later I heard the club's door open behind me and casually glanced back to see who would be walking through it. It was the stranger from the train. The one I had seen searching Kawamura.

I KEEP A NUMBER of unusual items on my key chain, including several rudimentary lock picks and a sawn-off dental mirror. The mirror can be held up to the eye unobtrusively, particularly if the user is leaning forward on an elbow and supporting his head with his hand. From this posture I was able to watch the stranger arguing with a scowling Mama as the second set began. No doubt she was telling him he wouldn't be able to stay. I saw him reach into his jacket pocket and produce a wallet, which he then opened. Mama looked closely, then smiled and gestured to the far wall. The stranger walked in the proffered direction and found a place to stand.

What could he have used to trump Mama? I watched him throughout the second set, but he gave no indication, leaning expressionless against the wall.

When the set ended, I had a decision to make. On one hand, I assumed he was here for Midori, and I wanted to watch him to see what I could learn. On the other, if he was connected with Kawamura, he might know that the heart attack had been induced, and he might recognise me from the train. Also, if I stayed to watch his interaction with Midori, I wouldn't be able to follow him when he left.

Although it was frustrating, I had to leave first. When the applause for the second set had ended, I watched the stranger shove off in the direction of the stage, and I headed towards the exit.

I stopped to thank Mama again.

'Why are you leaving so early? You don't come by nearly enough.'

'I'll have to remedy that. But tonight I have other plans.'

She shrugged, perhaps disappointed that her machinations had come to so little.

'By the way,' I said, 'who was that *gaijin,* that foreigner who came in during the second set? I saw you arguing with him.'

'He's a reporter. He's writing an article on Midori, so I let him stay.'

'A reporter? That's great. With what publication?'

'Some Western magazine. I don't remember.'

'Good for Midori. She really is going to be a star.' I patted her on the hand. 'Good night, Mama.'

I took the stairs down to the street, then crossed Roppongi-dori and waited in the Meidi-ya supermarket across the street, pretending to examine their champagne selection.

Out of habit I scanned the other spots that would make sense as set-up points if you were waiting for someone to emerge from Alfie. Cars parked along the street, maybe, but you could never count on getting a space. Or the phone booth just down from the Meidi-ya, where a crewcut Japanese in wraparound shades had been on the phone as I emerged. He was still there, I could see, facing the entrance to Alfie.

The stranger emerged after about fifteen minutes and made a right on Roppongi-dori. I stayed put for a moment, waiting for Telephone Man's reaction. Sure enough he hung up and started off down the street in the same direction.

I left the Meidi-ya and turned left onto the sidewalk. Telephone Man was already crossing to the stranger's side, not even waiting until he got to the crosswalk. He was following too closely, a mistake because it allowed me to fall in behind him.

They turned right onto Gaienhigashi-dori in front of the Almond Café, Telephone Man following by less than ten paces. I crossed the street to follow.

This is stupid, I thought. *You are in the middle of someone else's surveillance. If there's more than one and they're using film, you could get your picture taken.*

I imagined Benny, putting a B-team on Kawamura, playing me for a fool, and I knew I would take the risk.

I followed them for several blocks, noting that neither exhibited any concern about what was going on behind him. From the stranger I saw no surveillance-detection behaviour—no turns or stops that would have forced a follower to reveal his position.

At the fringes of Roppongi, the stranger turned into one of the Starbucks that are exterminating the traditional coffee shops. Telephone Man found a public booth a few yards further on. I crossed the street, entered the Freshness Burger, where I ordered their eponymous entrée, and took a seat at the window. I watched the stranger order and then sit down at a table.

My guess was that Telephone Man was alone. If he had been part of a team, it would have made sense for him to change places at some point to avoid detection. Also, my periodic checks as we progressed down the street hadn't identified anyone behind me.

I sat quietly watching the stranger sipping his beverage and checking his watch. Either he was waiting for someone to meet him there, or he was killing time before a meeting somewhere else.

After about half an hour had gone by, I was surprised to see Midori heading in our direction. She was checking storefronts as she walked, finally seeing the Starbucks sign and heading in.

Telephone Man pulled out a cellphone, pressed a key, and held the unit to his ear. Nice move for a guy standing in a public phone booth. He hadn't needed to input the whole number, I noted, so whomever he was calling was a speed dial.

The stranger stood up when he saw Midori approaching and bowed. The bow was good, and I knew this was someone who had been in Japan for some time. Midori returned his bow, uncertainty in her stance. I sensed that they were not well acquainted.

The stranger gestured for Midori to sit; she accepted, and he followed suit. He gestured to the counter, but Midori shook her head.

I watched them for about ten minutes. As their conversation progressed, the stranger's gestures took on an air of entreaty, while Midori's posture grew increasingly rigid. Finally she stood up, bowed quickly, and began to back away. Which one to follow now? I decided to leave the decision to Telephone Man.

As Midori exited the Starbucks, Telephone Man watched her go but held his position. So it was the stranger he wanted.

The stranger left shortly after Midori, returning to Hibiya Station on Roppongi-dori. Telephone Man and I followed, maintaining our previous positions. I stayed with them down to the tracks, waiting until an Ebisu-bound train arrived and we all boarded. I kept my back to them, watching in the reflection of the glass, until the train stopped in Ebisu and I saw them exit. I stepped off a moment after.

It was late, and there were only a half-dozen people leaving the station with us. I let them pull a good twenty yards ahead before emerging from the station entrance.

At the edge of Daikanyama, an upscale Tokyo suburb, the stranger turned into a large apartment complex. I watched him insert a key in the entrance door, which opened electronically and then closed behind him. Telephone Man also took obvious note, then pulled out his cellphone and spoke briefly. Then he lit a cigarette and sat down on the kerb.

I moved into the shadows at the back of a small commercial parking lot and waited. Fifteen minutes later a scarlet motorcycle roared onto the street. The driver pulled up in front of Telephone Man who got on the back of the bike, and they blasted off into the night.

A safe bet that the stranger lived here, but the building housed hundreds of units and I had no way of telling which was his. There would be at least two points of egress, as well, so waiting would be useless. I stayed until the sound of the bike had disappeared before checking the address. Then I headed back towards Ebisu Station.

I took the Hibiya line to Hibiya Station, where I would change to the Mita line and home. I never change trains directly, though, and I emerged from the station first to run an SDR.

I stopped in a Tsutaya music shop and strolled to the back of the store, glancing up to see who might be coming in behind me.

I browsed for a bit in the classical section, then moved on to jazz. On impulse I checked to see whether Midori had a CD. She did: *Another Time*. The cover showed her standing under a streetlamp. I didn't recognise the label—something small-time. She wasn't there yet, but I believed that she would be.

I started to return it, then thought, *It's just music. If you like it, buy it.* Still, an assistant might remember. So I also picked up a collection of jazz instrumentals and some Bach concertos. Chose a long line, harassed-looking assistant. Paid cash. All the guy would remember was that someone bought a few CDs, maybe classical, maybe jazz. Not that anyone was going to ask him.

I finished the SDR and took the CDs back to my apartment in Sengoku in the northeast of the city, what the natives call *Shitamachi*, the downtown. The area is antique, with no nightlife beyond the local watering holes, and no commercial district, so there aren't many transients. Most of its people are *Edoko*, the real Tokyoites, who live and work in its mom-and-pop shops and its restaurants and bars. 'Sengoku' means 'the thousand stones'. I don't know the origin of the name, but I've always liked it.

It's not home, but it's as close as anything I've ever had. After my father died, my mother took me back to the States. We settled in a town called Dryden in upstate New York, where she took a job as a Japanese instructor at nearby Cornell University.

Dryden was a predominantly white, working-class town, and my Asian features and non-native English made me a favourite with the local bullies. I received my first practical lessons in guerrilla warfare from the indigenous population: they hunted me in packs, and I struck back when they were alone and vulnerable. I understood the guerrilla mentality years before I landed at Da Nang.

My mother was distraught over my constant bruises and scraped knuckles, but was too distracted with her new position at the university and with trying to mend fences with her parents to intervene. I spent most of those years homesick for Japan.

So I grew up sticking out, only afterwards learning the art of anonymity. In this sense, Sengoku is an anomaly for me. It's the kind of place where everyone knows your name, thinks they know your business. At first it made me uncomfortable, and I thought about moving. But the old downtown has a magic to it. I like the walk from the subway to my apartment, up the little merchant's street painted red and green so that it always feels festive, even in the early darkness of winter. There's the middle-aged couple at the corner five-and-dime, who greet me '*Okaeri nasai!*'—Welcome home!—when they see me at night; there's the Octopus Woman who sells fried octopus from a streetside window. And there's the house of Yamada, the piano teacher, from which, on summer evenings, soft notes drift lazily down the street.

I listened to Midori's music that weekend. I'd get home from my office, boil water for a dinner of *ramen* noodles, then sit with the lights down and the music playing, unwinding, following the notes. Looking out of the window onto the quiet, narrow streets of Sengoku, I sensed the presence of the past but felt that I was safe from it.

The neighbourhood's rhythms and rituals have become part of me. Somehow a small step out of the shadows doesn't seem such a high price to pay for such indulgences. Besides, sticking out is an asset in some ways. Until Mom and Pop pull their wares back into their shops at night, they're always out there, watching over the street. If you don't belong in Sengoku people will notice. If you do belong—well, you get noticed in a different way.

I guess I can live with that.

THE FOLLOWING WEEK I arranged a lunch meeting with Harry at the Issan *sobaya*. I wasn't going to be able to let go of this little mystery, and I knew I would need his help to solve it.

Issan is in an old wooden house in Meguro. Utterly unpretentious, it serves some of the best *soba* noodles in Tokyo. One of the restaurant's petite waitresses escorted me to a low table in a small tatami room, then knelt to take my order. I selected the day's *umeboshi*, pickled plums, to crunch on while I waited for Harry.

He rolled in about ten minutes later. 'I guess it was too much to hope that you would pick Las Chicas again,' he said, looking around at the ancient walls and faded signs.

'I've decided it's time for you to experience more of traditional Japan,' I told him. 'Why don't you try something classic?'

The waitress came back and took our order: two *yuzukiri—soba* noodles flavoured with the juice of a delicate Japanese citrus fruit called the *yuzu*, and an Issan house speciality.

Harry told me he hadn't managed to unearth anything particularly revealing about Kawamura, just general biographical details.

'He was a Liberal Democratic Party lifer,' Harry explained. 'Graduated from the University of Tokyo in 1960, went straight to the government along with the rest of the cream of the crop. He started out at the Ministry of International Trade and Industry. MITI was working with companies like Panasonic and Sony to enhance Japan's position in the world economy, and Kawamura had a lot of power for a guy in his twenties. Steady promotions up the bureaucratic ladder, successful but not spectacular. After MITI he was transferred to the old Construction Ministry, and stayed with it as vice minister of Land and Infrastructure when Construction was merged into the Kokudokotsusho.'

He paused and ran his fingers through his unruly hair, doing nothing to improve its appearance. 'Look, mostly what I can tell you is basic bio stuff. I need to have a better idea of what I'm looking for, or I might not even recognise it if I see it.'

'Harry, don't be so hard on yourself. Let's just keep working at the problem, OK?' I paused, recognising that this would be dangerous, knowing that, if I wanted to solve this mystery, I would take the risk. I told him what I had seen at Alfie and afterwards, of following the stranger to the apartment in Daikanyama.

He shook his head. 'What are the chances that you would run into Kawamura's daughter like that? Unbelievable.'

I looked at him closely, not sure that he believed me.

'*Sekken wa semai yo*,' I said. It's a small world.

He shrugged. 'You think there's a connection with the break-in at Kawamura's apartment?'

'Could be. The guy on the train was looking for something on Kawamura. Couldn't find it. So he breaks into Kawamura's apartment. Still can't find it. Now he thinks the daughter has it.'

The waitress brought us the two *yuzukiri*. When we were done eating, Harry leaned back against the wall. 'What's your angle on this?' he asked.

I thought about telling him that I was doing it for a client, but I knew he wouldn't buy that. 'It reminds me of something that happened to me a long time ago,' I said, telling him the truth. 'Something I want to make sure never happens again. Let's leave it at that.'

He held up his hands. 'OK, the guy you followed, we can assume he lives in the apartment building. A good number of foreigners live in Daikanyama, but I can't imagine there are more than a dozen or so in that one building. So we're already in decent shape.'

'Good.'

'The mama-san said he told her he was a reporter?'

'I think he showed her a card, but it could have been fake.'

'It's a start. I'll try to cross-check the foreigners I find at that address against the declarations kept at the Nyukan, see if any of the people I identify are with the media.' The Nyukan is Japan's Immigration Bureau.

'While you're at it, see if you can get me the girl's home address.'

He looked down, as though trying to hide a smile.

'What?' I said.

He looked up. 'You like her.'

'Oh, for Christ's sake, Harry . . .'

'Is she pretty? Just tell me that.'

'I'm not going to give you the satisfaction.'

'So she's pretty. You like her.'

'C'mon, Harry, I need your help. That guy on the train was expecting Kawamura to be carrying something, which is why he patted him down. He didn't find it, though—otherwise, he wouldn't have been asking Midori questions. Now you tell me: Who currently has possession of all of Kawamura's belongings, including the clothes he was wearing and personal effects he was carrying when he died?'

'Midori, most likely,' he allowed with a small shrug.

'Right. She's still the best lead we've got. Get me the information, and we'll go from there.'

THE NEXT DAY I got a page from Harry, who used a preset numeric code to tell me that he had put something on the bulletin board we use. I figured it was Midori's address, and Harry didn't disappoint.

She lived in a small apartment complex called Harajuku Verdent Heights, in the shadow of the graceful arches of Tange Kenzo's 1964 Tokyo Olympic Stadium. Harry confirmed that Midori did not have a registered automobile, which meant that she would rely on trains: either the Japan Railway or one of the subway lines.

The problem was that the JR and subway stations were in opposite directions, and she was as likely to use one as the other. With no single choke point leading to both sets of stations, I had no basis for choosing either one. I would just have to find the best possible venue for waiting and watching.

Omotesando-dori, where the subway stations were located, fitted the bill. Known as the 'Champs Elysées of Tokyo', Omotesando-dori is a long shopping boulevard lined with elm trees. Its many bistros and coffee shops were designed with Paris-style people-watching in mind, and I would be able to spend an hour or two watching the street from various establishments without attracting attention. Even so, without a lot of luck, I would have been in for a very boring few days. But Harry had an innovation that saved me: a way of remotely turning a phone into a microphone.

The trick only works with digital phones with a speakerphone feature, where a line can be established even though the handset is in the cradle. The reception is muffled, but you can hear. Anticipating my next move, Harry had tested Midori's line for me and had let me know that we were good to go.

At ten o'clock on Saturday morning, I arrived at the Aoyama Blue Mountain coffee shop, equipped with a small unit that would activate Midori's phone and a cellphone for listening in. I took a seat at one of the small tables facing the street. Watching the morning crowds drift past, I flipped the switch on the unit and heard a slight hiss in the earpiece that told me the connection had been established. Other than that, there was silence. Nothing to do but wait.

A construction crew had set up a few yards down the road, repairing potholes. Four workers busied themselves—about two more men than were needed, but the *yakuza*, the Japanese mob, insists that workers be provided with work. The government, pleased at this additional avenue of job creation, is complicit.

As vice minister at the Kokudokotsusho, Midori's father would have been hip deep in a lot of this. It was not such a surprise that someone wanted him to come to an untimely end.

Two men left the coffee shop, and the aroma of hot gravel wafted over to my table. The smell reminded me of my childhood in Japan, of the late summer, when my mother would walk me to school for the first day of the new term. The roads always seemed to be in the process of being repaved at that time of year. To me this kind of construction still smells like a portent of a fresh round of bullying.

Sometimes I feel as though my life has been divided into segments. The first ends when my father was killed, an event that shattered a world of predictability and security, replacing it with vulnerability and fear. There is another break when I received the brief military telegram telling me that my mother had died, offering me stateside leave for the funeral. Along with my mother I lost an emotional centre of gravity and was left suffused with a new and awful sense of freedom. Cambodia was a further rupture, a deeper step into darkness.

Strangely, the time when my mother took me to the United States from our home in Japan does not represent a dividing line. I was an outsider in both places. Nor are any of my subsequent geographic ramblings particularly distinct. For a decade after Crazy Jake's funeral I wandered the earth a mercenary, daring the gods to kill me but surviving because part of me was already dead.

I was fighting alongside Lebanese Christians in Beirut when the CIA recruited me to train the mujahideen guerrillas battling the Soviets in Afghanistan. I was perfect: combat experience, and a mercenary history that made possible maximum governmental deniability. For me, there has always been a war, and the time before feels unreal, dreamlike. War is the basis from which I approach everything else. War is all I really know.

At a little after eleven, I heard sounds of movement within Midori's apartment. Footsteps, then running water, which I took to be a shower. Shortly before noon, I heard a closing door and the click of a lock, and I knew she was finally on the move.

I walked out onto Omotesando-dori, where I began to amble in the direction of JR Harajuku Station. I wanted to get to the pedestrian overpass. This would give me a panoramic view, but it would also leave me exposed, so I wouldn't be able to linger.

The timing was good. I only had to wait on the overpass for a minute before I caught sight of her. She was approaching from the direction of her apartment and made a right onto Omotesando-dori. Her hair was tied back in a ponytail, her dark eyes concealed by sunglasses. She was wearing snug black trousers, a black V-neck sweater and walked confidently, with purpose. I had to admit she looked good. *Enough of that. How she looks has nothing to do with this.* She was carrying a shopping bag from Mulberry. They had a store in Minami Aoyama, and I wondered if she was on her way to return something.

Midway to Aoyama-dori she turned into Paul Stuart. I could have followed her in, tried for our chance meeting there, but I decided to wait. I set up in the Fouchet Gallery across the street until she emerged, a Paul Stuart shopping bag in hand, twenty minutes later.

Her next stop was at Nicole Farhi London. From there, she continued onto a series of nameless Omotesando backstreets, periodically stopping to browse in one of the area's boutiques, until she emerged onto Koto-dori. I followed her on the opposite side of the street, until I saw her duck into Le Ciel Bleu.

Her taste was mostly European, it seemed. She seemed to be completing a circle that would take her back in the direction of her apartment. And she was carrying that Mulberry bag.

If she was indeed on her way to return something, I had a chance to be there first. It was a risk. But if I could be waiting at her next stop before she got there, the encounter would seem more like chance and less like the result of being followed. I cut across the street and ducked into Mulberry. I strolled over to the men's section, where I began to examine some of the briefcases on display.

Five minutes later she entered the store as I had hoped, removing her sunglasses. Keeping her at the limits of my peripheral vision, I picked up one of the briefcases. I felt her gaze stop on me and linger. I gave the briefcase a last once-over, then set it down and looked up. She was still watching me, her head cocked slightly to the right.

I blinked as though in surprise and approached her. 'Kawamura-san,' I said in Japanese. 'This is a nice surprise. I just saw you at Club Alfie last Friday. You were tremendous.'

She evaluated me silently for a long moment before responding. I sensed that this intelligent woman might have suspected, had I come in after her, that she had been followed.

'Yes, I remember,' she said finally. 'You're the one who thinks jazz is like sex.'

I looked into her dark eyes. 'Yes.'

'You enjoyed the performance?'

'Immensely. I have your CD, and have been meaning to catch you and your trio for the longest time. I travel a lot, though, and this was my first chance.'

'Where do you travel?'

'Mostly America and Europe. I'm a consultant,' I said. 'Nothing as exciting as being a jazz pianist.'

She smiled. 'You think being a jazz pianist is exciting?'

She had a natural interrogator's habit of reflecting back the last thing the other party had said, encouraging the speaker to share more. It doesn't work with me. 'Let me put it this way,' I said, 'I can't remember someone ever suggesting to me that consulting is like sex.'

She threw back her head and laughed then, not bothering to cover her open mouth with her hand in the typical Japanese woman's unnecessarily dainty gesture.

'That's good,' she said, conceding a small, lingering smile.

I smiled back. 'What's today? A bit of shopping?'

'A bit. And you?'

'The same. Time for a new briefcase. We consultants have to maintain appearances, you know.' I glanced down at the shopping bag she was carrying. 'I see you're a fan of Paul Stuart.'

'I know it from New York.'

'Have you spent much time in New York?'

'Some,' she said with a faint smile, looking into my eyes.

Damn, she's tough. Challenge her. 'How's your English?' I asked, switching from Japanese.

'I get by,' she said, without missing a beat.

'You want a cup of cawfee?' I asked, using my best Brooklyn accent.

She smiled again. 'That's pretty authentic.'

'So's the suggestion. The Tsuta coffee-house is round the corner.'

'I don't know it.'

'Then you've got to try it. Koyama-san serves the best coffee in Tokyo, and you can drink it listening to Bach or Chopin, looking out onto a wonderful secret garden.'

'What's the secret?' she asked, playing for time, I knew.

I gave her a sober look. 'Koyama-san says that if I tell you, I have to kill you. So it would be better if you were to see for yourself.'

She laughed again, cornered but seeming not to mind. 'I think I'd have to know your name first,' she said.

'Fujiwara Junichi,' I replied, bowing automatically. Fujiwara was my father's last name.

She returned the bow. 'It's nice to meet you, Fujiwara-san.'

'Let me introduce you to Tsuta,' I said, smiling, and we headed off.

The stroll over to Tsuta took less than five minutes, during which we made small talk about how the city had changed over the years. I enjoyed talking with her, and knew at some level that this was strange, even undesirable.

We were in luck, and one of Tsuta's two tables, each of which overlooks the establishment's secret garden through a single oversized picture window, was free and waiting for us. Alone, I typically enjoy a seat at the counter, but today I wanted an atmosphere more conducive to conversation. We each ordered the house demitasse, made with an intense dark roast, and sat at right angles to each other, so that we could both see the garden.

'How long have you lived in Tokyo?' I asked.

'On and off for my whole life,' she said. 'I grew up in Chiba, one town over. I used to come to Tokyo all the time when I was a teenager, to try to sneak into the live houses and listen to jazz. Then I spent four years in New York, studying at Julliard. After that, I came back. And you?'

'Same as you—off and on for my whole life.'

'And where did you learn to order coffee in a New York accent?'

I took a sip of the bitter liquid before me and considered how to answer. It's rare for me to share biographical details. The things I have done, and continue to do, have marked me, and, even if the mark is invisible to the wider world, I am always aware of it. Intimacy is no longer familiar to me. Probably, it is no longer possible. I haven't had a real relationship since my move into the shadows. Tatsu, and other friends I no longer see, sometimes tried to set me up with women they knew. But where were these relationships going to go, when the two subjects that most define me were unmentionable? Imagine the conversation: 'I served in Vietnam.' 'How did you manage that?' 'I'm half American, you see, a mongrel.'

There are a few women from the *mizu shobai*, the water trade, as Japan calls its demimonde, whom I see from time to time. They all assume I'm married and the assumption explains the suspended, on-again, off-again nature of our relationships, and my reticence.

But Midori had a reticence about her, too, a reticence she had just breached in telling me a bit about her childhood. I knew that if I failed to reciprocate, I would learn nothing more from her.

'I grew up in Japan and the States,' I said after a long pause.

Her eyes widened. 'How did you come to do that?'

'My mother was American.'

I was aware of a slight intensification of her gaze, as she searched for the Caucasian in my face.

'You must have inherited mostly your father's features.'

'It bothers some people that I look Japanese, but I'm really something else.'

I remembered the first time I heard the word *ainoko*, half-breed. I asked my father about it that night. He scowled and said only, *'Taishita koto nai.'* It's nothing. But pretty soon I got to hear the word while the school bullies were busy trying to beat the shit out of me, and I put two and two together.

She smiled. 'I don't know about other people. For me, the intersection of cultures is where things get most interesting.'

'Yeah?'

'Sure. Look at jazz. Roots in black America, branches in Japan and all over the world.'

'You're unusual. Japanese are typically racist.' I realised that my tone was more bitter than I had intended.

'I don't know that the country is so racist. It's just been insular for so long, and we're always afraid of what's new or unknown.'

Ordinarily I find such idealism in the face of all contrary facts irritating, but looking into her dark, earnest eyes, I couldn't help smiling. She smiled back, her full lips parting and lighting up her eyes, and I had to look away.

'What was it like to grow up in two countries?' she asked.

'It was difficult, actually. I had a hard time fitting in either place.'

'Where did you spend more time?'

'In Japan until I was about ten, then mostly in the States. I came back here in the early eighties.'

'To be with your parents?'

I shook my head. 'No. They were already gone.'

My tone rendered unambiguous the word *gone*, and she nodded in sympathy. 'Were you very young?'

'Early teens,' I said, averaging things out.

'That's terrible, to lose both parents so young. Were you close?'

'Fairly close, I suppose. They've been gone a long time.'

'Do you think you'll go back to America?'

'I did at one point,' I said. 'After returning as an adult, I spent ten years here always thinking I would stay just one more and then go back. Now I don't really dwell on it.'

'Does Japan feel like home to you?'

I remembered what Crazy Jake told me, just before I did what he asked of me. *There's no home for us, John. Not after what we've done.*

'It's become my home, I guess,' I said. 'What about you? Would you want to live in America again?'

'I really loved New York,' she said after a moment, 'and I'd like to go back to stay for a while. My manager thinks that the band isn't too far off. We've got a gig at the Vanguard in November that'll really put us on the map.'

The Village Vanguard, the Manhattan mecca of live jazz. 'The Vanguard?' I said, impressed. 'You could leverage that, and make New York your base, if you wanted to.'

'We'll see. I've lived in New York before. It's a great place, but it's like swimming under water. Eventually you have to come up for air. After four years, it was time for me to come home.'

That was the opening. 'You must have had indulgent parents, if they were willing to send you abroad for that long.'

She smiled faintly. 'My mother died when I was young—same as you. My father sent me to Julliard. He loved jazz and was thrilled that I wanted to be a jazz pianist.'

'Mama told me you lost him recently,' I said. 'I'm sorry.' She bowed her head in acknowledgment and I asked, 'What did he do?'

'He was a bureaucrat.' This is an honourable profession in Japan, and the Japanese word *kanryo* lacks the negative connotations of its English counterpart.

'With what ministry?'

'For most of his career, the Kensetsusho.' The Construction Ministry.

We were making some progress. The manipulation was making me uncomfortable. *Finish the interview*, I thought. *Then get the hell out. She puts you off your game; this is dangerous.*

'Construction must have been a stuffy place for a jazz enthusiast,' I said.

'It was hard for him at times,' she acknowledged. Somehow I knew she had been ready to say more and then had thought better of it. She glanced up. 'Can I ask you a question?'

'Sure,' I responded, not knowing what was coming.

'What did you mean, when you said we had "rescued" you?'

'Just trying to strike up a conversation,' I said. I saw immediately from her eyes that it was the wrong response. *You have to show her a little bit.* I sighed. 'I was talking about things I've done, things I thought were right,' I said, switching to English, which was more comfortable for me on this subject. 'But then later it turned out they weren't. At times those things haunt me.'

'Haunt you?' she asked, not understanding.

'*Borei no yo ni.*' Like a ghost.

'My music made the ghosts go away?'

I nodded and smiled, but the smile turned sad. 'It did. I'll have to listen to it more often.'

'Because they'll come back?'

Jesus, John, get off this. 'It's more like they're always there. *Sugita koto wa, sugita koto da.*' The past is the past.

'You have regrets?'

'Doesn't everyone?'

'Probably. But are yours like everyone else's?'

'That I wouldn't know. I don't usually compare.'

'But you just did.'

I chuckled. 'You're tough,' was all I could say.

She shook her head. 'I don't mean to be.'

I knew I would learn nothing more about her father or the stranger today without questions that would betray my true intention.

'Any more shopping today?' I asked.

'I've got to meet my manager in Jinbocho in less than an hour.'

I paid the bill and we walked back to Aoyama-dori. I had enjoyed myself much more than I had expected. I glanced over at Midori thinking, *What have I done to her? What am I doing?*

We walked, our footsteps echoing softly. Then she asked, 'Will you come to see me play again?'

'I'd like that.' Stupid thing to say but I didn't have to follow up on it.

'I'm at the Blue Note on Friday and Saturday.'

She flagged down a cab. As it pulled away from the kerb, she rolled down the window and said, 'Come alone.'

THE NEXT FRIDAY I received a page from Harry telling me to check our bulletin board. He had found out that the stranger on the train was indeed a reporter: Franklin Bulfinch, the Tokyo bureau chief for *Forbes* magazine. Bulfinch was one of only five male foreigners living in the Daikanyama apartment complex. Harry had cross-referenced the names in the local ward directory against the information on foreign residents kept by the Immigration Bureau, including age, birthplace, address, employer, fingerprints and a photograph. Harry had determined that the other foreigners failed to match the description I had provided. He had also uploaded Bulfinch's photo so I could confirm that we were talking about the same guy. We were.

Harry had recommended a look at forbes.com, where Bulfinch's articles were archived. I spent several hours reading Bulfinch's accounts of suspected alliances between the government and the *yakuza*, about how the Liberal Democratic Party uses threats, bribery and intimidation to control the press, about the cost of all this corruption to the average Japanese.

Bulfinch's English-language articles had little impact in Japan, and the local media were obviously not following up on his efforts. It was probably the reason I hadn't been tasked with removing him.

My guess was that Kawamura was one of Bulfinch's sources, hence the reporter's presence on the train. I felt some abstract admiration for his doggedness: his source is having a heart attack right in front of him, and all he does is search the guy's pockets.

Someone must have found out about the connection, figured it was too risky to take out a foreign bureau chief, and decided just to plug the leak instead. So they called me. All right, then. There had been no B-team. I had been wrong about Benny. I could let this one go.

I looked at my watch. I could easily get to the Blue Note by the time Midori's first set would begin. I liked her music and I liked her company. She was attractive, and, I sensed, attracted to me. Enticing combination.

Just go, I thought. *It'll be fun. Who knows what'll happen afterwards? The chemistry is there. Just a one-nighter. Could be good.*

But Midori didn't feel like a one-nighter. That was exactly why I wanted to see her, and exactly why I couldn't.

What's wrong with you? Call one of your acquaintances. Keiko-chan's usually good for a few laughs. A late dinner, some wine, a hotel.

For the moment, though, the prospect of a night with Keiko-chan was oddly depressing. Maybe a workout instead. I decided to head over to the Kodokan, one of the places where I practise judo.

Loosely speaking, judo is to Western wrestling what karate is to boxing. It is a system of throws and grappling, distinguished by an arsenal of brutal joint locks and deadly strangling techniques, all of which must of course be employed with great care in the practice hall. *Judo* literally means 'the way of gentleness'.

The Kodokan is housed in a surprisingly modern seven-storey building, just a few miles from my neighbourhood. I changed in one of the locker rooms and climbed the stairs to the *daidojo*, the main practice room, where the Tokyo University team was visiting. After I threw my first *uke* easily and made him tap out with a strangle, they all lined up to do battle with the seasoned warrior. They were young and tough but no match for old age and treachery; after about a half-hour of nonstop *randori*, practising throws, I was still consistently coming out on top.

I noticed a Japanese *kurobi*, or black belt, stretching out in the corner of the tatami mats. His belt was tattered and more grey than black, which indicated that he'd been wearing it for a lot of years. It was hard to guess his age. His hair was full and black, but his face was lined. Several times I sensed that he was aware of me, although I never actually saw him looking in my direction.

I needed a break and made my apologies to the college students. While I was stretching, I watched the guy with the tattered belt. He was practising with one of the students.

He finished, walked over to me and bowed. 'Will you join me for a round of *randori*?' he asked, in lightly accented English.

I noted an intense pair of eyes and a strongly set jaw. I was right about his watching me, even if I hadn't caught him. Did he spot the Caucasian in my features?

'*Kochira koso onegai shimasu*,' I replied. My pleasure. I was annoyed that he had addressed me in English, and I stayed with Japanese. '*Nihongo wa dekimasu ka?*' Do you speak Japanese?

'*Ei, mochiron. Nihonjin desu kara*,' he responded, indignantly. Of course I do. I'm Japanese.

'*Kore wa shitsure: shimashita. Watashi mo desu. Desu ga, hatsuon ga amari migoto datta no de . . .*' Forgive me. So am I. But your accent was so perfect that . . .

He laughed. 'And so is yours.' I was still annoyed, and also wary. I speak Japanese as well as I speak English, so trying to compliment me on my facility with either language is inherently insulting. And I wanted to know why he would assume that I spoke English.

We found an empty spot on the tatami and bowed to each other, then began circling. I feinted with a foot sweep, but he countered with a sweep of his own and slammed me down to the mat.

Damn, he was fast. I rolled to my feet and we took up our positions again. I had a solid grip on his right sleeve with my left hand, a nice set-up for *ippon seonagi*. But he'd be expecting that. Instead, I swept in hard for *sasae-tsurikomi-goshi*, but he'd anticipated the move, popping his hips free and blocking my escape with his right leg. I was off-balance and he hit me hard, drilling me into the mat.

He threw me twice more in the next five minutes. It was like fighting a waterfall. I was getting tired. I faced him and said, '*Jaa, tsugi o saigo ni shimasho ka?*' Shall we make this the last one?

'*Ei, so shimasho*,' he said, bouncing on his toes. Let's do it.

OK, I thought. *I've got a little surprise for you.*

Juji-gatame, which means 'cross-lock', is an arm-bar that leaves the attacker perpendicular to his opponent, with both players lying on their backs, forming the shape of a cross. One permutation is called flying *juji-gatame*, in which the attacker launches the lock directly from a standing position. Because it fails as often as it succeeds, this variation is not particularly well known.

If this guy wasn't familiar with it, he was about to receive an introduction. I circled defensively, breathing hard, trying to look more tired than I was. Three times I shook off the grip he attempted and dodged around him as though I was reluctant to engage. Finally he got frustrated, reaching a little too deeply with his left hand for my right lapel. As soon as he had the grip, I caught his arm and flung my head backwards, launching my legs. My head landed between his feet, my weight jerking him into a semicrouch, destroying his balance. For a split second, before he went sailing over me, I saw complete surprise on his face. Then we were on the mat and I had trapped his arm, forcing it back against the elbow.

He twisted away from me, but he couldn't get free. His arm was straightened to the limit of its natural movement. I knew that we had about a tenth of an inch before his elbow hyperextended. A quarter of an inch and his arm would break.

'*Maita ka*,' I said. Submit. He was grimacing in pain but he ignored me. It's stupid to fight a solid armlock. Even in Olympic competition, *judoka* will submit rather than face a broken arm. '*Maita ka*,' I said again but he kept struggling.

Another five seconds went by. I wasn't going to let him go without a submission, but I didn't want to break his arm. Finally he tapped my leg with his free hand, the *judoka*'s way of surrender. I released my grip instantly and pushed away from him. He rubbed his elbow for several seconds and regarded me.

'Excellent,' he said. 'I would request a rematch, but I don't think my arm will allow that today.'

'You should have tapped out earlier,' I said. 'You won the first four rounds. I'd trade your record for mine.' He was still using English; I was responding in Japanese.

When we stood up he said, 'I've never seen that variation of *juji-gatame* executed successfully in *randori*. Next time I'll know not to underestimate the risks you're willing to take.'

'Where do you practise?' I asked him.

'With a private club,' he said. 'I doubt that you would have heard of it. My . . . club is not generally open to foreigners.' He recovered quickly. 'But, of course, you are Japanese.'

I should have let it go. 'Yes. But you approached me in English.'

He paused. 'Your features are primarily Japanese, if I may say so. I thought I detected some trace of Caucasian, and wanted to satisfy myself. I am usually very sensitive to such things.' For a moment, I thought he looked oddly uncomfortable. Then he said, 'Would you mind if I were to speak frankly?'

'Have you not been?'

He smiled. 'You are Japanese, but American also, yes?'

My expression was carefully neutral.

'Regardless, I think you can understand me. I know Americans admire frankness. It's one of their disagreeable characteristics. And this disagreeable trait is now infecting even me! Do you see the threat America poses to Nippon?'

I regarded him, wondering if he was a crackpot rightist. You run into them from time to time—they profess to abhor America but they can't help being fascinated with it. 'Americans are . . . causing too many frank conversations?' I asked.

'I know you are being facetious, but in a sense, yes. Americans are missionaries, only now, they proselytise not Christianity, but the American Way. Frankness is only one, relatively trivial, aspect.'

Why not have some fun. 'You feel that you're being converted?'

'Of course. Americans believe in two things: first, that "all men are created equal"; and second, that complete trust in the market is the best way for a society to order its affairs. America has always needed such transcendental notions to bind together its citizens, who have come from different cultures all over the world. And Americans are then driven to prove the validity of these ideas by aggressively converting other cultures to them. In a religious context, this behaviour would be recognised as missionary in its origins and effect.'

'It's an interesting theory,' I allowed. 'But an aggressive outlook has never been an American monopoly. How do you explain the Japanese colonial history in Korea and China? Attempts to save Asia from the tyranny of Western market forces?'

He leaned forward. 'Japanese conquest in the first half of this century was a reaction to Western aggression. In earlier times there were other causes, even such base ones as the lust for power and plunder. War is a part of human nature, but we Japanese have never fought to convince the world of the rightness of an idea. It took America and its bastard twin, communism, to do that.'

He leaned closer. 'War has always been with the world and always will be. But an intellectual Crusade? Fought on a global scale, backed by modern industrial economies, with the threat of a nuclear auto-da-fé for the unbelievers? Only America offers this.'

Well, that confirmed the crackpot-rightist diagnosis. 'I appreciate your speaking frankly with me,' I said, bowing slightly. '*Ii benkyo ni narimashita*.' It's been an education.

He returned my bow. '*Kochira koso*.' The same here. 'Perhaps we will meet again.'

I watched him leave. Then, wanting to cool off before showering, I went down to an empty *dojo* on the fourth floor. I left the fluorescent lights off when I went in. This room was best when it was lit only by Korakuen Amusement Park, which twinkled and hummed next door. Standing in the quiet darkness, I looked out over Korakuen. I could hear the roller coaster ratcheting slowly up to its apogee, then the whoosh of its downward plunge and the screaming laughter of its passengers, the wind whipping away their cries.

I stretched in the centre of the room, the *judogi* uniform wet against my skin. It was past seven, too late for me to get to the Blue Note. Just as well.

I HAD NO SPECIAL PLANS the next day, so I decided to stop at an antiquarian bookstore in Jinbocho. The shop's proprietor was holding for me an old tome on *shimewaza*—strangles—that I had been trying to find for a long time, to add to my collection on the warrior arts.

I picked up the Mita subway line at Sengoku Station. Today there was a priest in Shinto garb collecting donations outside the station. It seemed like these guys were everywhere lately. I meant to leave Jinbocho Station at the exit nearest the Isseido Bookstore, but, distracted by thoughts of Midori and Kawamura, I wound up taking the wrong corridor. After turning a corner, I realised my error, turned, and rounded the corner again.

A podgy Japanese was moving quickly down the corridor, about ten yards away. I flashed his eyes as he approached but he ignored me. He was wearing a suit and a striped shirt. I glanced down and saw why I hadn't heard him coming: cheap shoes with rubber soles. But he was carrying an expensive-looking black attaché case. A businessman who knew good attachés but assumed no one would notice his shoes? Maybe. But this wasn't really the place for business. I knew the shoes would make for comfortable attire on a long walk—if following someone were part of the itinerary, for example.

I tensed as we passed each other. Something about him bothered me. I looked back and marked the way he walked. Faces are easy to disguise, clothes you can change in a minute, but not too many people can conceal their gait. I watched this guy's walk—short stride, bit of an exaggerated arm swing, slight side-to-side swaying of the head—until he turned the corner. Probably it was nothing, but I'd remember his face and gait, see if he showed up again.

Principles of Strangles was in excellent condition, as promised, with a price to match. I waited patiently while the proprietor carefully, almost ceremoniously, wrapped the book in heavy brown paper and string. This was his way of showing his appreciation for the sale and it would have been rude for me to hurry him.

I headed back to the Mita line to see if I could spot Attaché Man again. I waited on the platform while two trains pulled in and departed. Anyone trying to follow me would have had to stay on the platform, but it was deserted. Attaché Man was gone.

I thought of Midori again. It was her second night at the Blue Note and I wondered what she would think when I didn't show. She would probably assume that I hadn't been interested. It was unlikely that I would ever see her again, or if we did by chance bump into each other, it would be slightly awkward but polite, two people who met and started an acquaintanceship that somehow didn't take off. I wondered what it would have been like if we'd met under other circumstances. *It could have been good*, I thought again. I almost laughed at the absurdity. There was no room for anything like that in my life, and I knew it.

Crazy Jake again: *There's no home for us, John. Not after what we've done.*

That was about the truest advice I'd ever been given. *Forget about her*, I thought. *You know you have to.*

My pager buzzed. I found a payphone and dialled the number.

It was Benny. 'There's another job for you, if you want it.'

'I'm not known for turning away work.'

'You'd have to bend one of your rules on this one. If you do, there's a bonus.'

'I'm listening.'

'We're talking about a woman. Jazz musician.'

Long pause.

'You there?' he said. 'You want the details, you know where to find them.'

'What's the name?'

He cleared his throat. 'Same as a recent job. Related matter. Significant bonus if you want it.'

'What's significant?

'You know where to find the details. I need an answer within forty-eight hours, OK? This needs to be taken care of.'

I stood there for a moment afterwards, looking around the station, watching people bustling back and forth. Why Midori? A connection with Bulfinch, the reporter. He had sought her out, I saw that at Alfie, along with Telephone Man. So whoever Telephone Man worked for would assume that Midori had learned something she wasn't supposed to, or that her father had given her something, something Bulfinch was after. Something not worth taking any chances over.

You could do it, I thought. *If you don't, someone else will. You'd at least do it right. She wouldn't feel anything.* But they were just words. I wanted to feel that way but couldn't. What I felt like instead was that her world should never have collided with mine.

A Mita-sen train pulled in, heading in the direction of Omotesando and the Blue Note. *An omen*, I thought, and got on it.

At Omotesando I left the subway and took the stairs to the street. I walked to the Yahoo Café, a coffee shop with Internet terminals, paid the fee and logged on. It took just a few seconds to access the file Benny had posted. It included a few scanned publicity photos, Midori's home address, a concert schedule with tonight's appearance at the Blue Note, and parameters indicating that the job had to look natural. They were offering the yen equivalent of about $150,000—a substantial premium over our usual arrangement.

The reference to tonight's appearance at the Blue Note was ominous. If they wanted to take her out soon, tonight would be almost too good to pass up. On the other hand, Benny had told me I had forty-eight hours to get back to him. But even if she had that much time, I didn't see how I could parlay it into a reasonable life span. Warn her that someone had just put a contract out on her? I could try, but she had no reason to believe me. And even if she did, what then? Teach her how to improve her personal security?

Ludicrous. There was really only one thing I could do. Use the forty-eight hours to figure out why Benny's people had decided Midori was a liability and to eliminate the reasons behind that view.

I caught a cab and told the driver to take me down Koto-dori, then left to the Blue Note. Traffic was heavy as I had hoped, and I had a good chance to scope the area as we crawled past. In fact, the Blue Note isn't that easy a place to wait around unobtrusively. It's surrounded mostly by stores that were now closed. The Caffe Idee across the street would offer a clear enough view, but the Idee has a narrow external staircase that would afford access sufficiently slow as to make it an unacceptable place to wait.

On the other hand, you wouldn't have to linger long. You can time the end of a *Blue Note* set to within five minutes. The second set hadn't yet begun, so if anyone was planning on visiting Midori after the show tonight, they probably hadn't even arrived yet. Or they could already be inside, just another appreciative audience member.

I had the cab stop and walked the four blocks back to the Blue Note. I was careful to scope the likely places, but things looked clear.

At the ticket window I was told that the second set was sold out unless I had a reservation. Damn, I hadn't thought about that. But Midori would have, if she really had wanted me to come. 'I'm a friend of Kawamura Midori's,' I said. 'Fujiwara Junichi . . .?'

'Of course,' the clerk responded immediately. 'Kawamura-san told me you might be coming tonight. Please wait here—the second set will start in fifteen minutes.'

I stepped to the side. The crowd from the first set started filing out five minutes later, and as soon as they were clear I was taken down a wide, steep staircase and shown to a table in front of the empty stage.

No one would ever confuse the Blue Note with Alfie. The Blue Note has a high ceiling that conveys a feeling of spaciousness totally unlike Alfie's almost cave-like intimacy. The crowd is different too; the people at Alfie are there only for the music, whereas, at the Blue Note, people also come to be seen.

I looked around the room as the second-set crowd flowed in, but nothing set off my radar.

If you wanted to get to her where would you go? You'd stay close to one of the entrances. That would give you an escape route if you needed one and it would keep the entire room in front of you, so you could watch everyone from behind.

I swivelled and looked behind me as though searching for an acquaintance. There was a Japanese man, mid-forties, sitting in the left rear, near one of the exits. He was obviously alone, wearing a rumpled suit. His expression was bland, too bland for my taste. This was a crowd composed of enthusiasts, sitting in twos and threes, waiting eagerly for the performance. Mr Bland felt like he was deliberately trying to be unobtrusive. I filed him as a strong possible.

I swivelled in the other direction. Same seat, right rear. Three young women who looked like office ladies on a night out. No apparent problem there.

Mr Bland would be able to watch me throughout the performance, and I needed to avoid his mistake of being conspicuously alone. I told the people around me that I was a friend of Midori's and was here at her invitation; they started asking me questions, and pretty soon we were shooting the shit like old friends.

A waitress came by and I ordered a twelve-year-old Cragganmore. The people around me all followed suit. I was a friend of Kawamura Midori's, so whatever I had ordered, it must be cool.

Midori took her place at the piano. She was wearing faded blue jeans and a black velvet blouse, low cut and clinging, her skin dazzling white. She touched the keys and the audience grew silent.

She started slowly, with a coy rendering of Thelonious Monk's 'Brilliant Corners', but overall she played harder than she had at Alfie and with more abandon. The set lasted for ninety minutes, and the music alternated between an elegiac sadness and a giddy exuberance that shook the sadness away. Midori finished in a mad, exhilarated riff and the applause was unrestrained. Midori stood to acknowledge it. The drummer and bass guitarist were laughing and wiping sweat from their faces, and the applause went on and on. When finally it faded, Midori and her trio left the stage.

A few minutes later she reappeared and squeezed in next to me. Her face was still flushed from the performance. 'I thought I saw you here,' she said. 'Thank you for coming.'

'Thank you for inviting me. They were expecting me.'

She smiled. 'If I hadn't told them, you wouldn't have got in, and you can't hear the music from the street.'

'The reception is certainly better from where I'm sitting,' I said, looking around as though taking in the grandeur of the Blue Note, but in fact scoping for Mr Bland.

'Do you want to get something to eat?' she asked. 'I'm going to grab something with the band.'

I hesitated. I wasn't going to have a chance to probe for information with other people around. 'This is your big night,' I said. 'You probably want to just enjoy it yourselves.'

'I'd like you to come. We were thinking the Living Bar. Do you know it?'

Good choice, I thought. The Living Bar was close by, but we'd have to turn at least five corners to walk there, which would allow me to check and see if Mr Bland was following.

'Sure. It's a chain, isn't it?'

'The one in Omotesando is nicer than all the others. They serve a good selection of single malts. Mama says you're a connoisseur.'

'Mama flatters me,' I said, thinking that if I weren't careful, Mama would put together a damn dossier and start handing it out.

'Can you wait here for just a few minutes? I've got some things to take care of backstage.'

'Sure,' I said, getting up so that my back was to the stage and I could see the room. Too many people were milling about, though, and I couldn't spot Mr Bland.

Fifteen minutes later she reappeared. She had changed into a black turtleneck and slacks. Her hair was loose over her shoulders.

'You look great,' I said.

She smiled. 'Let's go! I'm starving.'

We headed out of the front entrance, passing a number of lingering fans who thanked her on the way. *If you wanted to get to her and could time it right*, I thought, *you would wait at the bottom of the stairs of the Caffe Idee, where you would have a view of both the front and side entrances.* Sure enough, Mr Bland was there, strolling away from us with studied nonchalance.

So much for Benny's forty-eight hours, I thought.

The drummer and bass guitarist were waiting for us. 'Tomo-chan, Ko-chan, this is Fujiwara Junichi,' Midori said, gesturing to me.

'*Hajimemashite*,' I said, bowing. '*Konya no euso wa saiko ni subarashikatta.*' It's good to meet you. Tonight's performance was a great pleasure.

'Hey, let's use English tonight,' Midori said, switching over as she did so. 'Fujiwara-san, these guys both spent years in New York. They can order a cab in Brooklyn as well as you can.'

'In that case, please call me John,' I said. I extended my hand to the drummer.

'You can call me Tom,' he said, shaking my hand and bowing simultaneously. He was dressed unpretentiously in jeans, a white shirt and a blue blazer. There was something sincere in the way he combined his Western and Japanese greetings and I liked him immediately.

'I remember you from Alfie,' the bassist said, extending his hand. He was dressed in black jeans, turtleneck and blazer, the sideburns and rectangular glasses all trying a bit too hard for the Look.

'And I remember you,' I said, taking his hand. 'Mama told me before the performance that you were all going to be stars, and I can see that she was right.'

Maybe he knew I was soft-soaping him, but he must have felt too good after the performance to care. He gave me a small but genuine-looking smile and said, 'Call me Ken.'

During the ten-minute walk we all chatted about jazz. Although I was ten years older than the oldest of them, conversation was easy enough. Periodically I was able to glance behind us as we turned corners. On several of these occasions I spotted Mr Bland in tow. I didn't expect him to move while Midori was with all these people, if that's what he had in mind.

The Living Bar announced its existence in the basement of the Scène Akira building with a discreet sign over the stairs. The crowd wasn't too dense for a Saturday night. Several groups of glamorous-looking women were sitting in high-backed chairs, wearing expertly applied make-up and Chanel. Midori put them to shame.

I wanted the seat facing the entrance, but Tom moved too quickly and I was left facing the bar. As we ordered, I saw Mr Bland walk over to the bar. He sat with his back to us, but there was a mirror behind the bar, and I knew he had a good view of the room.

While we waited for our order to arrive, I considered the merits of removing Mr Bland. He was part of a numerically superior enemy. If an opportunity presented itself to reduce that number by one, I would take it. If I did it right, his employers would never know of my involvement, and taking him out could buy me more time.

At some point, after much of the food had been consumed and we, along with Mr Bland, were on our second round of drinks, one of them asked me what I did for a living.

'I'm a consultant,' I told them. 'I advise foreign companies on how to bring their goods and services into the Japanese market.'

'That's good,' Tom said. 'It's too hard for foreigners to do business in Japan. In many ways it's closed to the outside world.'

'But that's good for John's business,' Ken added. 'Isn't it, John? Because, if Japan didn't have so many stupid regulations, if the ministries that inspect incoming products weren't so corrupt, you would need to find a different job, *ne?*'

'C'mon, Ken,' Midori said. 'We know how cynical you are. You don't have to prove it.'

I wondered if Ken might have had too much to drink.

'You used to be cynical, too,' he went on. He turned to me. 'When Midori came back from New York, she was a radical. She wanted to change everything about Japan. But not any more.'

'I still want to change things,' Midori said. 'It's just that you have to be patient, you have to pick your battles.'

'Which ones have you picked lately?' he asked.

Tom turned towards me. 'Ken feels like he sold out by doing gigs at established places like the Blue Note. Sometimes he takes it out on us.'

Ken looked at me. 'What about you, John? What's the American expression: "Either you're a part of the solution, or you're a part of the problem"?'

I smiled. 'There's a third part: "Or you're a part of the landscape."'

Ken nodded. 'That's the worst of all.'

I shrugged. He didn't matter to me, and it was easy to stay disengaged. 'The truth is, I hadn't really thought of what I do in these terms. Some people have a problem exporting to Japan, I help them out. But you make some good points.'

He wanted to argue and didn't know what to do with my agreeable responses. 'Let's have another drink,' he said.

'I think I've reached my limit,' Midori said.

As she spoke I noticed Mr Bland clicking a small device about the size of a disposable lighter in our direction. *A camera*, I thought.

He'd been taking Midori's picture, and I would be in the shots. This was the kind of risk I'd be taking if I stayed close to her now.

OK. I'd have to leave with the three of them, then invent an excuse, double back and catch him as he was leaving to follow Midori again. I wasn't going to let him keep that camera, not with my pictures on the film. But Mr Bland gave me another option. He got up and started walking in the direction of the men's room.

'I'm going to head home, too,' I said. 'Just need to hit the men's room first.' I eased away from the table.

I followed a few yards behind Mr Bland as he opened the men's-room door and went inside.

Two stalls, two urinals. I could see in my peripheral vision that the stall doors were open a crack. We were alone. He turned to face me, perhaps recognising me as one of the people who was with Midori, perhaps warned by instinct that he was in danger. My eyes were centred on his whole body, the position of his hips and hands, absorbing the information, processing it.

Without breaking my stride I stepped in and blasted my left hand directly into his throat, catching his trachea in the V created by my thumb and index finger. His head snapped forward and his hands flew to his throat. I stepped behind him and slipped my hands into his front pockets. From the left I retrieved the camera.

He was clawing ineffectually at his damaged throat, silent except for some clicking from his tongue and teeth as he tried to get air through the broken trachea and into the convulsing lungs. I took hold of his hair and chin and broke his neck with a hard clockwise twist. I dragged him into one of the empty stalls, sitting him on the toilet. With the door closed, anyone would just think the stall was occupied. With luck, the body wouldn't be discovered until long after we were gone.

I eased the door shut with my right hip and used my knee to close the latch. Gripping the upper edge of the stall divider, I pulled myself up and slid over to the stall on the other side. I used toilet paper to wipe the two spots that I had touched. I jammed the toilet paper in a pocket, took a deep breath, and walked out into the bar.

'All set?' I asked, walking up to the table.

'Let's go,' Midori said. The three of them stood up and we headed towards the cashier. Tom was holding the bill, but I insisted that they let me pay; it was my privilege after the pleasure of their performance. I didn't want to take a chance on anyone using a credit card and leaving a record of our presence.

As I was paying, Tom said, 'I'll be right back,' and headed towards the men's room. Ken followed him.

I imagined vaguely that the body could slide off the toilet while they were in there. Or that Murphy's Law would make an appearance in some other way. There was nothing I could do but relax and wait until they had returned.

'You want a walk home?' I asked Midori. She had mentioned during the evening that she lived in Harajuku, although of course I already knew that.

She smiled. 'That would be nice.'

Three minutes later, Tom and Ken returned. I saw them laughing as they approached, and knew that Mr Bland had gone undiscovered.

'My car's at the Blue Note,' Ken said when we were outside. He looked at Midori. 'Anyone need a ride?'

Midori shook her head. 'No, I'm fine. Thanks.'

'I'll take the subway,' I told him. 'But thanks.'

'I'll go with you,' Tom said to Ken, defusing the slight tension I could feel brewing as Ken did the maths. 'John, it was nice meeting you tonight. Thank you for coming, and for the dinner and drinks.'

I bowed. 'My pleasure, really.'

Tom took a step backwards, his cue to Ken, I knew, and we said good night.

Midori and I strolled slowly in the direction of Omotesando-dori. 'Was that OK?' she asked when Tom and Ken were out of earshot.

'I had a good time,' I told her. 'They're interesting people.'

'Ken can be difficult.'

I shrugged. 'He was a little jealous that you had invited someone else to tag along, that's all.'

'You know, I don't usually invite people I've only just met to come to a performance, or to go out afterwards.'

'We'd met before, so your guideline should be intact.'

She laughed. 'You feel like another single malt?'

'Always,' I said. 'And I've got a place I think you'll like.'

I took her to Bar Satoh, a tiny establishment nestled in a series of alleys. The route we took gave me several opportunities to check behind us, and I saw that we were clean. Mr Bland had been alone.

We took the elevator to the first floor of the building. A right turn, a step up, and there was Satoh-san, presiding over the solid cherry bar in the low light, dressed immaculately as always in a bow tie and waistcoat.

'*Ah, Fujiwara-san,*' he said in his soft baritone, smiling and bowing as he caught sight of us. '*Irrashaimase.*' Welcome.

I looked around, noting that his small establishment was almost full. 'Is there a possibility that we could be seated?'

'*Ei, mochiron,*' he replied. Yes, of course. Apologising in formal Japanese, he had the six patrons at the bar all shift to their right, creating room for Midori and me.

Thanking Satoh-san, we made our way to our seats. Midori's head was moving back and forth as she took in the decor: bottle after bottle of different whiskies, many obscure and ancient, adorning shelves throughout the room. As a complement to his whisky-only policy, Satoh-san plays nothing but jazz, and the sounds of singer Kurt Elling issued warm and wry from the back of the bar.

'I love this place!' Midori whispered to me in English as we sat down.

'Satoh-san is a former *sarariman* who got out of the rat race. He saved every yen he could until he was able to open this place ten years ago.'

Satoh-san strolled over, and I introduced Midori. 'Ah, of course!' he exclaimed. He reached under the bar for a copy of Midori's CD. Midori had to beg him not to play it.

'What do you recommend tonight?' I asked. Satoh-san makes four pilgrimages a year to Scotland and has introduced me to malts that are available nowhere else in Japan.

Satoh-san smiled. He took a clear glass bottle from in front of the mirror behind the bar. 'This is a forty-year-old Ardbeg,' he explained. 'From the south shore of Islay. Very rare. I keep it in a plain bottle because anyone who recognised it might try to steal it.'

He took out two immaculate tumblers, carefully poured off two measures of the bronze liquid and recorked the bottle.

'What makes this malt special is the balance of flavours,' he told us, his voice low and grave. 'There is peat, smoke, perfume, sherry, and the salt smell of the sea. It took forty years for this malt to realise the potential of its own character, just like a person. Please, enjoy.' He bowed and moved to the other end of the bar.

'I'm almost afraid to drink it,' Midori said, raising the glass before her and watching the light turn the liquid to amber.

'Satoh-san always provides a brief lecture on what you're about to experience. He's a student of single malts.' We touched glasses and drank. She paused, then said, 'Wow, that is good. Like a caress.'

'Like the sound of your music.'

She smiled. 'I enjoyed our conversation the other day,' she said. 'I'd like to hear more of your experiences growing up in two worlds.'

She was much more a listener than a talker, which would make my job of collecting operational intelligence more difficult. *Let's just see where this goes*, I thought.

'Home for me was a little town in upstate New York. My mother took me there after my father died so she could be close to her parents,' I said.

'Did you spend any time in Japan after that?'

'Some. During my junior year in high school, my father's parents wrote to me about a US/Japan high-school exchange programme that would allow me to spend a semester at a Japanese high school.'

'How was the semester?'

I shrugged. Some of these memories were not particularly pleasant. 'You know what it's like for returnees. It's bad enough if you're an ordinary Japanese kid with an accent that's been Americanised. If you're half-American on top of it, you're practically a freak.'

I saw a deep sympathy in her eyes that made me feel I was worsening a betrayal. 'You must have felt so alienated.'

I waved my hand as though it was nothing. 'It's all in the past.'

'And after high school?'

'After high school was Vietnam.'

'You were in Vietnam? You look young for that.'

I smiled. 'I was a teenager when I joined the army, and when I got there the war was already well under way.' I was aware that I was sharing more personal details than I should have. I didn't care.

'How long were you over there?'

'Three years.'

'I thought getting drafted meant only one year.'

'It did. I wasn't drafted.'

Her eyes widened. 'You volunteered?'

'I wanted to prove that I was American to the people who doubted it because of my eyes, my skin. And then, when I was over there, in a war against Asians, I had to prove it even more, so I stayed. I took dangerous assignments. I did some crazy things.'

We were quiet for a moment. Then she said, 'Are those the things that you said "haunt" you?'

'Some of them,' I said evenly. But this would go no further. We were getting close to places that even I can look at only obliquely.

Her fingers were resting lightly on the sides of her glass. Without thinking I took them into my hands, raised them before my face. 'I bet I could tell from your hands that you play the piano,' I said. 'Your fingers are slender, but they look strong.'

She twisted her hands round, so that now she was holding mine. 'You can tell a lot from a person's hands,' she said. 'In mine you see the piano. In yours I see *bushido*.'

Bushido means the martial ways, the way of the warrior. She was talking about the calluses on the first and second joints of all my fingers, the result of years of gripping and twisting the heavy cotton *judogi*. There was a gentleness in her touch and I felt electricity running all the way up my arms.

I withdrew my hands, afraid of what else she might read in them. 'These days just judo. Grappling, throwing, strangles—it's the most practical martial art. And the Kodokan is the best place for judo.'

'I know the Kodokan. I studied aikido at a little *dojo* nearby in Ochanomizu.'

'What's a jazz pianist doing studying aikido?'

'It was before I got really serious about the piano. I did it because I got bullied in school for a while.'

'Did the aikido help?'

'Not at first. But the bullies gave me incentive to keep practising. One day, one of them grabbed my arm, and I threw her with *san-kyo*. After that, they left me alone.'

I looked at her, imagining what it would be like to be on the *san-kyo* receiving end of the determination that was taking her to increasing renown, maybe to fame, in jazz circles.

She lifted her glass with the fingers of both hands, and I noticed an economy of movement to the simple act.

'You do *sado*,' I said, almost thinking out loud. *Sado* is the

Japanese tea ceremony. Its practitioners strive, through the refined, ritualised movements in the preparation and serving of tea, to achieve elegance in thought and movement.

'Not since I was a teenager,' she answered.

'I like the *sado*,' I said, fighting the feeling of being drawn into those dark eyes.

She smiled. 'What else do you like?'

Where is she going? 'I like watching you play.'

'Tell me.'

I sipped the Ardbeg, peat and smoke meandering across my tongue. 'I like the way you start calm, and then how, when you get going, it's as though the music is playing you. I always feel like you're looking for something while you're playing but that you can't find it. So you look harder, and the melody starts to get really edgy, but then it's as though you realise that you're not going to find it, and the music turns sad, but it's a beautiful sadness.'

I realised that there was something about her that made me open up too much. I needed to control it.

'It means a lot to me that you recognise that in my music,' she said after a moment. 'Because it's something that I'm trying to express. Do you know *mono no aware*?'

'I think so. "The pathos of things", right?'

'That's the usual translation. I like "the sadness of being human".'

'I hadn't thought of it that way,' I said quietly.

'I remember once I took a walk on a winter night. I sat in the playground of the school where I had gone as a girl and watched the silhouettes of the tree branches against the sky. I had a strong awareness that, one day, I was going to be gone, but the trees would still be here, the moon would still be above them, shining down, and it made me cry, but a good kind of crying. I had to accept it because that's the way things are. Things end. That's *mono no aware*.'

Things end. 'Yes, it is,' I said, thinking of her father.

We were quiet for a moment. Then I asked, 'What did Ken mean when he said that you were a radical?'

She took a sip of her Ardbeg. 'Look around you, John. Japan is incredibly screwed up. The LDP, the bureaucrats, they're bleeding the country dry.'

'There are problems,' I allowed.

'Problems? The economy's going to hell, families can't pay their property taxes, there's no confidence in the banking system. And you know why? Payoffs to the construction industry. The country is covered in concrete, there's nowhere else to build, so the politicians vote for office parks no one uses and bridges and roads no one drives on.'

'Ken was right,' I said, smiling. 'You are pretty radical.'

She shook her head. 'This is just common sense. Don't you sometimes feel like you're being screwed by the status quo?'

'Forgive me, but wasn't your father a part of that status quo?'

A long pause. 'We had our differences. For a long time we were pretty alienated.'

I nodded. 'Were you ever able to mend fences?'

She laughed softly, but without mirth. 'My father found out he had lung cancer a few months before he died. The diagnosis made him reassess his life, but that didn't give us long to work things out.'

The information caught me by surprise. 'He had lung cancer? But Mama mentioned a heart attack.'

'He had a heart condition, but always smoked anyway. To fit in. All his government cronies did.'

I took a sip of the whisky. 'Forgive me if I'm prying, but what do you mean when you say the diagnosis made him reassess his life?'

She was looking past me. 'In the end, he realised he had spent his life being part of the problem, as Ken would say. He decided he wanted to be part of the solution.'

'Did he have time to do that?'

'I don't think so. But he told me he wanted to do something, something right, before he died. The main thing was that he felt that way.'

'How do you know he didn't have time?'

'What do you mean?' she asked.

'Your father—he's diagnosed, he wants to do something to atone for the past. Could he have? In such a short time?'

'I'm not sure what you mean,' she said, and instantly I knew I had bumped up against that defensive wall.

'I'm thinking about what we talked about the other day. About regret. If there's something you regret, but you've only got a short time to do something about it, what do you do? What would your father have done?'

'I wouldn't know.'

But you do know. A reporter he was meeting contacted you. You know, but you're not telling me.

'What I mean is, maybe he was trying to do something, even if you couldn't see it. Maybe he told his colleagues about his change of heart, tried to get them to change theirs. Who knows?'

She was quiet, and I thought, *That's it, that's as far as you can possibly push it, she's going to get suspicious.*

But after a moment she said, 'Are you asking because of a regret of your own?'

I looked at her, disturbed by the truth of her question and relieved at the cover it afforded me. 'I'm not sure,' I said. 'I thought there'd be a lesson there for me. That's all. I'm sorry for pressing.'

She gave me a small smile. 'That's OK. This is all still a little recent.'

'Of course it is,' I said, recognising the dead end. I looked at my watch. 'I should get you home.'

This was tricky. On the one hand, we had undeniable chemistry, and it wasn't inconceivable that she would invite me up for a drink. If she did, I'd get a chance to make sure her apartment was secure, although I couldn't let anything stupid happen once we were inside.

On the other hand, if she wanted to go home alone, it would be hard for me to escort her without seeming like I was angling for a way to get into her bed. But I couldn't just turn her loose alone. They knew where she lived.

We thanked Satoh-san for his hospitality. I paid the bill and we took the stairs down into the now slightly chilly Omotesando night air. The streets were quiet.

'Which way are you heading?' Midori asked me.

'I'll go with you. I'd like to see you all the way home,' I said.

She smiled. 'OK.'

It was a fifteen-minute walk. I didn't observe anyone behind us. Not a surprise, given Mr Bland's departure from the scene.

When we reached the entrance of her building, she turned to me. '*Jaa* . . . Well, then . . .' It was a polite good night.

'Can I call you some time?' *In about five minutes, for example, to make sure there's no one waiting for you in your apartment.*

'I hope you will.'

I took out a pen and wrote the number she gave me down on my hand. I already knew it, of course, but I had to keep up appearances.

She was looking at me, half smiling. The kiss was there, if I wanted it.

'Good night, Midori.'

I turned and walked away, then paused to look back. But she had already gone inside, and the glass doors were closing behind her.

I SLIPPED into a parking area that faced the entrance. Hanging back beyond the perimeter of light cast from inside, I saw Midori waiting for an elevator. I watched her step inside, and then the doors closed.

No one seemed to be lurking outside. Unless they were waiting in her apartment or nearby, she would be safe for the night.

I took out Harry's unit and activated her phone, then listened in on my cellphone. Silence. A minute later, I heard her door being unlocked. Muffled footsteps. Then the sound of more footsteps, from more than one person. A loud gasp.

Then a male voice: 'Listen carefully. We're sorry to alarm you. We're investigating a matter of national security.'

Midori's voice, not much more than a whisper: 'Show me . . . Show me some identification.'

'We don't have time for that. We have some questions that we need to ask you, and then we'll leave.'

'Show me some ID,' I heard her say, her voice stronger now, 'or I'm going to start making a noise. And the walls in this building are really thin.'

My heart leapt. She had instinct and she had guts.

'No noise, please,' came the reply. Then the reverberation of a hard slap. They were roughing her up. I was going to have to move.

I heard her breathing, ragged. 'What the hell do you want?'

'Your father had something on his person around the time that he died. It is now in your possession. We need it.'

'I don't know what you're talking about.' Another slap. Shit.

I couldn't get into the building without a key. Even if someone entered or exited right then so that I could slip inside, I would never be able to make it into her apartment to help her.

I broke the connection and input her number on the cellphone. Her phone rang three times, then an answering machine cut in.

I hung up and repeated the procedure using the redial key, then again. And again. I wanted to make them nervous. If someone tried to get through enough times, maybe they would let her answer it to allay potential suspicions. On the fifth try, she picked up.

'Midori, this is John. I know you can't speak. I know there are men in your apartment. Say to me "There isn't a man in my apartment, Grandma." '

'There isn't . . .There isn't a man in my apartment, Grandma.'

'Good girl. Now say, "No, I don't want you coming over now. There's no one here." '

'No, I don't want you coming over now. There's no one here.'

They'd be itching to get out of her apartment now. 'Very good. Just keep arguing with your grandmother, OK? Those men are not the police, you know that. I can help you, but only if you get them out of your apartment. Tell them your father had some papers, but that they're hidden in his apartment. Tell them you'll take them there and show them. Do you understand?'

'Grandma, you worry too much.'

'I'll be waiting outside,' I said, and broke the connection.

Which way are they likely to go? I thought, trying to decide where I could set up an ambush. But just then an old woman emerged from the elevator, carrying out her trash. The electronic doors parted for her as she shuffled outside, and I slipped into the building.

I knew Midori lived on the second floor. I bolted up the stairwell and paused outside the entrance to her floor, listening. After about half a minute of silence, I heard the sound of a door opening from somewhere down the corridor.

I opened the door partway, then took out my key chain and extended the dental mirror through the opening until I had a view of a long, narrow hallway. A Japanese man was emerging from an apartment. He swept his head left and right, then nodded. A moment later Midori stepped out, followed by a second Japanese who had his hand on her shoulder, but not in a gentle way.

They started to move towards my position. I withdrew the mirror. There was a fire extinguisher on the wall, and I grabbed it. I aimed the nozzle face high. I heard their footsteps approaching, heard them right outside the door. I breathed shallowly through my mouth, my fingers tense around the trigger of the unit.

For a split second, in my imagination, I saw the door start to open, but it didn't. They had continued past it, heading for the elevators.

Damn. I had thought they would take the stairs. I eased the door open again and extended the mirror, adjusting the angle until I could see them. They had her sandwiched in tightly, the guy at the rear holding something against her back.

I turned and bolted down the stairs. When I got to the ground floor I cut across the lobby, stopping behind a pillar that they'd have to walk past. I braced the extinguisher against my waist and eased the mirror past the corner of the pillar.

They emerged half a minute later, bunched up in a tight formation. They were obviously afraid Midori was going to try to run.

I slipped the mirror and key chain back in my pocket, listening to their footsteps. When they sounded only a few inches away I bellowed a warrior's *kiyai* and leapt out, pulling the trigger and aiming face high. Nothing happened. The extinguisher hiccupped, then made a disappointing hissing sound.

The lead guy's mouth dropped open, and he started fumbling inside his coat. Feeling like I was moving in slow motion, I brought the butt end of the extinguisher up. Saw his hand coming free, holding a revolver. I jammed the extinguisher into his face like a battering ram, getting my weight behind the blow. There was a thud and he spilled into Midori and the guy in the rear, his gun clattering to the floor.

The second guy stumbled backwards, slipping clear of Midori. He was holding a gun in his hand and trying keep it in front of him.

I launched the extinguisher like a missile. He went down and I was on him, catching hold of the gun and jerking it away. Before he could get his hands up to protect himself I smashed the butt into his head, behind the ear. There was a loud crack and he went limp.

I spun and brought the gun up, but his friend wasn't moving. I turned back to Midori just in time to see a third goon emerge from the elevator, where he must have been positioned from the start. He grabbed Midori round the neck from behind with his left hand, trying to use her as a shield, while his right hand went to his jacket pocket, groping for a weapon. But before he could pull it free, Midori spun counterclockwise inside his grip, catching his left wrist in her hands and twisting his arm outwards and back in a classic aikido *san-kyo* joint lock. His reaction showed training: he threw his body in the direction of the lock to save his arm from being broken, and landed with a smooth *ukemi* break fall. But before he could recover I had closed the distance, launching a field-goal-style kick at his head with enough force to lift his whole body from the ground.

Midori was looking at me, her breath coming in shallow gasps.

'Are you OK?' I asked, taking her arm. 'Did they hurt you?'

She shook her head. 'They told me they were the police, but I knew they weren't. Why were they waiting in my apartment? How did you know they were in there?'

I started moving us through the lobby towards the glass doors, my eyes sweeping back and forth for signs of danger outside. 'I saw them at the Blue Note,' I said, urging her to increase the pace. 'When I realised they hadn't followed us back, I thought they might be waiting for you at your apartment. That's when I called.'

'You saw them at the Blue Note? Who are they? Who the hell are you?'

'I'm someone who's stumbled onto something very bad and wants to protect you from it. I'll explain later. Right now, we've got to get you someplace safe.'

'Safe? With you?' She stopped in front of the glass doors and looked at the three men, their faces bloody masks, then back at me.

'I'll explain everything to you, but not now. For now, the only thing that matters is that you're in danger, and I can't help you if you don't believe me. Let me just get you someplace where no one would know to look for you. A hotel, something like that.'

I wanted to search the men on the floor for ID or some other way of identifying them, but I couldn't do that and get Midori moving at the same time.

'How do I know I can believe you?' she said, but she was moving again. The doors opened.

'Trust your instincts. They'll tell you what's right.'

We moved through the doors, and I was able to see a squat Japanese man standing about five yards back and to the left. He had a nose that must have been broken many times. He was watching the scene in the foyer, and seemed uncertain of what to do. Something about his posture told me he wasn't a civilian. Probably he was with the three on the floor.

I steered Midori to the right, keeping clear of the flat-nosed guy's position. 'How could you know that there were men in my apartment?' she asked. 'How did you know what was happening?'

'I just knew, OK?' I said, turning my head, searching for danger, as we walked. I saw the flat-nosed guy go inside as we moved away from the scene, I assumed to help his fallen comrades.

They would have had a car. I looked around, but there were too many vehicles parked in the area for me to be able to pinpoint theirs.

All right, go, just keep on walking, they'll have to show themselves if they want to take you.

We cut across the dark parking lot, emerging onto Omotesando-dori, where we caught a cab. I told the driver to take us to the Seibu Department Store in Shibuya. There were few cars on the road, and none seemed to be trying to tail us.

What I had in mind was a love hotel. The love hotel is a Japanese institution, born of the country's housing shortage. With families, sometimes extended ones, jammed into small apartments, Mom and Dad need to have somewhere to go to be alone. Hence the *rabu hoteru*—places with rates for either a 'rest' or a 'stay', famously discreet front desk, no credit card required for registration, and fake names the norm.

The people we were up against weren't stupid, of course. They might guess that a love hotel would make an expedient safe house. But with about 10,000 *rabu hoteru* in Tokyo, it would take them a while to track us down.

We got out of the cab and walked to Shibuya 2-*chome*, which is choked with love hotels. *Chome* are small subdivisions within Tokyo's various wards. I chose a hotel at random, where we told the woman at the front desk that we wanted a room with a bath, for a stay, not just a rest. I put cash on the counter and she handed us a key.

We found our room at the end of a short hallway. I followed Midori in, locking the door behind me. We left our shoes in the entranceway. There was only one bed but there was a decent-sized couch in the room that I could curl up on.

Midori sat down on the edge of the bed and faced me. 'Here's where we are,' she said, her voice even. 'Tonight three men were waiting for me in my apartment. They claimed to be police, but obviously weren't. I'd think you were with them, but I saw how badly you hurt them. You asked me to go somewhere safe with you so you could explain. I'm listening.'

I nodded. 'You know this has to do with your father.'

'Those men told me he had something they wanted.'

'Yes, and they think you have it now.'

'I don't know why they would think that.'

I looked at her. 'I think you do.'

'Think what you want.'

'You know what's wrong with this picture, Midori? Three men are waiting for you in your apartment, they rough you up a little, I appear and rough them up a lot, and the whole time you've never once suggested that you want to go to the police.'

She sat facing me, her fingers drumming on the edge of the bed. *Goddamnit, what does she know that she hasn't been telling me?*

'Tell me about your father, Midori. I can't help you if you don't.'

She leapt off the bed and faced me squarely. 'Tell you?' she spat. 'No, you tell me! Tell me who you are, or I swear I will go to the police, and I don't care what happens after that!'

Progress, of a sort, I thought. 'What do you want to know?'

'Who were those men in my apartment?'

'I don't know.'

'But you knew they were there?'

She was going to pull hard at that loose thread until the entire fabric unravelled. I didn't know how to get round it. 'Yes, because your apartment is bugged.'

'Bugged, by who, by you?'

There it was. 'Yes.'

She looked at me for a long beat, then sat back down on the bed. 'Who do you work for?' she asked, her voice flat.

'It doesn't matter.'

Another long beat, and the same flat tone: 'Tell me what you want.'

I looked at her, wanting her to see my eyes. 'I want to make sure you don't get hurt. These people are coming after you because they think you have something that could harm them. I don't know what. But as long as they think you have it, you're not going to be safe.'

'But if I were to just give whatever it is to you . . .'

'Without knowing what the thing is, I don't even know if giving it to me would help. I told you, I'm not here for whatever it is. I just don't want you to get hurt.'

'Can't you see what this looks like from my perspective? "Just hand it over so I can help you." '

'I understand that.'

'I'm not sure you do.'

'Doesn't matter. Tell me about your father.'

I knew what she was going to say. 'This is why you were asking all those questions before. You came to Alfie and, God, everything . . . You've just been using me from the beginning.'

'Some of what you're saying is true. Not all of it. Now tell me about your father.'

'No.'

I felt a flush of anger. *Easy, John.* 'The reporter was asking, too, wasn't he? Bulfinch? What did you tell him?'

She looked at me, trying to gauge just how much I knew. 'I don't know what you're talking about.'

'Listen to me, Midori. You're the one who won't be able to sleep in her own apartment, who's afraid to go to the police, who can't go back to her life. Figure out a way to work with me on this.'

A long time, maybe a full minute passed. Then she said, 'Bulfinch told me that my father was supposed to deliver something to him on the morning he died, but that he never got it. Bulfinch wanted to know if I had it, or if I knew where it was.'

'What was it?'

'A computer disk. That's all he would tell me. He told me if he said more it would put me in danger.'

'He had already compromised you—he was being followed.' I pressed my fingers to my eyes. 'Do you know anything about this disk?'

'No.'

I looked at her. 'The people who want it aren't particularly restrained about the methods they'll use to get it.'

'I understand that.'

'OK, let's put together what we have. Everyone thinks your father told you something, or gave you something. Did he?'

'No. Nothing I remember.'

'Try. A safe-deposit key? A locker key? Did he tell you that he had hidden important papers somewhere?'

'No,' she said, after a moment. 'Nothing.'

She might be holding back. She had reason not to trust me.

'But you know something,' I said. 'Or you'd go to the police.'

She folded her arms across her chest and looked at me. 'It's not what you're hoping for,' she said.

'I'm not hoping for anything. Just what pieces you can give me.'

There was a long pause. Then she said, 'I told you my father and I were . . . estranged for a long time. It started when I was a teenager, when I started to understand Japan's political system and my father's place in it.' She got up and began to pace around the room, not looking at me. 'He was part of the Liberal Democratic Party machine and was made vice minister of Land and Infrastructure—of public works. Do you know what that means in Japan?'

'I know a little. The public-works programme channels money from the politicians and construction firms to the *yakuza*.'

'And the *yakuza* provide "protection". Did you know that construction outfits in Japan are called *gumi*?'

Gumi means 'gang', or 'organisation'—the same moniker the *yakuza* gangs use for themselves. The original *gumi* were groups of men displaced by the Second World War who worked for a gang boss doing whatever dirty jobs they could to survive. Eventually these gangs morphed into today's *yakuza* and construction outfits.

'I know,' I said.

'Then you know that, after the war, there were battles between construction companies that were so big the police were afraid to intervene. A bid-rigging system was established to stop these fights. The system still exists. My father ran it.'

She laughed. 'Remember in 1994 when Kansai Airport was built in Osaka? The airport cost fourteen billion dollars and everyone wanted a piece of it. Takumi Masaru, the Yamaguchi Gumi *yakuza* boss, was murdered that year for not sharing enough of the profits. My father ordered his death to appease the other gang bosses.'

'Christ, Midori,' I said quietly. 'Your father told you these things?'

'When he learned he was terminal. He needed to confess.'

I waited for her to go on.

'Every year during budget season, officials from the Ministry of

Finance and the Ministry of Land and Infrastructure meet politicians loyal to the industry to decide how to divvy up the pie. Do you know that Japan has four per cent of the land area and half the population of America, but spends a third more on public works? Some people think that in the last ten years ten *trillion* yen of government money have been paid to the *yakuza* through public works.'

Ten trillion? That's maybe a hundred billion dollars. 'Your father was going to blow the whistle?'

'Yes. When he was diagnosed, he called me. It was the first time we had talked in over a year. He told me he had to talk to me about something important, and he came over to my apartment. We hadn't talked in so long, I was thinking it was something about his health. He looked older when I saw him and I knew I was right. I made us tea, and we sat across from each other in my kitchen. Finally I said, "Papa, what is it?"'

'He smiled, his eyes warm but sad, and for a second he looked to me the way he had when I was a little girl. "I found out this week that I don't have very long to live," he said. "A month, maybe two. The strange thing is that when I heard this news it didn't bother me." Then his eyes filled up, and he said, "What bothered me wasn't losing my life, but knowing that I had already lost my daughter."'

'He told me about all the things he had been involved in. He told me he wanted to do something to make it right, that he would have done something much sooner but he had been a coward, knowing he would be killed if he tried. He also said that he was afraid for me, that the people he was involved with wouldn't hesitate to attack someone's family to send a message. He was planning to do something that would make things right, he told me, but if he did it I might be in danger.'

'What was he going to do?'

'I don't know. But I told him I couldn't accept being a hostage to a corrupt system, that he would have to act without regard to me.'

I considered. 'That was brave of you.'

She looked at me. 'Not really. Don't forget, I'm a radical.'

'Well, we know he was talking to Bulfinch, that he was supposed to deliver a disk. We need to figure out what was on it.'

'How?'

'I think by contacting Bulfinch directly.'

'And telling him what?'

'I haven't figured that part out yet.'

We were quiet for a minute, and I felt exhaustion setting in.

'Why don't we get some sleep,' I said. 'I'll take the couch, all right? And we can talk more tomorrow. Things will seem clearer then.'

I knew they couldn't become more murky.

I GOT UP EARLY the next morning and went straight to Shibuya Station, telling Midori that I would call her later on her cellphone. I had a few items hidden in my place in Sengoku, among them an alias passport, which I'd want if I had to leave the country suddenly. I told her to go out only when she really had to, knowing that she would need to buy food and a change of clothes, and not to use plastic for any purchases.

I took the Yamanote line to Ikebukuro, then got off and took a cab to Hakusan, a residential neighbourhood about a ten-minute walk from my apartment. I got out and dialled the voice-mail account that's attached to the phone in my apartment.

The phone has a few special features. I can call in any time from a remote location and silently activate the unit's speakerphone, essentially turning it into a transmitter. The unit is also sound activated: if there's a noise in the room it dials a voice-mail account. Before I go home, I always call the voice-mail number. If someone has been in my apartment in my absence, I'll know.

When the connection went through, I punched in my code. Every time I've done this, except for when I test the system, I've listened to a mechanical woman's voice say, 'You have no calls.' I was expecting the same today. Instead the message was 'You have one call.'

Son of a bitch. Barely breathing, I pressed the 'one' key.

I heard a man's voice, speaking Japanese. 'Small place. Hard to catch him by surprise when he comes in.'

Another man's voice, also in Japanese: 'Wait here. When he arrives, use the pepper spray.'

I knew that voice, but it took me a minute to place it—I was used to hearing it in English. Benny.

'What if he doesn't want to talk?'

'He'll talk.'

I was gripping the phone hard. *Benny. How did he track me down?* When did this message get recorded? What was that special-functions button . . . The mechanical woman informed me that this message was made at 7.00 this morning, maybe an hour ago.

OK, change of plan. I saved the message, hung up, and called Midori. I told her I had found out something important and would tell her about it when I got back, that she should wait for me even if

I was late. Then I backtracked to Sugamo, known for its red-light district and accompanying love hotels.

I picked the hotel that was closest to Sengoku. The room they gave me was dank. I didn't care. I just wanted a land line, and a place to wait. I dialled the phone in my apartment. It didn't ring, but I could hear when the connection had gone through. I waited. After a half-hour there still wasn't any sound and I started to wonder if they'd left. Then I heard a chair sliding against the wood floor, footsteps, and the unmistakable sound of a man urinating in the toilet. They were still there. I sat like that all day, listening in on nothing. The only consolation was that they must have been as bored as I was. I hoped they were as hungry.

At around 6.30, I heard a phone ring on the other end of the line. Benny answered, grunted a few times, then said, 'I have something to attend to in Shibakoen—shouldn't take more than a few hours.'

If Benny was going to Shibakoen, he'd take the Mita line from Sengoku Station. He wouldn't have driven; there's nowhere for non-residents to park in Sengoku. From my apartment to the station, he could choose more or less randomly from a half-dozen streets. I had to catch him leaving the apartment or I was going to lose him.

I bolted out of the room and flew down the stairs. When I hit the sidewalk I cut straight across Hakusan-dori, then made a left that would take me to my street. I was running fast while trying to hug the buildings I passed—if I timed this wrong, Benny was going to see me coming. I couldn't be certain that he wouldn't know my face.

When I was about fifteen yards from my street I slowed to a walk. At the corner I crouched low, eased my head out and looked to the right. No sign of Benny. No more than four minutes had passed since I'd hung up the phone. I was pretty sure I hadn't missed him.

There was a streetlight directly overhead, but I had to wait where I was. I had to be able to see him when he exited. Once I'd got my hands on him, I could drag him into the shadows.

My breathing had slowed to normal when I heard the external door to the building slam shut. I smiled. The residents know the door slams and are careful to let it close slowly.

I crouched down again and peered past the edge of the wall. A podgy Japanese was walking in my direction. The same guy I had seen with the attaché case in the subway. Benny. I should have known.

I waited, listening to his footsteps getting louder. When he sounded like he was about a yard away, I stepped out.

He pulled up short, his eyes bulging. He knew my face, all right.

Before he could say anything I stepped in close, pumping two upper-cuts into his abdomen. He dropped to the ground with a grunt. I stepped behind him, grabbed his right hand, and twisted his wrist in a pain-compliance hold.

'On your feet, Benny. Move fast, or I'll break your arm.' He wheezed and hauled himself up, making sucking noises.

I shoved him round the corner and patted him down. In his over-coat pocket I found a cellphone, which I took. I slammed him up against the wall. He grunted but still hadn't recovered enough wind to do more. I pinched his windpipe with the fingers of one hand.

'Listen very carefully.' He started to struggle, and I pinched his windpipe harder. He got the message. 'I want to know what's going on. I want names.'

I relaxed my grip a little. 'I can't tell you this stuff,' he wheezed.

'Benny, I'm not going to hurt you if you tell me what I want to know. But if you don't tell me, I've got to blame you, understand?' A little more pressure on the throat—this time, cutting off all his oxygen for a few seconds. I told him to nod if he understood, and after a second or two with no air, he did.

'Holtzer, Holtzer,' he rasped. 'Bill Holtzer.'

It was an effort, but I revealed no surprise at the sound of the name. 'Who's Holtzer?'

He looked at me, his eyes wide. 'You know him! From Vietnam, that's what he told me.'

'What's he doing in Tokyo?'

'He's CIA. Tokyo chief of station.'

Chief of station? Unbelievable. He obviously still knew just which asses to kiss.

'You're a damn CIA asset, Benny?'

'I needed the money,' he said, breathing hard.

'Why is he coming after me?' I asked. Holtzer and I had tangled when we were in Vietnam, but he'd come out on top in the end. I couldn't see how he'd still be carrying a grudge, even if I still carried mine.

'He said you know where to find a disk.'

'What disk?'

'I don't know! Holtzer didn't tell me. It's need-to-know.'

'Who's the guy in my apartment with you?'

'What guy . . .' he started to say, but I snapped his windpipe shut before he could finish.

'If you try to lie to me again, Benny, it's going to cost you. Who is the guy in my apartment?'

'He's with the Boeicho Boeikyoku. Holtzer just told me to take him to your apartment so we could question you.'

The Boeicho Boeikyoku is Japan's CIA.

'Why were you following me in Jinbocho?' I asked.

'Surveillance. Trying to locate the disk.'

'How did you find out where I live?'

'Holtzer gave me the address.'

'How did he get it?'

'I don't know. He just gave it to me.'

'What's your involvement?'

'Questions. Just questions. Finding the disk.'

'What were you supposed to do with me after you were done asking me your questions?'

'Nothing. They just want the disk.'

I pinched shut his windpipe again. 'Bullshit, Benny, you knew what was going to happen afterwards.'

It was coming together. I could see it. Holtzer tells Benny to take this Boeikyoku guy to my apartment to 'question' me. The little bureaucrat is scared, but he's caught in the middle. Maybe he rationalises that it's not really his affair. Besides, Mr Boeikyoku would take care of the wet stuff; Benny wouldn't even have to watch.

'OK, Benny,' I said. 'You're going to call your buddy. I know he has a cellphone. Tell him I've been spotted, and he needs to meet you at the station immediately. If I hear you say anything that doesn't fit with that message, I'll kill you. Do it right, and you can go.'

He looked up at me, his eyes pleading. 'You'll let me go?'

'If you do this letter-perfect.' I handed him his phone.

He did it just like I told him to. His voice sounded pretty steady. I took the phone back when he was done. 'I can go now?' he said.

Then he saw my eyes. 'You promised!' he panted. 'Please don't kill me! I was only following orders.' He actually said it.

'Orders are a bitch,' I said. I blasted the knife edge of my hand into the back of his neck. I felt the vertebrae splinter and he slumped to the ground.

I stepped over the body and took a few steps back to a parking area I'd passed. I heard the door to my building slam shut.

The front of the parking area was roped off across posts that were planted in sand. I grabbed a fistful of sand and returned to my position at the corner of the wall, peeking out past the edge. I didn't see Benny's buddy. Shit, he'd made a right down the narrow alley connecting my street with the one parallel to it. I had expected him to stick to the main roads. This was a problem. He was ahead of me now, and there was nowhere I could set up for him and wait. Besides, I didn't even know what he looked like. If he made it to the main artery by the station, I wouldn't be able to separate him from all the other people. It had to be now.

I sprinted down my street, pulled up short at the alley and saw a solitary figure walking away from me. I scanned the ground, looking for a weapon. Nothing the right size for a club. Too bad.

I turned into the alley, about seven yards behind him. He was wearing a waist-length leather jacket and had a squat, powerful build. Even from behind, I could see that his neck was massive. He was carrying something with him—a cane, it looked like. Not good. The sand had better do the trick.

I had closed the gap to about three yards when he looked back over his shoulder. This guy had sensitive antennae.

He turned and faced me, and I could see the confusion in his expression. Benny had said I'd been spotted at the station. I was coming from the other direction.

I saw his ears, puffed out like cauliflowers, disfigured from repeated blows. Japanese *kendoka* don't believe in protective gear; practitioners wear their scarred lobes, which they develop from bamboo sword blows in kendo, like badges of honour. Awareness of his possible skills registered at some level of my consciousness.

I moved to the left, took two more steps. Caught the recognition hardening on his face. Saw the cane start to come up in slow motion, his left foot driving forward to add power to the blow.

I flung the sand in his face and leapt aside. His head recoiled but the cane kept coming up; a split second later it snapped down in a blur. Despite the power of the blow he brought it up short when it failed to connect with his target, and then, with the same fluid speed, he cut through the air horizontally. I moved back diagonally, off the line of attack, staying on my toes. I could see him grimacing, his eyes squeezed shut. The sand had hit him squarely. He couldn't see. He could tell I was in front of him but he didn't know where.

He held his position, his nostrils flaring as though he was trying to catch my scent. *How is he keeping himself from wiping his eyes?* I thought. *He must be in agony*.

With a loud *kiyai* he leapt forward, slashing horizontally at waist level. But I was further back. Just as suddenly, he took two long steps backwards, his left hand coming loose from the cane and desperately wiping at his eyes.

That's what I'd been waiting for. I plunged in, raising my right fist for a hammer blow, but at the last instant he shifted slightly, his trapezius muscles taking the impact. Before I could get in another blow, he had whipped the cane round behind me and grabbed it with his free hand. Then he yanked me into him with a bear hug, the cane slicing into my back. He arched backwards and my feet left the ground. Pain exploded in my kidneys.

I fought the urge to force myself away, knowing I couldn't match his strength. Instead, I wrapped my arms round his neck and swung my legs up behind his back. The move surprised him and he lost his balance.

He took a step backwards, releasing the cane. I crossed my legs behind his back and dropped my weight suddenly, forcing him to pitch forwards. We hit the ground hard. I was underneath and took most of the impact. But now we were in my parlour.

I grabbed a cross grip on the lapels of his jacket and slammed in *gyaku-jujime*, one of the first strangles a *judoka* learns. He reacted instantly, going for my eyes. I whipped my head back and forth, trying to avoid his fingers, using my legs to control his torso.

The choke wasn't perfect. I had more windpipe than carotid, and he fought for a long time. But there was nothing he could do. I kept the grip even after he had stopped struggling, rotating my head to see if anyone was coming. Nobody. I released the grip and kicked out from under him. I stood up, my back screaming from the cane, my breath heaving in and out in ragged gasps.

I knew from long experience that he wasn't dead. People black out from strangles in the *dojo* with some regularity; if the unconsciousness is deep, like this, then you need to do a little CPR to get them breathing again. This guy was going to have to find someone else to jump-start his battery. I would have liked to have questioned him, but this was no Benny.

I squatted down and went through his pockets. Found a cellphone and the pepper spray. Other than that I came up empty.

I stood up, pulses of pain shooting through my back, and started walking towards my apartment. Two schoolgirls in their blue sailor uniforms were passing just as I emerged from the alley. Their mouths dropped when they saw me, but I ignored them. Why were they staring like that? I reached up with my hand and felt the wetness on my cheek. I was bleeding. He'd scratched the hell out of my face.

I walked to my building as quickly as I could, wincing as I went up the two flights of steps. I let myself in, then wet a facecloth at the bathroom basin and wiped the blood off my face. The image staring back at me from the mirror looked bad.

The apartment felt strange. It had always been a haven, now it had been exposed by Holtzer and the Agency—two ghosts from a past I thought I'd left behind. I needed to know why they were after me. Professional? Personal? With Holtzer, probably both.

I grabbed the things I needed and shoved them into a bag, turning once to glance around before leaving. Everything looked the same as always. I wondered when I would see the place again. I headed back to Midori. Maybe the cellphones would provide some clues.

BY THE TIME I reached the hotel, the pain in my back had become a dull throbbing. My left eye was swollen—he'd got a finger in there at one point—and my head ached.

I knocked on the door so Midori would know I was coming and then let myself in with the key.

She was sitting on the bed, and jumped when she saw my swollen eye and the scratches on my face. 'What happened?' she gasped, and the concern in her voice warmed me.

'Someone was waiting for me at my apartment,' I said. I let my coat fall off my back and eased myself onto the couch. 'It looks like we're both pretty popular lately.'

She knelt down next to me, her eyes searching my face. 'Your eye looks bad. Let me get you some ice.'

I watched her walk away from me. She was wearing jeans and a navy sweatshirt and I had a nice view of the proportions of her shoulders and waist, the curve of her hips.

She came back with some ice in a towel and I shifted on the couch, electric pain jolting through my back. She knelt down and held the ice against my eye, smoothing my hair back at the same time.

She eased me back on the couch and I grimaced, intensely aware of how near she was. 'Does that hurt?' she asked, her touch instantly becoming tentative.

'No, it's OK. The guy who cut up my face hit me in the back with a cane. It'll be OK.'

Midori held the ice against my eye, her free hand warm on the side of my head, while I sat stiffly, afraid to move and embarrassed at my reaction. The moment spun slowly out.

At one point she shifted the ice, and I reached to take it from her, but she continued to hold it and my hand wound up covering hers. The back of her hand was warm against my palm, the ice cold on my fingertips. 'That feels good,' I told her. She didn't ask whether I meant the ice or her hand. I wasn't sure myself.

'You were gone for a long time,' she said after a while. 'I didn't know what to do. I was going to call you, but then I was starting to think, maybe you and those men in my apartment set this up, to get me to trust you.'

'I can imagine how this must all seem to you.'

'It was starting to seem pretty unreal, actually. Until I saw you again.'

I looked at the towel, now speckled red where it had been pressed against my face. 'Nothing like a little blood to make things seem real.'

She pressed the towel against my face again. 'Tell me what happened.'

'You don't have anything to eat here, do you?' I asked. 'I'm starving.'

She reached for a bag beside the couch. 'I brought back some *bento*.'

I started wolfing down rice balls, eggs and vegetables. I washed it all down with a can of fruit juice. It tasted great.

When I was finished, I shifted on the couch so I could see her better. 'There were two of them at my apartment,' I said. 'An LDP flunky I know only as Benny. Turns out he's connected to the CIA. Would that mean anything to you? Any connection to your father?'

She shook her head. 'My father never said anything about a Benny or about the CIA.'

'OK. The other guy was a *kendoka*—he had a cane. I don't know what the connection is. I managed to get both their cellphones. Maybe it'll give me a clue who he is.'

I took the ice from her with one hand and leaned across the couch to reach my coat. I pulled the coat over, reached into the inside breast pocket and pulled out the phones. 'Benny told me the Agency is after the disk. I don't know why they're coming after me, though. Maybe they think I can prevent them from getting what they want.'

I flipped open the *kendoka*'s phone and pressed the recall button. A number lit up on the screen. 'This is a start. We can do a reverse phone number search. I've got a friend who can help us with this.'

I stood up, wincing. 'We need to change hotels. Can't behave any differently from the other patrons.'

She smiled. 'I suppose that's true.'

We changed to a nearby place called the Morocco, which seemed to be organised around some sort of Arabian Nights theme. It was the picture of Bedouin luxury, but there was only one bed, and sleeping on the couch was going to be like a night on the rack.

'Why don't you take the bed tonight?' she said, reading my mind.

I wound up accepting her offer, but my sleep was restless. I dreamed I was moving though dense jungle in southern Laos, hunted by a North Vietnamese Army counter-recon battalion. I had become separated from my team and was disorientated. The NVA had me surrounded, and I knew I was going to be captured and tortured. Then Midori was there. 'I don't want to be captured,' she was saying. 'Take the gun. Don't worry about me. Save my Montagnards.'

I snapped upright, my body coiled like a spring. *Easy, John. Just a dream.* I forced a long hiss of air out through my nostrils, feeling like Crazy Jake was right there in the room with me.

My face was wet and I thought it was bleeding again, but when I put my hand to my cheek I realised it was tears. *What the hell is this?*

Moonlight flowed in through the window. Midori was sitting up on the couch, her knees drawn to her chest. 'Bad dream?' she asked.

'How long have you been up?'

She shrugged. 'A while. You were tossing and turning.'

'I say anything?'

'No. Are you afraid of what you might say in your sleep?'

I looked at her, one side of her face illuminated by moonlight, the other hidden in shadow. 'Yes,' I said.

'What was the dream?' she asked.

'I don't know,' I said, lying. 'Mostly just images.'

I could feel her looking at me. 'You tell me to trust you,' she said, 'but you won't even tell me about a bad dream.'

I started to answer, then all at once felt irritated with her. I slid off the bed and walked over to the bathroom.

I don't need to take care of her, I thought. *Holtzer knows I'm in Tokyo, knows where I live. I've got enough problems.*

She was the key. Her father must have told her something. Or she had what whoever had broken into his apartment had been looking for. I walked back into the bedroom. 'Midori, you've got to try harder. Your father must have told you something or given you something.'

I saw surprise on her face. 'I told you, he didn't.'

'Someone broke into his apartment after he died. They couldn't find what they were looking for, and they think you have it.'

'Listen, if you want to take a look around my father's apartment, I can let you in.'

The people who had broken in had come up empty, and my old friend Tatsu had been there afterwards. I knew another look would be a dead end.

'That's not going to help. What would these people think that you have? The disk? Are you sure you don't have anything?'

I saw her redden slightly. 'I told you, I don't.'

'Well, try to remember something, can't you?'

'No, I can't,' she said, her voice angry. 'How can I remember something if I don't have it?'

'How can you be sure you don't have it if you can't remember it?'

'Why are you saying this? Why don't you believe me?'

'Because nothing else makes sense! And I don't like people trying to kill me when I don't even know why!'

She stood up. 'Do you think I like it? I didn't do anything! And I don't know why these people are doing this, either!'

I exhaled slowly, trying to rein in my anger. 'It's because they think you have the damn disk. Or you know where it is.'

'Well, I don't! I don't know anything!'

We stood staring at each other, breathing hard. Then she said, 'You don't give a shit about me.'

'That's not true.'

'It is true! I've had enough! You won't even tell me who you are!' She picked up a bag, started shoving her things into it.

'Midori, listen to me.' I grabbed the bag. 'I do care about you!'

'Why should I believe what you say when you don't believe me? I don't know anything!'

I yanked the bag out of her hands. 'All right, I believe you.'

'Like hell you do. Give me my case. Give it to me!' She tried to grab it and I moved it behind my back.

She looked at me, her eyes briefly incredulous, then started hitting me in the chest. I dropped the bag and wrapped my arms around her to stop the blows.

Later, I couldn't remember exactly how it happened. She was fighting me and I was trying to hold her arms. I became very aware of the feel of her body and then we were kissing.

We made love on the floor at the foot of the bed. The sex was passionate, headlong. At times it was like we were still fighting. My back was throbbing, but the pain was almost sweet.

Afterwards I reached up and pulled the bedcovers over us. We sat with our backs against the edge of the bed.

'*Yokatta*,' she said, drawing out the last syllable. 'That was good. Better than you deserved.'

I felt a little dazed. It had been a long time for me, a connection like that. It was almost unnerving.

'But you don't trust me,' she went on. 'That hurts.'

'It's not trust, Midori. It's . . .' I said, then stopped. 'I believe you. I'm sorry for pushing so hard.'

'I'm talking about your dream.'

I pressed my fingertips to my eyes. 'Midori, I can't.' I didn't know what to say. 'I don't talk about these things.'

She reached over and gently prised my fingertips from my eyes. 'You need to talk,' she said. 'I want you to tell me.'

I looked down at the tangled sheets and blankets. 'My mother was a Catholic. When I was a kid, she used to take me to church. I used to go to confession and tell the priest all my lascivious thoughts, the fights I'd been in, the kids I hated. At first it was like pulling teeth, but then it got addictive. But that was before the war. In the war, I did things . . . that are beyond confession.'

'If you keep them bottled up like this, they'll eat you like poison.'

I wanted to talk to her. I wanted to let it out.

What's with you? I thought. *Do you want to drive her away?*

Maybe that would be best. I couldn't tell her about her father, but I could tell her something worse. When I spoke, my voice was dry and steady. 'I'm talking about atrocities.'

'I don't know what you did,' she said, 'but I know it was a long time ago. In another world.'

I pressed my fingertips to my eyes again, the reflex useless against the images playing in my mind.

'A part of me loved operating in the North Vietnamese Army's back yard, not everybody could do that. I had over twenty missions in Indian country. People would say I had used up all my luck, but I just kept going.

'I was one of the youngest One-Zeros—SOG team leaders—ever. My teammates and I were tight. We could be twelve guys against an NVA division, and I knew that not one of my people would run. And they knew I wouldn't either. Do you know what that's like for a kid who's been ostracised because he's a half-breed?'

I talked faster. 'I don't care who you are. If you wade that deeply into the muck, you won't stay clean. Eventually everyone goes over the edge. Your people are blown in half by a Bouncing Betty mine. You're holding what's left of them, in the last moment of their lives, telling them, "It's going to be OK," they're crying and you're crying and then they're dead. You walk away, you're covered with their insides.

'You take more losses, and the frustration—the rage, the strangling, muscle-bunching rage—just builds and builds. And then one day, you're moving through a village with the power of life and death slung over your shoulder, sweeping back and forth, muzzle forward. You're in a declared free-fire zone, meaning anyone who isn't a confirmed friendly is assumed to be Vietcong and treated accordingly. And intel tells you this village is a hotbed of V.C. activity, they're feeding half the sector, they're a conduit for arms that are flowing south down the Trail. The people are giving you sullen looks, and some mama-san says, "Hey, Joe, you fuck mommie, you number ten," some shit like that. And two hours earlier you lost another buddy to a booby trap. Believe me, someone is going to pay.' I took two deep breaths. 'Tell me to stop, or I'm going to keep going.'

Midori was silent.

'The village was called Cu Lai. We herded all the people together, maybe forty or fifty, including women and children. We burned their homes down, shot all their farm animals. Catharsis. But it wasn't cathartic enough. Now what are we supposed to do with these people?

'The guy on the other end of the radio, I still don't know who, says, "Waste 'em." This was the way we described killing back then—so and so got wasted.

'I'm quiet, and the guy says again, "Waste 'em." Now it's one thing to be on the brink of hot-blooded murder, it's another to have the impulse coolly sanctioned higher up the chain of command. Suddenly I'm scared. I say, "Waste who?" He says, "All of 'em. Everybody." I say, "We're talking about fifty people here, women and children, too." The guy says again, "Just waste 'em." "Can I have your name and rank?" I say, because I'm not going to kill all these people just because a voice over the radio tells me to. "Son," the voice says, "you are in a declared free-fire zone. Now do as I say."

'I told him I wouldn't do it without being able to verify his authority. Then two more people, who claimed to be this guy's superiors, got on the radio. One of them says, "You have been given a direct order under the authority of the Commander in Chief of the United States Armed Forces. Obey this order or suffer the consequences."

'So I went back to the rest of the unit guarding the villagers. I told them what I had just heard. For most of the guys, it had the same effect it had on me: it cooled them down. But some of them were excited. "No way," they were saying. "They're *telling* us to waste 'em? Far out." Still, everyone was hesitating.

'I had a friend who everyone called Crazy Jake. All of a sudden he says, "Waste 'em means waste 'em." He starts yelling at the villagers. "Get down, everybody on the ground!" And the villagers complied. Jimmy doesn't even slow down, he shoulders his rifle, then *ka-pop!*

ka-pop! he starts shooting them. It was weird; no one tried to run away. Then one of the other guys shoulders his rifle, too. The next thing I knew we were all unloading our clips into these people, just blowing them apart.'

My voice was still steady, my eyes fixed straight ahead, remembering. 'If I could go back in time, I would try to stop it. I really would. And the memories dog me. I've been running for twenty-five years, but in the end, it's like trying to lose a shadow.'

I imagined her thinking, *I slept with a monster.*

'I wish you hadn't told me,' she said, confirming my suspicions.

I shrugged, feeling empty. 'Maybe it's better you know.'

She shook her head. 'That's not what I meant. It's an upsetting story. Upsetting to hear what you've been through. I never thought of war as so . . . personal.'

'Oh, it was personal. On both sides. There were special medals for NVA who killed an American. A severed head was the proof.'

She touched my face and I saw a deep sympathy in her eyes. 'You were right. You've been through horrors.'

'I didn't even tell you the best part. The intel on the village being a V.C. stronghold? Bogus. No tunnel networks, no rice or weapons caches. Not even any telltale tyre tracks, which we could have taken a second to check for before we started slaughtering people.'

'But you were so young. You must have been out of your minds with fear.'

I could feel her looking at me. It was OK. After all this time, the words sounded dead to me, just sounds without content.

She said, 'I have a friend named Mika. When I was in New York, she had a car accident. She hit a little girl who was playing in the street. Mika was driving at thirty miles per hour, the speed limit, and the little girl drove her bicycle out right in front of the car. There was nothing she could do. It was bad luck. It would have happened to anyone who was driving the car right there and right then.'

On a certain level, I understood what she was getting at. I'd known it all along, even before the psych evaluation they made me take at one point to see how I was handling the special stress of SOG. The shrink they made me talk to had said the same thing: 'How can you blame yourself for circumstances that were beyond your control?'

I remember that conversation. I remember listening to his bullshit, half angry, half amused at his attempts to draw me out. Finally, I just said, 'Have you ever killed anyone, Doc?' When he didn't answer, I walked out. I don't know what kind of evaluation he gave me but they didn't turn me loose from SOG. That came later.

'Do you still work with these people?' she asked.

'There are connections,' I responded.

'Why?' she asked after a moment. 'Why stay attached to things that give you nightmares?'

'It's a hard thing to explain,' I said slowly. I watched her hair glistening in the pale light, like a vertical sheet of water. I ran my fingers through it. 'After the war, I found I couldn't go back to the life I'd left behind. I wanted to come back to Asia, because Asia was where my ghosts were least restless, but it was more than just geography. All the things I'd done were justified by war. So I needed to stay at war.'

'But you can't stay at war for ever, John.'

'A shark can't stop swimming, or it dies.'

'You're not a shark.'

'I don't know what I am.'

We were quiet for a while, and I felt a pleasant drowsiness descend. I was going to regret all this. Some lucid part of my mind saw that clearly. But what was done was already done.

I slept, but the pain in my back kept the sleep fitful, and in those moments where consciousness briefly crested I would have doubted everything that had happened if she hadn't been lying next to me. Then I would slide down into sleep again, there to struggle with ghosts even more terrible than those which I had revealed to Midori.

PART TWO

The next morning I was sitting with my back to the wall in Las Chicas, waiting for Franklin Bulfinch to show himself.

It was a crisp, sunny morning, and I felt comfortable in my light-disguise Oakley shades, which I had picked up en route.

Midori was safely ensconced in the music section of the Spiral Building, close enough to meet Bulfinch quickly if necessary but far enough to be safe if things got hairy. She had called Bulfinch less than an hour earlier to arrange things. Most likely he was a legitimate reporter and would come to the meeting alone, but I saw no advantage in giving him time to deploy additional forces if I was mistaken.

Bulfinch was easy to spot as he approached the restaurant. He was wearing jeans and tennis shoes, dressed up with a blue blazer. He crossed the patio and stepped inside the restaurant proper, searching for Midori. His eyes passed over me without recognition.

He wandered in the direction of the separate dining space in the back. I knew he'd return in a moment, and used the time to watch the street. He'd been followed at Alfie, and it was possible that he was being followed now.

The street was still empty when Bulfinch returned a minute later. His eyes swept the space again. When they were pointed in my direction, I said quietly, 'Mr Bulfinch.'

He looked at me for a second. 'Do I know you?'

'I'm a friend of Kawamura Midori.'

'Is she coming?'

'That depends on whether I decide that it's safe.'

'Who are you?'

'As I said, a friend, interested in the same thing you are.'

'Which is?'

I looked at him through my shades. 'The disk.'

He paused before saying, 'I don't know about a disk.'

Right. 'You were expecting Midori's father to deliver you a disk when he died on the Yamanote three weeks ago. He didn't have it with him, so you followed up with Midori after her performance at Alfie the following Friday. You met her in the Starbucks on Gaienhigashi-dori, where you told her about the disk, because you hoped she might have it. You wouldn't tell her what's on the disk because you were afraid doing so would compromise her. Although you had already compromised her because you were followed. All of which will be sufficient, I hope, to establish my bona fides.'

He made no move to sit down. 'You could have learned most of that without Midori telling you.'

'And then I imitated her voice and called you an hour ago?'

He hesitated, then sat down. 'All right. What can you tell me?'

'I was going to ask you the same question.'

'Look, I'm a reporter. Do you have information for me?'

'Mr Bulfinch,' I said, 'the people who want that disk think that Midori has it, and they are willing to kill her to retrieve it. Your meeting her at Alfie, while you were being watched, is probably what put her in the danger she's in.'

He sighed. 'Assuming for a moment there is a disk, I don't see how knowledge of what's on it would help Midori.'

'I assume you would be interested in publishing the hypothetical disk's contents?'

'You could assume that, yes.'

'And I would also assume that certain people would want to prevent that publication?'

'That would also be a safe assumption.'

'OK. It's the threat of publication that's making these people target Midori. Once the contents of the disk are published, Midori would no longer be a threat. It seems we want the same thing.'

He shifted in his seat. 'I see your point. But I'm not going to be comfortable talking about this unless I see Midori.'

I considered for a moment. I pulled out a pen and small sheet of paper and started jotting down instructions. My gut told me he wasn't wired, but no one's gut is infallible.

My note read: *We'll walk out of the restaurant together. When we step outside, stop so I can pat you down for weapons. After that, go where I motion you to go. At some point I'll tell you where we're going. Starting now, do not say a word unless I speak first.*

I extended the note to him. When he was done reading, he pushed it across the table to me and nodded.

We got up and walked outside. I patted him down and was unsurprised to find that he was clean. As we moved down the street I was careful to keep him slightly in front of me. My head swept back and forth, looking for someone who might have followed Bulfinch and then set up to wait outside.

As we walked I called out 'left' or 'right' from behind him and we made our way to the Spiral Building. We walked into the music section, where Midori was waiting.

'Kawamura-san,' he said, bowing, when he saw her.

'Thank you for coming to meet me,' Midori replied. 'I'm afraid I wasn't completely candid with you when we met for coffee. I'm not as ignorant of my father's affiliations as I led you to believe. But I don't know anything about the disk you mentioned.'

'I'm not sure what I can do for you, then,' he said.

'Tell us what's on the disk,' I replied. 'Right now we're running blind. If we put our heads together, we've got a much better chance of retrieving the disk.'

'Please, Mr Bulfinch,' Midori said. 'I barely escaped being killed a few days ago by whoever is trying to find that disk. I need your help.'

Bulfinch looked at Midori and then at me. 'All right,' he said after a moment. 'Two months ago your father contacted me. He told me he read my column for *Forbes*. He told me who he was and said he wanted to help. A classic whistle-blower.'

Midori turned to me. 'That was about the time he was diagnosed.'

'I'm sorry?' Bulfinch asked.

'Lung cancer. He had just learned that he had little time to live.'

Bulfinch nodded. 'I didn't know that. I'm sorry.'

Midori bowed her head briefly. 'Please, go on.'

'Over the course of the next month your father briefed me extensively on corruption in the Construction Ministry and its role as broker between the Liberal Democratic Party and the *yakuza*. These briefings provided me with invaluable insight into the extent of corruption in Japanese society. But I needed corroboration.'

'Couldn't you just print it and attribute it to "a senior source in the Construction Ministry"?' I asked.

'Ordinarily,' Bulfinch replied. 'But there were two problems. Kawamura's position gave him unique access to the information he was providing. If we had published, we might as well have used his name in the by-line.'

'And the second problem?' Midori asked.

'Impact. We've already run a half-dozen exposés on the kind of corruption Kawamura was involved in. The Japanese press resolutely refuses to pick them up because the corporations provide over half the media's advertising revenues. So if a newspaper runs an article that offends a politician, the politician calls his contacts at the relevant corporations, who pull their advertising and the offending paper goes bankrupt. You see? No one here takes chances; Japan's press is the most docile in the world.'

'But with proof?' I asked.

'Hard proof would change everything. The papers would be forced to cover the story or else reveal that they are nothing but tools of the government. We could start a virtuous cycle that would lead to a change in Japanese politics.'

'The proof,' I said. 'What was it?'

Bulfinch looked at me. 'I don't know exactly. Only that it's hard evidence. Incontrovertible.'

'It sounds like that disk should go to the Keisatsucho, not the press,' Midori said, referring to Tatsu's organisation.

'Your father wouldn't have lasted a day if he'd handed that information over to the feds,' I said.

'Ever hear of Honma Tadayo?' Bulfinch said.

Midori shook her head.

'When Nippon Credit Bank went bankrupt in 1998,' Bulfinch went on, 'much of its one-hundred-and-thirty-three-billion-dollar loan portfolio had gone bad. The bad loans were linked to the under-world. To clean up the mess, a consortium of rescuers hired Honma Tadayo, the respected former director of the Bank of Japan.

'Honma lasted two weeks. He was found hanged in an Osaka hotel room. His body was cremated, without an autopsy, and the police ruled the death a suicide without even conducting an investigation.

'And Honma wasn't an isolated event. His death was the seventh "suicide" among ranking Japanese either investigating financial irregularities or due to testify since 1997, when the depth of bad loans affecting banks like Nippon Credit first started coming to light. Not one of these seven cases resulted in so much as a homicide investigation. The powers that be in this country don't allow it.'

I thought of Tatsu and his conspiracy theories, my eyes unblinking behind my shades.

'There are rumours of a special outfit within the *yakuza*,' Bulfinch said, 'specialists in "natural causes", who force victims to write wills at gunpoint, inject them with sedatives, then strangle them in a way that makes it appear that the victim committed suicide by hanging.'

'Have you found any substance to the rumours?' I asked.

'Not yet. But where there's smoke, there's fire. And I'll tell you something else. As bad as the problems are in the banks, the Construction Ministry is worse. Construction is by far the biggest contributor to the LDP. If you want to dig this country's corruption out by the roots, construction is the place to start. Your father was a brave man, Midori.'

'I know,' she said.

I wondered if she still assumed the heart attack had been natural.

'I've told you what I know,' Bulfinch said. 'Now it's your turn.'

I looked at him. 'Can you think of any reason why Kawamura would have not brought the disk?'

'No. This was the morning Kawamura was going to deliver the goods.'

'Maybe he couldn't download whatever he was going to down-load, and that's why he was coming up empty-handed.'

'No. He told me over the phone the day before that he had it.'

I felt a flash of insight. 'Midori, where did your father live?' Of course I already knew, but couldn't let her know that.

'Shibuya.'

I turned to Bulfinch. 'Where was Kawamura getting on the train that morning?'

'Shibuya JR Station.'

'I've got a hunch I'm going to follow up on. I'll call you if it pans out.'

'Wait just a minute . . .' he started to say.

'You're going to have to trust me,' I said. 'I think I can find that disk.' I started to move towards the door.

He took me by the arm. 'I'll go with you.'

I looked at his hand. After a moment it drifted back to his side.

'I want you to walk out of here,' I told him. 'Head in the direction of Omotesandro-dori. I'm going to take Midori someplace safe and follow up on my hunch. I'll be in touch.'

He looked at Midori, clearly at a loss.

'It's all right,' she said. 'We want the same thing you do.'

'I don't suppose I have much choice,' he said.

'Remember,' I said, gesturing to the street. 'Head in the direction of Omotesandro-dori. I'll be in touch soon.'

'You'd better be,' he said. He took a step closer and looked through the shades and into my eyes. I had to admire his balls. 'You just better.' He gave a nod to Midori and walked out.

Midori looked at me and asked, 'What's your hunch?'

'Later,' I said, watching him. 'We need to move now, before he gets a chance to double back and follow one of us.'

We flagged a cab heading in the direction of Shibuya. I could see Bulfinch, still walking in the other direction, as we drove away.

We got out and separated at Shibuya JR Station. Midori headed back to the hotel while I made my way up Dogenzaka—where Harry and I had followed Kawamura the morning he died, and where, if my hunch was right, he had ditched the disk.

I was thinking about Kawamura, about his behaviour that morning, about what must have been going on in his mind. More than anything else he's scared. Today's the day; he's got the disk that's going to flush all the rats out in the open. But he knows it will cost him his few remaining days if he's caught with it. In less than an hour he'll meet Bulfinch and unload the damn thing.

What if I'm being followed right now? he would think. He stops to light a cigarette, turns and scans the street.

Someone behind him looks suspicious. Why not? When you're hopped up on fear, the whole world is transformed. Every guy in a suit looks like a government assassin.

Get rid of the damn thing, and let Bulfinch retrieve it himself. Anywhere at all . . . the Higashimura fruit store, that'll do.

I stopped outside the store. If he had unloaded it on his way to see Bulfinch, this was the place.

I walked in. The proprietor acknowledged me then went back to reading his paper. The store was small, and the proprietor had a view of the whole place. Kawamura would have been able to hide the disk only in places where a patron could acceptably put his hands. It would only need to stay hidden for an hour or so, anyway, so he didn't have to find an incredibly secure spot.

Which meant it was probably already gone, I realised. But it was worth a try. Apples. I had seen an apple rolling out of the train as the doors had closed. I imagined Kawamura examining the apples, slipping the disk under them as he did so. I walked over and looked in the bin. It was only a few apples deep and easy to search. No disk. Shit. I repeated the drill with the adjacent pears, then the tangerines. Nothing. Damn it. I had been so sure.

I was going to have to buy something. I was obviously a discriminating buyer, looking for something special.

'Could you put together a small selection as a gift?' I asked the owner. 'Maybe a half-dozen pieces of fruit?'

'*Kashikomarimashita*,' he answered. Right away.

In the five minutes during which the proprietor was preoccupied with my request, I was able to check every place to which Kawamura would have had access that morning. It was useless.

The proprietor was just about finished. He pulled out a green moiré ribbon and wrapped it round the box he had used. It was actually a nice gift. Maybe Midori would enjoy it. I took out some notes and handed them over. He slowly counted out my change.

I waited for him to finish, then said, 'I know it's not likely, but a friend of mine lost a CD in here a week or so ago and asked me to check to see if anyone had found it. It's so unlikely but . . .'

'*Un*,' he grunted, kneeling down behind the counter. He stood up a moment later, a plastic box in his hand. 'I wondered whether anyone would claim this.' He handed it to me.

'Thank you,' I said, not a little bit surprised.

I FOLLOWED A SERIES of alleys that more or less paralleled Meiji-dori, the main artery connecting Shibuya and Aoyama. I had got up at first light, easing out of the bed as quietly as I could to let Midori sleep. She had woken anyway.

I had already taken the disk to Akihabara, Tokyo's electronics mecca, where I tried to play it on a PC in one of the enormous computer stores. No dice. It was encrypted.

Which meant that I needed Harry's help. The realisation wasn't comfortable: given Bulfinch's description of its contents—that it contained evidence of an assassin specialising in natural causes—I knew that what was on the disk could implicate me.

I called Harry from a payphone, using our usual code to tell him that I wanted to meet at the Doutor coffee shop in Roppongi. It was near his apartment, so he would be able to get there fast.

He was already waiting when I arrived twenty minutes later. He looked pale. 'Sorry to get you up,' I said.

He shook his head. 'What happened to your face?'

'You should see the other guy. Let's order some breakfast.'

'I'll just have coffee.'

'Sounds like it was a rough night.'

He looked at me. 'You're scaring me with the small talk. You wouldn't have used the code unless it was serious.'

'You wouldn't forgive me for getting you up otherwise,' I said.

We ordered coffee and breakfast and I filled him in on everything that had happened, beginning with how I met Midori, through the attack outside her apartment and then mine, the meeting with Bulfinch, the disk. I told him we were using a love hotel as a safe house. Looking at him there, I realised I trusted him. Not just because I knew that, operationally, he had no way to hurt me, but because he was worthy of trust. And because I wanted to trust him.

'I could use your help,' I told him. 'But you're going to need to know some fairly deep background. If that's not comfortable for you, all you need to do is say so.'

He reddened and I knew it would mean a lot to him that I needed him. 'It's comfortable,' he said.

I told him about Holtzer and Benny, the apparent CIA connection.

'I wish you'd told me earlier,' he said. 'I might have been able to help.'

'Just being careful, kid,' I said. 'It's nothing personal.'

'You saved my butt that time in Roppongi, remember? You think I'd forget that?'

'You'd be surprised what people forget.'

'Not me. Anyway, has it occurred to you how much I'm trusting you by letting you share this information with me, letting you make me a point of vulnerability? I know what you're capable of.'

'I'm not sure I understand what you mean,' I said.

He looked at me for a long time before he responded. 'I've kept your secrets for a long time. I'll continue to keep them.'

Never underestimate Harry, I thought. 'Now, enough of the I'm-OK-you're-OK routine. Let's work the problem. Start with Holtzer.'

'Tell me more about him.'

'I knew him in Vietnam. He was with the Agency then, attached to Special Operations Group. He wasn't afraid to go into the field, unlike some of the other bean counters I worked with out there. I liked that about him but even then he was nothing but a careerist. The first time we locked horns was after an ARVN—Army of the Republic of Vietnam, the South's army—operation. The ARVN had mortared the shit out of a suspected Vietcong base, based on intelligence from a source that Holtzer had developed. We were involved in the body count, as a way of verifying the intelligence.

'It was hard to identify the bodies—there were pieces everywhere. But there were no weapons. I told Holtzer this didn't look like Vietcong activity to me. He says, What are you talking about? Everyone here is Vietcong. I say, Come on, there aren't any weapons, your source was jerking you off.

'Back at base, he writes up his report and asks me to verify it. I told him to fuck off. There were a couple officers nearby. It got heated, and I wound up laying him out. The officers saw it, which is exactly what Holtzer had wanted, although I don't think he bargained for the rhinoplasty he needed afterwards. Ordinarily that kind of thing wouldn't have aroused much attention, but at the time there was some sensitivity to the way Special Forces and the CIA were cooperating in the field, and Holtzer knew how to work the bureaucracy. He made it sound like I wouldn't verify his report because I had a personal problem with him.'

I took a swallow of coffee. 'He caused a lot of problems for me after that. When I got back from the war I had some kind of black cloud over me, and I always knew he was the one behind it.'

'You never told me about what happened in the States after the war,' Harry said. 'Is that why you left?'

'Part of it.' I didn't want to go there.

Harry understood. 'What about Benny?' he asked.

'He was connected to the LDP—an errand boy, but trusted with some important errands. Apparently he was also a mole for the CIA.'

The word *mole* is still one of the foulest epithets I know. For six years, SOG's operations were compromised by a mole. Time and again, a team would be inserted successfully, only to be picked up in minutes. Some of these missions had been death traps but others were successful, which meant that the mole had limited access. An investigator could have quickly narrowed down the list of suspects.

But MACV—US Military Assistance Command, Vietnam—were

afraid of insulting the South Vietnamese government by suggesting that a South Vietnamese national might have been unreliable. Worse, SOG was ordered to continue to share its data with the ARVN.

In 1972, a traitorous ARVN corporal was uncovered, but this single, low-level agent couldn't have been the only source of damage for all those years. The real mole was never discovered.

I handed Benny's and the *kendoka*'s cellphones to Harry. 'Check out the numbers that have been called. See if there are any speed-dial numbers programmed, too, and try chasing them all down with a reverse directory. I want to know who these guys were talking to, how they were connected to each other and to the Agency.'

'No problem,' he said.

'Good. Now—' I took out the disk. 'What everybody is after is on this disk. Bulfinch says it's an exposé on corruption in the LDP and the Construction Ministry that could bring down the government.'

He held it up to the light. 'Why a disk?' he said. 'It would have been easier to move whatever's on here over the Net. Maybe a copy management program prevented that. I'll check it out.' He slipped it inside his jacket.

'Could that be how they knew we were onto Kawamura?' I asked. 'How they found out that he'd made the disk?'

'Could be. There are programs that will tell you if a copy has been made.'

'It's encrypted. Why would Kawamura have encrypted it?'

'I doubt he did. He probably wasn't supposed to have access. Whoever he took it from would have encrypted it.'

That made sense. 'OK,' I said. 'Page me when you're done. We'll meet back here. Use the usual code.'

He got up to leave. 'Harry,' I said. 'Don't be cocky now. There are people who would kill you to get that disk back.'

He nodded. 'I'll be careful.'

'Careful's not good enough. Be paranoid. Don't trust anyone.'

After he'd left I called Midori from a payphone. We had switched to a new hotel that morning. She answered on the first ring.

'When are you coming?'

'I'm on my way now.'

'Do me a favour, get me something to read. There's nothing to do in this room and I'm going crazy.'

Her tone was less strained than it had been when I first told her I had found the disk. She had wanted to know how, and I wouldn't tell her. Obviously couldn't.

'I was retained by a party that wanted it,' I finally said.

'Who was the party?' she had insisted.

'Doesn't matter,' was my response. 'If I wanted to give it to the party that paid me to find it, I wouldn't be here with it right now, discussing it with you. That's all I'm going to say.'

Not knowing my world, she had no reason to doubt that Kawamura's heart attack had been due to something other than natural causes. If it had been anything other than that—a bullet, even a fall from a tall building—I knew I would be suspect.

I headed to Suidobashi, where I began a thorough SDR by catching the JR line. I changed trains at Yoyogi and let two trains pass before I got back on. One stop later I exited at the east end of Shinjuku Station. I was still wearing shades to hide my swollen eye, and the dark tint gave the frenzied crowds a ghostly look. I let the mob carry me through one of the mazelike underground shopping arcades, then fought my way to the Isetan Department Store. I decided to buy Midori an oversized navy scarf and a pair of wraparound sunglasses that I thought would change the shape of her face.

Finally, I stopped at Kinokuniya, where I picked up a couple of magazines and a novel. I was waiting in line when my pager starting vibrating in my pocket. I pulled it out, expecting to see a code from Harry. Instead the display showed an eight-digit number with a Tokyo prefix. I paid for the magazines and the book then walked to a payphone. I punched in the number, glancing over my shoulder while the connection went through.

'John Rain,' a voice said on the other end. I didn't respond and the voice repeated my name.

'I think you've got the wrong number.'

There was a pause. 'My name is Lincoln. The chief wants to meet you.'

I understood then that the caller was with the Agency, that the chief was Holtzer. 'You must be joking,' I said.

'I'm not. There's been a mistake and he wants to explain. You can name the time and the place.'

'I don't think so.'

'You need to hear what he has to say. Things aren't what you think they are.'

I glanced back in the direction of Kinokuniya, weighing the risks and possible advantages.

'He'll have to meet me right now,' I said.

'Impossible. He's in a meeting. He can't get free before tonight.'

'I don't care if he's having open-heart surgery. If he wants to meet me, I'll be waiting for him in Shinjuku in twenty minutes. If he's one minute late, I'm gone.'

There was a long pause. 'Where in Shinjuku?'

'Tell him to walk out of the east exit of Shinjuku JR Station directly towards the Studio Alta sign. And tell him that if he's wearing anything besides trousers, shoes and a short-sleeved T-shirt, he'll never see me. OK?' I wanted to make it as hard as possible for Holtzer to conceal a weapon. 'Exactly twenty minutes,' I said, and hung up.

There were two possibilities. One, Holtzer might have something legitimate to say, the chances of which were remote. Two, this was an attempt to reacquire me to finish the job they had botched outside my apartment. But either way, it was a chance for me to learn more.

I had to assume there would be cameras. I'd keep him moving, but the risk would still be there. *What the hell. They know where you live, bastards have probably got a damn photo album by now.*

I crossed back to Shinjuku-dori and walked to the front of the Studio Alta building, where several cabs were waiting. I strolled over to one of the younger drivers who looked like he might be willing to overlook a strange situation if the price were right. I told him I wanted him to pick up a passenger who would be coming out of the east exit in about twenty minutes, a *gaijin* wearing a T-shirt.

'Ask if he's the chief,' I explained in Japanese, handing him a 10,000-yen note. 'If he answers yes, I want you to drive him down Shinjuku-dori, then make a left on Meiji-dori, then go left again on Yasukuni-dori. Wait for me in front of the Daiwa Bank.' I pulled out another 10,000-yen note and tore it in two pieces. I gave half to him, told him he would get the other half when he picked me up.

'Do you have a business card?' I asked him.

'*Hai*,' he answered, and produced one from his shirt pocket.

I took the card, then walked to the back of the Studio Alta building, where I took the stairs to the fourth floor. From there I had a good view of the east exit. I checked my watch: fourteen minutes to go. I wrote down an address in Ikebukuro on the back of the card and slipped it into my pocket.

Holtzer showed up one minute early. I watched him emerge, then walk slowly towards the Studio Alta sign. Even from a distance I could recognise the fleshy lips, the prominent nose. For a brief, satisfying moment, I remembered breaking it. He still had all his hair, although now it was more steel grey than the dirty blond I had known. I could tell that he was keeping in shape. He looked cold in the short-sleeved shirt. Too bad.

I saw the cab driver approach him. Holtzer followed him to the cab, and looked it over suspiciously before getting in. Then they moved off down Shinjuku-dori.

I headed back to the stairs, taking them three at a time until I got to the ground floor. Then I cut across to the Daiwa Bank, getting there just as the cab pulled up. I walked over to the passenger side. The automatic door opened, and Holtzer leaned towards me.

'John . . .' he started to say, in his reassuring voice.

'Let me see your hands,' I said, cutting him off. 'Palms forward, up in the air.' I didn't really think he was going to try to shoot me, but I wasn't going to give him the chance.

He hesitated, then leaned back and raised his hands.

'Now put your hands on the back of your neck. Then turn round and look out of the driver-side window.'

'Oh, come on, Rain—'

'Do it. Or I'm gone.' He glared at me and then complied.

I slid in next to him and gave the driver the business card with the Ikebukuro address, telling him to drive us there. I didn't want to say anything out loud. Then I patted Holtzer down. After a minute I moved away from him, satisfied that he wasn't carrying a weapon.

'Do you mind telling me where we're going?' he said.

I thought he might ask. 'You wearing a wire, Holtzer?' He didn't answer. *Where would it be?* I hadn't felt anything under his shirt.

'Take off your belt,' I told him.

'Like hell, Rain. This is going too far.'

'I'm not playing games with you. I'm about halfway to deciding that the way to solve my problems is to break your neck right here.'

'Go ahead and try.'

'*Sayonara*, asshole.' I leaned towards the driver. '*Tomatte, kudasa.*' Stop here.

'OK, you win,' he said. 'There's a transmitter in the belt. It's just a precaution. After Benny's unfortunate accident.'

Was he telling me not to worry, that Benny didn't even matter? '*Iya, sumimasen,*' I said to the driver. '*Itte kudasai.*' Sorry. Keep going.

'Good to see that you've still got the same high regard for your people,' I said to Holtzer. 'Give me the belt.'

'Benny wasn't my people,' he said. He handed me the belt. Sure enough, there was a tiny microphone under the buckle. I rolled down the window and pitched the belt out into the street.

He lunged for it, a second late. 'Goddamnit, Rain, you didn't have to do that. You could have just disabled it.'

'Let me see your shoes.'

'Not if you're planning on throwing them out of the window.'

'I will if they're wired. Take them off.' He handed them over. They were black loafers—no place for a microphone. I gave them back.

'Say what you've got to say,' I told him. 'I don't have much time.'

He sighed. 'The incident outside your apartment was a mistake. I want to apologise.' It was disgusting, how sincere he could sound.

'I'm listening.'

'I'm going out on a limb here, Rain,' he said. 'What I'm about to tell you is classified. For the last five years, we've been developing an asset in the Japanese government. Someone who knows where all the bodies are buried—and I'm not just being figurative here.'

If he was hoping for a reaction, he didn't get one, and he went on. 'We've got more and more from this guy over time, but never anything we could use as leverage. You following me?'

I nodded. Leverage in the business means blackmail. 'Well, we kept at him. Finally, six months ago, the nature of his refusals started to change. Instead of "No, I won't do that," we started hearing, "No, that's too dangerous." You know, practical objections.'

I did know. Good intelligence officers relish practical objections. They signal a shift from whether to how, from principle to price.

'It took us five more months to close him. We were going to give him a one-time cash payment big enough so he'd never have to worry again, plus false papers, settlement in a tropical locale where he'd blend in. In exchange, he was going to give us the goods on the Liberal Democratic Party—the payoffs, the *yakuza* ties, the killings of whistle-blowers. Hard evidence, the kind that would stand up in court.'

'What were you going to do with all that?'

'With that kind of information, we'd have every Japanese politician in our pocket. Think we'd ever get any grief again about military bases on Okinawa or at Atsugi? Think we'd have any trouble exporting as much rice or as many cars as we wanted? The LDP is the power here, and we'd have been the power behind the power.'

'What was your connection with Benny?' I asked.

'Poor Benny was a great source on LDP slime, but he didn't have the access, you know? The asset had the access.'

'But you sent him to my apartment.'

'Yeah, we sent him. Alone, to question you.'

'How did you find out what happened to him?'

'We had him wired for sound. So we heard everything, heard him blaming me, the little prick.'

'And the other guy?'

'We don't know anything about him.'

'Benny told me he was Boeicho Boeikyoku. That you handled the liaison.'

'He was right that I handled the Boeikyoku liaison, but he was full of shit that I knew his friend. We did some checking and Benny's pal wasn't with Japanese Intelligence. When Benny took him to your apartment, he was on a private mission, getting paid by someone else. You know you can't trust these moles, Rain. You remember the problems we had in Vietnam?'

I saw the driver looking at us in the rearview mirror, his face suspicious. The chances that he could follow our conversation in English were nil, but I could see that he sensed something was amiss.

'I'm not going to miss Benny,' Holtzer went on. 'You get paid by both sides, someone finds out, hey, you get what you had coming.'

Or at least you should. 'Right,' I said.

'But let me finish about the asset. Three weeks ago he's on his way to deliver the information, downloaded to a disk, and—can you believe this? He has a heart attack on the Yamanote and dies. We send people to the hospital, but the disk is gone.'

'How can you be so sure he was carrying the disk?'

'Oh, we're sure, Rain. But you want to hear the best part?' he said, leaning closer and smiling his grotesque smile. 'The best part is that it wasn't really a heart attack . . . someone iced him, someone who knew how to make it look like natural causes.'

'I don't know, Holtzer. It sounds pretty far-fetched.'

'It does, doesn't it? Especially because there are so few people in the whole world, let alone Japan, who could pull something like that off. Hell, the only one I know of is you.'

'This is what you wanted to meet me for?' I said. 'To suggest that I was mixed up in this kind of bullshit?'

'C'mon, Rain. I know exactly what you're mixed up in.'

'I'm not following you.'

'No? I've got news for you, then. Half the jobs you've done over the last ten years, you've done for us.'

What the hell?

He leaned closer and whispered the names of various prominent politicians, bankers and bureaucrats who had met untimely but natural ends. They were all my work.

'You can read those names in the paper,' I said.

He told me the particulars of the bulletin board system I had been using with Benny, the numbers of the Swiss accounts.

Goddamn, I thought, feeling sick. *You've been nothing but a fool for these people. It's never stopped.*

'Now look, we had access to the autopsy report. Kawamura had a pacemaker that somehow managed to shut itself off. The coroner attributed it to a defect. But we found out that a defect like that is just about impossible. Someone shut that pacemaker off, Rain. Your kind of job. I want to know who hired you.'

'It doesn't make sense,' I said.

'What doesn't?'

'Why go to such lengths just to retrieve the disk?'

His eyes narrowed. 'I was hoping you could tell me.'

'I can't. If I had wanted that disk, I could have found a lot of easier ways to take it.'

'Maybe it wasn't up to you,' he said. 'Maybe whoever hired you told you to retrieve it. I know you're not in the habit of asking questions about these assignments.'

'And have I ever been in the habit of "retrieving" items?'

'Not that I know of.'

'Then it sounds like you're barking up the wrong tree.'

'You were the last one with him, Rain. It doesn't look good.'

'My reputation will have to suffer.'

He looked at me. 'You know that the Agency is the least of your worries among the people trying to get the disk back.'

'What people?'

'Who do you think? The politicians, the *yakuza*, the muscle behind the whole Japanese power structure.'

I considered for a moment, then said, 'How did you find out about me? About me in Japan?'

He shook his head. 'Sorry, nothing I can discuss here. But I'll tell you what.' He leaned forward again. 'Come on in, and we can talk about anything you want.'

It was such a non sequitur that I thought I heard wrong. 'Did you say, "Come on in"?'

'Yes, I did. You'll see that you need our help.'

'I didn't know you were such a humanitarian, Holtzer.'

'We're not doing this for humanity. We want your cooperation. Either you've got that disk, or you've got information that might help us find it. We'll help you in exchange. It's as simple as that.'

But I knew these people, and I knew Holtzer. The simpler it looked, the harder they were about to nail you.

'Maybe I have to trust someone,' I said. 'But it's not going to be you.'

'Look, if this is about the war, you're being ridiculous. It was a long time ago. This is another time, another place.'

'But the people are the same.'

He waved his hand as though trying to dispel an offensive odour. 'It doesn't matter what you think about me, Rain, because this isn't about us. The situation is what matters, and the situation is this: the police want you. The LDP wants you. The *yakuza* wants you. And they're going to find you because your cover is blown. Now let us help you.'

What to do. Take him out right here? They knew where I lived, which made me newly vulnerable, and taking out the station chief could lead to retribution.

The car behind us made a right. I glanced back and saw the car that was following it, a black sedan with three or four Japanese in it, slow down instead of taking up the space that had developed. Not an effective strategy for driving in Tokyo traffic.

I waited until we were almost at the next light, then told the driver to make a left. The sedan changed lanes with us.

I told the driver that he should get back on Meiji-dori. He looked back at me, clearly annoyed, wondering what this was all about.

The sedan stayed with us as we made the turns.

'You bring some people with you, Holtzer?'

'They're here to bring you inside. For your protection.'

How could they have followed him? Even if he were wearing a transmitter in a body cavity, they couldn't have pinpointed the location in this traffic.

Then I realised. They had played me beautifully. They knew when "Lincoln" called that I would demand an immediate meeting. They didn't know where, but they had people ready to move the second they found out. They had twenty minutes to get to Shinjuku, and they could stay close enough to react to what they heard through the wire. Holtzer must have given them the name of the cab company, the car's description, the licence-plate number, and updated them about its progress until I got in. By then they were in position.

The light at the Kanda River overpass turned red. The cab started to slow down. I snapped my head right, then left, searching for an avenue of escape. The sedan crept closer, stopping a car length away.

Holtzer looked at me, trying to gauge what I was going to do. For a split instant our eyes locked. Then he lunged at me.

'It's for your own good!' he yelled, trying to get his arms round my waist. I saw the back doors of the sedan open, a pair of burly Japanese in sunglasses stepping out.

I tried to push Holtzer away, but his hands were locked behind my back. The driver turned round and started yelling. The two Japanese were approaching the taxi.

I wrapped my right arm round Holtzer's neck, holding his head in place against my chest, and slipped my left between my body and his neck, the ridge of my hand searching for his carotid. '*Aum da! Aum Shinrikyo da!*' I yelled at the driver. '*Sarin!*' Aum was the cult that gassed the Tokyo subway in 1995, and memories of the sarin attack can still cause panic.

Holtzer yelled something against my chest. I leaned forward, using my torso and legs like a walnut cracker. I felt him go limp.

'*Ei? Nan da tte?*' the driver asked. What do you mean?

One of the Japanese tapped on the passenger-side window. 'Those men! They're Aum—they have sarin! My friend is unconscious! Drive!' Getting the right note of terror in my voice wasn't a reach.

He might have thought that I was crazy, but sarin wasn't worth the chance. He snapped the car into gear and hauled the steering wheel to the right, doing a burning-rubber U-turn on Meiji-dori.

'*Isoide! Isoide! Byoin ni tanomu!*' Hurry! We need a hospital!

At the intersection the driver ripped through a light that had just turned red, braking into a sliding left-hand turn in the direction of the National Medical Centre. The G-force ripped Holtzer away from me. The flow of traffic closed in behind us a second later, and I knew the sedan would be stuck for a minute, maybe more.

Tozai Waseda Station was just ahead. Time for me to bail. I told the driver to pull over. Holtzer was slumped against the driver-side door, unconscious but breathing.

The driver started to protest, saying that we had to get my friend to a hospital, but I insisted he pull over. He stopped and I took out the half of the 10,000-yen note I owed him, then threw in one more. I grabbed the package I had bought for Midori, jumped out of the cab, and bolted down the steps to the subway. I knew I was safe for the moment. But they'd flushed me into the open, and the moment wouldn't last.

AN HOUR LATER I got Harry's page, and we met at the coffee shop per our previous arrangement. He was waiting for me when I got there.

'Tell me what you've got,' I said.

'Well, it's strange. This disk has some pretty advanced copy management protection built into it.'

'Can you break it?'

'Copy management is different to encryption. The disk can't be copied, can't be distributed electronically, can't be sent over the Internet. If you try, the data will get corrupted.'

'That explains a few things,' I said.

'Like what?'

'Like why they're so eager to get this disk back. They know it hasn't been copied or uploaded, so they know their potential damage is still limited to this one disk.'

'That's right.'

'Now tell me this. Why would whoever controls the data permit even a single copy to be made? Why not no copies?'

'Too risky. If something happened to the master, all your records would be gone.'

I considered. 'What else is there?'

'Ever hear of a lattice reduction?'

'I don't think so.'

'It's a kind of code. The cryptographer encodes a message in a pattern, like a symmetrical wallpaper design. But wallpaper patterns are simple—only one image in two dimensions. A more complex code uses a pattern that repeats itself at various levels of detail, in multiple mathematical dimensions. To break the code, you have to find the most basic way the lattice repeats itself—the origin of the pattern.'

'I get the picture. Can you break it?'

'I'm not sure. I did some work with lattice reductions at Fort Meade, but this one is strange because the lattice seems to be a musical pattern, not a physical one.'

'I'm not following you.'

'There's an overlay of what look like musical notes. I've got to tell you, John, I'm a little out of my element on this one.'

'All those years with the NSA, what could be out of your element?'

He blushed. 'It's not the encryption. It's the music. I need a musician to walk me through it. Someone who reads music, preferably someone who writes it.'

I didn't say anything.

'I could really use her help on this,' he said.

'Let me think about it,' I told him, uncomfortable. 'What about the cellphones? Anything there?'

He smiled. 'Ever hear of the Shinnento?'

'Not sure,' I said, trying to place the name. 'New Year something?'

'*Shinnen*, as in Conviction,' he said. 'It's a political party. The last call the *kendoka* made was to their headquarters in Shibakoen, and the number was speed-coded into both of the phones' memories.' He smiled. 'And just in case that's not enough to establish the connection, Conviction was paying the phone bill for the *kendoka*.'

'Harry, you never cease to amaze. Tell me more.'

'OK. Conviction was established in 1978 by a fellow named Yamaoto Toshi, who is still the head of the party. Yamaoto was born in 1949. He's the only son of a prominent family that traces its lines back to the samurai clans. His father was an officer in the Imperial Army, who after the war started a company that made portable communications devices. The father got rich during the Korean War, when the American Army bought his company's equipment.

'Yamaoto spent some years as a teenager in Europe training for classical piano. But his father sent him to the States to complete his education as a prelude to taking over the family business. When his old man died, Yamaoto returned to Japan, sold the business, and used the money to establish Conviction and run for parliament.'

'The piano training. Is there a connection with the way the disk is encrypted?'

'Don't know for sure. There could be.'

'Sorry. Keep going.'

'Conviction was a platform for Yamaoto's right-wing ideas. He was elected in 1985 to a seat in Nagano-ken, which he promptly lost in the next election.'

'You don't get elected in Japan because of your ideas,' I said. 'It's pork that pays.'

'That's exactly the lesson Yamaoto learned from his defeat. He ran again—this time focusing on the roads and bridges he would build for his constituents, the rice subsidies and tariffs he would impose. The nationalistic stuff was back-burnered. He got his seat back and has held on to it ever since.'

'But Conviction is a marginal player. I've never even read about the LDP using them to form a coalition.'

'Yamaoto has a few things going for him. One, Conviction is very well funded. Two, he knows how to dole out the pork. Nagano has a number of farming districts and Yamaoto keeps the subsidies rolling in. And three, he has a lot of support in the Shinto community.'

'Shinto,' I said, musing. Shinto is a nature-worshipping religion that Japan's nationalists turned into an ideology of Japaneseness before the war. There was something about the connection that was bothering me. Then I realised.

'That's how they found out where I live,' I said. 'No wonder I've been seeing priests begging for alms outside stations on the Mita-sen. I almost gave one of them a hundred yen the other day.'

'How would they know to focus on the Mita line?'

'They probably didn't, for sure. But if they placed me at the Kodokan, they would have assumed that I wouldn't live too far. There are only three train lines with stops within a reasonable distance. All they had to do was commit enough manpower.'

I had to give them credit; it was nicely done. Static surveillance is almost impossible to spot. It's like a zone defence in basketball: no matter where the guy with the ball goes, there's always someone new in the next zone to pick him up. If you can put enough people in place to make it work, it's deadly.

'What's the basis for the Shinto connection?' I asked.

'Shinto is a huge organisation, with priests running shrines that take in a lot of donations—so they're in a position to dispense patronage to the politicians they favour. And Yamaoto wants a bigger role for Shinto in Japan, which means more power for the priests.'

'So the shrines are part of his funding?'

'It's more than that. Shinto is part of Conviction's programme. The party wants it taught in schools; it wants to form an anti-crime alliance between the police and the local shrines. Don't forget, Shinto was at the centre of prewar Japanese nationalism.'

'You said Conviction headquarters is in Shibakoen,' I said.

'That's right.'

'OK, then. While you're having a crack at the lattice, I'm going to need some surveillance equipment—infrared and laser. And video. Also a transmitter in case I can get inside. I want to listen in on our friends at Conviction.'

'Why?'

'I need more information. Whose disk was this? Who's trying to get it back? Why? Without that, there's not much I can do to protect myself. Or Midori.'

'Why don't you just give me some time with the lattice? Maybe everything you need is already in it.'

'I don't have time. It might take you a week to crack the code, or you might not be able to crack it at all. In the meantime, I'm up against the Agency, the *yakuza*, and an army of Shinto priests. I've been flushed out into the open. Time is running against me.'

'Why don't you just leave the country? What's keeping you here?'

'For one thing, I've got to take care of Midori, and she can't leave under her own passport. I doubt she's got false papers handy.'

He looked at me closely. 'Is something going on between you two?' I didn't answer.

He shook his head. 'Is this why you don't want to let her help me with the lattice?'

'All right, I'll ask her,' I said, not seeing an alternative.

'I could use her help.'

'I know. I didn't really expect you to be able to decrypt something as complex as this without help.'

For a half-second his mouth started to drop in indignation. Then he saw my smile.

'Had you there,' I told him.

HARRY RENTED me a van from a place in Roppongi, using alias ID, while I waited at his apartment, a strange place, crammed with arcane electronic equipment.

When he came back, we loaded the equipment into the back of the van. It's sophisticated stuff. The laser reads the vibrations on windows that are caused by conversation inside, then feeds the resulting data into a computer, which breaks down the patterns into words. And the infrared can read minutely different temperatures on glass—the kind caused by body heat in an otherwise cool room.

When we were done, I parked the van and made my way back to Shibuya, conducting a solid SDR en route. I got to the hotel at a little past one o'clock. I had picked up some sandwiches, and Midori and I ate them while I filled her in on what was going on. I gave her the package I had brought, told her that she should wear the scarf and sunglasses when she went out. I gave her Harry's address, told her to meet me there in two hours.

When I arrived at Harry's, he was already running Kawamura's disk. A half-hour later the buzzer rang and I got up to check the window. I nodded and Harry pressed the button to open the front entrance. Then he walked over to his door, opened it a little and peered out. A minute later he opened the door wide and motioned Midori to come inside.

I said to her in Japanese, 'This is Harry. He's a little shy around people because he spends all his time with computers.'

'*Hajimemashite*,' Midori said, turning to Harry and bowing. Nice to meet you.

Harry was blinking rapidly, and I could see that he was nervous. 'Please don't listen to my friend. The government used him to test experimental drugs during the war, and it's led to premature senility.'

Harry? I thought, impressed with his sudden gumption.

Midori made a face of perfect innocence. 'It was caused by drugs?' Harry looked at me with a radiant smile.

'OK, I can see you're both going to get along,' I said. 'We don't have much time. This is the plan.' I explained to Midori what I was going to do.

'I don't like it,' she said. 'They could see you. It could be dangerous.'

'No one's going to see me.'

'You should give Harry and me some time with the musical code.'

'I've already been over this with Harry. You both do your jobs; I'll do mine. It's more efficient. I'll be fine.'

I DROVE THE VAN to the Conviction facility in Shibakoen. They occupied part of the first floor of a building on Hibiya-dori. I would use the laser to pick up the conversation in their offices, and then, based on Harry's analysis of what we picked up, I'd be able to guess which room or rooms would be the best candidates for a transmitter. The same equipment would tell me when the offices had emptied out, probably after dark, and that's when I'd go in to place the bug.

I parked across the street from the building. The spot was in a no-parking zone, but it was a good enough location to risk a ticket from a bored meter maid.

I had just finished setting up the equipment and targeting it at the appropriate windows when I heard a tap on the van's passenger-side window. I looked up and saw a uniformed cop.

Oh, shit. I made a conciliatory gesture, as though I was going to just drive away, but he said, '*Dete yo.*' Get out.

The equipment wasn't visible from the cop's vantage point. I would have to take a chance. I slid across to the passenger side, then stepped down onto the kerb.

There were three men waiting on the blind side of the van, where I couldn't see them until I was outside. They were armed with matching Beretta 92 Compacts and wore sunglasses and bulky coats—light disguise to change the shape of the face and the build. I took this to mean that they would shoot me if I resisted, counting on the disguises to confuse potential witnesses. I recognised the guy with the flat nose who had gone in after I had ambushed Midori's would-be abductors. One of them thanked the cop, who walked away.

They motioned me across the street, and there wasn't much I could do except comply. At least this solved the problem of how I was going to get into the building. I had an earpiece in my pocket, as well as one of Harry's custom adhesive-backed microtransmitters. If I saw the chance, I'd put the transmitter in place.

We took the stairs to the first floor. When we got to the landing, Flatnose shoved me up against the wall. One of his partners patted me down. He was looking for a weapon and didn't notice the small transmitter in my pocket.

When he was done, Flatnose suddenly kneed me in the balls. I doubled over and he kicked me in the stomach, then twice again in the ribs. I dropped down to my knees, sucking wind, pain shooting through my torso. One of them stepped between Flatnose and me, saying '*Iya, sono kurai ni shite oke.*' That's enough.

When I was able I stood up, and they took me down a short hallway. We stopped outside the last door. Flatnose knocked, and a voice answered, '*Dozo.*' Come in.

They took me into a room that was spacious by Japanese standards, furnished in the traditional minimalist fashion. Lots of light-hued wood, expensive-looking ceramics on the shelves. A small leather couch and armchairs in one corner of the room, arranged around a spotless glass coffee table. The overall appearance was clean and prosperous.

There was a wooden desk on the far side. It took me a second to recognise the guy sitting behind it. It was the *judoka* from the Kodokan. The one I'd fought in *randori*.

'Hello, John Rain,' he said, with a small smile. 'It's been a while.'

I returned his gaze. 'Hello, Yamaoto.'

He stood up and nodded to his men, told them in Japanese to wait outside. I watched them file out, Flatnose eyeing me as he closed the door behind them.

'Did I do something to offend the ugly one?' I asked, rubbing my ribs. 'I get the feeling he doesn't like me.'

'He has trouble controlling his temper. Ishikawa, the man you killed outside your apartment, was a friend of his.'

'Sorry to hear that.'

'Please, sit. Would you like something to drink?'

'I'm not thirsty. And I'm more comfortable standing.'

He nodded. 'I know what you are thinking, Rain-san. There are three armed men outside the door—in case you manage to get past me.' He smiled, a supremely confident smile, and remembering how things went at the Kodokan, I knew his confidence was justified. 'Why don't you make yourself comfortable, and we can think of a way to solve our mutual problem.'

'"Mutual problem"?'

'Yes. You have something that I want, or you know where it is. Once I have it, you will no longer be a liability, and we can "live and let live". But if I don't have it, the situation becomes more difficult.'

I walked over to one of the chairs facing the couch, putting my hands in my pockets as I did so, affecting an air of resignation. I switched on the transmitter. Regardless of how this turned out, Harry would at least hear everything. I sat down and waited.

'Tell me,' he said, sitting opposite me on the couch. 'How did you find me?'

I shrugged. 'Your man Ishikawa broke into my apartment and tried to kill me. I got his cellphone and used it to find out he's connected to you.'

'Ishikawa wasn't at your apartment to kill you. He was there to question you. We are not after you—only the disk.'

'Disk?'

'Please don't insult my intelligence. You're protecting Kawamura Midori.'

'What does she have to do with this?'

'I know that her father had the disk when he died. It is therefore likely that she has it now. And she is in hiding.'

'Of course she's in hiding. She had the same kind of welcome party at her apartment that I had at mine. She knows she's in danger but doesn't understand why.'

'Where is she?'

'I don't know. She took off after the ambush at her apartment. She thought I was with your people.'

'Really? She hasn't resurfaced.'

'Maybe she's staying with friends—in the country or something. She looked pretty scared to me.'

'I see,' he said. 'You understand, Rain-san, there is information on that disk that would be harmful to Japan, useful to her enemies, if revealed. These enemies are looking for the disk, too.'

I thought of Holtzer. One thing I didn't understand. 'Why the contact at the Kodokan?'

'Curiosity,' he said, his posture contemplative. 'I wanted to know what would drive a man with a history like yours.'

'What do mean, "history"?'

'A man of two such opposed countries and cultures. You wouldn't know, but I have retained your services from time to time.'

Through Benny, then. The little bastard really slept around.

'So you see, your interests and mine have always been aligned. If we can just clear up this matter, we can return to the status quo.'

'I don't know where this disk is,' I told him. 'If I did, I'd give it to you.'

He frowned. 'And Kawamura's daughter doesn't know, either?'

'How would I know?'

He nodded his head gravely. 'Until I have what I am looking for, Kawamura's daughter is a liability. It would be much safer for her if the item were returned to me.'

In that moment I was tempted to believe that there was some truth to what he was saying. But there were other parties after the disk, too, and they would have no way of knowing that Midori didn't have it any more.

'I don't think she has what you're looking for,' I said. 'Why would Kawamura have given her anything? He would have known it would put her in danger.'

'He may have given it to her inadvertently. The fact that she has not gone to the police is telling.'

I said nothing, waiting for him.

'Enough games,' he said finally. He stood up and took a suit jacket off a hanger. 'I have an appointment elsewhere. Tell me where I can find the disk, or tell me where to find Kawamura Midori.'

'I told you I don't know.'

'Rain-san, you are in a difficult position. You must understand that I will have what I want. If you tell me now, as a friend, you will be free to leave. But if my men have to acquire the information by other means, I may not be able to let you go afterwards. In fact, you may not be in a condition to go. Do you understand? If I don't have the disk, I am forced to do the next best thing: systematically eliminate every risk associated with it.'

I folded my arms across my chest. Inside my head I was playing a map of the hallway, the staircase, trying to find a way out.

Finally he called for his men. The door opened and I was surrounded and pulled to my feet. He barked some orders at them in Japanese. Find out where the disk is. And Midori. Whatever it takes.

They hauled me out of the room and back down the hallway. I noted the entrance as we went past double glass doors. The doors had opened outwards when we came in. If I hit them dead centre, the lock might give. If it didn't, I could try to go through the glass, hope not to get cut too badly. Lousy options, but they beat being tortured to death by Flatnose. I tried to emanate waves of fear and helplessness so their confidence would build. That might give me some small chance. Beyond that, I had only one advantage: considering what was coming, I was more motivated to escape than they were to hold me.

They took me to a room at the far end of the corridor, only about nine feet square. The door had a window of frosted glass in its centre and opened inwards, to the left. To the right was a small table with two chairs on either side. They pushed me into one of the chairs, my back to the door. I put my hands on my knees, under the table.

Flatnose was carrying a large wooden truncheon. He took a seat on the other side of the table, facing me. I heard the other two take up positions behind me. There were about three feet of empty space between Flatnose's back and the wall. Good.

They hadn't locked the door. Why bother? There were three of them. They knew they were in control.

I lifted the table a fraction with my knees. It was satisfyingly heavy. My heart was thudding in my ears.

Flatnose started to say something. As soon as the words began I sprang up, my arms catching the table from underneath, driving it up and into him. The force slammed him backwards into the wall.

The other two leapt forward. I shot my leg out into the guy coming in on my right. It caught him squarely in the gut. He went down and then the other one was on me.

He grabbed me from behind and tried for *hadaka jime*, a sleeper hold, but I turtled my neck in and his forearm closed across my mouth, the leading edge of his arm jammed between my teeth. Before he could twist free I bit down hard and heard him howl.

The grip loosened and I spun inside it, pumping uppercuts into his abdomen. He dropped his arms and I caught him with a solid palm-heel under the nose. He didn't fall, but he was dazed. I scrambled for the door and flung it open. It rocketed into the wall, the frosted glass exploding. I stumbled into the hallway, running like a man out of control. It took me only a second to reach the entrance doors. I hit them hard and they burst open at the centre. I bolted for the stairwell. When I reached the outer door I wrenched it open and plunged down the stairs four at a time. Just as I cleared the first riser, I heard the door slam open. They were already after me.

Shibakoen subway station was on the opposite side of Hibiya-dori. I bolted across the street, tyres screeching as I jumped in front of cars. Crowds of pedestrians were exiting at the top of the steps to the station—a train must have just come in. I glanced back as I hit the entrance and saw two of Yamaoto's boys sprinting after me.

I could hear another train pulling in. Maybe I could make it. I had no doubt that they would shoot me now if they could. In this crowd, no one would know where the shots had come from. I fought frantically for space, ducking past three old women blocking the stairway, and spun left at the bottom of the stairs. As I dodged past a concession stand I grabbed a palm-sized can of coffee. A hundred and ninety grams. Hard metal edges.

I shoved my way onto the platform. I was too late—the doors had already closed. The platform was crowded, but there was a clear passage alongside the train. I manoeuvred into it and saw one of Yamaoto's goons burst through the crowd.

I threw the can like a fastball, aiming for centre mass. It caught him in the sternum with a thud I could hear over the noise of the train. He went down hard. But his buddy was right behind him, his gun out.

I spun round. The train was picking up speed. I dropped my head and sprinted after it, my breath hammering in and out. I heard a gunshot. Then another. Two yards. One. I was close enough to reach out and touch the vertical bar at the back corner of the car, but I couldn't get any closer. For an instant, my speed was perfectly synchronised with the train. Then it started to slip away.

I leapt forward, my fingers outstretched. For one second I thought I'd come up short—then my hand closed round cold metal. My body fell forward and my knees smacked into the back of the train. My feet were dangling just over the tracks. Then the train entered the tunnel and I lost my grip.

I hit the tracks so hard that I actually bounced instead of rolling. There was one enormous shock all down my left side, then I felt a dull *whump!* and came to a sudden stop.

I was on my back, looking up at the ceiling of the subway tunnel. I lay there for a moment, wiggling my toes, flexing my fingers. Everything seemed to be working.

What the hell, I thought. *What the hell did I land on?*

I sat up. I was on a large sand pile to the left of the tracks. Beside it were two Japanese construction workers, their mouths agape. Next to the sand was a concrete floor that the workers were repairing, using the sand to mix cement. I realised that if I had let go of the train half a second later, I would have landed on concrete instead of sand.

I stood up and began brushing myself off. The shape of my body was imprinted in the sand like something from an over-the-top cartoon.

I saw that I was only a few yards inside the tunnel and started walking out. I considered what had happened. Yamaoto's men must have seen me go into the tunnel on the back of the train, but not seen me slip. So they were figuring that, in three minutes, I would be deposited at Mita Station, the end of the line. They must have bolted out of the station to Mita to try to intercept me.

I had a wild idea. I pulled out the earpiece I had pocketed before Flatnose and his crew had caught me in the van, slipped it into place. I felt in my pocket for the adhesive-backed transmitter. Still there. But was it still transmitting?

'Harry? Can you hear me? Talk to me,' I said.

There was a long pause, and just as I started to try again the earpiece came to life.

'John! What the hell is going on? Where are you?'

It felt great to hear the kid. 'Relax, I'm OK. But I need your help.' I hauled myself up onto the platform. Some people stared at me but I ignored them. 'Is the equipment up and running?'

'Yes, I'm getting a feed on all the rooms.'

'That's what I need to know. Who's still in the building?'

'Infrared says just one guy in the very last room on the right as you face the building—where the three men took you. He's been there since you got out.'

That would be Flatnose or one of his boys—he must have been in no condition to come after me. It felt good to know.

'OK, here's the situation. They think I'm on the back of a train to Mita, and that's where they're going to converge in about four minutes. It'll take them maybe another five to figure out that I'm not there and another five after that to get back to the Conviction building. So I've got fourteen minutes to get back in there and plant the bug.'

'What if they didn't all go to Mita? They could come back while you're still in there!'

'I'm counting on you to let me know if that's going to happen. You're getting a video feed from the van, right?'

'Yeah, it's still broadcasting.'

'Look, I'm practically at the building now—all clear?'

'Still all clear, but this is crazy.'

'I'm never going to get a better chance. I'm going in.'

I went through the stairway doors and jogged down the hallway to the entrance. They had left in a hurry and it was wide open.

Yamaoto's office was three doors down to the right. I was going to be in and out in no time.

The door was closed. I tried to turn the knob. 'It's locked.'

'Forget it—put the bug somewhere else.'

'I can't—this is where we need to listen.' I examined the lock, and could see that it was only a regular five-pin tumbler. Not a big deal. 'Hang on a minute. I think I can get in.'

'John, get out of there. They could come back.'

I didn't answer. I slipped out my keys and detached one of my homemade picks and the dental mirror. The latter's long handle made for a nice field-expedient tension wrench. I slipped the handle into the lock and gently rotated it clockwise. When the slack in the cylinder was gone, I eased in the pick.

I felt the fifth tumbler click, then lost it. Damn. I turned the mirror another fraction, tightening the cylinder against the pins. I felt the fifth pin click and hold. The next three were easy. Just one more.

The last pin was damaged. I couldn't feel the click. I worked the pick up and down, but couldn't get anything.

'C'mon, sweetheart, where are you?' I breathed. I held my breath and jiggled the pick. I never felt the tumbler click into place. But the knob was suddenly free. It twisted to the right and I was in.

The office was the same as when I'd left it. Even the lights were still on. I knelt next to the leather couch and felt its underside. It was covered with cloth. The edges were stapled to wood. Good backing to attach the bug. I pressed the transmitter into place. Anyone talking in this room was going to come through loud and clear.

Harry's voice in my ear: 'John, two of them just got back. Get out right now. Use the side exit.'

'The transmitter's in place. I'm not going to be able to respond to you once I leave this room. Keep talking.'

'They just stopped at the end of the walkway to the front entrance. Maybe they're waiting for the others. Go down to the side entrance and stay there until I tell you you're clear.'

'OK. I'm gone.' I relocked the door from the inside, then closed it behind me.

Flatnose was coming down the hallway. Animal sounds were rumbling up out of his chest. He was standing between me and the entrance. Nowhere to go but through him.

Harry again, a second late: 'There's one right in front of you! And the others are coming up the walk!'

Flatnose dropped his head, his neck and shoulders bunching, a bull about to charge. All he wanted was to get his hands on me.

He launched himself. As he lunged for my neck, I grabbed his bloodstained shirt and dropped to the floor, hurling him over me. He landed on his back with a thud. Using the momentum of the throw I rolled to my feet and leapt into the air, coming down hard on his prone torso. I felt bones breaking inside him and I knew he was done.

I lurched towards the corridor, then stopped. If they found him like this, they would know I'd been back here. They might look for a bug. I had to get him back to the room where it would look like he'd died by a freak shot from the table.

His legs were pointing in the right direction. I squatted between them and grabbed him round the knees. I leaned forward and dragged him, feeling like a horse yoked to a wagon with square wheels.

Harry's voice again: 'They're coming in the front entrance. You've got maybe twelve seconds to get clear.'

I dumped him in the room at the end of the hallway and raced out into the corridor. I reached the entrance to the side stairwell, yanked open the door and threw myself through it.

I squatted on the landing, holding the door open a crack and watching as three of Yamaoto's men walked into the corridor. One of them was doubled over—the guy I had nailed with the can of coffee. They walked out of my field of vision.

I heard Harry: 'They're back in the office. The front of the building is clear. Walk out of the side exit now.'

I went down the stairs quietly but fast. Stuck my head out of the exit door at the bottom, looked both ways. All clear. I shuffled down an alley and cut across the park. The sun felt good on my face.

PART THREE

'You are a maniac with a death wish, and I'm never working with you again,' Harry told me when I got to his apartment.

'I'm never working with me again, either,' I said. 'Have you been getting anything from the transmitter?'

'Yes, everything that went on while you were there and a short meeting that just ended. It's stored on the hard drive.'

'They say anything about the guy I ran into on my way out? I had a little encounter just after I put the transmitter in place.'

'Yes, they thought it happened when you busted out of interrogation. They didn't know you'd been back. You know, the guy is dead.'

'Yeah, he didn't look too good when I left him.'

He was watching me closely, but I couldn't read his eyes. 'You can do something like that, that fast, with just your hands?'

I looked at him, deadpan. 'No, I needed my feet, too. Where's Midori?'

'She went out to get an electronic piano keyboard. We're going to try playing what's on the disk for the computer—it's the only way to discern the patterns in the lattice.'

I frowned. 'She shouldn't be going out if we can avoid it.'

'We couldn't avoid it. Someone had to monitor the laser and infrared and save your ass before, and she isn't familiar with the equipment. That didn't leave a lot of alternatives.'

'I see what you mean.'

'She knows to be careful. She's wearing light disguise. I don't think there's going to be a problem.'

'OK. Let's listen to what you got from the transmitter.'

A few mouse clicks later I was listening to Yamaoto excoriating his men in Japanese. 'One unarmed man! And you let him get away! Useless, incompetent idiots!'

There was a long pause, and then someone spoke up: 'What would you have us do, *toushu*?'

'Focus on the girl. She is still our most promising lead.'

'She's underground now,' the voice said.

'Yes, but she's unaccustomed to such a life,' Yamaoto answered. 'She went into hiding suddenly. We can count on her to return. Put men in all the vital spots of her life—where she lives, where she works, her family. Work with Holtzer on this as necessary. He has the technical means.'

Holtzer? Work with *him?*

'And the man?'

There was a long pause, then Yamaoto said, 'The man is a different story. Unless we are lucky, I expect you have lost him.'

I could imagine heads bowed collectively in shame. One of the men spoke: 'We may spot him with the girl.'

'Yes, that's possible. He's obviously protecting her. We know he saved her from Ishikura's men outside her apartment.'

Ishikura? I thought.

'In any event,' Yamaoto continued, 'the girl poses more of a danger: she is the one Ishikura Tatsuhiko will be looking for, and he has as good a chance of finding her as we do—perhaps better. And if he finds the disk, he will know what to do with it.'

Tatsu? Tatsu is looking for the disk, too? Those were his men at her apartment?

'No more loose ends,' Yamaoto went on. 'When the girl resurfaces, eliminate her immediately.'

'*Hai*,' several voices replied in chorus.

'Unfortunately, in the absence of the disk's return, eliminating the girl will no longer provide us with complete security. It's time to remove Ishikura Tatsuhiko from the equation, as well.'

'But, *toushu*,' one of the voices said, 'Ishikura is not an easy man to eliminate without causing collateral problems. Moreover . . .'

'Yes, moreover, Ishikura's death will make him a martyr in certain circles by providing supporting evidence for all his conspiracy theories. But we have no choice. Do your utmost to make Ishikura's demise seem natural. Ironic, that at the moment we need him most, the man supremely capable of such art is unavailable to us.'

That was it. I looked at Harry. 'It's still transmitting?'

'Until the battery runs out. I'll keep monitoring it.'

I nodded, realising that Harry was going to hear things that would lead back to me. Hell, Yamaoto's comments were already damning if you were smart: the reference to having lost the services of the man 'supremely capable' of effecting death by natural causes.

'I don't think Midori should hear what's on that tape,' I said. 'I don't want to . . . compromise her further.'

Harry bowed his head. 'I completely understand.'

All at once, I knew that he knew.

'It's good that I can trust you,' I said. 'Thank you.'

He shook his head. '*Kochira koso*,' he said. The same here.

The buzzer rang. Midori. Harry hit the entrance buzzer, and we took up our positions, this time with me at the door and Harry at the window. A minute later I saw Midori walking down the hallway with a cardboard box in her arms. She covered the distance quickly, stepped inside and gave me a hug.

'Every time I see you, you look worse,' she told me, setting the box on the floor. 'What happened?'

'I'll give you the details in a little while. First, Harry tells me you're going to give us a piano recital.'

'That's right,' she said, stripping tape off the box. She slid out an electronic keyboard and handed it to Harry.

He plugged the keyboard into the computer and brought the scanned image of the notes up onto the monitor.

'The problem is that I can't play music and Midori can't run the computer. I think the short cut will be to get the computer to apply the patterns of sounds to the representation of notes on the page. Once it's got enough data to work with, the computer will apply the pattern to standard Japanese through a code-breaking algorithm I've set up, and we'll be in.'

'Right,' I said. 'That's just what I was thinking.'

Harry gave me his 'you-are-a-complete-knuckle-dragger' look, then said, 'Midori, try playing the score on the monitor.'

Midori lifted her fingers over the keyboard. 'Wait,' Harry said. 'You've got to play it perfectly. If you add or delete a note, or play one out of order, you'll create a new pattern, and the computer will get confused. Can you do that?'

'I'll need to run through it a few times first. Can you disconnect me from the computer?'

'Sure.' He dragged and clicked the mouse.

Midori looked at the screen for a few moments, Then she brought her hands down gently to the keys, and for the first time we heard the eerie melody of the information that had cost Kawamura his life.

I listened uncomfortably while Midori played. After a few minutes, she said to Harry, 'OK, I'm ready. Plug me in.'

Harry worked the mouse. 'You're in. Let it hear you.'

Again, Midori's fingers floated over the keys, and the room was filled with the strange requiem.

We watched the screen. After a half-minute or so, a strange, disembodied series of notes emanated from the computer speakers, shadows of what I had heard Midori play a moment earlier.

'It's factoring the sounds,' Harry said. 'It's trying to find the most basic pattern.'

We waited for several minutes. Finally Harry said, 'I don't see any progress. I might not have the computing power here.'

'Where can you get it?' Midori asked.

Harry shrugged. 'I could try hacking into a supercomputer, but it could take some time.'

There was a moment of frustrated quiet. Then Harry said, 'Let's think for a moment. How much do we even need to decrypt this?'

'What do you mean?' Midori asked.

'What are our objectives here? The disk is like dynamite; we just want to render it safe. The owners know that it can't be copied or electronically transmitted. We could render it safe by just giving it back to them.'

'No!' Midori said, standing and facing Harry. 'My father risked

115

his life for what's on that disk. It's going where he wanted it to go!'

Harry held up his hands. 'I'm just trying to think outside the box.'

'It's a logical idea, Harry,' I said, 'but Midori's right. Not only because her father risked his life to acquire the disk. We know now that there are multiple parties seeking its return—not just Yamaoto, but also the Agency, the Keisatsucho. Even if we were to give it back to one of them, it wouldn't solve our problems with the others.'

'I see your point,' Harry conceded.

'But I like your dynamite analogy. How do you render dynamite safe?'

'You detonate it somewhere safe,' Midori said.

'Exactly,' I said.

'Bulfinch,' Midori said. 'Bulfinch publishes it, and that's what makes it safe. And it's what my father wanted.'

Harry frowned. 'We don't know if he has the resources to decrypt it.'

I suppressed a smile at the slight hint of resentment I detected: someone was going to take away his toy.

'We can assume that *Forbes* can access the right resources.'

'I'd still like a better chance at decrypting it first.'

'So would I. But we don't know how long that would take. In the meantime we've got forces arrayed against us. The sooner Bulfinch publishes the damn thing, the sooner we can breathe easy again.'

Midori, not taking any chances, said, 'I'll call him.'

I HAD TOLD BULFINCH to meet me in Akasaka Mitsuke, with its profusion of hostess bars. It was raining and cold as I exited the subway station and paused to open the black umbrella I was carrying. I was over an hour early and decided to grab a quick lunch at the Tenkaichi ramen restaurant on the Esplanade. I ordered the *chukadon*—Chinese vegetables over rice—and ate while I watched the street through the window.

I had told Bulfinch that, at 2.00pm, he should start circling the block counterclockwise. There were more than a dozen alleys, so he wouldn't know where I'd be waiting until I made my presence known. It didn't matter if he came early. He'd just have to keep circling in the rain.

I finished at 1.50, paid the bill, and left. I crossed the Esplanade then cut into an alley opposite and waited under the overhang of some rusting corrugated roofing. Because of the hour and the weather, the area was quiet. I waited and watched sad drops of water falling in a slow rhythm from the rusted roof.

After about ten minutes I heard footsteps on the wet brick behind me, and a moment later Bulfinch appeared. He was wearing an olive trench coat and hunkering down under a large black umbrella. He couldn't see me and I waited until he had passed before speaking.

'Bulfinch. Over here,' I said quietly.

'Don't do that,' he said, turning to face me. 'You scared me.'

'You're alone?'

'Of course. You brought the disk?'

I observed the alley in both directions. All clear. 'It's nearby. Tell me what you plan to do with it.'

'You know what I plan to do. I'm going to write a series of stories with whatever's on there as corroboration.'

'How long will that take?'

'The stories are already written. All I need is the proof.'

I considered. 'Let me tell you a few things about the disk,' I said, and explained about the encryption.

'Not a problem,' he said. '*Forbes* has a relationship with Lawrence Livermore. They'll help us. As soon as it's cracked, we publish.'

'I want you to understand something,' I said. 'If you were to fail to publish, your failure might cost Midori her life. If that were to happen, I would find you and kill you.'

'I believe you.'

I looked at him a moment longer, then took out the disk. I handed it to him and walked back to the station.

I ran an SDR to Shinbashi, thinking about Tatsu. Until the contents of the disk were published, it wasn't just Midori who was in danger, it was also Tatsu. It had been a lot of years since I had seen him, but we had covered each other's backs once. I owed him a warning shot at least.

I called from a payphone. 'Do you know who this is?' I asked in English after they had put me through to him.

There was a long pause. '*Ei, hisashiburi desu ne.*' Yes, it's been a long time. Then he switched to English—a good sign, because it meant he didn't want the people around him to understand. 'Do you know that the Keisatsucho found two bodies in Sengoku? One of them had been carrying a cane. Your fingerprints were on it.'

My fingerprints were on file from the time I returned to Japan after the war—I was technically a foreigner, and all foreigners in Japan get fingerprinted.

'The best thing you can do,' he went on, 'is to come to the Keisatsucho. I will do everything I can do to help you. You make yourself look guilty by running.'

'That's why I'm calling, Tatsu. I've got information about this matter that I want to give to you.'

'Where and when?' he asked.

'Are we alone on this line?'

'Are you suggesting that this line could be tapped?' he asked. He was telling me to assume that it was.

'Lobby of the Hotel Okura, next Saturday, noon sharp,' I said. The Okura was a ridiculously public place to meet, and Tatsu would know that I would never seriously suggest it.

'Ah, that's a good place,' he answered, telling me he understood. 'I'll see you then.'

'You know, Tatsu, it sounds crazy, but sometimes I miss the times we had in Vietnam. Those useless weekly briefings—remember?'

The CIA head of the task force scheduled briefings for 16.30, leaving him plenty of time afterwards to chase prostitutes in Saigon.

'Yes, I remember,' he said.

'I was especially missing them just now,' I said, getting ready to give him the day to add to the time. 'Wished I had one tomorrow, in fact. I'm getting nostalgic in my old age.'

'That happens.'

'I'm sorry we lost touch. Tokyo's changed so much. I used to love that place where the mama-san made pottery. Remember?'

The place was in Ebisu. 'It's gone,' he said, telling me he understood. 'I strongly advise you to come in.'

'I'll think about it.' I hung up then, willing him to understand my cryptic message. I didn't know what I was going to do if he didn't.

THE PLACE I'D MENTIONED in Ebisu was a classic Japanese *izakaya* that Tatsu had introduced me to when I came to Japan after the war. *Izakaya* are tiny bars, usually run by an ageless man or woman, with only a red lantern outside the entrance to advertise their existence. Offering refuge from a demanding boss or a tedious marriage, *izakaya* serve beer and sake long into the night.

Tatsu and I had spent a lot of time at the place in Ebisu, but I had stopped going there once we lost touch. And now, according to Tatsu, the place wasn't even there any more. But I remembered where it had been, and that's where I would wait. I found the place. The dilapidated building was gone, replaced by an antiseptic-looking convenience store. No sign of Tatsu, but I was nearly an hour early. I circled round behind the new shopping mall, then came back through it, along a wide outdoor esplanade bright with chrome and glass. A couple of high-school kids passed me, laughing. They looked like they belonged there.

I saw a figure in an old grey trench coat coming towards me, and although I couldn't make out the face I recognised the gait. It was Tatsu, sucking a little warmth from a cigarette.

He saw me and waved, tossing away the cigarette. As he came closer I saw that his face was more deeply lined than I remembered, a weariness somehow closer to the surface.

'*Honto ni, shibaraku buri da na,*' I said, offering him a bow. It has been a long time. He extended his hand.

'Rain-san, what have you done this time?' he asked. 'You are a suspect in a double murder in which one of the victims was well connected in the LDP. I am under pressure to solve this, you know.'

'Aren't you even going to tell me it's good to see me?'

He smiled his sorrowful smile. 'You know it's good to see you. But I would wish for different circumstances.'

'How are your daughters?'

The smile broadened. 'Very fine. One doctor. One lawyer. Luckily they have their mother's brains, *ne?*'

We headed back across the mall and I got to the point. 'Yamaoto Toshi, head of Conviction, has put a contract out on your life.'

He stopped walking. 'How do you know this?'

'Sorry, no questions about how.'

We started walking again. 'You know, Rain-san, a lot of people would like to see me dead. Sometimes I wonder how I've managed to keep breathing for all this time.'

'Maybe you've got a guardian angel.'

He laughed. 'Actually, the explanation is simpler. My death would establish my credibility. Alive, I can be dismissed as a fool.'

'I'm afraid circumstances have changed.'

He looked at me closely. 'I didn't know you were mixed up with Yamaoto.'

'I'm not. There's a disk. My understanding is that it contains information implicating various politicians in massive corruption. Yamaoto is trying to get it. You know anything about this, Tatsu?'

He shrugged. 'I'm a cop. I know a little about everything.'

'Yamaoto thinks you know a lot. He knows you're after that disk. He's having trouble getting it back, so he's eliminating loose ends.'

'Why is he having trouble getting the disk back?'

'He doesn't know where it is.'

'Do you?'

'Tatsu, this isn't about the disk. I came here because I learned that you're in danger. I wanted to warn you.'

'But the missing disk is the reason I'm in danger, is it not?' he said, affecting a puzzled look. 'Find the disk; remove the danger.'

'I'll tell you this much,' I said. 'The person who has the disk is in a position to publish what's on it. That should remove the danger.'

He stopped and grabbed my arm. '*Masaka*, tell me you didn't give that disk to Bulfinch.'

Alarm bells started going off in my head. 'Why do you ask that?'

'Because Franklin Bulfinch was murdered yesterday in Akasaka Mitsuke, outside the Akasaka Tokyu Hotel.'

Outside the Akasaka Tokyu—100 yards from where I gave it to him. 'What time did it happen?' I asked.

'Early afternoon. Did he have the disk with him?'

'Almost certainly,' I told him.

His shoulders slumped, and I knew he wasn't play acting.

'Damn it, Tatsu. How do you know about the disk?'

There was a long pause before he answered. 'Because Kawamura was supposed to give the disk to me.'

I raised my eyebrows in surprise.

'I had been developing Kawamura. I had strongly encouraged him to provide me with the information that is now on that disk. It seems that, in the end, everyone trusts a reporter more than a cop. Kawamura decided to give the disk to Bulfinch instead.'

'How do you know?'

'Kawamura called me the morning he died. He said, "I'm giving the disk to the Western media."'

'How did you know it was Bulfinch?'

'Bulfinch is well known for his reporting on corruption. But I couldn't be sure until this morning, when I learned of his murder. And I wasn't completely certain until just now.'

'So this is why you've been following Midori?'

'Of course. Kawamura died almost immediately after he called me. His daughter had his things. She was a logical target.'

'And that's why you were investigating the break-in at her father's apartment?'

'My men performed that break-in, looking for the disk.'

'Two chances to look for it—the break-in, and then the investigation,' I said, admiring his efficiency. 'Convenient.'

'Not convenient enough. We couldn't find it.' He looked at me disapprovingly. 'You know, Rain-san, I had a man following her in

Omotesando. He had a most unlikely accident in the men's room of a local bar. His neck was broken.'

Hell, that was Tatsu's man. 'Really,' I said.

'On the same night I had men waiting at the daughter's apartment. Despite being armed, they were overcome by a single man.'

'Embarrassing,' I said, waiting for more.

He took out a cigarette. 'Academic,' he said, exhaling a cloud of grey smoke. 'It's over. The CIA has the disk now.'

'Why do you say that? What about Yamaoto?'

'I have means of knowing that Yamaoto is still searching. There is only one other player in this drama, besides me. That player must have taken the disk from Bulfinch.'

'If you're talking about Holtzer, he's working with Yamaoto.'

He smiled the sad smile. 'Yamaoto controls Holtzer through blackmail, as he controls all his puppets. But Holtzer is playing a double game. He plans to use that disk to bring Yamaoto down.'

'So Holtzer hasn't told Yamaoto that the Agency has the disk.'

He shrugged. 'As I said, Yamaoto is still looking for it.'

'Tatsu,' I said quietly, 'what's on that disk?'

He took a tired pull on his cigarette. 'Videos of extramarital sexual acts, audio of bribes and payoffs, records of illegal real estate transactions. Implicating everyone but Yamaoto.'

'Yamaoto uses this information as blackmail?'

'Why do you think we have had eleven prime ministers in as many years? Every one of them has either been an LDP flunky or a reformer who is immediately co-opted. This is Yamaoto, governing from the shadows.'

'But he's not even part of the LDP.'

'He doesn't want to be. When a politician displeases him, incriminating information is released, and the offending politician is disgraced. The scandal reflects only on the LDP, not on Conviction.'

'How does he get his information?'

'Wiretaps, video surveillance, and accomplices. Every time he traps someone new, the victim becomes complicit and assists him in furthering his network of blackmail.'

'Why would they help him?'

'Carrot and stick. Yamaoto has on his payroll a number of beautiful young women. Say he has one of his people videotape a member of parliament engaging in an embarrassing sexual act with one of these women. The politician is told it will be kept in confidence in exchange for his vote on certain measures and for his cooperation in entrapping his colleagues. The politician's fear of exposure is a significant motivator. As for entrapping his colleagues, there is psychology at work: by making others dirty, he feels less dirty by comparison. And Yamaoto offers an enormous slush fund that the politician can use to fund his next campaign. Yamaoto's influence runs so deep that, if you're not part of his network, you'll be defeated in the next election by being outspent by one of his puppets.'

'With all that power, why have I never heard of him?'

'Yamaoto's victims know only that they are being blackmailed, not by whom. Most of them believe it is the work of another LDP faction. Yamaoto manages things so that even the LDP believes the LDP is the power. But there is a power behind the power.'

I thought of Tatsu's conspiracy theories. 'But you've been focusing on corruption in the LDP yourself, Tatsu.'

His eyes narrowed. 'How would you know that?'

I smiled. 'Just because we've fallen out of touch doesn't mean I've lost interest.'

'Yes, I focus on corruption in the LDP. Yamaoto believes it serves his ends. And it would, if my reports were taken seriously.' There was a bitter set to his mouth as he said it.

I couldn't help but smile. 'Your real goal is Yamaoto. Now I understand why you wanted that disk.'

'You knew of my involvement, Rain-san. Why didn't you contact me?'

'Midori,' I said. 'If I'd given the disk to you, Yamaoto would still think it was missing, and he would keep after Midori. Publication was the only way to make her safe.'

We walked for a moment in silence, then I asked, 'How did Yamaoto get to Holtzer?'

'By offering him what every man wants. Power. How do you think that Holtzer rose so quickly to become Tokyo chief of station?'

'Yamaoto's been feeding him information?'

'Of course. It is my understanding that Mr Holtzer has been notably successful in Japan. He has been responsible for producing critical intelligence reports regarding corruption in the Japanese government, on which Yamaoto is of course an expert.'

'Holtzer knows that he's being played?'

'At first, he thought he was developing Yamaoto. Once he realised that the opposite was true, what were his options? Tell the CIA that the assets he had developed were plants? That would have meant the end of his career. The alternative was much more pleasant: work for

Yamaoto, who continues to feed the "intelligence" that makes Holtzer a star. And Yamaoto has his mole inside the CIA.'

Holtzer, a mole, I thought, disgusted. *I should have known.*

'What about Bulfinch,' I asked. 'How did Holtzer get to him?'

'By having him followed until you handed over the disk.' I heard the note of criticism in his voice—telling me it was stupid to give the disk to a civilian.

We walked silently for a few minutes. Then he said, 'Rain-san. What have you been doing in Japan all this time?'

'Nothing terribly new,' I said. 'Helping a few US companies find ways to import their products into Japan.'

'What I mean is, What are you still doing in Japan? I don't understand. I would like to.'

What could I tell him? *I needed to stay at war. A shark can't stop swimming, or it dies.* But it was more than that, I had to admit to myself. Sometimes I hate living here. Even after twenty-five years, I'm still an outsider. Despite my native features, my native linguistic level, what matters in the end is that inside I am half *gaijin.* I'm marked by an indelible stain.

'Maybe it's time for you to go home,' Tatsu said, gently.

'I wonder where that is,' I said.

He spoke slowly. 'There is a risk that, if you stay, we could learn we have opposing interests.'

'Let's not learn that, then.'

I saw the sad smile. 'We can try.'

Something occurred to me. I stopped walking and looked at him. 'It might not be over,' I said. 'Maybe we can still get the disk back.'

'How?'

'It can't be copied or transmitted electronically. Holtzer is going to need expertise to decrypt it. Either he has to take the disk to the experts, or the experts will have to come to him.'

He paused for only a second before taking out his cellphone. 'I need a schedule for visiting American government personnel,' he said into the phone. 'Particularly anyone declared from the NSA or CIA. Right away.'

The US and Japanese governments declare their high-level spooks to each other as part of their security treaty. It was a long shot, but it was something. And I knew Holtzer. He'd be billing the disk as the intelligence coup of the century. He'd be sure to hand it over himself.

We waited silently for a few minutes, then Tatsu said, 'Yes. Yes. Yes. Understood. Wait a minute.'

He held the phone against his chest and said, 'NSA software cryptography specialist, and the CIA director of East Asian Affairs. Both arriving from Washington tonight.'

'Where are they going? The embassy?'

'Hold on.' He put the phone back to his ear. 'Find out whether they've requested a diplomatic escort, and if so where they're going.' We waited. After a few minutes he said, 'Good.' The phone went back to his chest. 'Yokosuka US Naval Base. Thursday morning, straight from the Narita Airport Hilton.'

'We've got him, then.'

His expression was grim. 'How, exactly?'

'Hell, stop Holtzer's car, take the disk.'

'On what evidence, exactly? The prosecutors would want to know.'

'Tell them it was an anonymous source.'

'You're missing the point. What you've told me is not evidence. It's hearsay. What you are suggesting would be useless.'

I reddened. Somehow, Tatsu could always make me feel like a thickheaded *gaijin*. 'Well, what do you propose?'

'I can get the disk and protect Midori. But you will need to be involved. I will arrange to have Holtzer's car stopped outside the naval facility, perhaps on the pretext of needing to examine its undercarriage for explosive devices.' He looked at me drily. 'Perhaps an anonymous call could warn us of such an attempt.'

He intoned a phone number, which I wrote down on my hand. When I was done, he said, 'An officer will, of course, have to ask the driver to lower his window to explain.'

I nodded, seeing where he was going. 'Here's my pager number,' I said. 'Contact me when you've acquired the information on Holtzer's movements. Input a phone number, then five-five-five, so I'll know it's you. I'm going to need some equipment, too—a flashbang.' Flashbang grenades are just a big noise and a flash of light, so they temporarily disorientate, rather than kill and maim.

'How can I get it to you?' he asked.

'The fountain at Hibiya Park,' I answered. 'Drop it in on the side facing Hibiya-dori. Like this.' I drew a diagram on my hand to ensure that he understood. 'Page me when it is in position.'

'All right.'

'One more thing. Warn your people. I don't want anyone shooting at me by mistake.'

'I will do my best.'

'Do better than your best. It's my ass.'

'It's both our asses,' he said, his voice level. 'If you are unsuccessful.'

He had a point. Not that it was worth arguing over.

'You just stop the car,' I told him. 'I'll take care of the rest.'

He bowed with unsettling formality. 'Good luck, Rain-san,' he said, and walked off into the gathering darkness.

I LOVE TOKYO AT NIGHT. It's the lights, I think: more than the architecture, more, even, than its sounds and scents, the lights are what animate the city's nocturnal spirit. There is brightness: streets alight with neon, with the urgent blinking of constellations of pachinko parlours, streets where the store windows and the headlights of a thousand passing cars illuminate the road. And there is gloom: alleys lit by nothing more than the fluorescent glow of a lonely vending machine, streets lit only by the yellowish pall of lamplights spaced so widely that a passing figure and his shadow seem to evaporate in the dim spaces between.

I walked the gloomy backstreets of Ebisu after Tatsu departed, heading towards the Imperial Hotel in Hibiya, where I would stay until this thing was over. For near-suicidal audacity, what I was about to do would rank with any of the missions I had undertaken with SOG. I wondered if Tatsu's bow was some kind of epitaph.

You've survived missions before that ought to have been your last.

After our rampage in Cambodia, things started going bad for my unit. I knew what we had done at Cu Lai was wrong, but I rationalised by saying hey, we're at war; wrong things happen. Some of the other guys got gun-shy. Crazy Jake went the opposite way.

Crazy Jake was fanatically loyal to his Yards—short for Montagnards—and they responded to that. He eschewed army barracks, preferring to sleep in the Yard quarters. He learned their language and their customs, participated in their ceremonies and rituals. All this made the brass uncomfortable.

Frustrated with the Military Assistance Command, Vietnam's inability to root out the mole who was compromising SOG's operations, Jake started using Bu Dop as a staging ground for independent missions against the Vietcong in Cambodia. The Yards were happy to follow Crazy Jake on his forays. But SOG was being disbanded, and Vietnamisation—that is, turning the war over to the Vietnamese so that America could back out—was the order of the day. MACV told him to shut off the Cambodian ops, but Jake refused.

So MACV recalled him to Saigon. Jake ignored them. A detachment was sent in to retrieve him, and never returned. So they cut off his supplies. But Jake wouldn't cease and desist. MACV figured out that he was selling poppy to finance his operation. Jake had become his own universe. He had a self-sustaining, highly effective, fanatically loyal private army.

MACV knew about Jimmy and me. They brought me in one day. 'You're going to have to go in there and get him,' they told me. 'He's out of control. This is a public-relations fiasco if it gets out.'

'I don't think I can get him out,' I said.

'We didn't say, "get him out". We just said, "get him".'

There were three of them. Two MACV, one CIA. I was shaking my head. The guy from the Agency spoke up.

'Do what we're asking, and you've got a ticket home.'

'I'll get home when I get home,' I said, but I wondered.

He shrugged. 'We've got two choices here. One is, we carpet-bomb every hamlet in Bu Dop. That's about a thousand friendlies, plus Calhoun. Two is, you do what's right and save all those people, and you're on a plane the next day. Personally, I don't give a shit.'

I told them I would do it. They were going to grease him anyway. Even if they didn't, I saw what he had become.

I went in, told the Yards that I wanted to see Crazy Jake. I was known, so they took me to him. I didn't have a weapon.

'John,' he greeted me. 'You come in here to join me? We're the only outfit in this fucking war that the V.C. is actually afraid of.'

We spent some time catching up. By the time I told him they were going to bomb him it was already night.

'I figured they would, sooner or later,' he said.

'Why don't you just walk out?'

He gave me a sly look. 'I don't fancy going to jail, John. Not after leading the good life here.'

'Well, you're in a tight spot.'

He said, 'You supposed to kill me, man?'

'Yeah,' I told him.

'So do it.'

I didn't say anything.

'I've got no way out. They're going to vaporise my people otherwise, I know that. And I'd rather it be you than some guy I don't know. You're my blood brother, man.'

I still didn't say anything.

'I love these people,' he said. 'I really love them.' These were not just words. 'My Yards won't be happy with you. But you're pretty slippery. You'll get away.'

'I just want to go home,' I said.

He laughed. 'There's no home for us, John. Not after what we've done. It doesn't work that way. Here.' He handed me a side arm. 'Don't worry about me. Save my Yards.'

I thought of the recruiter, the one who'd given us twenty bucks to pay some woman to sign us into the army. I thought of Deirdre saying, *Watch out for Jimmy, OK?*

He picked up a CAR-15, a submachine-gun version of the M-16, and popped in a magazine. Clicked off the safety.

'C'mon, John. I'm not going to keep asking so nicely.'

The CAR-15 was swinging towards me. I thought of the swimming hole near Dryden, how you had just to forget about everything else and jump.

'Last chance,' Jimmy was saying. 'Last chance.'

Do what we're asking, and you've got a ticket home.

There's no home for us, John. Not after what we've done.

I raised the pistol, double-tapping the trigger. The two slugs slammed through his chest. Jimmy was dead before he hit the floor.

Two Yards burst into Jimmy's hooch but I cut them down and ran. I took some shrapnel but the wounds were minor. Back at base they told me, 'OK, soldier, that's your million-dollar wound. You're going home now.' Seventy-two hours later I was back in Dryden.

The body came back two days later. There was a funeral. Jimmy's parents were crying. Deirdre was crying. 'Oh God, John, I knew he wasn't going to make it back,' she was saying.

I left town a day later. Didn't say goodbye. Jimmy was right, there was no home after what we had done.

I tell myself it's karma, the great wheels of the universe grinding on. A lifetime ago I killed my girl's brother. Now I take out a guy, next thing I know I'm involved with his daughter. If it were happening to someone else, I'd think it was funny.

I had called the Imperial before the meeting with Tatsu and made a reservation. I keep a few things stored at the hotel in case of a rainy day: a couple of suits, identity papers, currency, concealed weapons. The hotel people think I'm an expat Japanese who visits Japan frequently, and I pay them to keep my things. The Imperial is big enough to be as anonymous as a love hotel, if you know how to play it.

I had just reached Hibiya Station when my pager went off. I saw a number I didn't recognise, followed by the 5-5-5 that told me it was Tatsu. I found a payphone. The other side picked up on the first ring. 'Secure line?' Tatsu's voice asked.

'Secure enough.'

'The two visitors are leaving Narita at oh-nine-hundred tomorrow. It's a ninety-minute ride. Our man might get there before them, so you'll need to be in position early.'

'OK. The package?'

'You can pick it up in an hour.'

'Will do.'

Silence. Then: 'Good luck.' Dead line.

I called the number Tatsu had given me in Ebisu. Whispering to disguise my voice, I said that there would be a bomb on the under-carriage of a diplomatic vehicle visiting the Yokosuka Naval Base tomorrow. That should slow things up in front of the guardhouse.

I looked pretty rough when I checked in at the hotel. No one seemed to notice my sleeve, wet from fishing Tatsu's package out of the fountain in the park. Anyway, I had just flown in from the East Coast of the United States—long trip, anything can happen.

My things were already waiting for me in the room, the shirts pressed and the suits hung neatly. I bolted the door and sat down on the bed, then checked a false compartment in the suitcase they had brought up, where I saw the dull gleam of the Glock. I opened up the toiletry kit, took out the rounds I wanted from a dummy can of deodorant, loaded the gun, and slipped it underneath the mattress.

At nine o'clock there was a quiet knock at the door. It was Midori, as expected. 'It's about time we stayed in a place like this,' she said. 'Those love hotels can get old.'

'But they have their advantages,' I said, putting my arms round her.

We ordered dinner from the room-service menu and I filled Midori in on my meeting with Tatsu, told her the bad news about Bulfinch.

After the food arrived, Midori said, 'I've been thinking about these people. They killed Bulfinch. They tried to kill you and me. They must have wanted to kill my father. Did he really have a heart attack?'

I poured sake into two small cups. My hands were steady. 'There are ways of killing someone that make it look like natural causes. And based on what they learned of your father's activities, they certainly would have wanted him dead.'

There was a cold fire in her eyes. 'I think they killed him,' she said.

There's no home for us, John. Not after what we've done. 'You may be right,' I said, quietly. Did she know? Or did her mind refuse to go where instinct wanted to take her? I couldn't tell.

'Your father was a brave man,' I said, my voice slightly thick. 'Regardless of how he died, he shouldn't have died in vain. That's why I have to get that disk back. I really . . .' I wasn't sure what I was going to say. 'I really want to do that.'

Warring emotions crossed her face. 'I don't want you to,' she said. 'It's too dangerous.'

'Less than it seems. My friend is going to make sure that the police know what's going on, so no one is going to take a shot at me.'

'What about the CIA people? You can't control them.'

I thought about that. Tatsu probably figured that if I got killed, he would use it as an excuse to order everyone out of the car, search for weapons, and find the disk that way. He was a practical guy.

'Nobody's going to shoot me. The way I've got it set up, they won't even know what's going on until it's too late.'

'I thought, in war, nothing goes according to plan.'

'That's true. I've made it this far by being a good improviser.' I took a swallow of sake. 'Anyway, we're out of alternatives. Yamaoto doesn't know that Holtzer has the disk, so he's going to keep coming after you if we don't get it back. And me, too.'

We ate for a few minutes in silence. Then she said, 'It makes sense, but it's still terrible.' Her voice was bitter.

She wandered over to the window. I watched her for a moment, then walked over, stopping close enough to smell the clean smell of her hair and some more exotic scent, and slowly, slowly let my hands rise so that my fingertips were just touching her shoulders.

Then my fingertips gave way to my hands, and when my hands made their way to her hips she eased back into me. Standing there with her, looking out of the window over Tokyo, I felt the weight of what I would face in the morning drift slowly away from me. There was nowhere on the whole planet that I would rather have been right then. The city around us was a living thing: the million lights were its eyes; the laughter of lovers its voice; the expressways and factories its muscles and sinews. And I was there at its pulsing heart.

I GOT UP JUST BEFORE DAWN, and stood looking out of the window as the lights came on in Tokyo and the city slowly emerged from its slumber. I showered and dressed in a grey flannel suit, a white cotton shirt and conservative blue tie. The shoes were handmade, the leather briefcase from a British manufacturer. The details are what make the disguise. *And who knows?* I thought. *If this doesn't go well, you could be buried in this outfit. You might as well look good.*

Midori sat on the bed while I dressed. 'I like you in a suit,' she told me. 'You look good.'

'Just a *sarariman* on his way to work,' I said.

I slipped the Glock into a custom holster at the small of my back, where it would be concealed by the drape of the flannel. Then I eased the flashbang up under my armpit where the natural compression of my arm held it in place. I moved my arm out a few inches and jiggled it hard, and the device slid down into my waiting hand. Satisfied, I put it back in position.

'OK. I've got to go. I'll be back some time in the evening. Will you wait for me?'

She nodded, her face set. 'I'll be here. Just come back.'

'I will.' I picked up the briefcase and left.

It was a brisk, clear morning: rare weather for Tokyo, and the kind I've always liked best. At Tokyo Station I bought a ticket to Shinbashi, where I transferred to the Yokosuka line, checking my back on the way. I got on the train at 7.00, and it eased out of the station four minutes later. Seventy-four minutes after that we pulled into Yokusuka Station, across the harbour from the naval base.

From the station I walked along the esplanade that follows the water line of Yokosuka Harbour. A cold wind sliced across the water into my face, smelling faintly of the sea. The sky was dark, in contrast to the clear weather in Tokyo.

The harbour surface was as grey and foreboding as the sky. I paused on a wooden walkway overlooking the harbour, watching the brooding US warships at rest, the clumps of hills behind them startlingly green against the grey of everything else.

I heard tyres crunching gravel, and turned round just in time to see the first of three black sedans brake to a stop a few yards from where I was standing. The rear doors flew open and a man got out on each side. All Caucasians. *Holtzer*, I thought.

The follow-on cars stopped to the left and right of the lead; with my back to the water, I was encircled. Two more men got out. All were brandishing compact Berettas.

'Get in,' the one closest to me growled.

'I don't think so,' I said evenly. If they were going to kill me, I'd make them do it here.

Six of them stood round me in a semicircle. One of them reached under his jacket and pulled out what I instantly recognised as a taser—a stun gun. Which meant they wanted to take me, not kill me. I heard the pop of the taser firing its twin electrical darts, felt them sink into my thigh, current surging through my body. I went down, jerking helplessly.

They let the current surge, standing around me while I spasmed like a fish on a deck. Finally it stopped, but I had no control over my limbs. I felt them doing a pat-down—ankles, thighs, lower back. I felt the Glock being taken from its holster. I waited for the pat-down to continue but it didn't. They must have been satisfied that they had found my weapon—an amateur mistake that saved the flashbang, which had stayed in place.

Someone handcuffed my arms behind my back. A hood was pulled over my head. Someone else moved in and I felt them pick me up, limp as a burlap sack. They dumped me onto the floor in the back of one of the cars and the car jerked into motion.

We drove for less than five minutes. During the ride I tested my fingers, wiggled my toes. Control was coming back, but my nervous system was still scrambled. I felt the car slow down and stop. Doors opened, and a pair of hands took me by each ankle and dragged me out. My head smacked the bottom edge of the door and I saw stars. They pulled me to my feet. Then they were pushing me up a short flight of stairs. I heard a door open, then slam shut. I was shoved into a chair and the hood was pulled off my head.

I was inside a construction trailer. Dim light came through a single window. A figure sat with his back to it. Holtzer.

'How did you get to me?' I said, deliberately radiating an air of defeat. Not so hard, under the circumstances.

'I knew you'd make another play for the disk. As a precaution, we set up checkpoints around the likely staging areas near the base. You walked right into one. You should have known you were going to come up short, John. You always do, when you're up against me.'

'Right,' I said. Without the handcuffs, I might be able to get past Holtzer and the two men at the door. With the handcuffs, I wasn't going anywhere.

'You don't even know what I mean by that, do you?' he went on. 'You've always been so blind.'

'What are you talking about?'

His fleshy lips twisted into a loathsome smile and he silently mouthed four words. *I was the mole.*

I dropped my head and fought for control. 'You never had the access. It was someone on the ARVN side.'

'You think so?' he said, his voice low so his men couldn't hear. 'Remember Cu Lai?'

The Cambodian village. I felt a sick feeling creeping in. 'What about it?' I said.

'Remember "Waste 'em"? You were tough, John! I had to use three sets of voices to convince you.'

Keep control. Focus on the problem. How do you get out of this?

'Why?' I asked.

'I had a source, a guy who could do a lot for me. I had to show him what I could do for him. Someone in the village had lent him a lot of money. I wanted to show him how I could make those kinds of problems go away.'

'So you massacred an entire village to get to one guy? Why not just give the source money to pay back the loan?'

He threw back his head and laughed. 'C'mon, Rain, the bean counters were paying more attention to the money than the bullets. Some dead villagers? Just a few more V.C. to add to the body count. It was easier to do it that way than to requisition funds.'

For the first time since the nightmares of the war, I could feel real despair starting to drill its way into my mind. I began to understand bone deep that in a very few minutes I would be dead, that Holtzer would have won, as he'd been winning all along. And while the thought of my own death no longer fascinated me, the knowledge that I had failed to stop him, at the same moment that I came to understand what he had caused me to do so long ago, was overwhelming.

'I don't believe you,' I said, playing for time. 'What were they giving you that would have been worth it? I know it wasn't money— you're still a government bean counter thirty-five years later.'

'You're such a farmer, Rain. There's the way of the world, and you just don't get it. You trade intel for intel, that's the game. The North wanted intel on SOG, and were willing to pay a lot for it with intel of their own. I was bartering pigshit for gold.'

I knew he was telling the truth. There was nothing I could say.

'Let me share one more titbit before these men dump your body in the harbour,' he went on. 'I know all about Crazy Jake. I volunteered you for the mission to get rid of him.'

My throat constricted. I couldn't speak.

'It was good luck that the problem of his little army came to my attention. But I knew just the guy to handle it—his old high-school pal, John Rain. No one else could get close enough.'

It was over. I was going to die. My mind started to drift, and a strange calmness descended.

'I got the word out afterwards. I made sure people knew.'

I found myself remembering the time I had climbed Mount Fuji with my father. We took turns wanting to go back, but the other always insisted on going on, and eventually we made it to the top. We laughed about it afterwards.

'It made people uncomfortable, John. What kind of man can top his own best friend? Not someone you could ever trust. Not someone you could promote. You've been nothing but a murderous little half-breed errand boy for your betters ever since.'

The old man had always liked to tell that story. And how glad he was that we had made it. It was a good memory. Not a bad one to have with you on your way out.

'Cat got your tongue, Rain?' He stood up and turned to the two men at the door. 'Don't kill him here—it's too close to the naval base. Take him somewhere else and dump him when you're done.'

One of the men opened the door for him, and he walked out. I heard car doors opening and closing, then two sets of tyres as they drove off. We had arrived in three cars, so only one was left. I didn't know if there were other men outside.

The two men remained at the door, their faces impassive.

Some deep part of me insisted on going out fighting. 'These cuffs are starting to hurt,' I said, standing up slowly.

One of them laughed. 'Don't worry, we'll take care of the pain in a few minutes.'

'But my arms hurt,' I said again, making a face and lifting my elbows to create space between my upper arms and my torso.

'Oh God, I think I'm losing circulation,' I moaned. I worked my shoulders in circles until the flashbang was poised over my sleeve, then started jiggling my arms violently. I felt the device ease into the upper part of the jacket sleeve.

I lowered my wrists and started bouncing on my toes as though I had to urinate. 'I need to take a leak,' I said.

The men at the door looked at each other, their expressions indicating that they found me pathetic.

Each bounce brought the device down another crucial inch. When it got past my elbow, I felt it slide smoothly down my sleeve and into my waiting hand. The device had a five-second timer. If I rolled it out too early, they might make it out of the door before it went off. If I waited too long, I would probably lose a hand. Not exactly how I was hoping to get the cuffs off.

I pulled the spoon free and counted. *One-one thousand . . .*

One of the men reached inside his jacket, started to slide out his gun. *Two-one thousand.* 'Wait a second, wait a second,' I said, my throat tight. *Three-one thousand.*

They looked at each other. They were thinking, *This is the hard case we'd been warned would be so dangerous?*

Four-one thousand. I squeezed my eyes shut and spun so that my back was to them, simultaneously shovelling the flashbang at them with a flick of my wrists. I heard it hit the floor, followed by a huge bang that concussed my entire body. My breath was knocked out of me and I collapsed onto the floor.

I rolled left, then right, trying to take a breath. I couldn't hear anything but a huge roaring inside my head.

Holtzer's men were on the floor, too, blinded, their hands gripping the sides of their heads. One of them pulled himself onto all fours and started feeling his way along the floor, trying to recover his gun.

I rolled onto my knees, concentrating on balancing. I planted a wobbly left foot forwards and tried to stand, but fell over again. I needed my arms for balance.

The man's groping fingers moved closer to the gun.

I rolled onto my back and plunged my hands downwards as hard as I could, forcing my cuffed wrists below the curve of my hips and buttocks and onto the backs of my thighs. I slid my wrists down the backs of my legs and got my hands in front of me.

I rolled onto all fours. Saw the man clutching the gun.

I closed the distance just as he was picking up the gun and kicked him in the face. The force of the kick sent him spinning away and knocked me over backwards.

I lurched to my feet just as the second man regained his footing. He reached inside his jacket, going for a weapon.

I stumbled over to his position just as he pulled free a pistol. Before he could raise it, I thrust the fingers of my cuffed hands hard into his throat, disrupting his phrenic and laryngeal nerves. Then I slipped my hands behind his neck and used the short space of chain between them to jerk his face down into my rising knee. He went limp and I tossed him to the side.

I turned towards the door and saw that the other one had got to his feet and was holding a knife. Before I could react, he charged. He thrust with the knife, but without focus I had already taken a half-step to the right, earlier than would have been ideal, but he couldn't adjust. The blade just missed me. I spun counterclockwise, clamping onto his knife wrist with both hands. I yanked his wrist in the other direction, popping my right elbow into his nose. Then I spun in fast, taking a headlock with my right arm. The knife hand came loose and I hip-threw him, my left hand coming in to strengthen the grip on his neck as his body sailed over me. When his torso had reached the extreme circumference of the throw, I jerked his neck hard in the other direction. A crack reverberated up my arms as his neck snapped and I released my grip.

I sank to my knees and tried to think. *Which one of them had the handcuff keys?* I frisked the first guy and found a set of car keys. With the other guy I hit pay dirt. A second later I was free. A quick search on the floor, and I was armed with one of their Berettas.

I stumbled into the parking lot. As I had expected, there was one car left. I slid the key into the ignition and raced out into the street.

I knew where I was—just three or four miles from the entrance to the naval base. Holtzer had left less than five minutes earlier. There might still be time. I knew the odds were massively against me, but I had one important advantage: I didn't give a shit whether I lived or died. I just wanted to watch Holtzer go first.

I wheeled left onto National Highway 16, working the horn to warn cars out of my way. I managed to buckle the seat belt as I drove, and noted with grim satisfaction that the car was equipped with an air bag. I had originally planned on tossing the flashbang into Holtzer's car as a means of gaining entry. As I had told Midori, I was going to have to improvise.

I was ten yards from the main gate when I saw the sedan turning right onto the access road. A Marine guard in camouflage uniform was approaching. There were a lot of guards doing checks ahead of the guard gate—the results of the anonymous bomb tip.

There were too many cars in front of me. I wasn't going to make it. The sedan's driver-side window was down. I leaned on the horn, but no one moved. I pulled out onto the sidewalk, knocking down trash cans. A pedestrian dived out of the way. A few yards from the access road I accelerated diagonally across the meridian, aiming for Holtzer's vehicle. I rammed the sedan into the driver-side rear door, spinning the car away from the impact and forming a two-car wreck shaped like the letter V. I was braced for the impact, and the seat belt and air bag, which deployed and deflated in a nanosecond, got me through.

It was only two steps to the sedan. I grabbed the steering wheel through the open window and hauled myself inside. I launched myself across the driver's lap, then dived into the back. Holtzer was in the left seat, obviously disorientated from the impact. One of Holtzer's aides sat next to him, a metal attaché case between them.

I grabbed Holtzer round the head with my left arm, pressing the barrel of the Beretta against his temple with my right. I saw one of the guards outside, his gun drawn. I pulled Holtzer's head closer.

'Get back, or I'll blow his head off!' I bellowed at him.

His expression was uncertain, but he kept the gun up.

'Everyone out of the car!' I shouted. 'Now!'

I reached all the way round Holtzer's neck with my hand and took hold of my own lapel. We were cheek to cheek. The Marine with the gun would have to have a hell of a lot of confidence in his marksmanship to get a shot off now.

'You!' I yelled at the driver. 'Roll up that window!'

The driver pressed a switch and his window went up. I yelled at him again to get out. He stumbled as he exited. 'You!' I yelled at the aide. 'Get out! Close the door behind you!'

The aide tried the door. 'It's jammed,' he said.

'Climb across to the front!' I shouted. 'Now!'

He scrambled forwards and got out, taking the attaché case.

'Us too,' I said to Holtzer. 'But first give me that disk.'

'Take it easy,' he said. 'It's in my left breast pocket.'

'Take it out. Slowly.'

He reached over with his right hand and carefully took out the disk. I slipped it into my jacket. 'Now we're going to get out. But slowly. Or your head is going to be all over the upholstery.'

He turned to me, his eyes hard. 'Put the gun down before the guards outside blow you away.'

'If you're not on your way in the next three seconds,' I snarled, 'I will shoot you in the balls.'

Something was nagging at me, something about the way he had turned over the disk. Too readily. Then I realised: It was a decoy. A disposable. He would never have given me the real disk so easily. *The attaché*, I thought.

'Now!' I yelled, and he reached for the door handle.

We were immediately surrounded by six Marines, all with guns.

'Stay back or I'll blow his head off!' I yelled, shoving the gun up under Holzer's jaw. I saw the aide standing behind the guards, the attaché case at his feet. 'You, over there! Open up that case!'

He looked bewildered. 'I can't. It's locked.'

'Give him the key,' I growled to Holtzer.

He laughed. 'Like hell.'

Six people had the drop on me. I yanked Holtzer to the left so they would have to re-aim, giving myself a split second to pull the gun away from his head and crack him in the temple with the butt. He sank to his knees, and I went down with him, staying close to his body. I patted his left trouser pocket and pulled out a set of keys.

'Bring the case over here!' I yelled. 'Or he's dead!'

The aide hesitated for a second, then picked up the case.

I tossed him the keys. 'Now open it.'

'I order you not to open that case!' Holtzer screamed. 'It's the US diplomatic pouch!' The aide froze, his face uncertain.

'Shut up!' I yelled, digging the barrel of the gun in under his chin. 'You think he's willing to take a chance on dying over the diplomatic pouch? Open it!'

'Shoot him!' Holtzer screamed suddenly at the guards.

'Open that case or you'll be wearing his fucking brains!'

The aide's eyes went from the case to Holtzer, then back. It seemed that everyone was frozen.

It happened suddenly. The aide dropped to his knees, fumbling with the key. The case popped open. Inside, clearly visible between two protective layers of foam, was Kawamura's disk.

A long second passed, then I heard a familiar voice from behind me. 'Arrest this man.'

I turned and saw Tatsu, three Japanese cops behind him.

The cops converged on me, one unclipping a set of handcuffs.

One of the Marine guards started to protest.

'We are outside the base,' Tatsu explained in fluent English. 'You have no jurisdiction. This is a domestic matter.'

My arms were bent behind my back, and I felt the handcuffs clicking into place. Tatstu held my eyes long enough for me to see the sadness in his, then turned and walked away.

THEY DROVE ME to Keisatsucho headquarters. I was photographed, fingerprinted, and put in a concrete cell. The cell wasn't bad. There was no window, and I kept time by counting the meals they brought me. Three times a day a taciturn guard dropped off a tray of food.

I was waiting for my sixteenth meal, trying not to worry about Midori, when two guards came for me. They took me to a small room with a table and two chairs. A naked bulb hung from the ceiling. *Looks like it's time for your interrogation*, I thought.

A few minutes later, Tatsu walked in, alone. After five days of solitary, it felt good to see someone I knew. We sat down with the table between us. He was silent and I waited for him to speak. I didn't find his reticence encouraging.

'I hope you will forgive your recent incarceration, which I know must have been unexpected.'

'I think a pat on the back would have been more in order.'

I saw the trademark sad smile. 'Appearances had to be maintained until I could straighten things out,' he said. 'To arrange for your release I had to have Kawamura's disk decrypted. After that, various phone calls had to be made, meetings arranged, levers pulled to secure your release. Evidence of your existence needed to be purged from Keisatsucho files. All this took time.'

'The disk met your expectations?'

'Exceeded them.'

He was holding something back. I waited for him to continue.

'Holtzer has been declared *persona non grata* and returned to Washington,' he said. 'He will be resigning from the CIA.'

'Just resigning? He's not being charged with anything? He's been a mole for Yamaoto, feeding false intel to the US government. Doesn't the disk implicate him?'

He sighed. 'The evidence on the disk is not the kind that will be used in court. There is a desire to avoid a public scandal.'

'And Yamaoto?' I asked.

'Yamaoto is a powerful enemy. To be fought obliquely, with stealth, over time.'

It hit me then. 'You're not going to publish it.'

'No.'

I was silent for a long moment as the implications set in. 'Then Yamaoto still thinks it's out there,' I said. 'And you've signed Midori's death warrant.'

'Yamaoto has been given to understand that the disk was destroyed by corrupt elements of the Keisatsucho. His interest in Kawamura Midori is thus substantially reduced. She will be safe for now in the United States.'

'You can't just exile her to America. She has a life here.'

'She has already left.'

I couldn't take it all in.

'You may be tempted to contact her,' he continued. 'I would advise against this. She believes you are dead.'

'Why would she believe that?'

'Because I told her.' His voice stayed matter-of-fact. 'Although I knew you were concerned for her, I didn't know, when I told her of your death, what had happened between you,' he said. 'From her reaction, I realised.'

He paused, then looked at me squarely. 'I deeply regret the pain you feel now. However, I am convinced that I did the right thing in telling her. It is better that she know nothing of your involvement in her father's death. Think of what such knowledge would do to her.'

'She didn't have to know,' I heard myself say.

'At some level, I believe she already did. Your presence would eventually have confirmed her suspicions. Instead, she is left with memories of the hero's death you died in completing her father's wishes.'

I realised, but somehow could not grasp, that Midori had already been made part of my past. It was like a magic trick.

'If I may say so,' he said, 'her affair with you was brief. There is no reason to expect her grief will be prolonged.'

'Thanks, Tatsu,' I managed to say. 'That's a comfort.'

He bowed his head.

'I still don't understand,' I said after a minute. 'I thought you wanted to publish what's on the disk. Bulfinch said that if the contents were made public, the Japanese media would have no choice but to follow up, that Yamaoto's power would be extinguished.'

He nodded slowly. 'There is some truth to that. But publishing the disk is like launching a nuclear missile. You only get to do it once, and it results in complete destruction.'

'So? Launch the missile. Destroy the corruption. Let the society breathe again.'

He sighed. 'In Japan, the corruption is the society. The rust has penetrated so deep that the superstructure is made of it. You cannot simply rip it all out without precipitating a collapse. Have you considered what would rise from the ashes?'

'What do you mean?'

'Put yourself in Yamaoto's place. Plan A is to use the threat of the disk to control the LDP. Plan B is to publish it—to destroy the LDP and put Conviction in power.'

'Because the tape implicates only the LDP,' I said, beginning to understand.

'Conviction seems a model of probity by comparison. Yamaoto would have to step out of the shadows, but he would finally have a platform from which to move the nation to the right.'

'I didn't know you were so liberal, Tatsu.'

'I am pragmatic. It matters little to me which way the country moves, as long as the move is not accompanied by Yamaoto's means of control.'

I considered. 'Yamaoto is going to figure out that the disk wasn't destroyed, that you have it. He was already coming after you. It's only going to get worse.'

'I am not such an easy man to get to, as you know.'

'You're taking a lot of chances.'

'I am playing for stakes.'

'I guess you know what you're doing,' I said, not caring any more.

He looked at me, his face impassive. 'There is another reason I must be careful. The disk implicates you.'

I had to smile at that. 'Really?' I asked.

'I had been looking for the assassin for a long time, Rain-san— there have been so many convenient deaths of "natural causes". And now I realise he is you.'

'What are you going to do about it?'

'That is for you to decide.'

'Meaning?'

'As I have told you, I have deleted all evidence of your activities, even of your existence, from the Keisatsucho's databases.'

'But there's still the disk. Is this your way of telling me that you're going to have leverage over me?'

He shook his head. 'You are free to return to your life in the shadows. But I must ask you, Rain-san, is this really the life you want?'

I didn't answer.

'May I say that I had never seen you more . . . complete than you were in Vietnam. And I believe I know why. Because at heart you are samurai. In Vietnam you thought you had found your master, your cause larger than yourself.'

What he said hit a nerve.

'You were not the same man when we met again in Japan after the war. Your master must have disappointed you for you to have become *ronin*.' A *ronin* is a person with no direction. A masterless samurai.

He waited for me to answer, but I didn't. Finally he said, 'Is what I am saying inaccurate?'

'No,' I admitted, thinking of Crazy Jake.

'You are samurai, Rain-san. But samurai cannot be samurai without a master. One cannot exist without the other.'

'What are you trying to tell me, Tatsu?'

'My battle with what plagues Japan is far from over. My acquisition of the disk provides me with an important weapon, but it is not enough. I need you with me.'

'I don't know, Tatsu. I don't know if I can trust you. You're manipulative. Look what you've been up to while I've been in jail.'

'Whether I am manipulative and whether you can trust me are two different matters,' he said.

'I'll think about it,' I told him.

'That is all I would ask.'

'Now let me out of here.'

He motioned to the door. 'You have been free to go since I came in.'

'I wish you'd said so sooner. We could have done this over coffee.'

I TOOK MY TIME getting back to Tatsu. There were a few things I needed to settle first. Harry, for one. He had hacked the Keisatsucho files, so he knew I'd been arrested and 'detained'. Several days later, he told me, all references to me had been deleted.

'I figured you were dead,' he said.

'That's what people are supposed to believe,' I said.

'Why?'

'They want my help with certain matters.'

'That's why they let you go?'

'Nothing for nothing, Harry. You know that.'

I told him about Midori.

'Maybe that's for the best,' he said.

He had most of the pieces, I knew.

'What are you going to do now?' he asked me.

'I haven't figured that out yet.'

'If you ever need a good hacker, you know where to find me.'

I FLEW OUT to Washington, DC, where they had shipped Holtzer. Processing his 'retirement' would take a few days and in the meantime he'd be in the Langley area.

I thought I'd be able to find him by calling all the hotels listed in the suburban Virginia Yellow Pages, but there was no guest named William Holtzer at any of them.

What about a car, though? I started phoning the major rent-a-car companies. It was William Holtzer calling, wanting to extend his service contract. Avis didn't have a record of a William Holtzer. Hertz did. The clerk was kind enough to tell me the licence-plate number of the car, which I told him I needed for some supplementary insurance. After that, all I had to do was search a DMV database to learn that Holtzer was driving a white Ford Taurus.

That night I drove through the parking lots of the major hotels closest to Langley, slowing to examine the licence plate of every white Ford Taurus I passed.

At about two o'clock that morning I found Holtzer's car in the garage of the Ritz Carlton. The spaces adjacent to the Taurus were taken, but there was an empty spot behind it to one side. I pulled in, nose forward so the van's sliding door would be facing Holtzer.

I checked my equipment. A 250,000-volt 'Thunder Blaster' guaranteed to cause disorientation upon contact and unconsciousness in less than five seconds. A medium-sized pink rubber 'Super Ball', available for eighty-nine cents at pretty much any drugstore. A portable defibrillation kit, small enough to tote around in an ordinary briefcase and considerably more expensive than the Super Ball.

HOLTZER SHOWED UP at 7.30. I watched him emerge from the elevator and head towards me. He was dressed in a grey suit, white shirt, dark tie. Standard Agency attire. His mind was elsewhere. I could see it in the way he failed to check the likely hot spots around his car. Shame on him, being so careless in a potential crime zone.

I slipped on a pair of black cowhide gloves. A click of the switch on the Thunder Blaster produced a sharp arc of blue sparks and an electric crackle. I was ready to go. I scanned the garage, satisfying myself that it was empty. Then I watched him move to the driver's side of the Taurus, where he paused to remove his suit jacket. *Good*, I thought. *Let's not get any wrinkles on your funeral suit.*

I waited until the jacket was just past his shoulders, then swung the van's side door open and moved in on him. He looked up when he heard the door open, but had no chance to do anything. Then I was on him, jamming the Thunder Blaster into his belly, propping him up while the shock scrambled his central nervous system.

It took less than six seconds to drag his dazed form into the van and slide the door shut behind us. I pushed him onto the ample back seat, then gave him another hit with the Thunder Blaster.

I buckled him in with the lap and shoulder belt. The hardest part was getting his shirt open and his tie out of the way so I could apply the paddles directly to his torso, where the conducting jelly would prevent any telltale burn marks.

As I applied the second paddle, his eyes fluttered open. He glanced down at his exposed chest, then looked up at me.

'Way . . . way . . .' he stammered.

'Wait?' I asked.

He grunted, I guessed to affirm.

'Sorry, can't do that,' I said, affixing the second paddle.

He opened his mouth to say something else and I shoved the Super Ball into it. I didn't want him to bite his tongue from the force of the shock—it could look suspicious.

I shifted to the side of the van to make sure I wasn't touching him when the shock was delivered. He watched me as I moved, his eyes wide. I flicked the switch on the unit. His body jerked forwards to the limit of the shoulder belt and his head arched backwards into the anti-whiplash head restraint. Cars are amazingly safe these days.

I waited for a minute, then checked his pulse to be sure he was finished. Satisfied, I removed the ball and the paddles, wiped off the residue of the conducting jelly with an alcohol swab, and fixed his clothes. I looked into his dead eyes and was surprised at how little I felt. I opened the door of the Taurus with his key, then placed it in the car's ignition. Using a modified fireman's lift, I scooped up the body and dumped it into the driver's seat.

That's for Jimmy, I thought. *And Cu Lai. They've all been waiting for you in hell.* And waiting for me. I wondered if Holtzer would be enough to satisfy them. I got into the van and drove away.

I HAD ONE MORE STOP to make. The Village Vanguard, Manhattan.

I knew that the Midori Kawamura trio was appearing from the first Tuesday in November through to the following Sunday. I made a reservation for the 1.00am set on Friday night. I didn't need to use a credit card, so I was easily able to use an alias: Watanabe, a common Japanese name.

I headed up Interstate 95. From the turnpike I could have picked up I-80 and gone on to Dryden, 200 miles and someone else's lifetime away. Instead I left the turnpike for the Holland Tunnel, where I entered the city and drove the quarter-mile to the Soho Grand Hotel on West Broadway. Mr Watanabe had reserved a suite for Friday night. He arrived before six o'clock and paid cash, counting out fourteen hundred dollar bills for the night. The staff, to their credit, evinced no surprise, probably guessing that the wealthy man with a passion for anonymity would be meeting his mistress.

The early arrival gave me time to shower, sleep for three hours, and enjoy an excellent room-service dinner.

I walked the mile or so to the Vanguard. It was cold, and I was glad of the gaberdine trousers, black cashmere turtleneck and navy blazer I was wearing. The charcoal trilby low across my forehead also provided some warmth, while obscuring my features.

I passed through the mahogany doors, taking a seat at one of the small round white tables at the back. Midori was already at the piano, wearing black like the first time I saw her. It felt good to watch her for the moment, unobserved, separated by a sadness that I knew she must have shared. She looked beautiful, and it hurt.

The lights dimmed, the murmur of conversation died away, and Midori brought the piano to life with a vengeance, her fingers ripping into the keys. I watched intently, trying to lock in the memory of the way she moved her hands and swayed her body, the expressions of her face. I knew I'd be listening to her music for ever, but this would be the last time I would watch her play.

I had always heard a frustration in her music, and loved the way it would at times be replaced by a deep, accepting sadness. But there was no acceptance in her music tonight. It was raw and angry, sometimes mournful, but never resigned. I listened, feeling the notes and the minutes slipping away from me, trying to find some solace in the thought that perhaps what had passed between us was now part of her music.

I thought about Tatsu. I knew he had done right in telling Midori I was dead. She would have figured out the truth eventually. He was right, too, about my loss not being a long-term issue for her. She had a brilliant career opening up in front of her. When you've known someone only briefly, even if intensely, death comes as a shock, but not a particularly long or deep one.

The set lasted an hour. When it was done, I exited through the wooden doors, pausing for a moment under a moonless sky.

'Excuse me,' a woman's voice came from behind me.

I turned, thinking, *Midori*. But it was only the coat-check girl. 'You left this behind,' she said, holding out the trilby.

I took the hat wordlessly and walked off into the night.

Midori. There were moments with her when I would forget everything I had done. But those moments would never have lasted. I am the product of the things I have done, and I know I will always wake up to this conclusion. What I needed to do was not deny what I was, but to find a way to channel it. Maybe, for the first time, into something worthwhile. Maybe something with Tatsu.

Midori. I still listen to her music. I hang on hard to the notes, trying to keep them from vanishing into the air, but each one dies in the dark around me like a tracer in a tree line. Sometimes I catch myself saying her name. I say it slowly, several times in succession, like a chant or a prayer.

Does she ever think of you? I sometimes wonder.

It doesn't matter. It feels good to know she's out there. I'll keep listening to her from the shadows. Like it was before. Like it's always going to be.

BARRY EISLER

A passion for judo and all things Japanese had a
significant impact on the young Barry Eisler when
he made his first career decisions. After graduat-
ing in law at Cornell University, he joined the US
State Department's Foreign Service in the hope
that he would be posted to Japan. Nothing was
forthcoming, however, so he moved to a law firm
in Washington, DC. In due course, he heard about a temporary post with
a Japanese law firm in Tokyo, and immediately requested leave of
absence. 'I persuaded my wife that this would be a good career move. It
would lead to a lot of international experience and I would improve my
Japanese.' He laughs. 'While none of that was untrue, my real reason was
to study judo at the Kodokan, the art's birthplace, and that's what I did five
or six times a week. It was a dream come true.'

After three years, Eisler had qualified as a black belt and was more
impassioned than ever about the Japanese way of life, as well as being
hooked by the city's jazz bars—a feature of Tokyo that he has woven into
Rain Fall. 'There's a lot to admire about Japan's society. If I had to identify
a single thing it would be their attitude of restraint. Unlike Americans and
certain other nationalities, Japanese rarely get upset in public over, for
example, getting cut up in traffic. After you've spent some time there, a lot
of the public displays you see elsewhere can seem childish by comparison.'

Eisler may admire Japanese society, but he has a different view of the
political scene. 'Although the depth of Japanese political corruption might
seem so outrageous that it must be fictional, it is all real. Over the course of
the last decade a number of would-be reforming politicians and bureaucrats
have died under mysterious circumstances and there are rumours in Japan
that there is a 'natural causes' assassin or assassins behind these events.'

Rain Fall was snapped up by ten publishers internationally and a sequel
is promised in 2003. 'John Rain is an interesting guy with massive contra-
dictions within his personality. The more time I spend with him, the more I
learn,' says Eisler, who now lives in the San Francisco Bay area. 'We'll have
to see whether he's going to go on killing. He's very conflicted about that.'

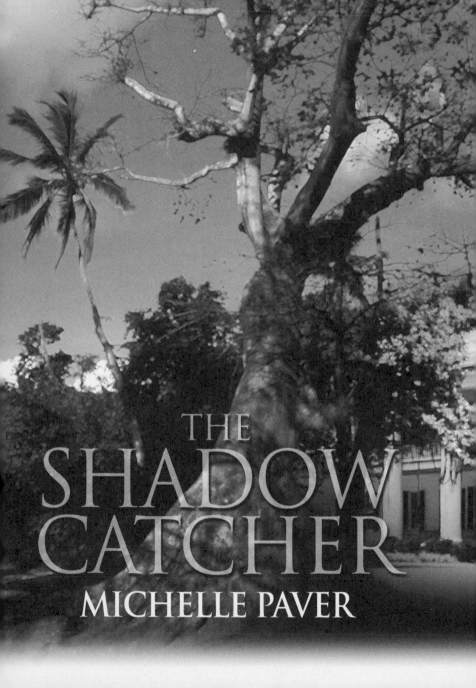

THE
SHADOW
CATCHER

MICHELLE PAVER

Eden. The ruined house stands in the heart of the Jamaican forest, the last reminder of a once great estate. Abandoned for decades, it still casts a spell, its empty hallways haunted by beauty and dreams, madness and magic.

For Madeleine it is the key to her mysterious past—and the gateway to her future.

CHAPTER ONE

Galloway, Scotland, March 1884

The important thing, her mother always said, is to think for yourself. Then she would bundle Madeleine into hat and coat and galoshes and send her out onto the beach—with orders to find ten kinds of seaweed. Come back when you're hungry, she would say.

Well, at least I am thinking for myself, Madeleine thought, as she stood at the edge of the Forbidden Kingdom. Although this probably wasn't what Mama had in mind. Her breath steamed in the frozen stillness and cold seeped through her boots. But she couldn't stamp her feet in case she alerted some guardian of the forest.

Before her the carriageway swept through the great iron gates and disappeared into the shadows beneath the trees. To her right the gatehouse loomed. Frost filmed its blind marble windows. Icicles waited to fall from the roof. In the pediment a marble crow hitched its wings to fly away, while a marble snake writhed in its claws.

Madeleine was vaguely aware of some story in the Bible about a snake. Her mother often said they must make a start on the Bible, but they never did. 'I'm sorry, Maddy,' she had said only the week before, 'I'm too ignorant and undisciplined to make a good teacher.' Madeleine strongly disagreed. Her mother knew all about photography and singing and tropical plants and animals; and she could tell stories about magic trees and talking spiders and a place called Eden, in the singsong language of Jamaica that she called *patois*.

There was a thud behind her. She spun round. A big black crow was watching her from a swaying branch.

'Go away,' she told it.

The crow gave a croak and flew off into the trees.

Through the gates, the woods were dark and haunted: warning her not to enter the Forbidden Kingdom. That was not, of course, its real name. Its real name was Strathnaw. The Forbidden Kingdom was merely what her mother called it when she was angry—because Papa had said that they must never visit it on any account. 'Then why on earth *take* a house two hours away from the wretched place?' Mama would blaze at him during one of their rows.

'Because it's secluded and within our means—'

'Nonsense. It's because you miss them, and you want to retain some sort of link, however tentative—'

'Rose, no.'

'Heaven knows, I understand. What I don't understand is why you won't allow us to make an approach, not even for Maddy's sake. She's never seen the place where you—'

'There would be no point.'

'Of course there's a point!'

And so it would go on. The last row had been a fortnight ago, just before Papa went back to his regiment. He had lost his temper and stormed from the house—but returned much later with an armful of hothouse lilies. Her mother had thrown them back at him and burst into tears. Madeleine had crouched against the banister, wondering what to do. Her mother never cried.

Dr Baines said it was just the usual 'morbid despondency of a lady near her time', and prescribed warm milk, and a little phial of cocaine drops for her sore gums. It didn't help. Recently, her mother's 'second bustle'—the one in front—had grown so big that her back ached constantly. And she'd become fretful and despondent. Hannah went about her work with a mouth pulled as tight as a drawstring, and muttered about giving in her notice.

In the end, Madeleine realised it was down to her. She couldn't let her mother stay so unhappy. She must go to the Forbidden Kingdom and talk to whoever lived there, and then perhaps they could all go to Jamaica, just as Papa was always promising they would.

For herself, Madeleine would much rather stay at Cairngowrie House, for she loved her lonely stretch of beach with its seals and its fulmars and its green-eyed cormorants. But she knew that her parents longed to go back to the land where they were born.

A harsh croak brought her back to the present. The crow was watching her from the gatehouse roof. She wished she were back at

Cairngowrie House. She wanted her father. She wanted the scratch of his whiskers and his spicy smell of moustache wax.

And yet, she reflected, he is the reason that you are here. It isn't fair of him to say 'I forbid it', and then go off to the army for months. He is always leaving us. It isn't fair.

She took a deep breath of the freezing air, and walked through the gates into the Forbidden Kingdom. The snow crunched beneath her boots like broken glass but she forced herself to walk slowly, to show the crow she was unafraid. It wasn't fooled. It followed her from branch to branch, its harsh laughter echoing through the wood.

She walked for what seemed like hours until she reached the edge of a vast park. The carriageway ran down past a frozen lake, then up a long white hill where a line of marble knights guarded the approach to a huge stone mansion. Madeleine hated it on sight.

The crow swept past her and perched on the helmet of the nearest knight. *Turn back*, it croaked.

If her mother were here, she would make a game of this. 'How would you photograph that house, Maddy? How would you show the way it makes you feel?'

The thought of her mother was a kernel of heat. The previous day, they had taken photographs with the new Instantograph, and Madeleine had tried on the stockinette 'abdominal binder' that Dr Baines had insisted her mother wear instead of stays. As Madeleine had pranced around the drawing room with a cushion for her second bustle, her mother had mimicked the doctor's rolling Scots tones— 'sup*poort* without *pray*ssure'—and they'd laughed till it hurt.

Halfway up the hill, a statue moved. Madeleine's heart jerked.

It was a knight on an enormous charger. His cloak of draped grey marble was dusted with snow. He was the guardian of the Forbidden Kingdom, come to spirit her away.

With a croak the crow flew off into the forest. The charger tossed its head and the statue resolved into an officer on a big grey horse.

Shakily, Madeleine breathed out. Nothing to be afraid of, she told herself. But her heart kept up its jerky rhythm.

'Who are you?' The officer's sharp voice carried through the freezing air. 'This is a private estate. What are you doing here?'

When she did not reply, he cantered down to her. He only reined in when he was practically upon her. The charger put down its nose to investigate her, and she took in a blast of its hot, musky breath.

She craned her neck to look up at the officer. He had thick fair hair, with darker brows and moustache, and no laughter lines. His eyes were light grey and startling in his sunburnt face. Madeleine had thought only farmers and fishermen got sunburn.

She wondered why he had no laughter lines, and whether he was unhappy, and what he would look like if he smiled. She felt nervous and uncertain as he contemplated her with his cool grey eyes, but curiously she didn't feel afraid. She just wanted him to like her.

He asked her what she was doing in the park.

She wasn't sure how to reply. She said, 'I need to see the people who live over there,' and pointed at the mansion on the hill.

'They are away. They generally are.'

She was appalled. It hadn't occurred to her that there might be no one at home.

'How did you get here?' he said with a slight frown.

'I came with Mr Ritchie,' she replied, 'the carter in Stranraer. He's gone on to Kildrochet with a parcel, but he'll be back in an hour to collect me.' She omitted to mention that she'd told her mother she was going to Stranraer to see the boats.

'Then you had better return to the gates,' said the officer, 'and wait for your Mr Ritchie there.'

She swallowed. She couldn't face going back on her own.

The officer glanced from her to the dark woods. He sighed. 'It might be quicker,' he said reluctantly, 'if you rode my horse.'

'Thank you very much,' she said politely.

He dismounted, lifted her beneath the arms and swung her into the saddle. Then he drew the reins over the horse's head so that he could lead, and started for the trees.

She was dizzyingly high up, and her legs were too short to reach the stirrups, so she had to clutch handfuls of mane to keep from sliding off. But the officer did not look round to check if she was all right, which made her feel grown up. And she liked the way his long grey cloak whispered over the snow.

It is dashing, she thought. Yes. He is a dashing officer.

She decided to start a conversation. She told him that her father was a soldier too, and that he'd been ordered to the Sudan. 'Papa,' she said to his back, 'is a major in the 65th York and Lancasters. To which regiment do you belong, sir?'

'The Borderers,' he said, still without turning round.

'Mm,' she said brightly, for want of more informed comment.

The crow appeared and began to follow them.

'My mother,' Madeleine went on doggedly, 'generally stays at home with me. She takes extremely good photographs, and she *detests* Scotland, for she can never get warm. But she pretends to like it for my sake. I was born here, you see, so it's different for me.'

By now she was desperate for him to respond. And she was dismayed when the gatehouse rose into sight.

As they emerged from the trees, the sun came out from behind a cloud and the crow took off with an indignant squawk. Madeleine laughed with delight, and at last the officer turned and looked up at her. He didn't smile, but his eyes were no longer cold; they were warm and vividly alive, like a restless sea with the sun on it.

He swung her out of the saddle and set her on the ground, and she thanked him for the ride. Flushed with the sense that the officer might at last be beginning to like her, she decided to ask him for tea. They seldom had any visitors so it would make a welcome change.

'I ought to introduce myself,' she said. 'My name is Madeleine Falkirk. My parents are Major and Mrs Falkirk of Cairngowrie House. Would you care to come to tea?'

The officer, who had been passing the reins back over his mount's head, stopped when she said her name. 'What did you say?' he asked quietly. She had a sudden terrible sense that the sun had gone in.

'M-Madeleine Falkirk,' she faltered.

The officer's face was rigid with shock. 'My God,' he murmured. 'How could they do it? To send a *child.*'

She swallowed. 'Nobody sent me,' she said.

Plainly he did not believe her. 'Your name isn't Falkirk,' he said between his teeth. He mounted his horse.

Madeleine had to step back smartly to avoid his spurs. She didn't understand what had gone wrong. She sensed that without knowing it she had tricked him in some shameful way.

'Tell your parents,' he said, 'that this will never work.'

'They don't know I'm here,' she whispered. 'And they wouldn't trick anyone. They—'

'Your parents wrecked lives. Don't you know that yet?'

For the first time, he looked her full in the face. His eyes were glassy with anger. 'Tell them they're dead to me,' he said in a quiet voice that made her go cold inside. 'And dead to the old man. Tell them they ought to have the courage—the decency—to stay dead.'

He yanked the horse's head round and dug in his spurs, and the great hind hoofs churned the snow inches from her feet.

She stood there until the officer was swallowed up by the dark beneath the trees. And behind her the crow thudded down onto the gatehouse roof and filled the air with raucous laughter.

IT WAS BEGINNING to get dark when Madeleine climbed down from Mr Ritchie's wagon and started along the path to Cairngowrie House. She let herself in to the silent, dim hall. Hannah must have forgotten to turn up the gas. She tugged off her hat and coat and mittens and struggled out of her boots, then padded angrily into the drawing room. It was empty, and only feebly lit by the dying fire.

The clock on the mantelpiece said four, but there was no sign of tea. There was no sign of anyone. And she had been counting on tea to make things normal again.

She had a horrible churning feeling of guilt and bewilderment and loss. She should never have gone to the Forbidden Kingdom. She should never have told the officer her name. But why had he been so angry? *Your parents wrecked lives*, he had said. What did he mean?

A thump shook the ceiling, and the gasoliers' crystal fringes chimed. A moment later she heard her mother ringing for Hannah. But no irritable 'Coming, coming' issued from the kitchen.

Wretched Hannah. With a sigh Madeleine stalked upstairs.

When she opened the bedroom door, she saw her mother—her elegant, unpredictable, beautiful mother—crouching on the rug on all fours, panting and baring her teeth like an animal. She looked as if she had been dressing to go out when she had fallen to her knees. The collar of her walking coat was twisted and her blue velvet bonnet had slid down her back and become snarled in her hair. Then Madeleine saw the great wet patch on the rug. She was horrified.

Her mother raised her head and saw her. 'Ah, there you are,' she said, bizarrely calm.

'Are you unwell?' Madeleine mumbled.

'Much better now, thank you. Dr Baines said that being on all fours might ease the backache.' She gave a mock grimace. 'I know it looks odd, but he's right. I—' She broke off with a sudden hiss as some sort of spasm seized her.

Madeleine gripped the doorknob.

'Now here's a thing,' her mother gasped. 'They're coming rather more quickly than I'd expected. You'd better fetch Hannah.'

Madeleine fled. She ran down to the kitchen, but to her dismay it was in darkness. So was the dining room, and the scullery, pantry, cloakroom and cellar. Mewing like a kitten, she raced upstairs. She checked the bedrooms and the bathroom, and finally the attic.

'I can't find her,' she panted when she'd rejoined her mother.

While she was away, her mother had struggled out of her coat, tossed the bonnet in a corner and climbed into bed. She looked pale.

'I can't find Hannah,' Madeleine said in a calmer voice. 'Her trunk's padlocked with a note on top. I think she's gone.'

Her mother shut her eyes. 'That bloody, *bloody* girl.'

Then, without warning, another spasm took hold of her. This time she had to suck in her lips to keep from crying out. Helplessly Madeleine waited for it to end. If only Dr Baines were here.

'Don't be frightened,' her mother said at last. 'These pains are supposed to happen.'

Madeleine looked at her in disbelief. 'Why?' she demanded.

'They simply mean that the baby has decided to arrive a little earlier than we expected.'

'The *baby*? Can't it wait? I'll fetch Dr Baines tomorrow.'

Her mother's lip curled. 'I'm afraid not. And from the way this is going, I think we're going to need him tonight. You'd better run up the path and tell Mr Ritchie to fetch him.'

Madeleine swallowed. 'Mr Ritchie's not at home,' she said. 'He went to his daughter's in Portpatrick for a fortnight. He just left.'

Her mother had shut her eyes and gone frighteningly pale.

Madeleine said, 'I can go for Dr Baines.'

'No, you can't. Not all the way to Stranraer.'

'Yes, I can. I can take a lantern—'

'Maddy, it's four miles, it's snowing, it's pitch-dark, and you're only ten years old. Absolutely not.'

There was a long silence. At last her mother opened her eyes. She licked her lips. 'Well, Maddy,' she said quietly. 'There's nothing for it. We'll just have to do this on our own. Can you help me?'

Madeleine gripped the bedpost and gave a doubtful nod. She had no idea what 'this' actually meant.

'That's my brave girl. Now in the bottom drawer of my dressing table you'll find a little red booklet. Bring it to me.'

Madeleine went to the dressing table and, after some fumbling, found a thin, much-thumbed booklet. Its gilded lettering announced it to be *The Wife's Handbook by Dr Archibald Philpott—Or How a Woman Should Order Herself During Pregnancy and Delivery*.

'That's the one,' said her mother. Another spasm took hold, and this time it went on for longer. Madeleine swallowed tears.

'I think,' panted her mother at last, 'you had better read it aloud.'

Madeleine's teeth began to chatter. 'I can't.'

'Yes, you can. Come on, Maddy. You'll feel better with something to do. Now there's an index at the back. Find the section headed "Labour", and start reading from there.'

'"WHEN THE PAINS grow severe,"' Madeleine read, '"loop a roller towel round the bedpost and give the ends to the woman to pull on, while she braces her feet against the footboard."'

'We haven't got a roller towel,' panted her mother. 'Fetch a sheet from the linen cupboard.' Then she was off on another wave of pain.

Madeleine raced for the linen cupboard.

An hour before, when the pains were not as close together, she and her mother had gone through Dr Philpott's list of *Equipment for the Lying-in Room*. Reassuringly, her mother seemed to have some idea of what was going on. She knew the right position she ought to adopt even before Madeleine read Dr Philpott: 'on the woman's left side, with her knees drawn up', and she knew that 'the woman must refrain from crying out'. She even managed it most of the time. But she wouldn't let Madeleine help her out of her gown, and flatly refused to raise her nightgown to her knees, as Dr Philpott said she should. 'No, Maddy, absolutely not. You're far too young as it is. And for goodness' *sake*, look away when I tell you to.'

The gaps between the spasms were narrowing, and her mother looked exhausted. Sweat plastered her hair to her temples. 'What wouldn't I give,' she muttered, 'for a stiff dose of chloroform.'

'What's chlor—what's that?' said Madeleine.

'It's why I've put up with Dr Baines all these months.' She looked at Madeleine. 'My poor darling. You oughtn't to know any of this. It wasn't supposed to happen for another three weeks.'

'Is that why it hurts?'

'No. It's supposed to hurt.' Her face twisted, and she sucked in her breath. 'If anything happens—don't remember me like this.'

Madeleine shied away from what she meant.

This time the pain went on for longer. Then another one came, and another, and suddenly there were no more gaps. Her mother started crying out bad words, and Madeleine dropped Dr Philpott, but her mother shouted at her to keep reading, keep bloody *reading*.

Madeleine snatched Dr Philpott from the rug and retreated to the foot of the bed. She couldn't find the right page. The words kept jumping about. 'It says—it says—to bear down and push.'

'I *am* pushing! *Aaah* . . .'

'"After one final push,"' Madeleine shouted, '"the head appears, and a minute or two after this, the body."' She stole a fearful glance at her mother's long white foot pressed against the footboard.

'Turn *away*,' gasped her mother. 'Don't *look*!'

Then she screamed, a terrible, wrenching scream, and Madeleine clapped her hands over her ears and dropped Dr Philpott again.

Then there was nothing. Silence reverberated round the room. Madeleine kept her ears covered and her eyes tight shut.

From behind her came another cry, smaller than her mother's, but just as piercing. It went on and on, rhythmic and unvarying, as if from a pair of bellows being tirelessly worked.

She turned round.

Her mother lay with her eyes closed and her pale lips slightly parted. Her face was shiny with sweat, her eyelids looked fragile like pastry rolled too thin. The nightgown still tented the second bustle— as well as a smaller, twitching lump below it.

The baby, Madeleine thought numbly. The rhythmic cries came at her in waves. The nightgown was splotched with red.

'Mama,' Madeleine said in a small voice. 'You're wounded.'

To her bewilderment her mother smiled. 'It's all right. It's all right,' she said. 'It was easy. So much easier than the first time.'

Easy? thought Madeleine.

'Pass—the scissors and thread, Maddy. Read the bit about cutting the cord. And—back turned. I mean it.'

Madeleine passed the scissors and the worsted, then stooped reluctantly for Dr Philpott. She didn't want to read any more. She felt shaky and sick. She wanted to put back her head and howl. If the wretched baby could do it, why couldn't she?

Turning her back and wiping her eyes with her fingers, she scanned the page. 'Um. "With the worsted, tie off the cord about two inches from the navel. Then tie it off two inches below that and cut."'

Through the shrill rhythmic cries she heard the rustle of the nightgown and the soft flump of her mother subsiding onto the pillows. 'You can turn round now,' she said.

What Madeleine saw when she lifted the nightgown made her recoil in horror. It wasn't a baby; it was a devil. A slimy, spindly, crumpled, *angry* little devil, smeared with blood.

Black dots floated before her eyes. Her stomach heaved.

'It's all right,' her mother said calmly. 'When you were born you looked just the same, Maddy, I promise. Fetch one of those napkins you left to warm over the fender and wrap her in it.'

Madeleine did as she was told.

'Now give her to me. Put one hand under her neck to support the head—carefully. That's it.' She seemed unable to stop smiling and giving delighted little spurts of laughter. 'We've done it, Maddy. We've done it! You have a sister. A perfect, *beautiful* little sister.'

MADELEINE WAS JOLTED awake by the baby crying. It seemed no time at all since she had crawled into bed beside her mother and fallen asleep, listening to her mother's deep, even breathing. The baby was lying wrapped in her mother's paisley shawl, on a pillow in a bureau drawer that she had placed at the foot of the bed.

Madeleine lay on her back wondering when the crying would stop. She could see daylight through a gap in the curtains. She must have slept all night.

Then she became aware of a chilly dampness down her right side, and a strange coppery smell. It must be the baby, she thought in disgust. She wished it had never arrived.

Beside her, her mother still slept. Her face was waxy and her expression strangely absent, as if she were dreaming a deep dream.

Madeleine touched her arm but she didn't wake up. The arm felt hard, like a doll's. Madeleine struggled out from under the bedclothes and knelt beside her. Gently she put her finger to her mother's cheek. The flesh was cool and firm, like an unripe plum.

Madeleine's stayed kneeling on the bed. Her frock was cold and damp down the side that had lain against her mother, and when she put her palm to her thigh it came away glistening red. She shuffled off the bed and peeled back the blankets.

Her mother lay in a great crimson stain that surrounded her like a monstrous butterfly.

The baby was still crying. She wondered how to make it stop. She padded into her own room and changed her frock. Dr Baines would come soon, she told herself. He would deal with the baby. Then she remembered that Dr Baines came once a week on Tuesdays, and that he'd already been the day before yesterday, so he wouldn't come again for another five days.

She decided to go downstairs and wait until someone came. The stairwell was freezing, and when she reached the bottom she couldn't remember what she was doing there. She sat on the stairs, blinking. On the mat by the front door she saw a letter. She went and picked it up. It was for her mother. She replaced it on the mat.

Someone would come soon. And they would look after her and the baby, and—and everything. Her thoughts skittered away from what 'everything' meant. She was hazily aware that her mother wasn't going to wake up again, but whenever she started to think about that, a smooth blank wall rose up in her mind and shut it out.

And the baby was still crying. It didn't sound as if it would stop.

She went back upstairs and into her mother's room. Dr Philpott was lying on the floor by the bed. Keeping her eyes averted from her mother, she crossed the room and picked it up, then retreated to the dressing table and sat down on the stool.

The dressing table was covered with the familiar clutter: the ivory brush set, the Japanese lacquer ring-tray, the jewel casket. She pushed everything to one side to make room for Dr Philpott, then turned to the index. After searching for some time, she found what she was looking for: *Infant, Management Of — Page 57*.

She turned to page fifty-seven and started to read.

CHAPTER TWO

Northern Sudan, 12th March, 1884

As Cameron Lawe shouldered his way through the Suakin bazaar, he cursed once again the vagueness of the orders that had brought him here. *Report to the Muhafaza at Suakin with the utmost dispatch.* He was to be transferred to 'special duties' with another regiment. Special duties. What the devil did that mean? No doubt it was just another glorious army muddle which had sent him on a headlong rush from Scotland for no reason at all.

As he passed a spice-grinder's stall he caught a heady wave of cumin and cloves, and without warning homesickness had him in its grip. Wherever he turned he saw reminders of Jamaica. The dust, the glare, the gaudy robes fluttering in the furnace wind: saffron, crimson and emerald. The clamour of voices, the teeming black and brown faces. Why now? he thought angrily. There isn't time for this.

But if he was honest, he knew why Jamaica was so much in his thoughts. Because on his last day at Strathnaw he had taken a farewell ride in the park, and met a little girl in the snow.

It had taken just one word—Falkirk—and all the anger, the pain, had come boiling to the surface. There is no *justice*, he had thought as he looked down into the child's fearless, eager little face. Your father isn't 'Alasdair Falkirk'. He's Ainsley Monroe. Ainsley Randolph Falkirk Monroe, of Fever Hill, Jamaica. And this isn't some storybook playground for you to explore. It's the ancient seat of the family that your father dragged through the mud.

He had been appalled at the violence of his feelings. For twelve years he had done all he could to drive Ainsley from his mind. But all it took was a single word to break down the wall.

At last the bazaar was left behind, and he walked out into the heat and glare of the Keff, the jumble of flat-roofed houses where the army was encamped. Swarms of tiny flies wavered and settled and rose again. Down an alley stinking of goats, he found the Muhafaza, the Governor's House: a run-down old building of battered white coral. Ducking beneath the lintel, he entered the shadowy interior, and came face to face with Ainsley Monroe.

He felt as if he'd been kicked in the chest.

Ainsley had been writing at a rickety little desk by the window, his bright gold head bowed over his papers and lit by a shaft of sunlight from a half-open shutter.

Of course, thought Cameron. The child in the park said that her father was a major in the 65th. Why didn't you think of that before?

Ainsley raised his head and saw him, and blinked once. He rose to his feet, came round to the other side of the desk and put out his hand. Cameron ignored it. Ainsley gave him an uncertain smile.

'My God, Cameron, but this is a fine thing!' His voice shook with emotion. 'You've grown so tall! I have to look up to you now.'

At one stroke Cameron was a boy again, shocked and bewildered when this man whom he'd loved as a brother had shattered his world. He gave a stiff salute. 'Captain Lawe reporting for duty, sir.'

Ainsley gave a startled laugh and returned the salute.

It had been twelve years, but Ainsley hadn't changed at all. Those warm blue eyes. That wide mouth always ready for laughter. Cameron watched him take a sheet of orders from the desk.

'Here you are,' he said, still smiling. 'These are for you.'

Cameron took the papers in silence. *Cameron Lawe, Captain, 'B' Company, 25th King's Own Scottish Borderers: special attachment to the 65th York and Lancasters under Major Alasdair Falkirk, until such time as the relief of Tokar has been accomplished.*

He folded the paper and put it in his tunic pocket. 'Sir, on whose initiative was this arranged?'

Ainsley looked surprised. 'On mine, of course.' He paused. 'I couldn't believe it when I saw your name in the transport lists. It was like a gift from God.'

'I want a transfer back to my own corps.'

Ainsley's smile faltered. 'I'd forgotten how blunt you can be.'

'I prefer to call it straightforward.'

'Then I'll be straightforward, too. Your request is denied.'

'On what grounds?'

'I understand you speak Arabic. I need an interpreter.'

'I'd be of no use to you, sir,' Cameron said crisply. 'In this region they speak a corrupt version of the tongue. A sort of—bastard version. If you will.'

Their eyes locked.

Ainsley said, 'You can make this easy for yourself or you can make it hard. It's your choice.'

'What if I simply refuse to serve under you?'

'Then I shall have you court-martialled for insubordination.'

Cameron decided that he meant it. Ainsley had always had a ruthless streak. 'Why are you doing this?' he said.

Ainsley gave him a hooded look. 'I have my reasons.'

IT WAS NEARLY SIX in the evening, and stillness reigned: the peculiar taut stillness before a battle. They had set out from Suakin in the chill of the night, and had joined the main column at an oasis where they struck camp. They flung up a line of zeribas with walls of thorn-scrub and camel saddles, and camped inside: the officers in tents, the men in what shade they could create from sacking and store boxes. They would rest here until nightfall, march by moonlight, and engage the enemy some time after dawn.

Cameron couldn't sleep. He told himself it was just the pain in his hand, for he'd taken a sabre-cut across the palm in a skirmish during the night, but he knew it was more than that. Something ugly was churning away inside his chest.

Eventually he gave up and went for a walk. He left the zeriba and climbed a goat-track up the bluff, and sat down in a patch of shade beneath a boulder near the top. He sat for an hour or so, and below him the column began to wake up. Blue smoke rose from cookingfires. Men yawned and stretched in the eerie copper light.

At the foot of the bluff a group of Hussars crouched in a ring, urging a scorpion into battle against a yellow tarantula. As Cameron watched the spider's delicate circling, he was back in Jamaica, nineteen years before. It was his first week at Fever Hill, and he was six years old, crying beneath the guango tree, for he couldn't understand why his parents had left him and his baby brother on their own. He had reached the hiccupping stage when Ainsley had wandered up: a gangly fifteen-year-old, but a god to a small boy. Ainsley had pretended not to notice the tears, and had said simply, 'Would you care to see my pet tarantula?'

Angrily, Cameron got to his feet and threw a stone as hard as he could across the bluff. *God*, why must you think about that now?

He needed to be doing something—anything, so long as it didn't involve Ainsley. Back at the zeriba he spoke to the officer with the next watch, and negotiated an exchange. Then he retrieved his kit, found a store box to sit on, and buckled on his spurs.

Or rather, he tried to buckle them on, but his injured palm made him clumsy, and he couldn't get them fastened. He cursed savagely.

'Trouble?' said a voice that made the back of his neck prickle.

'No,' he said without looking up.

Ainsley sat on the store box next to his. 'Those spurs were my father's, weren't they?' he said quietly.

And now they're mine, thought Cameron. For Jocelyn no longer has a son. He flexed his injured hand to make the pain flare. It was a good, clean pain. Nothing like the sick churning in his chest.

'We missed you at dinner,' Ainsley said. 'The colonel asked where you were. He's a bit of a stickler for the conventions.'

Cameron made no reply, but wrestled with the buckle and wished Ainsley to blazes.

Ainsley said, 'I handled it badly yesterday. You must have thought I was making light of things. I wasn't. I was just so glad to see you.'

At last Cameron succeeded with the spurs. He stood up.

'Where are you going?'

'I have the patrol.'

'I'll ride with you.'

'I'd rather you didn't.'

Ainsley gave a lopsided smile. 'I'm aware of that.'

They rode at the head of the detail, out of earshot of the other men. When they were clear of the camp Cameron said, 'I think you ought to tell me what the fellows know about you in the mess.'

Ainsley glanced behind him. 'As far as they're concerned I'm Alasdair Falkirk. Have been for the past twelve years. They don't even know I'm from Jamaica.' He paused. 'I thought that best. For the family as well as myself.'

'Indeed,' said Cameron drily. 'Family honour has always been close to your heart.' It gave him a sick satisfaction to see Ainsley flinch. 'How could you do it?' he said. 'Break the heart of a fine old man. Desert your wife and child.'

Ainsley let out a long breath. 'When I left Jamaica I didn't know that Clemency was with child.'

'Would it have made a difference if you had?'

Ainsley did not reply. Behind them the men were casting them curious glances. Cameron put his mare forward, and heard the rattle of pebbles as Ainsley brought his horse level.

'Cameron, try to understand. I was young.'

'You were weak. You've always been weak.'

He gave a twisted smile. 'I can see you've never been in love.'

Cameron snorted.

'Well, it may surprise you to learn that Clemency at least has forgiven me. Oh, yes, it's true. She wrote to me. Years ago.' He patted his tunic pocket. 'I keep her letter with me always.'

'Whatever for?'

'I suppose to remind me that there is such a thing as forgiveness.'

'You never could face up to your responsibilities,' Cameron said. 'You ran off and left your wife, and now you've left your mistress.'

'I have not left Rose,' Ainsley said between his teeth.

'You're in the army. It amounts to the same thing.'

Ainsley sighed. 'You've changed. You used to be able to listen to both sides of an argument, then make your own choice.'

'In some things there is no choice. In matters of honour.'

'You sound just like my father.'

'Well, God damn it,' snarled Cameron, 'he brought me up!'

He hadn't lowered his voice, and behind them all heads turned.

'I didn't accompany you,' Ainsley said quietly, 'to have an argument. I came because I need to ask you something.'

'Then tell me and have done with it.'

Ainsley looked out across the burning plain. 'I have a daughter,' he said. 'A girl of ten. And God willing, another child on the way.'

Cameron thought about the little girl in the park. 'And what is that to me?' he said.

Ainsley gave him a hard look. 'I don't care what you think of me,' he said. 'All I care about is that you help me to help my children.'

'What the devil do you mean?'

'When this campaign is over, I intend to resign my commission and take my family back to Jamaica.'

Cameron stared at him in disbelief. 'You can't mean that.'

'It's our home, Cameron. It's where we belong. Don't worry, I shan't live openly with Rose. I shall establish her somewhere far from Fever Hill—near Kingston perhaps. As far as Society is concerned, I shall be returning to Jamaica after some years of "delicate health". Isn't that what Father gave out?' He gave a wry smile. 'So there won't be any scandal.'

They began their descent down the bluff, and the horses jostled for position on the narrow track. Cameron said, 'You seem to have everything worked out. Why bother to tell me?'

'Because I need you to tell my father. He returns all my letters unopened. Just like you. He doesn't even know he's a grandfather.' He paused. 'I'd rather not have him learn of my return in the *Daily Gleaner*.'

Cameron wanted to grab Ainsley by the throat and shake him till he saw sense. Couldn't he see that his plan was impossible? Had he no idea what things had been like after he left? Having to watch poor, soft, obedient Clemency cradling her dead baby in her arms. Proud old Jocelyn humbling himself to buy the silence of her upstart brother. The odious May taking control with unspeakable relish.

He remembered that beautiful little girl in the snow at Strathnaw. Why had Clemency's child died, while the bastard had thrived? There is no justice, he thought.

They were nearing the zeriba, and men were coming forward to take the horses. 'We must be civilised about this,' said Ainsley. 'I need you to help me. And, by God, you shall—'

'*Enough*,' said Cameron. 'I've heard enough.' He dismounted and tossed his reins to his man and walked away.

'Cameron, come back! Damnit, man, that's an order!'

'Go to the devil,' said Cameron.

DR BAINES NEVER came back to Cairngowrie House. Perhaps he forgot. Perhaps he fell ill. Whatever the reason, the days passed and the snow kept falling, and nobody came.

Madeleine didn't greatly mind, for she was safe inside her shell. Her smooth, shiny, unbreakable Easter-egg shell, which allowed her to see and hear and smell and taste, but only in a muffled sort of way, as if she were under water.

She didn't like the baby any more than when it had first arrived, but it had proved impossible to ignore. It gazed at her with eyes as dark and deep as a seal's, and when she left the room its outraged howls followed her through the house.

From Dr Philpott she had learned how to look after it. Dressing was the easiest task because there were lots of baby-clothes, and it was very like dressing a doll. Bathing was easy too, because the baby liked it. But to begin with, feeding had been impossible. Dr Philpott said that 'If the mother is unable to suckle, the baby should have a few dessertspoonsful of warm water and sugar every two hours. On the second day, good cow's milk may be added, or tinned milk.'

There was plenty of sugar and Nestlé's Condensed Milk in the pantry, but the problem was getting it into the baby.

'If a baby is brought up by hand, the feeding bottle must be kept very clean.' Madeleine emptied a pretty blue glass bottle of syrup of figs, thoroughly washed it and filled it with sugar-water. The baby howled and batted it away. She tried pouring sugar-water into the baby's mouth from a teaspoon, but it spluttered and coughed it back again. She was on the point of giving up when she had the idea of soaking a corner of her best handkerchief in the sugar-water. The baby's mouth fastened on it like a magnet. From then on feeding was easy, although it always took a long time.

The section on *changing* puzzled Madeleine at first, but she quickly realised why it came straight after *feeding*. Cleaning up the mess was a horrible task, and the napkins had a tendency to leak.

The final challenge was to choose somewhere for the baby to sleep. In the end, Madeleine dragged the cot from the nursery into the spare room. She slept there too. She preferred it to her own room.

All this left her with little time for herself, but she was safe inside her shell, and didn't need much looking after. There was bread in the pantry and seed cake and a ham, so when she felt dizzy she chewed a piece of ham, or toasted bread on the spare-room fire.

Sometimes, when the baby was clean, fed and asleep, Madeleine would sit on the spare-room bed and look out of the window. The garden was a white, humped smoothness leading down to the beach. The seals and the cormorants had gone. Everyone had gone. Perhaps there was no one left in the world except herself and the baby. Why had her mother left her all alone like this? Why had she left her to look after the baby by herself? It wasn't fair. Mothers weren't supposed to do that sort of thing. If it hadn't been for the shell, she would have felt angry with her.

ON THE MORNING of the tenth day there was a knock at the door. Madeleine was in the spare room, adding coal to the fire. When she heard the noise she froze. Visitors never came to Cairngowrie House. So who could be knocking? The postman never knocked. And it didn't sound like Dr Baines's ebullient tattoo.

She glanced at the baby, which was fast asleep, then went quietly downstairs and opened the door, letting in a blast of cold, clean air.

An unknown couple stood on the porch: a short, plump gentleman with damp jowls, and a tiny rigid lady in a quilted purple cape and a Tirolean hat adorned with half a dead pheasant.

The lady's close-set eyes fastened on Madeleine. 'What is your name?' she demanded.

Madeleine said her name. The lady and gentleman exchanged glances and walked past her into the drawing room. She followed.

Briskly the lady divested herself of hat, cape and gloves to reveal a grimly elaborate gown of green and violet tartan. 'I am Mrs Fynn,' she declared. 'You shall address me as Cousin Lettice. This'—she indicated the damp-jowled gentleman—'is Mr Fynn, whom you shall address as Cousin Septimus. Where is your mother?'

Madeleine said her mother was upstairs in her room.

She waited in the hall while the lady and gentleman ascended to her mother's room. Moments later, Cousin Lettice came back onto the landing with a handkerchief clamped over her mouth. Cousin Septimus followed, looking clammy and outraged.

Madeleine felt obscurely at fault.

When they were back in the drawing room, Cousin Lettice tucked her handkerchief in her cuff. 'When did this occur?' she asked.

'A bit more than a week ago,' said Madeleine.

'Where are the servants?'

'We only had one, but she had left.'

Cousin Lettice looked Madeleine up and down. 'Did not your mother receive my letter?' she asked with a frown.

Madeleine wondered what she meant. Then she remembered the letter on the doormat. She went into the hall and retrieved it from the mat, and handed it to Cousin Lettice.

Cousin Lettice's gaze went from Madeleine to the letter and back again. 'How,' she demanded, 'have you survived?'

Madeleine told her about the ham, the seed cake and Dr Philpott.

'Dr Philpott? So there has *been* a doctor. Where is he now?'

Until then, Madeleine had been holding Dr Philpott against her chest. Now she held him out to Cousin Lettice.

Cousin Lettice took Dr Philpott and read the title. Her head snapped up. 'How much of this have you read? Tell me the *truth*.'

'All of it,' said Madeleine. 'But the first part had nothing to do with babies, so I only read it once.'

Upstairs in the spare room, the baby began to cry. Cousin Septimus turned to Cousin Lettice with a horrified stare.

Cousin Lettice went yellowish grey. 'The infant survived?'

Madeleine nodded.

This time Cousin Septimus stayed below, while Madeleine took Cousin Lettice upstairs to show her the baby. They stood together beside the cot. Cousin Lettice scrutinised the crying baby, but made no move to touch or comfort it.

'It survived,' she said between her teeth. 'It were better had it died.' Suddenly she turned on Madeleine. 'You,' she said accusingly, 'were born with a terrible burden. The infant carries it too.'

Madeleine cast the baby a doubtful glance. How could it carry anything when it couldn't even stand up?

'Your mother was *wicked*,' Cousin Lettice declared. 'She enticed your father away from his lawful wife. Your mother was *degenerate*. And so are you. Do you know what that means?'

Madeleine shook her head.

'It means that your blood is tainted.'

Madeleine pictured little grey blotches floating in scarlet, like the dust devils she sometimes found beneath the bed.

'It *means*,' Cousin Lettice went on, 'that the wickedness grows worse with each succeeding generation. Depravity. Insanity. Disease. It is all in the blood.' She drew herself up. 'But God has delivered you to me. It will be my duty to teach you the life of penitence and obscurity for which you are destined. For God is *just*.' She paused for breath. 'Henceforth,' she declared, 'you will live with us. You will take the name of Fynn.'

Madeleine was confused. 'But my name is Falkirk. Madeleine Falkirk. And my sister is . . .' She glanced at the books on the shelf: *The Water Babies* and *Les Malheurs de Sophie*. 'Sophie. She's called Sophie Falkirk.'

'No. Falkirk is a false name. Your parents were never married. Henceforth, for the sake of decency, you will be Fynn.'

Madeleine frowned. 'Miss Lettice,' she said, 'I don't believe Papa will like it if I change my name.'

That brought Cousin Lettice to a halt. 'Of course,' she muttered. 'She has not been told.'

Madeleine put her hand on the cot. The baby turned its head and stared at her severely.

'Your father has been killed in battle,' said Cousin Lettice. 'It is a visitation on him. We will never speak of him again.'

Madeleine let go of the cot and sat down heavily on the floor.

CAMERON IS RIDING slowly over the battlefield, picking off the strag-glers. He feels the heat of the sun on his shoulders and smells the bitterness of smoke. He sees the gutted horses and the sodden scarlet tunics, but he doesn't experience any of it. All he really feels is the fierce, sick joy of having killed and come through alive.

It's nearly noon, and soon it will be too hot to carry on. His horse picks its way across the bodies and between the jagged black rocks that jut from the sand like dragons' teeth. Some distance ahead, he sees Ainsley leading a small recovery detail. Thank God, he thinks. He's come through it too. Thank God.

Behind him a shout, and he turns to see one of the men bayoneting a wounded tribesman. These Arabs like to fox dead, then rise up and make a last-ditch stand.

When he turns to go on, Ainsley is in trouble. A trio of dervishes has risen from the dead and butchered his detail to a man, and Ainsley is surrounded. His horse is on its haunches, screaming, its hind leg shattered, but his spur is caught in the stirrup and he can't jump free. He has lost his helmet, and his bright hair is vivid against the smoke as he struggles to right himself, and draws his revolver and drops one of the Arabs. The other two circle behind him.

Cameron sees it happening as if through water. He hauls his horse to a halt and levels his revolver, takes aim and shoots one of the Arabs through the head. He fires again and drops the other with a shot in the throat. 'All right now,' he mutters, 'it's all right now.' He spurs his horse on and at last he understands that the anger of the night before has no meaning; that he would rather be killed himself than watch Ainsley die.

But as he closes the distance between them he sees Ainsley is still fighting to untangle his spur from the stirrup as his mount crashes down onto the rocks, with him beneath.

Cameron jumps off his horse and runs to where Ainsley is lying, and drops to his knees in the stinking black sand. He looks down into the blue eyes and watches the dullness come, like the bloom on a grape. A small wind tosses black sand across the waxy features and Cameron tries to brush it away, but the sand keeps coming, gently sifting into mouth and nostrils, sugaring the staring eyes.

Someone is shaking him by the shoulder. 'Captain Lawe. Captain Lawe. Sir. Wake up.'

Cameron woke up. It was dark in the zeriba, for the moon had not yet risen. He felt hot tears on his cheeks.

'The colonel wishes to see you in his tent, sir,' said the orderly.

Cameron lay on his back, blinking at the stars. It wasn't a dream, he thought. He is dead. And it's too late to make anything right.

He kicked his way out of his blanket-bag and got to his feet. Straightening his uniform, he followed the orderly through the sleeping camp to the colonel's tent. The colonel sat on a canvas stool before a small field desk covered with papers. A staff officer Cameron didn't know sat beside him with a notebook and pencil.

Cameron had a vague sense that he was in trouble. He swayed, and tried to assume an expression of respectful attention.

'A report has reached me,' said the colonel, 'that the day before yesterday you disregarded a direct order of your CO, the late Major Falkirk. For reasons which pass understanding, Major Falkirk let that go unpunished.' A pause. 'I take it that it was a personal matter. Some kind of . . . bad blood between you?'

Behind his back Cameron flexed his injured palm, and the new scab cracked. Bad blood. Odd way of putting it. The truth is, there was no blood between us, good or bad. Yet I never stopped thinking of him as a brother. Why didn't I tell him when I had the chance?

He dragged himself back to the present. He squared his shoulders. 'Yes, sir,' he said. 'Bad blood.'

'I shouldn't normally trouble myself with what was clearly a personal matter.' The colonel frowned. 'However, it is my duty to investigate a second report. A report of an extremely grave nature.'

The staff officer bent his head and scribbled furiously.

'Yesterday,' the colonel went on with his eyes on Cameron, 'shortly after Major Falkirk fell, you were seen systematically rifling the pockets, then extracting a piece of paper from the breast of the major's tunic. To put it baldly, despoiling the body.' He paused. 'Well? What have you to say? Do you deny it?'

Again Cameron swayed. 'No, sir. I don't.'

The colonel's narrow face was incredulous. 'Are you telling me that these reports are true?'

'Yes, sir.'

'This paper, where is it now?'

'I burnt it, sir.'

'You burnt it,' repeated the colonel. 'What was it? A promissory note? Gambling pledge? Letter from a woman?'

'I'd rather not say, sir. It's a private matter.'

'Not any more,' snapped the colonel. 'Not when it results in one of my officers publicly desecrating the body of a brother in arms—his own CO, God damn it. Not when . . .'

Cameron stopped listening. He was back on the battlefield, kneeling by Ainsley's body with Clemency's letter in his hand. If the letter were found, Ainsley would be exposed as a scoundrel who had deserted his wife and deceived his brother officers for years. But if the letter disappeared, the world would honour Alasdair Falkirk, a good soldier and a pure-hearted man who gave his life for his country.

'Captain Lawe. Are you listening to me?'

Cameron studied him for a moment. 'Yes, sir,' he said.

'Because I wish there to be no mistake about the gravity of your position. I am ordering you to provide me—now—with a complete explanation of your conduct in this affair.'

The staff officer raised his head and waited, his pencil poised.

Cameron licked his dry, cracked lips. 'Sir, I can't tell you anything.'

The colonel leaned forward. 'Captain Lawe. Explain yourself.'

Cameron met the colonel's eyes. 'No,' he said.

LETTER FROM CAPTAIN CAMERON LAWE, Carysfort Military Prison, Suakin, to his guardian, Jocelyn Monroe, Fever Hill Estate, Parish of Trelawny, Jamaica, 18th March, 1884.

Dear Jocelyn,

By the time this reaches you, you may already have seen accounts of an incident arising from the death of my Commanding Officer, Major Alasdair Falkirk, as a result of which I have been the subject of a General Court-Martial. I am writing to report the circumstances in so far as I can, and the sentence of the court, which Her Majesty has today confirmed.

Cameron set down the letter and put his elbows on his knees and pressed the heels of his hands into his eyes.

Discharge with ignominy from Her Majesty's Service. Forfeiture of all field medals and decorations. Committal to a public prison for a term of not less than two years.

He remembered Jocelyn's face on the day he had received his commission. He had been so proud. This was going to tear him apart.

Cameron took his hands from his eyes and stared at the rough wall of his cell. Through the shutters came the steady roar of the bazaar and the smell of cumin and palm oil and goat.

He pictured the old man receiving the news. He would be on the great north verandah at Fever Hill, sitting in his favourite rattan armchair. At his elbow there would be the usual Scotch and soda, and beside it the tarnished daguerreotype of Kitty, the young wife who had been dead for thirty-five years. The fierce, sunbleached eyes would be scanning the columns of his weekly *Times*. He would spot the familiar names: ... *A notable casualty of the Battle of Tamai was Major Alasdair Falkirk of the 65th York and Lancasters. It is this correspondent's painful duty to report the horrifying news that one*

Captain Cameron Lawe, a brother officer on special attachment from the King's Own Scottish Borderers, was observed in the aftermath of the hero's fall despoiling the body . . . persistently refused to explain his actions . . . immediate Court-Martial on grounds of insubordination and conduct unbecoming an officer and a gentleman . . .

The hearing had been conducted in the mess hall at Fort Euryalus, the one place in Suakin large enough to accommodate the regulation bench of thirteen officers together with twelve witnesses, three short-hand writers, and a throng of spectators.

Cameron had found it hard to keep his mind on the proceedings. *Your parents are dead to me*, he had told the little girl in the park. Why had he said that? Had he *wanted* Ainsley dead? Irrational to imagine that wishes can influence events. But he felt that. He felt responsible. If he had got a transfer back to his own regiment, per-haps Ainsley would not have been preoccupied as he rode across the battlefield. Perhaps he would have survived. Compared with that, what did it matter what they said about him at the hearing?

He had soon given up listening to the prosecutor. Fort Euryalus, he mused. Wasn't there a Euryalus who fought at Troy? Jocelyn would know. *The Iliad* was his Bible. When they were small, he used to read them a passage every night. They didn't understand a word, but they adored it just the same, because it was Jocelyn. He was the only father they had ever really known, for he had come for them on the day of the accident that had killed their parents. Cameron had been barely six and his brother Sinclair just a baby.

The white house at Arethusa had been in uproar that day. Rooms echoing to the piercing *ai ai ai* of Negro mourning. Bare feet slap-ping on hardwood floors. Young Cameron, forgotten in the chaos, had wandered out onto the verandah, where his mother used to sit. The servants said his mother was gone for ever. He had wondered what would happen now. Was he old enough to look after himself?

Then Jocelyn had come. Cameron had watched the tall, unsmiling gentleman riding slowly up the carriageway. The man had barked at the servants to get back to work, dispatched the baby and its nurse in a buggy, and finally hoisted Cameron before him on his horse and set off for Fever Hill. He never said a word, but he held Cameron fast.

And when they reached the great house on the hill, Jocelyn sat him down on a verandah overlooking a vast rippling valley of cane and had the housekeeper bring out a tumbler of coconut milk and a bowl of red pea soup. Cameron demolished them both in seconds.

Then Jocelyn had spoken of the centuries-old friendship between the Monroes and the Lawes. 'Our families are bound together,' he said, 'and your father was my best friend. Henceforth I shall be as a father to you. You belong here now. At Fever Hill.'

Cameron stood up and ran his fingers over the coral windowsill. The old man gave you a home, he thought. See how you have repaid him. For the first time in his life he saw himself as he truly was. Arrogant. Self-righteous. Intolerant. With an ungovernable impulse to violence that until now he had never questioned. He remembered that last ride with Ainsley at the oasis. The raw, churning anger in his chest. He had been so certain that he was right.

On the old crate that he used as a makeshift desk, the letter to Jocelyn waited for his signature. The stilted account had taken hours to draft, but he still hadn't found a way to explain or even hint at what he had taken from the body of 'Major Falkirk'. Others would read the letter before it reached Jocelyn, so he must be circumspect.

On a separate sheet he had penned a few equally guarded lines about 'Mrs Falkirk' and her children. *A child of ten, I believe, and an infant yet to be born. Needless to say, something must be done for them, as I understand that the major's means were but moderate.*

Hypocrite, he told himself. You don't give a damn about Rose Durrant or her children. You can't even think of them without anger.

Cameron suddenly thought about the little girl in the snow. *Tell them they're dead to me*, he had said. He had frightened her. A despicable thing to do, to frighten a child. But God damn it, why think of her at all? Why think of any of them? What's the use?

Cameron went back to the desk and picked up the sheet on which he had written about Rose and her bastards. All he cared about now was Jocelyn. Surely he needn't be told about them just yet.

He folded the sheet in half and tore it up.

CHAPTER THREE

London, March 1894 — ten years later

Ben Kelly should of never gone near that shop. If he hadn't, his whole bloody life would of been different. And Robbie's too.

But it's half past six and they're up the Portland Road, and it's foggy and freezing cold and there's bugger all to click—so what's he to do? Here's this nice little empty shop, door unlocked, gas on low, like the shopkeeper just nipped out. *Rennard & Co*, it says in the window, P-h-o-t-o-g-something-or-other. So in they go.

Queer kind of shop it is, and all. Golden chairs, and this plaster column with red velvet hanging over. Straight off Ben spots this little Box Brownie. Get a bob for that at the coffee-house down Endell Street. Should of just clicked it and cut the lucky out of there. But then he spots the bowl of apples on the counter.

Him and Robbie are stuffing their pockets with apples when all of a sudden this nobby voice goes, 'Stop, thief!' and there's this bint behind the counter with a sodding *rifle* pointed straight at him. And then this second bint, a little one, pops up beside her.

'What have you got in your pockets?' says the one with the rifle. She's a pretty bit of muslin, nineteen or twenty, cloudy black hair, big black eyes and a curvy red mouth. But she puts Ben in mind of his big sister Kate, and that gives him a pain in his chest, 'cos Kate's dead, and he swore he'd never think of her again.

'What have you got in your pockets?' goes Black-hair again.

So him and Robbie put the apples on the counter. Well, she's got the gun, and all.

She frowns. 'What were you going to do with those?'

'Eat them,' snaps Ben. 'What d'you think?'

'But they're rotten. We were going to throw them away.'

'Shows how much you know,' he goes.

Something flickers in her face, like he's hit a nerve. Then she darts a look at the little bint, who gets out this big paper bag and pours out these new apples and pears.

'They're props,' she mumbles. 'We use them for photographs.'

She's ten or so, with long yellow hair, but he can tell straight off that they're sisters. They got that way of talking without talking.

'Take some,' Black-hair tells him. 'We can buy some more.'

That's when he knows she's not going to shoot; she never was. She's scared of him. Shows some sense, that does.

So now there's nothing to stop him cutting the lucky, except that Robbie's pounced on the apples, and chomping away. The bints are staring at his ugly little mug with their mouths open. Well, he's a bit of a sight, is Robbie, with his carroty hair and his greasy old jacket stretched over his hump, and his kickseys that peter out at the shins, and his scabby black feet.

'How old is he?' Black-hair asks Ben.

'Seven,' he growls, 'and he can speak for hisself.' Just because Robbie's one button short of a row, it don't mean he's an idiot.

'How old are you?'

'I dunno. Thirteen? What's it to you?'

He can't make her out. Why don't she just chuck them out or call the bluebottles? What's she after?

He goes, 'You never work in a shop, you're too posh.'

'This is just a hobby,' she says. 'I help out from time to time but I don't get paid. Mr Rennard couldn't afford it.'

'Bit early for helping,' he goes. 'Seven in the morning.'

'Sometimes I take my own photographs before we open.'

'And sometimes,' chimes in Yellow-hair, 'as a *special* treat, Maddy lets me come along too.'

Crikey, thinks Ben, that her idea of a treat?

Yellow-hair's not as pretty as her sister, but she'll do—although them eyebrows spell trouble. Straight and dark. *Watch out*, they seem to say, *or you're in for a fight*.

'You ought to go,' says Black-hair. 'Mr Rennard will be here soon.'

'Oh, not *yet*,' goes Yellow-hair.

'Sophie . . .'

'Oh, *please*.' She turns to Robbie, and points at his woolly dog that Ben clicked from the toyshop, and goes, 'What's his name?'

Robbie looks well worried. He's had the sodding thing a couple of years, but never thought to give it a name. 'Dog?' he mumbles.

She nods. 'Dog. Well, I'm Sophie, and that's Maddy—Madeleine, actually. Maddy chose my name when I was born. She got it off a book, but we never told Cousin Lettice.'

Robbie's got his mouth open, he can't believe she's talking to him like a proper person. And Black-hair's watching him with this little half-smile; not sneery, just kind. It makes Ben go all prickly.

'It was my birthday last week,' goes Yellow-hair. 'I didn't have a party, as we don't know anyone. So it's very nice to meet you—'

'Sophie, that's enough—' goes her sister.

'Maddy gave me *Black Beauty*,' goes Yellow-hair, regular chatter-basket. 'I've read it twice already.' She fetches this book from behind the counter.

'So you can read. So what?' says Ben.

She's taken aback. 'But everyone can read.' She puts her hand to her mouth. 'I'm awfully sorry, I didn't mean—um, can't you read?'

'I know my letters,' snaps Ben. And he does, give or take.

'I do apologise,' goes Yellow-hair, and then she's off again ferreting behind the counter. Her sister looks down to see what she's up to, and that's when Ben whips off his cap and stows the Brownie inside, and clutches the cap to his belly like he's just remembered his manners. Nobody sees nothing. Beautiful.

Yellow-hair chucks a questioning look at her sister, and gets the nod, and holds out this picture book to Ben. 'Maddy keeps a few books for clients' children, to keep them amused. I thought you might care to have one to read.'

He's all hot and prickly again, and sick to his stomach. Who the hell does she think she is? *Giving* him things?

'It's about a cavalry horse in the Crimean War,' she says. 'And when you finish it, you can come back and I'll give you another.'

'You cracked?' he says. 'Why would I come back?'

That's better. Now she looks like she's going to cry. Light brown eyes with little bits of gold in them, all swimming in tears.

That's when Black-hair shoots him this look. Plain as day it says to him: *Don't you dare go upsetting my sister*.

He glares back at her, but inside he thinks, fair enough. 'Come on, Robbie,' he goes. 'It's high time we was off.'

But they're just out the door when Black-hair knocks him for six. 'You know, Ben Whatever-your-name-is, you're not as sharp as you think you are.' She hoists the rifle, and grins. 'It's just a fake. Made of wood. Gentlemen like to be photographed with it, so that they can pretend they're lords on a grouse moor.'

Quick as a flash Ben goes, 'And you're not as sharp as you think neither! What's to stop me thrashing the stuffing out of you now?'

Course he don't do no such thing, he just cuts the lucky out of there. But it bothers him that she blabbed about that gun. It's like she was trusting him or something.

Serve her right about the Brownie. Serve her bloody well right.

HE TELLS HISSELF he's had a lucky escape, but he don't know what from. So what's he do? He only goes and sees them again.

It's Robbie's fault, as per usual. One day in August they're up their place in Shelton Street, and Robbie's patching over the window with bits of card to keep out the smell of some dead cab-horse down St Giles, and Ben's on the bed, working his way through the last of the book about Blacky the charger.

'Them posh bints,' goes Robbie. He's been on and on about them for months; keeping tabs on them and all. 'I heard their old man croaked and left them stony-broke.'

'So?' growls Ben.

'Can we go and see them? See if they're all right?'

'Shut it, Robbie,' he says. But then he gives in to Robbie's badgering and they set off for Madeleine's place in Wyndham Street.

When they get there and he sees how nobby it is, he gives Robbie a cuff that sends him flying. 'You said they was broke,' he snarls.

Broke? In a street like this? Housemaids scrubbing the steps, and a bloke with a water-cart laying the dust? And Madeleine's house has got these big columns, and railings painted green and steps up to a porch with blue and red tiles. But her basement gate's wide open and the kitchen door's ajar, and Ben's shocked. Anybody could walk in off the street. He'll have to have a word with her about that.

Robbie says they got no more money for domestics, and sure enough, when they nip down the steps, there's Madeleine standing at this big gas range, stirring this big stewpan and frowning at the thickest book Ben's ever seen. And Sophie's on the table swinging her legs and chattering nineteen to the dozen.

Him and Robbie go in, and Sophie gives them this big grin like they're long lost friends. 'Maddy, *look*! It's Ben and Robbie!'

Madeleine shoots Ben a cool look and tells him to shut the door.

Robbie's gawping at Sophie, and she asks to see Dog, and they fall to chattering, or Sophie does. Ben stays by the door.

He says to Madeleine, 'I heard your old man went all to smash.'

'He was our cousin,' she goes, still stirring. 'After he died we learned that he'd been embezzling from the bank where he was a director.' She says it matter-of-fact, like she's not surprised.

Sophie pipes up. 'Cousin Lettice is in a state of *collapse*, and has taken to her room.'

'Cousin Lettice,' mutters Madeleine, 'will outlive us all.' She shuts the book with a thump, catches him eyeing it and twists that curvy red mouth of hers. 'I had no idea how to cook, so I thought I should consult Mrs Beeton.' She and Sophie swap one of their sister-looks that's nearly a smile, then she tells Sophie to lay the table.

Sophie hops to the dresser. Four of everything, he can't help noticing. He gets that hot prickly feeling again. He watches Robbie and Sophie sitting at the table, and Madeleine dishing out soup. And all of a sudden he's back at Sunday dinner in the old days, with Kate laying the table and yelling at him to run down the pump and sluice.

His chest hurts. He's got to get out of here. But he can't. He watches Madeleine eating neatly like a cat, and Robbie slopping milk in his soup, and Sophie chatting for England.

All of a sudden she hikes her frock up to her knees and goes, 'Look, Ben, I've got a bruise. I fell down the steps.'

'Sophie . . .' says Madeleine, but Sophie peels back her black stocking to reveal a faint pink swelling on her knee.

'That's no bruise,' he sneers.

'Yes it jolly well is,' she flashes back, 'and it hurts, too.'

Crikey, he thinks. I was right about them eyebrows.

The smell of the soup's making him dizzy, so after a bit he sidles over and pulls up a chair where Madeleine's set a bowl for him. Lumps of meat and onions and barley. Best grub he's ever had.

Robbie looks up, soup on his chin, and goes, 'Ben clumped a geezer.'

'Shut it,' mumbles Ben.

'This geezer calls me a cripple,' goes Robbie, 'and Ben goes I'll get you, and the geezer laughs 'cos he's as big as a shed. But Ben tips this barrel on him, and the geezer falls under a dray and the wheels go on his legs, and Ben goes, now who's the cripple, eh?' Robbie roars.

Sophie's staring at Ben. 'Didn't you get told off?'

'Who by?'

'Um. Your parents?'

He snorts. 'Dead and gone.'

'That's a coincidence; so are ours.'

They go back to their soup. Then Sophie asks Robbie what their mother looked like, and he's off.

'She had red hair, like me, but Pa's was black like Ben's, and Pa knocked her about so she died. Then Ben took me away and Pa died too and Ben said good riddance.'

Sophie goes, 'I've never seen a picture of my mother. Cousin Lettice burned them all before we left Scotland.'

Ben says to Madeleine, 'This Cousin Lettice. She all you got left?'

She nods. 'Mother died when Sophie was born, and Father was killed in the Sudan. He was a soldier.'

Sophie pipes up. 'His name was Major Alasdair Falkirk and he came from Jamaica and deserted his young wife to run off with our mother. Her name was Rose, but that's all we know and we're not supposed to talk about them.'

'Why?' says Ben.

Sophie shoots Madeleine a look. Madeleine gets up and puts her bowl in the sink. 'We're illegitimate,' she says.

Ben don't know what that means, but it's plain they think it's bad.

'It means,' says Madeleine, 'our father never married our mother.'

'Is that all?' says Ben. 'Where I live you don't get spliced. Only toffs get spliced, 'cos only toffs got to worry about who gets the house and the jewels and that.'

Maddy looks at him as if he's said something deep.

Robbie asks Sophie if she wants to play stick and goose, and she says what's that, and Madeleine sends them out into the garden, calling after Sophie to put on her hat.

'Proper garden they got,' Robbie shouts down from the steps. 'Grass and flowerpots and a tree.'

When they're gone, Madeleine goes to the dresser and fetches a book and plonks it down in front of him.

'What's this?' he says.

'*The Downfall of the Dervishes*. We thought you might like it.'

He looks at the front cover and he realises she's had that book waiting all along, like she knew he was coming. He hates that. He goes, 'I never read the last one. Sold it. I'll do the same with this.'

'Do what you like. It was cheap enough.'

'Cheap?' he snaps. 'Nothing's cheap if you can't pay for it. Don't you know that yet?'

She sits down across from him and puts her hands on the table. 'You think we're rich, but soon we'll have nothing. We've got to sell the furniture to pay off the debts, and I'll have to work to support us.' She pauses. 'Mr Rennard can't afford to give me a job. I can't be a governess because I never went to school. I could be a lady's companion or a shop assistant, but that won't keep us alive.'

'So?' says Ben. 'Why tell me?'

'I thought you might be able to help.'

He's outraged. 'Me? I don't help nobody.'

'Then why are you here?'

'That was Robbie's idea.'

She don't say nothing. Just makes patterns on the table with her fingernail. The answer's as plain as the nose on her face, but she can't see it 'cos she's a toff. They're all the same.

After a bit he says, 'You could make a fortune on your back.'

She don't even blink, just gives him this long, slow look, like she's been thinking the same thing. Bit of a surprise, that.

'Cousin Lettice,' she goes, 'would say that it's in my blood.'

'You what?'

'That it's what I was meant to do. Because of who I am.'

Ben don't know about that, so he says, 'What about your family? If they're in Jamaica, they're rich, yeh?' He knows that 'cos Jamaica means sugar barons and darkie slaves.

But she's well narked. Shaking her head, with a face like thunder. 'I'm not asking them for help.'

'Why not?'

'For one thing, I don't even know who they are. Lettice would never tell me my father's real name.'

'Get out of it!'

'It's true. And I don't care. Why should I?'

'The point is, they won't want a couple of by-blows mucking things up for them, so they'll shell out a bit to keep you quiet.'

She's still shaking her head. 'Why should I go begging to them?'

It's his turn to get narked. 'Oh, that's beautiful, that is! You say you're broke, but you won't do bugger all about it. Well, I can't be doing with that.' He grabs the book and yells for Robbie, and they're out the door and up the steps, with Madeleine and Sophie standing in the kitchen looking shocked.

And what really pisses him off is that in among all them stewpans and whatnot, he never clicked nothing. Not even a spoon.

IT'S THE END of September but still baking hot, and the wind's in the south, so there's this choky stink of the knacker's yard down Garratt Lane. Ben's on the bed reading *The Downfall of the Dervishes*, when in comes Madeleine, right here in his place.

It's horrible having her here. She's all poshed up in that black dress of hers, with gloves and a hat, and him in nothing but his kickseys. But she don't seem to notice. She looks all in.

She gives Robbie a bag of cherries and his jaw drops and he's off like a lamplighter into the corner, chomping away.

Ben goes, 'How'd you find us, then?'

'Robbie told Sophie, then I asked around.' She paces about and turns, and smooths her hair. 'I did what you suggested: I tried to contact the family. I went to Septimus's attorney. He wouldn't tell me anything except that all this time it was the *family* that's been paying for us, not Septimus. There was some sort of trust, but now there's nothing left in it. Septimus stole the lot.'

'So? What d'you want me to do about it?'

She wraps her arms round her waist and takes these deep breaths like she can't get any air. 'Sophie has tuberculosis.'

Robbie looks up from his cherries. 'What's that?'

'The con,' snaps Ben. 'How long's she got, then.'

She looks at him like she can't believe what he just said. 'It's not consumption,' she says in a shaky voice. 'Her lungs are perfectly fine. The doctor says it's tuberculosis of the bones.' She swallows.

Ben shakes his head and starts picking at a scab on his elbow.

'It probably started with that bump on her knee. In a sanatorium, with good food and sunshine and a special splint, she might get better, completely better. But if she isn't treated soon—if the disease goes to her lungs—she won't survive the winter.'

He flicks the scab at the wall. 'Poor little cow.'

'She's not going to die,' she says between her teeth. 'I won't let her.'

'Oh yeh?' he goes. 'How d'you work that out? A bloody *san*? D'you know how much they cost?'

'Yes. Twenty guineas a month,' she snaps, 'with three months payable in advance. That's why I'm here.'

He shoots her a look.

'You said I could make a fortune on my back. Well, that's what I need. A fortune.'

He narrows his eyes. 'So?'

'Help me. Show me what to do.'

'Leave it out, Madlin.'

'I'll give you a cut on everything I make.'

'Now you're talking,' he says.

HOW COULD LIVES change so fast? Madeleine thought, as she dressed behind the screen. The month before, she had been photographing flowers in the garden, while Lettice was off to Maples to see the latest electric globes, Septimus voting to ban Americans from his club, and Sophie composing a pamphlet on the plight of the Regent's Park cab-horses. Now Septimus was dead, the money all gone, and her garrulous, infuriating little sister was mortally ill.

'*Why* won't you say where you're going?' asked Sophie. She was lying in bed, propped up against the pillows, looking furious.

'I did. I'm going to see Mr Rennard.'

'That's just what you told Cousin Lettice.'

Madeleine did not reply.

'You're meeting Ben and Robbie. Aren't you? You're meeting them and leaving me out. You're horrible. I hate you.'

She had been impossible ever since Dr Wray had fitted the splint two days before. A hideous device of steel hoops and bars covered in boiler felt, it encircled her left leg from the upper thigh to a couple of inches below her foot. A patten screwed to the other boot was supposed to even up the difference in heights. Dr Wray had assured her it was easy to stand on, but she had burst into tears of frustration after just five minutes.

Yet she was so determined to be grown up. When Madeleine had retrieved her beloved stuffed donkey from the attic, she had pushed him away for being too babyish. After Madeleine had explained that he wasn't a toy but a mascot, Pablo Grey had been allowed to stay.

The church bells struck the quarter-hour. Madeleine finished buttoning her blouse and came out from behind the screen. 'You're right,' she said. 'I am going to see Ben. But don't breathe a word to Lettice.'

Sophie nodded, and picked at the buckle on her splint.

She doesn't look ill, thought Madeleine. How can she be ill?

It had begun with that bump on the knee, then a touch of feverishness in the evenings. Lettice had put it down to growing pains, and dosed her with calomel. It was only when she grew languid in the mornings that they became alarmed.

Dr Wray had made a brisk diagnosis and prescribed prolonged rest in the famous splint along with plenty of beef and mutton suet, and lots of sunshine and fresh air in a sanatorium in the country.

Lettice had been outraged. To her, disease was a sign of moral turpitude, stemming from bad blood. But Dr Wray had explained to Madeleine that tuberculosis was caused by thousands of invisible organisms called bacilli. That night, she had lain awake and pictured them as a procession of tiny tombstones in her sister's blood.

Buttoning her jacket, she caught sight of herself in the looking glass. Her mother's dark eyes stared back at her. What if Dr Wray was wrong and Lettice was right? What if the disease *was* the taint, working its way out?

She couldn't think about that now. Today was Friday, and by Monday she needed twelve pounds. Twelve pounds for food, a month's rent in advance, and a carter to take the three of them to the dingy little rooms she had found in the North Wharf Road.

BEN WAS WAITING for her outside a fruiterer's on the corner of Titchfield Street and the Portland Road. He was flirting with a pock-faced little laundress with a basket of washing on her hip.

Madeleine liked Ben. He was filthy and foul-mouthed, and his green eyes were sharp with a knowledge gained far too soon. But she liked him. She understood his loneliness and his mistrust, and his passionate attachment to a younger brother who trusted too much.

And now she stood in the sun, watching him cracking jokes with the skivvy. Suddenly he put his hand behind the girl's head and drew her face close to his, and kissed her. The girl sank her fingers into his greasy black hair, and her body arched against his.

Madeleine's cheeks flamed. Was this what Lettice called vice?

When they drew apart, both were breathing fast. Ben studied the girl for a moment, his face expressionless. Then he looked round and caught sight of Madeleine, and left the skivvy without a backward glance.

'What's up, Madlin. Thought you wasn't coming.'

Her hands tightened on her reticule. 'What do we do now?'

He threw her an appraising glance. 'Little tour. Help you get your bearings.'

They crossed the road and started south, and as they walked he gave her a rapid-fire lesson in geography. At the bottom of the pile were the night-houses in Betty Street, which were despised for giving the profession a bad name. Then there were the accommodation houses around Seven Dials and the Haymarket, where business was transacted in doorways at sixpence a time. Above that was Marylebone, and then the pinnacle of Mayfair, where the houses were fearsomely discreet. Word would simply go out of a new arrival, and an interested client would have her sent round to his rooms in a cab. A girl could get twenty guineas for her first time. No scandal and no disease. All clean and topper and nice.

'Stop,' said Madeleine. They were outside the Coliseum, and she had to raise her voice above the rattle of the trams. 'I need you to tell me what this involves.'

He frowned. 'That's what I been—'

'No. I mean what one actually does. What one—does.'

He blinked. 'Shit. You mean you don't know?'

Just then, a commotion of yelps erupted down the street, followed by a good deal of raucous laughter. Outside a pub stood a brewer's dray with four black shire horses between the shafts, their ears pricked in mild curiosity at a pair of mongrels mating in the gutter.

Ben pointed at the dogs. 'There you are.'

Madeleine looked at him, then back to the dogs. 'That?'

He shrugged. 'Give or take.'

It wasn't the first time she had seen two dogs thus engaged, but she had never imagined that such behaviour applied to people. Lettice and Septimus? Her father and mother?

Two dogs mating in a gutter. Is that all there is?

But in a way, she thought as they carried on along the street, what's so surprising about that? If giving birth means blood and sweat and pain, why should the act of conception be any different?

She found herself scrutinising every man she passed and tried to picture herself doing 'it' with them.

I can't, she thought in sudden panic.

Why not? said another voice inside her head. It's in your blood.

I can't I can't I can't.

'I can't do this,' she told Ben. 'Not now. Not—today.'

Ben flicked her a glance. 'I know,' he said. 'I got a better idea.'

'Ben—'

'It'll work. You'll see. And you won't have to touch nobody.'

'WILL I HAVE to take *all* my clothes off?'

Madeleine was looking at a card that Ben had just handed to her. It was a photograph of a plump girl with wavy blonde hair lying on a couch. She was completely naked, and dreamily contemplating a single rose laid across her dimpled thighs.

'Well, why not?' Ben said. 'You don't got to do nothing.'

He had brought her to a little shop whose sign proclaimed it in cracked gold lettering to be *Venables & Co, Specialist Books & Photographs*. Ben waited downstairs while the photographer, a plump young man with a bad case of acne and a shock of blond curls, showed Madeleine into his surprisingly spacious studio.

'If you need to shave your legs,' he said, 'there's a razor behind the screen. I don't run to soap.'

Madeleine shook her head and went behind the screen. Over one corner hung a purple robe of imitation silk. Nobody's going to touch you, she told herself as she struggled out of her clothes.

The robe felt horribly insubstantial when she put it on, but when she emerged from behind the screen she was relieved to see that the photographer was busy draping grubby white sheets over the backs of chairs arranged in a semicircle about a blue plush couch. He must be using them as reflectors, she thought.

At length he noticed her and fetched her a mug of black tea from a gas ring in the corner. She perched on the edge of the couch and sipped her tea while he rooted around in a stack of cartons. To break the silence, she asked what he thought about the new handheld cameras. She had noticed that he favoured an old-fashioned view camera, with half-size plates and a sturdy tripod.

'Snapshots?' He snorted. 'I tell you, if I wasn't such an artist I'd be out of the biz.' He scowled into a carton of plates. 'Know a bit about it, do you?'

She told him about helping at Mr Rennard's, and soon he was telling her about the new flash powders he'd been trying out, and his hopes for panchromatic plates—the way of the future, dear, or it would be if it wasn't so bloody *expensive*, pardon my French.

He peered into the viewfinder and slotted a plate into the camera.

'Now when you're ready, we can just get rid of that robe. I thought we'd get those hands clasped, or the shaking'll spoil the pics. And a bit of gauze over the face—sort of like a shroud? Be amazed how many of the gentlemen like that kind of thing.'

THE GIRL IN THE TEA SHOP asked Lettice if she was still feeling seedy, and Lettice replied that she was better thank you, and the girl nodded and hurried off to attend to another customer.

Lettice blinked at her cold tea. Even though the sharp pain in her breast had subsided, all she could see before her was Madeleine and that—creature—disappeared into that appalling little shop.

Why had God forsaken her? She had always done His will. Always. When Mama had said how can you think of accepting that Mr Fynn, he is scarcely a gentleman, Lettice had married him, for she had known that she was too plain to turn down the only offer she was likely to get. She had borne a childless union to a vulgar man, and when Mama cut them off without a shilling, and Septimus cooled towards her, she had borne that too, for it was God's will.

Then, one dark February morning, she had opened the letter from Rose Durrant. She had long known that this woman's wickedness had brought shame to the family. But it was a shock to see that infamous name proudly scrawled in bold black script.

Please forgive me for writing, but Ainsley is in the Sudan, and I fear for my daughter and for the little one to come, should anything occur while he remains overseas. Then the bald request: if 'the worst' should occur, would Lettice care for the children until their father's return? Please send an assurance as soon as convenient.

Enclosed with the letter was a photograph of a beautiful woman seated on a chair, with a handsome, fair-haired man smiling down at her, and a lovely little girl on her lap. *Look at me*, said the peerless dark eyes. *All my life I have been wicked. And see how God has rewarded me.* Why had God allowed it? Where was the *justice*?

For a fortnight she had agonised about what to do. Then she had dashed off a curt response, seeking details of the lying-in. She never received a reply. Ten days later she had seen the piece in *The Times*: 'Gallant major slain . . . captain held, pending court-martial.' She had been shocked, but also horribly soothed. God had spoken. The world was just after all. She had overruled her husband's objections and they had travelled to Scotland.

Rose Durrant had died too, because she was wicked. God had given her Rose's children because she was good, and for ten years she had clung to that truth as to a rock.

She picked up her cup and took a sip of cold tea. It tasted bitter. All her life she had struggled to do God's will, and now He had forsaken her. She didn't know what to do.

One thing is certain, she told herself. You cannot manage this on your own. You are only a woman.

She took another sip of tea.

Yes. That is it. You must find a man to take control.

WALKING THE PAVEMENTS back to Wyndham Street, Madeleine had felt as if everyone was staring at her. What did they see? Could they tell what she had just done?

She let herself into the house. The hall was dim and empty, and her footsteps echoed as she crossed the tiles. She felt exhausted and nauseous. She wanted to go upstairs and curl up beneath the covers.

She was taking out her hat pins when she noticed Lettice sitting on the stairs, her bony yellow hands clutching her knees.

Anxiety gripped Madeleine. 'Is Sophie all right?'

'Asleep,' said Lettice.

Madeleine let out a long breath. She turned away and took off her hat, wishing Lettice would stop watching her and leave her alone.

With a stiff rustle of skirts Lettice rose to her feet. 'Tell me what you did. With that—creature.'

The hall was completely silent.

'I saw you,' said Lettice. 'I followed you.'

'That was underhand.'

'I followed you quite openly. You were too involved with that creature to notice.'

Madeleine glanced down at the hat in her hand.

'Tell me the truth,' said Lettice. 'What did you do?'

'Nothing,' she replied.

'A lie.'

'If you wish it, I'll swear on the Bible.'

'The Bible,' spat Lettice, 'means nothing to you.'

Again Madeleine said nothing. Lettice was right.

'I have tried to make you decent, respectable,' said Lettice.

'But I'm not respectable. You made sure I never forgot that.'

'You can *seem* respectable. You can *pass* for respectable among decent people—'

'I don't know any decent people. You never let me meet any. Except for Mr Rennard, and he's a shopkeeper so he doesn't count.'

Another silence. Lettice drew herself up. 'I can do nothing more with you. Someone else must try. I have failed.'

'What do you mean, someone else?'

Lettice hesitated. 'Your grandfather's adopted son. A churchman. You must apply to him for guidance.'

'My *grandfather*? Why didn't you tell me this before?'

'Because he doesn't want you!' spat Lettice. 'He never wanted you!' Her bony breast rose and fell. 'Ten years ago,' she said more quietly, 'I felt it my duty to break a long silence. I wrote to him. Jocelyn Monroe. Your father's father. My cousin. Yes, you and I are related after all. To my lasting shame.' She paused for breath. 'I thought it my duty to inform him of your existence. He replied that he wished to know nothing about you. Nothing.'

It was Madeleine's turn to sit on the stairs.

Lettice stood looking down at her. 'His adopted son is a churchman. The Reverend Sinclair Lawe. I understand that he has an address in Fitzroy Square. You must go to him and confess all.'

'Fitzroy Square? But—that's practically round the corner! Why hasn't he ever visited us?'

'Because the head of the family *commanded* me to keep you separate. Besides, I have never met the Reverend Lawe. Indeed I doubt he even knows I exist.' She paused. 'As you very well know, my contact with my family was all but ended by my marriage.'

Madeleine was silent for a moment. Then she said, 'This Reverend Lawe. What makes you think that he'll see me?'

Lettice leaned over her. 'Sinclair Lawe is a man of God,' she hissed. 'Have you any conception of what that means?'

'But, Lettice, I can't just—'

'Go to him. Throw yourself on his mercy. I can do nothing more with you.'

WHAT DOES GOD want from me? wondered the Reverend Sinclair Lawe in despair. He took the nailbrush from the washstand and scrubbed his fingers till the water turned pink. Why had he succumbed again? Why had God allowed him to pollute himself?

As he reached for a napkin to dry his hands, his eye was caught by a flash of colour outside the window. He froze. The bathroom was three floors up, and not overlooked—and yet there, on the neighbouring roof, crouched a chimney sweep's boy.

Breathlessly Sinclair took in the stick limbs, the vivid copper hair and the blackened face. The creature had seen everything.

He shut his eyes, and when he looked again the creature was gone. And that was worse. Already evil gossip might be spreading.

He willed himself to be calm. He replaced the napkin on the rail and straightened his smoking jacket. Then he went downstairs to his study, rang for Mary and ordered a glass of hot milk.

But he could not forget the apparition on the roof. Perhaps it was some sort of sign? Perhaps God intended some great change in his fortunes? Oh, let it be so. His life had become intolerable.

Everyone was urging him to do the one thing that he never could. Even the Dean was becoming impatient. 'Now that you have turned thirty,' he had said at their last encounter, 'I presume that you will shortly be delighting us with news of your engagement to an appropriate young lady.'

There was no answer to his dilemma. There could *be* no answer. And yet he must marry, to gain his inheritance. Great-Aunt May was clear enough in her letters. *You must marry at once*, she had told him, *and produce a son, or Fever Hill will never be yours. Your brother will find some means of worming his way back into the old man's affections, and you will be disinherited. Cameron may be an outcast and a recluse, but he lives in Jamaica. You do not.*

Wearily he took out the little grey booklet from the secret compartment of his desk and reread the familiar page. It was not that he needed to be reminded of the text, but he clung to some hope that this time he might derive a meaning less absolute.

Of course he never did. *Plain Words to Young Men on an Avoided Subject* was exactly that. 'If once a young man succumbs to the imbruted cravings of lust, and wastes his substance in solitary indulgence, the fatal habit is acquired . . . Should such a man be wicked enough to marry, he risks passing the dreadful malady to his wife. His progeny are born dead, or exist only in brief suffering.'

He passed a shaky hand over his face. With such a secret, how could he marry? How risk exposure and ruin?

At that moment he heard footsteps on the porch. A rap at the door. He sucked in his breath. The chimney sweep? He pictured the creature waiting on the doorstep, plotting blackmail.

When Mary announced 'a lady', Sinclair shuddered with relief, and was unconcerned that he did not recognise the caller's name.

The girl whom Mary showed in was no parishioner. Sinclair would have remembered her, for she was handsome—although her features were too decided for truly feminine beauty. And she was in trouble; he could tell that at once. He wondered why.

He offered her a chair by the fireplace and took the one opposite, and ordered tea. He noticed that her manners were ladylike, but that when she drew off her gloves to pour, her fingers were reddened at the tips. Ah. A lady in reduced circumstances. He could always tell.

And she was hiding something. He stopped listening to her tale of misfortune. 'Forgive me for interrupting,' he said, 'but I have many demands on my time, and I confess to being surprised that you should come to me for assistance, while concealing the truth.'

A hit, a palpable hit. Her dark eyes widened with shock.

He gave her a brief, reassuring smile. 'I am sorry if I startled you, but my calling has made me expert in these matters. You come to me with a tale of a bankrupt guardian and an invalid sister, and an urgent need for guidance, which'—he forestalled her protest with an upheld palm—'I assure you I do believe. But you make no reference to what prevents you from seeking the obvious solution.'

She looked perplexed.

'Why, marriage, of course. A young lady with—permit me—your advantages should not find it difficult to secure a match.'

'Oh, no, that's out of the question. I can never marry.'

'And why is that?'

She glanced at her lap and frowned.

'Forgive me,' he said, 'but does your concern over marriage derive from some—inherited weakness in your family?'

She did not reply. He sensed that he was nearing the truth.

He swallowed. 'Permit me to guess. There is some defect in the physical constitution—perhaps of a nervous indisposition?'

'Not exactly.'

'Perhaps—some flaw in the circumstances of your birth?'

She went still.

So that was it. The girl was illegitimate. And as he studied her reserved features, he was overwhelmed by a tremendous elation. It was as if he stood on the verge of a great revelation that in some mysterious way would alter his destiny. But what could it be?

'Mr Lawe,' she began in her curiously direct way, 'I regret having to ask you this when you've been so kind—but . . .' She bit her lip. 'You see, I need ten pounds. I need it today. If I don't get it, I don't know what I shall do.' She coloured, and he guessed that she knew exactly what she would do.

Money. Of course! Why hadn't he thought of it before?

'God has indeed brought you to the right place, my dear. I happen to be the trustee of a small charity conceived to help just such unfortunates as yourself.' He went to his desk, unlocked the money drawer and withdrew four five-pound notes, which he placed on the blotter. 'I have doubled the amount, to avoid your having to remove to those inferior lodgings you mentioned.'

She looked at the money. 'You are very generous,' she muttered.

'However,' he added. 'I feel it my duty to impose one condition.'

She raised her eyes to his.

'You must return tomorrow, and every day thereafter. That we might pray together for your salvation.'

She looked from him to the money, then back again.

'Have I your word,' he said, 'that you will return?'

She rose to her feet. 'You have my word.'

When Mary had shown her out, he stood at the window and watched her walk away down the street. What was the cause of this extraordinary elation he felt? This sense that she held the key to his destiny? God had sent her for a purpose. But what was it?

He was turning away from the window when a flash of red on the pavement caught his eye.

It was the chimney sweep. The creature stood on the other side of the road, openly watching the house. It had found time to shed its brushes and scrub the soot from its evil little face—but its red hair was unmistakable. And beside it loitered an associate: taller, thinner, with dark hair and sharp, malevolent features.

Slowly, as in a dream, the dark-haired urchin turned its head and looked Sinclair in the eye.

He gripped the curtain and turned away.

There could be only one interpretation of that look. The red-haired imp had told his evil associate what he had witnessed on the roof. And now they meant to tell the world.

THE STREET SMELT of rain, wet horses and coal-dust as Madeleine descended the steps of the Reverend's elegant little town house and started walking home. With twenty pounds in her reticule she ought to feel relieved. Instead she felt humiliated. She was so lost in thought she forgot that Ben and Robbie had been waiting for her on the opposite pavement.

'So,' said Ben, when he had caught up with her, 'the parson give you any dosh?'

She told him about the twenty pounds.

He whistled. 'Bugger me. That'll cost you.'

'I don't know what you mean,' she said coldly.

'Oh yeh? Course you do!'

'He wants me to go back tomorrow. To pray with him.'

He spluttered. '"To pray"? I never heard it called that before.'

'For heaven's sake, it's not like that. He's a clergyman. You were the one who said I should ask the family for help. Well, now I have.'

'Oh yeh? But I bet you didn't tell him you *was* family.'

There was no answer to that. And she had been shocked by the ease with which she had deceived the clergyman. But she had been brought up to lie, and she knew that the best deceptions are the ones that stay closest to the truth. Thus she referred to her guardian simply as her aunt, while Sophie remained her sister, and their parents still fell victim to childbirth and war. All she had done was fillet out any references to Falkirk, Durrant, Monroe and Jamaica.

Ben said, 'So what's he like, the parson?'

She wondered how to reply. The first thing that had struck her about the Reverend Lawe was his beauty. His features were narrow and severely well proportioned; the eyes an unblinking cobalt, the lips fine and very red beneath the clipped blond moustache. It was the face of a saint or a zealot or a madman.

Which, she told herself sternly, is absolute nonsense. The poor man behaved with delicacy, courtesy and great generosity. What more could you possibly ask?

'So what's he like?' Ben said again.

She frowned. 'He's—very correct. And rather secretive, I think.' She decided that she didn't like him. She had a sense that he might be a liar. Being one herself, she could usually tell.

Ben spat in the gutter. 'So you're going back there tomorrow.'

'I must. I gave my word.'

'Oh, well, in that case,' he said sarcastically. He called to his brother, 'Come on, Robbie. Time we was off.'

'Ben, don't go off in a mood. Won't you come and see Sophie?'

He shook his head and the scruffy figures melted into the crowd.

She told herself it didn't matter, but it did. They needed him.

A few minutes later Madeleine turned into Wyndham Street, saw the doctor's carriage outside their house, and forgot about Ben. She picked up her skirts and ran. She met Dr Wray coming down the steps, his face grave.

'Is Sophie—?' she panted.

'Not Sophie,' he said. 'Mrs Fynn.'

IT HAD TAKEN PRAYER and mortification, but at last Reverend Lawe understood. He understood his strange elation over the young woman's illegitimacy. He understood why she alone among females held no terror for him. The answer was better than his wildest dreams.

And if any doubts remained, they were quashed by the death of the aunt. So now Miss Fynn was quite, quite alone. She had no family left—except for the invalid sister, who didn't count. It was proof positive of God's design.

The aunt's funeral took place on an unseasonably cold Thursday afternoon. At Miss Fynn's request, the clergyman did not attend. She had said that she did not wish to trouble him, and he was happy to oblige. But when the day came he could not contain his impatience, and went to wait for her at the lich gate outside the church.

She was the only mourner. He watched her black-veiled figure standing by the grave as the vicar rattled through the service. He watched her stoop for a clod of earth and toss it in. Then she turned and took the path that skirted the churchyard.

As he watched her walk towards him, he thought how overwhelmed she would be when he revealed his purpose. How could she not be overwhelmed? The beauty of God's plan was breathtaking. How could he have doubted his Redeemer for an instant?

And yet he *had* doubted. During the long years of darkness he had believed himself polluted and unfit to mate. But the Lord had given him a creature who had been compromised *from birth*. With such a creature he need feel no guilt—for she had already sinned. He need fear no exposure—for she had no kin. It was perfection.

Finally she saw him and quickened her step. As she drew near, she put back her veil to reveal a pale face unmarked by tears.

He took her hand. 'This has been a great shock for you.'

'It was—rather sudden. The doctor didn't hold out any hope after the first seizure, but when the end came it was still a shock.'

Sinclair offered her his arm and they moved out into the street. 'Allow me to offer you a moment of prayer before you return home. If you will accompany me to my—'

'You are very kind, but I can't. My sister is alone.'

He repressed a movement of impatience. 'My house is but two steps away. And I have something particular to impart.'

That caught her attention, as he had known it would.

He waited until they were settled in his study, and the tea had been brought and Mary sent away. 'Miss Fynn,' he said. 'It has been—what, eleven days since you first sought my guidance.'

She looked at him with solemn dark eyes.

'And during that time we have prayed together, and I have provided such modest financial assistance as lies within my power.'

'Mr Lawe,' she said in a low voice, 'I do appreciate—'

'No, no'—he held up his hand—'it was not my intention to solicit your thanks. I was merely referring to the manner in which our acquaintance has developed.' He leaned back. 'May I speak plainly?'

She nodded.

'With the passing of your aunt,' he went on, 'I understand that you—and your unfortunate sister—are entirely alone.'

The slightest of nods.

'I have been loath to tell you about my own circumstances, for fear of deepening your despondency at this difficult time. But I must now inform you that I intend shortly to take up a living in Jamaica.'

He was gratified to see her face drain of blood.

'I am troubled,' he went on, 'by the thought of what will become of you. Forgive me for raising a painful subject, but remember that I have nothing but your best interests at heart.' He was silent for a moment. 'You have provided only the barest particulars of your unfortunate parentage—and, please, I would not have it otherwise. But we cannot deny that you were begotten in godlessness.'

She coloured.

'Consider then the perfect *circularity* of a scheme whereby the godless one begets the godly.'

He waited for her to respond, but she merely looked puzzled.

'I have found a way for you to be redeemed. The All-perfect has vouchsafed it to me. You shall become my helpmeet.'

'Your helpmeet? You—you want me to go to Jamaica and help in your missionary work?'

He met her eyes. 'You shall do more than that. You shall *be* more than that. You shall be my companion. My fellow labourer.'

'Your fellow—'

'My wife.'

'HE WANTS *WHAT*?' demanded Ben. He was crouching on the basement steps, watching Madeleine watering Lettice's ferns. 'Oh, *Madlin*. You're never taken in by that! It's the oldest trick in the book.'

Madeleine put down the watering can and kneaded her temples. She hadn't slept all night. 'It's not a trick,' she muttered.

'Course it's a trick. Think about it. If you say yes, he gets it for nothing. And you—'

'And Sophie goes to Jamaica,' she snapped, 'where there's sunshine and sea air and a sanatorium up in the mountains.'

Ben took off his cap and scratched his head. 'What's his game, that parson? Toff like him, with a sodding great house in Fitzroy Square. He could marry anyone he wants. So who's he go and ask? A bastard with no money. You tell me how that makes sense.'

She couldn't. As always, he had put his finger on the weak spot. Her only explanation was that the clergyman had developed some sort of regard for her. Which didn't seem very likely.

'Course,' Ben went on, 'soon as he knows who you really are, he'll run a mile.'

She pushed a strand of hair behind her ear and straightened up. 'He won't find out,' she said, 'unless I tell him.'

'Don't be daft, Madlin,' Ben said. 'You'd be play-acting for the rest of your life. You'd never bring it off.'

He was right. What was she thinking of? To deceive an innocent young churchman into wedding the bastard offshoot of his own adoptive family? It was unthinkable. Unconscionable.

But she *was* unconscionable. She knew that already. She had posed for those photographs, hadn't she?

Ben got to his feet. 'You'll never do it. Will you?'

For a moment he looked very young, and it occurred to her that if she went through with it, he and Robbie would be alone again.

'If I don't, what happens to Sophie?'

They stood glaring at one another, while a gust of wind over-turned a fern and rolled it across the tiles.

Ben jammed on his cap. 'I got to go,' he muttered.

'Come back tomorrow. I need you to help me decide.'

He shrugged. 'See what I can do.'

When Ben had gone, she found herself hoping fiercely that he would come tomorrow. She needed his sharpness, and his flat-on view of the world, to help her decide.

IT'S THREE IN THE MORNING and Ben's just woken up, and for a bit he don't remember nothing, and everything's fine. Then it all comes back in a rush and he wants to die. He grinds his knuckles in his eyes, but he can't stop seeing it, over and over.

It was yesterday—only yesterday? Day after he had that row with Madeleine down in the basement. Him and Robbie are heading off to her place, like he said he would, when Ben sees Constable Hatch standing on the pavement. He's got his hands on his hips and he's looking about slowly, like he means business. Then he spots Robbie—*Robbie*—and he blows his whistle and shouts, 'Stop, thief!' And Robbie's going, 'What? What?' and Ben's thinking, Christ, this is the only time we *ain't* done a bloody click.

So off they go, him and Robbie, up the alley, up the drainpipes, over the roofs. It's one of his best routes; Hatch ain't got a chance.

But Hatch won't leave off. He's tracking them on the ground, and he's got two other bluebottles with him.

It's tricky on them roofs, and Ben steps on a loose tile and nearly goes over, and it's forty feet down. He calls to Robbie to watch that tile, and there's no answer, so he looks over his shoulder, and Robbie's not there. Must of taken a wrong turn. So Ben goes back for him, but he can't find him nowhere. Then he looks over the edge and sees this little crowd on the pavement. Then Hatch pushes back the crowd and that's when Ben sees what's on the ground.

He has to shove his fist in his mouth to keep from yelling out. It's like he's a bird swooping down, he sees it so close and sharp. Robbie's on his back, all twisted like a doll. Dog sticking out of his pocket. Pool of blood round his head.

Constable Hatch is looking up at the roof to see where Robbie fell, so Ben edges back. He don't know how long he stays there, fist still in his mouth, but when he looks again, Robbie's gone. Crowd's gone too, and so is Constable Hatch.

All day long Ben stays on the roof. He can't go back to Shelton Street, 'cos Hatch will be watching it. So he heads off east until he finds an empty space behind a chimney-stack. Soon as he curls up, he feels it rising up inside him, clawing at his gullet, fighting to get out. He can't go on without Robbie. He wants to die.

But you can't, says this voice inside his head. If you top yourself now, who's going to make sure Robbie's not shoved in a pauper's grave without Dog? You got to fix that, Ben. After that we'll see.

Then he thinks, hang about, there's more. It was that parson as put the coppers onto you. You got to fix him too.

Soon as he thinks it, he knows it's true. He can see just how it went. This nobby young parson asks Madeleine to marry him. He thinks she'll fall at his feet, but she wants time to consider. Nasty shock, that. So the parson gets to thinking, and he thinks, Ay ay, maybe them two lads I seen outside my house been putting ideas in her head. I didn't like the look of them. So I think I'll do for them.

And being a nob, it's easy to fix it with the bluebottles, and that.

The only thing Ben can't understand is why the parson put Hatch onto Robbie instead of him. 'Cos that's what happened, he's sure of it. When Hatch shouted Stop thief, he was looking at Robbie. But why?

Ben's eyes are hot again, and he stabs them with his knuckles. Shut it, Ben. You know what you got to do. First you got to find Robbie and get him settled with Dog. Then you got to see about the parson.

IT WAS AN OVERCAST October day, and Madeleine was sitting on the window seat in the morning room. Beside her was Lettice's prayer book and on her lap was Lettice's writing-case. She had taken out a fountain pen and a sheet of paper. *Dear Mr Lawe*, she wrote.

She put down the pen. Yes or no? She still didn't know. She picked up the prayer book. Please God, she thought, what should I do?

A letter slipped from between the pages and fell to the floor.

It was old, and had obviously been unfolded and refolded many times. The handwriting was large, sprawling, and hard to read, but the signature was clear. *Cameron Lawe*.

Madeleine felt a coldness in the pit of her stomach. She had once asked the Reverend if he had any siblings. 'Only a brother,' he had said with a tightening of the lips. 'It pains me to speak of him. For I am a man of God, but Cameron is a man of violence. He was discharged from the Service—for a crime too shameful to repeat.'

She had pictured a gambler and a rake: the sort of black sheep who could make a clergyman blanch. And that same Cameron Lawe had written to Lettice, whom his own brother didn't know.

She wondered why Lettice had kept it all these years: a short note from a disgraced ex-soldier. It was dated December 1886.

Dear Mrs Fynn,

I was surprised to receive your letter—not least because I didn't know that I had a cousin in England. But you are right to apply to me: better that than to have written to Jocelyn. As you know, he took the death of his son hard—although he would never admit that.

Why not? thought Madeleine angrily. The death of his only son? My God, what sort of family is this?

As you are also aware, Jocelyn wants nothing to do with Ainsley's progeny. Neither do I. But I feel it my duty to contribute what I can. My attorneys will contact you shortly, with a view to amplifying the trust which Jocelyn set up two years ago. I would simply ask that you do not mention this to him, as I see no point in causing him further distress.

The letter was blunt to the point of discourtesy. And Cameron Lawe's distaste for 'Ainsley's progeny' showed in every line. Like her grandfather, he had been only too ready to pay money in order to sweep the inconvenient bastards under the carpet.

Madeleine crumpled the letter and threw it across the room. She took a fresh sheet of writing paper, and Lettice's fountain pen. *Dear Mr Lawe*, she wrote. *I accept your offer. Yours, Madeleine Fynn.*

CHAPTER FOUR

Jamaica, March 1895

Cameron is back in his cell at Millbank prison. It's the first day of his sentence. He's lying on the planks in the cold and the stink, and the black sand is blowing in from the desert, and somewhere down a distant corridor a child is crying. Black sand stops his mouth and sugars his eyes. He can't see. Can't find what he's looking for. And all he can hear is that black sand hissing and that lost child crying in the dark.

He took a shuddering breath and woke up.

It was dawn. He was lying in his own bed on the verandah at Eden. The sky showed blue through the hole in the roof. He breathed in, and smelt the wet red earth. Usually this was his favourite time, when he was at his most optimistic. But the dream had left an after-taste of longing and regret that he couldn't shake off.

He wondered why he'd had it again. It only came when things went wrong. When croptime was late or there was a fire in the boiling house. What was it this time? Was it because Sinclair was back in Jamaica?

He heard the click of claws across the tiles, then felt a blast of hot breath on his shoulder, and Abigail's rasping tongue. She climbed on top of him, and when he could no longer breathe—for she was big even for a mastiff—he pushed her off and sat up.

He grabbed the old sheet he used for a towel, and in his nightshirt he made his way down the steps and through the dripping garden to the river. The green water was stingingly cool when he dived in, yet he could not erase that strange, indefinable sense of loss.

He had bought Eden to make his peace with Ainsley's ghost. It hadn't worked out that way, but he couldn't leave Eden now. He had fallen in love with her. She was beautiful, dangerous and infuriating. Sometimes he would ask himself what he was doing here. Why didn't he just give up and let her slip back into the wilderness that she'd been when he found her? But in the end he always stayed.

Back at the house he shaved, flung on clothes, and ate a plate of akee and saltfish before riding to Maputah. For the past three months he'd been racing to get in the cane before the rains made the tracks impassable, and now it was piled high in the works yard. The mill and the boiling house were running day and night, and he and his men were red-eyed with fatigue.

As the morning slipped away, his frustration deepened. It would take decades to haul Eden into the present. The mill was still powered by the centuries-old aqueduct from the Martha Brae. Oxen still toiled with agonising slowness to bring in the cane. Who was he deceiving? Over at Parnassus, old Addison Traherne had laid down a tramway *twenty-five years* before.

At midday he returned to the house for a hasty meal of curried goat, then rode the eight miles north to Falmouth to order kerosene and candles at Ryle's, and a crate of Scotch and a box of cigars at Doran's. Finally he decided to make a quick call on Olivia Herapath. She usually helped to put things in perspective.

The 'Closed' sign was up on the studio door, but Etheline let him in and showed him through to the salon at the back. The little room was dim and fugged with tobacco smoke. For the next twenty minutes Olivia indulged her passion for gossip, and she made him laugh despite himself. She was shrewd and coarse as only an aristocrat can be, and she knew 'everyone who mattered'. Society matrons flocked to her. For where else could they have their photographs taken and their friends dissected by a genuine noblewoman—even if she had dropped her title on marrying a commoner?

'I've been wondering,' she said at last, 'how long you think you're going to get away with never mentioning your brother.'

Cameron's heart sank.

'Heaven help us, Cameron, he's been back for nearly four months!'

'So I've heard.'

'And he's acquired a wife.'

'I've heard that too.'

'Have you seen them yet?'

'You know I haven't. I don't see any of them. Ever.'

She snorted. 'Well, I have. I left my card on her the morning they arrived.' She bared her small yellow teeth in a grin. 'Sinclair doesn't care for me, but he dared not send his regrets. He's such a snob.'

She waited for him to speak. At last he gave in.

'So,' he said. 'What do you think of my new sister-in-law?'

Her eyes glittered. 'Now *there's* a puzzle. Good lines, a tolerable taste in dress—but *no accomplishments*! No French, no music. Can't even ride. Although I hear that Jocelyn's been giving her lessons. But it's frightfully *odd*. One wonders where Sinclair found her. And most provoking of all is that she's far too good for him.'

Cameron was surprised. 'You mean you like her?'

'I know, isn't it singular?' She paused to draw on her pipe. 'For one thing, she knows her photography. Oh, yes. She's set up a darkroom in the undercroft. Of course, Sinclair doesn't approve at all, but what can he do, when she buys her supplies from a baron's daughter?' She shook her head. 'Damned intriguing. I cannot imagine why she married him, except of course for his money.'

He got to his feet and picked up his hat. 'Well then, it seems he's got what he deserves.'

Usually, seeing Olivia Herapath lifted his spirits, but as he rode out of Falmouth he felt an odd sense of betrayal. Olivia was *his* friend, dammit. Why did she have to approve of Sinclair's wife?

He was telling himself not to be so childish when he reached the crossroads over the Martha Brae and turned south for Eden. The afternoon heat was still intense, so he kept to the shade of the poinciana trees. He had not gone far when he heard the rattle of wheels behind him, and turned to see a smart new trap crossing the bridge and heading west along the Fever Hill Road.

Sinclair wore a white linen suit and a Panama hat, and he drove briskly, staring straight ahead. The young woman at his side wore a dust-coat of russet silk and a wide straw hat. Like Sinclair, she was staring straight ahead. Neither of them saw Cameron.

He only caught a glimpse of the girl as they swept past, but it was a shock. He had imagined Sinclair's wife to be slight and blonde, with a pinched mouth. This girl had a chignon of rich dark hair, an olive flush to her cheek, and an extravagantly curved red mouth.

It was an unpleasant surprise to find himself admiring his brother's choice. Despite the heat, he kicked his horse to a canter. He spent two hours at Maputah, snapping at everyone, then returned to the house for a stiff rum and water.

As evening came on, his mood darkened and he went out to the garden and picked a couple of mangoes and washed them down with another rum and water. Abigail heaved herself of the verandah and followed him. The air was heavy with the scent of datura and star jasmine, but Cameron hardly noticed.

Whenever he thought of his brother it was with a sense of defeat and irritation. Sinclair hated him. Cameron had long given up wondering why. And now Sinclair was back in Jamaica, living with Jocelyn at Fever Hill with a handsome young wife. He had everything a man could want. Someone to share things with, to work for.

Next to that, what had he, Cameron, achieved in eight years at Eden? What was the point of his efforts? Who was he doing this *for*?

In disgust, he turned to go back into the house, and was startled to see that he was not alone. Grace McFarlane was standing at the foot of the steps, watching him. Her two children were hiding behind her.

'Hello, Grace,' said Cameron.

He caught the brilliance of her smile as she inclined her head in greeting. 'Mas' Camron,' she said. 'Lang time me nuh see you.'

'A long time,' he agreed.

He was not in love with Grace, nor she with him. They had settled that years ago. And these days she only made the journey from Fever Hill when she was looking for birds' eggs, or visiting one of her relations in the hills. He pictured her striding barefoot along the moonlit track: tall, uncompromising and completely unafraid.

'How have you been, Grace?' he asked.

She tilted her head in a gesture that could have meant anything. 'An you, soldier-man? What I hear, you in one a your *black* moods.'

He made no reply, but studied the strong planes of her face. The broad cheekbones, the slanted eyes, the generous, well-shaped mouth.

'You don' glad Mas' Sinclair back,' she said.

'Glad?' he said. 'What to glad fe, girl?'

She grinned. She liked it when he spoke *patois*. 'Preacher-man fixing to cut you out de fambly.'

'I don't care about that. I don't have any right to Fever Hill, and neither does Sinclair. It belongs to the Monroes, not to the Lawes.'

She cocked her head. 'Maybe so. But preacher-man not only ting troubling you. Eh, soldier-man?'

No hiding from Grace, not even in the dark.

She drew her finger down his cheek. 'You wait. Preacher-man reckon widout Gracie McFarlane. She fix it so he get no boy-child.'

'Grace,' he said sharply. 'Don't go touching him.'

The smile widened to a grin. 'Oh, I don' need fe go *touching* him, soldier-man. Don' trouble yourself about dat.'

'That's not what I meant . . .'

But she had gone, melting into the darkness and calling to her children, Evie and Victory, as she went.

SEVENTH OF MARCH, Eighteen Ninety-Five.

Maddy has given me this beautiful writing book for my birthday, so I am starting a Journal.

I ADORE Jamaica. It has sugar cane, magic and alligators, and vultures called john crows. It is exceedingly hot, and there is no rain, for it is the dry season; but there is a sea breeze in the morning and a land breeze at night, which keeps us tolerably cool.

I don't think Maddy cares for Jamaica. Or perhaps it is just Fever Hill she doesn't like. I ADORE Fever Hill. Sometimes it smells of rum from the New Works, and always of orange peel from the floor polish, and everything about it is strange. There is no gaslight, only kerosene lamps and candles, and the house is dark and mysterious even in daytime. The walls are wooden, with slats to let through the breeze, so one can hear what is said three rooms away. Maddy calls it a House of Whispers.

When we first arrived, she was dismayed to learn that we would be living here with the family. She is only allowed to go for walks at night, for Great-Aunt May disapproves of ladies going out during the day. The gazetteer that Maddy bought me in London says that white ladies go about unaccompanied at all times in Jamaica nowadays, and it is perfectly safe and respectable. What a shame for Maddy! She says the darkness and confinement are what turned Clemency mad.

My room here is PERFECTION. Actually my real *room is just for clothes, I mean the gallery outside it where I live!! A gallery is Jamaican for a verandah which is enclosed by louvres to keep out the sun. This makes it shadowy and hard to see out, but luckily for me, three of the louvres in front of my bed are broken!*

Fever Hill was once the greatest estate on the Northside, but now most of the cane-fields are let to the Trahernes or left in ruin. Sinclair says that Uncle Jocelyn has lost heart. I believe that is because of Sinclair's wicked brother, but no one will talk of him. Maddy says she doesn't care to know about the past. But I do.

Ninth of March

Sinclair has just found an egg beneath his bed, and is greatly perturbed. It was only a little pale blue egg, but he wouldn't touch it and nor would the helpers, and there was quite a to-do. Eventually Daphne took it to the cook-house and threw it in the oven. She said she is too old to be frightened of obeah.

My new friend Evie says obeah is Jamaican black magic, and that an egg is a bad obeah sign. I asked what it signifies, but she said she didn't know, which is Jamaican for I'm not telling.

Twelfth of March—After supper

Maddy has just gone to dinner. She looked BEAUTIFUL in her amber evening gown. She says the talk at dinner is always of sugar and how hundreds of estates have been abandoned because they freed the slaves too soon, which is embarrassing in front of the helpers. Sinclair says they don't understand, but I bet they do. Kean is the butler, and very clever and quiet; Maddy calls him the 'eyes and ears of Fever Hill', as he reports everything to Great-Aunt May. Maddy's maid, Jessie, is also a sneak, but the others are nicer.

Fourteenth

I can see across the lawn to the duppy tree. The English name for it is a silk-cotton tree. It is tall and wide like an oak, with creepers hanging down, and spiky wild pines clinging to the branches. In the dark they look like giant spiders.

Evie says that on nights with no moon, all the duppy trees transport themselves to the deep woods to hold secret conferences. Tonight I woke myself up, to check that our duppy tree was still in place.

Seventeenth—After tea

What a day! I have just had my first walk on the lawns with my new crutches!!!! I was very wobbly and it only lasted five minutes, but I did get a good look at the outside of Fever Hill.

The house faces north towards the sea, and has two storeys with galleries all round, and a great flight of marble steps down to the carriage-drive. On the outside the louvres are peeling, and eaten by termites, which makes the house look ruined, and boarded up.

Clemency says there was once a Rose Walk and an aviary, but Uncle Jocelyn had them destroyed when his wife, Kitty, died, after they were married just a year. Sometimes Clemency goes down onto the lawns at night, if she hears her baby crying in Hell. I asked her why the baby is in Hell, and she said that the Reverend Grant arrived too late to baptise him before he died, so the baby went to Hell. Clemency blames herself.

Beyond the lawns I can see the duppy tree, and behind it there is a rise, on the other side of which I understand there is the Burying-place with all the family graves. I wish I could see the Burying-place, for it is the one place at Fever Hill that Sinclair's wicked brother, Cameron, is allowed to visit. He goes there once a month. Uncle Jocelyn thought the world of him until he did something unspeakable and got sent to prison.

Somewhere beyond the Burying-place there is a ruined 'hothouse', which is Jamaican for slave hospital. Evie says it is a very bad place, and she wouldn't go there at night for anything, because of the duppies. A duppy is an evil ghost which appears when someone dies. Evie says that no matter how nice a person was when they were alive, when they die their duppy is always horrid. Beyond the hothouse there are cane-fields and cattle pastures, and on the edge of the estate there is an old hunting lodge called Providence. Beyond that is the Cockpit Country, a terrible place where runaway slaves used to hide, and their descendants still live there. It has no roads, rivers or streams: just ravines and sink-holes, where they used to leave disobedient slaves to die of thirst.

Twentieth of March
I asked Uncle Jocelyn if white people become duppies and he said that black people's magic doesn't work on white people. Uncle Jocelyn is seventy-three, extremely tall, lean and stiff. He has a silver moustache and bushy eyebrows. He likes Maddy, and sometimes comes out to the gallery to hear her read aloud. I don't know what she thinks of him.

Great-Aunt May is seventy-six and wears tight grey gowns and grey kid gloves. Great-Aunt May is in fact Uncle Jocelyn's aunt. She is narrow and straight and has angry eyes. She used to be a Beauty, but she never married. She doesn't like me.

Clemency is my FAVOURITE person (apart from Maddy!!!). She is forty-three but still pretty, although she dyed her hair grey when her baby died. It is a great shame that she has no other children, for she would have been an extremely good mother.

Clemency is the widow of Uncle Jocelyn's only son, Ainsley. He did something bad, like Cameron Lawe, and no one mentions him either. Clemency told me she can hardly remember Ainsley, and that she only married him because her brother, Cornelius Traherne, told her to.

Twenty-fifth of March
Black people are healthier than white people, and have more fun, even though they do all the work and have no money. They go about in the sun, sing a lot, and swim in the river. Black ladies do not need husbands in order to have babies. For example, Grace who does the laundry has never had a husband. She has never told anyone who is the father of Evie and Victory. They don't even know themselves.

Evie is twelve, and the PRETTIEST little girl I ever saw. She's a lovely caramel colour. I only got to know her a few weeks ago, when Maddy started paying her a quattie an hour to sit with me. Now she is my friend. Victory is six, and has curly eyelashes. Evie and Victory live with Grace down in the ruined slave village by the Old Works that got burnt down sixty years ago in the Christmas Rebellion. Nobody else will live there because of the duppies, but they don't bother Grace because she is a witch and knows about black magic, which is called obeah, and white magic, which is called myalism. Mostly she does good magic, I think.

Evie says that when a person gets sick, it's because someone has stolen their shadow and nailed it to a duppy tree, and that only a shadow catcher can catch it and put it back inside the person to make them well again. She says that someone must have stolen my shadow, which is why I am so ill. But I don't see how someone could have nailed it to a duppy tree, because I became ill before we came to Jamaica, and there are no duppy trees in England.

Sophie put down her pen and listened to the crickets' rasp. Around her the house lay dreaming in the heat. Maddy was in the darkroom, Uncle Jocelyn in his library, Great-Aunt May and Clemency were resting in their rooms, and Sinclair was writing in his study.

Since the wedding, Maddy had changed. She didn't talk as much. Perhaps she found the secrecy tiresome. It must be hard, having to remember that not even Sinclair must know that their parents came from Jamaica. Sophie found it hard too, although she had grown up with secrets, for Cousin Lettice had always forbidden them to mention their parents to anyone.

Then it occurred to her that perhaps Maddy had secrets from her too. The thought made her skin prickle.

ON THE MORNING of the visit to Falmouth, Madeleine awoke before dawn to find that her monthly courses had begun. Oh *no*, she thought. Once again she would have to tell Sinclair that she would not be giving him a son, and they would have to do *that* again.

He slept beside her curled in a ball. Since the episode of the egg, he had taken to dosing himself with a sleeping draught every night. She wondered what dreams he had.

She drew aside the mosquito curtain, slipped out of bed and crept to the dressing room. When she was dressed she went out into the gallery and down the steps to the undercroft. As she opened the darkroom door she took a deep, reassuring breath of the familiar chemical smell. This was her place. Nothing could reach her here.

Madeleine lit the kerosene lamp, and shadows flared. Faces leapt from the prints pegged on the line to dry. She walked slowly down the line, choosing prints to show to Mrs Herapath that afternoon. Sophie and Pablo Grey ('I know it's babyish, but he's a mascot, really'). A stark, unforgiving profile of Great-Aunt May. Jocelyn in the library with his books and his framed map of the Northside.

It still surprised her that she liked the old man. Sometimes she had to remind herself who he was: not just a proud, lonely old gentleman who admired her photography and was wary of Sophie, but the grandfather who had dusted off his hands and forgotten them.

There were so many questions that she wanted to ask him. Did you mourn your son at all? Why isn't he buried with the rest of the family at the Burying-place? Do you ever think of your grandchildren in England? Do you ever think of us?

She looked down again at the prints in her hand. In the steady glow of the lamp she caught a trace of her mother in Sophie's wilful mouth. Her father gazed out through Jocelyn's hooded eyes.

Go *away*, she told them silently. I don't want you. I never wanted you. Why can't you leave me alone?

Her sanctuary wasn't safe any more. They had followed her in.

SHE HAD GIVEN Sinclair the bad news just after luncheon, when he had withdrawn to his study to work. He had looked at her steadily, then suggested that she have a bed made up on the gallery until she was clean again. They had parted with polite ill will.

She intended to lie down until it was cool enough to start for town, but on the way to their bedroom she decided to risk universal disapproval and go to see Mrs Herapath now, in the blazing sun.

For once, luck was on her side. By the time she and Sophie were ready to leave, Sinclair was closeted in the library with Jocelyn, and Great-Aunt May and Clemency had gone upstairs to rest.

The royal palms lining the carriageway gave little shade, and as they started off the heat was like a wall. Sophie was unusually quiet but for once Madeleine didn't try to talk her out of it.

Five days, she thought. Six at the most. Then I'll be 'clean', and we'll have to do it again. Four times in as many months, and each time as messy and humiliating as the wedding night.

The wedding night. Whenever she thought of it her spirits sank. Neither of them had known what to expect, and in their different ways they had both been profoundly shocked. Not by the act itself, but by the blood.

Sinclair had been terrified. '*Blood*,' he had whispered, his face grey with shock, his lips taut with disgust. He had retreated to an armchair and drawn up his legs, like a small boy after a nightmare. Nothing she had said could persuade him back to bed.

It had been different for her. One look at those scarlet blotches on the sheets and she had been a child again, staring at her mother's body in the crimson butterfly, feeling the bewilderment of loss.

The following month they had tried again. This time there was no blood, but by then, for Sinclair, the damage had been done.

She was unclean.

Angrily, she flicked the whip across the pony's rump and the trap swept on across the Martha Brae towards Falmouth.

THEY FOUND MRS HERAPATH in the salon, two-thirds of the way through a bottle of manzanilla. As she poured a glass of sherry for Madeleine, who was busy settling Sophie in an armchair, Mrs Herapath muttered, 'I'm afraid I'm in one of my moods today. Wretched day. Wedding anniversary. Twenty-fifth.'

'Oh no. We shouldn't have come.'

'No, no. I invited you. And we had a good innings, Hector and I.' Blinking furiously, she gestured to a photograph of a stout gentleman above the desk. The eyes held a dry intelligence, but the whiskered cheeks suggested a hamster.

'Did Mr Herapath become a duppy?' asked Sophie.

'Not as such,' said Mrs Herapath. 'He ascended to a higher state of being.'

'Do you know about shadows, Mrs Herapath?'

'Sophie . . .' said Madeleine.

'It's quite all right,' said the older woman. 'Sweet child. I take it you mean the Jamaican kind?'

Sophie nodded.

'As it happens, I don't. But you might find a book in the studio, if you care to look. That is'—a questioning glance at Madeleine—'if she's allowed to move about?'

Madeleine nodded. Dr Pritchard had said that, since the knee was so much better, Sophie should start learning to use her crutches.

When Sophie had hobbled laboriously out, Mrs Herapath turned back to Madeleine. 'You seem out of sorts, my dear. What's the matter? Some sort of spat with Sinclair?'

Madeleine shook her head. 'I'm fine.'

Mrs Herapath gave an ill-tempered smile. 'Ah, young love! Strongest force in the world. And the most destructive. You just ask that twisted lot up at Fever Hill.'

'I'd rather not,' said Madeleine.

Mrs Herapath threw her a curious glance. 'I'd noticed that.

Whenever I get anywhere near the Scandal About Which We're Not Supposed To Know, you close up like a limpet.'

Madeleine did not reply.

Mrs Herapath drained her glass. 'It's just that it *bothers* me to see that old man mouldering away up there, missing poor dear Cameron so terribly—and he does, you know. If we could just get the two of them *together*, just once, then I'm sure at least that part of the wretched muddle could be sorted out.'

'They're grown men,' said Madeleine stiffly. 'I'm sure they can sort it out for themselves.'

Mrs Herapath gave a mirthless laugh. 'My dear, how little you know about men!'

She heaved herself to her feet and refilled their glasses. 'I knew Rose Durrant, you know. Oh yes. I suppose you've heard of Rose?'

Madeleine kept her eyes on the sherry glass in her hand. It was slightly shaking, but if she concentrated, she could make it go still.

'She used to help me in the studio,' said Mrs Herapath, subsiding back onto the sofa. 'Quite a talent for composition. But wild, of course. All the Durrants were. Impulsive. Passionate. And such a temper! Still. I adored her. *Such* a blow when she ran off like that. Why, my dear, you've gone quite pale.'

'I'm fine.'

Mrs Herapath put her head on one side and studied her with narrowed eyes. 'You know, it's a part of the family history. You ought to take more of an interest.'

Madeleine felt herself growing hot. 'Why should I want to know about something that happened twenty years ago?'

Mrs Herapath looked startled. 'But—I'm sorry. I had no idea that you felt so strongly.'

'I don't.'

'Then you *are* out of sorts.'

There was an irritable silence between them. Mrs Herapath picked up her glass and scowled at it. Madeleine put hers down.

'I'm sorry,' they both said at the same time.

Madeleine smoothed her skirt over her knees. 'You're right,' she said, 'I am out of sorts. I'm a little—indisposed.'

Mrs Herapath leaned over and patted her hand.

Madeleine blinked back tears and rose quickly to her feet. 'Sophie's been awfully quiet. I ought to go and see—'

'Oh dear, now I've chased you away.'

'No, you haven't. It's time we were off.'

'Shall you come again? Soon?'

'If I'm permitted.' She leaned down and kissed Mrs Herapath on the cheek, then hurried out to find Sophie.

Sophie wasn't in the studio at the front of the house, but outside on the verandah, watching what was going on in the square.

Madeleine hung back in the studio. She needed to be alone. It had been horrible to hear her mother spoken of with such easy familiarity. It made her feel shaky and exposed.

'Oh, yes,' came Sophie's voice from outside, 'I do so agree.'

Oh, no, thought Madeleine. Just for once, she wished her sister hadn't managed to strike up an acquaintance with whomever she happened to have met in the street.

Softly she moved closer to the door, and saw Sophie leaning against the balustrade, stroking the nose of a large bay gelding.

The owner of the horse was tying the reins to the hitching-post, and Madeleine couldn't see his face, but from his clothes she guessed him to be a planter of the not-so-profitable kind. His top boots hadn't been polished in years and his riding breeches and shooting jacket looked as if he'd slept in them.

In no mood for new acquaintances, she backed into the shadows.

'His name is Pilate,' said the gentleman.

'Pilate?' said Sophie. 'You mean, like Pontius Pilate?'

'I suppose so, yes.'

'But that's not fair. Pontius Pilate was horrible. Your horse doesn't deserve a name like that. He didn't *do* anything.'

'You're right,' said the gentleman. He had an agreeable voice, and Madeleine could tell that he was smiling. 'But he was called that when I bought him, and horses don't care to have their names changed.'

'Like people,' said Sophie.

'Like people,' agreed the gentleman.

Pilate bent his neck and nuzzled Sophie's chest. She squealed with delight, and would have toppled over if the gentleman hadn't put out a sunburnt hand to steady her. As she regained her balance, she glanced indoors and spotted Madeleine.

'Oh, there's my sister! Maddy, come and meet Pilate the horse!'

Madeleine's heart sank. But it was too late to escape now. Assuming a social smile, she moved out into the light.

The gentleman turned to face her, and the sun went in as she recognised the officer in the snow at Strathnaw.

Ten years fell away in a heartbeat. He hadn't changed. Perhaps he was a little more lined than she remembered, and considerably less well groomed. But the vivid grey eyes were the same, and the brief lightening of the sunburnt features that was almost a smile.

Her heart was thudding against her ribs. He doesn't recognise you, she told herself, and it was true. His manner showed nothing more than the courtesy that any gentleman might extend to any well-bred young woman whom he had only just met.

Sophie sucked in her cheeks and announced, 'Maddy, this is Mr *Cameron Lawe*. His estate is called Eden. Isn't that a lovely name? It's only eight miles away from us, up in the hills. I'm to go there for tea and meet Abigail, his dog, and the parrots in his garden . . .'

Madeleine stopped listening. How could she not have seen this coming? How could she have been so stupid?

She realised that the silence was becoming embarrassing, and that he was offering her his hand. When she didn't respond, he withdrew it, and his face became carefully expressionless.

She cleared her throat. 'I'm Madeleine Lawe. That is, I'm Mrs Sinclair Lawe.'

'Yes, I know,' he said bluntly. 'I saw you with my brother.'

'When?'

'A few weeks ago? You were out driving.' He frowned at his hat, and muttered, 'You'd gone past before I had time to call out.'

'Indeed,' she said. 'Sinclair will be sorry to have missed you.' That was such a blatant lie that she felt herself colouring.

He threw her a glance and then looked quickly away, and she wondered with a stab of alarm if something had jogged his memory.

With his hat he gestured towards the studio. 'I wonder, do you know if Mrs Herapath is—'

'Indisposed,' she replied. 'I don't believe she'll see anyone today.'

'I'm sorry to hear that. Well. Perhaps you'd tell her I called?'

'Yes.'

He raised his head and studied her face for a moment. Then he gave her a curt nod, and went down the steps to untie his horse.

'YOU WERE SO RUDE to him,' said Sophie as they were driving home. She sat with her legs propped up on the cushions.

'I was not rude,' said Madeleine, giving the reins a snap.

'You were,' Sophie insisted. 'You didn't smile, you hardly said a thing, and you *refused* to shake hands.'

'I didn't refuse. I forgot.'

'You practically cut him dead. Just because he went to prison.'

'That has nothing to do with it. Do be quiet, and let me drive.'

After an uncomfortable silence lasting nearly twenty minutes, the gatehouses of Fever Hill loomed into sight. As they drove past, Madeleine caught sight of a stone serpent between the leaves of a strangler fig. Another reminder of Strathnaw. As if she needed one.

In retrospect it struck her as extraordinary that in all the years since that encounter in the snow, she had never once asked herself who the officer might have been. It was impossible now to think of him as Sinclair's brother, the infamous Cameron Lawe, the author of that brusque, unfeeling little note in Lettice's prayer book.

That doesn't matter, she told herself firmly. What matters is that he didn't recognise you. And he didn't, did he? She found herself going over everything he had said, every nuance and expression. The more she thought about it, the more she wondered.

Oh God, she thought. Don't let him have recognised me.

CHAPTER FIVE

She didn't tell Sinclair of her encounter with his brother, but by the time she had settled Sophie in the gallery, and taken a bath and dressed for dinner, he already knew. Dinner was eaten in uneasy silence, and when Madeleine asked Sinclair what was wrong, he denied that anything *was* wrong. What could conceivably be wrong?

She gave up, and went to say good night to Sophie. She found her wide-eyed and anxious, convinced it was all her fault. It turned out that Sinclair had questioned her while Madeleine was taking a bath.

That night she slept in the gallery. The wind howled through the house, and behind her in the bedroom she heard Sinclair pacing the boards. Around midnight he came to the door and she felt him watching her. She pretended to be asleep and he returned to bed.

The next morning she waited for the inevitable dressing-down, but it never came. A day passed. And another, and another. The house crackled with tension but nothing was said. When she tried to clear things up, to make Sinclair understand that she'd scarcely spoken two words to Cameron Lawe, he cut her short and walked away.

Two nights later, they made a fifth attempt to conceive a son. It was a disaster.

'I can't! I can't!' gasped Sinclair, collapsing beside her.

They lay side by side, staring into the darkness, while outside the owls hooted and the crickets rang in their night song.

'It's this confounded heat,' he muttered. 'It saps my vitality. Ever since we arrived I have been out of sorts. That filthy Negro charm.'

Madeleine turned to look at him. 'It was only a bird's egg. I'm not sure what it could have—'

'You never try to understand. You only contradict and ridicule.'

He got up and went to the looking glass. His reflection was pale and drawn. 'This is your fault,' he said without turning round. 'I should have known it would turn out like this. You are just like him.'

'Like whom?' But she already knew. These days, his brother was never far from his thoughts.

'You are coarse,' he said. 'You have no life of the spirit.'

She sat up and pushed her hair behind her ears. 'So this is my fault. Because I spoke to your brother. Once. A week ago.'

He raised a hand for silence. 'We will *not* speak of it again.'

The following day, the atmosphere of unspoken censure was even worse than before.

At last the rains came. Every afternoon for four weeks, great silver downpours rattled the slates, pounded the lawns, and made the carriageway run red. In the humid shadows of the great house, Madeleine and Sinclair circled each other with a cold courtesy that set her teeth on edge. Eventually she could stand it no longer. She would have to have it out with him or go insane.

She chose a teatime when Jocelyn was in his library and Sophie was asleep, but Clemency and May would both be present. She needed witnesses.

'I'm not sure what crime I'm supposed to have committed,' she said as she stirred her tea, 'but I think this has gone on for long enough, and that I should be given a chance to lodge a defence.'

Clemency froze with her cup halfway to her lips, while May serenely finished pouring and handed Sinclair his tea.

'You know, I didn't intend to speak to your brother,' Madeleine continued. 'At first I didn't even know who he was. It was a chance encounter. And one which I've no desire to repeat.'

That was a lie. Today was Cameron Lawe's day for visiting the Burying-place, and all morning she had been wondering whether to go and confront him. She knew it would be the height of folly, but she needed to know whether he had finally remembered her.

Sinclair put his cup to his lips, then replaced it in the saucer and set it on the side table. 'My brother,' he said, 'is not a respectable man. *That* is the reason for my objection.'

'I thought he'd served his sentence,' said Madeleine. 'I thought it was our Christian duty to forgive.'

'It might interest you to learn that we *have* forgiven him. That we pray daily for him to mend his ways. Sadly, that has not come to pass. Therein lies my objection to your conduct.'

'I don't understand. You mean he's done something else?'

'Of course, you do not understand.' He turned to Clemency and May. 'My apologies for trespassing on a matter of some indelicacy.'

Clemency looked up in bemusement. May inclined her head.

Sinclair turned back to Madeleine. 'Something happens to the white man when he cohabits with the Negress.'

She was startled. 'What do you mean?'

'The nature of the white man,' he went on, 'becomes coarsened by such an association. Animalised by the imbruted cravings of the creature with whom he has thrown in his lot.'

'Are you asking me to believe that you object to my having talked to your brother because he has a black mistress?' said Madeleine. 'As I understand it from Mrs Herapath, that rules out conversation with three-quarters of the planters on the Northside.'

Sinclair pressed his red lips together. 'The wife of a man of God can never be too vigilant when it comes to her character.'

'A few words on a verandah don't—'

'You were seen with a compromised individual. You injured yourself and you injured me. Moreover, you injured your sister.'

'Sophie? Oh, now really, I can't agree with that!'

'Which matters not at all, since you are not her legal guardian.'

Alarmed, she met his gaze. His blue eyes were glittering. He was enjoying himself.

She glanced down at her hands, tightly clenched in her lap. She saw now that she hadn't *done* anything wrong. This was about control. It was about ramming home the fact that he was the husband, and she the wife. Until he had her public acknowledgment of that, he would not let up.

'Well then,' she said, struggling to keep her voice steady. 'Let's bring this war of attrition to an end, shall we? I apologise. Wholly and without reservation. There. Is that better?'

May folded her ringless fingers in her lap. Clemency laughed her noiseless little laugh and clapped her hands.

Sinclair gave Madeleine a considering look. '*Thank* you,' he said. 'Henceforth we will speak no more of this. I would simply ask that in the future you exercise greater discretion.' He rose to his feet. 'I shall be writing in my study for the rest of the afternoon. It would be a *great* indulgence if I were not disturbed.'

After he had gone, Great-Aunt May turned to Madeleine and remarked, 'Sinclair has the most perfect respect for the proprieties of any being I know. Others would do well to emulate him.'

'What sound advice,' Madeleine said crisply, rising in her turn. 'I shall take a walk about the lawns, the better to reflect upon it.'

THE WIND HAD DROPPED by the time Madeleine made her way out onto the lawns, still buttoning her dust-coat in her haste to get away. She glanced back at the house, and caught a glint of sunlight on the upper gallery. That would be Great-Aunt May, donning her steel-rimmed spectacles. Take a good long look, Madeleine told her silently. This ought to give you something to talk about.

She turned and made her way over the rise to the Burying-place. It was a peaceful, sunny clearing, where a dozen raised barrel tombs dreamed away the decades in the long silver grass.

It was deserted. Cameron Lawe had not yet arrived. She took a deep breath and smelt the sharp green tang of the asparagus ferns among the graves. Around her the grass buzzed with crickets. Above her the poinciana tree was brilliant with vermilion flowers.

Some of her anger and frustration seeped away, leaving in its place a distant sadness. To her right stood the little white marble tomb of Clemency's baby, lovingly adorned with fresh flowers. *Elliot Fraser Monroe, died 1873, aged two days.* Her half-brother.

And before her she could just make out the inscription on her grandmother's tomb: *Here lies Catherine Dorothy Monroe, née McFarlane, 1831–1850, and with her the blasted expectations of an adoring husband. Death, thou hast obtained thy victory.*

She thought about the love that had made Jocelyn stay faithful to a memory for a lifetime, then she thought about her cramped and haunted existence with Sinclair.

You *chose* this life, she told herself. You went into it with your eyes open. Now you must make the best of it.

Yes, but how?

A movement at the edge of her vision made her start. She turned to see Cameron Lawe standing near the trees, watching her.

What was he thinking? Was he remembering that long-ago meeting in the snow? She stared back at him across twenty feet of silver grass and barrel tombs. Her heart was hammering against her ribs.

'I'd quite forgotten,' she lied, 'that it's your day for visiting.'

'That's all right,' he said.

'I expect you'd rather be alone.'

'No, no, I—' He frowned at the flowers in his hand: an artless bunch of large spiky white ginger lilies and heliconia, its great scarlet claws tipped with gold. 'I did rather wonder if you'd be here.'

A cold wave washed over her. 'Why? What do you mean?'

'I suppose—only that I hoped you might be.' He tossed his hat and riding crop in the grass and ran a hand through his hair. 'I'm sorry, that wasn't very proper. But it's the truth.'

She didn't know how to take that. What did he mean? To break the silence she said, 'How did you get here? I didn't see you arrive.'

He gestured towards the old slave hospital. 'The track down there joins the road up to my estate. That's where I left my horse.'

'Ah.' She realised that she was twisting her hands together. She thrust them into the pockets of her dust-coat. She said, 'Sophie tells me that I was rude to you the other day.'

'No, no,' he said unconvincingly.

'She says that I practically cut you dead.'

For a moment some of the tension left his features and he gave her a smile. 'Your sister has strong views.'

'Yes. Yes, she does.'

He hesitated. 'Those crutches of hers. What is it, polio?'

'Tuberculosis of the knee.'

'Ah. And—is she—'

'Getting better. Oh yes.' But she sounded more certain than she felt. Sophie's progress seemed unaccountably to have slowed.

She watched him approach the tomb on the other side of Kitty's, and place the ginger lilies at the head. The inscription read: *Alice Amelie Monroe, née Vavasour, 1821–83*. What, she wondered, had Jocelyn's mother to do with Cameron Lawe?

'She was my great-aunt,' he said as if she'd spoken aloud. 'When I was a boy, she was a widow, living up at Providence. She used to swoop down and snatch us away from our lessons, and take us for long rides in the hills. I adored her.'

'So does that mean—was your mother a Vavasour?'

'Yes. I'm sorry, I thought you knew that.'

'Sinclair never speaks of his parents.'

'Ah.'

Vavasour was a Huguenot name. Like Durrant. It was an unsettling feeling to know that they both came of the same stock.

'In Jamaica,' he explained, 'everyone's related to everyone else. For instance, Jocelyn married a McFarlane, whose grandmother married a Traherne, whose daughter married a Barrett, whose cousin married a Durrant—' He broke off.

There was an awkward silence. A gust of wind stirred the feathery leaves of the poinciana tree.

Cameron Lawe glanced up at the grey sky. 'Rain on the way. I should be going.' He thought for a moment, then held out the heliconias to her. 'I wonder, would you mind? These are for Ainsley.'

The ground tilted in front of her. '*What?*'

He gestured at the blue slate behind her. 'Ainsley Monroe? Jocelyn's son. That's the grave . . . I'm sorry, I thought you knew.'

She pulled in her skirts from the slab on which she'd been sitting moments before. 'B-But—there's no inscription,' she stammered.

'The old man had the stone turned over, so that he wouldn't have to look at the inscription.'

She put her hand on Kitty's tomb to steady herself.

'Are you all right?' he said. 'You've gone quite pale.'

The buzz of the crickets was loud in her ears, the sun fierce on her back. She felt sick. 'His own son. He did that to his own son.'

He moved round to her side, went down on one knee and placed the heliconias on the hot blue slate. 'You'll soon find out,' he said, 'that forgiveness isn't a very marked trait in that family.'

He glanced at the heliconias and smiled. 'Those were his favourites. When I was little he used to call them dragon's claws.'

It had never occurred to her that he had grown up with her father. That he might have cared about him. The thought threw everything into disarray. And as she watched him silently contemplating her father's grave, she felt a lightening inside her, as if something tight had worked itself loose. This man had loved her father, and her father had loved him. In the end that was all that mattered.

She cleared her throat. 'You know,' she said, 'I didn't really come up here by accident.'

He kept his eyes on Ainsley's grave. 'I did wonder about that.'

'Sinclair made a fearful row when he heard that I'd spoken to you at Mrs Herapath's. It's too ridiculous for words. So I thought I'd really give them something to row about.'

He turned his head and looked at her, and his light grey eyes were warm. 'That wasn't a very good idea.'

'No. I don't suppose it was.'

They exchanged tentative smiles.

Above the Cockpits a thick cord of lightning split the sky. A few seconds later there came a terrific crack of thunder.

Cameron Lawe stood up. 'It's strange,' he said, 'but you're not at all what I expected of Sinclair's wife.'

'What did you expect?'

'Oh. Someone little and blonde and pious, I suppose.' He coloured. 'I'm sorry, I didn't mean to imply that you're not pious.'

'That's all right,' she said, biting back a smile. 'I'm afraid I've never cared very much for the Bible.'

He looked at her for a moment. 'That's very direct.'

She made no reply.

Another ripple of thunder. He glanced up at the sky, then back to her. 'You should go in or you'll get wet.'

'I don't care about that.'

'Well, I do.' He stooped to retrieve his hat from the grass.

Suddenly she didn't want him to go. She wanted him to stay and talk to her about Eden. And she found herself wondering what dreadful crime he had committed. She said, 'According to Sinclair, you did something "unspeakable". Can that really be true?'

He turned his hat in his hands. 'Quite true, I'm afraid.'

'What did you do?'

'Surely Sinclair's told you by now?'

'He never talks about you. Nobody does. But—sometimes I get the feeling that you're all they think about.'

He rubbed a hand over his face and blew out a long breath. 'I was in the Sudan,' he said without looking at her. 'Ainsley was my CO.'

'You were in the Sudan? With him? You saw him die?'

'Of course. My God, hasn't Sinclair told you anything?'

'I told you, no. That's why I need you to tell me now.'

He cast around for some means of escape. 'We were on the battle-field,' he said shortly. 'Ainsley had just been killed. I despoiled the body. I rifled through the pockets while he was still warm.' He looked down. 'Conduct unbecoming. Discharge with ignominy. Two years at Her Majesty's pleasure. There. Now you know.'

Ninth of July—written while Maddy is at luncheon
I have had a slight cough for the past three days, and Maddy has imposed strict inactivity. She has been out of sorts since she met Cameron Lawe at the Burying-place—even though by her own admission she got off astonishingly lightly, with no telling off from Sinclair. She says that he doesn't know what to do when one simply defies him, then owns up to it and apologises straight away.

Eleventh of July
Cough persisting. Maddy very worried.

I have been thinking a great deal about why this is happening to me. When I first became ill, Maddy told me about the little bacilli, which she said are the cause of the disease. The question is, WHO SENT THE BACILLI? Maddy says that no one sent them, they simply came, but I think that someone stole my shadow and nailed it to the duppy tree. That's why the bacilli came.

Fourteenth of July
Cough very nearly gone!

Everyone is busy with preparations for the Trahernes' ball on the twentieth. Maddy doesn't care to go, but Sinclair says that they must, for the Trahernes' July Ball is THE event on the Northside.

After lunch I had an argument with Sinclair. I asked him about the paragraph in my gazetteer on the branding of slaves. I said that branding must have hurt a great deal, and is surely <u>proof</u> that slavery was a bad thing. Sinclair said I was misinformed. He fetched a small silver branding iron which he keeps for a paperweight on his desk. He said that if the iron were heated until red-hot, and applied to skin previously anointed with sweet oil, the pain was minimal and fleeting.

I had no answer to that, but I mean to test it for myself.

Fifteenth of July
Sinclair is wrong. Last night I anointed my forearm with coconut oil, and then held a quattie in the flame of my lamp and applied the hot coin to my forearm. It hurt <u>extremely</u>, and I now have a nasty red burn. I can't show it to anyone, because Maddy would be distressed and Sinclair would only say that I didn't do it correctly, or some such thing.

Evie says that black people sometimes give duppy trees presents of rum if they want a favour. She says that if I give her my pocket money she will buy me a bottle of rum at Pinchgut market. That is nice of her.

Seventeenth of July
Evie procured the rum, which I hid under the croton bush by the steps. I intended to give it to the duppy tree and ask it to make me well again, but unfortunately I got caught by Grace.

I waited till extremely late, and went across the lawn on my crutches in the moonlight. The duppy tree was enormous and scary with creepers, and then I saw a shape, and dropped the rum in fright, but it was Grace. Evie had told on me. She is a <u>sneak</u>.

Grace was EXTREMELY angry. She said I had no business messing with powers I didn't understand. She grabbed my arm and I cried out, and that's when she saw the burn. She said what is that? So I told her how Sinclair had said that branding didn't hurt, but that I'd tried it and it jolly well did. After that she fetched an aloe leaf to put it on my burn. It REALLY helped, which is proof that she is a good witch.

But when I asked if she would fetch my shadow back from the duppy tree, she said no—BECAUSE IT ISN'T THERE.

If the duppy tree doesn't have my shadow, then where is it? I have to find it. If I don't get my shadow back, I shall die. Perhaps I shall ask Maddy if she would ask Grace to make me a charm-bag like the one Evie wears round her neck. That might help.

EVENING-TIME, and Grace is taking her ease out on her step, and everything going silk. Hogs and chickens fed, and she's been cooking up fufu for supper, and waiting for the children to come home after their chores. Smoking little pipe, drinking little bush tea, with a drop of that rum in it of Missy Sophie, to warm up the blood.

Yes, Grace, she tells herself, smiling. Everything going silk.

Then the chickens start up a squabble, and she sees a figure coming down the path from the aqueduct. But what is this? Jesum Peace. Is Miss Maddy walking quick, quick, with her skirts trailing out behind her like a fishtail. What in hell she doing down here?

Grace dislikes Miss Maddy. Oh, she speaks nice and sweet, and she seems soft and weakly, like all buckra woman. But she different. She hiding something. Grace can't make out what. And right now she's got some worry-head in her, Grace can see that straight.

'You walking late, Miss Maddy,' says Grace, getting to her feet.

'I don't have much time,' Miss Maddy says. 'I need to get back, to dress for dinner.'

Now why in hell, thinks Grace, Miss Maddy come all this way when she could a sent for Grace up at Master Jocelyn house? Maybe Miss Maddy don't want that husband of hers to know.

'I need you to make one of those little charm-bags,' says Miss Maddy, simple straight. 'Like the ones your children wear?'

Grace give her the blank eye. 'I don't know, ma'am,' she says.

'Yes, you do. It's a little bag with rosemary and spirit weed and Madam Fate. And probably other things besides.'

Now Grace getting on suspicious. How Miss Maddy know a thing like that? 'You fooling me up, Miss Maddy,' she says. 'Black people medicine for buckra lady? Cho!'

'It isn't for me,' says Miss Maddy. 'It's for Missy Sophie.'

Grace spits. 'That child sick bad, ma'am. She flaking away. Needs strong tea, and maybe a bush-bath. Then she pick up again.'

'Perhaps. But right now what she thinks she needs is that charm. Will you make her one?'

Grace considers a while. She thinking, White people always calling black people magic 'witchcraft', and saying it *bad*. Then they want a piece of black people magic for them own self. But that little Missy Sophie, she all right. Grace says, 'I think pon it a while, ma'am.'

'Think on it quickly,' Miss Maddy says sharp.

Grace decides have a little fun. 'You come from foreign, ma'am, but you understand potwah good. I know some buckra ladies, live here roundabout long time, never understand as good as you.'

Miss Maddy colours right up, like she just been found out. She hiding something. Sure as sin.

Grace takes a pull on her pipe. 'You bring trouble to the house, Miss Maddy. You not who you say.'

Miss Maddy tight up her hand, but not turn way her eye. She not to frighten easy, that true to the fact. She says, 'You're impertinent, Grace. You should watch your tongue.'

Grace decides have little more fun. 'You understand potwah,' she says. 'Well, I speak buckra talk, you know.' She straightens up and says in buckra talk, 'That is, when I have a mind to do so.' She cracks a laugh. 'Oh, yes. Master Cameron teach it to I.'

But look me trouble, what all this? Soon as Grace says soldier-man name, Miss Maddy she opens her mouth like she got a sudden thought, and dislikes how it taste. What the hell this all about?

'I'll pay you one shilling,' Miss Maddy says, strict and sharp. 'Bring the charm tomorrow. Bring it to me and no one else. Do it for Missy Sophie.'

'We see about it, ma'am,' says Grace.

She watches Miss Maddy go, and she thinks, Well, all right. I bring the charm tomorrow for the little girl child, so maybe she pick up some. But you, Miss Maddy. You better watch out, now. Gracie McFarlane and Master Cameron they gone their separate ways from long, long time—but Gracie still watches out for him. Don't you go make trouble for him, Miss Maddy. Or I make trouble for you.

MADELEINE CLOSED Mrs Herapath's blue morocco folder and tied it up with the pink satin ribbon. The folder contained newspaper cuttings from the *Pall Mall Gazette* of 22nd March, 1884, reporting the proceedings of the General Court-Martial of Captain Cameron Anthony Lawe of the 25th King's Own Scottish Borderers.

She tried to picture the court-martial in the stuffy little fort at Suakin. She could almost hear Cameron Lawe infuriating the prosecutor with his blunt, unhelpful replies. Wilfully, almost perversely calling down on himself the full wrath of the army. As if he no longer cared what became of him.

She kneaded her temple. What was she doing here, sitting on Mrs Herapath's sofa with this lovingly assembled file of cuttings on her lap? What was she hoping to find? She didn't know. All she knew was that in the weeks since she had seen him at the Burying-place, she had found herself going over and over every word, every expression, every glance that had passed between them.

'Well?' said Mrs Herapath, handing her a cup of tea and dragging her back to the present. 'What do you think?'

Madeleine coloured. She was glad that the older woman couldn't guess her thoughts. 'What do I think?' she said. 'I think—he kept quiet to protect Ainsley. That's it, isn't it? So that the world wouldn't discover that Alasdair Falkirk, the "gallant officer", was in fact Ainsley Monroe, the man who deserted his wife.'

'And didn't it work *splendidly*?' said Mrs Herapath.

'But surely,' said Madeleine, 'people guessed that Alasdair Falkirk was Ainsley Monroe? I mean, Falkirk's a family name.'

'Oh, doubtless a few of them did, but the point is, Cameron made it possible for people to behave as if they *hadn't* guessed.'

All these rules, Madeleine thought. They weren't her rules. She felt like an interloper in an alien tribe.

'What about the piece of paper he took from—the body. What was it? Do you know?'

'Letter from Clemency,' mumbled Mrs Herapath through a mouthful of scone. 'Granting Ainsley absolution. As it were.'

'How do you know all this?' Madeleine asked, stirring her tea.

'Why, Cameron told me, of course. A few months after Hector died.' Mrs Herapath shook her head. 'Desperate time. Desperate. But that darling boy used to come down out of the hills every week, just to see me. We just sat and smoked and talked about Hector. Such a tonic.' A flush rose to her cheeks, and she blinked rapidly. 'You know, I've always believed that he told me his story as a sort of *distraction*. And it worked beautifully. For of course, as soon as he told me the bare bones, I simply had to know everything.'

'But I still don't understand,' said Madeleine. 'Why won't Jocelyn see him? Surely *he* must have guessed why Cameron did it?'

'Oh, undoubtedly.' Mrs Herapath spread her tapered fingers. 'But disgrace is disgrace, my dear. Discharge with ignominy. Scarcely the sort of career that Jocelyn had planned for him.'

'But—Cameron did it to protect him. I can't believe Jocelyn—'

'Believe it, my dear. There's granite in that old man.'

'I suppose,' Maddy said, 'none of this would have happened if Ainsley hadn't married Clemency. But from what she's told me, he wasn't in love with her. Or she with him. So why did they marry?'

Mrs Herapath gave a bark of laughter. 'My dear! What an astonishingly naive question.'

Madeleine flushed.

'I'm rather afraid that poor dear Jocelyn forced Ainsley into it. Of course, he genuinely believed that he was acting for the best.'

'But he detests the Trahernes.'

'Well of course he does. We all do. But they're still vastly preferable to the Durrants.'

'The D— I don't understand.'

'Why, my dear, if it hadn't been for that marriage to Clemency, Ainsley and Rose would have eloped.'

'*Eloped?* But—I thought the affair with Rose began *after* he married Clemency.'

'Good heavens, no! Ainsley and Rose had been in love since they were children. But Jocelyn couldn't let Ainsley marry a *Durrant*. Two hundred years of dissolution and *crimes passionnels* and goodness knows what else? Oh, no, that would never have done.'

'Did you correspond with Rose? After she went to England?'

Mrs Herapath looked outraged. 'Good heavens, no!'

'But I thought she was your friend.'

'She *was*. But she forfeited that when she ran off with Ainsley.' She sighed. 'It would have been perfectly possible for her to have carried on seeing him after he married Clemency, if they'd been *discreet*. Happens all the time. But Rose couldn't do that. She had to run off with him, and make it impossible for us all to ignore.'

So that was her crime, thought Madeleine. It wasn't that she broke the rules, but that she broke them in such a way that it was impossible to ignore. It seemed such a terrible punishment, to be cut off for ever from everyone she had known, and exiled from this lush, ruined, bewitchingly beautiful island.

There was an uncomfortable silence.

'It's just such a *shame*,' Mrs Herapath burst out, 'that the whole wretched muddle had to whiplash onto Cameron. Attractive boy like that.' She plucked a crumb from her lap and frowned at it. 'You want to be careful, my dear. This sudden interest in courts-martial and whatnot. I'm not at all sure that it will do.'

Madeleine felt herself colouring. 'You were the one who suggested I should learn more about the family.'

'This isn't what I meant.'

'Yes, it is. He's family, isn't he? I don't see the harm.'

'That,' said Mrs Herapath, 'is rather my point.'

NINETEENTH OF JULY

Evie has found out where my shadow is. She went and asked a great many black people (not Grace, of course), and finally learned that my shadow is in the hothouse—where I can't go. I had suspected it was there, for the hothouse is full of duppies, as it was once the slave hospital.

Victory has offered to go and fetch it for me, which is SO brave, but of course I said no. Victory is only six; it wouldn't be fair. Besides, he wouldn't know which shadow is mine.

Despite what Evie says, I bet I CAN get to the hothouse on my crutches. And for protection, I have the charm that Grace made for me.

The best time to go will be extremely early in the morning, when the duppies are still asleep. The morning after the Trahernes' ball will be the best, for then everyone will stay in bed until very late.

CHAPTER SIX

Madeleine hadn't expected Cameron Lawe to be at the Trahernes' ball. She had been with Mrs Herapath, crossing the marble entrance hall towards the ballroom, when she had seen him, standing silently amid a throng of gentlemen.

As if suddenly conscious that he was being watched, he had turned his head, and their eyes had locked. She had known by his stillness, that he was as sharply, intensely aware of her as she was of him.

Then one of the gentlemen clapped him on the shoulder, and for a second he was distracted. Madeleine seized her chance and swept on towards the Trahernes' enormous shimmering ballroom.

And that is where she now stood, as she had stood all evening, longing to be safely back home with Sophie. It was one o'clock in the morning, and Sinclair had declared it their duty to stay until three. So far she had danced with him once, and once with Cornelius Traherne, and once with Jocelyn. She had smiled until her cheeks were stiff, and listened to a river of Mrs Herapath's imperious gossip. All the while she had kept a silent watch for Cameron Lawe, and been both relieved and disappointed when he did not appear.

According to Mrs Herapath, Cornelius Traherne had crowned himself emperor of Northside society by betrothing his elder daughter to an Irving of Ironshore and he had spared no expense to celebrate his triumph. Parnassus, the first great house in Trelawny to be wired for electricity, was a blaze of light. The grounds had been newly landscaped by English gardeners, the state rooms repanelled in satinwood, and a thirty-piece orchestra shipped out from Vienna.

The waltz ended, and Madeleine watched the Irving boy leading his fiancée to a little gilt sofa, and bringing her a rosewater ice and gazing into her eyes before a score of watchful relations.

She turned to find Sinclair watching her from across the room, his gaze unsmiling. In his dress coat he looked severely beautiful, but there were shadows beneath his eyes. Despite the chloral he had not been sleeping well, and there were nights when he awoke ten times, and knelt on the floor to check beneath the bed for charms. And in some way that she didn't understand, he blamed her for his malaise. What was it about her that horrified him? Why had he married her?

Suddenly the music was loud in her ears; the ballroom hot and airless. She had to get out. She muttered an excuse to Mrs Herapath and went through into the crowded gallery.

She descended the steps to the lower terraces and finally reached a pergola that opened onto the lawns and was mercifully empty. She took a deep breath. The air was warm and still and heavy with the scent of cinnamon and stephanotis, and the bitter haze from the Spanish braziers that kept the mosquitoes at bay.

Above her head, through gaps in the pergola, she glimpsed the people on the upper terraces. They seemed a world apart.

Suddenly an image came to her of Ben Kelly kissing the little skivvy in the Portland Road. Then another image took over. Grace McFarlane. *I speak buckra talk*, she had said, looking Madeleine up and down. *Oh yes. Master Cameron teach it to I*. Beautiful, independent, knowing Grace, with her frank, uninhibited ways.

Madeleine snapped off a stephanotis flower and, as she crushed its waxy white petals in her palm, she wondered what it would be like to be kissed by a man. The flower stained her white kid evening glove and released a heavy, funereal perfume. I wish I was old, she thought savagely, with everything behind me. I wish I was old and terrifying, like Great-Aunt May.

Like a sorceress summoned by an incantation, Great-Aunt May appeared on the upper terrace. She looked magnificent, in a forbiddingly tight gown of pewter *peau de soie*.

'Brought up to snare a duke,' Mrs Herapath had told Madeleine at supper. 'Punishing childhood. Backboards. Tight-lacing. Governess used to make her practise walking across a ballroom for hours. Sandbag on the head. It was all part of the plan. Her destiny. To be presented at Court and become a Beauty, and snare a duke. Turned out that dukes were in short supply.'

Looking up at her now, Madeleine caught a glimpse of what had shaped the old despot. When the predestined match failed to appear, she had resolved to have no one. She had decided to despise the world, and everything she did expressed her disdain. The savage tight-lacing. Collars boned to the jaw. The rigid adherence to form.

I wonder if I'll end up like that, thought Madeleine. A fearsome old witch who hasn't touched another human being in years. Her throat tightened. Her eyes grew hot. She left the pergola and went out onto the lawn.

About thirty feet ahead of her, a man was walking up and down in the moonlight, smoking a cigar. She knew him instantly by his height and his fair hair and the set of his shoulders. He turned his head and saw her, and for a moment they faced one another in silence.

She had wanted to see him again, but not like this. Not when she was in this strange angry mood, on the brink of tears. She turned and walked back through the pergola, across the lower terrace, round the west wing, and into the gardens at the front of the house.

A flight of shallow steps led down into a sunken parterre. She found a bench near the steps, and sat down. There were no illuminations. There didn't need to be. Moonlight flooded the parterre with silver-blue radiance. She was not invisible.

She turned and watched him appear at the corner of the house, as she had known he would. He made no pretence of finding her by chance. He walked swiftly through the garden and down into the parterre, halting at the foot of the steps.

'Please go,' she said. 'I don't wish to talk to you.'

'Then why did you come out here?' he said in a low voice. 'You could have gone back into the house. But you didn't. You knew I'd follow you.'

For a moment they regarded each other in silence. He was better groomed than before, but not by much. His dress coat looked as if it had spent several years inside a chest, his waistcoat seemed to date from the previous decade, and he had mislaid his gloves.

'You ought to be careful, you know,' he said, then frowned. 'I mean, there aren't any braziers out here. If you were bitten, you might catch a fever.'

'I'm fine,' she said.

'No. I don't think you are.'

She was horrified to feel her eyes growing hot again. She glanced down at her fists clenched in her lap.

'Madeleine—'

'I'm *fine*,' she said again. And nearly broke down.

'PLEASE *DON'T* FEEL sorry for me,' she said, when she had brought herself under control.

She was asking the impossible. Watching her fighting back the tears had been horrible. He had never felt so powerless. She wore a gown of amber silk with a low, square neck, and when she turned away he saw the little smooth bumps at the top of her spine. It was a physical effort to keep from reaching out and touching her.

'I can't help it,' he replied. 'I should feel sorry for any woman married to my brother.'

There was a moment of appalled silence.

He shut his eyes. What had possessed him to say that? It might be the truth, but it sounded facetious and cruel.

'I suppose,' she said, 'you think you can get away with remarks like that because of your past.'

'You're right. I apologise. I left my manners in prison.'

'How convenient. But I didn't think ex-convicts attended balls.'

'Only this one,' he said. 'Cornelius likes to hedge his bets.'

'I don't understand.' Now that they had shifted to neutral ground, she seemed calmer, and more inclined to talk.

'I once obliged his father,' he told her, 'by taking Eden off his hands. As there's still a chance that I might make a go of it, I always receive an invitation.' And I always send my regrets, he thought, and stay away. Until tonight.

She remarked that she hadn't appreciated that the Trahernes had once owned Eden. 'I thought it was the Durrants',' she said.

It seemed an odd topic to pick. Why should she want to know about that? Or was she making small talk to regain her composure?

'It was indeed the Durrants',' he told her. 'But they weren't too good at being planters, so they mortgaged the place to the hilt, and it ended up with old Addison Traherne, who let it fall into ruin. A couple of decades later I bought it.'

'Why?'

He hesitated. He didn't want to mention Ainsley. 'It was cheap.'

She gave a slow nod. 'And you live there on your own?'

'Yes. Well. I have a cook, and a stableboy.' By now he was convinced that this wasn't small talk. Beneath the generalities she had more personal concerns.

Another nod. 'And you love it there.'

'Yes.' He frowned. 'Ask me what you really want to ask.'

She flicked him a glance, then turned and laid her black silk fan in her lap. 'Very well,' she said. 'Is Grace McFarlane your mistress?'

There was a taut silence. A gust of wind rustled the lime trees.

He cleared his throat. 'No,' he said. 'She isn't.'

She opened and shut the fan, and smoothed its black silk tassel over her knee. 'Was she your mistress in the past?'

He swallowed. 'Yes.'

Her profile remained impassive. Was she shocked? Presumably she would be. He wished she would turn and look at him.

'When?' she said, still looking down at her lap.

'About five years ago.'

'Is Evie your daughter?'

Colour rose to his cheeks. 'Of course not. She's twelve years old.'

'Is Victory your son?'

'No. He's six.' He was beginning to feel giddy. It was bizarre of her to question him like this. He didn't want it to end.

'She's beautiful, isn't she?' she said. 'Grace, I mean.'

So are you, he told her silently.

'Isn't she?' she repeated, frowning slightly.

'I—suppose so. Yes.'

Still she wouldn't turn and look at him.

'Why are you always so honest with me?' she said at last. She sounded almost accusatory.

He ran his hand over the balustrade. 'I think,' he said, 'that's one question too many.'

For the first time she turned and smiled at him. Not her meaningless social smile, but a proper one that made him catch his breath. He told himself that he ought to leave right now, this very minute. Instead he went and spoilt it all.

'I think,' he said, 'that it's my turn to ask a question.'

She inclined her head in silent assent.

'However did you come to marry my brother?'

Her smile faded. She looked wary. 'He lived in the parish next to ours,' she said. 'I went and asked him for money.'

God, she was blunt.

'Our guardian had died,' she went on. 'We had nothing. I didn't know what else to do.'

'So you applied to the Church. And the Church asked you to marry him.'

'Yes.' She frowned. 'I still don't know why.'

Cameron stole a glance at her face and thought, Well, I could hazard a guess.

She raised her chin and met his eyes. 'I married Sinclair for his money,' she said. 'That's what you wanted to know, isn't it? Well, that's the reason. That's the truth.'

Not the whole truth, he thought. She hadn't mentioned her sister. He said, 'Why do you make yourself out to be worse than you are?'

She rose to her feet. 'You don't know enough about me to form that opinion. No one does.'

'What does that mean?'

She pressed her lips together. 'Please, I think you should go now.'

Standing, she came no higher than his chin. He had an urge to lift her onto the step so that he could kiss her. He could sense that she wanted him to—although if he tried, she would push him away.

'Cameron,' she said. It was the first time she had spoken his name. 'This isn't helping.'

'I know,' he said. 'I do know.' The urge to touch her was almost overwhelming.

She said, 'You'd better go in first. I'll follow in a little while.'

He nodded, but didn't move. There was one last question he had to ask her. 'About Grace,' he said. 'Are you—shocked?'

She glanced down, turning the black silk fan in her fingers. 'I don't know,' she said at last. 'I suppose I must be.'

It wasn't the answer he wanted.

He turned on his heel and left her in the parterre, with the wind from the sea stirring her amber skirts about her.

He went back through the garden almost at a run, fought his way through the throng on the terraces and took a hasty leave of the Trahernes. Then he went out to the stables and called for his carriage.

As he waited, he saw his brother making purposefully towards him. Sinclair was pale, and there were red patches on his chin as if he'd been rubbing it.

God damn it to *hell*, thought Cameron.

'OFF SO SOON?' said Sinclair.

'It's two o'clock,' snapped his brother. 'I've got to be up at five.'

Yes, of course you must, thought Sinclair. For you are the man of action, aren't you? The soldier, the planter, the lover of Negro whores. The defiler of other men's wives.

He smiled. 'How commendably hard you work. I have no doubt that you shall reap your reward.'

His brother snorted.

In his mind Sinclair saw again what he'd just witnessed in the parterre. His wife and his brother alone together.

He felt better than he had done in weeks. Clearer in his mind and more certain of his purpose—for at last he understood what had been going wrong. He understood why he had been unable to possess his wife. It was because she was unfaithful. Therefore, God would not allow him to possess her. *It was God's way of keeping him pure.*

A stableboy ran up with the pony-trap, and his brother went round to the other side. He gave the horse an absent caress. The gesture seemed to sum up everything Sinclair loathed about his brother. The physicality. The lack of reflection. The ease.

He forced himself to appear calm. 'It is a great pity,' he said, 'that you have not had the chance to become acquainted with my wife.'

His brother did not reply.

'I had particularly hoped,' Sinclair went on, 'to introduce you.'

His brother adjusted the harness. 'We've already met.'

Yes, indeed, thought Sinclair. And what legions of untruths are concealed behind that simple statement. 'Because you see,' he said as if his brother hadn't spoken, 'my wife requires—protection.'

'From whom?'

'Why, from herself.'

His brother straightened up and looked at him across the horse's back. 'What do you mean?'

Sinclair hesitated. 'There are aspects about her character,' he said, 'and background, which are—little short of indelicate.'

His brother opened his mouth to protest, and Sinclair raised his hand. 'No, no, do not ask me to elaborate. It is too painful.'

His brother threw the reins on the seat and came round to his side. He was a good head taller, and Sinclair was forced to take a step back. 'All right, Sinclair,' he said, 'let's stop circling, shall we? You saw us together. I know a jealous husband when I see one.'

'*Jealous?*' Sinclair could hardly breathe. 'You could scarcely be more wrong! No, brother, I came out here to warn you.'

'About what.'

'About my wife. She is not—not as innocent as she seems.'

His brother's eyes became glassy. 'You mustn't speak of her like that.'

'And you,' said Sinclair, 'must not speak of her at all.'

For a moment they faced one another in silence. Then his brother dropped his gaze. 'You're right,' he said shortly. 'But it was my fault I met her tonight, not hers. I sought her out. She didn't want to talk to me. It won't—it won't happen again.' He jumped up into the trap and snapped the reins on the horse's rump. The trap moved off.

Sinclair raged inwardly at his brother's departing back. *It won't happen again*, you say. Ah, my brother, in that you are more correct than you can imagine. I shall see that it never happens again.

IT WAS FOUR in the morning by the time the carriage swept through the gates of Fever Hill.

'At least that's over for another year,' said Jocelyn.

Madeleine, sitting opposite, thought how old he looked tonight.

Beside him, Great-Aunt May turned her head to survey the darkened cane-pieces. 'I could not but remark,' she said, 'that Cameron was among the guests.'

At her side, Madeleine felt Sinclair tense.

'Did you speak to him?' May asked Jocelyn.

'Of course not,' he replied.

'I cannot imagine,' she said, 'why Cornelius invited him.'

Madeleine said, 'Someone told me it's because Cameron is doing rather well with his estate, and Cornelius likes to hedge his bets.'

'Doing rather well, is he?' said Jocelyn, his face studiedly blank.

'That's what I heard.'

Sinclair's gloved hands tightened on his cane. 'You should not believe everything you hear.'

She made no reply. It gave her a quiet satisfaction to repeat what Cameron had said, and to add a positive twist of her own. But a moment later her spirits plunged. What was the point? A petty rebellion that could never come to anything. What on earth was the point?

When they had reached the house and said their good nights, and attained the relative privacy of their room, Sinclair sent Jessie and his man away. He folded his arms and paced up and down.

'Your colour is rather high,' he said. 'Parnassus has always been prone to putrid airs. I trust that you have not taken a fever.'

'I'm just tired,' she said, unbuttoning her gloves. 'I don't feel unwell.'

Another lie. Her face felt stiff, her eyes hot and scratchy. She wanted to go to sleep and never wake up.

'You have overtaxed yourself,' he asserted. 'You need rest, or you will bring on a brain fever.'

She met his gaze, and wondered where this was leading.

'It would be best,' he said, 'if you were to stay on the property for the next few months. Very quietly. To regain your strength.'

She moved past him into the dressing room, sat down at her dressing table and began letting down her hair. 'As you wish,' she said.

In the looking glass she saw him blink. Perhaps she had surprised him. 'No more visits to town,' he said.

'Very well.'

No doubt he was longing for her to protest, but for once their wishes were the same. She would miss her outings to Falmouth, but it was time to make a clean break. No more driving about the countryside pretending she was free. No more talks in the moonlight. She was not free. Trying to pretend otherwise only hurt.

She took off her dancing slippers and began to unfasten her bodice, and asked Sinclair if he was coming to bed.

In the looking glass she saw him take a deep breath. 'Later,' he said. 'I need to take a turn about the lawns.'

What I need, thought Madeleine, is chloral.

No thinking. No dreaming. Just sleep.

ON THE RIVER BANK something rustled in the ginger lilies and Abigail barked. 'All right, girl,' Cameron told her. 'Settle down.'

They were sitting on the steps that led down into the garden. Cameron was still in his evening coat, with a bottle of Scotch at his elbow. It would be dawn soon, and he would regret the Scotch, but he didn't care. He didn't care about much any more.

No. That wasn't true. He *wanted* not to care. He wanted it to be croptime again, so that he could work round the clock and think about nothing except rum yields and striking points. He took another pull at the bottle, and felt the whisky's clean, cauterising burn.

He wished he could wash away the last twelve hours from his mind. Everything. The way she had smiled at him. Her face as she'd admitted that she was shocked. His brother's pale, feverish features as he'd slandered her. *She is not as innocent as she seems.*

In the instant after he'd said it, Cameron had wanted to grab him by the hair and beat out his brains on the carriage wheel.

He set down the bottle and studied his palms. How could you think it, even for a moment? Your own brother.

He got to his feet, and the bottle overturned. Whisky leaked out onto the steps. Abigail put down her head and sniffed.

Cameron pushed her away. 'Not for you, Abby. And not for me either.' He stooped for the bottle and lobbed it into the bushes.

To the devil with everything, he thought.

SINCLAIR KNELT in the darkness of the hothouse, gasping and shuddering with relief. In the distance a mule brayed. He leaned back against the mossy wall and shut his eyes. He felt light and clean and calm again. Powerful. At last he understood. What he had just done was not self-pollution. It was self-*purification*. God had seen this and permitted it, *for God approved. It was keeping him pure.*

And to think that there had been a time when he had wanted her. Thank God that was all in the past. He had been shown the way.

He flexed his shoulders, drew a deep, calm breath and opened his eyes. And met the gleam of another's in the gloom.

A child was crouching in the furthest corner of the cell. It was a pickney: a small boy pickney, very dark, and huddled into a ball. The whites of its eyes glistened with fright.

For a long, appalled moment they stared at one another.

It was in here all the time, thought Sinclair, his heart hammering in his chest. It had crouched in that corner and seen everything—*everything*. Dear God, what do I do now?

Keeping his eyes on the pickney, Sinclair got slowly to his feet. He brushed the dirt off his knees and straightened his linen. Then he backed out of the cell. The pickney watched, but didn't move.

Sinclair stepped back through the doorway, and paused. The pickney still watched with huge, unblinking eyes.

Sinclair grasped the heavy bulletwood door. Swung it shut. After a moment he put his ear to the door and listened. No sound from within. He pictured the pickney crouching in the darkness. Silent. Obedient to its fate.

The sun was nearly up and the air tasted clean and pure. A new dawn. He found a lump of cut-stone, and wedged it under the door.

AS SHE WATCHED Sinclair wading away through the long grass, Sophie swayed on her crutches and nearly fell. Her heart was still thudding from the fright of seeing him emerge from the hothouse. What had he been doing inside?

She had been so sure that everyone was asleep before she'd ventured out. She had lain awake and listened to them returning from the ball. The snort of the horses, the rattle of harness. And she could have sworn that they were all in bed and fast asleep by the time she had let herself out of the gallery and hobbled down the steps and across the lawns.

The hothouse was a well of darkness when she reached it, and she hung back beneath an ironwood tree, one hand gripping Grace's charm about her neck. That was when she'd seen the duppy emerge from the doorway. *A duppy*. Leaving its lair to come and get her.

Then the duppy had turned, and resolved into Sinclair. The relief was like a wave of warm water washing over her.

But something was wrong with him. His face was pale and glistening, his eyes vacant. What had he seen in there?

There could be only one answer. He had seen a duppy. Or a whole nest of duppies. That was why he'd looked so terrified as he'd closed the door and wedged it shut.

And now she was all alone with a nest of duppies not ten feet away. There was nothing for it but to hobble all the way back to the house as quickly as she could, and hope that Sinclair had shut the door securely enough to stop the duppies getting out.

As she started off, she blinked back tears. Once again she had tried to recover her shadow, and once again she had failed. Perhaps after all it was time to ask Victory for help.

Tuesday, 23rd July

Victory has run away, and has been gone for three days. At first Grace was vexed, but on the second day she asked Uncle Jocelyn to send a field-gang to search Clairmont Hill and Pinchgut. They even dragged the pond below the Old Works. But they didn't find anything.

There is a horrid feeling in the house, and the night before last Clemency heard her baby crying in Hell, but much louder than before. Clemency said it is a bad sign, but Maddy was vexed, and told her to keep her fancies to herself, did she want Grace to hear?

I think that when Sinclair was at the hothouse he failed to lock up the duppies securely enough, and they escaped. Maybe they chased Victory away. Maybe they got him.

But Victory can run extremely fast, so I am hopeful that he got away and is hiding somewhere, afraid to come out.

THE NEWS CAME to Fever Hill in the middle of the night. The garden boy had found Victory's body in the hothouse.

Maddy dressed immediately and set off for the old slave village. On the steps, Sinclair tried to stop her.

'This is preposterous,' he said. 'These people do not feel as we do. You should leave that woman to her own kind.'

'Her own kind,' said Madeleine, picking up the basket that the cook had prepared, 'are too frightened to go near her. And it'll be tomorrow before any of her relations arrive.'

Sinclair compressed his lips, but made no further objection.

Madeleine followed the aqueduct to the old slave village. It was a cool night and damp air wafted off the stagnant water. She shivered. My God, she thought, what if it had been Sophie?

Jocelyn had told her that, from the condition of the body, the boy must have died some time that morning. 'It was probably thirst that killed him,' he had said, shaking his head.

'I told you I heard crying,' Clemency had said to Madeleine in her matter-of-fact way when she'd heard the news. Then she'd taken Sophie into her bed and reached for a jar of ginger bonbons.

I told you I heard crying.

As on her previous visit, it was a shock to come upon Grace's orderly yard amid the tangled wilderness. A glow of lamplight came from the open doorway of Grace's cottage.

As Madeleine climbed the steps, the sweet, alien smell of death hit her like a wall. She fought the urge to retch.

The room looked as if a storm had blown through it. The floor was littered with shattered earthenware, shredded lizard skins, bright, mangled feathers and the tiny crushed skulls of birds. Grace must have destroyed her entire stock in trade.

The black woman crouched beside a low wooden bedstead on which lay her son. His skin was a bluish-grey, his belly marbled green and purple as if the blood vessels had risen to the surface.

'Is who dat?' said Grace without turning round.

Madeleine set down the basket inside the door. 'It's Miss Maddy,' she said. 'I've brought you some things for the laying-out.'

Grace turned and looked at her. Her eyes were swollen and her blink was slow, as if exhausted by grief and rage.

'Why you come to I house, ma'am? Why you bring dese tings?'

'The helpers are too scared.'

Grace spat on the floor. 'Of what to frighten? Of duppy chile?'

'Of you, I think.'

That seemed to put a little spirit into her. 'They *should* to frighten. Who done dis, die soon. I self gwine see to dat.'

Madeleine was not surprised that Grace had assumed that her son's death had been no accident. The garden boy had said that the hothouse door had been blocked from the outside.

But surely it must have been an accident. No one would do such a thing to a child. Somehow a stone must have rolled in front of the door. But it was no use telling his mother that. She wanted blood.

Grace gazed at her with swollen, exhausted eyes. 'Why you not frighten too, ma'am?'

'I've seen death before.'

For a moment the black woman held her gaze. Then she turned back to the body on the bed. The dismissal was clear.

As she went down the steps, Madeleine heard hoofbeats. She looked up to see Cameron reining in his mount at the entrance to Grace's yard. He saw her and took off his hat.

'Doshey told me what happened,' he said as he tethered his horse to the fence. 'But I don't understand. He said the boy was shut in.'

'Yes. Some kind of accident. A stone rolled in front of the door. Clemency heard him crying, but I didn't believe her. I told her to be quiet, in case Grace heard and became upset.'

He put out his hand to touch her, then withdrew it.

For the first time in her adult life, she wanted to be close to a man. She wanted to put her arms round his waist and lean against him and bury her face in his chest. Grace is allowed to do that, she thought. A flash of pure jealousy went through her.

My God, you are despicable, she told herself. You'd begrudge that poor woman her only comfort, because you want him.

'Madeleine,' he said.

She looked up at him.

'You look cold. You'd better go back up to the house.'

TWO DAYS AFTER THE PICKNEY was found in the hothouse, Jocelyn drove Sophie to Falmouth. They made good speed from Fever Hill and were soon within sight of the sea. She sat very straight beside him in the trap, with her splinted leg sticking out in front and one thin hand clutching the guardrail. The other hand held a book on her lap, while tucked beneath her arm was the ever-present toy donkey.

Over the past few weeks her face had regained the invalid sallowness that Jocelyn had hoped was gone for good. But as he flicked the reins on the horse's rump, he decided that his idea of cutting through to the coast road had been really rather inspired. The sea air had brought a little colour back into her cheeks.

Above them, a flock of emerald parakeets exploded from the trees and flew away, furiously beating their stubby little wings. Sophie's jaw dropped. 'Those were real parrots,' she said.

He felt irrationally proud, as if he had conjured up the parakeets especially for her.

Madeleine would be pleased. She had approached him after breakfast as he was preparing for the magistrates' meeting, and asked if, as a special favour, he would take the child with him into town. 'I can't go myself,' she had said, and explained Sinclair's wish that she should remain on the property.

Jocelyn had been surprised. Madeleine was not the woman to be cowed by a weaselly little fellow like Sinclair. But perhaps she had lost confidence after this dreadful business of the pickney. In that she was not alone. The whole estate still lay under a pall.

'I'm worried about Sophie,' she had said. 'She won't talk about it, but I know it's all she thinks of. She needs a distraction.'

Jocelyn had already noticed the unaccustomed silence in the house. He had never known a child who loved talking as much as Sophie. Her voice had become one of the background noises of the house, like the crickets and the crows. And when it had fallen silent, Jocelyn had been surprised and a little dismayed.

'She'll be no trouble,' Madeleine had said. 'You can leave her with Mrs Herapath, or if she isn't at home, just put her on the bench outside the courthouse. There's always plenty to see on market day.'

And since it was Madeleine who asked, of course Jocelyn had given in. 'I should be delighted,' he had said. And Madeleine had given him a wry smile, for she knew he was lying.

He threw Sophie a worried glance now, and wondered what she was thinking. There had been times during the drive when she had looked as if she were puzzling something out: something far too big for her to manage. And then, out of the blue, she had asked him a question which, for whatever reason, clearly mattered enormously:

'Will the policemen come about Victory?' she had asked, and Jocelyn had said no, for it had been an accident, and since he himself was a magistrate he could sort things out on his own.

He wondered whether his answer had laid to rest whatever child-ish anxieties were plaguing her. And for the tenth time he wished that he didn't have to go to Kingston the following day. Of all the times to be needed at the Assembly. This dreadful affair of the pickney, and now this child beside him, clearly in need of help.

She was gazing solemnly ahead of her, thinking heaven knew what disquieting thoughts. In desperation he asked the title of the book on her lap.

'*The Gods of Ancient Greece,*' she said. She explained that she had borrowed it from Mrs Herapath.

Now he really did feel bad. Thousands of volumes at Fever Hill, and she was compelled to borrow one from Olivia Herapath. It wouldn't do. How could he in all conscience persist in keeping the library out of bounds?

At last they reached the market square, but as soon as Jocelyn saw it his heart sank. Usually he enjoyed market day, but this morning all he could see were the pickneys: dodging the traffic, hitching rides, pestering their mothers. He saw Sophie gazing at them, and silently cursed.

'Uncle Jocelyn?' she said in a small voice.

'Yes?'

'How will they stop Victory becoming a duppy?'

Good Lord. What could he say to that? Dismiss it all as balderdash? The trouble was, he knew that it wasn't. Or rather, that if enough people believe in a thing, it acquires a reality of its own.

'They can't,' he said. 'The trick is to stop the duppy walking. Stop him, er, bothering people. D'you see?'

'How do they do that?'

He blew out a long breath. 'Well. They put slices of lime on the, er, eyes. Rub the body with lime juice and nutmeg. Sew up the pockets.' He glanced at her, hoping he'd said enough. But she was waiting for him to go on.

He cleared his throat. 'Then, nine days after the, er, passing, they hold something called a nine-night. That's like a wake, when they do all sorts of things to send the duppy to sleep. Sing songs. Tell stories. Have a decent supper. Can be rather jolly, I believe.'

But Sophie was not to be deflected by jollity. 'Does it work *every* time? Does the duppy always go to sleep?'

He paused. The answer was no, or why would there be duppy stories? But he was dashed if he was going to tell her that. 'It does when Grace McFarlane has anything to do with it,' he said. 'Very powerful woman, Grace. Extraordinarily good at nine-nights. Never been known to fail.'

To his relief some of the tension left the small face.

They pulled up outside Olivia's studio. More pickneys. More gleaming ivory smiles and plump, shiny black limbs.

That poor little boy, he thought. What a ghastly, lonely death. He glanced over at the solemn little girl beside him.

God help me, he thought, what if it had been her?

CHAPTER SEVEN

There's something about markets that gives Ben Kelly the hump. Maybe it's all them darkies laughing and chattering and calling each other 'sistah' and 'breddah' and 'muddah', like they're one big sodding family.

Today he's feeling hot and dizzy on account of being off his feed, and his chest is all tight after that dream. Last night he was kipping out on this beach past Salt Wash when he had that dream again.

Him and Robbie are having larks on the beach. The sea's like blue glass in the sun, and the sand's so bright you can't hardly look. And him and Robbie are all clean, not a louse between them, and they're running along chucking sea-grapes at each other. Do they laugh!

When Ben wakes up he's making these little jerky moans like he wants to cry. He *hates* that. When Robbie got killed he never cried once, not once. And he's not going to start now.

He's coming into Falmouth. Not many whites about, but Ben don't mind, 'cos he knows he blends in all right. He's got his dungarees and his calico shirt and his tatty straw hat, and them rope-soled shoes that round here they call bulldogs. So to the darkies he's just another walkfoot buckra what can't afford a jack-mule. He learned some of the darkie talk from this cook on the boat coming out, and that helps with the blending in.

He's in Duke Street now, and as he goes past the church he spits it a good one, 'cos churches mean preachers, and preachers mean the parson what killed Robbie.

When he thinks of the parson he gets this cold feeling in his belly, like he's swallowed a stone. He's only seen him once since he got here, just a flash as the carriage rattled past, but it was enough. Parson sitting inside so upright and proper in his chimney-pot hat and his little red screwed-up mouth. Soft as shit and twice as nasty.

Ben goes hot and cold just thinking about him. And about that gun, too. He's left it tucked up safe in that tree out on the Eden road—but even now, when he's miles away, he can feel it watching him. It's like it owns him or something. And he's only had it a week.

He was padding the hoof a few miles to the south when he come upon this village, and seen this pony-trap stopped under a tree. Nobody about; must be a doctor on his rounds or something. And he wanders closer, and there's this little handgun poking out from under a cushion, just asking to be clicked. So over he goes, and stuffs it down his front in a brace of shakes, and cuts the lucky out of there. Then he finds out the bloody gun's got no *bullets*. That doctor must of kept it just for show. Bloody marvellous! So now it's off to the market for Ben Kelly, and maybe this time he can click a *loaded* gun—or at least a few sodding bullets.

When he reaches the square, the market crashes over him like a wave. Spicy dust smells and horse sweat; pickled mangoes and salt-fish fritters. And all them people yelling and joking and haggling.

He's decided he don't much like these Jamaican darkies. Back in Shelton Street he never paid darkies no mind. They had a bad time of it in London, and all. But out here they're so happy and polite. What they got to be so happy about? Sodding darkies with their big happy sodding families.

But deep down, he knows it's not the darkies he hates. It's him. Ben Kelly. 'Cos here he is, walking along in the sunshine, all warm and clean—and Robbie's dead.

And for the first time he thinks about what it'll be like to kill the parson. And every time a pony trap goes by, his chest gets all tight in case it's Sophie or Madeleine. Course it never is, and he's well narked at hisself, 'cos he don't want to see them again, not ever. She went and married the parson, didn't she? She's the enemy now.

But he can't help wondering what'll happen to them when he kills the parson. What if the parson's family chucks her out, and she's poor, and Sophie gets worse and dies, and it's all on account of him?

Everything's so mixed up. He can't get it straight in his head.

And so far, no bullets at this sodding market. Just chickens hanging by their feet, and darkie girls with trays of hog plum jelly on their heads, and darkie men with baskets of swamp oysters and parrotfish.

He's pushing his way through the commotion when somebody calls his name. *His* name, 'Ben, Ben!', right out loud above the din.

Something in his chest shifts painfully.

He looks up and there she is on the verandah of the courthouse, not ten yards away. Long yellow hair pulled back in a black velvet ribbon. Frilly white pinafore over a tartan frock. A couple of crutches, and that clumpy iron thing still on her leg. And she's waving her big straw hat and yelling, *'Ben! Ben! Over here!'*

He shoves his hands in his pockets and hunches up his shoulders. No harm in saying hello, is there? And it'll stop her yelling.

He pushes his way through the crowd and jumps up onto the verandah. Sits down on the bench. 'What's up, Sophie?' he goes.

She sits down too—more like falls down, on account of her splint and the crutches and all—and she's laughing and crying, and so glad she can't hardly breathe. 'Ben, you've grown so tall! And brown! And you've got new clothes—and, and everything—'

'And I don't pong no more,' he puts in, seeing as she's too polite to mention it.

She giggles.

And again that something shifts in his chest, and makes him wince. 'And look at you,' he goes. But then he can't think what else to say, 'cos up close she looks so done in that it fair gives him a turn. She's nothing but a bag of bones.

She says, 'Oh, Ben, I thought I'd never see you again. You never came to say goodbye.'

'Couldn't. Got the bluebottles after me.'

'Bluebott— oh, you mean policemen. I guessed it must have been something like that. Is it all right now?'

He turns away and looks out over the market. No, he thinks. It'll never be all right now.

Then she says what he hoped she wouldn't. 'Where's Robbie?'

His chest goes tight again and he sucks in his breath to keep from crying out. 'He's not here,' he goes.

She shoots him a look, and don't ask no more. She's all right, is Sophie.

For a bit they don't say nothing. Then she goes, 'How did you find us, Ben? How did you get to Jamaica?'

He just shrugs and says, 'I worked on a boat.'

'Gosh, how exciting. Did you get seasick?'

He shakes his head.

'I didn't, either. Or Maddy. But Sinclair did, a little.' She twists her hands together in her lap. 'Oh, Ben,' she says, 'I'm so glad you're here.' Then she bursts into tears.

Shit, he hates watching her cry. *Hates it.* What's he supposed to do? 'What's up, Sophie?' he goes.

After a bit she stops sobbing. Just hiccups for a bit. Nose pink, eyelashes all spiky. Then she ups and tells him what's bothering her.

To begin with it's hard to follow, but soon he gets to the meat of it.

And he can't hardly believe it. First the parson done for Robbie, and now he's gone and done for this little darkie that was Sophie's mate. *Why?* It don't make no sense.

'I'm sure he didn't *mean* to do it,' she says. 'He couldn't have done, could he?'

She searches his face with her big brown eyes, but he don't say nothing. No point scaring her, is there?

Then he gets a thought that makes him go cold all over. If the parson gets wind that Sophie saw him shut up that little darkie, then—well, Ben don't like to finish that particular notion.

'Here, Sophie,' he goes. 'Who else d'you tell about this?'

'No one. Only you.'

'Good. Keep it like that. Don't go breathing a word. And don't tell nobody about me, neither. You never seen me, all right?'

She looked puzzled. 'Can't I even tell Maddy?'

'You cracked, or what? She's *married* to him!' He takes her arm. 'Listen,' he says. 'Nothing won't bring your mate back now. So you got to forget about him and start thinking about getting better, girl.'

To his surprise she shakes her head. 'It's not that easy, Ben. I was getting better. But then someone took my shadow.' She bites her lip. 'I think—I think Victory was trying to get it back for me.'

Then she tells him a queer little story about shadows and darkie magic and that. When she's finished she gives him this worried look, like she don't know what he'll make of it.

Truth is, he don't know *what* to make of it. He learned a bit about darkie magic off of the cook on the *Marianne*, and as far as he's concerned it's all bollocks. But Sophie don't think so. And if she don't watch out, she'll fret herself to an early grave.

'Right,' he says, sounding a lot cockier than he feels. 'You leave it to me. I'll get your shadow back, and I'll sort it out about the parson, too. But you got to do your bit. All right?'

She nods. 'What do I do?'

'You don't say nothing to nobody, you stop fretting, and you start getting better.'

SINCLAIR PICKED UP the little silver branding iron from his blotter and turned it in his fingers, and wondered what this unsettling news that Kean had brought from town could possibly mean.

'A white boy,' Kean had said, 'cheaply dressed, with black hair and a sharp, wicked-looking face. He seem to know Missy Sophie well.'

It was impossible. Inconceivable. Those urchins in London had been seen to; the officer had assured him of that. And yet—to whom had the sister been talking if not one of them? And why?

A soft knock at the door.

'Enter,' he said.

Kean came in and bowed low. Missy Sophie, he said, had been woken, and was expecting Master Sinclair. Miss Maddy was taking her bath.

Sinclair rose to his feet. 'Very good,' he said.

The child was sitting up in bed when he went out to her. She was still dazed with sleep. After the visit to town, his wife had insisted that she should go straight to bed for a nap.

Sinclair stood looking down at her. In a low, gentle voice he said, 'You were seen outside the courthouse, talking to an undesirable.'

A hit, a palpable hit. He watched her face drain with shock.

He gave her a kindly smile. 'A wastrel and yet you knew him? I think you ought to tell me who he was, and what was said.'

She swallowed. 'He was asking the way,' she said.

'He was asking the way,' he repeated. 'For a quarter of an hour?'

She nodded.

He leaned over her: close, but not so close as to inhale the effluvium of her disease. 'I am surprised that you, of all people, should attempt to deceive a man of God. You must know that you have not long to live. You could go to Hell for that.'

Beneath the dressing gown her bony breast rose and fell.

He straightened up. 'I will leave you now, to reflect upon what you have done. When you decide to tell me the truth, you shall find me an attentive audience.' He walked down the gallery and paused at the door. 'And do not imagine that you shall go unpunished.'

The effect on her was immediate and astonishing. 'Oh, no, please!' she cried. 'Don't lock me up! I couldn't bear it, I should go mad!'

Lock her up? Whatever did she mean?

'I won't tell anyone ever,' she cried, 'I swear on the Bible! Just don't lock me up in the hothouse!'

He forced himself to take a deep, slow breath, then he walked back across the gallery, drew up a chair beside her and sat down.

'Tell me,' he said gently. 'Tell me what you think you saw.'

WITH LUCK, no one would see her leave. Jocelyn had gone to Kingston early that morning; Great-Aunt May was taking her afternoon rest; Clemency's spinal irritation had kept her in bed in a fog of laudanum; and Sinclair had gone to town on business of his own.

Sophie was fast asleep in the gallery. Yesterday's trip with Jocelyn had been an enormous success, but it had clearly worn her out.

By the time the house was finally quiet, it was four in the afternoon. Madeleine calculated that it would take her about an hour to ride to Eden. That should leave her with just enough time to say her piece to Cameron and make it back before Sinclair returned.

Nearly a week had gone by since the ball at Parnassus, and every day she felt worse about deceiving him. She had tried to tell herself that he deserved to be lied to. Hadn't he written that note to Cousin Lettice? Hadn't he washed his hands of Ainsley's children?

It didn't work. He had been honest with her, and she must be honest with him. She must tell him who she was. Then he could make of it what he would, and she could put it all behind her.

She slipped out through the back of the house to the stableyard, where she asked Doshey to wait with Kestrel, the little grey mare that Jocelyn had given her when he'd taught her to ride.

The groom was shaking his head. 'You better hurry wid dat ride, Miss Maddy. Rain go come in a hour or so.'

He was right. The air was hot and heavy, the eastern sky thickening to a dirty grey as she put Kestrel into a trot along the track that led south, along the muddy stream they called the Green River.

After half an hour she saw the ancient guango tree that marked the turning into the Eden road. As she approached it, a slight figure stepped away from the trunk and moved out into the road. It stood there unmoving, waiting for her.

She was still too far away to make out his face. He looked like a field-hand, in dungarees and tattered straw hat—more than a boy but not quite a man—and yet something about him was familiar. The thin face was wary and unsmiling as he watched her approach.

Her stomach turned over. No, she thought. It can't be.

'Hello, Madlin,' said Ben.

SHE'S NOT PLEASED to see him like Sophie, he can tell. She's horrified. Or maybe scared. Maybe she thinks that he's after the money; that he wants paying for not telling no one about them photos.

He should of stayed hid. She's a grand lady now, with a feather in her hat and her glossy white horse. And she's in a hurry, too, like she's off somewheres important. But he couldn't just let her ride past.

He watches her bring her horse about and jump down. '*Ben*,' she says in that low voice of hers. 'God. *Ben*.'

Without thinking, he takes the bridle and ties it to a tree root.

'Ben,' she says again. 'What are you *doing* here?'

He shoves his hands in his pockets and shrugs. 'Sophie didn't tell you nothing, then?'

'Sophie? What do you mean?'

'Saw her in Falmouth, didn't I? Outside the courthouse.' He tries to grin. 'Ben Kelly sitting outside a courthouse. Fancy that.'

She don't smile back.

'Anyway,' he goes, 'what was Sophie doing there in the first place? I never thought to ask her, and all.'

'She was waiting for Jocelyn,' she says. 'He was at a magistrates' meeting. But tell me about—'

'Jocelyn. The one she calls Uncle Jocelyn?'

She nods.

'Is he your grandpa, then?'

She shoots a glance over her shoulder, like she thinks there might be someone watching her or something. 'Yes,' she goes. 'My father was his son. Ainsley Monroe. But nobody knows that here.'

'Not even Sophie?'

She shakes her head.

Behind them the horse is kicking up a fuss, like a hornet's got at it or something, so he goes and talks to it to calm it down.

A rumble of thunder up ahead. They're in for a storm. He watches her looking up at the sky. She wants to be off. It gives him a turn to see how much. 'Cos he don't want her to go.

'Ben?' she goes. 'Where's Robbie?'

He opens his mouth to fob her off, but no sound comes out. Nothing. Just opens and shuts his mouth like a bloody fish.

'Ben? What's the matter? What happened? Where's Robbie?'

He backs away from her and trips on this tree root and sits down hard, still gaping like a fish.

She gets down on her knees beside him in the dust. Up close, she's not the grand lady no more, she's just Madeleine.

He takes this big gulp of air to steady hisself, and then he tells her everything. Out it all comes. He tells her how the parson paid this bloke to follow him and Robbie back to Shelton Street, to see where they lived, and then called the bluebottles and fingered them for a click: a big one, silver plate and all. When he gets to the bit about Robbie getting killed, he can't look at her no more. He just looks at this twisted tree root, and he hears his voice telling her what happened, and it's like it's not Ben Kelly talking, but somebody else.

And then he's past Robbie, and out the other side to the docks and the *Marianne* and that. But even then he can't stop, it's like he's a train or something, chugging along. He tells her about the gun and the plan. The only thing he don't tell about is that little darkie that was Sophie's mate and died, in case it gets Sophie into trouble.

When he gets to the end he's shivering like it's the middle of winter, even though it's stinking hot. She tries to put her hand on his shoulder but he twitches away. If she touches him he'll crack into pieces.

Gently, like she's talking to a baby, she says, 'Oh, Ben. I'm so sorry.' He spits. 'Well,' he goes. 'Way of the world.'

There's a silence. High above them a john crow circles in the sky.

'Ben,' she goes, and this time she sounds different. More grown-up. 'The gun. Show me the gun.'

He don't even think about refusing. Gets up and goes to the tree and finds the special place, and takes it out.

She looks at it without touching. 'Do you know how to use this?'

He nods. Been doing a bit of target practice down by the river.

'You can't, Ben,' she says in her low voice. 'You can't do this.'

'Yes, I can. I—'

'No. No. Listen to me. I'm not thinking about Sinclair, God forgive me for that. I'm thinking of you. You'd be caught, Ben. They'd hang you for it.'

He tries to shrug. 'Who cares?'

'Robbie.' She fixes him with her dark eyes. 'Robbie cares.'

'Robbie's dead,' he snarls.

'But what if he weren't? What if it were the other way round, Ben? What if you were the one who'd fallen from that roof, and he'd survived? Would you want him to stay alive and make something of his life? Or would you want him to get himself hanged?'

Ben don't answer. He can't, can he? He's got a great big lump of something stuck in his throat. 'R-Robbie,' he blurts out, 'would of never got out here. Not on his own.'

She puts her hand on his back and smooths it up and down, and he wants to tell her to lay off, but he can't.

And all of a sudden it comes so strong upon him that he can't hold it back no more. Right up from deep inside him it comes, and cracks him wide open, and out come these great big jerky hee-hawing sobs, and he can't stop for nothing, he just can't, and it hurts, it really hurts.

MADELEINE WRAPPED the revolver in her scarf and stowed it gingerly in her saddlebag. She had no idea what she was going to do with it. All she knew was that it was imperative to get the thing away from

Ben. His bizarre notion of 'paying back the parson' could get him killed or deported, or thrown into prison at the very least.

Hunched amid the tree roots, he looked so alone, so completely out of his depth. How could she ride off and leave him? She had tried to give him money, but been snarlingly rejected. He was doing all right, he told her. This country was easy pickings. She didn't believe a word of it. He looked as if he hadn't eaten for weeks.

A flurry of wind stirred the Spanish moss in the guango tree. She glanced up at the sky. The rain was approaching fast. If she didn't get going soon, she'd have to turn back.

'Here,' she said. She knelt beside him and took her card-case from her pocket and wrote a few words on the back of one of her cards. 'This is the address of a good friend of mine in Falmouth. Mrs Olivia Herapath. Go and see her as soon as you can. She'll find you a job. I'll send her a line, so that she'll know to expect you.'

He wiped his nose on the back of his hand, and took the card and scowled at it.

'Ben,' she said. 'Promise me you'll go to see her.'

He glanced up, his eyes unfocused, and she wondered if he'd even heard. 'I have to go now,' she said. She stood up and dusted off her skirts. 'Would you help me onto my horse?'

That seemed to bring him back to himself, as she had hoped it would. He struggled to his feet and pocketed the card, then untied Kestrel and helped her into the saddle.

'Rain coming,' he said. To her relief he sounded almost his old self. 'Where you off to, Madlin, in such a hurry?'

'Just making a call,' she said.

He glanced up the road. 'Not much up there,' he said.

She did not reply.

A moment later his face changed. 'Bloody hell. The brother. That's it, isn't it? You and the parson's brother?'

She flashed him a look, but he was shaking his head and gazing up at her with new respect. 'Sodding hell,' he said. 'What a mess.'

She gave him a twisted smile. 'As you say.' She gathered the reins and turned Kestrel's head. 'Look after yourself, Ben Kelly. Stay away from Fever Hill. And don't get mixed up in this.'

THE FIRST SPOTS of rain were pitting the red dust as she cantered south towards the Martha Brae. She kept her eyes on the road as she passed the ruins of the slave village at Romilly, which had often featured in her mother's stories. Suddenly the woods were left behind.

Cane-pieces opened out on either side of her, acid green in the stormy light. A rainstorm in July? Who ever heard of that? Up ahead, the hills loomed shockingly close: the start of the Cockpits.

Cameron was speaking to a tall Negro field hand when Madeleine brought Kestrel to a halt outside his property.

'I have to talk to you,' she said, raising her voice above the noise of the rain, which had started to come down in force.

He stepped towards her and gave her a concentrated look that she couldn't read. 'Does Sinclair know you're here?'

'Of course not.'

A terrific peal of thunder. Her horse sidestepped in alarm.

He glanced over his shoulder at the field hand, then back to her. 'Come into the house.'

He showed her into a dim and shuttered 'spare room', then left her to go and see to her horse.

She removed her hat and her sodden dust-coat and threw them on a chair. Her hair was wet, her riding habit damp, but there was nothing to be done about that now. Besides, it was too hot to catch a chill.

As her eyes adjusted to the gloom, she made out more of her surroundings. The room must once have been beautiful, but the window hangings were mildewed, the wall panelling was worm-eaten, and the canopied bed had collapsed into a pile of mouldy planks.

A crash of thunder and a brilliant flare of lightning, and the rain on the shingles became deafening. She moved to the window.

Against the broken louvres the fronds of an enormous fern trembled in the rain. She looked down over a steep slope of wind-tossed trees and saw stables and a cookhouse, smothered by creepers and bougainvillea. It was hard to tell whether the buildings supported the greenery or the other way round.

As she moved from the window, the rain ceased with tropical suddenness. Blue sky began to show through the hole in the roof and sunlight outlined the ferns with gold.

She opened the door into the hall and emerged into a large empty space made airy by high open rafters, louvred fanlights, and several more holes in the roof. How can he live like this? she wondered. *Where* does he live?

She moved through to the sitting room, which was empty except for an ancient, battered chest of drawers, and walked towards a louvred doorway. She opened the doors, expecting a dim, shuttered chamber like the gallery at Fever Hill. Instead she found herself on a wide, open verandah in a blaze of light.

A flock of parakeets exploded from the trees and filled the sky with emerald wings. The sun shone green through tree ferns dripping beneath the eaves, and purple grenadilla invaded the broken fretwork balustrade. At the foot of the slope, the jade-green river slid by, and far in the distance lay the grey-blue glitter of the sea.

The air was buzzing with life. The rasp of crickets, the piping of frogs, the twittering of wild canaries. Then she heard footsteps behind her, and turned to see Cameron coming out onto the verandah.

'It used to be a proper gallery,' he said, as if he felt he must apologise, 'but the wood ants got into the louvres. It seemed simpler just to open the whole thing up.'

She crossed her arms round her waist. 'It's beautiful.'

There was an uneasy silence. She noticed that he remained by the doors, a safe distance away, awkward and on edge.

Then two things happened at once. An enormous mastiff hurtled up the steps and launched itself at Cameron, and an ancient black man with unsteady yellow eyes emerged from the house bearing a tray with an earthenware pitcher, two tumblers, and a bottle of rum.

Helper and mastiff narrowly missed one another, and Madeleine, grateful for the diversion, found a rickety cane chair near the steps, and sat down. She took a tumbler from the helper's tray.

The question of where Cameron lived was finally solved. He lived out here. Behind him was a cot-bed hastily covered by a moth-eaten grey blanket, and flanked by an elderly washstand and a large, iron-bound campaign chest. On the chest was a stack of battered ledgers, an ancient kerosene lamp, and a corner of silvered mirror-glass.

He caught the direction of her glance, and coloured. 'Sorry about this. You must think I've gone bush.'

She shook her head.

'It's just that there's always so much to do on the estate. I haven't had time for the house.' As he spoke the mastiff trotted over to investigate her. She sniffed Madeleine's hand, then trotted back to Cameron and slumped at his feet.

She said, 'I take it that's the famous Abigail. Sophie will be annoyed to have missed the introductions.'

Another silence, while they both thought how unlikely it was that Sophie would ever be allowed to visit Eden.

Madeleine took a sip of her drink. It was freshly pressed cane juice: pearl-grey and fragrant and wonderfully steadying.

'Would you like some rum in that?' said Cameron. 'You must have got rather wet.'

'No. Thank you. But you go ahead.'

He poured rum into his own glass and added a splash of cane juice from the pitcher, then took a chair by the campaign chest.

She ought to tell him now why she had come. Just tell him and get it over with. But she couldn't do it yet. Let him have a drink first. Yes, let him have a drink. He was going to need it.

Behind him on the campaign chest stood a leather travelling frame containing a pair of photographs. In one of them she recognised a younger Jocelyn, much less rigid and hawk-like. In the other, a young man with wavy fair hair. He looked happy and handsome and unafraid. He was her father.

Cameron said something, but she didn't hear.

She had forgotten what her father looked like when he smiled. How could she have forgotten something as important as that?

'Madeleine? What's wrong?'

She dragged her gaze away. 'Is that Ainsley?'

'I'm sorry? Oh. Yes, that's Ainsley. Just before he took off with Rose.'

'What was he like?'

'He was clever. Imaginative. Enormously self-critical. Which could be infuriating. And kind.' He paused. 'I think that's why he could never be happy after what he did. Because of all the people he'd hurt.'

'Have you really forgiven him?' she said.

He glanced at her in surprise. 'Of course. He was so young when it happened.'

'Have you forgiven Rose?'

'She was young too.'

'That's not an answer.'

He considered that. 'I was thirteen when they left, and a little bit in love with her myself. But, yes. Of course I've forgiven her. It's strange. I still—' He broke off with a frown.

'What were you going to say?'

'It's just that I still dream of him. Ainsley. And they're not peaceful dreams. I don't know why.'

Don't you? she thought. He had never once mentioned Ainsley's children. He seemed to have driven them from his mind.

She said, 'Do you still miss him?'

'Imagine how you'd feel if Sophie went away and never came back.'

In the garden a flock of crows settled squabbling in a mango tree. Abigail hurtled down the steps to see them off.

Madeleine asked, 'Why have you never tried to make it up with Jocelyn?'

He made no reply.

'I think,' she said, 'that you've become accustomed to living like this. It's become a way of life. Just as it has for Jocelyn. You're so alike. You could be father and son.'

She watched him pour himself another drink and look at it, and put it down untasted. His hair was still damp and as he wasn't wearing a necktie she could see the droplets of rainwater trickling down his neck. Heat rose to her cheeks.

'Madeleine,' he said, 'why did you come here?'

'I needed to see you.'

'It only makes things worse.'

'I know.' Now was the time to tell him and have done with it.

She tried to imagine what he would say when he knew that she had been lying to him. She looked at him sitting there with his elbows on his knees. He seemed so capable and strong, but he could be hurt. Especially by her. How could she do it?

She shook her head. She couldn't tell him. It was cowardly and wrong, but she couldn't do it.

He rubbed his hand over his face. 'That night at the Trahernes',' he said, 'I wanted to kill Sinclair. My own brother. And I wanted to kill him for what he said about you.'

'What did he say?'

'He said you're not as innocent as you seem.'

She got up and went to the balustrade. 'He's right,' she said.

'I don't believe that.'

'It's true.'

She heard him get to his feet and come to stand beside her. Again she felt herself growing hot. She wanted to touch him, to feel the warmth of his skin.

He said, 'If things had been different, we'd be living here together, you and I.'

'Don't say that.'

He turned to her. 'Leave him. Leave him and come to me.'

'I can't.'

'Yes, you can. You can break the rules. I know, I've done it.'

'Well, I can't. He's Sophie's guardian.'

'Bring her with you. She'd love it here. She'd get better.'

'He'd take her away. He'd have the law on his side.'

'So you have thought about it?'

'Of course I have.'

'So what are you saying, that there's nothing to be done?'

She paused. 'The only way out,' she said, 'would be to run away. Just like Ainsley and Rose. But that would only start the whole wretched cycle over again, and I won't do it. So, yes, I am saying that there's nothing to be done. And you know it, too.'

He opened his mouth to reply, then shut it again. She was right.

Rainwater dripped from the eaves. An egret sped upriver, brilliant white against searing green.

She glanced at his hand on the railing. He had rolled back his shirtsleeves and she looked at the broad wristbone and the fine fair hairs on his forearm. Why shouldn't she touch him, just once, so that she'd have something to remember?

She reached over and put her fingers on the back of his hand. She felt his grip tighten on the balustrade; she felt the tension in him, the holding back. She put her hand on his shoulder and raised herself on her toes and kissed him. She had meant to reach his mouth, but in her nervousness her lips found the roughness of his cheek. He smelt of rum and cool, rain-washed skin.

He put one hand on her waist and the other on the nape of her neck, and bent and kissed her mouth. Softly at first, just finding her lips. Then more deeply.

Startling, unfamiliar. She was spiralling down into heat and strength and closeness, unbelievable closeness; no barriers. She put her arms round his neck and felt his damp hair, and his grip about her tightening. She didn't want it to end. She wanted to drown in him and never wake up.

At last they had to draw apart for breath. They stood with their heads together, taking in each other's scent.

'I don't understand you,' he said. 'Is this what you came to tell me? That you want to be with me but can't?'

'Yes,' she said. 'That's why I came.'

'You know I'll never accept that.'

'You don't have a choice.'

'There's always a choice. Madeleine—'

'It's getting late,' she said. 'I've got to go back.'

His arms tightened about her. 'You can't go. Not after this.'

'Cameron. I'm sorry. Let me go.'

'I don't understand you. It's always as if there's something missing.'

'I know. I do know.'

'Why won't you tell me?'

She put both hands on his chest. 'I have to go,' she said again. 'It's late. Please. Fetch my horse.'

IT WAS SIX O'CLOCK by the time Sinclair returned from town, greatly calmed by his interview with Dr Valentine. But he was granted no time to dwell on that, for as he brought the pony-trap to a halt outside the house, Kean descended the steps with a note from Great-Aunt May: *I must speak to you. The west grounds, forthwith. We must not be overheard.*

A cold sweat broke out on Sinclair's forehead. What could possibly be so momentous that Great-Aunt May would break the rule of a lifetime and go into the grounds in daylight? He hurried round to the back of the house, where two straight-backed chairs had been set on the hard brown grass. In one, beneath an enormous black sun-umbrella, sat Great-Aunt May: rigid, unmoving, and armoured against the sun by a floor-length dust-coat of flint-grey silk.

She did not seem to be angry; at least, not with him. If he hadn't known her better, he would have said that she was excited.

'This afternoon,' she began, as soon as he was seated, 'Kean overheard an exchange between two persons on the Eden road. Your wife and another. An undesirable.'

He opened his mouth to protest, but she quelled him with a glance. 'Regrettably,' she went on, 'Kean did not hear all, for he was disturbed by field workers and forced to move on. But he heard enough.' She paused. 'Your wife has not been honest with you, Sinclair. She is not who she says she is.' She folded her long narrow hands in her lap. 'Your wife is Jocelyn's granddaughter.'

CHAPTER EIGHT

Power and knowledge fizzed in Sinclair's veins as he rode out in the early morning to see his brother. For now at last he understood. He understood why God had given him this woman to wife. He understood the trials that God had made him undergo. *They were to prove his worthiness for the great office that was his destiny.*

Looking about him at the rain-washed cane, he thought, Who on earth can stop you now? It is all so clear. Dr Valentine will cure her of her condition, and she will be a proper wife at last. She will gratify your needs and bear you a son, and your inheritance will be secure.

The old man's granddaughter. Ainsley's child. His inheritance made flesh.

It no longer mattered that she was intransigent and unwomanly, *for that was not her fault*! He understood that now. He understood from yesterday's providential visit to Falmouth that she was simply ill. 'An exhaustion of the nerve power', the doctor had called it.

'There is much room for hope, Mr Lawe. For there is a regimen which I myself have used for many years to treat just such cases as this. Depend upon it, my dear sir. After three months of the isolation cure—that is to say, of bed-rest, seclusion and sedation—your wife will be a different woman. Obedient, well regulated, and properly eager to take her place at your side as your helpmeet and comforter.'

Smiling, Sinclair looked about him at Eden's shimmering cane-pieces. Yes, yes, my brother, you may toil all you wish, but it will always be in vain. You can never surpass me now.

He rode on up the muddy track, and at last he came to a sprawling, untidy compound populated by the usual gaggle of blacks. Croptime was long over, but there must have been a tail end of milling in progress, for the ground was white with trampled cane-trash and the air was thick with the stench of burnt sugar and rum.

Sinclair dismounted and gave his horse to a pickney, then strolled over to where his brother was supervising a group of blacks unpacking equipment from an ox-wain.

When at last his brother saw him, he made no attempt to conceal his displeasure. 'What are you doing here?'

Sinclair took off his hat and put on a jaunty smile. 'And a good morning to you too, brother,' he said gaily. 'Working on a Saturday? However did you prevail upon our dusky brethren?'

'I paid them,' Cameron snapped. 'Now what d'you want?'

With his riding crop, Sinclair indicated the track. 'Walk with me. I have something to impart.'

'I don't have time.'

'I assure you, it will not take long.'

'All the same, I—'

'Please.' Sinclair held up his hand. 'This is of some moment. Indeed, I should call it little short of a revelation.'

'Really,' said his brother, sounding unimpressed. 'Concerning?'

Sinclair turned and met his eyes. 'Concerning my wife.'

THE DOGCART CLIPPED smartly along beneath the giant bamboo, and Sophie hugged Pablo Grey and thought what a difference a day could make. Everything would be all right now. Ben would find a way to retrieve her shadow, and she would get better at last. And the accident with Victory had, after all, been exactly that: an *accident*.

Sinclair had explained it all. *Of course* he hadn't known that Victory was inside the hothouse. In fact, he'd closed the door to *stop* little children from wandering in and getting into difficulties.

It was such a relief. She'd wanted to tell Maddy straight away, but Sinclair had said no, we shall wait until we're all at Providence together, and then you can tell her. It had been his idea to arrange the holiday at Providence as a surprise for Maddy. That morning, after he'd returned from his ride, he had suggested to her that she might care to go into town to see Mrs Herapath, and Maddy had jumped at it, for she had been out of sorts lately. Then, while she was gone, they had packed Sophie's valise, and left for Providence—for it was Sinclair's idea to take her there a day ahead, so that she could supervise the housekeeper in making the house nice for Maddy, as part of the surprise.

As the afternoon wore on, Sophie began to wonder if they would ever reach Providence. Soon the road became steeper, and they left the river behind. The hills were suddenly much closer. The Cockpits at last? She longed to consult the little volume in her valise that Clemency had given her: *Tales of the Rebel Maroons of the Cockpits*. The very thing for a holiday in the hills.

She would miss Clemency. She had helped with the packing, and fussed and not wanted Sophie to leave, just like a proper mother. To cheer her up, Sophie had told her about Ben, and made her swear to keep him secret, and Clemency had been touched.

At last they came to a pair of tall iron gates, and Sinclair reined in and spoke to the gatekeeper. The gates swung open and they trotted up the carriageway.

Sophie knew that Providence was a hunting lodge, so she'd been expecting something cosy and rustic. But the house that rose before them was even larger than Fever Hill. It had pointed gables like a witch's dwelling, and blank, unfriendly louvres painted dark grey.

Helpers in grey uniforms ran down and took charge of the dogcart and Sophie's valise, and one of them picked her up and carried her up the steps and set her down in a shadowy gallery with her crutches. The gallery was extremely clean, with a floor of brown linoleum like the scullery at Wyndham Street, and it stank of Lysol.

Then Sinclair mounted the steps and swept past her along the corridor, and told her to hurry. She had no choice but to start after him on her crutches, with Pablo Grey swinging from her wrist by his halter. At the end of the corridor a door opened, and a tall lady came out and ushered them into a study with an enormous desk and two hard black leather visitors' chairs.

The lady was deferential to Sinclair, and Sophie wondered if she was the housekeeper. She wore a grey silk dress like Great-Aunt May's, only plainer. She took the crutches from Sophie, along with Pablo Grey. 'This will have to go,' she said, holding the donkey by one ear. 'Toys are not permitted. They harbour dust.'

'Oh, he's extremely clean,' said Sophie. 'I brush him every day.'

The lady did not reply. She crossed to the other side of the room and laid Pablo Grey on a chair. Then she gave Sophie a book and told her to study it while she talked to the Reverend Lawe.

By now Sophie was convinced she was missing something. She didn't like this place, and was sure Maddy wouldn't like it either.

Sinclair and the lady were talking in low voices about 'registration', so Sophie stopped listening and looked down at the book in her lap. The cover said: *Rules for Patients. Burntwood Private Clinic for Afflictions of the Lungs.*

'SHE'S *WHERE*?' said his wife.

Quietly, Sinclair repeated what he had just said. 'Be seated,' he said, 'and calm yourself.'

'I will not "calm myself" until Sophie's back where she belongs.'

'She belongs where I choose to place her. Now calm yourself!' This time he allowed the steel to enter his voice, and it had its effect.

His wife sat down. He could see the effort it took to restrain herself. 'Sinclair,' she said in a voice shaking with emotion, 'don't take this out on Sophie. She's done nothing to you.'

'You misunderstand. I have only her best interests at heart. Your sister's condition requires constant nursing. That has made you ill. Yes, ill. It is futile to deny it.'

'This is because of Cameron, isn't it? You've sent Sophie to that awful place to punish me. Burntwood is a hospice for consumptives. People go there to die. I won't allow you to do this. I—'

'*You* will not allow *me*?' He gave an incredulous laugh. 'If I were a less forgiving man, I might do as many a wronged husband has done before me, and have you committed to an asylum. Dr Valentine has confirmed that I could have you committed right now.'

Ah, now he had her attention. 'Dr Valentine? And who is he?'

'Dr Valentine is my physician.'

'He's never even met me. How can he say that I'm mad?'

With weary patience he kneaded his temples. 'He predicted that you would react like this. He warned me that contentiousness is one of the symptoms.'

'Symptoms of what?'

'Exhaustion of the nerve power.'

She snorted. 'Nonsense! There's nothing wrong with my nerves.'

'Dr Valentine would disagree. And since he is the physician and you are not, it is his opinion that decides the matter.'

She sat back in her chair, and he watched her struggling to take it in. The grandfather clock struck seven.

Sinclair rose to his feet. 'You must hasten and dress for dinner. We must not keep Great-Aunt May waiting.'

She was shaking her head in disbelief. 'But can't you see that this is pointless? In a fortnight Jocelyn will be back from Kingston. He won't allow her to stay at Burntwood.'

'Oh yes he will. The old man would never come between a man and his wife. Or between a man and his legal charge. He may not *like* my decision, but he will most certainly respect it.'

She saw the force of that. Yet she opened her mouth to protest.

'*Enough!*' he cried. 'I am not to be moved! Do as you are told and dress for dinner. And after dinner you shall pack your trunk, for tomorrow morning, directly after church, we leave for Providence.'

'*What?* But I can't possibly—'

'And I warn you, if you defy me, I shall have you sedated.'

'Sedated? But, Sinclair—'

'Sedated,' he repeated, raising his voice to conquer hers. 'But if you obey me, and do all that Dr Valentine requires, then I may decide, in time, to permit your sister to join us. The choice is yours.'

That found its mark. At last she grasped that further disobedience would only delay her sister's return. And delay was not something she could afford, for Sophie was among consumptives, and would not last long once the disease had taken hold of her lungs.

In fact, he was counting on it.

THE REVEREND GRANT was not known for the brevity of his sermons, but this morning he outdid himself. He spoke until Madeleine wanted to scream. A quarter past ten o'clock, and she still had no plan for getting Sophie out of Burntwood.

She had lain awake all night, as schemes whirled through her mind. Steal a horse and make her way across country. Send for the police. Kill Sinclair. She could do that, couldn't she? She was a Durrant; wasn't that what Durrants did?

But when morning came, the hopelessness of her position became apparent. She had no allies at Fever Hill. She was watched constantly by Sinclair and Great-Aunt May, and the helpers had orders not to let her anywhere near the stables. Clemency was too frightened to help, and Olivia Herapath wouldn't dream of interfering in what she would regard as a purely family affair.

Which left Cameron. But how could she get a message to him? He never came to church, and was probably in some distant cane-piece right now, with no idea of what had happened.

At last the sermon ended, and the final prayers were said. With agonising slowness, the congregation filed out. Sinclair preceded Madeleine into the porch, and paused to say a few words to the Reverend Grant. Great-Aunt May drew down her veil and put up her parasol to protect herself from the sun on the way to the carriage.

Madeleine went out into the glare and stared blankly at the parishioners talking in the churchyard. This couldn't be happening.

She turned, and saw Cameron standing on the other side of the road, looking straight at her. He was in his work clothes.

Relief washed over her. It'll be all right now, she told herself. He'll get her out. She went to Sinclair and touched his arm. 'Your brother is here,' she whispered.

He glanced across the street. 'Ah, to be sure,' he murmured. To her surprise he did not look dismayed, but quietly pleased.

'I must speak to him,' she said. 'I need . . . to . . .'

'To say goodbye?' he supplied. To her astonishment, he inclined his head in assent. 'You seem surprised. Why? I have no objection to your speaking to your brother-in-law after church.'

She didn't wait for him to change his mind, but crossed the street almost at a run.

'I haven't much time,' she told Cameron as she drew near.

'Walk with me,' he said.

They started slowly up Duke Street, keeping to the shade beneath the trees. Acquaintances nodded at them.

'I need to speak to you,' he said when they were out of earshot. 'I need to—'

'Sophie's in Burntwood,' she broke in. 'Sinclair took her there yesterday when I was in town. You've got to get her out.'

He stopped and turned to her. His expression was strangely withdrawn, and she felt a prickle of unease.

'Just get her out,' she said, 'and bring her home. Or better still, keep her at Eden until Jocelyn returns.'

Still he did not reply. Still that unnerving scrutiny.

'Cameron? What is it?'

He glanced up and down the street. When there was no passer-by within earshot he said, 'Sinclair told me who you are.'

Outside sounds receded. She felt herself sway. Sinclair knows, she thought. God. Sinclair knows.

She glanced back and saw him standing in the churchyard, watching her. 'He knows,' she said aloud.

'Which, I imagine, is why he let you come and talk to me. It's his little game. Letting you find out from me. I always knew there was something wrong between us. Something more than just Sinclair.' He gave a little half-smile that was painful to see. 'I still can't believe it. Ainsley's daughter. The little girl in the park. You know, I always felt bad about frightening a child.'

'I know. I never blamed you for it.'

He put his hands behind his back and studied the ground. 'But if that were true, I think you'd have told me sooner.'

Oh God, she thought. He doesn't believe me. She said, 'You think I'm saying it now to persuade you to help Sophie.'

'I think you'd do anything for your sister. Yes.'

'Cameron—'

'Tell me,' he said, 'why did you marry him? Was it some kind of revenge? Revenge against the family?'

'Of course not. You asked me before, remember? And I told you the truth. I married him for money. For Sophie.'

He looked unconvinced.

'We had no money, Cameron. Can't you understand? Oh, there was a trust, but Septimus took it all, and when he died there was nothing left. Then Sophie fell ill, and suddenly we needed a great deal of money, very soon, or she wouldn't survive. What was I to do? If I'd been a man I'd have got a job, or something. As it was, the only plan I could come up with was to become a prostitute.'

She saw his shock, but it was too late to pull back now. 'Then Lettice told me where Sinclair lived, so I went to borrow money from him instead. It all happened just as I told you. I wanted to borrow money, but he asked me to marry him. So I did.'

'You were planning to sell yourself?' he said. 'How could you even think it?'

'Well,' she flashed out at him, 'what was I supposed to do, let Sophie die? It's no good looking at me like that. What choice did I have? And has it occurred to you,' she added, unable to stop, 'that if you and Jocelyn hadn't been so eager to slough off the black sheep's inconvenient bastards, none of this would have happened? But it did happen, and I was left to sort it out on my own, so I did.'

She drew a deep breath and forced herself to be still.

An Indian rattled by on a bicycle, trailing a plume of dust.

'You're right,' said Cameron. 'This is our fault, not yours.'

She shut her eyes. 'I didn't mean to blame you.' She turned her head away. 'I lied to you. I admit that. I lied to everyone. I married a man I despised for his money. But women do that all the time. We marry for money, or position, or because some man tells us to, because we're not allowed to do anything else.'

Cameron said, 'What about the old man? Does he know?'

She shook her head. 'Not unless Sinclair told him; and I don't think he has. I was going to tell Jocelyn myself. When the time was right.'

'Yes,' he said. 'As you were going to tell me.'

She shot him a look, but his face gave nothing away. She said, 'Try to understand. The only reason I lied was to protect Sophie. Is that so different from what you did at your court-martial? You kept quiet to stop my father's story coming out.'

He studied her for a moment. Then he said, 'We should turn back. They're waiting for you.'

Madeleine began to feel sick. None of this mattered next to Sophie, and he had brushed that aside as if he didn't care.

They turned and started walking back, and she saw that while Great-Aunt May was waiting in the carriage, Sinclair was still in the churchyard, watching them.

'All right,' she said, 'don't forgive me. But don't make Sophie pay for what I did. I'm the one who lied. Not her. She doesn't even know that she's Ainsley's daughter.' She paused. 'His daughter, Cameron. For eight years you've been in your self-imposed exile in the hills, having those nightmares about him and wondering why. You say you've forgiven him, but if you really had, would you have visited his sins on his children by denying their very existence?'

'Madeleine—'

'Because that's what you did, isn't it? You sent off a cheque and made sure that we'd never trouble you again.'

He looked appalled.

'She's his *daughter*, Cameron. She's eleven years old, and she's stuck in that dreadful place among a whole lot of dying people. You're the only one who can get her out.'

He rubbed a hand over his face, and she could see the emotions warring in him. Finally, he shook his head. 'Even if I could get her out,' he said, 'he'd only put her back again. He's her guardian, Madeleine. He has the law on his side.'

'But—'

'No.' He put up a hand as if to ward off some imaginary blow. 'I'm sorry. I'm sorry. I can't help.'

So this is Fever Hill, thinks Ben. This is where the parson lives. Bugger me, what a pile. It gives him the jitters, all them shutters peering down at him.

Evie cocks her head at Ben, and he follows her up the steps. In the gallery he looks out for Sophie or Madeleine, but they're not there. Oh well, that's not why he's come. This 'Miss Clemmy' has got a job for him; that's what Evie said. And a job at Fever Hill gets him closer to the parson, and that's the point.

It's been three days since he seen Madeleine. Bloody Madeleine. It's all very well her telling him what Robbie would of wanted. 'Get on with your life,' she said. All right. But how?

He's thinking on that when Evie pulls him into this sitting room and hisses at him to wait while she fetches 'Miss Clemmy'.

Queer sort of room he's in. Golden couch and chairs and lots of silky cushions, all purple and grey, like in a coffin. And everywhere these little black bows, hundreds of them, even round the photos.

Footsteps, and in comes Evie with this old lady. No, she's not old—no wrinkles, nice figure on her—but she's got grey hair, and these staring blue eyes that go right through you, then skitter away.

'You must be Ben,' she whispers, with a queer little smile.

He whips off his hat.

'I'm Mrs Monroe,' she whispers, 'but you shall call me Miss Clemmy. I take it that no one saw you come in?'

He swallows and shakes his head.

'Good. Good. Because you see, Great-Aunt May doesn't care for me to have visitors.' That whispering's giving Ben the jitters.

She sits herself down on the couch, and tells him to 'be seated'. He looks round and picks this little footstool. So he's sitting there and she's twisting her hands in her lap, like she's scared out of her wits. Then she takes this deep breath and tells him what she wants. It seems the parson's put Sophie in a san. A san for lung jobs; the kind where they carry you out in a box. Sod it. *Sod* it.

'Of course,' whispers Miss Clemmy, leaning towards him, 'I'm *convinced* that Sinclair only meant the best for her. And Aunt May *thoroughly approves* . . . And yet,' she bursts out, 'I cannot bear to think of that poor child in that dreadful place!'

So now he knows what's going on. Somehow, the parson's got wind that Sophie knows about the little darkie, so he's packed her off to the san. And Miss Clemmy's gone behind their backs. Got a bee in her bonnet about Sophie but she's frightened silly of this Aunt May.

'What about Madeleine?' he pipes up. 'She got something to say about this, or what?'

'That's the *thing*,' she whispers. Then she tells him how the parson's taken Madeleine off into the hills, and she's not coming down again for months. 'Sinclair says she's neurasthenic'—Ben guesses that's posh for mad—'but he once said the same about me, and I'm rather sure that I'm not.'

Don't know about that, thinks Ben, shifting uneasily on his footstool. And sure enough, what she says next only goes to show. Barmy idea she's got, barmy, about him, Ben Kelly, padding the hoof all the way to this Burntwood, and 'rescuing' Sophie; all on his lonesome—or maybe with that brother of the parson's—how's that going to work? Apples to ashes he'll just end up in the clink.

So he picks up his hat and gets to his feet and tells Miss Clemmy he can't do nothing about it.

She's not expecting that. Hands start going all aflutter, big blue eyes all staring. 'B-But—Sophie said you were her *friend*.'

Sophie, he thinks angrily, should of never told nobody nothing. You try anything, Ben Kelly, and *you're* the one that gets into trouble. Besides, it'll all get sorted without you sticking your nose in, you wait and see.

Madeleine's the best bet. Bloody tiger she is, when it comes to Sophie. Yeh, Madeleine'll get it sorted. No doubt about it.

SHE IS AT CAIRNGOWRIE HOUSE, curled up on the window seat, watching the snow covering the garden. Smooth white garden. Soft white sky. White surf on the beach. Everything peaceful and soft.

The window seat begins gently to rock. A man's voice says, *Mrs Lawe. Mrs Lawe. Wake up. Open your eyes.*

She doesn't want to open her eyes. She wants to stay on the window seat, where it's peaceful and safe.

'Mrs Lawe,' says Dr Valentine in his deep, firm voice. 'Wake up.'

Slowly, hazily, she opens her eyes.

The doctor is leaning over her—commandingly, of course—and his face is so close that she can count the pores on his nose. But he doesn't frighten her. She can handle him with her eyes shut. In fact she's doing it right now, by making him think that she's fast asleep.

She gives him a drowsy little frown.

He pats her hand. 'Good girl. Now tell Dr Valentine how you feel.'

Slowly, dazedly, she blinks at him. Then she gives him a weak, scared, tremulous little smile. A sort of Clemency-smile. Yes, that's it. Let's pretend to be Clemency.

Out loud she whispers in a soft, trembly Clemency-voice, 'Th-Thirsty, Doctor . . . Very thirsty . . . Where am I?'

He gives a satisfied nod. 'To be sure, to be sure, of course you are thirsty. You shall have a large glass of goat's milk.'

How perfectly horrid, she thinks. Out loud she murmurs, 'Thank you, Doctor,' in a grateful Clemency-whisper.

'Excellent,' he says. 'Now you must be very good and lie here quietly. By and by, you shall begin to feel better.'

'Yes, Doctor,' she whispers, and snuggles into the pillow. Your little Clemency-patient is so sleepy, Doctor, and so confused.

He takes her pulse and feels beneath her jaw, and she restrains an urge to bite him on the wrist. Finally, with a satisfied 'Capital, capital,' he leaves the room, and she hears the key turn in the lock.

Yes, Doctor, she thinks, I shall do exactly as you say. I shall drink my horrid goat's milk, then when it's night-time and you and Sinclair are asleep, I shall clamber out of that window and sneak round behind the croton bushes and find my trunk and my clothes, and steal Sinclair's horse—and that's the last you'll be seeing of me.

She stifles a spurt of laughter.

Is it the laudanum, making her silly? Oh well. It's really rather nice. But watch out, Sinclair. Your wife has become a drug fiend.

'Drug fiend,' she giggles helplessly into her pillow.

ELIPHALET TAIT been stumbling round all night long in this damn dark Providence Wood, trying to poach little something to take for Free Come party over at Disappointment.

Lord, but it *dark* in here! Still, his luck's starting to sugar, for he's just caught himself three little bald-pates, all nice and fat.

And now he's at the edge of the wood, looking down on buckra house in the moonshine. And he's just deciding to go rest up in the stables till old Aaron come awake, when out the house he sees a woman in white come creeping soft, soft, towards the stable door.

Lord Master God! Is what all this now? *Buckra* woman creeping about at three o'clock in the night? And she's walking strange, like she's all liquored up. Eliphalet wonders if maybe she's the wife of that pinch-mouth parson over at Fever Hill who maintains she's gone moonshine mad. Hn, he thinks. Mad, I don't know. But she wants bad to get away from her man.

He sees her go into the stable, then come out again riding horse. Peculiar strange, he tells himself. And he sits down in the deep darkness behind the rockstone to consider awhile.

He must a fell in sleep, for when he comes awake, Brother Sun's starting up into the big blue. And down at the buckra house there's a lot, lot a trouble. Old Aaron's running fast as he can for the stables, and that parson's pacing in the yard, yelling for his horse.

Eliphalet swallows hard, and stays careful still. Don't you get tangle-up in this, he tells himself. You stand up soft now, and run like black ant back to your own self yard. And you keep one careful fact in that head you got. Far as you concern, you never was here.

THE DEW HAD BEEN heavy overnight, so his wife's trail was easy to follow. For an hour Sinclair had tracked her, and despite the heat and the discomfort he had almost enjoyed the ride, for with every passing moment he felt more certain that he would find her.

He reached a fork in the track and reined in. Curious. She should have turned left, heading down through the hill pastures towards Fever Hill. Instead she had taken the right-hand track, heading southeast up a narrow path that wound into the Cockpits.

Was this some kind of broken-backed attempt to reach Eden across country? Or had she simply lost her way? He dismounted, unhooked his water bottle from the saddle, and sat in the shade of a thorn tree. After drinking deeply, he glanced up at the towering, eerily conical hills of the Cockpits and, for the first time since he had started out, he felt a flicker of real unease.

He had always hated the Cockpits. It enraged him when Mrs Herapath held forth about their 'untamed beauty—their savage and desolate allure'. What allure? They were the mouth of hell.

Still, he told himself, what of that? It's such rough country, she'll make slow progress. She can't be far ahead now.

He remounted and kicked his horse to a trot. Soon the track became steeper and narrower, forcing him to slow to a walk. Twisted thorn trees clung to the slopes. Beneath them the ground was a dreary confusion of tumbled boulders and spiky wild pine and the rampant, dusty creeper the blacks called hogmeat.

He wished Dr Valentine was with him. But the doctor had

returned to town the previous evening, and Sinclair had been alone when the housekeeper had roused him with the news that his wife had stolen the carriage-horse and gone. But how? And *why*?

It hadn't taken long for the suspicion to take root that somehow she had learned the truth about the pickney's death. Perhaps her sister had told her; perhaps she had found out by some other means. It didn't matter. The point was he had to find her. Take her back.

Ahead of him the track led down into a rocky hollow like a small natural amphitheatre, before snaking up the other side. He put his horse cautiously forward. Wasn't there, he wondered, something familiar about this place? Something vaguely unsettling? But what?

He was trying to remember when he rounded a spur, and came upon Madeleine. She was sitting with her back to him beneath a calabash tree: head down, arms about her knees, as if exhausted, or taken ill. She hadn't heard his approach, but her horse, tethered a few yards behind her, pricked up its ears.

Mouth dry, heart pounding, Sinclair slid from the saddle and tied his horse to a thorn bush, and moved silently forward. He was no more than twenty feet away from her when she turned and saw him. He froze. For a moment they stared at one another in silence.

'You,' she mouthed. Her lips formed a perfect O of alarm.

She was bizarrely dressed: a wide straw hat with white silk roses round the brim; a pair of cream calfskin ankle-boots; and a wildly unsuitable morning dress of white muslin. When she got to her feet, he saw how she swayed. She was still drugged. Thank God.

'Why did you run?' he said.

She backed away. 'After what you did? How can you ask?'

A cold weight sank within him. Now he was sure. 'You cannot run from me,' he said. 'You have nowhere to go.'

She threw a rapid glance over her shoulder, and took another step down the slope, stumbling on the uneven ground.

He held out his hand. 'Come. We will forget all about this.'

She shook her head.

Still holding out his hand, he took a step towards her. 'I can't let you tell anyone,' he said. 'Come. Be reasonable.'

She took another step back and lost her footing, and fell to her knees in a clump of hogmeat. The ground seemed to sag beneath her. 'Sinclair . . .' she said. She sounded surprised.

'Come,' he said again.

The next few seconds seemed to stretch, and he took in the details with extraordinary clarity. He saw the earth crumble beneath her. He saw her grab at the creepers with both hands. He heard the vegetable snap as they gave way, and the rattle of falling pebbles.

She looked up at him, her face blank with shock. 'Sinclair—I can't—' She clutched at the creepers and slid down, down, and disappeared into a choking cloud of red dust.

The dust was blinding, all-enveloping. He whipped out his handkerchief and covered his mouth, and dropped to his knees and crawled towards the edge. Through the red haze he made out a ragged hole some ten feet across and, as the dust slowly settled, he saw her at the bottom, lying in a mound of creepers and rubble. He leaned over as far as he dared. 'Madeleine? Are you all right?'

She coughed, and sat up, wiping her eyes. She touched her forehead and winced, and finally nodded. 'I—I think so. Yes. What—is this place, Sinclair?'

'It must be a sinkhole. They're everywhere around here. The creepers grow over the edge, so it's hard to see them. We were never allowed to come here as boys.'

Still probing her forehead with her fingertips, she got unsteadily to her feet. 'How am I going to get out?'

He had been wondering that himself. The walls were nearly sheer, and about eighteen feet deep. Far too deep for him to reach her by leaning over. He looked around for some creeper that might bear her weight but saw only hogmeat: as thin and brittle as honeysuckle.

Then an idea came to him. Sights and sounds fell away. He sat back on his heels and wiped his face with his handkerchief.

'Sinclair,' his wife called out. 'Do you have any rope?'

He peered down at her again. 'Only my belt. And that's not long enough.'

'Well, then. I suppose you'd better go for help.'

Above her, there was a lengthy pause. 'Yes,' he echoed. 'I shall go for help.'

She looked up at him. His face was dark against the glare. 'Come back soon,' she said.

MADELEINE LISTENED to the clatter of hoofs disappearing down the track. Hot, bruised and thirsty, she found a patch of ground without too many rocks, and sat down to wait. The sun was directly overhead and there was no shade to be had. Thank God she still had her hat. But why hadn't she had the sense to unearth her dust-coat and riding habit from the trunk instead of this ridiculous morning dress?

After a while, a thin rind of shade appeared at the other side of the sinkhole. As she crawled over to it, something crunched beneath her hand. She remembered the passage on sinkholes in Sophie's gazetteer. Recalcitrant slaves left down here to die. She wondered if what had crunched beneath her hand was bones.

Don't be absurd, she told herself. That was sixty years ago; they'd be dust by now. Besides, she had more pressing concerns. Thirst was becoming a problem. Why hadn't she had the sense to make Sinclair throw down his water bottle?

The afternoon wore on, and the rind of shade grew wider. She curled up against the wall and tried to doze.

When she opened her eyes, she was alarmed to see that the shade had eaten up most of the sinkhole floor. Soon it would be dark.

That was when it hit her. Sinclair wasn't coming back.

CHAPTER NINE

Cameron woke before dawn, still drunk from the bottle of rum he had got through the night before. Three days had passed since he'd left Madeleine outside the church. Three days and three nights that had brought him no answers, only more questions.

The ride to Maputah took him past some of his best cane-pieces, but the sight did nothing to lighten his mood. He had thought that by rescuing Eden he was making peace with Ainsley's ghost. What a shameful piece of self-deception that had been.

For ten years he had scarcely given Ainsley's children a thought. When he remembered them at all it had been with a sense of distant relief. He'd done the right thing by them, hadn't he? He'd given them half his patrimony; what more did they need?

And that dream. Why had he never grasped its meaning, when it was staring him in the face? Simply because he hadn't wanted to?

How could he have been so *blind*? She even looked like Rose. The same rich colouring, the same dark, almond-shaped eyes. And the same extraordinary blend of candour and secretiveness and naiveté. Sinclair had told him once that she was not as innocent as she seemed. Well, perhaps that was true—but surely not in the way that Sinclair had meant. She didn't even know how to kiss.

The thought made him reach for his hip flask and take a long, burning pull of Scotch.

The night before he had been so angry with her that a red haze had misted his vision. She had lied to him, led him on. What *right* had she to ask him to help her sister?

He was still carrying that anger inside him when he reached Maputah. There he threw himself into work supervising the new still. The hours flew by. Gradually, some of the anger leached away.

After all, what crime had she committed? What had she done, except to make an already confounded mess even worse? None of this was her fault. It was his fault, his and Jocelyn's. If they hadn't been so eager to sweep Ainsley's 'inconvenient bastards' under the carpet, none of this would have happened. Septimus would not have emptied the trust and left them with nothing. Sophie would not have fallen ill. And Madeleine would not have married Sinclair.

But what could be done about that now? Nothing. Try to forget.

The bell tolled for the noonday break, and as the men settled down in the shade with their lunchpails, Cameron noticed a stranger loitering under the poinciana tree at the entrance to the yard. The stranger was small and thin, maybe thirteen or fourteen years old, in tattered dungarees and crumpled straw hat: plainly one of the poor white vagrants who wandered the countryside in search of casual work.

Cameron put his hands in his pockets and made his way across the yard. 'There's no work for you here,' he told the stranger. 'You'd better be on your way.'

'Din't come for a job, did I?' came the sharp retort. 'I got somethink to tell you.'

Cameron was intrigued. A cockney street Arab on the Northside of Jamaica. What were the odds on that? And what are the odds, he reminded himself, that this wily little urchin isn't on the lookout for something to steal? He gave the boy a hard look. 'What's your name,' he said, 'and what are you doing on my land?'

The boy met his gaze. 'Don't matter who I am,' he snapped. He flicked a sideways glance at the men in the yard, and lowered his voice. 'It's about Sophie. Missy Clemmy told me. She's in Burntwood san. That's what I come to tell you. You got to get her out.'

Cameron was astonished. 'Are you claiming some acquaintance with Miss Sophie Lawe?' he asked.

'Well, I can't get her out of there, can I?' the boy said, dodging the question. 'And the grandpa's in Kingston and won't be back—'

'The grandfather?' Cameron cut in.

Impatiently, the boy tossed his head. 'Yeh. Madlin's and Sophie's. The old man. The one they call Uncle Jocelyn.'

Cameron ran a hand through his hair. 'Did Mad— did Mrs Lawe send you?'

'Course not. How could she? Parson's gone and locked her up.'

'*What?*'

'Some place called Providence. Up in the hills. He says she's cracked, and he's put her on some kind of cure.'

'Who told you this? Who are you? How do you know Mrs Lawe?'

The boy clenched his fists. 'Who cares who I am?' he muttered. 'Point is, Madlin can't do nothink for Sophie.' He seemed genuinely anxious. 'That's why I come. To tell you she's in the san. So you can go and get her out. Yeh?'

As Cameron stood there in the sun, the lunacy of the situation came crashing in on him. 'What do you expect me to do?' he said, feeling his temper rise. 'Ride up to Burntwood like some medieval champion, and break down the door?'

For the first time, the boy was lost for words.

'Perhaps you're not aware,' Cameron went on, 'that Miss Sophie Lawe is my brother's responsibility. He is her legal guardian, which means that he's the only one who can get her out.'

The boy was staring at him with his mouth open. 'You *knew*,' he said. 'You already knew she's in the san. And you done nothink.'

'I don't need you,' said Cameron between his teeth, 'to teach me my duty. Now be off with you. I've got work to do.'

The boy was shaking his head. 'I thought you was different. I thought, if Madlin likes him, he can't be the same as them others. Shit. I should of known.'

Cameron gave the boy a look that made him flinch. 'I've let you have your say,' he said in a low voice, 'but I'll not tolerate disrespect. Now do as you're told and get off my land.'

But the boy stood his ground, though he threw a quick glance over his shoulder to make sure of his escape. 'You're narked at Madlin,' he said. 'That's it, innit?'

'How dare you, you little—'

'You're narked at her, so you're taking it out on Sophie. You think Madlin done it for fun? All she ever done, she done for Sophie. Don't you know that yet?'

And then the boy turned and ran.

SHE HAD TRIED everything she could think of, but nothing had worked. She had tried making steps in the sinkhole walls by hammering wedges of rock into cracks, but the limestone splintered beneath her weight. She had tried ripping up her gown and plaiting a rope then throwing the 'rope' over a sapling that jutted halfway up the sinkhole wall, but the sapling gave way before she could haul herself more than a few feet off the ground. Finally, she had tried shouting for help. She had given that up soonest of all. It was frightening to hear her voice buffeted from wall to wall, with no reply.

She forced herself to sit down and think. How long since Sinclair had left? Five hours? Six? It was becoming difficult to think of anything but water. She'd had nothing since well before dawn. *Why* hadn't she thought to take anything with her?

But if she had, it would be out of reach now.

Just like that wretched gun. If she had it now, everything would be different. She could fire off shots that would be heard for miles. She remembered taking it from the trunk with her clothes and then finding it in the saddlebag when she'd stopped to rest beneath the calabash tree. She'd put it on the ground and stared at it. Why had she taken it? What had she imagined she could do with it?

No doubt Sinclair had found it when he'd gone to fetch her horse; and no doubt it would help him justify what he had done. *She had a gun*, he would tell himself. *She meant to shoot me. I had no choice.*

She kept seeing his face as he peered over the edge. Those bright, dispassionate eyes: like a child watching a minnow in a pail. *Look at the funny little creature I have caught. I wonder how long it will live.*

How long will it live?

She pictured Sinclair riding down to Fever Hill to sound the alarm. She pictured Northside society tut-tutting over its afternoon tea. *Too dreadful, one can hardly bear to think of it. Apparently it was neurasthenia, and she simply wandered off. Poor Reverend Lawe!*

She wondered how Cameron would feel when he heard the news. And Jocelyn. And Sophie. God, Sophie. Who would tell her? Would she even live long enough to find out?

When she opened her eyes, she saw that some of the blue had leached from the sky. How long till it got dark?

She put out her hand and studied it. Her fingers were swollen, the skin so taut that it hurt to make a fist. If she didn't get out tonight, she would be too weak to do anything by morning.

Setting her teeth, she struggled to her feet and forced herself to begin again, to search for more stones that might serve as wedges.

She found the rock she had been using as a hammer, and went to the part of the wall where about four feet of her rudimentary ladder had survived. She found a crack about five feet up and started hammering in a wedge. This time it went more smoothly, and half an hour later she'd made a zigzag of hand- and footholds snaking roughly halfway up the wall. From there on up she'd have to carry her hammer and the rest of the wedges with her and put them in as she went along. She made a sack of her petticoat, slung it over her shoulder and filled it with stones.

She was five feet up before a wedge snapped. She went down, landing heavily on her side, and pain shot through her shoulder.

Winded, she lay where she had fallen. Her throat was swollen, her lips sore. It hurt to swallow. It hurt to move. She wanted to cry, but the tears wouldn't come. She curled into a ball and dug her knuckles in her eyes. What do I do? she thought. What do I *do*?

No answer came. No heaven-sent voice whispering salvation in the wilderness. Eventually, she opened her eyes. In the twilight she was surprised to see a long gash down her left forearm. She groped beneath her for the rock that had done it.

Her swollen fingers closed on it painfully. But it wasn't a rock. It was a shackle. Rough with corrosion but solid, and unmistakably a leg-iron: part of the section that encircles the ankle.

Heart pounding, she sat up. Her skin prickled with the sense of being watched. Someone had been here before her. She strained to make out shapes in the gloom. And after a while they began to move, as shadows do when you look at them for long enough.

'I don't want to harm you,' she whispered. 'I just want to get out.'

The shadows stopped moving and became a listening stillness.

She felt warmth and wetness on her arm and glanced down. The cut had bled freely but was already forming a scab. She crawled over to her petticoat and tore a strip with her teeth to make a rough bandage. When she had finished binding the cut, her fingers were sticky and glistening. She sat cross-legged in the dust and she thought about waking up in her mother's cold bed at Cairngowrie House, and peeling back the blankets to reveal the great scarlet stain.

She scowled at the blood on her hands.

Her mother had been wild, self-indulgent, undisciplined and brave. She had made enormous mistakes in her life, and when she'd got into trouble she had never blamed anyone but herself. She'd simply done her best to get herself out. *Well, Maddy, we'll just have to do this on our own.*

A noise above her made her start. A john crow had alighted at the edge, and was peering down at her, its eyes bright and dispassionate. She reached for a stone and aimed for the edge of the sinkhole. It tumbled harmlessly back to earth. With a squawk the john crow spread its wings and flew away.

'Come back tomorrow,' she shouted. 'I'm not dead yet.'

UP IN THE RAFTERS, a spider is spinning its web. It will finish soon, unless a helper comes and brushes it away.

The web disappears behind a shiny black face. 'Now, chile,' says the nurse, 'be quick an take you medicine. I don' got all day.'

The medicine is oily and brown and tastes of ash, but the child swallows it in one gulp, for she is a good child, and doesn't want to go without supper again.

The inside Sophie watches the child take the medicine, and knows that it tastes of ash, but she doesn't say a word. The inside Sophie watched when they strapped the child to the bed, and gave her injections that made her jangly all over. She watched when they burnt Pablo Grey in the incinerator. She watched when the child screamed and screamed until they gave her morphine which made her sick. The inside Sophie saw it all, but never said a word. She never speaks. If she did, the nurses would find her and take her away.

The child's bed is in the south gallery, with the rest of the female patients. She can't see out because of the louvres, but below them there are gaps between the balusters and she can see down into the yard, to the incinerator where they burnt Pablo Grey, and the twisty black flakes flew up and up and crumbled to nothing.

The child sleeps all the time now, except when she is woken by the nurses to take her medicine or her semolina, or by somebody coughing. After the medicine, everything becomes fuzzy. Fuzzy shadows and fuzzy strips of sunlight on the floor. Fuzzy noises too.

Until now, there hasn't been much noise, except for coughing and sometimes the gurgly noise of a person trying to breathe. But now there is a great deal of noise. The nurses are shouting and running about, and there are footsteps in the gallery: not the footsteps of the nurses in their cotton slippers, but someone in boots.

The child turns her head and sees a tall gentleman at the other end of the gallery. The nurses are crowding round him and waving their arms, and the inside Sophie can tell that they are frightened, although she can't make out what they are saying.

The tall gentleman walks the length of the gallery very fast, with the nurses trailing after him, and now he is standing over the child, looking down. The inside Sophie can tell that he is extremely angry.

The tall gentleman is undoing the straps on the child's arms and leg and round her splint, and wrapping her in a blanket and lifting her up and carrying her along the gallery and down the steps and out into the sunlight, which makes the child blink. Then the tall gentleman turns, and the child sees the nurses huddled on the steps, frightened.

Carefully, so as not to jar her splint, the tall gentleman passes the child to a helper. The helper lifts her high, high, and the tall gentleman takes her before him on his horse, and they are moving off down the carriageway. She can't see much because of the blanket wrapped round her, but she can smell the horse and hear its hoofs, and see the tips of its glossy black ears.

Pilate, she thinks. The horse's name is Pilate.

After a while they reach the great iron gate, and it's shut, and the gatekeeper runs out and shouts and waves his arms. Then the tall gentleman tells the gatekeeper a very bad thing, and after that there is no more shouting, and the gates open up, and they pass through.

The inside Sophie wants to tell the tall gentleman that she is glad he came for her, but she can't, for the inside Sophie never speaks. If she did, the nurses would find her and take her away.

As CAMERON DROVE the borrowed trap through the gates of Fever Hill, he glanced at the reddening sky and gave the reins an impatient flick. It would be dark soon, and he needed to see Sophie to safety before he could think of starting for Providence.

The sensible thing, of course, would be to postpone Providence until the morning. But he couldn't do that. After what the street Arab had said, he needed to know that Madeleine was all right.

A mongoose shot across the carriageway, and Pilate swerved and tossed his head. 'He's just making a fuss,' Cameron explained to Sophie beside him, 'because he doesn't like pulling a trap.'

She turned her head and gave him her unblinking stare. The sedatives were wearing off, but she still hadn't said a word.

Soon after leaving Burntwood, he had realised the impossibility of taking her all the way to Fever Hill on horseback. So he'd stopped at the first settlement they reached—a straggling little slum village called Simonstown—hoping to borrow a trap.

The village was heaving with preparations for Free Come eve. Men were stacking green pimento wood by the barbecues, pickneys were racing about and women were stoking the fires beneath great bubbling yabbas of gungo peas stew. The whole village smelt of cloves and wood smoke and anticipation.

They welcomed him like a holiday novelty that had arrived a day early. A man ran off to petition old Mowat for his pony-trap, and another took Pilate to be fed and watered. Cameron bought a tumbler of rum punch for himself, and watched in relief as Sophie worked her way with painful concentration through a beaker of guava syrup and a bowl of stewed okra and yam.

He wondered now what she had been through in that place. She was there for . . . five days? Surely that wasn't long enough for permanent harm? He shot her an anxious glance. She was watching the cane-pieces whip past, her lips slightly parted, her eyes dull.

Ainsley's daughter. He still couldn't believe it. And yet all the evidence was before him. The fair hair. The straight, intelligent dark brows. The hint of her grandfather in the determined set of her chin.

He remembered what Madeleine had said outside the church. *You say you've forgiven him, but if you really had, would you have visited his sins on his children by denying their very existence?*

I have forgiven you, Ainsley, he told the rippling cane-pieces. Look. Here's your daughter. I'm bringing her home.

It had been ten years since he'd driven up this carriageway. Ten years since he'd been anywhere near the house. He wondered what sort of reception he would receive. Jocelyn was safely in Kingston, but what about May? And Clemency?

The carriageway in front of the house was empty, but a groom ran round from the servants' quarters and took charge of the trap while Cameron carried Sophie up the steps and into the gallery.

A wave of emotion swept over him. The gallery hadn't changed at all. The same slatted amber light. The same battered old rattan chairs. The same scent of cigar smoke and orange-oil polish. This gallery had been the centre of his world when he was growing up. When he'd had nightmares, he would come out here and curl up with the dogs. When there was a storm, he would stand here with Jocelyn and watch the rain sweeping the cane-pieces.

He put Sophie in the nearest armchair, and fetched a footstool to support her splint. As he did so, the grandfather clock in the ballroom struck half past seven. It would be dark soon and he would be lucky to reach Providence by midnight.

As he was straightening up, a woman hurried round the corner of the gallery, feverishly searching for something. She was dressed in a travelling-costume of crisp white brocade and a sumptuous hat brimming with white chiffon roses. In one hand she clutched a pair of white kid gloves, and over her arm hung a cloak of snowy silk damask.

Cameron saw with a pang that she had hardly aged since he'd last seen her. Still the same pretty features beneath the startling chignon of dyed grey hair. 'Hello, Clemmy,' he said.

She gave a violent start, and her face froze guiltily, as if she'd been caught in some crime. Then guilt gave way to round-eyed astonishment as she recognised him. 'Cameron, is that you?'

He reached for her free hand. 'How are you, Clemmy?' he asked. She opened her mouth, but no words came. Cameron tried again. 'I got your message, Clemmy. I went to Burntwood and brought S—'

'I can't find my purse!' she burst out. 'It was here a minute ago, I know it was, and now it's simply vanished! Oh, it's all such a *muddle*!' Her lips quivered. She still hadn't noticed Sophie.

Cameron gestured to the girl and said, 'Look, Clemmy. See whom I've brought back.'

At last Clemency saw her. Her hand flew to her cheek. 'Oh, I prayed for this to happen—but May will be so vexed!'

Cameron suppressed a flicker of impatience. 'Forget about May. I need you to look after Sophie. She needs you. Don't let her down.'

Her face worked. 'I don't know what to *do*. May will—'

'May will what?' said Great-Aunt May.

Oh hell, thought Cameron.

Great-Aunt May stood at the entrance to the ballroom, her hands serenely clasped at her waist. Despite the heat she wore a high-collared gown of grey moiré, and long gloves of pewter kid.

Her inflamed blue gaze flickered over Sophie, then locked with Cameron's. 'What,' she said, 'is the meaning of this?'

'I should have thought that was obvious,' he said. 'I've brought Sophie home.'

May permitted herself the slight tightening of the lips that was her version of a smile. 'Against her guardian's wishes, no doubt.'

'Well, of course.'

'Then she shall be returned in the morning.'

He opened his mouth to contradict her, but Clemency got there before him. 'Oh no!' she exclaimed. 'No no *no*! I absolutely will not allow that!' She rustled over to Sophie and plumped herself down in the adjacent chair. Then she realised whom she had just countermanded, and her jaw dropped.

'That will do, Clemency,' said Great-Aunt May, keeping her eyes on Cameron. 'Now go and dress yourself appropriately for dinner.'

Clemency drew a deep breath, and sat her ground. After a moment she frowned and reached beneath her, and pulled out a small rectangle of white plush embroidered with pearls. 'Why, *here* it is! Look, Sophie, my evening purse! Isn't it beautiful?'

Cameron glanced from her to Great-Aunt May, and realised with a sinking feeling that he couldn't leave Sophie with them. Which meant that he would have to take her all the way to Olivia Herapath before he could even make a start for Providence. He was wondering whether he could persuade Doshey to give him a fresh horse from the old man's stables when he heard the familiar tapping of a cane approaching. My God, he thought, but he's in Kingston. Isn't he?

Then Jocelyn walked into the gallery, and when he caught sight of Cameron he drew himself up like a battered old eagle. 'What the deuce,' he said, 'is all this rumpus?'

Plainly, he had only just arrived, for he hadn't had time to change out of his travelling clothes. He looked dusty and exhausted, and very much his age. But he took in May's glacial expression, Clemency's extraordinary outfit, and Sophie's sallow, unsmiling presence without a flicker. Finally, his gaze returned to Cameron.

For ten years Cameron had thought about this moment. He had worked out what he would say, and how he would act. Now all that deserted him. 'I thought you were in Kingston,' he muttered.

'Evidently not,' snapped the old man. 'I came back when I received a wire from Clemency. Now answer the question.'

Cameron gestured at Sophie, whose head was still bowed over the evening purse. 'Sinclair sent her to Burntwood. I—'

'I know that,' barked Jocelyn. 'It's a rum do, but there we are. You seem to have forgotten that he is her legal—'

'I don't care about that. What he did was wrong.'

'Wrong? And I suppose you're the man to decide that?'

Cameron bit back a retort. My God, he thought, all it takes is two minutes, and we're at each other's throats. But if I don't cut the Gordian knot soon, we'll be here till next week. 'I don't have time to argue,' he said. 'So I'm just going to tell you the truth, and then you can work out what to do.' He glanced at Sophie, then back to the old man. 'That's your grandchild. That's Ainsley's daughter.'

Jocelyn's eyes never wavered from his own.

From the corner of his vision, Cameron saw May go very still.

'Jocelyn,' she said calmly, 'Sinclair is the only one who—'

'Be *quiet*,' snapped Cameron. 'Haven't you done enough harm?'

May's eyes widened with shock.

'You knew who she was,' Cameron told her. 'You've known for days. But you didn't see fit to tell Jocelyn—or, heaven help us, to get her out of that godawful place.'

May opened her mouth to reply, then shut it again.

Cameron turned back to the old man. 'I need your assurance that Sophie stays here. No matter what Sinclair says.'

Jocelyn's shoulders seemed to have lost some of their parade-ground stiffness. He grasped the back of a chair. Scowling at the floor, he muttered, 'You've said your piece. Now go.'

'Not until you promise that Sophie stays here.'

Jocelyn made no reply. Cameron wondered if he'd heard.

'Jocelyn,' said May, 'this has gone far enough. I will not tolerate—'

'*Enough!*' barked Jocelyn, and May dropped her gaze. If it had been any other woman, Cameron would have pitied her.

Still grasping the back of the chair, the old man turned and looked at Sophie. There was no softening of his expression.

'What will you do?' said Cameron.

'I told you to leave.'

'Dammit, Jocelyn, if you mean to send her back to that place, I'll take her to Olivia Herapath right now.'

The old man ignored him. He couldn't take his eyes off Sophie.

She raised her head from Clemency's evening purse and gave him her solemn stare. Her lips moved, but no sound came.

'What's that you say?' Jocelyn said sharply. 'Speak up.'

She frowned and tried again. 'Uncle Jocelyn,' she said.

The old man blinked. His hand tightened on the chair.

'They burnt Pablo Grey.'

There was a silence. Then Jocelyn cleared his throat. 'Did they,' he said. He let go of the chair, and squared his shoulders. 'Well. I dare say it was quick.'

Sophie's eyes never left his face. 'Can we build a monument?'

THE JOHN CROW had been back three times, but after the moon had risen it hadn't come again. Patoo had taken over, his soft hoo-hoos echoing from hill to hill. In Jamaica the country people believe that if an owl flies into the house, a death will follow soon. Patoo frightens them. He didn't frighten Madeleine. Nothing frightened her now. Not even the ghost that crouched in the corner, watching her hammer flat the last section of leg-iron.

She put down the stone and sat back on her heels to catch her breath. At the edge of her vision, the ghost watched. A shape out of darkness, it only took form when she looked away, and dissolved into rubble when she turned to stare.

There had been a time when it had frightened her. But now she felt no more fear. No more hunger. No more pain from the gash in her arm. Even thirst had become just another companion. Nothing was left except the stone in her hand and the fragments of iron she had found in the rubble, and her determination to get out.

Before dark, she had added as much as she could to the crude progression of hand- and footholds from which she had fallen some hours before. She had managed about ten feet of it: four small ledges of stone, and three of iron, all wedged in securely enough to take her weight. Above that, the slope of the wall became gentler, which ought to make it easier—if she could get that far.

She got to her feet, and from its corner the ghost watched in silent approval. She acknowledged it with a nod. Then she shouldered the petticoat pouch and began to climb.

HE KEPT SEEING his wife's face peering up at him. There had been something animal in her expression. Yes, an animal in a trap, with no true awareness of its fate. But it was better so. Wasn't it?

Still in his riding clothes, he lay on the bed at Providence and longed for sleep. He had never felt so exhausted. And yet he couldn't relax. When would this torment end? He had never wanted her harmed. He had never wanted anyone harmed.

He rolled onto his side and reached for the small amber phial, and poured enough chloral into an inch of water to put him out. He drank it in one slow swallow, and lay back and waited.

The first wave was always the best. Soft warm radiance warming his flesh. Clarity and confidence suffusing his limbs. Power in his veins. He shut his eyes and drifted away.

The chimes of the clock wrenched him back to consciousness. He was in darkness. He rolled off the bed and stumbled to the window. Outside, the moon had risen, and all was peaceful and still. The housekeeper and the stableboy had gone to spend the Free Come holiday with their families. So when he heard the skitter of a horse's hoofs down below he froze, breathless and horrified. No one ever came this way. The track ended at Providence. Nor could it be a messenger from Fever Hill, for no black would ride like that in the dark.

He cast about for a weapon, and saw the candlestick beside the bed. He took hold of it and softly made his way through the house towards the gallery.

A man had just climbed the steps. He was tall, with unruly fair hair, and, though his back was turned, Sinclair knew him at once.

His dismissal of the servants now seemed the purest madness. He was alone with a man who coveted his wife and wished him ill.

Then he saw the familiar horse tethered to the mounting-stone at the foot of the steps: a big, clean-limbed grey hunter from Fever Hill. The old man's horse. His brother must have been at Fever Hill, and had so contrived to worm his way back into the old man's affections that he had come away with one of his horses.

Sinclair's skin prickled with loathing. His hand on the candlestick became slick with sweat. In that moment he understood the urge to kill. He understood Cain.

His brother turned and saw him. 'You're not going to do much damage with that,' he said, indicating the candlestick.

'A curious notion,' said Sinclair. 'I was seeking a fresh candle.' He put the candlestick on a side table, and placed both hands on the back of a chair. Calm, calm, he told himself. This fool is no match for you. Out loud he said, 'What brings you here at this hour?'

'I was worried about Madeleine,' his brother said, matching his conversational tone. 'I didn't like the sound of your rest cure.'

How blunt, thought Sinclair. 'I don't see why,' he replied. 'It is entirely appropriate. And under strict medical supervision.'

'Where is she?' asked his brother.

Sinclair moistened his lips. 'My wife is no longer here.' He was gratified to see his brother's astonishment. 'She left,' he volunteered. 'She took a horse and left.'

'When? Where did she go?'

The exchange had put fresh heart into him. This was going to be easy. 'I imagine that she has returned to Fever Hill.'

His brother shook his head. 'I've just come from there.'

Sinclair allowed a silence to grow. Then he said, 'And what took you to Fever Hill?'

His brother threw him an impatient look. 'I brought Sophie back. And, yes, I know you're her guardian, but I told the old man who she is, so from now on I don't think he'll be so ready to let you play the autocrat.'

Sinclair swayed. The child and the old man. Together. The child knew about the pickney. If she told the old man— He felt sick. Terror buzzed in his skull like an angry wasp. No. Wait. If she had said anything, then his brother would be crowing about that too. Calm, calm. He ran his fingers over his throat, his thoughts racing.

'What's the *matter* with you?' said his brother.

'What?'

'I've asked you three times, when did she leave?'

Sinclair thought for a moment. 'Some time around dawn.'

'*Dawn?* What the hell have you been doing?'

'I've spent all day looking for her,' he said, indicating his dusty riding clothes. 'I've only just returned.'

This was easy. All he had to do was keep his nerve.

His brother rubbed his hand over his face. 'D'you have any idea where she was heading?'

'North,' said Sinclair without hesitation. 'A field hand saw her heading north. Which is why I assumed she was making for Fever Hill. She must have taken a wrong turn.'

His brother swallowed it whole. It was beautiful. 'Saddle your horse,' he said. 'We're going to find her.'

'In the dark?'

'There's a moon.'

Sinclair studied him for a moment. 'Very well,' he said. 'I shall fetch my hat.'

Why had he worried? This sugar-planter was no match for him. He would pass the test that God had sent him, and he would prevail.

STILL SOME HOURS till the sun comes up, and Evie has dropped asleep in the house, and Grace is out on her step, sitting in the moonshine and looking at that fresh grave at the back of the yard.

She got her pipe ready for a little smoke, and she got her bankra ready to do a little obeah, to ask again for a sign who kill her boy. She asked before, but no sign came. If only she could clean up this confusion in her heart. But she so tangle-up with mourning and worry and black monster hate, she about reaching her rope end.

Strange, the way things work out. Usually on the eve of First August everybody singing and partying, to mark the day they mancipate the slaves. But not this night; not here. This First August eve, they been too busy keeping nine-night for Victory.

Last week, soon as word of the death went out, everybody came for the burying. Brother, sister, cousin, aunt. From all over Trelawny and from foreign they came. And now, on the nine-night, everybody arrived again. Brought lot, lot a food. Curried land crab and pepperpot, bammy cakes and hot pickle. Rum and ginger wine. And Grace and Evie were cooking since dawn. Hard-dough and roast breadfruit, jerked hog and chocho pie. And duppy own feast, too besides.

Dark falls, and everybody sitting round in the dead room, eating, singing, telling story. Waiting for duppy to come. Duppy feast spread out on banana leaf in the middle, nobody touch.

And roundabout midnight, old Cecilia said, 'I feel him oh I feel him: hot wind rushing through.' And people started to shiver and shake, and Evie was near to crying.

And old Cecilia felt him—but Grace she *seen* him too. And he was one dirty little duppy. No shoe, no Sunday best for him. Just the saggy old blue pants and yellow shirt he liked so much.

So then came the time for Grace to shoo him out to the graves, to tell him: Go way and never come back. But she couldn't do it, not with her own self son. And old Cecilia seen that and took it on, to give Grace time to get her spirit back.

'Duppy,' said Cecilia loud and polite, 'we know you come. We glad you come. See, duppy, we give you feast. Boil fowl and white rice and good white rum. We do everything for you.'

Then Cecilia looked to Grace, to see if she better yet. And Grace nodded, for she was ready to take it on from here. But it *hard*. Hardest thing she ever did in life. She stood up straight, and she said, 'Duppy! Go on to you rest now, and not to do we no harm. We no want to see you again, duppy. So no come back.'

After that they removed the duppy feast into the yard, and put cross-mark charcoal on the door—and then it done, and people left. Cecilia said, 'Well, Grace, we done with Victory now. We shooed him to the grave and planted him good. Now he at peace.'

True. Victory at peace now. But Grace never know peace again.

Out of her bankra, she takes an old syrup bottle of earth from the new grave, and some parrot bones, and scrip-scraps of lizard parts. Still some few hours till the sun comes up, so she's getting ready to ask again for a sign who done this thing. Could be any sort of a sign. Bird on the roof. Man in the road. Mark in the dirt. She'll know it when it comes.

CHAPTER TEN

Madeleine lay back, gasping and staring at the moon. She was so relieved that she wanted to retch.

A trickle of pebbles rattled down into the sinkhole, warning her that she was still on the edge. She rolled onto her front and half-crawled, half dragged herself away until it was safe to stand up. Her head was swimming. She took a deep breath of the warm night air, and smelt sweat and dust and the coppery tang of blood.

Beneath the ring of crickets was the faint, continuous roar of a river. She held her breath. The Martha Brae had its source in the Cockpits. Was that what she could hear? If it was, and if she could find it, she could follow it out of the hills.

Twenty feet ahead, the calabash tree loomed in the moonlight. She made out the boulder where she had rested, a lifetime ago. Around it thorn bushes, and the spiky rosette of a wild pine.

In Sophie's gazetteer it said that if country people get lost, they can sometimes get a little moisture from a wild pine. She stumbled over to it and fell to her knees in the dust. She broke off an outer leaf, and then another. A trickle of moisture ran into her palm. It was no more than an eggcupful, stale and gritty with midges, but she gulped it down. She snapped off another leaf and sucked the bitter sap. It would have to do until she reached the river.

As she twisted herself round to rest against the trunk of the calabash tree, something tilted beneath her heel. She looked down and saw a faint metallic gleam. She reached out, and her fingers closed on the cold steel of Ben Kelly's gun.

THE CANE-FIELDS can be eerie at night. The ghostly white slash of the marled track cutting through the dark. The tall, whispering cane. Yes, in the cane-fields at night, it's easy to believe in duppies, and in the sorcery that can take a man's shadow and nail it to a tree.

Cameron led his horse down to the irrigation ditch, and thought about Madeleine out here on her own. Why had he allowed Sinclair to take her to Providence? Why had he wasted so much time?

For two hours they had been working their way north through the hill-pastures of Turnaround and Corner Pen—*No, sah, nobody see Miss Maddy heah about*—and always Sinclair rode beside him: silent, and very slightly aggrieved. As if this were some elaborate game that had gone on for just a little too long.

Cameron glanced over his shoulder and saw his brother standing at the top of the ditch, watching him. He can't have done anything to her, Cameron told himself. He isn't capable of that. Of many things, perhaps. But not of that. So why did he feel this tightening in his chest, this feeling that events were veering out of control?

Above him, Sinclair tapped the reins against his thigh. 'This is pointless. I'm going back. I shall start again when it's light.'

Cameron led his horse back up the side of the ditch. 'For a man whose wife is missing, you're showing remarkably little concern.'

'Why? Because I don't indulge in vulgar displays of emotion?'

'What's wrong with you? Don't you care?'

'Not nearly as much as you.'

That's when Cameron lost his temper. One moment he was watching Sinclair gather the reins, and the next he was grabbing him by the belt and hauling him out of the saddle and throwing him to the ground with a *whump* that sent the dust flying up.

A red haze misted his vision. He looked at Sinclair lying on his back, and as if it were really happening, he saw himself flipping him over and pounding his face to a pulp. It took a massive effort to put his hands behind his back and step away.

Sinclair sat up gingerly, coughing the dust from his lungs. 'Have you completely lost your reason?' he said.

'Tell me where she is.'

Still coughing, Sinclair brushed the dust from his riding jacket. 'I don't *know* where she is,' he spat.

Cameron reached down and grabbed him by the collar and hauled him to his feet, and Sinclair's arm flashed out, and Cameron felt warmth and wetness opening up across his chest. He looked down and saw a dark diagonal stain blotting his shirt.

He took a step back. Christ, he thought, he's got a knife.

He put a hand to his ribs, and it came away wet. A long, shallow slash that already burned like the devil.

Sinclair had staggered back, and was staring down at the knife.

'Put that thing down,' said Cameron.

'*You* attacked *me*,' muttered Sinclair. 'It wasn't my fault.'

'It never is,' snarled Cameron. 'Now put the bloody thing down.'

Sinclair shot him a look of pure hatred. 'You're glad I did it, aren't you? Now you can run squealing back to the old man, and tell him how wicked I am, how unfit to inherit—'

'Oh, for Christ's sake. Take it! Take the whole bloody estate! I don't want it! I just want to find Madeleine!'

'Oh, you do want it,' cried Sinclair. 'It's all you ever think about!'

Cameron moved forward and made a feint with his right hand, and Sinclair went for it, and with his left Cameron grasped his brother's wrist and gave it a vicious twist, and with a howl Sinclair dropped the knife, and Cameron caught it.

Now it was his turn to look down at the knife in his hands.

'You'd do it, wouldn't you?' cried Sinclair, cradling his wrist. 'Your own brother. You'd kill me like a dog in the road.'

Cameron looked from his brother's clammy face to the dull grey metal in his hand. He remembered as if it were yesterday what it had felt like to kill. The terror and the disgust and the incredible feeling of power. And he turned and flung the knife as far as he could into the cane. 'Get out of my sight,' he said.

SINCLAIR RODE BACK to Providence shaking with humiliation and rage. His mind teemed with fearful images. His wife's animal gaze. The crippled child telling the old man everything. The mockery in his brother's eyes as he threw away the knife.

By four o'clock the hunting lodge at Providence loomed into sight. He ran up the steps to the gallery and poured himself a brandy and soda, and drank it pacing up and down. He had been tempted to go straight to Fever Hill—he'd even started to ride that way, to throw his brother off the scent. But he knew that first he had to see for himself that she was dead. Then he would be free to go to Fever Hill and deal with the child. Only then would he know peace.

The thought of going back into the Cockpits, alone and in darkness, was almost more than he could bear. But he told himself that this, too, was part of God's great test.

DAY JUST ABOUT commence to light, and Grace must a dozed asleep, but then she comes awake with a start.

At first she thinks that everything fine: she sitting out on her step, neck little stiff, but everything fine. Then she sees the new grave by the garden cherry tree, and she knows that it never be fine again.

Then she hears someone out in her yard. Who got the nerve to intrude on Victory nine-night? She starts up, hot and vex. 'Who there?' she yells out. 'Go way! Get out a me yard!'

A boy moves out from the shadows. Grace about to yell again, when she astonished to see that he buckra boy. Hat in hand, he comes over, and she sees that he whistle-thin and ripped about, with face tight-stretch and full of mourning, though he not like to show. And peculiar strange, him eye *green*, like puss-eye. Grace starts to consider if he some sort of sign.

Then she thinks again. This boy no sign. This just a damn intruding disrespectful buckra boy.

'Didn't I just tell you?' she blazes at him. 'Get out a me yard!'

But he just stands before her. 'Sorry to trouble you, ma'am,' he says, nice and polite. 'But Grace McFarlane the name you got?'

Grace so surprise, she near forgets to stay vex. Cho! She says, 'Where you from, boy, that you not know Grace?'

'I from foreign, ma'am,' he says. 'Ben Kelly the name I got.'

He talks damn peculiar when he tries talk potwah. Grace dislikes when buckra do that, for they only do it to crack a laugh—except for Cameron soldier-man, who talk it since a boy. But this boy only does it for respect. And that all right.

She sits again on her step, and lights her pipe. She says, 'You walking late, puss-eye boy. This a bad place for buckra. Full a skull laughter and evilness and duppy.'

'Duppy?' he says. 'That's like a ghost, yeh?'

Hn! He not frighten easy; but he *un*easy, that plain to see. He takes deep breath and says, 'I got a deal to do with you, ma'am.'

Grace so surprise, she near to choke on her pipe. What sort a deal she going to do with a meagre down-class mocho like this?

She about to blaze into him again, and he sees it, and still he decides to take a chance on what he got to say. 'You know the girl Sophie?' he says. 'The sick girl up at the buckra house? Well, she thinks she's lost her shadow, and I need for you to get it back.'

Grace gives him a long, hard look. She says, 'You fooling me up, boy. Buckra begging after black medicine? Cho!'

'No, ma'am,' he says, still respectful. 'I not fooling you up.'

But Grace wants no more talk about little buckra girl. All of a sudden her heart so full up with mourning and destroyful feeling, she about ready to burst. 'Go *way*,' she says. 'Get out a me yard. Why I should help buckra child when my own self son dead?'

By now Grace getting hot and vex, and wishing to hell this damn boy just get out a her yard. But then she remembers that little buckra girl playing with her boy. Talking a stream, and telling him story. Making him laugh. And one time that crazy child put hot quattie on her arm, just to discover whether buckra books tell the truth about if branding not to hurt.

So all this raises a crazy black confusion in her head till she don't know *what* to think. So she snaps out at him, 'So now you tell Grace why she *should* help little buckra girl.'

And buckra boy looks at her long, long, and never turns way him eye. 'Because,' he says, 'I got something you want.'

That so surprises Grace, for first time in days she cracks a laugh. She looks him up and down, and she says, 'Boy, you got nothing I want. In a year or two, maybe. But not this day. Oh, no.'

But buckra boy just looks at her steady with him green puss-eye, and he says, 'Ma'am, you're wrong about that. You get Sophie's shadow back, and I'll tell you who killed your boy.'

SHE WAS DIZZY with hunger, and it was becoming harder to think in straight lines. There was something important she had to do, but she couldn't remember what. The heat had become oppressive. Like an underwater swimmer she waded through the hot green shade. The crickets were deafening.

Strange how quickly the thirst had returned. Hours before, when she'd found the river, she had stumbled down the crumbling red banks and into the fast-flowing water, and in a few long, cool green swallows, the thirst had become a distant memory.

But then she'd forced herself back onto the track and started off again, and something had gone wrong. She'd been so absorbed in pushing through the undergrowth that she hadn't noticed the track veer away from the bank. Now she couldn't even hear the river any more. She was alone in the high forest, with no idea where she was.

She had been walking for hours, since it had started to get light. The revolver in its pouch bumped against her thigh. Why was it still there? She remembered standing on the river bank and deciding to throw it in. After that, nothing.

At last she reached a clearing where dragonflies swam in the dusty sunlight. She stumbled out into the sharp, splintered light, and the rank smells of growth and decay. She crossed the clearing to the shade on the other side, and stopped for breath beneath an ironwood tree. She tried to go on, but her legs wouldn't move.

Just a little rest, she told herself. And then you can go on.

She curled up among the ferns beneath the tree and shut her eyes. She took deep breaths of the warm green air. She slept.

She dreamed she was back in the Forbidden Kingdom. She was curled up in the snow, watching Cameron riding away. He had almost disappeared when she saw him turn and start back for her. She watched him dismount and come towards her through the long grass. 'I knew you would come,' she said.

'Thank goodness I've found you,' said Sinclair.

With a cry she woke up.

He stood on the path about eight feet away, looking tense and frightened. His eyes flickered over her, then darted away.

Sweat trickled down her sides. She sank her fingers into the leaf mould, and felt a tree root beneath her hand. Something to hold on to. 'You left me,' she said. 'You left me there all night.'

He blinked. 'I was delayed. When I reached Providence there was a message about your sister. She wanted to come home. I had to make arrangements to bring her back to Fever Hill.'

Did he truly expect her to believe that?

Behind him the clearing was weirdly peaceful. Sinclair's horse put down its head and cropped the grass.

'Your sister is well,' Sinclair said, as if she had asked a question. 'Come. I shall take you to her.' He put out his hand.

She pressed back against the tree. 'Why did you leave me in that place?'

'I didn't "leave" you.'

'Sinclair—'

Irritably he tossed his head. 'Why won't you believe me? Why won't you accept that what happened to that child was an accident?'

A cold wave washed over her. 'You said Sophie was safe. You—'

'And so she is,' he snapped. 'You're always so eager to believe the worst! It's your duty as my wife to accept what I say.'

She was hardly listening. *What happened to that child was an accident.* What did he mean? What had he done?

'I forgot about him,' he said tetchily. 'That's all. It wasn't my fault. Why must you be so determined to tell the world?'

Her thoughts rearranged themselves in a swift, seismic falling into place. Victory in the hothouse. *I forgot about him.* She remembered Sophie's silence after the little boy's death, and Sinclair's sudden decision to send her to Burntwood. She remembered what he had said at the sinkhole. *I can't let you tell anyone.* It had a weird kind of logic, but it couldn't be true, could it?

'Enough of this nonsense,' he snapped. 'Come with me at once.'

She drew her legs closer beneath her, and as she did so, the revolver in its pouch nudged her side.

Until then she had forgotten about it. But now in a heartbeat she took in its weight against her hip, and the fact that she was alone with a man who had taken a life, and who perceived her as a threat; the fact that she had a weapon, and that she was going to have to use it. *Well, Maddy, we'll just have to do it on our own.*

I can't, she thought. I can't I can't I can't.

Yes, you can, came the reply inside her head. You're a Durrant. This is what Durrants do. It's in your blood. No one will blame you for it. He left you to die, didn't he? And if you do it, Sophie is safe.

All this raced through her mind in the seconds while he waited on the path. She slid her hand into the pouch and her fingers closed on the smooth steel. With a sense of disbelief she drew out the revolver and pointed it at him.

At any other time his astonishment would have been comical.

His blue eyes widened, and his mouth fell open.

With her back against the tree she struggled to her feet. She was shaking so much that she had to grasp the revolver in both hands to keep it steady. 'Turn round,' she said as levelly as she could, 'and go back the way you came. Walk. I'm taking the horse.'

He looked from her to the revolver, and back again. He seemed more vexed than alarmed. 'Have you taken leave of your senses? Give that to me at once.'

'Do as I say.'

'Don't be ridiculous. You're not going to—'

'I mean it, Sinclair.'

And what frightened her most was that she *wanted* to do it. All she had to do was squeeze the trigger and Sophie would be safe, and she would be free.

'Do you realise,' he said, 'that you've just signed your own committal papers? A deranged, half-naked woman pointing a weapon at her own husband? They'll lock you up for ever. You'll spend the rest of your life in a straitjacket.'

'Go away,' she said.

'A straitjacket,' he repeated, and started towards her.

She took aim and fired.

CAMERON FOUND HER in a clearing, curled up beneath an ironwood tree. In the green shade her face had an underwater pallor. He thought she was dead.

Then she opened her eyes and gave him a dark, unfocused stare, and the world tilted back into place.

He left his horse and fell to his knees beside her and gathered her into his arms. 'My God,' he said, 'my God.'

He wanted to tell her what it had been like to see her lying there dead, but his throat had closed, and he couldn't get out the words.

She twisted out of his arms and touched his face with her fingers. Then she saw the scab on his ribs. 'What's this?'

'Nothing. I—got in a fight.'

Only then did he register that she was dressed in some kind of cambric undergarment, its elaborate pin-tucks and satin ribbons bizarrely at odds with the scratches on her arms and shins.

'A fight?' she said. 'When? With whom?'

He took off his shooting jacket and put it round her shoulders. 'It doesn't matter. It's all right now. It's all right.' He knew that he was saying that to reassure himself.

For hours he had lived with the terror that she was dead. From that first moment when he'd stumbled down to the edge of the sinkhole and seen the crumpled muslin at the bottom and thought it was her. Then tracking Sinclair, knowing his brother was tracking her.

Still sick with relief, he went to his horse and unhooked the water bottle. When he gave it to her, she drank with the concentration of an animal. Then he took out his handkerchief and soaked it in water, and gently cleaned the blood from her hands.

He said, 'I heard a shot. What happened?'

She picked up a pouch that had been lying beside her, and gave it to him. Then she sat back on her heels and clasped her arms about her waist. 'I thought I could kill him,' she said. 'But I couldn't. I'm not—not who I thought I was. So I shot the tree instead.'

He opened the pouch. Inside was a small Lee-Remington service revolver. In disbelief he emptied the chamber into his palm. There was one round missing. He looked up and scanned the empty clearing. 'What happened then?' he asked.

She hunched her shoulders against the memory. 'He was terrified. He ran back to his horse and rode away.'

'Where? Where did he go?'

'I don't know. Didn't you meet him on the path?'

He hesitated. 'Perhaps he took a different one. There are several in this part of the forest.'

She was watching him as he said it, and he saw understanding dawn in her face. 'You don't believe me, do you?' she said, her teeth chattering. 'It's because I lied to you, isn't it? I lied to you, so you don't believe me now.'

'No,' he said, 'no, that's not it at all.'

'I told you why I lied. I tried to explain—'

'Madeleine, *look* at me. No, look at me. What happened before doesn't matter. All that matters is that you're safe.'

She was looking at him as if she wanted to believe him, but couldn't.

'Sophie's safe too,' he told her. 'I took her out of Burntwood, she's with the old man. We'll go down to Eden, and get you some food and some clothes, and then we can go to Fever Hill and see her. Everything will be sorted out.'

'How?' she said harshly. 'He'll tell them one version, and I'll tell them another. He'll say I'm mad, he'll say I'm making it up.'

'Madeleine—'

'He can do what he likes, Cameron. He has all the power.'

'Not after what he did—'

'Yes! Even then! Don't you see? What he did won't have any consequences. It won't *matter*. That's how it works.'

'Everything has consequences,' he said.

SINCLAIR WAS ENORMOUSLY relieved when he reached the edge of the forest. But as he emerged blinking into the glare, he was startled to find that he didn't recognise the way ahead.

Still, he thought, no harm done. A glance at the sun gave him a rough idea of a northward course, and he put his horse forward along the most likely track.

Despite the heat of the afternoon, he was in excellent spirits. The moment she had brought out that revolver, he had known that he was saved. A half-naked madwoman brandishing a gun. Even if she survived, no one would believe a word she said. And the sister would be tarred with the same brush—insanity in the family. Poor, handsome young Reverend Lawe. All Society would sympathise after what he'd endured. It would be easy to find another wife. And she would bear him a son, and his brother would be vanquished, and he would come into his inheritance at last.

As he rounded a bend, an animal shot across the track. His horse reared and he lost his stirrups and fell. For a moment he lay winded, listening to his horse galloping off down the track. Then he sat up, wincing and rubbing his head. There seemed to be no serious harm done. A bruised hip, a slight contusion at the back of the head. His horse, however, was nowhere to be seen. He got to his feet and brushed himself off. Glancing round, he saw with a start that a little pickney girl, a mulatto, was crouching on the slope above, watching him.

A stroke of luck, he thought. Here's just the creature to run and retrieve the horse. He called to her to come down, but to his surprise she did not respond. He repeated the command more sharply. Still no response. It was a confounded nuisance, but he would have to make his way on foot.

It was another hour before he could admit to himself that he was lost. Instead of leaving the Cockpits, he seemed to be heading deeper into them. The track had become treacherous: to his left the ground rose steeply, but to his right it fell away into a dizzying ravine.

He stopped to rest by a thorn tree. The air shimmered with heat. The glare off the white rocks pained his head. The rasp of crickets assailed his ears—and behind it, a great, watching silence.

Once again he struggled to his feet, and this time his heart leapt to see a man on the track, some distance ahead. He was saved: the man was white. True, he was as ragged and filthy as any backwoods black, but he was a white man nonetheless.

'You there!' Sinclair shouted. 'Come down here at once!'

To his consternation, the man made no move to obey. He stood on the track with his hands at his sides, silently watching.

Outraged, Sinclair started up the slope towards him. But as he drew nearer he saw that the 'man' was in fact just a boy, with an unsettling resemblance to the urchin from Fitzroy Square.

Which, he told himself angrily, is arrant nonsense. Yet he couldn't help glancing about him for that other one, the hunchback with the flame-coloured hair. And for one unnerving moment he even thought he saw him, some twenty yards behind. But it was only the little mulatto girl who had watched him earlier.

This time she was accompanied by two tall blacks: hill Negroes, by the look of them. Relief washed over him. Now there were grown men to assist him instead of children.

He turned to find that the white boy had also been joined by blacks: a full-grown male, and three squat and ancient Negresses.

A scatter of pebbles behind made him spin about, and he overbalanced and nearly fell. Some thirty feet above him, another Negress stood looking down with her hands on her hips. She was younger than the others, and slender; but although her skin was mahogany, not sable, the glare was too bright to make out her face.

'You there!' he shouted. 'Come down and help me at once!'

She made no reply. She just stood there with her hands on her hips, a pose he found astonishingly insolent.

He opened his mouth to administer a sharp rebuke. But as he did so, she began to pick her way down the slope towards him, and as she drew nearer, he recognised her. And understood.

CHAPTER ELEVEN

March 1896 — eight months later

The service had ended and the congregation was filing out. Through the dust of departing carriages Cameron spotted Cornelius Traherne on the other side of the road, talking to Jocelyn, Clemency and Sophie. Madeleine was nowhere to be seen. God damn it to hell. She hadn't slipped away already, had she? Not *again*.

Sophie caught sight of him and waved so vigorously that she nearly fell over. She was wearing her new light walking-splint, of which she was immensely proud. 'Dr Pritchard has pronounced my lungs quite sound, and the tuberculosis practically *vanquished*,' she had told him on her last visit to Eden—which had been an historic one, for Clemency had brought her all on her own and had driven the trap herself. 'I shall have a limp,' Sophie had told him, as if it were a badge of honour, 'but Grandpapa says it will take more than that to keep me from whatever I put my mind to.'

Clemency had spotted him too, and shyly lifted a hand in greeting. He tipped his hat to her and forced a smile. She was gaining daily in assurance, now that May had taken to spending all her time upstairs. And her health had improved immeasurably since Jocelyn had transferred the management of the house to her.

Cameron turned and made his way up the church path, taking off his hat as he reached the porch. St Peter's was empty, except for the curate and a trio of lady volunteers tidying the flowers. No Madeleine. He swore under his breath. The curate shot him a look.

Cameron went back into the glare of the churchyard. Since Sinclair's death he had seen her exactly seven times, always in the company of others. For the most part she was edgy and monosyllabic, or worse: polite. Since the funeral she hadn't left Fever Hill except to go to church. Nothing out of the ordinary there. No respectable widow would make calls for at least a year after her husband's death. Except that with Madeleine, he felt there was more to it than that.

In his darker moments, Cameron cursed his brother. He wished he could honestly grieve for Sinclair, but he was too conscious that, for his brother, death had been an escape. He would have been crushed by the public disclosure of his guilt. As it turned out there had been no disclosure. Grace had been content to let it lie.

Cameron had gone to her and told her who had killed her son as soon as Madeleine had told him, the week after the funeral. 'In a sense,' he had said to Grace, 'one might regard Sinclair's death as—I don't know, perhaps an act of God?' Grace had studied his face for a long time, her features unreadable. 'Maybe so,' was all she had said.

He rounded the corner of the church, and saw Madeleine standing before the Lawe family plot, where a new stone commemorated the death of Sinclair Euan Lawe, suddenly in a riding accident at the age of thirty-one.

With a spasm of anger Cameron saw that she was still wearing the dull black crepe of deepest mourning. He'd been blunt about that the last time they'd met. 'I don't understand you, Madeleine. What is this about? You didn't love him.'

'No,' she had sombrely agreed. 'No one did.'

To begin with, he had wondered if in some perverse way she felt responsible for Sinclair's accident. 'Why should you feel guilty because he lost his way and fell down a ravine?'

Then he realised that it was not the manner of his brother's death that had brought about her withdrawal, but the fact of it. Sinclair's death had given her back her freedom. She had benefited from it. How could she not experience guilt?

Madeleine had seen him, and was waiting composedly beneath her parasol of dull black silk. He had to admit that black suited her. She gave Cameron a meaningless smile and offered him her hand. He took off his hat and pressed her black-gloved fingertips and bowed. For a while they walked without speaking.

To break the silence he said, 'Sophie looks well.'

'She is,' she replied. 'And she can't wait to show you her new treasure. Mrs Herapath gave it to her. It's a photograph of our mother.' She seemed perfectly at ease with him when they kept to neutral ground. It made him want to shake her. Here they were, making small talk when all he wanted to say to her was, *Marry me. Promise that you'll be my wife. I can't go on like this.*

'Cameron, I'm sorry,' she said with disarming suddenness.

He coloured. 'For what,' he muttered.

'I've treated you appallingly. But I needed to think about things. To make sense of what happened. I know it's been hard for you.'

'It doesn't matter.'

'Yes, it does.'

They exchanged glances, and his heart leapt.

They had reached the overgrown part of the churchyard, and were drawing near to the Durrant graves. Cameron watched her stop to read the legend on her maternal grandfather's tomb. *Aristide Durrant, 1813–1868. Of Your Charity, Pray for His Soul.*

'Madeleine,' he said, 'it's been eight months.'

Her eyes remained stubbornly fixed on the tomb.

'Eight months,' he repeated, 'and you've never allowed me to say it. Well, this time you can't stop me.' He reached out and gently took her hand in his. She tried to pull away, but he kept his hold. Slowly he turned it palm upwards and unbuttoned the three little black jet buttons of her glove. Then he bent and kissed the soft, pale skin on the inside of her wrist. He heard the sharp intake of her breath.

Dizzily, he straightened up. 'You know that I love you,' he said, still holding her hand. 'And I thought—at least I hoped—that you—' He broke off. 'Marry me. I want you to marry me.'

She made no reply. Her head was bowed. She was biting her lip.

He drew her closer to him. 'If you want a long engagement,' he said, 'then you shall have it. I just—I just need you to tell me that some day, in the future, you will be my wife.'

At last she raised her head and looked at him. Her face was pale and agitated, her eyes bright with tears. 'Not here,' she said.

'Madeleine—'

'Not here.' She twisted from his grasp and stepped away.

A terrible realisation swept over him. If he could not bring her to accept him now, he would lose her for ever. He would end up like Jocelyn: hopelessly longing for a love he had lost decades before.

'If you've stopped loving me,' he said, struggling to keep his voice steady, 'it would be kinder to tell me now. I'll never trouble you again. But God damn it, Madeleine, just tell me.'

'I haven't stopped loving you,' she said over her shoulder. 'You know I haven't.'

'Then *what*? You can't put it off any longer.'

At last, to his incredulous relief, she nodded. 'You're right,' she said. 'We can't put it off any longer. Come. Let's walk.'

They turned and took the path that ran the length of the church-yard. Patiently he waited for her to begin. 'When two people marry,' she said at last, 'neither of them has any real idea whether it will work. And if it goes wrong, there's no way out. It's irrevocable.'

'True,' he said slowly. 'But I don't see what—'

'That's what happened with Sinclair. We made each other miser-able, but we were trapped.' She caught her lower lip in her teeth. 'I couldn't bear it if that happened with you. I couldn't—'

'But why should we make each other miserable? I'm not Sinclair.'

She gave him her quick wide smile. 'Of course you're not.' Then the smile faded. 'It's not you I'm worried about.'

'What do you mean?'

But she shook her head, and turned away.

He felt mystified. She seemed to be blaming herself for something she couldn't bring herself to name. 'Madeleine,' he began, 'I don't pretend to have understood Sinclair. But whatever went wrong between you, it wasn't your fault. There was something in him that wasn't right. And it began a long time ago. Long before he met you.'

'I'm not sure about that,' she put in, startling him.

'What do you mean?'

She dug at the gravel with her heel. 'Sinclair had a horror of me from the very first night we were married. No, don't interrupt. I know it's true. Something about me truly horrified him.'

That was so absurd that he nearly laughed. 'Well, I can assure you that there's nothing about you which "truly horrifies" me.'

'But you don't know that, do you?' she said quickly. 'And you *won't* know for sure until we're married. And then it'll be too late.'

He cleared his throat. 'Well,' he began awkwardly, 'as regards—um, that side of things—one can usually sort of—I mean, if there's real regard, if there's love . . .'

'But there's no guarantee,' she insisted.

'Well—I suppose not, but—'

'I won't take that risk. I won't have you look at me the way he did. As if I were some sort of monster.' Her tone was decided.

His heart sank. He felt as if he stood at the edge of a high cliff, looking down over the edge. 'Then what do you suggest we do?' he said. 'You can't possibly want to end things between us simply because of some theoretical risk that it might go wrong.'

They had reached the end of the path, where the silk-cotton tree towered overhead. She came to a halt, and stood there stabbing at the gravel with the point of her parasol.

'Madeleine,' he said. 'Whatever it is, you've got to tell me—'

'I'll only marry you,' she broke in with peculiar intensity, 'if we find out beforehand whether it's going to be all right.'

He blinked. Then understanding dawned. 'Are you telling me that you'll marry me if we—if we sort this side of things out first?' he said.

She nodded. 'And *only* if it turns out that it's all right.'

He raised his head and looked up into the branches of the silk-cotton tree: at the vivid emerald leaves and the creamy white flowers against the brilliant, tender blue of the sky. How beautiful, he thought. The most beautiful sight he'd ever seen.

He turned back to her, and reached out and took her hand in his. Then he met her eyes, and gave her a slight smile. 'I think,' he said, 'I can agree to that.'

MICHELLE PAVER

'I think of my books as very detailed day-dreams,' says Michelle Paver. 'The sort of things I used to think about when I was on my way to court during a long trial.'

Until 1998, she earned her living as a lawyer and was forced to confine her writing to weekends and early mornings. But after an encouraging response to an early draft of *Without Charity*, Paver bravely gave up her job before she received a publishing contract for the book. It was a decision she says she had to make. 'I had got to the point where I felt I had to make my dream of becoming a writer happen.'

Three books later she has absolutely no regrets about leaving the law. 'I earn a fraction of what I made in a big City law firm, but I have about ten million times more fun.' Part of the fun is travelling, and Paver spent three weeks out in Jamaica researching the background to *The Shadow Catcher*. She stayed with her cousin, Alec, who organised a guide to take her round the island.

'I wrote pages and pages of notes because I didn't want to forget anything. I took a few photographs but I didn't really use them. For me it's not just the view I want to be able to remember but also smells, sounds, and the way things feel. There's no substitute for actually being there, surrounded by all that incredible, exuberant vegetation, gazing up at the tree ferns, smelling the lilies, listening to the parrots . . . and getting soaked in a tropical downpour, then bitten by mozzies!'

She especially remembers her first glimpse of a silk-cotton tree, known as a duppy tree in Jamaican folklore, on the driveway of her cousin's estate. 'Duppies are evil ghosts that sometimes take up residence in the tree trunks. This particular tree had a number of rusty old nails embedded in the bark, a clear sign, as I knew from my research, that someone had been casting spells. To actually see that was fascinating.'

PETER ROBINSON

THE SUMMER THAT NEVER WAS

Luke Armitage and Graham
Marshall. Two very different
boys from very different
times, both missing in
mysterious circumstances.

One of them is a new case
for Chief Inspector Alan
Banks's team, the other was
his childhood friend. Banks
is determined to see justice
done for both.

1

Trevor Dickinson was hung over and bad-tempered when he turned up for work on Monday morning. His mouth tasted like the bottom of a birdcage, his head was throbbing like the speakers at a heavy-metal concert, and his stomach was lurching like a car with a dirty carburettor. He had already drunk half a bottle of milk of magnesia and swallowed four extra-strength paracetamol, with no noticeable effect.

When he arrived at the site, Trevor found he had to wait until the police had cleared away the last of the demonstrators before he could start work. There were five left, all sitting cross-legged in the field. *Environmentalists*.

He looked around for some clue as to why anyone would want to save those particular few acres. The fields belonged to a farmer who had been put out of business by mad cow disease and foot-and-mouth. As far as Trevor knew, there weren't any rare pink-nippled fart warblers that couldn't nest anywhere else in the entire country; nor were there any ivy-leafed lark's turds lurking in the hedgerows. There weren't even any trees, unless you counted the shabby row of poplars that grew between the fields and the A1, stunted and choked from years of exhaust fumes.

The police cleared away the demonstrators by picking them up bodily and carting them off to a van, then they gave the go-ahead to Trevor and his fellow workers. The weekend's rain had muddied the ground, which made manoeuvring difficult, but Trevor was a skilled operator, and he soon got his dipper shovel well below the topsoil, hoisting his loads high and dumping them into the waiting lorry. He handled the levers with dexterity, scooping as much as the power shovel could hold, then straightening it so as not to spill any when he lifted it up and over to the lorry.

Trevor had been at work for well over two hours when he thought he saw something sticking out of the dirt.

Leaning forward and rubbing condensation from the window of the cab, he squinted to see what it was, and when he saw, it took his breath away. He was looking at a human skull, and what was worse was that it seemed to be looking right back at him.

ALAN BANKS DIDN'T FEEL in the least bit hung over, but he knew he'd drunk too much ouzo the night before when he saw that he had left the television on. The only channels it received were Greek, and he never watched it when he was sober.

Banks groaned, stretched, and made some of the strong Greek coffee he had become attached to during his first week on the island. While the coffee was brewing, he put on a CD of Mozart arias, picked up one of last week's newspapers he hadn't read yet, and walked out onto the balcony. The sun was shining in a perfect blue sky, the way it had done every day since he had arrived. He could smell wild lavender and rosemary in the air. A cruise ship had just dropped anchor, and the first launches of the day were carrying their loads of excited tourists to the harbour, gulls squawking in their wake.

After looking at the newspaper, Banks thought he would walk down to the village for a long lunch, maybe have a glass or two of wine, pick up some fresh bread, olives and goat's cheese, then come back for a nap and a little music, before spending his evening at the taverna on the quayside playing chess with Alexandros, as had been his habit since his second day.

There was nothing that interested him in the newspaper, apart from a brief report on a skeleton uncovered by a construction worker at the site of a new shopping centre by the A1, not far from Peterborough. He only noticed it because he had spent a good part of his early life in Peterborough, and his parents still lived there.

He put the paper aside and watched the gulls swoop and circle. They looked as if they were drifting on waves of Mozart. Drifting, just like him. He thought back to his second conversation with Alexandros. During their game of chess, Alex had paused, looked seriously at Banks and said, 'You seem like a man with many secrets,

Alan, a very sad man. What is it you are running from?'

Banks had thought about that a lot. Was he running? Yes, in a way. Running from a failed marriage and a botched romance, and a job that had threatened to send him over the edge with its proximity to violent death and all that was worst in people. He was seeking a temporary escape, at least.

Or did it go deeper than that? He had answered only, 'I wish I knew,' before making a rash move and putting his queen in jeopardy.

DETECTIVE INSPECTOR Michelle Hart of the Cambridgeshire Constabulary, Northern Division, entered the forensic anthropology department of the district hospital. She was looking forward to this morning. Usually at post-mortems she found herself disturbed by the contrast between the bright reflective surfaces of utilitarian tile and steel and the messy slosh of stomach contents, the dribbles of blackish blood running into the polished gutters, between the smell of disinfectant and the stench of a punctured bowel. But this morning all that Dr Wendy Cooper, the forensic anthropologist, had to examine was bones.

Dr Cooper and her assistant, David Roberts, were bent over the partial skeleton, arranging the small bones of the hands and feet in the correct order. Dr Cooper was in her fifties, a stout figure with short grey hair, silver-rimmed glasses and a no-nonsense manner.

'Got anything for me yet?' Michelle took out her notebook.

'A little bit. As you can see, we're still trying to put him together again,' said Dr Cooper.

'Him?'

'Oh, yes. The skull and pubis bear it out. Northern European, too, I'd say.' She turned the skull sideways. 'See that straight facial profile, the narrow nasal aperture? All signs.'

'Not very tall, though, is he?' said Michelle.

Dr Cooper looked at the bones. 'Tall enough for his age, I'd say.'

'Don't tell me you know his age?'

Dr Cooper nodded. 'Only a rough guess, mind you. The fusion of ilium, ischium and pubis is in its early stages. That process usually takes place between the ages of twelve and seventeen.'

'So you're saying he's how old?'

'I'll say between the ages of twelve and fifteen.'

'That's amazing. How long ago was he buried there?'

'Impossible to say. There's no remaining soft tissue or ligaments, the bones are discoloured and there's some flaking, so I'd say more than a decade or two, but beyond that it's anyone's guess until I've done more rigorous tests.'

'Any sign of cause of death?'

'Not yet. I need to get the bones cleaned up. Sometimes you can't see knife marks, for example, because of the encrusted dirt.'

'Where's the stuff we found with the body?'

Dr Cooper gestured towards the bench beside the far wall and turned back to the bones. David Roberts spoke for the first time. He seemed embarrassed in Michelle's presence, as if he fancied her. She knew that her combination of blonde hair and green eyes had a captivating effect on some men, but this was ridiculous. Michelle had just turned forty and David couldn't be more than twenty-two.

She followed him to the bench, where he pointed to a number of barely recognisable objects. 'All these were gathered within a short radius of the body,' he said. Michelle could make out scraps of material, perhaps fragments of clothing, coins, a small, round-edged triangular shape, and several round objects. 'What are those?' she asked.

'Marbles.' David rubbed one with a cloth and handed it to her.

'Summer, then,' Michelle said, almost to herself.

'Beg your pardon?'

She looked up at David. 'Oh, sorry. I said summer. Boys usually played marbles in summer. Outdoors, when the weather was good. What about the coins?'

'A few pennies, half a crown, a sixpence. All before decimalisation.'

'So that's pre-1971.' She picked up the triangular object. 'What's this?'

David polished away some of the grime and revealed a tortoise-shell pattern. 'I think it's a plectrum,' he said. 'For a guitar.'

'A musician, then?' Michelle picked up a chain bracelet, crusted and corroded, with a flat, elongated oval at its centre.

Dr Cooper came over. 'Yes, I thought that was interesting. It's an identity bracelet. They became popular with teenage boys during the sixties. You can read part of the name if you look closely. Here, use this.' She passed Michelle a magnifying glass. Michelle looked through it and was able to make out the faint edges of some of the engraved letters: GR–HA–.

'If I'm right,' said Dr Cooper, 'you're looking for a boy named Graham, aged between twelve and fifteen, who went missing at least twenty or thirty years ago, maybe in summer. Oh, and he played marbles and the guitar. I'll bet there can't be too many matching that description in your files.'

BANKS WALKED DOWN the hill and through the village's winding streets at about seven every evening. One or two of the shopkeepers greeted him as he passed. He had been on the island for a little over two weeks now, which was longer than most tourists stayed, and while he wasn't *accepted* his presence was at least acknowledged. It was much the same as in a Yorkshire village, where you remain an incomer until you have wintered out several years. Maybe he *would* stay here that long, learn the language, merge into the rhythms of island life. He even looked a bit Greek, with his lean frame, closely cropped black hair and tanned skin.

He picked up the two-day-old English newspapers that came on the last boat of the day and carried them to Philippe's quayside taverna, where he spent most of his evenings at an outside table overlooking the harbour.

Banks sipped ouzo and nibbled some olives as he settled on fish à la grecque and a green salad for dinner. The last of the tourists had returned to their cruise ship, and as soon as he had cleared away his stock Alex would come by to play chess. In the meantime, Banks turned to the newspapers. His attention was caught by an article on the bottom right of the front page, headed DNA CONFIRMS IDENTITY OF LONG-BURIED BODY. Intrigued, Banks read on:

> A week ago the skeleton of a boy was unearthed by workers digging the foundations of a new shopping centre next to the A1 west of Peterborough, Cambridgeshire. Information discovered at the scene led to a narrow list of possibilities. When police came up with one strong candidate, Graham Marshall, the boy's parents were approached for DNA samples, and the testing proved positive. Graham Marshall disappeared on Sunday, August 22, 1965, at the age of fourteen, while walking his regular newspaper round in Peterborough. 'The police at the time exhausted every possible lead,' Detective Inspector Michelle Hart of the Cambridgeshire Constabulary told our reporter, 'but there's always a chance that this discovery will bring new clues.' Asked if there was likely to be a new investigation into the case, DI Hart would only state that, 'Missing persons are never written off until they are found, and if there's the possibility of foul play, then justice must be pursued.'

Banks felt his stomach clench. He put the paper down and stared out to sea, where the setting sun was sprinkling rose dust over the horizon. Everything around him began to shimmer and feel unreal.

The taverna, the harbour, the brittle laughter of other diners all seemed to vanish, and there was only Banks with his memories and the stark words in the newspaper.

'Alan? What is it you say: a penny for them?'

Banks looked up and saw the dark, squat figure of Alex standing over him. 'Alex. Sorry. Good to see you. Sit down.'

Alex sat, looking concerned. 'You look as if you've had bad news.'

'You could say that.' Banks lit a cigarette and stared out over the darkening sea. Alex gestured to the waitress, and in moments a bottle of ouzo appeared on the table in front of them. Alex took his portable chess set from its leather bag and arranged the pieces.

Banks knew Alex wouldn't press him. It was one of the things he liked about his new friend. Alex had been born on the island and after university in Athens had travelled the world as an executive for a Greek shipping line, before deciding to pack it all in ten years ago at the age of forty. Now he made a living from tooling leather belts, which he sold to tourists on the quayside. Of course, Banks hadn't told Alex what *he* did for a living. He had found that telling strangers you were a policeman tended to put them off.

'Perhaps it's not a good idea tonight,' Alex said, and Banks noticed he was putting the chess set away. It had always been a mere back-drop to conversation, anyway, as neither man was a skilled player.

'I'm sorry,' said Banks. 'I just don't seem to be in the mood.'

'It's all right, my friend. Clearly there is something troubling you.' Alex stood to leave, but Banks reached out and touched his arm. 'No, stay,' he said, pouring them both a generous glass of ouzo. Alex looked at him for a moment and sat down again.

'When I was fourteen,' said Banks, looking out at the lights in the harbour, 'a schoolfriend of mine disappeared. There was a general assumption at the time that he had been abducted by a paedophile and done away with. The thing is, about two months earlier I was playing by the river when a man grabbed me and tried to push me in.'

'What happened?'

'I was wiry and slippery enough to wriggle free and run off.'

'But you never told the authorities?'

'I never even told my parents.'

'Why not?'

'I was playing truant from school. I didn't want to get into trouble.'

Alex poured more ouzo. 'So, when your friend disappeared, you assumed it was the same man, and you've been carrying the guilt all these years?'

'I suppose so. It's like an old wound that never quite heals. I don't know. I think it was partly why I—'

'Why you became a policeman?'

Banks looked at him in astonishment. 'How did you know?'

'I've met a few in my time. You get to recognise the signs.'

'Like what?'

'Oh, watchfulness, curiosity, a certain way of walking and sitting. Little things. But please go on.'

Banks tapped the newspaper. 'They've found him. Buried by the roadside about eight miles from where he disappeared.'

'So perhaps the assumptions were right?'

'Yes.'

'And that makes you feel bad all over again, does it?'

'Terrible. What if it *was* the same man? If I'd spoken up—'

'Even if you had reported what happened, it doesn't mean he would have been caught.' Alex shook his head. 'But I'm not foolish enough to believe one can talk a man out of his guilt when he's set on feeling it. I have a feeling I'm going to miss you, my friend.'

'Are you trying to tell me you think I ought to go back?'

Alex smiled. 'I'm not the one who thinks you ought to go back.'

Banks looked out at the sea. Alex was right; he *would* have to go. He had been carrying his guilty secret around for so long now that it was a part of him, and he could no more put the discovery of Graham Marshall's bones out of his mind than he could all the other things he had thought he'd left behind: Sandra and her pregnancy, Annie Cabbot, the Job.

He felt terribly sad because he knew it was all over now, this brief sojourn in paradise, knew that this would be the last time he and Alex would spend a companionable evening together in the Greek warmth. He knew that tomorrow he must go down to the harbour early, take the morning ferry to Piraeus and get on the first flight home. And he wished to hell he didn't.

UP IN YORKSHIRE, two days later, the sky was far from cloudless. The sun had not, in fact, shone since Banks had left for Greece, reflected Detective Inspector Annie Cabbot as she pushed yet another pile of paperwork aside and put her feet up on the desk. It was as if the bugger had gone and taken all the sunshine with him. And this was August. Where was summer?

Annie had to admit that she missed Banks. She had ended their romantic relationship, but there was no one else in her life, and she enjoyed his company and professional insight. In her weaker moments, she sometimes wished they had remained lovers, but it wasn't a valid option, given his family baggage and her renewed interest in her career. Too many complications involved in sleeping with the boss.

Not that she couldn't understand *why* Banks had gone. The poor sod had simply had enough. He needed to recharge his batteries, gird his loins before he entered the fray once more. A month should do it, Assistant Chief Constable Ron McLaughlin had agreed.

At least Banks's temporary absence meant a quick transfer for Annie from Complaints and Discipline back to CID at the rank of detective inspector, which was what she had been angling for.

There hadn't been much more crime than sun in Western Division lately, either, which was why Annie, bored with looking over reports, mission statements, circulars and cost-cutting proposals, pricked her ears up when she heard the tapping of Detective Superintendent Gristhorpe's walking stick approaching the office door. She took her feet off the desk, as much so that Gristhorpe wouldn't notice her red suede ankle boots as anything else, tucked her wavy chestnut hair behind her ears and pretended to be buried deep in paperwork.

Gristhorpe walked over to her desk. He'd lost quite a bit of weight since he shattered his ankle, but he still looked robust enough. 'Owt on, Annie?' he asked.

Annie gestured to the papers strewn over her desk. 'Not a lot.'

'Only there's this boy gone missing. Schoolboy, aged fifteen.'

'How long ago?'

'Didn't come home last night.' Gristhorpe put the misper report in front of her. 'Parents have been calling us since yesterday evening.'

Annie raised her eyebrows. 'A bit soon to bring us in on it, isn't it, sir? Kids go missing all the time. Fifteen-year-olds in particular.'

'Not ones called Luke Armitage, they don't.'

'Luke Armitage? Not . . .'

'Aye. Martin Armitage's son. Stepson, to be accurate.'

'Oh, shit.' Martin Armitage was an ex-footballer, who in his time had been one of the major strikers of the Premier League. Since retiring from professional sport he had become something of a country gentleman. He lived with his wife and stepson, Luke, in Swainsdale Hall, a magnificent manor house perched above Fortford.

His wife, Robin Fetherling, had once been a celebrated model, well enough known in her field as Martin Armitage was in his, and her exploits, including drugs, wild parties and affairs with a variety of rock stars, had provided plenty of fodder twenty years ago or more.

Robin Fetherling and Neil Byrd had been a hot item, the beautiful young couple of the moment, when Annie was at university. She had even listened to Neil Byrd's records in her student flat, but she hadn't heard his name, or his music, in years. She remembered reading that Robin and Neil had had a baby out of wedlock about fifteen years ago. *Luke*. Then they split up, and Neil Byrd had committed suicide while the child was still very young.

'Oh, shit, indeed,' said Gristhorpe. 'I'd not like to think we give better service to the rich and famous than to the poor, Annie, but perhaps you could go and try to set the parents at ease. The kid's probably gone gallivanting off with his mates, run away to London or something, but you know what people's imaginations can get up to.'

'Where did he disappear from, sir?'

'We don't know. He'd been into town yesterday afternoon, but when it got late and he still wasn't home they started to worry. The lad carried a mobile with him, so they're sure he would have rung if anything came up.'

'That *does* sound odd. Have they tried ringing him?'

'No signal. They say his phone's switched off.'

Annie stood up. 'I'll go over there and talk to them now.'

Gristhorpe nodded. 'Good.'

BANKS REMEMBERED the days surrounding Graham Marshall's disappearance more clearly than he remembered most days that long ago, he realised, as he closed his eyes and settled back in the aeroplane seat.

Just over a week after he had returned from a holiday in Blackpool with the Banks family, Graham Marshall had disappeared during his Sunday-morning paper round out of Donald Bradford's newsagent's shop, a round he had been walking for about six months, and one that Banks himself had walked a year earlier.

As Banks leaned back in his seat, he tried to reconstruct that Sunday. It would have begun the normal way. At weekends, Banks usually stayed in bed until lunchtime, when his mother called him down for the roast. During lunch they would listen to the radio comedies on the Light Programme: *The Navy Lark* and *Round the Horne*, until *The Billy Cotton Band Show* drove Banks outdoors to meet up with his friends on the estate.

Sometimes, the five of them—Banks, Graham, Steve Hill, Paul Major and Dave Grenfell—would go to the local park, staking out an area of grass near the playing fields, and listen to Alan Freeman's *Pick of the Pops* on Paul's tranny, watching the girls walk by.

Other Sundays they'd gather at Paul's and play records, which was what they did on the day Graham disappeared, Banks remembered. Paul had a new Dansette, which he would bring outside on the steps if the weather was good. That Sunday everyone was there except Graham, and nobody knew why he was missing, unless his parents were keeping him in for some reason. They could be strict, Graham's parents, especially his dad. Still, whatever the reason, he wasn't there, and nobody thought too much of it.

There they would be, then, sitting on the steps, wearing their drainpipe trousers, tight-fitting shirts and winkle-pickers, hair about as long as they could grow it before their parents prescribed a trip to the barber's. No doubt they played other music, but the highlights of that day, Banks remembered, were Steve's pristine copy of the latest Bob Dylan LP, *Bringing It All Back Home*, and Banks's *Help!*

Dave left early, saying he had to go to his grandparents' for tea. Steve headed off a few minutes later, taking his LP with him. Banks couldn't remember the exact time, but he was certain he and Paul were listening to 'Everyone's Gone to the Moon' when they saw the Ford Zephyr cruising down the street. Paul started whistling the *Z Cars* theme music. The police car stopped at number 58, Graham's house, and two uniformed officers got out and knocked on the door.

Banks remembered watching as Mrs Marshall opened the door, and the two policemen took off their hats and followed her into the house. After that, nothing was ever quite the same on the estate.

ANNIE TURNED OFF the B road between Fortford and Relton onto the gravel drive of Swainsdale Hall. Built of local limestone and millstone grit in the seventeenth century, the hall was a long, two-storey building with stone-mullioned windows. Though Martin Armitage had bought the place for a song, so the stories went, the cost of upkeep was crippling, and Annie could see that parts of the flagstone roof were in a state of disrepair.

A dog barked inside the house as Annie parked and approached the door. More of a cat person herself, she hated the way dogs rushed up when visitors arrived, jumped at you and sniffed your crotch.

However, the young woman who opened the door got a firm grip on the dog's collar before it could drool on Annie's skirt, and another woman appeared behind her. 'Miata!' she called out. 'Behave! Josie, would you take Miata to the scullery, please?'

'Yes, ma'am.' Josie disappeared, half dragging the frustrated Doberman along with her.

Annie introduced herself.

The woman held out her hand. 'I'm Robin Armitage. Come in.'

Annie followed Robin down the hall and through a door. The room was enormous, with antique furniture scattered round a Persian rug and a stone fireplace bigger than Annie's entire cottage.

The man who had been staring out of the back window over a lawn the size of a golf course turned when Annie entered. Like his wife, he looked as if he hadn't slept all night. He introduced himself as Martin Armitage and shook her hand. His grip was firm and brief.

Martin Armitage was over six foot tall, handsome in a rugged, athletic sort of way, with his hair shaved almost to his skull. Even his casual clothes, jeans and a loose hand-knitted sweater, looked as if they cost more than Annie's monthly salary.

'Detective Superintendent Gristhorpe told me about Luke,' Annie said.

'Yes.' Robin Armitage tried to smile, but it came out like the twentieth take of a commercial shoot.

'I know how upsetting something like this can be,' said Annie, perching on the edge of an antique chair, 'but in ninety-nine per cent of cases there's nothing to worry about. You'd be surprised how many mispers we get—sorry, that's police talk for missing persons—and most of them turn up none the worse for wear.'

'*Most* of them?' echoed Martin Armitage.

'I'm just telling you that statistically he's likely—'

'*Statistically?* What kind of—'

'Martin! Calm down. She's only trying to help. I'm sorry,' Robin said to Annie, 'but neither of us has had much sleep. Luke's never done anything like this before, and we really are quite frantic with worry.'

Martin Armitage ran his hand over his head, sighed and flopped down on the sofa. 'Yes, of course,' he said. 'And I apologise. My nerves are a bit frazzled, that's all.' When he looked right at her, she could see the concern in his eyes and she could also see the steely gaze of a man who usually got what he wanted.

'When did you first start to believe something was wrong?'

Martin looked at his wife. 'When was it, love? Early evening?'

Robin nodded. 'He's always home for tea. When he wasn't back by seven and we hadn't heard from him, we started to get worried.'

'We tried to call him on his mobile,' Martin said, 'but it was switched off.'

'Then what?'

'Well, at about eight,' Robin said, 'Martin went looking for him.'

'Where did you look, Mr Armitage?'

'I just drove around Eastvale. A bit aimless, really. But I had to do something. Robin stayed at home in case Luke rang or turned up.'

'How long were you gone?'

'Not long. I was back, oh, around ten.'

'Do you have a recent photograph of Luke?' Annie asked.

Robin went over to one of the low polished tables and picked up a package of prints. She thumbed through them and handed one to Annie. 'This was taken at Easter. We took Luke to Paris for the holidays. Will it do?' Annie looked at the photograph. It showed a tall, thin young man, dark hair curling around his ears and brow, who looked older than his fifteen years, even to the point of having the fluffy beginnings of a goatee. He was standing by a grave in an old cemetery looking moody and contemplative, but his face was close enough to the camera to be useful for identification purposes.

'He insisted on visiting the Père Lachaise cemetery,' Robin explained. 'That's where all the famous people are buried. Chopin. Balzac. Proust. Luke's standing by Jim Morrison's grave there.'

Robin Armitage's golden tresses hung over her narrow shoulders and shone every bit as much in real life as they did in her magazine adverts for shampoo. Annie guessed she was in her early forties, and she still had a striking figure. Despite signs of strain and worry, hardly a line marred her smooth, pale complexion.

'This'll do fine,' said Annie, slipping the photo into her briefcase. 'I'll get it circulated as soon as I get back. What was he wearing?'

'The usual,' said Robin. 'Black T-shirt and black jeans.'

'I'd like more information about Luke himself, anything you know about his friends, interests or acquaintances that could help us work out where he may be. First of all, was everything all right between you? Had there been any arguments recently?'

'Not that I can think of. I mean, nothing serious,' Robin answered.

'Was there something he wanted to do that you wouldn't let him. Friends you didn't like him being with. That sort of thing.'

Martin Armitage shook his head. 'I think we're pretty liberal parents,' he said. 'And Luke's a quiet, shy sort of boy. He keeps to himself.'

'He's very creative,' Robin added. 'He loves to read and he writes stories and poems.'

'What about girlfriends?' Annie asked.

'He never mentioned anyone,' said Robin.

'I don't know how to put this diplomatically,' Annie said, 'but I understand you're not Luke's biological father, Mr Armitage?'

'He's my stepson. But I've always thought of him as my own son. Robin and I have been married ten years now. Luke has our name.'

'Tell me about Luke's father, Mrs Armitage.'

Robin glanced over at her husband. 'Actually, I'm surprised you don't know already, given the inordinate amount of interest the gutter press took in the whole affair at the time. It's Neil Byrd.'

'Oh, I know who he was and what happened. I just don't remember the details. He was a pop singer, wasn't he?'

'A pop singer? He'd have been disgusted to hear himself called that. He thought of himself more as a sort of modern troubadour, more of a poet than anything else.'

'How long were you together?' Annie asked.

'About five years. Luke was only two when Neil walked out on us. Just like that. No warning. He said he needed his solitude and couldn't afford to be burdened with a family any longer. But why do you need to know all this? Neil's been dead for twelve years.'

'I'm just trying to get as much background as I can,' Annie explained. 'You never know what might be important to missing persons, what might trigger them. Does Luke know who his father was?'

'Oh, yes. I told him when he was twelve.'

'How did he react to the news?' Annie asked.

'He was confused, naturally,' said Robin. 'Martin is the only father he had known. He asked a lot of questions, but didn't talk about it much afterwards.'

'Do you still have any contact with any of Neil Byrd's friends or relatives?'

'Lord, no. Neil's parents both died young—it was one of the things that haunted him—and I don't move in those circles any more.'

'May I see Luke's room?'

'Of course.' Robin led Annie out into the hall, up a flight of worn stone stairs to the upper floor, where she turned to the left and opened the heavy oak door of the second room along.

Annie turned on the bedside light. It took her a few moments to register that the room was black except for the carpeted floor.

One wall was covered with posters of rock stars and, moving closer, Annie noted the names: Kurt Cobain, Jeff Buckley, Ian Curtis, Jim Morrison. Most of them were vaguely familiar to her, but she thought Banks might know more about them than she did. No sports personalities, she noticed.

An electric guitar stood propped against an amplifier under the window, a computer sat on a desk, and next to the wardrobe was a stereo system and a stack of CDs. She opened the violin case on top of the dresser and saw that it did, indeed, contain a violin.

Annie flipped through the CDs. Most of the bands she'd never heard of, but she recognised some oldies like Nirvana and REM. There was even some old Bob Dylan.

There was nothing by Neil Byrd. Again, Annie wished Banks were here; he'd be able to read something into all this.

Annie glanced at the contents of the bookcase: a lot of novels, a number of poetry anthologies, an oversized book on Pre-Raphaelite art, and that was about it.

Other than that, the room revealed remarkably little. There was no address book, at least none that Annie could find. Robin told her that Luke carried a battered leather shoulder bag around with him, wouldn't go anywhere without it, and anything important to him would be in there, including his ultralight laptop.

Annie did find some manuscripts in a drawer, short stories and poems, and she asked if she could borrow them to look at later. She could tell that Robin wasn't keen, mostly, it seemed, for the sake of Luke's privacy, but a little prodding in the right direction worked wonders. She didn't think the creative work would tell her much, but it might give her some insight into Luke's character.

They went back downstairs, where Martin Armitage was still sitting on the sofa.

'I understand Luke goes to Eastvale Comprehensive. Is he happy there?'

'He's never complained,' said Martin. 'No more than any kid would. You know, he doesn't like his geography teacher, doesn't like games. That sort of thing.'

'He's not a sports fan?'

'Unfortunately, no,' said Martin. 'I've tried to get him interested, but . . .' He shrugged.

'What about the other boys at school? Even if he is, as you say, a bit of a loner, he must have *some* contact with his classmates?'

'I suppose so, but I've never seen any evidence of it.'

'He's never brought friends to the house?'

'Never.'

'What did Luke do yesterday?' Annie asked.

'He went into the town centre,' said Martin.

'How did he get there?'

'Bus. There's a good service, at least until after teatime.'

'Did he have any particular reason to go to Eastvale yesterday?'

'No,' Robin answered. 'He just loves hunting for secondhand books, and he wanted to look at some new computer stuff.'

'Have there ever been any threats against you?' Annie asked.

'No,' said Martin. 'Why do you ask?'

'Celebrities often attract the wrong sort of attention.'

Martin snorted. 'We're hardly Beckham and Posh Spice. We're not much in the public eye these days. We both keep a very low profile.'

'Did it cross your mind that someone might have thought Luke was worth kidnapping?' she asked.

'Despite what you think,' Martin said, 'we're actually not all that wealthy.' He gestured around. 'The house, for a start . . . it just eats up money. We'd be very poor marks for a kidnapper, believe me.'

'The kidnapper might not know that. And just to be on the safe side, do you think we could arrange to have any phone calls intercepted, in case of ransom demands?'

Martin nodded. 'Very well. If you must.'

'Thank you, sir. I'll arrange for the technician to drop by later this morning.' Annie stood up to leave. 'I won't keep you any longer.' She passed her card to Robin, who was closer. 'My mobile number's on there, too.' She smiled and added, 'When you can reach it.' Cellphone coverage was spotty in the Dales, to say the least. 'If you hear anything at all, you won't hesitate to call me, will you?'

'No,' said Robin. 'Of course not. And if—'

'You'll be the first to hear. Don't worry, we'll be looking for him, I can assure you.' Annie gave them her best, most confident smile and left, not feeling confident at all.

2

DI Michelle Hart locked up her grey Peugeot outside 58 Hazel Crescent and took measure of the neighbourhood. As council estates went, the Hazels, as the locals called it, wasn't particularly bad. Built in the early sixties before the 'new town' expansion, its terraces of brick houses behind low walls and privet hedges were now home to a mixed crowd of unemployed people, teenage mothers, pensioners, and a growing Asian population.

Michelle knocked on the dark green door. Mrs Marshall, a frail-looking woman, stooped and grey-haired, face lined with care, answered and led her into a small living room and bade her sit on a plum velours armchair. Michelle had met the Marshalls before, during the identification process, but hadn't yet visited them at home. Everything in the room was so tidy and spotless that she felt a momentary twinge of guilt over her own unwashed breakfast dishes and unmade bed. Still, who was there to see them but her?

Bill Marshall, incapacitated by a stroke, looked at Michelle, blanket over his knees, walking stick by his side, slack-jawed, a little drool collecting at the corner of his mouth, one half of his face drooping lower than the other. He had been a big man, that much was obvious, but now his body had withered. His eyes were alive, though, the whites a little cloudy, but the grey irises watchful. Michelle said hello to him and thought she saw his head move just a fraction in greeting. Though he couldn't speak, Mrs Marshall had assured Michelle that he could understand everything they said.

Among the framed photographs on the mantelpiece above the electric fire was one of a boy, aged about thirteen or fourteen, hair in a 'Beatle' cut popular in the early sixties, standing on a promenade with the sea in the background. He was a good-looking kid, Michelle noticed, perhaps a little feminine, soft and delicate in his features, but he'd probably have grown up to be a heartbreaker, nonetheless.

Mrs Marshall noticed her looking. 'Yes, that's our Graham. It was taken on the last holiday he had. We couldn't go away that year— Bill had a big job to finish—so the Bankses took him to Blackpool with them. Their lad Alan was a good mate of his. Mr Banks took that photo and gave it to us when they came back.' She paused. 'No more than a week or so later and Graham was gone for ever.'

Michelle nodded. 'I don't want to bother you for long,' she began, 'but I need to ask a few more questions, if that's all right?'

'You've got your job to do, love. Don't worry about us. We did our mourning years ago. Most of it, anyhow.'

'I haven't seen the reports yet, but I understand there was a full investigation in 1965, when Graham first disappeared?'

'Oh, yes. They searched high and low. Jet Harris himself was in charge, you know. At his wits' end he was when all their efforts turned up nothing. He even came to search our house for clues himself.'

Detective Superintendent John Harris—nicknamed Jet after both his speed and his resemblance to the Shadows' bass guitarist—was still a legend around divisional headquarters. Even Michelle had read the biographical pamphlet published by one of the local bobbies with a literary bent, and she had been impressed by it, from his

Distinguished Conduct Medal with the commandos in the Second World War, his rise through the ranks to detective chief superintendent, and his legendary retirement party in 1985. His framed photograph hung on the wall near the front entrance, and his name was mentioned only with suitably hushed awe. Michelle could imagine how his failure to solve the case must have galled him. Harris had a reputation for closing cases quickly, and for not letting go until he got a conviction. Since his death from cancer eight years ago, he had become even more revered. 'It'll have been done properly, then,' she said.

'I've got no complaints. They turned over every stone they could find, but who'd think to dig there, eight miles away? I mean, they could hardly dig up the whole county, could they?'

'I suppose not,' Michelle agreed.

'And there were those missing kids out Manchester way,' Mrs Marshall went on. 'What they later called the Moors Murders. It wasn't until a couple of months after our Graham disappeared, though, that Brady and Hindley got caught.'

Michelle knew about Ian Brady and Myra Hindley, the Moors Murderers, even though she had been only a child at the time. She hadn't realised, though, just how closely their crimes were linked chronologically with Graham Marshall's disappearance. It might have been natural for Detective Superintendent Harris at least to assume that Graham's disappearance could somehow be linked with Brady and Hindley. On the other hand, Peterborough was over 130 miles from Manchester, and Brady and Hindley tended to stick to their own neck of the woods.

Before Michelle could formulate her next question, another woman walked into the room. She bore a strong facial resemblance to the boy in the photograph. She wore her grey-streaked hair long, tied in a ponytail, and was casually dressed in a dark blue T-shirt and jeans. The stress of recent events showed in her features, as it did in Mrs Marshall's.

'This is Joan, my daughter,' Mrs Marshall said.

Michelle stood up and shook Joan's limp hand.

'She lives in Folkestone, teaches at a comprehensive school there,' Mrs Marshall added with obvious pride. 'She was going on her holidays, but when she heard . . . well, she wanted to be with us.'

'I understand,' said Michelle. 'Were you and Graham close, Joan?'

'As close as any brother and sister with two years between them can be in their teens,' said Joan, with a rueful smile. 'Actually, I'm not being fair. Graham wasn't like most other boys his age. He even bought me presents. He didn't tease me. If anything, he was very protective.'

'Was Graham a tough lad?'

'Not really,' said Mrs Marshall. 'Mind you, he never backed away from a fight. When we moved here, there was a bit of bullying—you know, the way they always like to test the new kid—but in his first week our Graham took on the school bully. He didn't win, but he put up a good fight, so nobody bothered him after that.'

Michelle was wondering how difficult it would be for someone to abduct and murder Graham Marshall if he could put up a good fight. Was it someone he knew and went with willingly? 'You said you moved up here? Would that be from the East End of London?'

'It still shows, does it, after all these years? Once a cockney, always a cockney, I suppose. Yes, we came from Bethnal Green. We moved around a fair bit because of Bill's work. He's a bricklayer. Or he was. We'd only been here a year or so when it happened.'

'But you stayed on after.'

'Yes. There was plenty of work, what with the new town business.'

'Mrs Marshall,' said Michelle. 'I know it's a long time ago, but can you tell me what sort of things Graham was interested in?'

'Oh, the usual boys' stuff. Football. Cricket. And he was pop music crazy. We've still got his old guitar upstairs. Practised chords for hours, he did.' She paused. 'What's going to happen now, Miss Hart? I mean, surely you don't think you can catch whoever did this? Not after all this time?'

'I don't know,' said Michelle. 'I certainly wouldn't want to make any rash promises. But when something like this happens, we do our best to go over the ground again and see if we can find something someone missed the first time around. A fresh pair of eyes. It works sometimes.'

'You know,' said Mrs Marshall, 'the way things happened, we never . . . I mean, our Graham never had a proper funeral. Do you think we could do that? You know, the bones . . .'

'I'll talk to the forensic anthropologist,' Michelle said. 'I'm sure she'll do her best to release the remains as soon as possible.'

'Really? Oh, thank you so much, Miss Hart. You don't know how much it means to us. Do you have any children of your own?'

Michelle felt herself tense up, the way she always did when people asked her that. Finally, she got the words out. 'No. No, I don't.'

Mrs Marshall saw her to the door, and Michelle walked down the path to her car taking deep breaths, shaken, flooded with memories she'd been blocking out, memories of Melissa and of Ted.

BANKS MET ANNIE at the Woolpack, a quiet pub in the tiny village of Maltham. On his way home from Manchester Airport, he had decided he wanted to talk to someone about what he had just learned, and Annie was the only person he had told about the incident with the pervert down by the river. It shocked him to realise he hadn't even told his ex-wife Sandra, though they had been married for over twenty years.

It was drizzling when he pulled up in the car park shortly before nine o'clock. Annie's purple Astra was nowhere in sight. He obeyed the sign and stepped on the disinfectant pad before entering the pub. Though there hadn't been an outbreak of foot-and-mouth disease near Maltham itself, strict measures had been brought in by the Ministry. Many footpaths had been closed and access to the countryside limited. Also, as local farmers used the village pubs and shops, many of the owners had placed disinfectant mats on their doorsteps.

Banks bought a pint of Black Sheep bitter and a packet of cheese and onion crisps and sat down near the door. It opened and Annie entered in tight jeans and a light blue sleeveless top, bag slung over her shoulder. She pecked Banks on the cheek and sat down. Banks felt a momentary rush of desire for her, but that part of their relationship was over; they had moved on to something different. He went back to the bar and bought her a pint.

'Look at that tan,' Annie said when he sat down again, her laughter lines crinkling. She patted his arm. 'It's good to see you, Alan.'

'You, too.'

'So come on, then. Tell. How was Greece?'

'Magnificent. Magical. Paradisiacal.'

'Then what the bloody hell are you doing back in Yorkshire?' Annie leaned back in her chair and stretched out her legs, crossing them at the slender ankles, where the thin gold chain hung, sipped some beer and almost purred. 'Anyway, you're looking well. Less stressed. Even half a holiday seems to have had some effect.'

Banks considered for a moment and decided he did feel better than when he had left. 'It helped put things in perspective. And you?'

'Swimmingly. Thriving. The job's going well. I'm getting back into yoga and meditation. And I've been doing some painting again.'

'I kept you away from all that?'

Annie laughed. 'Well, it's not as if you twisted my arm, but when you've got as little time as people in our line of work have, then something has to go by the wayside.'

Banks was about to make a sarcastic reference to that something being him this time, but he bit his tongue. He wouldn't have done that two weeks ago. The holiday really must have done him good. 'Well,' he said, 'I'm glad you're happy. I mean it, Annie.'

Annie touched his hand. 'I know you do. Now, what brings you back here in such a hurry? I hope it's not serious.'

Banks explained about the discovery of Graham Marshall's bones.

Annie listened, frowning. When Banks had finished, she said, 'I can understand why you're concerned, but what can you do?'

'I don't know,' Banks said. 'If I were the local police, I wouldn't want me sticking my nose in, but when I heard . . . I don't know. It was a big part of my adolescence, Annie, Graham disappearing like that, and I suppose it's a big part of me now, always has been. I told you about the man by the river, the one who tried to push me in?'

'Yes.'

'If it was him, then maybe I can help them find him, if he's still alive. I can remember what he looked like. Odds are there could be a photo on file.'

'And if it wasn't him?'

'Even if it's nothing to do with the man by the river, *someone* killed Graham and buried his body. Maybe I can remember something, something I missed at the time. If I can cast my mind back . . .'

'So when are you going down there?' Annie asked.

'First thing tomorrow morning.'

'And you're going to do what, exactly? Present yourself at the local nick and offer to help them solve their case?'

'Something like that. I haven't thought it out yet.'

'Well, it's a pity you're not sticking around. We might be able to use your help up here.'

'Oh? What's on?'

'Missing boy. This one disappeared a bit more recently than Graham.'

'How old?'

'Fifteen.'

That was almost Graham's age when he disappeared, Banks thought, sipping his beer. 'What were the circumstances?'

Annie told him. 'And there's another thing. He's Luke Armitage.'

'Robin's boy? Neil Byrd's son?'

'Martin Armitage's stepson. Do you know him?'

'Martin Armitage? Hardly. Saw him play once or twice, though. But I've got a couple of CDs by Neil Byrd. They did a compilation three or four years ago, and they've just brought out a collection of outtakes and live performances. He really *was* very good, you know.'

Annie brought out her notebook and named the subjects of Luke's posters. 'I mean, I know Kurt Cobain was in Nirvana and killed himself, but what about the others?'

Banks frowned. 'They're all singers and they all either committed suicide or died under mysterious circumstances.'

'Interesting.' Annie's mobile buzzed. Excusing herself, she walked over to the front door and stepped outside. When she came back two minutes later she looked puzzled.

'Not bad news, I hope?' said Banks.

'No, not at all. Quite the opposite. That was Robin. Robin Armitage. Apparently, Luke just rang them. He says he just needed some space, that he'll be back home tomorrow.'

'Did he say where he was?'

'Wouldn't tell them.'

'What are you going to do?'

Annie finished her drink. 'I think I'd better go to the station, scale down the manhunt. You know how expensive these things are. I don't want Red Ron on my back for wasting our time and money.'

'Scale down?'

'Yes. Call me suspicious, but I'm not going to call off the search completely until I see Luke Armitage with my own eyes.'

'I wouldn't call that suspicious,' said Banks. 'I'd call it sensible.'

ON THE SURFACE, it seemed a simple enough question: where were the Graham Marshall case files? In reality, it was like searching for the Holy Grail, and it had taken Michelle and DC Nat Collins the best part of two days.

What complicated matters was that the original forces—Cambridge, Peterborough, Ely and Huntingdon—had amalgamated into the Mid-Anglia Constabulary in 1965, necessitating a major overhaul and restructuring, and had become the present-day Cambridgeshire Constabulary in 1974.

Michelle was about to throw in the towel around lunchtime. She'd drunk too much wine the previous evening—something that was happening rather too often these days—and didn't feel a hundred per cent.

When she finally did track the paperwork down, she could have kicked herself. It was deep in the bowels of Divisional HQ, not more than thirty feet below her office, and the records clerk, Mrs Metcalfe, proved to be a mine of information and let her sign out a couple of files. Why hadn't Michelle thought to look there in the first place? Easy. She had been at Thorpe Wood only a short time, and no one had given her the grand tour; she didn't know that the basement was the repository for much of the county force's old paperwork.

Michelle put on her reading glasses and opened the first folder, which contained maps and photos of the Hazels estate, along with a summary of any relevant witness statements that helped to pin down Graham's progress on the morning of August 22, 1965.

One hand-drawn map showed Graham's paper round, listing the houses he delivered to. At the eastern end of the estate, Wilmer Road separated the Hazels from an area of older houses, soon to be demolished. It was at the T-junction between Wilmer Road and Hazel Crescent that Graham had delivered his last newspaper.

The next delivery was supposed to be to one of the houses across the road, but nobody in Wilmer Road received a newspaper that morning. The anonymous map-maker had calculated that it would have been around 6.30am when Graham, who started at 6.00am, got to that part of his round—daylight, but still very early in the morning for any sort of traffic, including pedestrian. It was a Sunday, after all.

Michelle tucked some strands of blonde hair, which had been tickling her cheek, behind her ears and chewed at the end of her pen as she read over transcripts of the initial interviews.

Detective Superintendent Benjamin Shaw, now one of the senior officers at Thorpe Wood, was named once or twice as a detective constable on the case. Maybe she should have a word with him, see if he had any theories that hadn't made it into the files.

It seemed that the first person to miss Graham Marshall was his employer, Donald Bradford, owner of the newsagent's shop. Bradford lived some distance away from the shop and employed a local woman to open up, not arriving himself until eight o'clock. According to Bradford's statement, when Graham hadn't returned by 8.15 that Sunday, half an hour late for his second round on a neighbouring estate, Bradford drove around the Wilmer Road estate in search of him. He found nothing. Whatever had happened to Graham, his papers and his canvas bag were missing too.

After that, Bradford called at Graham's house to see if the lad had become ill and hurried home without stopping to report in. He hadn't. Graham's parents, now also worried, searched the estate for their son and found nothing. With news of the Manchester child abductions still fresh in the minds of the public, the Marshalls were soon concerned enough to call in the police. Detective Superintendent Harris was put in charge the following day, when still no trace had been found of Graham.

Police had interviewed everyone on Graham's round, along with all his friends, family and teachers. None of it led anywhere. Nobody on Wilmer Road had seen or heard anything unusual that morning—though one person said he had heard a car door bang at around half past six. All the evidence, especially the missing newspaper sack, suggested that Graham had most likely got into a car willingly, with someone he knew. But who? And why?

ANNIE CABBOT DROVE out to Swainsdale Hall mid-morning to tie up a few loose ends with the Armitages. The sun had come to the Yorkshire Dales at last, and wraiths of mist rose from the roadsides and the fields that stretched up the dalesides.

Josie, the Armitages' housekeeper, answered the door and seemed surprised to see her.

'Sorry I didn't phone ahead,' Annie said. 'Are they in?'

Josie stood aside and let Annie walk through to the same large living room she had been in yesterday. Only Robin Armitage was there this time, sitting on the sofa and flipping through a copy of *Vogue*. She jumped to her feet when Annie entered. 'What's happened? Is something wrong?'

'Nothing's happened,' said Annie. 'I came to see if you're all right.'

'Of course I am. Why shouldn't I be? Luke's coming home.'

'May I sit down?'

'Please.'

Annie sat, but Robin Armitage stayed on her feet, pacing. 'I'd have thought you'd be relieved,' Annie said.

'I am,' said Robin. 'It's just that . . . well, I'll be a lot more settled when Luke's back home again. I'm sure you understand.'

'Have you heard from him again?'

'No. Only the once.'

'And he definitely said he's coming home today?'

'Yes.'

'Mrs Armitage, you told me yesterday that Luke said he needed some space. Do you know why?'

'I hardly think that's relevant now, do you, Detective Inspector Cabbot?' Annie turned to see Martin Armitage standing in the doorway, briefcase in hand. 'Why are you here? What is it?' Despite his commanding presence, he seemed edgy to Annie, like his wife.

'Nothing,' she said. 'Just a friendly visit.'

'I see. Well, thank you for your efforts and your concern. We appreciate it, but I can see no point in your badgering us with more questions now that Luke's safe and sound, can you?' He glanced at his watch. 'Anyway, I'm afraid I have to hurry to a business meeting. Thank you again, Inspector.'

'Yes, thank you,' echoed Robin.

Dismissed. Annie knew when she was beaten. 'I only wanted to make sure everything was OK. I didn't mean to cause offence.'

'Well, as you can see,' said Martin, 'everything's fine. Luke will be back this evening, and it will be as if none of this ever happened.'

'Oh, just one more thing.' Annie paused in the doorway.

'Yes?'

'You said Luke rang you last night.'

'Yes. And immediately afterwards my wife rang you.'

'Yes, but I'm wondering why Luke's call wasn't intercepted. After all, the technician had set everything up.'

'That's easy,' said Martin. 'He called me on my mobile.'

'Ah, I see,' said Annie. 'Problem solved. Goodbye, then.'

They both bade her a perfunctory goodbye and she left. At the end of the drive, she turned right and parked in a lay-by just round the corner from the Armitages' drive. Annie sat for a moment in her car trying to figure out the meaning of the tension she had sensed in the room. Something was going on; Annie only wished she knew what. Neither Robin nor Martin had behaved like a couple who had just heard that the son whose life they feared for was now safe and would soon be home.

When Martin Armitage's BMW shot out of the driveway spraying gravel a minute later, Annie had an idea. As far as she knew, Martin Armitage had no idea what car she drove, so he would hardly be suspicious that a purple Astra was following him at a respectful distance.

As BANKS DROVE down the A1 and entered the landscape of bright new shopping centres that had replaced the old coal mines and slag heaps of West Yorkshire, he thought about the way the country had changed since Graham's disappearance.

Most people now seemed to have what they wanted, but what they wanted was mostly of a material nature—a new car, a DVD player, a pair of Nike trainers—and people were being mugged, even murdered, for their mobile phones.

But were things so very different back in the mid-sixties? Banks asked himself. Wasn't consumerism just as rife back then? That Monday evening in August 1965, when the knock came at their door, the Banks family was settling down to watch *Coronation Street* on their brand-new television set, bought on hire purchase just the previous week. Banks's father was in work then, at the sheet-metal factory, and if anyone had predicted that he would be made redundant seventeen years later, he'd have laughed in their face.

The one thing that entered nobody's mind when Arthur Banks answered the door, because it was such a disturbance of the normal routine, was that Joey, Banks's budgie, was out of his cage having his evening constitutional. When Banks opened the front door to admit the two detectives, Joey seized the moment and flew away, never to return. More fuss might have been made over Joey's escape had the visitors not become the centre of everyone's attention. They were the first plain-clothes policemen ever to enter the Banks household.

One of them, the one who did most of the talking, was about the same age as Banks's father, with slicked-back dark hair, a long nose, a general air of benevolence and a twinkle in his eye, the sort of kindly uncle who might slip you half a crown to go to the pictures and wink as he gave it to you. The other one was younger and more nondescript, with ginger hair, freckles and sticking-out ears.

Banks's father turned off the TV. Nine-year-old Roy just sat and gawped at the men. The kindly uncle asked his questions and the other took notes. Banks couldn't remember the exact wording after so many years, but imagined it went along the following lines.

'You know why we're here, don't you?'

'It's about Graham, isn't it?'

'Yes. You were a friend of his, right?'

'Yes.'

'Do you have any idea where he might have gone?'

'No.'

'When did you see him last?'

'Saturday afternoon.'

'Did he say or do anything unusual?'

'No.'

'What did you do?'

'Went shopping in town.'

'What'd you buy?'

'Just some records.'

'Was anything bothering him?'

'He was just like normal.'

'Did he ever talk about running away from home?'

'No.'

'Any idea where he might go if he did run away?'

'No. But he was from London. I mean, his parents brought him up from London last year.'

'Have you seen any strange men hanging around the area lately?'

'No.' Banks probably blushed as he lied.

'All right then, son, that's it for now. But if you can think of anything at all, you know where the police station is, don't you?'

'Yes.'

'And I'm sorry about your budgie, really I am.'

ANNIE WAITED until Martin Armitage's BMW had got a respectable distance ahead, then let a local delivery van get between them before she started to follow. At the village of Relton he turned right and followed the B road that ran about halfway up the valley-side.

They passed through tiny Mortsett, which didn't even have a pub or a general store, and Annie got stuck when the delivery van stopped to make a call at one of the cottages. The road wasn't wide enough for her to pass.

She got out and prepared to show her warrant card and ask the driver to get out of the way—there was a passing area about twenty yards further along—when she noticed Armitage pull over and halt about half a mile beyond the village. She brought out the binoculars she kept in her glove compartment and watched him.

Armitage got out of the car with his briefcase, looked around and started walking towards a squat stone shepherd's shelter about eighty yards off the road, and she didn't think he was nervous because he was breaking the government foot-and-mouth regulations.

When he got there he ducked inside the shelter, and when he came out he wasn't carrying his briefcase. Annie watched him walk back to his car and drive off in the direction of Gratly.

The delivery man drove off too and Annie got back into her car. Armitage was long gone by the time she reached the spot where he had stopped, and there were no other cars in sight.

Annie was the one who felt nervous now. Was someone watching her the way she had watched Armitage? She hoped not. If this was what she thought it was, it wouldn't do to reveal police interest. She ignored the posted warnings and made her way to the shelter. The place smelt musty and acrid inside. Enough light spilled through the gaps in the dry-stone for her to see the used condom, the empty cigarette packet and crushed lager cans. A local lad's idea of showing his girlfriend a good time, no doubt. She could also see the briefcase, the inexpensive, nylon kind.

Annie picked it up. It felt heavy. She opened the Velcro strips and inside, as she had expected, found stacks of money, mostly ten- and twenty-pound notes. She guessed it must be somewhere in the region of ten or fifteen thousand pounds.

She put the briefcase back and returned to her car. She couldn't just sit there waiting for something to happen, but she couldn't very well leave the scene either. In the end, she drove back to Mortsett and parked. Before she headed out on foot to find a good spot from which to watch the shelter without being seen, Annie picked up her mobile to ring the station and let DS Gristhorpe know what was going on.

And, wouldn't you know it, the damn mobile didn't work. Out of range. Bloody typical. *Damn!* Unwilling to take her eyes off the shelter for too long, Annie knocked on some doors, but nobody seemed to be home. She would have to take to the high ground.

As she climbed, she kept glancing behind her at the shepherd's shelter, but nobody approached it. She could only hope that she hadn't been spotted, that the kidnapper, if that was what this was all about, wasn't watching her from a comfortable distance.

She found a spot where she could lie on her stomach and keep a close eye on the shelter without being seen from below. How long should she wait? she wondered. The money was just lying there. What if he didn't come before nightfall and the lovers returned, more important things than foot-and-mouth on their minds? Several thousand quid as well as a quick bonk would be an unexpected bonus for them.

Annie trained the binoculars on the shelter. Waiting. Watching.

3

As Banks approached the turnoff to Peterborough, he wondered what to do. He had rung his parents to let them know he was coming, so perhaps he should go straight there. On the other hand, he was closer to police HQ, and the sooner he introduced himself to DI Michelle Hart, the better. So he headed for the police station.

In the reception area, he asked to speak to the detective in charge of the Graham Marshall investigation, introducing himself only as Alan Banks, a childhood friend. He didn't want to appear to be pulling rank or even introduce himself as a fellow copper, at least not at first, not until he saw which way the wind was blowing.

After he had been waiting about ten minutes, a young woman opened the locked door that led to the main part of the station. Conservatively dressed in a navy-blue suit, skirt below the knees, she was petite and slim, with shoulder-length blonde hair parted in the middle and tucked behind small, delicate ears. She had a jagged fringe that came almost down to her eyes, which were a startling green. Her mouth was slightly down-turned at the edges, which made her look a bit sad, and she had a small, straight nose. All in all, she was a very attractive woman, Banks thought, but he sensed a severity and a reserve in her—a definite 'No Entry' sign—and there was no mistaking the lines that suffering had etched round her haunting and haunted eyes.

'Mr Banks?' she said, raising her eyebrows.

Banks stood up. 'Yes.'

'I'm Detective Inspector Hart. Please follow me.' She led him to an interview room. Though it was a different county, the basics were still the same as in every interview room he had ever seen: table and chairs bolted to the floor, high window covered by a grille, institutional green paint on the walls, and that unforgettable smell of fear.

DI Hart put on silver-rimmed, oval reading glasses and shuffled the papers around in front of her, as Banks had done many times himself, to draw out the tension. It was a bit heavy-handed to talk to him in an interview room. He had come in voluntarily and he was neither a witness nor a suspect. She could have found an empty office and sent for coffee. But what would he have done? The same as her, probably; it was the us and them mentality, and in her mind he was a civilian. *Them.*

DI Hart stopped playing with her papers and broke the silence. 'So you say you can help with the Graham Marshall investigation?'

'Perhaps,' said Banks. 'I knew him.'

'Have you any idea at all what might have happened to him?'

'I'm afraid not.' Banks had intended to tell her everything but found it wasn't that easy. Not yet. 'We just hung around together.'

'What was he like?'

'Graham? It's hard to say,' said Banks. 'I mean, you don't think about things like that when you're kids, do you?'

'Try now.'

'He was deep, I think. Quiet, at any rate. Most kids joked around, did stupid stuff, but Graham was always more serious, more reserved. You never felt you were fully privy to what was going on in his mind,' he added. 'There was a secretive side to his nature. Look, I should probably have done this before, but . . .' He took out his warrant card, and laid it on the desk in front of her.

Michelle looked at it, then slid it back across the desk to Banks. 'Prick,' she whispered.

'Come again?'

'You heard me. Why didn't you tell me at the start you were a DCI?'

'Because I didn't want to give the impression I was trying to interfere. I'm simply here as someone who knew Graham. Besides, why did you have to come on so heavy-handed? I came here to volunteer information. There was no need to put me in an interview room and use the same tactics you use on a suspect. I'm surprised you didn't leave me here alone to stew for an hour.'

'You're making me wish I had.'

They glared at one another in silence for a few moments, then Banks said, 'Look, I'm sorry. I had no intention of making you feel foolish. And you don't need to. It's true that I knew Graham. We were close friends. But this isn't my case, and I don't want you to think I'm pushing my nose in or anything. That's why I didn't announce myself at first. I'm sorry. You're right. I should have told you I was on the Job right from the start. OK?'

Michelle gazed at him through narrowed eyes for a while, then twitched the corners of her lips in a brief smile and nodded. 'Your name came up when I was talking to his parents. I would have got in touch eventually.'

'The powers that be not exactly overwhelming you with assistance, then?'

Michelle snorted. 'You could say that. One DC. It's not a high priority case, and I'm the new kid on the block. New *girl*.'

'I know what you mean,' Banks said.

'Anyway,' she went on, 'I didn't know you were a copper. I suppose I should call you "sir"? Rank and all?'

'Not necessary. I'm not one to stand on ceremony. Besides, I'm on your patch here. You're the boss. I do have a suggestion, though.'

'Oh?'

Banks looked at his watch. 'It's one o'clock. I drove down from Eastvale without stopping and I haven't had a thing to eat. Why don't we get out of this depressing interview room and talk about Graham over lunch? I'll pay.'

Michelle raised an eyebrow. 'You're asking me out to lunch?'

'To discuss the case. Yes. Know any decent pubs around here?'

'OK. I know a place,' she said. 'But I'm paying my own way.'

MICHELLE DROVE BANKS to a pub she knew near the A1. She was intrigued to meet a friend of Graham Marshall's, especially as this Banks, despite a touch of grey in his closely cropped black hair, didn't look old enough. He was slim, perhaps three or four inches taller than her five foot five, had an angular face with lively blue eyes and a tan. He showed no great clothes sense but was dressed in basic Marks & Sparks casuals—light sports jacket, grey chinos, a blue denim shirt unbuttoned at the collar—and the look suited him.

'Is it to be DI Hart, then?' Banks asked.

'I suppose you can call me Michelle, if you want.'

'Michelle it is, then. Nice name.'

'Just as long as you don't start singing the old Beatles song.'

'I never sing to a woman I've just met.'

Michelle graced him with a smile.

The pub had parking at the back and a lawn with tables and chairs where they could sit out in the sun. Michelle watched the children play as Banks went inside to get the drinks. One of them was about six or seven, head covered in lovely golden curls, laughing unselfconsciously as she went higher on the swings. *Melissa*. Michelle felt as if her heart was breaking up inside her chest as she watched. It was a relief when Banks came back with a pint for himself and a shandy for her, and set two menus down on the table.

'What's up?' he asked. 'You look as if you've seen a ghost.'

'Maybe I have,' she said. 'Cheers.' They clinked glasses. Banks was diplomatic, she noted, curious about her mood, but considerate enough to leave well alone and pretend to be studying the menu. Michelle ordered a prawn sandwich. Banks ordered a huge Yorkshire pudding filled with sausages and gravy.

When their orders were in, Banks drank some beer and lit a cigarette. He looked in good shape, Michelle thought, for someone who smoked, drank and ate Yorkshire puddings and sausages. But how long would that last? If he really was Graham Marshall's contemporary, he'd be around fifty now, and wasn't that the age that men started worrying about their blood pressure, not to mention the prostate? Still, who was she to judge? True, she didn't smoke, but she drank too much and ate far too much junk food.

'So what else can you tell me about Graham Marshall?' she asked.

'He lived a few doors down the street, and for the year I knew him there was a small gang of us who were pretty much inseparable.'

'David Grenfell, Paul Major, Steven Hill and you. I've only had time to track down and speak to David and Paul on the phone so far, though neither of them was able to tell me very much. Go on.'

'I haven't seen them since I left for London when I was eighteen.'

'You only knew Graham for a year?'

'Yes. His family had moved up from London the summer before he disappeared. You probably weren't around then.'

'I certainly wasn't here.'

'Where, if you don't mind my asking?'

'I grew up in Hawick, border country. Spent most of my early police career with Greater Manchester, and since then I've been on the move. I've only been here a couple of months. Go on.'

'That explains the accent.' Banks paused to sip his beer. 'I grew up here, a provincial kid. Graham seemed sort of cool, exotic, different. He was from *London*, and that was where it was all happening.'

'What do you mean by "cool"?'

'He seemed sort of worldly-wise beyond his years.'

'When did you last see Graham?' Michelle asked.

'Just the day before he disappeared. Saturday.'

'What did you do?'

Banks gazed away into the trees before answering. 'Do? What we usually did on Saturdays. In the morning we went to the Palace, to the matinée. *Flash Gordon* or *Hopalong Cassidy*, a Three Stooges short.'

'And the afternoon?'

'In town. There was an electrical shop on Bridge Street that used to sell records. Long gone now. Three or four of us would sometimes crowd into one of those booths and smoke ourselves silly listening to the latest singles.'

'And that night?'

'Don't remember. I think I just stayed in watching TV. Saturday nights were good. *Juke Box Jury*, *Dr Who*, *Dixon of Dock Green*.'

'Anything odd about the day at all? About Graham?'

'You know, for the life of me I can't remember anything unusual. I'm thinking perhaps I didn't know him very well, after all.'

Michelle was getting the strong impression that Banks *did* know something, that he was holding back. She didn't know why, but she was certain that was the case.

'Twelve?' A girl carrying two plates wandered into the garden.

'Over here,' Banks said.

She delivered the plates. Banks tucked into his Yorkshire pudding and sausages, then said, 'I used to do Graham's paper round before him, before the shop changed owners and Bradford bought the shop.'

'Ever have any trouble on the paper round?'

'There was one bloke, near the end of Hazel Crescent. He was about the only one ever awake at that time, and I got the impression he hadn't even gone to bed. He'd open the door in his pyjamas and ask me to come in for a smoke or drink or whatever, but I always said no.'

'Harry Chatham,' Michelle said.

'You *have* done your homework.'

'He came under suspicion at the time, but he was on holiday in Great Yarmouth. Didn't get back until that Sunday night. Plenty of witnesses. Jet Harris gave him the third degree, I should imagine.'

Banks smiled. '*Jet Harris*. Haven't heard his name in years. You know, when I was a kid growing up around there, it was always, "Better keep your nose clean or Jet Harris will get you and lock you up." We were terrified of him, though none of us had ever met him.'

Michelle laughed. 'It's still pretty much the same today,' she said.

'Surely he must be dead by now?'

'Eight years ago. But the legend lingers on.' She picked up her sandwich and took a bite. It was good. 'Was there anything else?'

She noticed Banks hesitate. He had finished his Yorkshire pudding, and he reached for another cigarette. A temporary postponement. This man definitely had something on his conscience. Michelle sensed that she couldn't hurry matters by pushing him, so she let him put the cigarette in his mouth and fiddle with his lighter for a few moments. And she waited.

ANNIE LAY on her belly in the grass keeping an eye on the distant shepherd's shelter. She glanced at her watch and realised she had been lying there over four hours and nobody had come for the money.

She felt bathed in sweat. All she wanted to do was walk under a nice cool shower and luxuriate there for half an hour. But if she left her spot, what would happen? On the other hand, what would happen if she stayed there?

The kidnapper might turn up, but would Annie go running down the daleside to make an arrest? No, because Luke Armitage certainly wouldn't be with him. Would she have time to get to her car in Mortsett and follow whoever picked up the money? Possibly, but she would have a much better chance if she were already in the car.

In the end, Annie decided that she should go back down to Mortsett, still keeping an eye on the shelter, and try again to find someone home with a telephone, then sit in her car and watch from there until relief came from Eastvale.

It was a plan, and it beat lying around up here melting in the sun.

NOW THAT IT WAS TIME to confess, Banks was finding it more difficult than he had imagined. His mouth felt dry and the words stuck in his throat. 'We were playing down by the river,' he said.

'Who was playing with you?'

'Just Paul and Steve. We were throwing stones in the water, skimming, that sort of thing. Then we moved down a bit and found some big stones and bricks. We started chucking those in to make a bigger splash. At least I did. Steve and Paul were a bit further down. Anyway, I was holding this big rock to my chest with both hands—it took all my strength—when I noticed this tall, scruffy sort of bloke walking along the riverbank towards me.'

'What did you do?'

'Held on to it,' said Banks. 'So I didn't splash him. Always the polite little bugger, I was. I remember smiling as he got nearer, you know, showing him I was holding off dropping the rock until he was out of range. Next thing I knew, he'd grabbed hold of me from behind and I'd dropped the rock.'

'What happened? What did he do?'

'We struggled. I thought he was trying to push me in, but I managed to dig in my heels. I might not have been very big, but I was wiry and strong.'

Michelle took her notebook out. 'Can you give me a description?'

'He had a ragged dark beard. His hair was greasy and long, longer than usual back then. It was black. Like Rasputin. And he wore one of those army greatcoats. I remember thinking that he must be hot in it.'

'When was this?'

'Late June. It was a nice day, sort of like today.'

'So what happened?'

'He tried to drag me away, towards the bushes, but I managed to squirm out of his grasp, one arm at any rate, and he swung me round, swore at me and punched me in the face. The momentum broke me loose, so I ran.'

'Where were your friends?'

'Back up by the road by then. A good hundred yards away.'

'Didn't they help you?'

'They were scared.'

'They didn't call the police?'

'It all happened so fast. When I got free, I ran off and joined them and we never looked back. We decided not to say anything to our parents because we were supposed to be at school. We thought we'd get into trouble.'

'Why do you see a connection with what happened to Graham?'

'It seemed too much of a coincidence, that's all,' said Banks. 'First this pervert trying to drag me into the bushes, then Graham disappearing like that.'

'Well,' said Michelle, closing her notebook, 'I'd better go and see if I can find any trace of your mystery man, hadn't I?'

SHOWERED AND DRESSED in crisp, clean clothes, Annie presented herself at Detective Superintendent Gristhorpe's office that afternoon, as requested. There was something austere and headmasterly about the room that always intimidated her. Partly, it was to do with the tall bookcases, mostly filled with legal and forensics texts. And partly it was Gristhorpe's appearance: big, bulky, red-faced, unruly-haired, hook-nosed, pockmarked. Today he wore grey flannel trousers and a tweed jacket with elbow patches.

'Right,' said Gristhorpe after he had asked her to sit down. 'Now, tell me what the hell's going on out Mortsett way.'

Annie felt herself flush. 'It was a judgment call, sir.'

Gristhorpe waved his large, hairy hand. 'I'm not questioning your judgment. I want to know what you think is happening.'

'I think Luke Armitage has been kidnapped, sir. Someone communicated a ransom demand to the family last night, and Martin Armitage rang me to cancel the search for Luke.'

'But you didn't?'

'No, sir. Something wasn't right. In my opinion, Luke Armitage wasn't to be considered "found" until I'd seen him with my own eyes and talked to him.'

'Fair enough. What happened next?'

'I went out to see the family again this morning. I got the impression that something was going on.' Annie explained about following Martin Armitage and watching the shelter by herself for hours.

'Do you think he saw you? The kidnapper.'

'It's possible,' Annie admitted. 'If he was hiding somewhere nearby and watching through binoculars. It's open country up there. But it's my impression that he'll either wait until nightfall—'

'And risk leaving the money out there all day?'

'It's off the beaten track. And most people follow the government regulations.'

'Go on. What else do you think might have happened?'

'Maybe something has gone wrong.'

'Like?'

Annie swallowed and looked away. 'Like Luke's dead, sir. He tried to escape, struggled too hard . . .'

'Possibly.' Gristhorpe looked at his watch. 'Who's up there now?'

'DC Templeton, sir.'

'Organise a surveillance rota. I'll ask for permission to plant an electronic tracking device in the briefcase. Someone can put it there under cover of darkness. Go carefully, Annie. And don't give up on the kid. It's early days yet.'

'Yes, sir,' Annie said, though she wasn't at all certain about that.

THE OLD STREET looked much the same as it had when Banks lived there, except that everything—the brickwork, the doors, the slate roofs—was a bit shabbier, and satellite dishes had replaced the forest of TV aerials on just about all the houses, including his parents'. That made sense. He couldn't imagine his father living without Sky Sports.

The house stood near the western edge of the estate. Banks paused for a moment and took in the terraced houses   rows of five, each with a little garden, wooden gate, low wall and privet hedge. He opened the gate, walked up the flagstone path and knocked on the door. He saw his mother approach through the frosted-glass pane. She opened the door and gave him a hug. 'Alan,' she said. 'Lovely to see you. Come in.'

Banks dropped his overnight bag in the hall and followed his mother through to the living room. His father was sitting in his usual armchair, the one with the best straight-on view of the television. He didn't get up, only grunted, 'Son. How you doing?'

'Not bad, Dad. You?'

'Mustn't complain.' Arthur Banks had been suffering from mild angina and an assortment of less specified chronic illnesses for years, ever since he'd been made redundant from the sheet-metal factory. Other than that, and the damage booze and fags had wreaked on his liver and lungs, he had always been fit as a fiddle. Short, skinny and hollow-chested, he still had a head of thick dark hair with hardly a trace of grey. He wore it slicked back with lashings of Brylcreem.

Banks's mother, plump and nervy, with pouchy, chipmunk cheeks and a haze of blue-grey hair hovering around her skull, fussed about how thin Banks was looking. 'I don't suppose you've been eating properly since Sandra left, have you?' she said. 'In for tea?'

'Yes. I'll just take my bag up,' Banks said, heading for the stairs.

Though Banks hadn't stayed overnight since he had first left for London, somehow he knew his room would be just as it always had been. And he was right. It was the same wardrobe, the same small bookcase, the same narrow bed he had slept in as a teenager, sneaking his transistor radio under the covers to listen to Radio Luxembourg.

Banks dropped his bag at the bottom of the bed and unpacked his shirt to hang up in the wardrobe. The other clothes in the wardrobe were unfamiliar, but Banks noticed several cardboard boxes on the floor. He pulled one out and was stunned when he saw it was full of his old records: singles, as those were all he could afford back then.

The records here represented the beginnings of his musical interests. When he left, he had soon gone on to Cream, Hendrix and Jefferson Airplane, then later discovered jazz and, later still, classical, but these . . . Banks dipped his hand in and lifted out a stack, flipping through them. Here they were in all their glory: Dusty Springfield's 'Goin' Back', The Shadows' 'The Rise & Fall of Flingel Bunt', Cilla Black's 'Anyone Who Had a Heart' and 'Alfie', 'Nutrocker' by B. Bumble and the Stingers, 'House of the Rising Sun' by the Animals and 'As Tears Go By' by Marianne Faithfull. What a treasure trove of nostalgia, all the stuff he listened to between the ages of about eleven and sixteen.

For the moment, he put back the box and pulled out another one, this one full mostly of old toys. There were model aeroplanes—Spitfires, Wellingtons, and a Messerschmitt with a broken wing—a couple of Dinky toys, and a small clockwork Dalek that said 'Ex-ter-min-ate! Ex-ter-min-ate!' as it rolled along like an upturned dustbin.

The third box he opened was full of old school reports, magazines, letters and exercise books. Banks pulled out a handful of small notebooks and found they were his old diaries. The one that was of most immediate interest to him was a *Photoplay* diary with a photo of a different film star facing each page of dates. The first was Brigitte Bardot, for the week starting Sunday, December 27, 1964, the first full week of his diary for 1965, the year Graham disappeared.

MICHELLE TOOK OFF her reading glasses and rubbed the bridge of her nose, where she sensed a headache beginning to form between her eyes. She suffered from headaches frequently these days—her psychiatrist told her that it was probably just stress and 'coping'.

The air quality in the archives office didn't help either but she wanted to get an idea of the crimes occurring around the time of Graham's disappearance, to see if she could come up with any links to Banks's mysterious stranger. Mrs Metcalfe, the records clerk, had directed her to the logbooks that indexed and recorded all complaints and actions taken, day by day.

There were certainly plenty of incidents before and after Graham Marshall's disappearance, Michelle was fast discovering, but none of them seemed to have anything remotely to do with Banks's riverbank adventure. In July 1965, police had investigated complaints about a local protection racket modelled on the East London Kray gang's operation, allegedly led by a man called Carlo Fiorino, but no charges were brought. In August, two alleged homosexuals had been questioned in connection with lewd goings-on at the country mansion of local bigwig, Rupert Mandeville, but the anonymous informant couldn't be located, and all charges had later been dismissed for lack of evidence. Hard to believe that it was a crime to be gay, Michelle thought, but 1965 was back in the dark ages, before homosexuality had been legalised in 1967.

Reading the crime reports, she sensed rather than heard someone approaching the office, and when she looked up she saw it was Detective Superintendent Benjamin Shaw.

Shaw's bulk filled the doorway. 'What you up to, DI Hart?'

'Just checking the old logs, sir.'

'I can see that. What for? You won't find anything there, you know.'

'I was trying to get some context for the Marshall case. Actually—'

'*Context?* Is that one of those fancy words they taught you at college? Bloody time-wasting sounds more like it.'

'Sir, I was talking to one of Graham Marshall's friends earlier,' she said. 'He told me he was approached by a strange man on the riverbank about two months before the Marshall boy disappeared. I was just trying to see if any similar incidents were on file.'

Shaw sat on the edge of the desk. 'And?' he asked. 'I'm curious.'

'Nothing so far, sir. Do you remember anything odd like that?'

Shaw frowned. 'No. But who is this "friend"?'

'Alan Banks, sir. Actually, it's Detective Chief Inspector Banks.'

'Is it, indeed? Banks? The name sounds vaguely familiar. I take it he didn't report the incident at the time?'

'No, sir. Too scared of what his parents might say.'

'I can imagine. Look, about this Banks chap,' he went on. 'I think I'd like a little word with him. Can you arrange it?'

'I've got his phone number, sir. But . . .' Michelle was about to tell Shaw that it was *her* case and that she didn't appreciate his poaching her interviews, but she decided it wouldn't be diplomatic to alienate one of her new senior officers. Besides, he might be helpful, having been involved in the original investigation.

'But what?'

'Nothing, sir.'

'Good.' Shaw stood up. 'We'll have him in, then. Soon as possible.'

After Shaw left, Michelle went back to the files. Nineteen sixty-five hadn't been a bumper crime year for Peterborough, but the fast-growing city had its share of some of the national problems. Cannabis was beginning to insinuate its way into the lifestyles of the young and rebellious and the pornography trade was blossoming in the shape of tons of German, Danish and Swedish magazines.

She flipped through file after file and tossed them aside in frustration. Finally, as her eyes were starting to tire, she struck gold.

4

Banks walked into the Coach and Horses with his father at eight o'clock that night, his mother's steamed pudding and custard weighing heavily in his stomach. This was Arthur Banks's local. He had been coming here almost every day for forty years, and so had his cronies, Harry Finnegan and Norman Grenfell, Dave's father.

After Banks and his father had settled themselves at the table, pints in front of them and introductions made, Norman Grenfell started the ball rolling. 'We were just saying, Alan, what a terrible thing it is about the Marshall boy. I remember you and our David used to play with him.'

'Yes. How is Dave, by the way?'

'He's doing fine,' said Norman. 'He and Ellie still live in Dorchester. The kids have grown up now, of course.'

'They're still together?' Ellie was, Banks remembered, Dave's first girlfriend; they must have started going out together around 1968.

'Some couples stick it out,' muttered Arthur Banks.

Banks ignored the remark and asked Norman to pass on his regards to Dave next time they spoke.

'Well,' he continued, raising his glass. 'Here's to Graham. In the long run, I suppose it's best they found him. At least his parents can lay his bones to rest now.'

'True enough,' said Harry.

'Amen,' said Norman.

'Didn't Graham's father used to drink here?' Banks asked.

Arthur Banks laughed. 'Yes. He was a rum customer, Bill Marshall.'

'In what way was he rum?' Banks asked.

There was a pause, then Arthur Banks looked over at Harry Finnegan. 'He was shifty, wouldn't you say so, Harry?'

'He was indeed. Always an eye for a fiddle, and not above a bit of strong-arm stuff. And he was a big talker, too.'

'What do you mean?' Banks asked.

'Well,' his father said, 'you know the family came from London?'

'Yes.'

'Bill Marshall worked as a bricklayer and he was a good one, too, but when he'd had a drink or two he'd start letting things slip about some of his other activities in London.'

'I still don't understand.'

'He was a fit bloke, Bill. Strong. Big hands, powerful upper body.'

'What your Dad's saying,' explained Harry, leaning forward, 'is that Bill Marshall let slip he used to act as an enforcer for gangsters down the Smoke. Protection rackets, that sort of thing.'

The Smoke? Banks hadn't heard that term for London in years. 'Did you tell the police?'

The men looked at one another, then Arthur looked back at Banks, his lip curling. 'Bill Marshall might have been a bit of a wild man, but he didn't go round killing young lads, especially not his own son.'

'I didn't say I thought he did it,' Banks said. 'If there was any truth in what Bill Marshall said about his criminal background in London, then isn't it possible that something he'd done there came back to haunt him?'

'But nobody hurt *Bill*.'

'Doesn't matter, Dad. These people often have more devious ways of getting back at their enemies. Did he ever mention any names?'

'What do you mean?'

'I mean in London. The people he worked for.'

Harry Finnegan gave a nervous laugh. Arthur shot him a glance. 'As a matter of fact,' said Arthur, pausing dramatically, 'he did.'

'Who?'

'The Twins. Reggie and Ronnie Kray.'

'Bloody hell!'

Arthur Banks's eyes shone with triumph. '*Now* do you see why we just thought he had a big mouth on him?'

FOR THE SECOND TIME that day Annie turned up at Swainsdale Hall. Josie answered the door, as usual, holding back a barking Miata. Robin and Martin were both in the garden sitting at a wrought-iron table, but neither of them seemed to be enjoying the beautiful evening. Both seemed pale, tense and preoccupied, the mobile perched on the table like an unexploded bomb.

'What are you doing here?' Martin Armitage said.

'I take it Luke's not arrived yet?'

'No.'

'Heard from him again?'

'No.'

Sighing, Annie sat down. 'Look,' she said, 'I know what's going on.'

'I don't understand what you mean.'

'Come off it. After I left this morning I waited in a lay-by and followed you to the shepherd's shelter. What were you doing there?'

'None of your bloody business. Why, what are you going to do? Charge me with disobeying government regulations?'

'Let me tell you what you were doing, Mr Armitage. You were leaving a briefcase full of money. Old bills. Tens and twenties for the most part. Around ten thousand pounds, at a guess, maybe fifteen.'

Armitage was red in the face. Still, Annie pressed on. 'And now let me tell you what happened. They got in touch with you last night on your mobile, said they'd got Luke and you were to hand over the money. You told them you couldn't lay your hands on that much cash until the banks were open, so they gave you until this morning. They said no police, which is why my arrival scared you.'

'I've told you—'

'Martin.' Robin spoke for the first time. 'Can't you see? She knows.'

'But he said—'

'They don't know who I am,' said Annie. 'And I'm pretty certain they didn't see me around Mortsett this morning.'

'Pretty certain?'

Annie looked him in the eye. 'I'd be a liar if I said I was a hundred per cent certain.' In the silence that followed, she held Martin Armitage's gaze until she saw it waver and finally wane into defeat. His shoulders slumped.

Robin leaned over and put her arm round him. 'It's all right, darling,' she said. 'The police will know what to do. They'll be discreet.'

'But he said no police,' Martin said. 'He said if we brought in the police he'd kill Luke.'

'What did you say?' Annie asked.

'I told him I'd already reported Luke missing.'

'And what did he say to that?'

'He was quiet for a moment, then he said that was fine, but to tell you Luke had rung to say that he was coming home. Which I did.'

'It was a man who made the call, then?'

'Yes.'

'What time did you receive the call?'

'About half past nine. Just before Robin rang you.'

'How much did he ask for?'

'Ten thousand.'

'Accent?'

'None, really. He didn't have a strong accent. Sort of bland.'

'And his voice? High or low? Husky, reedy, whatever?'

'Just ordinary. I'm sorry, I'm not good at this sort of thing, especially recognising voices on the telephone.'

Annie favoured him with a smile. 'Not many people are. Think about it, though. It could be important if there's anything at all you remember about the voice. Did he let you speak to Luke?'

'No, he said Luke was being kept somewhere else.'

'And he called you on your mobile?'

'Yes. At first, I thought it was Luke because his name came up.'

'So the kidnapper used Luke's mobile to call you?'

'I suppose so. Why does it matter?'

'It tells us he's in an area where there's a signal. Or he was when he made the call. Also, if he's used it at other times, we'll be able to get the information from the phone company. It might help us pinpoint him.'

'Tell me,' said Robin, 'in your experience, in how many cases do they . . . how many times do the victims . . .'

'I don't have any statistics offhand,' Annie admitted. 'But if it makes you feel any better, kidnappers are essentially business people. They're in it for the money, not to hurt anyone. There's every chance that this will be resolved and that you'll see Luke back here safe and sound.' Annie could feel her nose growing as she talked. Too much time had passed, she suspected, for a happy ending.

THE KRAYS, Banks thought as he lay in his narrow bed that night. Reggie and Ronnie. He didn't remember the exact dates, but he had an idea they were flying high in the mid-sixties, part of the swinging London scene, mixing with celebrities, pop stars and politicians.

It was hard to believe that Graham's dad had anything to do with them, but the Marshalls came from the East End of London, Kray territory in the mid-sixties, and Banks now remembered that he had felt afraid around Mr Marshall.

If Bill Marshall had done anything for the Krays, it had obviously

been low level, going round exuding physical menace, maybe clob-
bering the occasional informer or double-dealer in a dark alley.

He would have to tell DI Hart. Michelle. She had left a message
with Banks's mother while he was out, asking him to drop by Thorpe
Wood at 9.00am the following morning. It was her case, after all. If
there was a connection, he was surprised it hadn't come out in the
investigation. Usually the parents come under very close scrutiny in
missing-child cases, no matter how grief-stricken they appear.

Banks picked up his *Photoplay* diary. He flipped to the Saturday
before Graham disappeared. August 21: *Went into town with
Graham. Bought* Help! *with Uncle Ken's record token.*

On Sunday he had written: *Played records at Paul's place. Saw
police car go to Graham's house.* On Monday: *Graham's run away
from home. Police came. Joey flew away.*

Interesting he should assume that Graham had run away from
home. But of course he would at that age. The alternatives would
have been too horrific for a fourteen-year-old boy to contemplate.

Tired, Banks put the diary aside and turned out the light. It felt odd
to be back in the same bed he had slept in during his teenage years, the
same bed where he had had his first sexual experience, with Kay
Summerville, while his parents were out visiting his grandparents.

He put on his headphones and turned on his portable CD player,
listening to Vaughan Williams's second string quartet, and settled
back to more pleasant thoughts of Kay Summerville. But as he
approached the edge of sleep his thoughts jumbled, mixing memory
with dream. It was cold and dark, and Banks and Graham were walking across a rugby field, cracking spider-web patterns in the ice as they
walked, their breath misting the air. Banks must have said something
about the Krays being arrested—was he interested in criminals, even
then?—and Graham just laughed, saying the law could never touch
people like them. Banks asked him how he knew, and Graham said he
used to live near them. 'They were kings,' he said.

Puzzled by the memory, or dream, Banks turned the light on again
and picked up the diary. If what he had just imagined had any basis
in reality, then it had happened in winter. He glanced through his
entries for January and February 1965. But no mention of the Krays
until March 9, when he had written: *Krays went to trial today.
Graham laughed and said they'd get off easy.* So Graham *had* mentioned them. It was flimsy, but a start.

He turned off the light again, and this time he drifted off to sleep
without further thoughts of either Graham or Kay Summerville.

WHEN BANKS ARRIVED at Thorpe Wood the following morning and asked to see Detective Inspector Hart, he was surprised when a man came down to greet him. The telephone call that his mother had told him about when he got back from the pub had been from Michelle.

'Mr Banks, or should I say DCI Banks? Come with me, please, if you would.' He stood aside and gestured for Banks to enter.

'And you are?'

'Detective Superintendent Shaw. We'll talk in my office.'

Shaw looked familiar, but Banks couldn't place him. As soon as they got to Shaw's office, Shaw disappeared, saying he'd be back in a couple of minutes. Old copper's trick, Banks knew. And Shaw knew he knew.

There wasn't likely to be anything of interest in the office if Shaw was willing to leave Banks there alone, but he had a poke around nonetheless. There was a framed photograph on the wall, quite a few years old by the look of it, showing a younger Shaw and Jet Harris standing by an unmarked Rover looking for all the world like John Thaw and Dennis Waterman in *The Sweeney*. The bookcase held a few legal texts and an American textbook called *Practical Homicide Investigation*. Banks was browsing through this and trying not to look at the gruesome illustrations when, after half an hour, Shaw came back, followed by a rather embarrassed-looking DI Michelle Hart.

'Sorry about that,' said Shaw, sitting opposite Banks. 'Something came up. You know how it is.' Michelle sat to one side looking uncomfortable.

'I know.' Banks put the book aside. 'What can I do for you, Superintendent Shaw?'

'You don't remember me, do you?'

Shaw stared at Banks, and Banks searched through his store of faces for a match. The ginger hair was thin on top, hardly any eyebrows, freckles, pale blue eyes, the face filled out and jowly, the fleshy, red-veined nose of a seasoned drinker. He was familiar, but there was something different about him. Then Banks knew.

'You've had your ears fixed,' he said. 'The wonders of modern medicine.'

Shaw reddened. 'So you *do* remember me.'

'You were the baby DC who came to our house after Graham disappeared.' It was hard to believe, but Shaw would have been about twenty-one at the time, only seven years older than Banks, yet he had seemed an adult, someone from another world.

'Tell me,' said Shaw, leaning forward across the table so Banks could smell the minty breath of a man who drinks his breakfast, 'I've always wondered. Did you ever get your budgie back?'

Banks leaned back in his chair. 'Well, now we've got all the pleasantries out of the way, why don't we get on with it?'

Shaw jerked his head at Michelle, who slid a photograph across the desk to Banks. She looked serious with her reading glasses on. Sexy, too, Banks thought. 'Is this the man?' she asked.

Banks stared at the black and white photo and felt a rush of blood to his brain, ears buzzing and vision clouding. It all flooded back, those few moments of claustrophobia and terror in the stranger's grip.

'Are you all right?'

It was Michelle who spoke, a concerned look on her face.

'I'm fine,' said Banks. 'It's him.'

Shaw nodded, and Michelle took the picture back.

'Why?' Banks asked, looking from one to the other. 'Who is it?'

'James Francis McCallum,' Michelle said. 'He went missing from a mental institution near Wisbech on Thursday, June 17th, 1965.'

'When was he caught?' Banks asked.

'That's just it,' Michelle went on. 'He wasn't. McCallum's body was fished out of the River Nene near Oundle on July 1st.'

Banks felt his mouth open and shut. 'Dead?' he managed.

'Dead,' echoed Shaw. 'Nearly two months before your friend disappeared. So you see, DCI Banks, you've been labouring under an illusion for all these years. Now, what I'm really interested in is why you lied to me and DI Proctor in the first place.'

Banks felt numb from the shock he had just received. *Dead.* All these years. The guilt. And all for nothing. The man on the riverbank *couldn't* have abducted and killed Graham. He should have felt relieved, but he only felt confused. 'I didn't lie,' he muttered.

'Call it a sin of omission, then. You didn't tell us about McCallum.'

'Doesn't seem as if it would have mattered, does it?'

Shaw scratched his chin. 'I remember thinking at the time that you knew something, that you were holding something back. I'd like to have taken you to the station, had you down in the cells for an hour or so, but you were a minor and Reg Proctor was a bit of a softy, when it came right down to it. What really happened to your friend?'

'I don't know. Graham just disappeared.'

'Are you sure you and your mates didn't set on him?'

'What the hell are you talking about?'

'Maybe a fight broke out and Graham got killed. Maybe fell and smashed his skull, or broke his neck? I'm not saying you *intended* to kill him, but it happened, didn't it? Why don't you come clean with me, Banks? It'll do you good to get it off your chest after all these years.'

'Sir?'

'Shut up, DI Hart. Well, Banks? I'm waiting.'

Banks stood up. 'You'll have a bloody long wait, then. Goodbye.' He walked towards the door. Shaw didn't try to stop him. As he turned the handle, he heard the superintendent speak again and turned to face him. Shaw was grinning. 'Only teasing, Banks,' he said. Then his expression became serious. 'My, but you're sensitive. The point I want to make is that you're on *my* turf, and it turns out you can't help us any more now than you could all those years ago. So my advice to you, laddie, is to bugger off back up to Yorkshire and forget about Graham Marshall. Leave it to the pros.'

'Bloody good job the pros did last time,' said Banks, leaving and slamming the door behind him. Outside the station he kicked a tyre, lit a cigarette and got in his car. Maybe Shaw was right and he should head back north. He still had over a week's holiday left and plenty to do around the cottage, whereas there was nothing more he could do down here. Turning up the volume on Cream's 'Crossroads', he sped out of the police car park, daring one of the patrol cars to chase him. Nobody did.

THEY LOOKED TIRED, Annie thought, as the Armitage team gathered in the boardroom of Western Division late that morning.

DS Gristhorpe sat at the head of the table. Also present were DCs Templeton, Rickerd and Jackman. It was the DCs who had borne the brunt of the previous night's surveillance.

'So we're not much further ahead,' Gristhorpe opened.

'No, sir,' said Annie. 'Except we've checked with the phone company and got Luke's records. The ransom call to Martin Armitage was the only call made after Luke's disappearance and it was local.'

'Anything else?'

'We've got a fair idea of Luke's movements until five thirty the day he disappeared. He arrived at the bus station by the Swainsdale Centre at a quarter to three. We've been looking at some of the CCTV footage, and he walked round the centre for a while. That takes us up until half past three. He appeared in that small computer shop on North Market Street at a quarter to four. He stayed there half an hour, then he visited the music shop at the corner of York Road and Barton Place.'

'And next?' Gristhorpe asked.

'The Used Book Shop on the market square. Then he walked out of CCTV range at half past five, and we haven't found anyone who admits to seeing him since. Oh, and he was also seen talking to a group of lads in the square after coming out of the book shop. One of them took the parcel of books from his hand and they tossed it around to one another while he flailed around trying to get it back.'

'What happened in the end?'

'One of them threw it to him and they went off laughing.'

'Classmates?'

'Yes. We've had a chat with them. They've all got alibis.'

'Which direction did he walk off in?' Gristhorpe asked.

'Down Market Street. South.'

Gristhorpe scratched his chin. 'What do you make of it, Annie?'

'I don't know, sir. He's been gone three nights now and nobody's seen hide nor hair.'

'He's probably dead, sir,' cut in DC Winsome Jackman.

'But why hasn't the kidnapper gone for the money?'

'Because he knows we're watching,' Annie answered. 'It's the only explanation. He must have seen me when I went up to the shelter to check the briefcase. Unless . . .'

'Aye, lass?'

'Well, a couple of things puzzle me about all this. In the first place, why did the kidnapper wait so long before getting in touch with the Armitages and making his demand? Luke disappeared some time late on Monday, yet the demand didn't come until after dark on *Tuesday*.'

'What else?' Gristhorpe asked.

'Well, Martin Armitage told me that when he asked to speak to Luke, the kidnapper said Luke was somewhere else. Isn't it usual for kidnappers to let the people they want the money from speak to their loved ones? Isn't it an incentive to pay? Proof of life?'

'So we've got two unusual variations on the formula,' said Gristhorpe. 'First, the time delay, and second, no proof of life. Anything else?'

'Yes,' said Annie. 'The ransom demand is nowhere near enough.'

'The Armitages aren't as rich as people think,' argued DC Kevin Templeton.

'My point exactly, Kev. So they're struggling to maintain the lifestyle they've become accustomed to. We know that now, but it wasn't common knowledge. If you kidnapped the son of a famous ex-model and a famous ex-footballer living in a place like Swainsdale Hall, how much would you *think* they were worth? How much would you ask them for the life of their son? I'd go to a hundred thousand, myself. I certainly wouldn't start at ten.'

'So maybe the kidnapper knew they were on their uppers?' Templeton suggested. 'Maybe it's someone who knows the family?'

'Then why kidnap Luke at all? Why not go for someone who had more money?' Annie looked at Gristhorpe.

'What are your conclusions, Annie?' Gristhorpe asked.

'Either it's an amateur job,' Annie answered. '*Very* amateur, like some junkie who saw the chance to get enough money for his next few fixes and now he's too scared to go through with it. Or it's something else entirely. A set-up, a diversion, the ransom demand merely to deflect us, confuse us, and something else is going on.'

'Like what?' Gristhorpe asked.

'I don't know, sir,' Annie answered. 'All I know is that in either scenario the outcome looks bad for Luke.'

ANDREW NAYLOR, the man from the Ministry, drove over the disinfectant pad at the entrance to the unfenced road above Gratly. It was part of Andrew's job to collect water samples from local lakes, ponds and reservoirs, and these were later tested for contaminants. Because some of these bodies of water were surrounded by open country, Andrew was one of the few with a special dispensation to visit them.

That day, his last call was Hallam Tarn, a hollowed-out bowl of water on the very top of the moor. The deepest part of the tarn ran close to the road and a dry-stone wall separated it from children, drunks and anyone else foolish enough to wander around up there in the dark. To access the water, you had to drive a few yards further on, cross the stile and take a footpath that led to its shallow shore.

Andrew walked along the narrow dirt path to the edge of the tarn and squatted by the waterside to fill his sample jar. Because he had to take samples from various depths, he then got in his small dinghy and began to row.

When he neared the wall, he noticed some material snagged on the roots of an old tree. The tree was gone, but gnarled roots still jutted out of the bank. Curious about the material, he rowed closer.

When he got near enough, he stretched out his arm and tried to free the material from the root. It was heavier than he thought, and as it jerked free, the dinghy tipped and Andrew, off-balance, fell into the tarn. He was a strong swimmer, so drowning didn't worry him, but what chilled his blood was that the thing he was holding as tightly as a lover in a slow dance was a dead body, and from its ashen face, open dead eyes looked directly into his.

Andrew let go of the burden, mouth full of bile. He struggled back into the dinghy and rowed back to shore, where he stopped only long enough to be sick, before squelching back to his van.

BANKS STILL felt angry when he pulled up outside his parents' house. He found his father in front of the TV and his mother in the kitchen.

'I'm heading home this afternoon,' he said, popping his head round the kitchen door. 'Thanks for letting me stay.'

'There's always a bed for you here,' his mother said. 'You know that. By the way, there was a phone call for you while you were out.'

'Who was it?'

'Same woman as last night. Have you got a new girlfriend already?'

Already? Sandra had been gone nearly two years, was pregnant with another man's child and about to marry him.

'No, Mum,' he said. 'It's one of the local coppers. You already know that from last night. What did she say?'

'To ring her back when you had a moment. I wrote down the number in case you'd forgotten it.'

The number scribbled on the pad by the hall telephone wasn't familiar. It certainly wasn't Thorpe Wood. Curious, Banks dialled.

'DI Hart here. Who's speaking?'

'Michelle? It's me. Alan Banks. Is this your mobile number?'

'That's right. Look, first off, I'm sorry about DS Shaw this morning.'

'That's all right. Not your fault.'

'I just felt . . . well, anyway, I'm surprised he's taking such an inter-est. It's not even his case. I had him marked down as just putting in time till his retirement, now he's all over me like a dirty shirt.'

'What did you want to talk to me about?'

'Are you going home?'

'Yes.'

'When?'

'I don't know. This afternoon. This evening.'

'I was wondering if you'd like to meet up for a chat before you go.'

'Yes, OK. Why not?'

'Shall we say half past five in Starbucks, Cathedral Square?'

'Half five it is. That'll give me plenty of time to pack. See you there.'

ANNIE AND GRISTHORPE arrived at Hallam Tarn in time to see two police frogmen haul up the body. Once on shore, they laid it on the grass at the feet of Dr Burns, the police surgeon. It was Luke Armitage. No doubt about it. He was wearing the black T-shirt and jeans that Robin had said he had on when he went to Eastvale, and Annie recognised his face.

Dr Burns turned the body over and pointed to the back of Luke's head. Annie could see the signs of a blow. 'Would that have been enough to cause death?' she asked.

'Hard blow to the cerebellum?' said Dr Burns. 'Certainly.' He began to examine the body. 'He's cold and there's no rigor.'

'What does that tell you?'

'Usually a body is cold after eight to ten hours in the water. As for the rigor, given the obvious effects of water on his skin, it must have come and gone.'

'How long does that take?'

'In water? Anything from two to four days.'

Two days, Annie thought. It was Thursday afternoon now, and the ransom demand had come two days ago, on Tuesday evening. Was Luke already dead by then? If so, his death was nothing to do with her rash actions in following Martin Armitage. If that were the case, then the kidnapper was trying to cash in on Luke's death, which could have come about for other reasons.

The sound of an approaching van interrupted Annie's thoughts, and she looked across to see scene-of-crime officers jumping the stile. Well, she thought, maybe the experts would be able to tell her more.

BANKS FOUND STARBUCKS and sipped a latte while he waited.

Michelle arrived five minutes late, cool and collected, wearing black slacks and a slate-grey jacket over a cream blouse. She went to the counter for a cappuccino then sat down opposite Banks.

'Bit of a shock for you, wasn't it, this morning?' she said.

'I suppose so,' Banks said. 'After all these years . . . I don't know, I suppose I'd allowed myself to believe there had to be a connection.'

'You've got a bit of froth on your lip.' Before Banks could wipe it away, Michelle reached out her finger and did it for him.

'Thanks,' he said.

Michelle blushed and let out a little giggle. 'I don't know why I did that. My mother used to do it when I drank milkshakes.'

'Haven't had a milkshake in years,' said Banks.

'Me neither. What next?'

'Home. And you?'

'Dunno. The leads are hardly jumping out at me.'

Banks thought for a moment. 'I've heard rumours that Graham Marshall's dad was connected with the Krays in London just before the family moved up here.'

'Connected? In what way?'

'Strong-arm man. Enforcer. It might be worth delving into.'

'But what could they have to do with Graham's murder?'

'Probably nothing,' Banks said. 'They didn't operate outside London much, but if Bill Marshall did work for them, then there's always the chance he left them reason to bear a grudge, and the twins had a long reach. Anyway, it's not only that. If Bill Marshall did work as a strong-arm man for the Krays, what was he doing up here? You know as well as I do that people don't just walk away from that line of work. Maybe he got himself fixed up with someone local.'

'So you're saying he might have been up to the same tricks here and that might have had something to do with Graham's death?'

'I'm just saying it's possible, that's all. Worth investigating.'

'There was a reference to a protection racket in the old crime logs,' Michelle said. 'Someone called Carlo Fiorino. Ring any bells?'

'Vaguely,' said Banks. 'Maybe his name was in the papers when I was a kid. Anyway, it's something to think about.'

'So why didn't it come up in the original investigation?'

'Didn't it?' said Banks. 'Dunno. But as your boss made clear this morning, it's none of my business.'

Michelle frowned. 'Yeah, I know. I keep thinking he's looking over my shoulder, even now, in here.'

'I don't want you to get into trouble for talking to me.'

'Don't worry. I wasn't followed. I'm only being paranoid.'

'It doesn't mean you're not being followed. Will you keep in touch, let me know if you come up with anything?'

'I shouldn't, but I will.'

'And, look, Graham's mother mentioned a funeral, when the remains have been released. I think I'd like to come down for it. Will you let me know when it will be?'

'Of course.'

'And, lastly, will you answer another question for me?'

Michelle nodded but looked wary and shuffled in her seat.

'Are you married?' Banks asked.

'No,' she said. 'No, I'm not.' And she got up and walked out without even saying goodbye.

Banks was about to go after her when his mobile rang. Cursing, he answered the call.

'Alan? It's Annie. Hope I haven't called at a bad time.'

'No, not at all.'

'Only we could use a bit of extra help, if you've finished your business down there.'

'Pretty much,' said Banks. 'What's up?'

'Know that missing kid I told you about? Luke Armitage?'

'What about him?'

'It looks as if it's just turned into a murder case.'

'Shit,' said Banks. 'I'm on my way.'

5

'Strictly speaking, you know,' said Banks, 'this is your case. It has been from the start. Are you sure you want me muscling in?'

'I wouldn't have rung you if I didn't, would I?' said Annie. 'Anyway, you can help me just as long as you don't treat me like a skivvy.'

'Have I ever?'

'This is a pretty good start.'

Banks's car was in the garage for servicing and wouldn't be ready until after lunch, so they had signed out a department car that morning, and Annie was driving; something Banks liked to do himself.

'I was thinking I could sort of get to like it,' said Banks. 'There's a lot to be said for having a chauffeuse.'

Annie shot him a look. 'Feel like getting out and walking?'

'No, thanks.'

As Annie drove, Banks told her about McCallum turning out to be an escaped mental patient who drowned before Graham disappeared.

'I'm so sorry, Alan,' she said, touching his knee. 'After all those years feeling guilty and responsible . . . But you must be relieved . . . I mean, knowing it couldn't have been him, so it wasn't your fault?'

'I suppose I must. You know, apart from the police down there, you're the only other person I've ever told about what happened by the river that day.'

'You never told Sandra?'

'No.'

'Why?'

'I don't know.'

Banks felt Annie retreat into silence beside him and knew he'd done again exactly the sort of thing that caused her to end their romantic relationship. It was as if she offered him something warm, soft and sensitive, yet when he reached out and touched it, she shot back into her hard, impenetrable shell.

Before either of them could think of anything else to say, they arrived at the end of the Armitages' drive, where reporters clamoured around them with cameras. The officer on duty lifted the tape and let them through.

'Impressive,' said Banks, when the building's solid, symmetrical architecture came into view. 'I've only seen the place from the riverside walk before.'

Annie sighed. 'I'm not looking forward to this.'

Banks turned to look at her. 'Who dealt with the identification?'

'Winsome did. Last night.'

'So you haven't seen the parents since the boy's body was found?'

'No.'

'If you don't think I'm being patronising, why don't you let me deal with them?'

'Be my guest. Fresh approach and all that.'

Josie answered the door almost the moment they rang the bell and led them into the living room, where Banks introduced himself.

'What is it now?' Martin Armitage asked, glaring at Annie. Neither he nor his wife looked as if they had had much sleep.

'A murder investigation,' said Banks. 'Or so it seems. And we need your help.'

'I don't see how we can help any more than we have done already. We cooperated with you, against the kidnapper's wishes, and look what happened.' He glanced towards Annie again, voice rising. 'I hope you realise this is your fault, that Luke's death is *your* responsibility. If you hadn't followed me to the shelter, the kidnapper would have picked up the money and Luke would be home safe and sound.'

'I'm sorry for your loss,' Banks said, 'but it's no good flinging blame about. We don't know how or why Luke died yet. We don't even know where or when. So until we've been able to answer some of those basic questions we're not in a position to jump to conclusions.

'I'm sure you know,' Banks continued, 'that Luke's death changes the way we proceed in the investigation, and we're going to have to go over much of the same ground again. Firstly, we'll need to have a look at Luke's room and then we'd like to talk to your housekeeper and her husband.'

MICHELLE HAD BEEN JOKING when she told Banks she was getting paranoid, but she was beginning to think that every time she visited the archives, Mrs Metcalfe rang Detective Superintendent Shaw. Here he was again, preceded by the dark chill of his shadow, on the threshold of the tiny room.

'Any progress?' he asked, leaning against the door.

Michelle paused. She had to be careful what she said because she didn't want Shaw to know that Banks had tipped her off to the Kray connection. That would send him into a tantrum she could well do without. 'I was reading over the reports on a protection racket investigation in July 1965, and Graham's dad's name came up.'

'So? Where's the connection?'

'A club on Church Street called Le Phonographe.'

'I remember that place. It was a disco. Owned by a nasty piece of work called Carlo Fiorino. Used to like to pretend he was Mafia, wore the striped, wide-lapel suits, pencil-thin moustache, spats and everything—very Untouchables. Plenty of local villains hung out there.'

'Including Bill Marshall?'

'Yes.'

'So you knew about Bill Marshall's activities?'

'Of course we did. He was strictly a minor presence. We kept an eye on him. It was routine.'

'What was this Carlo Fiorino's game?'

'Bit of everything. Soon as the new town expansion was under way he turned Le Phonographe into a casino. He also owned an escort agency. We think he got into drugs, prostitution and pornography, but he was always clever enough to stay one step ahead, and he played both sides against the middle. Most of the time.'

'What do you mean, sir?'

'Got himself shot in a drug war with the Jamaicans in 1982.'

'But he never did time?'

'Never got charged with anything, far as I remember.'

'Doesn't that strike you as odd, sir?'

'Odd?' Shaw seemed to snap out of his reminiscing mood and become his grumpy old self again. 'I'll tell you what's bloody odd, DI Hart. It's you asking these questions. None of this can possibly have anything to do with what happened to Graham Marshall. You're muckraking. I don't know why, but that's what you're doing.'

'But, sir, doesn't it seem odd to you that when Graham Marshall disappeared, his father never came under close scrutiny, even though he had recently been implicated in a criminal ring?'

'You think you can do better than us, do you?' said Shaw. 'Think you can out-detect Jet Harris?'

'I didn't say that, sir. It's just the advantage of hindsight, that's all.'

'Look, we worked our bollocks off on that case, Jet Harris, Reg Proctor and me. It's about time you stopped nosing about down here and got back on the bloody job.' And he turned and stalked out.

Michelle noticed her hands were shaking when he left, and she felt her breath held tight in her chest. She didn't like confrontation with authority. But Shaw's rage seemed out of proportion to the situation.

Back in her office, she found a message slip on her desk informing her that Dr Cooper had rung and wanted her to drop by the mortuary. No time like the present, she thought, heading out to her car.

THE SEARCH OF LUKE'S ROOM didn't reveal much except a cassette tape marked *Songs from a Black Room*, which Banks, with Robin's permission, slipped in his pocket to listen to later. Banks was surprised at the range of Luke's musical tastes. There was the usual stuff, of course, but among the grunge, metal and hip-hop, he had found other oddities, such as Benjamin Britten's setting of Rimbaud's *Les Illuminations* and Miles Davis's *In a Silent Way*. There were also several indie CDs, including, Banks was thrilled to see, his son Brian's band's first recording, *Blue Rain*. Not your usual listening for a fifteen-year-old. But Banks was coming to believe that Luke Armitage had been a far from typical fifteen-year-old.

He had also read some of the stories and poems Annie had collected from her first visit, and in his humble opinion they showed real promise. They didn't tell him anything about what might have happened to Luke, or his feelings about his father or stepfather, but they revealed a young mind preoccupied with death and social alienation.

Unlike Annie, Banks wasn't surprised by the room's decor. Brian hadn't painted his room black, but he had stuck posters on the walls and surrounded himself with his favourite music. Annie had no children, so Banks could imagine how the black room would seem more outlandish to her. The only thing that disturbed him was Luke's apparent obsession with dead rock stars, and with the absence of anything to do with his famous father, Neil Byrd. Something was definitely out of kilter there.

Brian had gone on to make a career of music, and now his band was on the verge of recording for a major label. After getting over the initial shock that Brian wasn't going to follow any safe paths in life, Banks had come to feel very proud of him. Banks wondered if

Luke had been any good. Maybe the tape would tell him.

Josie Batty and her husband Calvin lived in their own self-contained apartment at the far end of Swainsdale Hall. Josie looked as if she could be quite an attractive young woman if she tried, Banks thought. But as it was, her hair seemed lifeless and ill-cut, her clothes plain and her complexion pale and dry. Her husband was short and thickset with dark colouring and heavy eyebrows that met in the middle.

'What exactly are your duties here?' Banks asked the two of them when they were settled in the living room.

'General, really. I do most of the washing, ironing, cleaning and cooking. Calvin does odd jobs, takes care of the cars and garden.'

'Did any of your duties involve taking care of Luke?'

'I'd make sure he was well fed if sir and madam had to go away.'

'What did Luke do when he was left alone in the house? Did he ever have his friends over? That sort of thing.'

'He didn't have no friends to ask over, did he?' said Calvin.

'You know that's not true,' said his wife.

'So he did entertain friends?'

'Not here.'

Banks took a deep breath. 'Who were these friends, Mrs Batty?'

'Just someone I saw him with, that's all.'

'Where?'

'In Eastvale. Swainsdale Centre.'

'How old? His age? Older? Younger?'

'Older. She wasn't no fifteen-year-old, I can tell you that.'

'What age?'

'Young woman.'

'How young? Late teens, early twenties?'

'Aye, around that.'

'Taller or shorter than him?'

'Shorter. Luke were a big lad for his age. Tall and skinny.'

'What did she look like?'

'Dark.'

'You mean she was black?'

'No, her skin was pale. She just dressed dark, like him. Her hair was dyed black and she had them studs and chains all over t'place. And she had a tattoo,' she added in a hushed tone, as if saving the greatest sin for last.

Banks glanced at Annie, who, he happened to know from experience, had a butterfly tattoo just above her right breast. Annie gave him a look. 'Where?' she asked Josie.

Josie touched her upper left arm, just below the shoulder. 'There,' she said. 'She was wearing one of them leather waistcoats over a T-shirt.'

'What was the tattoo?' Annie asked her.

'Couldn't tell,' said Josie. 'Too far away.'

This woman shouldn't be too difficult to find if she lived in or near Eastvale, Banks thought. There was only one club, the Bar None, which catered for such a crowd. 'Would you mind if we sent a sketch artist over to work on an impression with you?' he asked.

'I suppose not,' said Josie. 'But I didn't get a close look.'

'Can you tell us anything more about her?' Banks asked.

'No. It was just a quick look. I were having a coffee at the food court when I saw them walk by and go into that there big music shop.'

'HMV?'

'That's the one.'

'What were they doing?'

'Just walking.'

'Close together?'

'They weren't holding hands, if that's what you mean.'

'But you knew they were together? How?'

'You just know, don't you?'

They got no further with the Battys.

IT WAS ONLY a short drive from police HQ to the district hospital, and Michelle parked in the official visitors' area and made her way to pathology.

'Ah, DI Hart,' Dr Cooper greeted her in her office, standing up and shaking hands. 'Good of you to come.'

'Not at all. You said you had something to tell me?'

'Show you, actually. It's not much, but it might help. Follow me.'

Michelle followed her into the lab, where Graham Marshall's bones were still laid out on the table and Tammy Wynette was singing 'Stand by Your Man' on Dr Cooper's portable cassette player. Though still a dirty brownish-yellow, the bones were a lot cleaner than they had been a few days ago, she noticed. The body looked asymmetrical, though, and Michelle wondered what was missing. When she looked more closely, she could see it was the bottom rib on the left side. Hadn't they been able to find it? But no, there it was on the bench Dr Cooper led her towards.

'We couldn't see it before because of the dirt,' Dr Cooper explained, 'but once we'd cleaned it up, it was plain as daylight. Look.'

Michelle bent closer and looked. She could see a deep, narrow notch in the bone. It was something she had come across before. She looked at Dr Cooper. 'Knife wound?'

'Very good. That's what I'd say.'

'Cause of death?'

Dr Cooper frowned. 'I can't say for certain. I mean, there could have been lethal poison in the system, but I can say that the wound would have been sufficient to cause death. If you follow the trajectory of the blade to its destination, it pierces the heart.'

'Front or behind?' Michelle asked.

'Does it matter?'

'If it was done from behind, it could have been a stranger. If it happened from the front, someone had to get close enough to the boy to do it without his knowing what was going to happen.'

'Yes, I see,' said Dr Cooper, picking up the rib. 'Judging from the position of the cut on the bone and by the straightness I'd say that it was done from in front, the classic upthrust though the rib cage and into the heart. Harder to be that accurate from behind.'

'So it had to be someone he would let get close to him.'

'Close enough to pat him on the shoulder, yes.'

'What kind of knife?'

'That I can't tell you, except that it was very sharp and the blade wasn't serrated. There's an expert I know who can probably tell you. His name's Dr Hilary Wendell. I can try to get him to have a look.'

'Could you?'

Dr Cooper laughed. 'I said I'd *try*. Hilary's all over the place.'

'Any idea when the coroner can release the bones for burial?'

'He can release them now as far as I'm concerned.'

'I know the Marshalls are anxious for some sense of closure. I'll give them a ring and say it's OK to make arrangements.'

'Funny thing, that, isn't it?' said Dr Cooper. 'Closure. As if burying someone's remains actually marks the end of the pain.'

'It's very human, though, don't you think?' said Michelle, for whom closure had simply refused to come, despite all the trappings.

'I suppose so. What about this, though?' Dr Cooper pointed to the rib on the lab bench. 'It could end up being evidence in court.'

'Well, I don't suppose the Marshalls will mind if they know Graham's being buried with a rib missing. Especially if it might help lead us to his killer. I'll get their permission, anyway.'

'Fine,' said Dr Cooper. 'I'll talk to the coroner this afternoon and try to track Hilary down in the meantime.'

BANKS DROVE OUT in his own car to the crime scene late that afternoon, listening to Luke Armitage's *Songs from a Black Room*.

There were only five short songs on the tape, and lyrically they were not sophisticated, about what you'd expect for a fifteen-year-old. But the remarkable thing was how much Luke's voice resembled his father's. He had Neil Byrd's broad range, though his voice hadn't deepened enough to handle the lowest notes yet, and he also had his father's timbre, wistful but bored, and even a little angry, edgy.

The last song on the tape stood out; it was a love song of sorts:

> He shut me out but you took me in.
> He's in the dark but you're a bird on the wing.
> I couldn't hold you but you chose to stay.
> Why do you care? Please don't go away.

Was it about his mother, Robin? Or was it the girl Josie had seen him with in the Swainsdale Centre? Along with Winsome Jackman and Kevin Templeton, Annie was out showing the artist's impression around the most likely places. Maybe one of them would get lucky.

The scene-of-crime officers were still at Hallam Tarn, the road still taped off, as was a local TV van, along with a gaggle of reporters who barely kept their distance. Banks pulled up by the side of the road. Detective Sergeant Stefan Nowak was in charge.

'Stefan,' Banks greeted him. 'Anything interesting?'

'Maybe,' said Stefan. 'We tried to pin down the exact point on the wall where the body had been dropped over, and it matches the spot where these stones stick out here like steps. Makes climbing easy. Good footholds.'

'I see. Could one person have done it?'

'Certainly. It's also possible the killer scratched himself climbing up.'

'You've found blood on the wall?'

'Minute traces. But we don't even know if it's human, yet.'

'Any chance of footprints?'

Stefan shook his head. 'Don't get your hopes up.'

'Do I ever? Tyre tracks?'

'Too many, and it's not a good road surface. But we're looking.'

'Wonderful.'

AFTER TRACKING DOWN a retired detective inspector who had worked out of West End Central, and persuading him to talk to her in London the following day, Michelle stopped off to rent the video of *The Krays* on her way home.

She had been living in her riverside flat for two months now, but it still felt temporary, just another place she was passing through. She didn't know why she hadn't settled in more; it was one of the nicest places she had ever lived in, if a bit pricey. But what else did she have to spend her money on?

As usual there was nothing edible in the fridge, so she went round the corner to the Indian takeaway and got some prawn curry and rice. Sitting with a tray on her lap and a bottle of South African Merlot beside her, she felt ready to watch *The Krays*.

When it had finished, Michelle didn't feel she knew much more about the Kray twins than before it had begun. She didn't really believe that the Krays had anything to do with Graham Marshall's murder, any more than she believed Brady and Hindley had.

If Bill Marshall had any serious criminal aspirations, they hadn't done him much good. He never got out of the council house.

Perhaps he swore off crime. Michelle had checked subsequent police records and found no further mention of him, so he had gone either straight or uncaught. She would guess the former, given his standard of living. Graham's disappearance must have shaken him. Maybe he sensed a connection to the world he had been involved in, so he severed all ties. She would have to have an even closer look at the old crime reports, dig out old action books and the notebooks of the detectives involved. But that could wait until after the weekend.

There wasn't enough wine left in the bottle to be worth saving, so she topped up her glass. As it so often did around bedtime, the depression seemed to close in on her like a dense fog. She sipped her wine and listened to rain tapping against her window. God, how she missed Melissa, even after all this time. She missed Ted, too, but mostly she missed Melissa.

Her thoughts went back to the day it happened. It was a movie that ran in her mind, as if on a constant loop. She wasn't there—that was a big part of the problem—but she could picture Melissa outside the school gates, her golden curls, little blue dress with the flowers on it, the other kids milling around, vigilant teachers nearby, then Melissa seeing what she thought was her father's car pulling to a stop across the road, though they always picked her up on *her* side. Then she pictured Melissa waving, smiling, and, before anyone could stop her, running right out in front of the speeding lorry.

Before getting into bed, she took Melissa's dress, the same dress she had died in, from her bedside drawer, lay down, held it to her face and cried herself to sleep.

6

Michelle got off the Intercity train at King's Cross at about half past one the following afternoon and walked down the steps to the tube. She had never worked on the Met, although she had thought of moving there after Manchester, after Melissa had died and Ted had left. Instead she had moved around a lot over the past five years and taken numerous courses, convincing herself that it was all for the good of her career. She suspected, though, she had just been running.

The tube was crowded and she had to stand all the way to Tottenham Court Road, where retired Detective Inspector Robert Lancaster had agreed to talk to her over a late lunch in Dean Street.

Though it was a pub, Michelle was pleased to see that it looked rather more up-market than some establishments, with its hanging baskets of flowers outside, stained glass and shiny dark woodwork. She had dressed about as casually as she was capable of, in a mid-length skirt, a pink V-neck top and a light wool jacket, but she would still have looked overdressed in a lot of London pubs. This one, however, catered to a business luncheon crowd. It even had a separate restaurant section, with table service, no less.

Lancaster, recognisable by the carnation he told Michelle he would be wearing in his grey suit, was a dapper man with a full head of silver hair and a sparkle in his eye. Perhaps a bit portly, Michelle noticed as he stood up to greet her, but definitely well preserved for his age, which she guessed at around seventy.

'Mr Lancaster,' she said, sitting down. 'Thank you for seeing me.'

'The pleasure's mine entirely,' he said, traces of a cockney accent in his voice. 'It's not every day I get to come down the West End and have lunch with a pretty girl like yourself.'

Michelle smiled and felt herself blush a little. A *girl*, he'd called her, when she had turned forty last September. For some reason, she didn't feel offended by Lancaster's particular brand of male chauvinism; it had such a quaint, old-fashioned feel to it. A waitress appeared with her order book.

'What would you like to drink?' Lancaster asked.

'Just an orange juice, please.'

'And I'll have another pint of Guinness, please,' Lancaster said.

The waitress fetched their drinks and asked them for their orders. 'I'll have the Cumberland sausage and mashed potatoes, please,' Michelle said. Lancaster ordered the roast beef.

He paused for a few moments, drumming his fingers on the table. Michelle could sense him changing gear, from old-fashioned gallant to seasoned street copper, wondering what she was after and whether it could harm him. She could see it in his eyes, their gaze sharpening, becoming more watchful.

'The bloke that put you onto me said you wanted to know about Reggie and Ronnie,' he said, when the waitress had wandered off.

'Sort of,' Michelle said. 'But let me explain.'

Lancaster listened, nodding here and there, as Michelle told him about the Marshalls and what had happened to Graham.

'So, you see,' she finished, 'it's not really the Kray twins, or not *just* them, anyway, that I'm interested in.'

'Yes, I see,' said Lancaster. Their food arrived and they both took a few bites before he spoke again. 'I knew Billy Marshall. We grew up just round the corner from one another. Thing is, it could've gone either way for me. I ran a bit wild when I was a kid, got into a scrap or two. I could easily have used my street-smarts for criminal purposes like Reggie and Ronnie or . . .' He let the sentence trail and ate some more roast beef.

'You're saying morality doesn't come into it?' Michelle asked. 'The law? Justice? Honesty?'

'Words, love,' Lancaster said. 'When it came down to it, when you stood at the bar of your local, and someone like Billy came in, someone you knew was a bit dodgy, well, then it was just a job you did. Everybody knew it. Nothing personal. We mixed, tolerated one another, hoped our paths never crossed in a serious way, a professional way. And remember I was working out of West End Central then. The East End wasn't my manor. I just grew up there, lived there. Of course, we were all aware there was a barrier between us, at least one we'd better not breach in public, so it was all, "Hello, Billy. How's it going? How's the wife and kid?" "Oh, fine, Bob, can't complain. How's things down the nick?" "Thriving, Billy boy, thriving." "Glad to hear it, mate." That sort of thing.'

'I can understand that,' said Michelle.

'Just wanted to get it clear,' said Lancaster, 'so you wouldn't go away thinking I was bent or anything.'

'Why would I think that?'

He winked. 'Oh, there were plenty that were. Vice, Obscene

Publications, the Sweeney. Oh, yes. It was all just getting going then, '63, '64, '65. It was the beginnings of the rise of organised crime in this country. Porn was coming in by the lorryload from Denmark, Germany, Sweden, the Netherlands. Someone had to control distribution, wholesale, resale. Same with drugs.'

'Did Bill Marshall work for Reggie and Ronnie?' Michelle asked.

'Billy was a boxer. Amateur, mind. And so were the Krays. They met up at one of the local gyms. Billy did a few odd jobs with them.'

'But he wasn't regularly employed, not on their payroll?'

'That's about it. An occasional encouragement to pay up, or deterrent against talking. You know the sort of thing.'

'What do you remember about him?'

'Nice enough bloke, if you didn't cross him. Bit of a temper, especially after a jar or two. Like I said, he was strictly low-level muscle.'

'I wonder if all this could have had any connection with Graham's death. If Billy did something to upset his masters, then—'

'If Billy Marshall had done anything to upset Reggie or Ronnie, love, he'd have been the one pushing up daisies, not the kid.'

'They wouldn't have harmed the boy to make a point?'

'Not their way, no. Direct, not subtle. They had their faults, and there wasn't much they wouldn't do if it came down to it. But if you crossed them, it wasn't your wife or your kid got hurt, it was you. It was a man's world. There was a code. Unwritten. But it was there. Reggie and Ronnie were like Robin Hood, Dick Turpin and Billy the Kid all rolled into one as far as most East Enders were concerned.'

'And you were the sheriff of Nottingham?'

Lancaster laughed. 'Hardly. I was only a DC, a mere foot soldier. But you get the picture.'

'I think so. And after the day's battles you'd all adjourn to the local and have a jolly old drink together and talk about football.'

Lancaster laughed. 'Something like that. You know, maybe you're right. Maybe it was a bit of a game.'

'I think Billy Marshall took the game to Peterborough with him. Ever hear of a bloke called Carlo Fiorino?'

Lancaster's bushy eyebrows knitted in a frown. 'No. But I've already told you, Billy didn't have the brains to set up an operation. He didn't have the authority, the charisma. Now that lad of his, he was another matter.'

Michelle pricked up her ears. 'Graham? What about him?'

'If anyone in that family was destined to go far, I'd have said it would've been him.'

'What do you mean? *Graham* was a criminal?'

'No. Well, not apart from a bit of shoplifting, but they all got into that. No, it was just that he had brains—though God knows who he got them from—*and* he was what they call street-smart these days. Never said much, but you could tell he was taking it all in, looking for the main chance.'

'You're saying *Graham* might have been involved with the Krays?'

'Nah. Oh, he might have run an errand or two for them, but they didn't mess around with twelve-year-old kids. Only that he watched and learned. There wasn't much got by him. Sharp as a tack. Billy used to leave him outside the local, sitting in the street playing marbles with the other kids. And some pretty shady customers went in there. No flies on young Graham Marshall, that's for sure. I'm just sorry to hear he came to such an early end, though I can't say as it surprises me that much.'

UNTIL THE POST-MORTEM, Banks thought his time would be well spent talking to some of Luke's teachers, starting with Gavin Barlow, the head teacher of Eastvale Comprehensive.

Barlow was weeding the garden of his north Eastvale semi, dressed in torn jeans and a dirty old shirt, as Banks entered through the garden gate. Gavin Barlow took off a glove, wiped his hand on his jeans and offered it. Banks shook hands and introduced himself.

'Yes, I've been expecting a visit,' said Barlow. 'Terrible business. Let's go inside.'

They went into a small kitchen. Banks sat at a breakfast nook with a red-and-white-checked tablecloth while Barlow made some coffee.

'Daddy, who's this?' A girl of about sixteen appeared in the doorway, all long blonde hair and bare leg.

'It's a policeman come to talk about Luke Armitage, Rose. Off you go.'

Rose pouted, then made a theatrical about-turn and sashayed away, wiggling her hips.

'I'm not sure I can tell you much about Luke,' he said, bringing over two mugs of coffee and sitting opposite Banks. 'It's usually only the troublemakers who come to my attention.'

'And Luke wasn't a troublemaker?'

'Good heavens, no! You'd hardly know he was there if he didn't move once in a while.'

'Did Luke have any close friends at school, any other pupils he might have confided in?'

'I really can't say. He always seemed to be a bit of a loner. We encourage group activities, of course, but you can't *force* people to be sociable, can you?'

Banks opened his briefcase and slipped out the artist's impression of the girl Josie Batty had seen going into HMV with Luke. 'Do you recognise this girl?' he asked, not sure how close a likeness it was.

Barlow squinted at it, then shook his head. 'No,' he said. 'I can't say as I do. I'm not saying we don't have pupils who affect that general look, but not very many, and nobody quite like this.'

Banks returned the sketch to his briefcase. 'What about his schoolwork? Did he show any promise?'

'Enormous promise. His work in maths left a lot to be desired, but when it came to English and music he was remarkably gifted.'

'Were there any teachers Luke was particularly close to?' Banks asked. 'Anyone who might be able to tell me a bit more about him?'

'Yes. You might try Ms Anderson. Lauren Anderson. She teaches English and art history. Luke was way ahead of his classmates in his appreciation of literature, and in its composition, and I believe Ms Anderson gave him extra tuition.'

Lauren Anderson's name had come up in the company's records of Luke's cellphone calls, Banks remembered. 'Is that something the school does often?'

'If the student seems likely to benefit from it, then yes, certainly.'

'Is there anything else you can tell me?' Banks asked, standing to leave.

'I don't think there is,' said Barlow. 'All in all, Luke Armitage was a bit of a dark horse.'

As they walked through to the hall, Banks felt certain he caught a flurry of blonde hair and long leg ducking through a doorway, but he could have been mistaken. Why would Rose Barlow want to listen in on their conversation, anyway?

THE RAIN SEEMED to have settled in after a short afternoon respite, when Annie did the rounds of Luke's final ports of call. She found out nothing from the HMV staff. No one recognised the sketch. Besides, as one salesperson told her, black clothing wasn't exactly unusual as far as HMV's customers were concerned, nor were body piercing or tattoos.

She fared little better at the computer shop. Gerald Kelly, the sole proprietor and staff member, remembered just about all his customers, but he had seen no one resembling the girl in black with

Luke, who had always been alone on his visits to the shop.

Annie had just one last call. Norman's Used Books was a dank, cramped space down a flight of stone steps under a bakery, one of several shops that seemed to be set right into the church walls in the market square. Annie herself had shopped there once or twice, looking for old art books.

The owner, Norman Wells, was just a little over five foot tall, with thin brown hair, a bulbous sort of face and rheumy eyes. Because it was so cold and damp down there, no matter what the weather was like up above, he always wore a moth-eaten grey cardigan, woolly gloves with the fingers cut off and an old Leeds United scarf.

Norman Wells glanced up from the paperback he was reading and nodded in Annie's direction. He seemed surprised when she showed her warrant card and spoke to him.

'I've seen you before, haven't I?' he said, taking off his reading glasses, which hung on a piece of string round his neck.

'I've been here once or twice.'

'Thought so. I never forget a face.'

Annie showed him a photograph of Luke. 'Remember him?'

'Course I do. He's the lad who disappeared, isn't he? One of your lot was around the other day asking about him. I told him all I know.'

'I'm sure you did, Mr Wells, but things have changed. It's a murder investigation now and we have to go over the ground afresh.'

'Bloody hell. I hadn't heard. Who'd . . .? He wouldn't say boo to a goose.'

'Did you know him well, then?' asked Annie.

'Well? No, I wouldn't say that. But we talked.'

'What about?'

'Books. He knew a lot more than most kids his age. His reading level was way beyond that of his contemporaries.'

'How do you know?'

'I . . . never mind.'

'Mr Wells?'

'Let's just say I used to be a teacher, that's all. I know about these things, and that lad was bordering on genius.'

'How often did Luke call by?' she asked.

'Whenever he was out of something to read. We got chatting the first time he dropped in—'

'When was that?'

'Maybe eighteen months or so ago. Anyway, we got chatting and he came back. He liked those old Penguin Modern Classics. Real paperbacks, not your trade size. You can't buy those at Waterstone's.'

'Did Luke ever come in here with anyone else?'

'No.'

Annie took her copy of the artist's impression out and set it on the table. 'What about her?'

Wells leaned forward, put his glasses on again and examined the sketch. 'It *looks* like her,' he said.

'But you told me Luke never came in with anyone else,' Annie said.

'Who said she was with him? No, she came in with another bloke, same sort of clothing and piercings.'

'Who are they?'

'I don't know. They must have been a bit short of money, though.'

'Why do you say that?'

'Because they came in with an armful of brand-new books to sell. Stolen, I thought. Plain as day. Stolen books. So I sent them packing.'

7

Before he cut into Luke Armitage's flesh, Dr Glendenning, the Home Office pathologist, made a thorough examination of the body's exterior. Banks watched as the doctor examined the head.

'Back of the skull splintered into the cerebellum,' the doctor said.

'Enough to kill him?'

'At a guess.' Glendenning squinted at the wound. 'And it would have bled quite a bit, if that's any use.'

'Could be,' said Banks. 'Blood's harder to clean up than most people think. What about the weapon?'

'Looks like some sort of round-edged object,' the doctor said. 'Smooth-sided.'

'Like what?'

'Well, it's not got a very large circumference, so I'd rule out something like a baseball bat. I can't see any traces—wood splinters or anything—so it could have been metal or ceramic. Hard, anyway. It's the angle that puzzles me.'

'What about it?'

'See for yourself.'

Banks bent over the wound, which Dr Glendenning's assistant had shaved and cleaned. There was no blood. A few days in the water would see to that. He could see the indentation clearly. The wound was oblique, almost horizontal.

'You'd expect someone swinging an object to swing downwards from behind, or at least at a forty-five degree angle, so we'd get a more vertical pattern,' Dr Glendenning said. 'But this was inflicted from sideways on, not from in front or behind.'

'Maybe the victim was already bent double from a previous blow?' Banks suggested. 'Which side did the blow come from?'

'Right side. But I'm not happy with this, Banks. In the first place, it's hardly a sure-fire way to kill somebody. Head blows are tricky. You can't count on them, especially just one.'

'So our killer's an amateur who got lucky.'

'Could be. We'll know more when I get a look at the brain tissue.'

'But could this blow have been the cause of death?'

'Can't say for certain. It *could* have killed him, but he might have been dead already. You'll have to wait for the full toxicology report to know whether that might have been the case.'

Banks watched patiently, if rather queasily, as Dr Glendenning's assistant made the customary Y-shaped incision and peeled back the skin and muscle from the chest wall with a scalpel. Next the assistant took a bone-cutter to the rib cage, finally peeling off the chest plate and exposing the inner organs. When he had removed these *en bloc*, he placed them on the dissecting table and reached for his electric saw. Banks turned his attention to Dr Glendenning, who was dissecting the organs, paying particular attention to the lungs.

'No water,' he announced. 'Or minimal.'

'Meaning Luke was dead when he went in the water?'

'I'll send the tissues for diatomic analysis, but I don't expect they'll find much.'

The electric saw stopped and Banks heard a grating and sucking sound, and knew it was the top of the skull coming off. The assistant then cut the spinal cord and the tentorium and lifted the brain out. Dr Glendenning had a quick look.

'Aha,' he said. 'I thought so. Look, Banks, do you see that damage there, to the frontal lobes?'

Banks saw it. And he knew what it meant.

If a blow is delivered while the victim's head is stationary, then the damage is limited to the point of impact—bones splintered into the brain—but if the victim's head is in motion, then the result is a *contre coup* injury: additional damage *opposite* the point of impact. *Contre coup* injuries are almost always the result of a fall.

'Luke *fell?*'

'Or was pushed,' said Glendenning. 'But as far as I can tell, there are no other injuries. And if there was bruising, if someone hit him, say, knocked him over, then unless there are any small bones in the cheek broken, we won't be able to tell.'

'Can you give me any idea about time of death?'

'I've looked over Dr Burns's measurements at the scene. Rigor's been and gone, which indicates over two days at the temperatures noted. Water preserves, delays putrefaction. There's no lividity, and I'm afraid it'll be almost impossible to tell whether there was any other bruising. But there's the discoloration around the neck. That indicates the beginnings of putrefaction. In bodies found in water, it always starts at the root of the neck.'

'After how long?'

'That's just it,' Dr Glendenning said. 'Not until at least three or four days, not at the temperatures Dr Burns recorded.'

Banks made a mental calculation. 'Bloody hell,' he said. 'Even at the outside, that means Luke had to have been killed just after he went missing.'

'Some time that very night, by my calculations. Taking everything into account, between about eight in the evening and eight in the morning.'

In which case, Banks thought, Luke had died before Annie had even paid her *first* visit to Swainsdale Hall, let alone before she had followed Martin Armitage to the site of the drop.

BEFORE SHE WENT off duty Annie had made a few enquiries round the bookshops, asking after the couple who had tried to sell Norman Wells books he believed were stolen, but she drew a blank. Before meeting Banks for a drink at the Queen's Arms, she had also checked recent shoplifting reports but turned up nothing there either. The artist's impression would be in the evening paper, so she would see what happened after that. There was something else she had intended to do, but it was like that name you can't quite remember. If she put it out of her mind, it would come to her eventually.

Banks was already waiting for her at a corner table. She bought herself a pint of bitter and walked over to him. 'So what was that mysterious message about your wanting to see me?' she asked.

'Nothing mysterious about it at all,' Banks said. 'I just wanted to deliver a message myself, in person.'

'I'm all ears.'

'It looks as if you're off the hook as far as Luke Armitage's death is concerned. Dr Glendenning pegs time of death before the first kidnap call even came in.'

'How? He didn't drown, did he?'

'No,' Banks said. 'Pending tox results, it looks as if cause of death was a blow to the cerebellum, quite possibly the result of a fall.'

'A struggle of some sort, then?'

'Exactly what I thought. Perhaps with the kidnapper, very early on. Or whoever he was with.'

'And that person decided to try and collect anyway?'

'Yes. But that's pure speculation.'

'So Luke died somewhere else and was dumped in the tarn?'

'Yes. Probably wherever he was being held—*if* he was being held. Anyway, there'd have been a fair bit of blood, the doc says, so there's every chance of our still finding evidence at the original scene.'

'If we can find the scene.'

'Exactly.'

'So we *are* making progress?'

'Slowly. What about the girl?'

'Nothing yet.' Annie told him about her meeting with Norman Wells.

'Whoever they are,' Banks said when she'd finished, 'if Wells is right and they had been shoplifting, then that tells us they're short of money. Which gives them a motive for demanding a ransom if they were somehow responsible for Luke's death.'

'More speculation?'

'Yes,' Banks admitted. 'Let's assume they got into a fight over something or other and Luke ended up dead. Maybe not intentionally, but dead is dead. They panicked and drove out and dumped him into Hallam Tarn.'

'They'd need a motor, remember, which might be a bit of a problem if they were broke.'

'Maybe they "borrowed" one?'

'We can check car-theft reports for the night in question.'

'Good idea. Anyway, they know who Luke's parents are, think they might be able to make a few bob out of them.'

'Which would explain the low demand.'

'Yes. They're not pros. They've no idea how much to ask. And ten grand is a bloody fortune to them.'

'But they were watching Martin Armitage make the drop and they saw me.'

'More than likely. Sorry, Annie. They might not be pros, but they're not stupid. They knew the money was tainted then.'

Annie paused to digest what Banks had said. She *had* made a mistake, had scared the kidnappers off, but Luke had already been dead by then, so his death wasn't down to her. 'Have you ever thought,' she said, 'that maybe that was why they befriended him in the first place, and why they had to kill him? Because he knew who they were.'

'Yes,' said Banks. 'But too many things about this seem hurried and ill thought out. No, Annie, I think they just took advantage of an existing situation.'

'So why kill Luke, then?'

'No idea. We'll have to ask them.'

'If we find them.'

'Oh, we'll find them, all right, but we need to keep an open mind as regards other lines of enquiry.'

'Such as?'

'I'm not sure yet. There might be something even closer to home. I want to talk to a couple of teachers who knew Luke fairly well.'

'Shit,' said Annie, getting to her feet. She had remembered the task that had been eluding her all evening.

'What?'

'Just something I should have checked out before.' She looked at her watch. 'See you later.'

MICHELLE SAT BACK in her seat on the train and watched the fields drift by under a grey sky, rain streaking the dirty window. She thought back to her lunch with ex-Detective Inspector Robert Lancaster. It was interesting what he had said, she thought. She had never considered that it might have been Graham's *own* criminal activities that got him killed. Not that fourteen-year-olds were immune to criminal activity. But if Graham Marshall had been involved in something that was likely to get him killed, wouldn't somebody have known and come forward? Surely Jet Harris or Reg Proctor would have picked up the scent?

The problem, though, was how she could gather any more information about Graham. She could go through the statements again, read the investigating detectives' notebooks and check all the actions allocated, but if none of them focused on Graham himself as a possible line of enquiry, then she would get no further.

Michelle realised that if Graham had been involved in anything untoward, there was one person who might know something, even if he didn't know he did: *Banks*. And thinking of him made her regret the way she had left him at Starbucks the other day. True, she had resented his intrusion into what she regarded as her private life, but she had perhaps overreacted a tad. After all, he had only asked her if she was married: a perfectly innocent question in its way, and one you might ask a stranger over a coffee. It didn't have to mean anything, but it was such a raw-nerve point with her that she had behaved rudely. Well, she wasn't married. Melissa had died because she and Ted had got their wires crossed. She was on surveillance and thought *he* was picking up their daughter after school; he had a meeting and thought *she* was doing it. Possibly no marriage could survive that amount of trauma—the guilt, blame, grief and anger—and theirs hadn't. Six months after Melissa's funeral they had agreed to separate, and Michelle had begun her years of wandering from county to county trying to put the past behind her. Succeeding to an extent, but still haunted, still in some ways maimed by what had happened.

She hadn't had the time or the inclination for men, and that was another thing about Banks that bothered her. He was the only man, beyond her immediate colleagues on the Job, with whom she had spent any time in years, and she liked him, found him attractive. The problem was that part of her wanted him, against all her common sense and all the barriers she had built inside, and the result flustered and confused her. Banks might be one of the few people who could help her reconstruct Graham Marshall's past, but could she bear to face Banks again in the flesh?

She would have no choice, she realised as the train pulled up and she reached for her briefcase. Graham Marshall's funeral would be taking place soon, and she had promised to call and let him know about it.

Michelle could have walked to her flat in Rivergate, it wasn't that far, but it wasn't a pleasant walk and the rain was still pouring down, so she decided to treat herself to a taxi from the station.

The first inkling she got that something was wrong in the flat was when she heard the creaking door of her 'Mystery' screensaver. She knew she had turned her computer off after she'd checked her email that morning. Also, someone had pulled some books out of one of the boxes that she hadn't unpacked. They were piled up on the floor beside the box.

Michelle jogged the mouse and the computer returned to its regular display. Only it was open at Michelle's file of notes about the Marshall case, and she knew she hadn't opened that since the previous night.

With the hairs prickling at the back of her neck, Michelle

strained her ears for any odd sounds in the flat. Nothing except the clock ticking and the humming of the refrigerator. She took her old side-handled baton from her uniform days out of the closet by the door. Gripping that, she went to explore the rest of the flat.

The kitchen light was on, and items that she knew she had put back in the fridge that morning—milk, butter, eggs—lay on the countertop.

Her bathroom cabinet stood open, and the various pills and potions she kept there were not in their usual order. Her bottle of aspirins sat on the edge of the sink, top off and cotton wool missing. Michelle wondered what the hell all this was about. Clearly, whoever had done this had done it to scare her—and they were succeeding.

She went into the bedroom. What she saw there made her drop her baton and put her hands to her mouth.

Spread out neatly on the bed lay Melissa's dress. When Michelle reached out to pick it up, she found it had been cut into two halves.

Michelle staggered back against the wall, half the dress clutched to her chest. As she did so, her eye caught the writing on the dressing-table mirror: FORGET GRAHAM MARSHALL, BITCH. REMEMBER MELISSA. YOU COULD JOIN HER.

8

Norman Wells sat in the interview room with his arms folded and his lips pressed tight together. If he was scared, he wasn't showing it. But then, he didn't know how much the police already knew about him. Banks and Annie sat opposite him, files spread out in front of them. Banks felt well rested after a day off. He had done nothing on Sunday but read the papers and go for a walk, stopping for a pub lunch on the way.

'Norman,' said Banks. 'Detective Inspector Cabbot here has been doing a bit of digging around in your background, and it turns out you've been a naughty boy, haven't you?'

Wells said nothing. Annie pushed a file towards Banks and he opened it. 'You used to be a schoolteacher at a private school in Cheltenham, am I right?'

'Yes.'

'How long ago?'

'I left seven years ago.'

'Why did you leave?'

'I grew tired of teaching.'

Banks glanced at Annie, who frowned. 'Norman,' Banks went on, 'I think I ought to inform you that we spoke to your old headmaster. He was reticent at first, but when we informed him that we were conducting a possible murder investigation, he was a little more forthcoming. We know all about you, Norman.'

Wells seemed to deflate and shrink in his chair. 'What do you want from me?' he whispered.

'The truth.'

'I had a nervous breakdown.'

'What caused it?'

'The pressures of the job. You've no idea what teaching's like.'

'Stop beating about the bush, Norman,' Annie cut in. 'Does the name Steven Farrow mean anything to you?'

Wells paled. 'Nothing happened. False accusations.'

'According to the headmaster, Norman, you were infatuated with this thirteen-year-old boy. So much so that on one occasion—'

'Enough!' Wells slammed his fist down on the table. 'It was pure. A pure love.' He rubbed his teary eyes with his forearm. 'But you wouldn't understand that, would you? To people like you, anything other than a man and a woman is dirty, abnormal, *perverted*.'

'Try us, Norman,' said Banks. 'Give us a chance. You loved him?'

'Steven was beautiful. An angel. All I wanted was to be close to him, to be with him. What could be wrong with that?'

'But you touched him, Norman,' said Annie. 'He told—'

'I never touched him! He was lying. He turned on me. He wanted money. Can you believe it? My little angel wanted *money*.'

'What happened?' Banks asked.

'I refused, of course. Steven went to the headmaster and . . . I was asked to leave, no questions asked, no scandal. All for the good of the school, you see. But word got round. On the scrapheap at thirty-eight. One foolish mistake.' He shook his head.

'Surely you couldn't expect them to keep you on?' Banks said. 'In fact, you're bloody lucky they didn't bring in the police. And you know how we feel about paedophiles.'

'I am not a child molester! I would have been content just . . . just to be with him. Have you ever been in love, Chief Inspector?'

Banks said nothing. He sensed Annie glance at him.

'Luke Armitage,' Annie cut in.

Wells leaned back and licked his lips. He was sweating profusely,

Banks noticed. 'I wondered when we'd be getting round to him.'

'You were among the last people to see Luke Armitage on the day he disappeared, Norman,' Annie went on. 'When we found out about your past, wasn't it only natural that we should want to talk to you?'

'I know nothing about what happened to him.'

'But you were friends with him, weren't you?'

'Acquaintances. He was a customer.'

'He was an attractive boy, wasn't he, Norman? Like Steven Farrow.'

Wells sighed. 'The boy left my shop. I never saw him again.'

'Are you certain?' Banks asked. 'Are you sure he didn't come back, or you didn't meet him somewhere else? Your house, perhaps?'

'I never saw him again. Why would he come to my house?'

'Did he come back to the shop? Did something happen there? Did you kill him and then move him? Maybe it was a terrible accident. I can't believe you meant to kill him. Not if you loved him.'

'I didn't *love* him.'

'I suppose the money was an afterthought, was it?' Banks went on. 'But why not make a little money out of what you'd done? I mean, you could do with it, couldn't you? Look at the dump you spend your days in. A crappy used-book business in a dank, cold dungeon can't be making much money, can it? An extra ten thousand quid would have set you up nicely.'

'I have done nothing wrong,' said Wells, crossing his arms again.

The problem was, as Banks and Annie had already discussed, that the closed-circuit television cameras corroborated Wells's story. Luke Armitage had entered Norman's Used Books at two minutes to five and left—alone—at five twenty-four.

'What time did you close that day?' Banks asked.

'Half past five, as usual.'

'And what did you do?'

'I went home.'

'Number 57 Arden Terrace? That's off Market Street, isn't it?'

'Close, yes.'

'Do you live alone?'

'Yes.'

'Do you own a car?'

'Yes. A secondhand Renault.'

'Good enough to get you out to Hallam Tarn and back?'

Wells hung his head in his hands. 'I haven't been near Hallam Tarn in months. Certainly not since the foot-and-mouth outbreak.'

'What did you do after you went home?'

'Had my tea. Watched television. Read for a while, then went to sleep.'

'Has Luke Armitage ever visited your house?'

'No.'

'Did you ever give him a lift anywhere?'

'No.'

'So Luke has never been in your car?'

'Never.'

'In that case,' said Banks, 'I'm sure you won't mind if our forensic experts have a close look at your house and your car. We'd also like to take a DNA sample, just for comparison.'

Wells hung his head. 'Fine,' he said. 'Go ahead. Do what you will. I don't care any more.'

AFTER A SLEEPLESS NIGHT on Saturday, Michelle had spent Sunday getting over the shock of what had happened in her flat and trying to rein in her emotional response in favour of more analytical thought.

That someone had gained entry and arranged things in order to frighten her was obvious enough. Why was another matter entirely. That the interloper knew about Melissa surprised her, though she supposed people could find out anything about her if they really wanted to. But, given that he knew, it would have been evident when he searched her bedside drawers that the little dress was Melissa's, and that its desecration would cause her a great deal of anguish. In other words, it had been a cold, calculated assault.

Though it went against Michelle's nature not to report the break-in to the police, in the end she decided against it. The intrusion was meant to frighten her off the case, and the only people who knew she was working on it, apart from the Marshalls themselves, were other police officers, or people connected with them. True, Michelle's name had been in the papers when the bones had first been found, so technically anyone could know she was on the case, but she felt the answers lay closer to home.

The question was, Was she going to be frightened off the case? The answer was, No. She had, however, found a locksmith and arranged to have a chain and an extra deadbolt lock put on her door.

As a result of her weekend experience, Michelle felt drained and edgy on Monday morning and found herself looking at everyone in divisional headquarters differently, as if they knew something she didn't. Creeping paranoia, she told herself, and tried to shake it off.

She went down to the archives to check out the old notebooks and action allocations. An officer's notebooks could be invaluable when trying to reconstruct the pattern of an investigation, as could the action allocations, records made of all the instructions issued to investigating officers by the senior investigating officer. By looking at the actions you could determine which areas of enquiry had been pursued and which had not, and by reading the notebooks you could unearth impressions that might not have made it into the formal reports.

Mrs Metcalfe showed Michelle where the notebooks were filed, and Michelle went first to Ben Shaw's. But no matter how many times she flipped through the boxes, checked and rechecked the dates, in the end she had to admit that if there had been notebooks covering the day of Graham Marshall's disappearance, August 22, 1965, and the next month or two, then they had vanished.

Michelle asked for Mrs Metcalfe's help, but after half an hour even the poor records clerk had to admit defeat. 'I can't imagine where they've got to, love,' she said.

'Could someone have taken them?' Michelle asked.

'I don't see who. Or why. I mean, it's only people like you who come down here. Other police.'

Exactly what Michelle had been thinking. Someone had gained entry to her flat and tried to scare her off the case, and now she found that nearly two months' worth of notebooks had somehow disappeared. Coincidence? Michelle didn't think so.

Half an hour later, when they had run into the same problem with the action allocation book for the Graham Marshall case, Michelle knew in her bones that the actions and the notebooks were gone for ever, destroyed most likely. But why? And by whom?

'THANK YOU for seeing to the release,' Mrs Marshall said. 'We'll be holding the funeral service at St Peter's the day after tomorrow. You'll be there?'

'Yes, of course,' said Michelle. 'There's just one thing.'

'What's that, love?'

Michelle told her about the rib they needed for evidence.

Mrs Marshall frowned and thought for a moment. 'I don't think we need worry about a little thing like a missing rib, need we? Especially if it might help you. Is there any more news?'

'No, I'm afraid not. Only more questions.'

'I can't understand what else I can tell you, but please go ahead.'

Michelle leaned back in her chair. This was going to be difficult, she knew. To find out about any mischief Graham might have been up to without suggesting that he got up to mischief—which his mother would never accept—was almost to attempt the impossible.

'Was Graham ever away from home for any periods of time?'

'He missed his tea from time to time, and once or twice he missed his nine o'clock curfew. And many's the occasion we didn't see hide nor hair of him from dawn till dusk. Not during term-time, mind. Just weekends and school holidays he could be a bit unreliable.'

'Did you have any idea where he'd been when he turned up late?'

'Playing with his pals. Sometimes he'd have his guitar with him, too. They were practising, see.'

'How much pocket money did you give him?'

'Five shillings a week. It was all we could afford. But he had his paper round and that made him a bit extra.'

'So he didn't go short of anything?'

'No. Not so's you'd notice. Why? What are you trying to get at?'

'I'm just trying to get a picture of his activities, Mrs Marshall. It'll help me try to work out who might have stopped and picked him up.'

'You think it was somebody he knew?'

'I didn't say that, but it's possible.'

Mrs Marshall fiddled with her necklace. The idea clearly upset her.

'And you know nothing about any unsavoury company Graham might have been keeping?' Michelle went on.

'No. I don't understand what you're trying to say.'

'It's all right,' said Michelle. 'I'm not sure I understand it, myself. I suppose all I really want to ask is whether Graham had any friends you disliked, or spent time with anyone you didn't approve of.'

'Oh. No. They were all just regular lads. We knew their mums and dads. They were just like us.'

'And Graham never seemed to have more money than you expected him to have?'

Mrs Marshall's expression sharpened and Michelle knew she'd gone too far. She also knew that she had touched a raw nerve.

'Are you suggesting our Graham was a thief?'

'Of course not,' Michelle backtracked. 'I just wondered if he maybe did other odd jobs he didn't tell you about, other than the paper round, perhaps when he should have been at school.'

Mrs Marshall still eyed her suspiciously. Bill Marshall seemed to be taking everything in, his beady eyes moving from one to the other as they spoke, but they were the only things moving in his face. If only he could talk, Michelle thought. And then she realised that would be no use. He wouldn't tell her anything.

'I suppose it's just a mark of my frustration with the case,' Michelle admitted. 'After all, it was so long ago.'

'Jet Harris always said it was them Moors Murderers, the ones who were tried the year after.'

'He told you that, did he?' said Michelle. She was fast coming to the conclusion that DS Harris had run the case with blinkers on, and Mrs Marshall, like so many mothers, hadn't a clue what her son was up to most of the time. Michelle took a deep breath and plunged in.

'I understand your husband used to work for the Kray twins back in London.'

There was a short silence, then Mrs Marshall said, 'Bill didn't *work* for them. He used to spar with them down the gym. We grew up in the same neighbourhood. Everybody knew Reggie and Ronnie. Always polite to me, they were, no matter what anybody says about them, and I've heard some stories as would make your hair curl. But they were basically good lads. People don't like it when others get a bit above their station, you know.'

Michelle could feel her jaw dropping. There was nothing more to be gained here, she realised, and if she was going to solve this case she was going to do so without the family's help, and without Ben Shaw's. And perhaps in peril of her life. *Remember Melissa. You could join her* . . . Promising again that she would be at the funeral, Michelle excused herself and hurried off.

THAT EVENING AT HOME, Banks slipped Bill Evans's *Paris Concert* into the CD player, poured himself a couple of fingers of Laphroaig and flopped down on the sofa with his 1965 *Photoplay* diary. As he flipped the pages once again, he was struck by how many records he had bought and films he had seen. Banks saw that his diary did, in fact, have its moments, and as he read the trivial or cryptic entries, he was able to fill in the rest with his memory and imagination.

In the first week of August 1965 the Banks family had set off for their annual holidays. That year they went to Blackpool and they took Graham Marshall with them. Graham's dad had just started on a large building project, it didn't look as if the Marshalls would get a holiday that year, so Graham was allowed to accompany them.

They would have piled their cases into the back of Arthur Banks's Morris Traveller and headed north, arriving in time for tea at Mrs Barraclough's boarding house.

Most evenings after tea they spent watching television in the guests' lounge. Banks hadn't recorded it in his diary, but no doubt there would have been some adult wanting to watch *Sunday Night at the London Palladium* instead of *Perry Mason*, which was only to be expected of adults. So Banks and Graham would go up to their room and pore over the dirty magazines Graham seemed to get hold of in abundance.

Of course, they didn't spend every minute together. Graham had been moody at times, unusually quiet, and looking back Banks suspected he had been preoccupied with some problem or other. At the time, though, he hadn't given it a second thought, had simply gone his own way on occasion.

As the holiday progressed, Banks and Graham did all the usual things, some with the rest of the family and some by themselves. When it was warm enough, they spent time lounging with Banks's mother and father on the beach in their swimming trunks. They even went in the sea once or twice, but it was cold. Mostly they just lay there, plugged into their radios, hoping to hear the Animals singing 'We've Gotta Get Out of This Place' or the Byrds doing 'Mr Tambourine Man', and surreptitiously eyeing the girls in their bathing costumes.

The highlight of the week, though, was the two girls. One fine evening Banks and Graham headed down to the Pleasure Beach. As they were walking round trying to decide which ride to go on first, they noticed two girls about their own age who kept looking at them, whispering to one another and giggling, the way girls did.

Eventually, Banks and Graham approached them and, Graham being the silent, moody type, Banks offered them cigarettes and started chatting them up. Tina was short with rather large breasts, a dark complexion and long wavy brown hair. Her friend, Sharon, was a slender blonde.

They went on the Ghost Train first, and the girls got scared when phosphorescent skeletons jumped out in front of the slow-moving cars. After the Ghost Train they were holding hands, and Graham suggested they ride on the Big Dipper, a roller coaster, next. Graham paid.

That was something Banks remembered as he read through his diary. Graham often paid. He always seemed to have plenty of money, always enough, even back in Peterborough, for ten Gold Leaf and a double bill at the Gaumont. Maybe even some Kia-Ora and a choc-ice from the woman who came round with the tray during the intermission. Banks never wondered or asked where he got it from at the time; he just assumed that Graham got plenty of pocket money from his dad in addition to his paper-round money. Looking back now, though, it seemed odd.

They went out with Sharon and Tina twice more, once to see *Help!*

and once to the arcades, Graham as usual supplying most of the cash.

Remembering their holiday had made him also remember other things, and some of them started to ring alarm bells in his policeman's mind. Quiet at first, then getting louder and louder.

But soon, it wasn't an inner alarm bell, it was the telephone that was ringing. Banks picked it up.

'DCI Banks?' A woman's voice, familiar, strained.

'Yes.'

'It's DI Hart. Michelle.'

'I haven't forgotten your name yet,' Banks said. 'What can I do for you? Any news?'

'Are you busy?'

'Just after you left me in Starbucks a missing persons case turned into a murder, so yes, I am.'

'Look, I'm sorry about that. I mean . . . This is so difficult.'

'Just tell me.'

'Today I discovered that Ben Shaw's notebooks and actions allocations are missing. There's a gap from August 15 to October 6, 1965.'

Banks whistled between his teeth.

'There's something else, too. Something that happened over the weekend. But I don't want to talk about it on the phone.' She gave a nervous laugh. 'I suppose I'm asking you for advice. I don't know what to do.'

'You should tell someone.'

'I'm telling you.'

'I mean someone in your station.'

'That's the problem,' she said. 'I just don't know who I can trust down here. That's why I thought of you. I know you have a personal interest in the case, and it would be helpful for me to have another professional around. One I know I can trust.'

Banks thought it over. Michelle was right; he did have an interest in the case. And the way it sounded, she was out on a limb by herself down there. 'I'm not sure what I can do to help,' he said, 'but I'll see if I can get away. Any news on the funeral service?'

'Day after tomorrow.'

'I'll get away as soon as I can,' he said. 'Maybe tomorrow. In the meantime, don't say or do anything. Just carry on as normal. OK?'

'OK. And, Alan?'

'Yes?'

'Thanks. I mean it. I'm in a jam.' She paused. 'And I'm scared.'

'I'll be there.'

LAUREN ANDERSON LIVED in a small semi not too far from where Banks used to live with Sandra before their separation. He hadn't passed the end of his old street in a long time and it brought back memories he would rather forget. He felt cheated, somehow. The memories should have been good—he and Sandra *had* had good times together, had been in love for many years—but everything seemed tainted by her betrayal and now by her forthcoming marriage to Sean. And the baby, of course. The baby hurt a lot.

It was as fine a summer's day as they had seen in a while. They were in Banks's car this time. He parked and they got out of the car. Annie pressed the doorbell and a few seconds later saw the shape coming towards them through the frosted glass.

Lauren Anderson was dressed in jeans and a thin V-neck jumper, and she wore no make-up. Younger than Banks had expected, she was willowy, with full lips, a pale oval face and heavy-lidded pale blue eyes, all framed by long auburn hair spilling down over her shoulders. As she stood in the doorway, she wrapped her arms around herself as if she were cold.

'Police,' Banks said, holding out his warrant card. 'May we come in?'

'Of course.' Lauren stood aside.

'In here?' Banks asked, pointing towards what looked like the living room.

'If you like.'

Banks found a comfortable chair and sat down. 'It's a nice place,' he said. 'Do you live here alone?'

'I do now. I used to share it with one of the other teachers, but she got her own flat a few months ago. I think I prefer it by myself.'

'I don't blame you,' said Banks. 'Look, the reason we're here is that we heard you used to give Luke Armitage extra tuition in English, and we wondered if you could tell us anything about him.'

'I'm not sure I can tell you anything about him, but, yes, I used to tutor Luke.' Lauren sat on the small sofa with her legs tucked under her. 'He was so far ahead of the rest of his class he must have been bored silly at school. He was far ahead of me most of the time.' She flicked some troublesome locks of hair out of her face.

'That good?'

'His enthusiasm made up for what he lacked in formal training.'

'I gather he was a talented writer, too.'

'Very. Again, he needed discipline, but he was young, raw. He'd have gone far if . . . if . . .' She rubbed her sleeve across her eyes. 'I'm sorry,' she said. 'I just can't get over it. Luke. Dead. Such a waste.'

Annie passed her a tissue from the box on one of the bookshelves.
'Thank you,' she said, then blew her nose. She shifted on the sofa
and Banks noticed her feet were bare and her toenails painted red.

'Did Luke ever talk about himself?'

'Sometimes he might let his guard drop a little, yes.'

'And what did he talk about then?'

'Oh, the usual. School. His parents.'

'What did he have to say about them?'

'He hated school. He didn't like the discipline, the formality.'

Banks thought of the boys who had tormented him in the market
square. 'What about bullying?'

'Yes, that too. But it wasn't serious. Mostly teasing.'

'What did he say about his parents?'

Lauren paused for a moment before answering. 'Not much. It was
clear he wasn't happy at home. He said he loved his mother, but he
gave me the impression he didn't get along with his stepfather.'

'What was he going to do about his problems?'

'Nothing. What could he do? He was only fifteen.'

'Did Luke ever talk about Neil Byrd?'

'Hardly ever. He got very emotional when the subject came up.
Angry, even. Luke had a lot of unresolved issues.'

'Was there anything that might have been bothering him recently?'

'No. The last time I saw him, at the end of term, he was excited
about the summer holidays. I assigned him some reading.'

'You felt very close to Luke, am I right?'

'In a way, I suppose. If you really *could* be close to him. He was
slippery, chameleon-like, often moody, quiet and withdrawn. But I
liked him and I believed in his talent, if that's what you mean.'

'We don't know where Luke went after about five thirty the day he
disappeared. But he was last seen walking north on Market Street.
Would that have brought him to your neighbourhood, eventually?'

'Yes, but . . . I mean . . . why would he come here?'

'Are you sure Luke never came to see you the Monday before last?'

'Of course I'm sure. He had no reason to.'

'You were only his tutor, right?'

Lauren stood up and anger flashed in her eyes. 'What do you mean?'

Banks held his hand up. 'Whoa. Wait a minute. I was only thinking
that he might have considered you as a friend and mentor, someone
he could go to if he was in trouble.'

'Well, he didn't. Look, as it happens, I wasn't even home the
Monday before last.'

'Where were you?'

'Visiting my brother, Vernon.'

'And where does Vernon live?'

'Harrogate.'

'What time did you leave?'

'About five. Shortly after.'

'And what time did you get back?'

'I didn't. As a matter of fact, I had a bit too much to drink. Too much to risk driving, at any rate. So I slept on Vernon's sofa.'

Banks glanced at Annie, who put her notebook aside and pulled the artist's impression out of her briefcase. 'Have you ever seen this girl, Ms Anderson?' she asked. 'Think carefully.'

Lauren studied the drawing and shook her head. 'No.'

'We think she might have been Luke's girlfriend,' Banks said.

Lauren shot Banks a glance. '*Girlfriend?* But Luke didn't have a girlfriend.'

'How do you know? You said he didn't tell you everything.'

She fingered the collar of her V-neck. 'But . . . but I'd have *known*.'

Banks and Annie stood up to leave. Lauren walked to the door with them.

'Thanks for your time,' Banks said.

'I do hope you catch whoever did this,' Lauren said.

'Don't worry,' said Banks, with much more confidence than he felt. 'We will.'

9

Michelle had been down in the archives again first thing that morning on another fruitless search. She needed to think about what it all meant, so she decided to drive over to the Hazels estate and walk Graham's route.

She parked in front of the row of shops opposite the estate and looked at the newsagent's, now run by Mrs Walker. That was where it had all begun. Michelle entered the shop and found the sturdy, grey-haired old lady arranging newspapers on the counter.

'Are you Mrs Walker?'

'Yes, love,' the woman said with a smile. 'What can I do for you?'

'I don't know if you can do anything,' said Michelle, presenting her warrant card, 'but you might have heard we found some bones—'

'The lad who used to work here? I read about it. Terrible business. But I don't see how I can help you. It was before my time.'

'When did you come here?'

'My husband and I bought the shop in the autumn of 1966.'

'Did you buy it from Mr Bradford, the previous owner?'

'As far as I know we did. The estate agent handled all the details, along with my husband, of course, bless his soul.'

'Mr Walker is deceased?'

'A good ten years now.'

'I'm sorry. Did you meet Mr Bradford?'

'Oh, yes. He was very helpful. Showed us the ropes and everything.'

'What was he like?'

'I can't say I knew him well. My husband had most dealings with him. But he seemed all right. A bit stiff and military in his bearing. I remember he was something important during the war, a member of some special unit or other in Burma. But he was helpful.'

'Did he ever mention Graham?'

'Oh, yes. That's why he left. Partly, at any rate. He said his heart hadn't been in the business since the boy disappeared, so he wanted to move away and try to forget.'

'Do you know where he moved to?'

'The North, or so he said. Carlisle.'

'I don't suppose you had a forwarding address, did you?'

'Didn't you know? Mr Bradford died. Killed in a burglary not weeks after he moved. It was in all the local papers at the time.'

'Indeed?' said Michelle, curious. 'No, I didn't know.' It probably wasn't relevant to her enquiry, but it was suspicious. One of the last people to see Graham alive had, himself, been killed.

Michelle went back outside. She crossed the road and started walking along Hazel Crescent, the route Graham would have taken all those years ago. She was almost certain that Graham *knew* his attacker and that he got in a car willingly, taking his canvas bag of papers with him. If someone had tried to force him into a car, he would have struggled and dropped the papers, and the abductor was unlikely to stick around and pick them up.

As Michelle stood in the street, she thought again about the missing notebooks and actions and was struck by a notion so obvious she could have kicked herself for not seeing it earlier.

That the missing notebooks were DS Shaw's disturbed her for a different reason now she realised what she should have seen straight away. Shaw was a mere DC, a junior on the case, so what on earth could he have had to hide? He had no power; he wasn't in charge, and he certainly hadn't assigned the actions. He had simply been along taking notes of DI Reg Proctor's interviews; that was all.

Michelle had focused on Shaw mostly because she resented the way he had been treating her, but when it came right down to it, the person in charge of the case, the one who might have had the most to hide in the event of a future investigation was not Shaw but that legend of the local constabulary, Detective Superintendent John Harris.

Thinking about Jet Harris, and what he might possibly have had to hide, Michelle walked back to where she had left her car parked in front of the shops. Perhaps she was a little distracted by her thoughts, and perhaps she didn't pay as much attention as she usually did to crossing the road, but on the other hand, perhaps the beige van with the tinted windows really *did* start up as she approached, and perhaps the driver really *did* put his foot on the accelerator when she stepped into the road.

Either way, she saw it coming—fast—and just had time to jump out of the way. The side of the van brushed against her hip as she stumbled and fell onto the tarmac. By the time Michelle realised what was happening, the van was out of sight. One thing she did remember, though: the number plate was so covered in mud it was impossible to read.

'CAN YOU MANAGE by yourself for a day or so?' Banks asked Annie over a lunchtime pint in the Queen's Arms.

Annie put her glass down. 'Course I can,' she said. 'What's up?'

'It's Graham Marshall's funeral tomorrow. There'll likely be some old friends around. I'd like to go down this evening.'

'No problem. Have you asked the boss?'

'DS Gristhorpe has given me permission to be absent from school for two days. I just wanted to clear it with you.'

'I've got plenty to keep me occupied. By the way, Winsome ran a check on all cars reported stolen in the Eastvale area the night Luke disappeared. There are two possibilities, one abandoned near Hawes, in Wensleydale, and the other in Richmond.'

'We'd better have Stefan's team check them both for signs of blood.' Annie made a note. 'OK.'

The server brought their lunches over: a salad sandwich for Annie and lasagne and chips for Banks.

'Talking about cars,' Banks said, after pausing for a few mouthfuls, 'how are forensics coming on with Norman Wells's?'

'Nothing yet. Do you really expect anything?'

'Maybe not. But it's got to be done.'

'Do you think we should have detained him?'

'We've nothing to hold him on,' Banks said. 'And he does have his business to run. Besides, I don't think Mr Wells is going anywhere.'

'What about Lauren Anderson?'

'Methinks the lady did protest too much.'

'What do you mean?'

'Just that her reaction to a simple question seemed extreme.'

'She did sound awfully close to Luke. Emotionally, I mean.'

'But she does have an alibi. Ask Winsome to check with the brother, Vernon, just to be certain, but I can't imagine she'd risk lying about that. And it was a man's voice on the ransom call.'

'I'm not suggesting she *did* it—she certainly seemed genuine in her regard for him—just that she might know more than she's letting on about what Luke was up to.'

'You're right,' said Banks. 'We shouldn't rule her out. Maybe you could get Winsome and young Templeton to run background checks on everyone we know who was connected with Luke, and that includes the Battys, Lauren Anderson and the mystery girl, if we ever find her.'

'What about forensic checks on the Anderson woman's house?'

Banks shook his head. 'We can't afford to send forensic teams to everyone's house. With Wells we had good reason—his history, for a start. Besides, we know Luke has been in Lauren Anderson's house.'

'You'll stay in touch?'

'I'll leave my mobile on all the time. I'm not deserting you, Annie.'

Banks still couldn't help feeling a little guilty—and it wasn't because he was leaving the case to Annie, but because he would be seeing Michelle again, and the idea appealed to him.

Annie touched his sleeve. 'I know you're not.' She grinned. 'You go and pay your respects and have a piss-up with your old mates. You'll have a lot to catch up on. When did you last see them?'

'Not since I went to London, when I was eighteen. We lost touch.'

Banks considered telling Annie about Michelle's phone call but decided against it. Why complicate matters? Annie had enough on her plate. Besides, he wasn't sure there was much he could do about Michelle's concerns. If there had been some sort of cover-up, then it would have to be investigated by an outside force, not some maverick from north Yorkshire. Yet a part of him wanted to get involved, to get to the bottom of Graham's death as well as Luke's. They were linked in his mind in some odd way. Not technically, of course, but two very different boys from very different times had ended up dead before their time, and both had died violently. Banks wanted to know why, what it was about these two children that had attracted such cruel fates.

EARLY IN THE AFTERNOON Annie showed the artist's impression of the mystery girl around the Swainsdale Centre and the bus station again. At the end of an hour she was beginning to wonder whether the girl existed or whether she was just a figment of imagination.

She walked along York Road enjoying the sunshine, glancing in the shop windows as she walked. The market square was clogged with cars trying to find parking space. A large group of tourists stood gazing up at the sculpted figures of saints above the doors of the Norman church.

One of the the cars, she noticed—partly because it screeched straight into a disabled parking space and almost hit a young woman—was Martin Armitage's BMW. What the hell was he doing here? And what was he doing in a disabled parking spot? But when she saw him jump out of the car, slam the door and head for the shops built into the side of the church, she knew what was going on.

Annie pushed her way through the tourist crowd by the church and got there just in time to see Armitage disappearing down the stairs into Norman's Used Books. She dashed down behind him, but he already had Wells by the throat and judging by the blood pouring from the little man's nose had punched him at least once.

'Mr Armitage!' Annie called out as she grabbed his arm. 'Martin! Stop it. This won't get you anywhere.'

Armitage shook her off as if she were a troublesome insect. 'This pervert killed my son,' he said. 'If you lot can't do it, I'll get a bloody confession, even if I have to shake it out of him.' He started to shake Wells again and slap him back and forth across the face.

Annie tried to wedge herself between them. Armitage was strong. He pushed her and she staggered back into a table.

Gathering all her strength, Annie launched herself towards the struggling men, but Armitage saw her coming and swung his fist beyond Wells's head, connecting directly with Annie's mouth. The blow stunned her and she fell back again, in pain this time. Armitage was still shaking Wells and was paying her no mind now, so she managed to edge behind him to the door and dash up the steps. The police station was only yards away, and nobody asked her any questions when she rushed in the door, blood streaming from her mouth.

Two burly PCs followed her back to the shop, and it took both of them to subdue Armitage, wrecking the place in the process. They got the handcuffs on him and marched him up the stairs. Annie got Wells's arm round her shoulder and helped him stumble up into the fresh air.

IT HAD BEEN a while since Banks had spent much time in his office. He had just settled into whittling away at the pile of paperwork on his desk when his phone rang.

'Alan, it's Stefan.'

'Good news, I hope?'

'Depends on how you look at it. Your man Norman Wells is clean. We were pretty thorough, and I'm sure if there'd been any traces of Luke Armitage in his car or house we'd have found something.'

'OK. Anything positive?'

'The blood on the dry-stone wall. It's definitely human and it doesn't match the victim's.'

Banks whistled. 'So there's a good chance it could belong to whoever dropped Luke over the wall?'

'A pretty good chance, yes. But don't get your hopes up too high. It *could* belong to anyone.'

'But you'll be able to match it with any samples we can get?'

'Of course.'

'OK. Thanks, Stefan.'

'My pleasure.'

Banks wondered who he should ask to provide DNA samples. Norman Wells. Lauren Anderson. And the parents. DNA could be processed in two or three days now, but it was an expensive proposition. Banks would just have to see how much he could get away with. Then there was the mystery girl, of course. They would definitely need a sample from her if they ever found her, if she existed.

His phone rang again. This time it was the duty constable. Someone to see him in connection with Luke Armitage. A young woman.

'Send her up,' said Banks, wondering if *this* could be the mystery woman. She must know that she was wanted by now, and if she did then her failure to show up was suspicious in itself.

A minute or so later a uniformed constable ushered the girl into Banks's office. Banks recognised Rose Barlow immediately. She strutted into his office all blue-jeaned leg, blonde hair and attitude.

'I'm Rose,' she said. 'Rose Barlow.'

'I know who you are,' said Banks. 'What can I do for you?'

'It's more a matter of what *I* can do for *you*,' Rose said, sitting down.

'And what can you do for me?' Banks asked.

'Have you talked to Miss Anderson yet?'

'Lauren Anderson? Yes.'

A mischievous glint lit Rose's eyes. 'And did she tell you about her and Luke?'

'She told us she gave him extra tuition in English because he was ahead of the rest of the class.'

Rose laughed. '*Extra tuition*. That's a good one. And did she tell you where she gave this tuition?'

'At her house.'

Rose leaned back and folded her arms. 'Exactly.'

'I'm not sure what you're getting at,' said Banks, who was perfectly sure but wanted her to get there by herself.

'They were having it off, weren't they?'

'You know that for a fact?'

'Stands to reason.'

'Why?'

'She's nothing but a slut, that Miss Anderson, and a cradle-snatcher.'

'What makes you say that?'

'Well, she didn't give anybody *else* tuition in her home, did she?'

'I don't know,' said Banks.

'Well she *didn't*.'

'Tell me, Rose,' Banks said, 'what did you think of Luke?'

Rose twirled some strands of hair. 'He was all right, I suppose.'

'Pretty good-looking, wasn't he?'

Rose made a face. 'Ugh! I wouldn't have gone out with him if he was the last boy on earth.'

'I don't think you're telling me the truth, Rose, are you?'

'What do you mean?'

'You know very well what I mean. You and Luke.'

'We went to McDonald's a couple of times, but that's all.'

'Rose, do you have any evidence at all to support your accusation that Luke and Lauren Anderson were having an affair?'

'If you mean was I watching at her window, then no. But why else would she spend her spare time with someone like him?'

'But *you* spent time with him.'

'Yeah. Well . . . that was different.'

'What happened?'

'Nothing. He just sort of . . . like he got *bored* with me or something. Like I didn't read all those stupid books he was always carrying around, and I didn't listen to the same lousy music. I wasn't good enough for him. He was a snob. Above the rest of us.'

'And because of this you assumed he was having sexual relations with a teacher. That's a bit of a far stretch, isn't it?'

'*You* didn't see them together.'

'Did you see them kissing, touching, holding hands?'

'Of course not. They were too careful in public, weren't they?'

'What then?'

'The way they looked at each other. The way she always left him alone in class. The way they talked. The way he made her laugh.'

'You were just jealous, weren't you, Rose? That's why you're saying all this. You couldn't get along with Luke, but Miss Anderson could.'

Before Rose could respond, two things happened in quick succession. First, there came an urgent tap at his door and Annie Cabbot walked in, a handkerchief to her mouth covered with what looked like blood. But before Annie could speak, Kevin Templeton poked his head round the door behind her, and said to Banks, 'Sorry to interrupt you, sir, but we think we've got a positive ID on you know who.'

Banks knew who he meant. The mystery girl. So she *did* exist.

'Better than that,' Templeton went on, 'we've got an address.'

MICHELLE DISCOVERED from DC Collins that Shaw had gone home after lunch, complaining of a stomach upset. Collins's tone was such as to suggest it might be more a matter of the number of whiskies Shaw had downed at lunch. He had been taking quite a lot of time off lately. At least that left the coast clear for Michelle.

It was time to follow up on what she had learned from Mrs Walker. Michelle managed to reach one of the retired Carlisle police sergeants who had looked into the death of Donald Bradford, the newsagent: ex-DS Raymond Scholes, now living on the Cumbrian coast.

'I don't know what I can tell you after all this time,' Scholes said over the telephone. 'Donald Bradford was just unlucky.'

'What happened?'

'Surprised a burglar. Someone broke into his house, and Bradford got beaten so badly he died of his injuries.'

Michelle felt a chill. The same thing might have happened to her on Saturday if she'd been home earlier. 'Ever catch the burglar?'

'No. He must have taken Bradford by surprise, though.'

'Why do you say that?'

'Because he was a pretty tough customer, himself. Way it looks is the burglar must have heard him coming and hid behind the door, then bashed the back of Bradford's head in with a cosh.'

'What was taken?'

'Wallet, a few knick-knacks, by the looks of it. Place was a mess.'

'Did it appear as if someone had been *looking* for something?'

'I never really thought about that. As I say, though, it was a mess. Turned upside-down. Why the sudden interest?'

Michelle told him a little bit about Graham Marshall.

'Yes, I've read about that. I hadn't realised there was a connection.'

'Was Bradford married?'

'No. He lived alone.'

Michelle could sense him pause, as if he was going to add something. 'What?' she asked.

'Well, we had to have a look around the house after, and we found pornographic magazines. A bundle of them. And some blue films. I won't go into detail, but they covered quite a range of perversions.'

'Including paedophilia?'

'Well, there were some pretty young-looking models involved, I can tell you that. Male and female.'

'What happened to all this stuff?'

'Destroyed. We didn't let anything slip at the time,' he went on, 'because . . . well, the bloke *had* just been killed, after all. There seemed no point in blackening his name with that sort of thing.'

'Thank you, Mr Scholes,' Michelle said. 'You've been a great help.'

'Think nothing of it.'

Michelle hung up. She had a lot to discuss with Banks.

PC FLAHERTY, who had tracked down the mystery girl's address, had been asking around Eastvale College, thinking that a girl who looked like she did must be a student. As it turned out, she wasn't, but her boyfriend was, and one of the people he spoke to remembered seeing her at a college dance. The boyfriend's name was Ryan Milne and the girl was known as Elizabeth Palmer. They lived together in a flat above a hat shop on South Market Street, the direction in which Luke Armitage had been walking when he was last seen.

Annie insisted she felt well enough to make the call. She was damned, she told Banks, if she was going to be excluded after all the footwork she'd done just because some over-testosteroned lout had punched her. Banks decided he would make the call with her before setting off for Peterborough. He phoned Michelle and arranged to meet her in a city-centre pub at nine o'clock, just to be on the safe side.

Martin Armitage was cooling off in the custody suite and Norman Wells was in Eastvale General Infirmary. They could charge Armitage with assaulting a police officer, after they had visited the mystery girl.

Within twenty minutes of getting the address, Banks and Annie climbed the lino-covered stairs and knocked on the door. Seconds later a young woman opened the door. *The* young woman.

'DCI Banks and DI Cabbot,' Banks said. 'We'd like a word.'

'You'd better come in then.' She stood aside.

One reason why it had taken so long to locate her was obvious to Banks: she didn't look anywhere near as *weird* as the description Josie Batty had given of her.

The pixyish facial features the artist had drawn were right enough, the heart-shaped face, large eyes and small mouth, but she was far prettier than Josie Batty had indicated, and she had a pale, flawless complexion. The small tattoo on her upper arm was a simple double helix, and there was no sign of body piercing anywhere except silver spider-web earrings. Her short black hair was dyed and gelled, but there was nothing weird about that.

The flat was clean and tidy, not a filthy crack house full of sprawled drug-addled kids. Banks and Annie walked around the small room, checking it out, while the girl arranged beanbag cushions for them.

'Elizabeth, is it?' asked Banks.

'I prefer Liz.'

'OK. Ryan not here?'

'He's got classes.'

'When will he be back?'

'Not till after teatime.'

'What do you do, Liz?'

'I'm a musician.'

'Make a living at it?'

'You know what it's like . . .'

Banks did, having a son in the business. But Brian's success was unusual, and even that hadn't brought in heaps of money. He moved on. 'You know why we're here, don't you?'

Liz nodded. 'About Luke.'

'You could have come forward and saved us a lot of trouble.'

Liz sat down. 'But I don't know anything.'

'Let us be the judge of that,' said Banks, pausing in his examination of her CD collection. He had noticed a cassette labelled 'Songs from a Black Room' mixed in with a lot of other tapes.

'How was I to know you were looking for me?'

'Don't you read the papers or watch television?' Annie asked.

'Not much. Mostly I practise, listen to music or read.'

'How old are you, Liz?' Banks asked.

'Twenty-one.'

'And Ryan?'

'The same. He's in his last year at college.'

'He a musician, too?'

'Yes.'

Annie sat down on one of the beanbags, but Banks went to stand by the window, leaning the backs of his thighs against the sill.

'What was your relationship with Luke Armitage?' Annie asked.

'He's . . . he *was* in our band.'

'Along with?'

'Me and Ryan. We don't have a drummer yet.'

'How long have you been together?'

She thought for a moment. 'We've only been practising together since earlier this year, after we met Luke. But Ryan and me had been talking about doing something like this for ages.'

'How did you meet Luke?'

'At a concert at the college.'

'How did Luke get into a college concert? He was only fifteen.'

Liz smiled. 'Not to look at. Or to talk to. Luke was far more mature than his years. You didn't know him.'

'And then?'

'Well, we found out he was interested in music, too, looking to get a band together. He had some songs.'

'What about who his real father was? Did you know that?'

Liz looked away. 'He didn't tell us that until later. He didn't seem to want anything to do with Neil Byrd and his legacy.'

'How did you find out?' Banks asked. 'I mean, did Luke just come right out and tell you who his father was?'

'No. No. He didn't like to talk about him. There was something on the radio while he was here, a review of that new compilation. He got upset about it and it just sort of slipped out. It made a lot of sense.'

'What do you mean?' Annie asked.

'That voice. His talent. There was *something* that rang a bell.'

'What happened after you knew? Did it make a difference?'

'Not really.'

'You had Neil Byrd's *son* in your band. You can't expect us to believe that you weren't aware that would make a big difference commercially.'

'OK,' said Liz. 'Sure, we were all aware of that. But the point is that we weren't *anywhere* commercially at that time. We're still not. We haven't even played in public yet. And now, without Luke . . .'

'Did you have a relationship with Luke? Other than musical?'

'What do you mean?'

'Did you sleep with him?'

'I'm not a bloody cradlesnatcher. Besides, I'm perfectly happy with Ryan, thank you very much.' Liz's face was red.

'So there's no chance that Ryan caught the two of you in bed together and ended up killing Luke, then deciding he might as well cash in on it?'

'I don't know how you can even suggest something as horrible as that.' Liz seemed close to tears and Banks was starting to feel like a shit. She seemed a good kid. But *seemed* wasn't good enough.

'It happens,' Banks said. 'You'd be surprised. Maybe it was an accident, you just couldn't see any other way out.'

'Nothing like that happened. Luke was in the band, that's all.'

'When did you last see Luke?' Annie asked.

'About a week before he disappeared. Band practice.'

Annie struggled to her feet. 'Where do you practise?'

'Church basement, down the street.'

'And you haven't seen Luke since?'

'No.'

'Has he ever been here?' Banks asked. 'In this flat?'

'Sure. Plenty of times.' Liz stood up.

'Did he ever leave anything here?'

'Like what?'

'You know, notebooks, poems, stories, clothes, that sort of thing.'

'He sometimes left tapes of songs. And some lyrics, maybe. But . . .'

'Could you collect them all together for us?'

'Do you mean right now? Can't you come back later?'

'Now would be best,' said Banks. 'We'll help you look, if you like.'

'No! I mean, no. It's all right. I'll find them.'

'Is there something here you don't want us to see, Liz?'

'No, nothing. There's only a few tapes and some poems, notes for songs. I don't see how they can help you. Look, will I get them back?'

'Why would you get them back?' Annie asked. 'They were Luke's property, weren't they?'

'I suppose. But he brought them for us. The band. To share.'

'They'll still most likely go to the family,' Banks told her.

'Luke's family! But they don't care.'

'Can't be helped. It's the law.'

Liz shifted from foot to foot, arms folded, as if she needed to go to the toilet. 'Look, couldn't you go away and come back, just for a while, give me just a bit of time to get everything together?'

'We can't do that, Liz. I'm sorry.'

'So you'll just take everything and give it to Luke's parents, just like that? You won't even give me time to make copies.'

'This is a murder investigation,' Annie reminded her.

'But still . . .' Liz sat down, close to tears again. 'It doesn't seem fair. It seems such a waste . . . I don't know. His parents don't care.'

Banks felt sorry for her. He suspected she wanted to hang on to Luke's tapes and writings for selfish reasons, so the band could one day ride on Luke's and his father's coattails to success. That Luke had been murdered would also, no doubt, help boost the public interest. Banks didn't think particularly ill of Liz for this and didn't think it lessened her genuine feelings for Luke. There was something else that bothered him; the way she had reacted when he had offered to help look around. He glanced at Annie. It was one of those rare moments when each knew what the other was thinking.

'Mind if we have a little look around?' Annie asked.

'What? Why? I'll give you everything.' She got up and went over to the tapes, picking out three. 'These for a start. The writings are in—'

'Why are you so jumpy, Liz?'

'I'm not jumpy.'

'Yes, you are. I think we should have a look around the place.'

'You can't do that. You need a search warrant.'

Banks sighed. 'Are you sure you want that? Because we can get one.'

'Go do it then. Get one.'

Banks looked at Annie. 'DI Cabbot, will you please go—'

Liz looked from one to the other. 'Not just *her*. Both of you go.'

'It doesn't work like that,' said Banks. 'One of us has to stay here to make sure you don't interfere with anything. We'd hardly be doing our jobs if we let drug dealers flush their stuff down the toilet, would we?'

'I'm not a drug dealer.'

'I'm sure you're not. But there's something you don't want us to find. I'll stay here while DI Cabbot gets the warrant, then she'll come back with four or five constables and we'll tear the place apart.'

Liz turned so pale Banks was worried she might faint. 'What's it to be, Liz? Will you give us consent to look around now, or do we do it the hard way?'

Liz's eyes brimmed with tears. 'I told Ryan he was stupid to keep it.'

'What, Liz?'

'It's in the cupboard by the door, under the sleeping-bag.'

Banks and Annie opened the cupboard by the door and moved

aside the sleeping-bag. Underneath it was a battered leather shoulder bag, exactly the kind that Luke Armitage had been carrying when the bullies taunted him in the market square.

'I think you and Ryan have got quite a bit of explaining to do, don't you?' said Banks.

10

Annie's face was starting to ache when she went to interview Liz Palmer. She'd taken a couple of paracetamol earlier, but the effect was wearing off. She took another two and probed a loose tooth with her tongue. That bastard Armitage. His high-priced lawyer had been down the station like a shot and he'd been bound over until the following day and sent off home. Annie would have liked to see him cooling his heels in the custody suite overnight.

Because the Luke Armitage murder was a high-profile case, Gristhorpe and DC Jackman were interviewing Ryan Milne at the same time next door. So far, since they had picked him up at the college, Milne had been about as forthcoming as Liz.

Banks had left for Peterborough and so Annie took DC Kevin Templeton with her into Interview Room 2. She made sure Liz was clear about her rights and started the tape recorders. As yet, Annie explained, no charges had been brought and nobody was under arrest. She simply wanted an explanation as to how Luke Armitage's shoulder bag had got into Liz's hall cupboard. The bag and its contents were already with forensics.

'You told me you last saw Luke at band practice in the church basement about a week before he disappeared, right?' Annie began.

Liz nodded. She slumped in her chair and worked at a fingernail.

'Did he have the shoulder bag with him?'

'He always had it with him.'

'Then what was it doing in your cupboard?'

'I've no idea. Must've been since band practice.'

'He came to the flat first?'

'Yes.'

'Problem is, Liz,' Annie went on, 'that the market square CCTV cameras caught Luke before he disappeared a week ago yesterday, last Monday, and he had the bag with him then.'

'It must've been a new one.'

'No,' Annie said. 'It was the same one.' She couldn't be certain of that, of course—perhaps Luke *had* left his bag and bought a new one—but it was unlikely Luke would have left all his things there, too. After all, it wasn't the bag itself that counted, but the possessions it contained: his notebook, his laptop computer, tapes and CDs.

Liz frowned. 'Well, I don't see how . . .'

'Me, neither. Unless you're not telling us the truth.'

'Why would I lie?'

'Oh, come off it,' Kevin Templeton butted in. 'Luke's dead. I'd say that's a pretty good reason to lie, wouldn't you?'

Liz jerked forward. '*I* didn't kill him! You can't think I killed him?'

'I don't know what we're supposed to think,' said Annie, spreading her hands. 'Luke and his bag go missing, then Luke turns up dead and we find his bag in your cupboard.'

'I've told you, I don't know when he put it there.'

'Where were you the Monday afternoon Luke disappeared?'

'I don't know. Home, I suppose.'

'Are you sure he didn't call at the flat, then perhaps forget his bag when he went off somewhere else?'

'I didn't see him.'

'Maybe it was Ryan,' Kevin Templeton suggested.

Liz looked confused. 'Ryan? What do you mean?'

'Well,' Templeton went on, 'let me tell you what I think happened.' Annie gave him the nod. 'I think Luke went to your flat after he'd been in the market square. It was late afternoon. Ryan was out and the two of you thought you had time for a roll on the bed.'

'No! That didn't happen. It wasn't like that!'

'But Ryan came home and caught you at it. The two of them got in a scuffle and one way or another Luke ended up dead.'

'It's all lies. Nothing like that happened.'

'Look,' said Templeton, 'we can check, you know. Our forensics people are very good.'

'What do you mean?'

'I mean they'll go through your flat, and if there's any evidence of wrongdoing, even a drop of Luke's blood, they'll find it.'

'He's right,' Annie said. 'If there's any trace of Luke's blood on the carpet, between the floorboards, down the sink, we'll find it.'

Liz bit her lip. Annie could tell she'd touched a nerve. What was it? The mention of blood? Did Liz know they'd find traces of Luke's blood in the flat? 'What is it, Liz?' she asked. 'Something to tell me?'

Liz shook her head.

'What about the ransom demands?'

'What about them?'

'Whose idea was that? Was it Ryan's? Did he see it as an easy opportunity to make some money now that Luke was dead anyway?'

'I don't know what you're talking about.'

Annie stood up and Templeton followed suit. 'Right,' Annie said, switching off the tapes. 'I'm fed up with this. Have her taken to the custody suite, Kev, and arrange for the taking of intimate samples. Maybe we'll get a DNA match with the blood on the wall. And get a search warrant. We'll have forensics in her flat within an hour.'

IT WASN'T OFTEN that DS Gristhorpe visited the Queen's Arms, but after they had finished the interviews with Ryan Milne and Liz Palmer, he suggested to Annie that they discuss the results over a bite to eat. Hungry and thirsty, Annie thought it a good idea.

Gristhorpe returned from the bar with a pint of bitter for her and a half of shandy for himself. They glanced over the menu on the blackboard, and Annie went for a vegetarian lasagne, which ought to be easy on her loose tooth, while Gristhorpe settled on fish and chips.

'Now what about the Palmer girl?' he asked. 'Anything interesting?'

Annie recounted what little she had got from Liz Palmer, then Gristhorpe sipped some shandy and told her about Ryan Milne's interview. 'He said he knew nothing about the bag, just like his girlfriend. He told me he was out that day and didn't see Luke at all.'

'Do you think they did it, sir?'

'I don't know. Milne's got an old banger, so they had the means of transport. Like you, I suggested some sort of romantic angle, something going on between Luke and Liz, but Milne didn't bite, and to be honest I didn't notice any signs I'd hit the nail on the head.'

'So you don't think there was any romantic angle?'

'As I remember, the last thing a twenty-one-year-old woman would want is a fifteen-year-old boyfriend. Now maybe if she were forty-one . . .'

'I don't know,' said Annie. 'The head teacher's daughter told DCI Banks she thought Luke was having it off with his English teacher, and she's pushing thirty.'

'Lauren Anderson?'

'That's the one.'

'Does the Anderson woman have a jealous boyfriend?'

'Not according to Winsome. She did a bit of digging. Only bit of dirt on Ms Anderson is that her brother Vernon's got a record.'

Gristhorpe raised his bushy eyebrows. 'Oh?'

'Nothing really nasty. Just dodgy cheques.'

'I've written a few of those myself, according to my bank manager.'

When their food arrived, both were hungry enough to stop talking for a while and eat, then Gristhorpe slowed down. 'Any ideas of your own about how Luke's bag ended up where it did, Annie?' he asked.

Annie finished her mouthful of lasagne, then said, 'I think Luke went there after his run-in with a group of lads in the market square. What happened after that, I don't know, but either he died there or something happened that made him run off without his bag, which I don't think he'd do under any normal circumstances.'

'So *something* happened there?'

'Yes. Certainly.'

'What about his mobile?'

'One of those tiny models you can just flip open and shut. Probably carried it in his pocket. Anyway, it hasn't been found yet.'

'Anything valuable in the bag?'

'There's still a thriving Neil Byrd industry, a dozen years after his death. Luke inherited some of his father's talent, and, if Liz and Ryan wanted to milk the connection, I'm sure there are plenty of song ideas and fragments on the laptop and in his notebooks.'

'So, whether the two of them killed Luke or not, they somehow found themselves with a gold mine of material and thought they might as well hang on to it until they could use it?'

'It's a thought, sir.'

'Would Liz and Ryan have killed Luke for his stuff?'

'That's the problem. Whichever way you look at it, they'd be far better off with Luke alive. *He* would have been the real draw. Without him, well . . . they're simply doing the best they can.'

'So they had nothing to gain by killing him?'

'Not unless he was intending to walk out on them and take all his works with him. One of them could have lost it with him then.'

'I suppose so. Let's just give them a bit of time, hope forensics turn up something, and have at them again in the morning.'

'Good idea, sir.' Annie finished her pint.

MICHELLE WAS FIVE minutes late, and Banks had already settled at a corner table with a pint of bitter. She was wearing tight black trousers and a green blouse tucked in at the waist. She carried a tan suede jacket slung over her shoulder. Banks had never seen her dressed so casually before. Hadn't seen her looking as good, either. She'd had her hair done, he noticed: nothing drastic, just tidied up a bit, the fringe trimmed, highlights renewed. And she wore a little make-up, just enough to accentuate her green eyes and high cheekbones.

She seemed self-conscious about her appearance because she wouldn't meet his eyes at first. Only when he had offered her a drink did she favour him with a shy smile. 'Thanks for coming,' she said, when Banks placed the dry white wine in front of her and sat down.

'My pleasure,' said Banks. 'Any more news?'

Michelle gave him the gist of her conversation with retired DI Robert Lancaster in London, especially his remarks about Graham seeming streetwise beyond his years.

'So your ex-copper thought Graham had a future in crime, did he?' Banks said. 'Interesting, that.'

'Why? Have you remembered something?'

'Nothing, really. Just that Graham never seemed short of money, and I'd no idea where he got it from.'

'There's something else,' Michelle said. She seemed hesitant.

'Yes?'

'Someone was in my flat on Saturday, while I was in London.'

'Anything taken?'

'Not as far as I can tell, just a few things out of place. But whoever it was had also been having a good look at my computer files.'

Banks got the impression that she wasn't telling him everything, but he didn't pursue it. If there was something she was omitting, it was probably for a good reason, such as embarrassment. She'd hardly want to tell him if someone had been going through her undies, would she?

'Anything there?'

'Not much. Personal notes. Speculations about the case.'

'Did you report the break-in?'

'Of course not. Under the circumstances.'

'Anything else?'

'Maybe. Yesterday, as I was crossing the road near the Hazels, I was almost hit by a van. I couldn't be certain, but I thought it was deliberate.'

'Any idea who?'

'The number plate was obscured.'

'A guess?'

'Well, I hesitate to say it, but after the missing notebooks and actions, my mind can't help but wander towards Shaw.'

'Shaw was teamed up with DI Proctor, right?'

'Reg Proctor, yes. He took early retirement in 1975 and then died of liver cancer in 1978. He was only forty-seven.'

'Any rumours, hints of scandal?'

Michelle sipped some wine and shook her head. 'Not that I could uncover. Seems to have had an exemplary career.'

'Shaw and Proctor were the detectives who came to our house. For some reason someone wanted rid of *Shaw*'s notes. Shaw himself?'

'He was only a DC at the time,' said Michelle.

'Right. What could he have to hide? There must have been something in his notebooks that incriminated someone else. The actions would show us how the investigation was managed. Most of them probably came from Jet Harris himself. They'd show the direction the investigation took, or didn't take, the shape of it.'

'We keep getting back to this blinkered approach,' Michelle said. 'DS Shaw even hinted that they all knew Brady and Hindley did it.'

Banks laughed. 'They operated miles away. No, there's something else going on. Something we can't figure out because there are still too many missing pieces. Another?'

'I'll go.'

Michelle walked to the bar and Banks sat wondering what the hell it was all about. So far, all they had was an investigation that had concentrated on only one possibility—the passing paedophile. Now they had Bill Marshall's relationship with the Krays and with Carlo Fiorino, and the fact that Banks remembered Graham often had money enough to pay for their entertainment. And now the missing records. There were links—Graham, Bill Marshall, Carlo Fiorino— but where did it go after that? And how did Jet Harris fit in? It was possible that he'd been on the take, paid by Fiorino to head off trouble. Jet Harris, bent copper. That would go down well at headquarters. But how did it relate to Graham and his murder?

Michelle came back with the drinks and told him about Donald Bradford's death and the pornography that had been found in his flat.

'It's a bit of a coincidence, isn't it?' Banks said.

'It is indeed.'

'What if Bradford was using the newsagent's shop as an outlet for distributing porn?' Banks suggested.

'And Graham delivered it?'

'Why not? He always seemed to be able to get his hands on it. That's another thing I remember.'

'Maybe he just found out about it. Maybe Bradford was working for a wholesaler with even more at stake?'

'Someone like Carlo Fiorino?' suggested Banks. 'And Harris was on Fiorino's payroll? It's possible, but still speculation. And it doesn't get us a lot further with the missing notebooks.'

'Unless Proctor and Shaw hit on the truth during their interviews, and it was recorded in Shaw's notebooks. I don't know how we'd find out, though. It's not as if we can talk to Harris or Proctor.'

'Maybe not,' said Banks. 'But we might be able to do the next best thing. Were they married?'

'Harris was. Not Proctor.'

'Is his wife still alive?'

'As far as I know.'

'Maybe she'll be able to tell us something. Think you can find her?'

'Piece of cake,' said Michelle.

'And let's delve a little deeper into Donald Bradford's domain, including the circumstances of his death.'

'OK.'

'Are you going to the funeral tomorrow?'

'Yes.'

'Good.' Banks finished his drink. 'Another?'

Michelle looked at her watch. 'No. Really. I'd better go.'

'OK. I suppose I should go, too.' Banks smiled. 'I'm sure my mum'll be waiting up for me.'

Michelle laughed. It was a nice sound. Soft, warm, musical. Banks hadn't heard her laugh before. 'Can I give you a lift?' he asked.

'Oh, no. Thank you,' said Michelle, standing up. 'I'm just round the corner.'

'I'll walk with you, then.'

'You don't need to. It's quite safe.'

'I insist. Especially after what you've just told me.'

They walked out into the darkness, crossed the road and neared the riverside flats. Banks walked Michelle up to her door.

'Well,' she said, fumbling for her key, giving him a brief smile over her shoulder. 'Good night, then.'

'I'll just wait and make sure everything's OK.'

'Until you're sure there are no bogeymen waiting for me?'

'Something like that.'

Michelle opened her door and did a quick check while Banks stood in the doorway and glanced around the living room. It seemed a bit barren, as if Michelle hadn't put her stamp on it yet.

'All clear,' she said, emerging from the bedroom.

'Good night, then,' said Banks, trying to hide his disappointment that she didn't even invite him in for a coffee. 'See you tomorrow.'

'Yes.' She gave him a smile. 'Tomorrow.' Then she closed the door gently behind him, and the sound of the bolt slipping home seemed far louder than it probably was.

BANKS WALKED DOWN the stairs and tried to shake off his sense of disappointment. Just round the corner from the flats, he stopped to light a cigarette. Before he got his lighter out of his pocket, he felt something thud into him from behind. He staggered forward and turned to face whoever had hit him. He got only a quick glimpse of a pug nose and piggy eyes before a blow to the face upset both his vision and his balance. Another blow knocked him to the ground. Next he felt a sharp pain in his ribs and a kick to his stomach made him retch.

Then he heard a dog barking and a man shouting, felt rather than saw his attacker hesitate and heard him whisper, 'Go back where you came from, or there'll be more of that,' before he ran off into the night.

Banks got to his knees and felt sick, head hanging on his chest. He tried to stand, but his legs still felt too wobbly. Then a hand grasped his elbow and he managed to get to his feet.

'Are you all right, mister?' Banks swayed and took a couple of deep breaths. That felt a little better. His head was still spinning, but his vision had cleared. A young man stood beside him, Jack Russell terrier on a leash.

'Thank you,' said Banks. 'That was very brave. You saved my bacon.'

'Is there anything else I can do? Call you a taxi or something?'

Banks looked towards the flats. 'No,' he said. 'No, thanks. I've a friend lives just over there. I'll be fine.'

'If you're certain.'

'Yes. And thanks again.'

The young man shrugged. 'No problem. Come on, Pugwash.' And they wandered off, the man casting backward glances as he went.

Still a bit wobbly, Banks made his way back to Michelle's flat and pressed the intercom. A few moments later her voice crackled into the night air. 'Yes? Who is it?'

'It's me, Alan,' said Banks.

'What is it?'

'I've had a little accident. I wonder if . . .'

But before he could finish Michelle buzzed him in and he made his way up to her door. She was already standing there, looking concerned, and came forward to help him onto the sofa.

'What happened?' she asked.

'Someone jumped me. Thank God for dog walkers or I'd probably be in the river by now.'

Michelle handed him a glass. 'Drink,' she said.

He drank. Cognac. As the fiery liquor spread through his limbs he started to feel better. His mind came into sharper focus and he was able to assess the damage. Not much, really. His ribs felt tender but he didn't feel as if anything was broken. He looked up and saw Michelle standing over him.

'How do you feel now?'

'Much better, thank you.' Banks sipped some more cognac. 'Look,' he said, 'I'd better call a taxi. I don't feel much like driving in this condition, especially not after this.'

'OK,' she said. 'But you must let me see to your nose first.'

'Nose?' Banks realised his nose and upper lip felt numb. He put his hand up and it came away bloody.

'I don't think it's broken,' Michelle said, leading him towards the bathroom, 'but I'd better clean you up and put something on it before you go. There's a small cut on your lip, too. Whoever hit you must have been wearing a ring or something.'

The bathroom was small, almost too small for two people to stand without touching. Banks stood with the backs of his legs against the toilet as Michelle used a damp facecloth to wipe away the blood then looked in the cabinet and came up with some TCP liquid antiseptic, which she carefully applied to his lip. It stung and made him gasp. Michelle took the cotton wool away.

'It's all right,' he said.

She dropped one bloodstained swab into the bin and prepared another. Banks watched her face close to his, the look of concentration as she applied the cotton wool, tip of her tongue nipped between her teeth. She caught his eye and blushed. 'What?'

'Nothing,' he said. She was so close he could feel the warmth of her body, smell the cognac on her breath.

'Go on,' she said. 'You were going to say something.'

'It's just like *Chinatown*,' Banks said.

'What do you mean?'

'The film, *Chinatown*. Jack Nicholson gets his nose cut by Roman Polanski, and Faye Dunaway, well . . . she does what you're doing now.'

'Puts TCP on it?'

'Well, I don't think it was TCP—I don't think they have that in America—but the idea's the same. Anyway, it's a very sexy scene.'

'Sexy?' Michelle paused. Banks could see her flushed skin, feel the hcat from her cheeks. The bathroom seemed to be getting smaller. She dabbed at him again. Her hand was trembling. 'I don't see how putting TCP on a cut could be sexy. I mean, what happens?'

She was so close to him now that he could feel her breast touching ever so lightly against his arm. He could have leaned further back but he stood his ground. 'First, they kiss,' he said.

'But wouldn't it hurt?'

'It was just his nose that got cut. Remember?'

'Of course. How silly of me.'

'Michelle?'

'What? What is it?'

Banks took her trembling hand by the wrist and moved it away from his mouth, then he put his other hand under her chin and cupped it gently so she was looking at him, her brilliant green eyes questioning but holding his gaze, not looking away now. He could feel his heart thudding in his chest and his knees wobbling as he pulled her closer to him and felt her yield.

'YOU WERE LATE BACK last night,' Banks's mother said, without turning from the kitchen sink. 'Tea's fresh.'

Banks poured himself a cup of tea and added a splash of milk. His mother had probably lain awake until two in the morning listening for him the way she did when he was a teenager.

Ida Banks turned. 'Alan! What *have* you done to your face? It's all bruised. And your lip's cut. What have you been up to?'

Banks turned away. 'It's nothing.'

'Were you fighting? Was it some criminal you were arresting?'

'Something like that,' Banks said. 'I had a bit of business to take care of. Look, I'm sorry I didn't ring, but it was late. I didn't want to wake you.'

His mother sniffed and nodded. 'Well,' she said. 'I suppose you'll be hungry. Bacon and eggs?'

Banks wasn't that hungry, but he couldn't deal with the protests he knew he'd get if he asked for just cereal. He was also in a hurry. Michelle had suggested he come down to headquarters to search through the mugshots for his attacker. Still, Mother comes first. 'If it's no trouble,' he said. 'Is the paper around?'

'Your dad took it down to the allotment with him.'

'I'll just nip over the road, then.'

Banks's mother sighed, and he headed out. As he entered the newsagent's, he remembered the way it used to be: the counter in a different place, racks arranged differently. Different magazines and covers back then, too: *Film Show*, *Jackie*, *Honey*, *Tit-Bits*.

Banks remembered his conversation with Michelle in the pub about Donald Bradford and his collection of porn and wondered if he really had acted as a distributor. While Banks couldn't imagine Graham slipping a porn magazine between the pages of the *People* and putting it through Number 42's letterbox, he *could* imagine Bradford keeping his stock under the counter or hidden in the back. And maybe Graham had stumbled upon it.

It hardly seemed something worth murdering over, but if it was a part of something bigger—the Kray empire, for example—and if Graham had got involved in it way beyond his depth, then there might be a link to his murder.

Tapping a newspaper against his thigh, Banks crossed the road and hurried back home before his bacon and eggs turned cold.

DESPITE HER LATE NIGHT, Michelle was at her desk long before Detective Superintendent Shaw was likely to see the light of day. If he bothered coming in at all. Maybe he would take another sick day. There were people around the office, so she and Banks hadn't had a chance to do much more than say a quick hello before they got down to business. She had given him a choice of the computer versions of the mugshots or the photo albums, and he had chosen the albums.

She had felt a little shy when he walked in and could still hardly believe that she had slept with him. She didn't know what Banks's personal situation was, except that he was going through a divorce. He hadn't talked about his wife, or his children, if he had any. Michelle found herself curious. She hadn't told him about Melissa and Ted either, and she didn't know if she would. Not for a while, anyway.

Putting aside her thoughts, Michelle got to work. She had a couple of things to do before Graham Marshall's funeral service that afternoon, including tracking down Jet Harris's wife and ringing Dr Cooper. But before she could pick up the phone, Dr Cooper rang *her*.

'Dr Cooper,' said Michelle. 'Any news?'

'Sorry it took so long to get the information you wanted, but I told you Hilary Wendell's a tough man to track down.'

'You've got something?'

'Hilary has. He won't commit himself to this absolutely, so he'd be very unwilling to testify if it ever came to a court case.'

'It probably won't, but the information might be useful.'

'Well, from careful measurement of the nick on the underside of the rib, he's made a few projections and he's pretty certain it's a military knife of some kind. His money's on a Fairbairn-Sykes.'

'What's that?'

'British commando knife. Introduced in 1940.'

'A commando knife?'

'Yes. Is that of any use?'

'It might be,' said Michelle. 'Thanks a lot.'

'You're welcome.'

'And please thank Dr Wendell from me.'

'Will do.'

A *commando knife*. In 1965 the war had been over for only twenty years and plenty of men in their early forties would have fought in it and had access to such a knife. What worried Michelle most of all, though, was that the only person she *knew* had served as a commando was Jet Harris; she remembered it from the brief biography she had read when she first came to Thorpe Wood.

After about an hour, Banks poked his head out of the interview room, then carried one of the books over. 'I think that's him.'

Michelle looked at the photo. The man was in his late twenties, with medium-length brown hair, badly cut, a stocky build, piggy eyes and a pug nose. His name was Des Wayman, and according to his record he had been in and out of the courts ever since his days as juvenile car thief, progressing from that to public disorder offences and GBH. His most recent incarceration, a lenient nine months, was for receiving stolen goods. He had been out just over a year.

'I'll go and have a word with him.'

'Want me to come along?'

'No. I think it would work better if I could question him without you there. After all, it might come to an identity parade. If any charges are brought, I want to make sure this is done right.'

'Fair enough,' said Banks. 'But he looks like a tough customer.' He rubbed his jaw. 'Feels like one, too.'

Michelle looked across the office, to where DC Collins sat talking on the phone. Could she trust him? He was almost as new as she was, for a start, and that went in his favour. She had never seen him hanging around with Shaw, either, another plus. In the end, she decided she *had* to trust someone, and Collins was the man.

'I'll take DC Collins,' she said, then lowered her voice. 'Look, there's a couple of things I need to talk to you about, but not here.'

'After the funeral this afternoon?'

'OK,' said Michelle.

ANNIE PORED over Luke Armitage's notebooks and computer files in her office that morning. Though her jaw was still throbbing a bit, it didn't hurt anywhere near as much as it had.

One thing that intrigued her about Luke's jottings was the increasing eroticism mixed in with the vague classical references to Persephone, Psyche and Ophelia. Then she remembered that Ophelia wasn't a character from classical mythology, but Hamlet's girlfriend, driven mad by his rejection of her. She remembered from somewhere the image of Ophelia floating down a river surrounded by flowers. Did Luke feel guilty about rejecting someone, then? Had he been killed out of revenge, by 'a woman scorned'? And if so, who? Liz Palmer? Lauren Anderson? Rose Barlow?

Her phone rang just as she was turning off Luke's computer.

'Annie, it's Stefan Nowak. The lab hasn't finished trying to match your DNA samples with the blood on the dry-stone wall yet, so I can't tell you about that, but my team *did* find blood at Liz Palmer's flat.'

'How much?'

'Only a small amount. And not where you'd expect. Smeared under the bathroom sink.'

'As if someone gripped it while leaning over?'

'Could be, yes. But there are no prints or anything.'

'Is it enough for analysis?'

'Oh, yes. We're working on it now. All the lab has been able to tell me so far is that it matches Luke Armitage's blood type and that it doesn't match the samples we took from Liz Palmer or Ryan Milne.'

'That's fantastic, Stefan! It puts Luke bleeding in Liz Palmer's flat.'

'Maybe. But it won't tell you *when*.'

'For the moment, I'll take what I can get.'

'There's more.'

'What?'

'I've just been talking to Dr Glendenning, and he tells me the tox screen on Luke shows an unusually large amount of diazepam.'

'Diazepam? That's Valium, isn't it?'

'That's one name for it. But the point is it was mostly undigested.'

'So he died very soon after taking it?'

'Yes.'

'But it's not the cause of death?'

'No way.'

'Would it have been enough to kill him?'

'Probably not.'

'Anything else?'

THE SUMMER THAT NEVER WAS

'In the flat? Yes. Drugs. Some marijuana, LSD, Ecstasy.'
'Dealing?'
'No. Not enough. Just for personal use, I'd say. And no diazepam.'
'Thanks, Stefan. Thanks a lot.'

11

According to his file, Des Wayman lived in a council house on Hazel Way. It was mid-morning when Michelle and DC Collins parked outside and walked down the path. Michelle was glad Collins was with her. He played second row for the police rugby team and his solid presence was enough to put anyone off trying anything.

Michelle knocked at the door of Number 15. Des Wayman opened it wearing grubby jeans, with his shirt hanging out.

'Who are you?' he said, with a leer. 'I'm off out. But seeing as you're here, how about coming with us for a drink?'

Michelle showed her warrant card and DC Collins followed suit. The man's expression became wary.

'Mr Wayman?' Michelle said.

'And what if it is?'

'We'd like a word, sir. Mind if we come in?'

'Like I said, I'm just on my way out. Can't we talk down the pub?'

'It'd be better here, sir,' Michelle insisted. When Wayman made no move, she walked past him into the house. He followed her into his living room, DC Collins right behind him. The place was a tip. Empty beer cans littered the floor, along with overflowing ashtrays. Wayman picked up a can from the table and ripped the tab. Michelle looked around and saw no surface she felt comfortable sitting on, so she stood by the window. 'You're in a bit of trouble, Des,' she said, aware of DC Collins paying careful attention. She hadn't explained much to him in the car; all she had said was not to take notes.

'Last night at approximately ten fifty-five, you assaulted a man outside a riverside flat.'

'I did no such thing,' said Wayman.

'Des, he saw you. He picked you out of the villains' album.'

'He must be mistaken,' he said. 'His word against mine.'

Michelle laughed. 'Is that the best you can do? Where were you?'

'I was having a bevvy or two in the Pig and Whistle.'

'Anyone see you?'

'Lots of people. It was very busy.'

'That's not far away from where the attack took place,' said Michelle. 'What time did you leave?'

'Dunno. After closing time.'

'Sure you didn't sneak out early and then go back for last orders?'

'Not me, miss.'

'Show me your hands, Des.'

Wayman stretched his hands out, palms up.

'Turn them over.'

Wayman did as she asked.

'Where'd you get that skinned knuckle?'

'I don't know,' said Wayman. 'Must have brushed it against the wall or something.'

'And that ring you've got,' Michelle went on. 'Sharp, I'll bet. Sharp enough to cut someone. I bet there'll still be traces of blood on the metal,' she said. 'Enough to identify as your victim's.'

Wayman lit a cigarette and fell silent. 'Trouble is, Des,' Michelle said, 'the man you attacked, the man who recognised you, he's a copper. What was it you said earlier? His word against yours? Whose word do you think the judge is going to believe, Des?'

'Nobody told me—'

'Told you what?'

'Shut up. I've got to think.'

'You've not got long. Assaulting a police officer. That's a serious charge. You'll go down for a lot longer than nine months on that.'

Wayman laughed. 'You know,' he said, puffing out his chest, 'I'm practically one of you lot, myself. I don't know where you get off pinning this assault on me when it's police business to start with.'

'What are you talking about?'

'You know damn well what I'm talking about. I was on police business. Undercover. Sometimes a little tap on the head and a few words of warning work wonders. It's the way they used to do things in the old days, so I hear. And don't tell me you don't know what I'm talking about. Your boss certainly does.'

'Boss?'

'Yes. *Numero uno*. Detective bloody Superintendent Ben Shaw.'

'*Shaw?*' Michelle had half suspected that Shaw was behind the attacks on her and Banks, but was stunned to have it confirmed.

'Wait a minute. Are you telling me you're an undercover police officer following Detective Superintendent Shaw's orders?'

'Well, maybe I'm not exactly what you'd call an undercover officer, but I've done your boss a little favour from time to time.'

'Do you own a beige van?' Michelle asked.

'What? I don't own a van at all. Dark blue Corsa.'

'Ever done time for burglary?'

'You've read my form. Did you notice anything about burglary?'

Michelle hadn't. So Wayman most likely wasn't responsible for the damage to her flat and the attempt on her life. 'Look,' she said, 'it's up to you where it goes from here. It could go to the station, to the lawyers, to court eventually. Or it could end here.'

'You promise?'

'Only if you tell me what I want to know.' Michelle looked at DC Collins, who looked lost. 'This bloke you assaulted last night, what did Shaw tell you about him?'

'That he was a small-time villain from up North looking to get himself established on our patch.'

'And what did Detective Superintendent Shaw ask you to do?'

'Nip it in the bud.'

'Can you be more specific?'

'Most people understand a thump on the nose.'

'And how did you know where he was that evening?'

'I got a call on my mobile in the Pig and Whistle.'

'From who?'

'Who do you think?'

'But how did he . . . Never mind.' Michelle realised that Shaw must have been using his whole network of informers to keep an eye on the comings and goings in the Graham Marshall investigation. But why? To hide the truth, that the great local hero Jet Harris was a murderer?

'What's going to happen now? Remember what you promised.'

Michelle looked at DC Collins. 'What's going to happen now,' she said, 'is that you're going to the pub to drink yourself into a stupor. And if you ever cross my path again, I'll make sure they put you somewhere that'll make the Middle East look like an alcoholic's paradise. That clear?'

'Yes, ma'am.'

'Do you think you can tell me what all that was about?' asked DC Collins when they got outside.

Michelle took a deep breath and smiled. 'Yes, of course, Nat. I'm sorry for keeping you in the dark so long, but I think you'll understand when you hear what I have to say. I'll tell you over a pie and a pint. My treat.' She looked round. 'But not in his local.'

'I'M ALAN BANKS, Mrs Marshall. I'd like to offer my condolences.'

'Alan Banks. Well, I never! Glad you could come, Alan,' said Mrs Marshall, sticking out her black-gloved hand. 'I hope you'll come back to the house for drinks and sandwiches.'

They were standing outside the chapel after Graham's funeral.

'Of course,' Banks said, shaking Mrs Marshall's hand. Then he saw Michelle walking down the path. 'Excuse me a moment.'

He hurried after Michelle and put his hand gently on her shoulder. Michelle turned to face him and smiled.

'You said you wanted to talk to me.'

'Yes.' Michelle told him about Dr Wendell's identification of the Fairbairn-Sykes knife and Harris's wartime record as a commando.

'It's hard to believe that Jet Harris might have killed Graham.'

'He's not the only candidate. Mrs Walker—the woman in the newsagent's—said something about Donald Bradford being in a special unit in Burma. I checked. Turns out it was a commando unit.'

'Bradford, too? That complicates things.'

'Well, at least we know that Bradford had some sort of involvement with pornography. We don't have any evidence that Harris was bent yet,' said Michelle. 'Only Shaw's behaviour. Which brings me to our interview with Des Wayman.' Michelle told him about Wayman's assertion that Shaw was behind last night's attack. 'He'd deny he ever said it if we challenged him, and I'm certain Shaw will deny it, too.'

'But *we* know it's true,' said Banks. 'That gives us an edge. What about the burglary at your flat and the van that tried to run you down?'

Michelle shook her head. 'Wayman knows nothing about them. Shaw must have got someone else, maybe someone a bit brighter.'

'You think we should have a chat with Shaw?'

'Soon. It'd be nice to know a bit more about Harris first.'

'I'll call you later.'

'OK.' Michelle turned and carried on walking down the path.

'RIGHT, LIZ, are you going to tell us the truth now?' Annie asked once the interview room was set up and the tapes turned on.

'We didn't do anything wrong, Ryan and me,' Liz said.

'You know we found drugs in your flat, don't you?'

'Are you going to arrest us for that?'

'Depends on what you tell me. I just want you to know you're in trouble already. You can make it better by telling me the truth, or you can make it worse by continuing with lies. What's it to be, Liz?'

'I'm tired.'

'Maybe it would help,' said Annie, 'if I told you we found traces of Luke's blood under your bathroom sink.'

Liz looked at her, wide-eyed. 'But we didn't kill Luke. Honest!' She started crying. Annie passed her some tissues and waited till she calmed down.

'Did Luke call at your flat the day he disappeared?'

After a long silence, Liz said, 'Yes.'

'Good,' breathed Annie. 'Now we're getting somewhere. What time did he arrive?'

'Time? I don't know. Early in the evening. Maybe sixish.'

'So he must have come straight from the market square?'

'I suppose so. He was a bit upset because some of the kids from the school had pushed him around in the square, so maybe he had.'

'Was Ryan in the flat when Luke arrived?'

'Yes.'

So that put paid to Annie's theory that Ryan had interrupted something between Liz and Luke. 'What did the three of you do?'

'We just talked, went through a few songs.'

'And then?'

Liz fell silent and her eyes filled with tears. 'Ryan rolled a joint. Luke . . . he'd . . . like he was a virgin, you know, when it came to drugs. I mean we'd offered to share before but he always said no.'

'Not that night?'

'No. That night he said yes. The first time.'

'What happened?'

'He got all giggly at first, then he went sort of introspective.'

'So what went wrong?'

'It was when Ryan put that Neil Byrd CD on. You know, that new compilation, *The Summer That Never Was*.'

'He did *what*?' Annie could imagine what effect something like that might have on Luke if he was under the influence of cannabis. Maybe it wasn't a seriously dangerous drug, but it could cause paranoia in people, and it intensified and exaggerated emotions. Reining in her temper, Annie asked, 'How did Luke react to the music?'

'He freaked. Ryan thought it would be a neat idea to do a Neil Byrd song, you know, with Luke singing. I mean, it'd get a lot of attention.'

'Didn't you realise how confused Luke was about his real father? Didn't you know he *never* listened to Neil Byrd's music?'

'Yes, but we thought this was a good time to try it. We thought his mind was open to new things, mellow from the dope, that it was more likely he'd see how *beautiful* his father's work was.'

'When he was disorientated, ultrasensitive?' Annie shook her head in disbelief. 'You're more stupid than I thought you were. Or so selfish and blinkered it amounts to the same thing. What happened next?'

'Luke knocked the guitar out of Ryan's hand and went over to the CD player and took the CD out and started trying to break it in two. Ryan struggled with him, but Luke was, like, *possessed*.'

'What about the blood?'

'In the end Ryan just punched him. That was where the blood came from. Luke ran into the bathroom. I was just behind him, to see if he was all right. There wasn't much blood, it was only like a nosebleed. I tried to calm him down, but he pushed past me and left.'

'Neither of you went after him?'

'No. We figured he just wanted to be by himself.'

'A disturbed fifteen-year-old having a bad drug experience? Oh, come on, Liz. Surely you can't be *that* stupid?'

'Well, *we* were stoned, too. I'm not saying we were, like, the most *rational* we could be.' She lowered her head and sobbed.

'Do you know where he went after he left your flat?' Annie asked.

'No. We never saw him again. I'm sorry. I'm so sorry.'

'Did you or Ryan give Luke Valium, to calm him down, perhaps?'

Liz frowned. 'No. We didn't do stuff like that.'

'So you never had any Valium in the house?'

'No.'

'And there's nothing more you can tell me?'

'I've told you everything. Can I go home now? I'm tired.'

Annie stood up and called for a uniformed officer. 'Yes,' she said. 'But don't wander too far. We'll be wanting to talk to you again.'

'ANOTHER DRINK, ALAN?'

Banks had just arranged to go out drinking that evening with his old friends Dave Grenfell and Paul Major, so he declined Mrs Marshall's offer.

'I'm glad we did this,' Mrs Marshall said. 'The service. I know it probably seems silly, after all this time, but it means a lot to me.'

'It doesn't seem silly,' said Banks. 'I think it meant a lot to all of us.'

'Thank you,' Mrs Marshall said tearfully, moving away.

Feeling the call of nature, Banks went upstairs.

When he had finished in the toilet, he noticed that the door to Graham's old room was open and was surprised to see that the space-rocket wallpaper he remembered from years back was still on the walls. Drawn by the sight, he wandered into the small bedroom.

Of course, everything else had changed. The only familiar object stood in a case leaning against the wall. Graham's guitar.

Certain that no one would mind, Banks sat down on a chair and took the guitar out of its case. Graham had been so proud of it, he remembered. Banks strummed a C chord. Way out of tune. He moved to put the guitar back in its case. As he did so, he thought he heard something slip around inside it. Gently, he shook the guitar, and there it was again: something scraping inside.

Curious, Banks loosened the strings so that he could slip his hand inside. With a bit of juggling and shaking he managed to grab hold of what felt like a piece of stiff, rolled-up paper. Carefully, he pulled it out, noticing the dried Sellotape Graham had used to stick it to the inside of the guitar. That made it something he had tried to hide.

And when Banks unrolled it, he saw why.

It was a photograph: Graham sprawled on a sheepskin rug in front of a large, ornate fireplace, arms behind him, hands propping him up, legs stretched out in front. He was smiling at the camera in a flirtatious and knowing manner.

And he was absolutely stark naked.

MICHELLE FOUND a parking spot near the former Mrs Harris's pretentious pile of mock Tudor on Long Road, Cambridge.

It hadn't been too hard to track down Jet Harris's ex-wife. The biographical pamphlet told Michelle that she had been married to Harris for twenty-three years, between 1950 and 1973, and that she was ten years his junior. A few discreet enquiries around the office yielded the information that a retired civilian employee, Margery Jenkins, visited her occasionally, and she was happy to give Michelle the address. She also told her that the former Mrs Harris had remarried and was now called Mrs Gifford.

A slim, elegantly dressed, grey-haired woman answered the door, and Michelle introduced herself. With a puzzled but interested expression, Mrs Gifford led Michelle to her living room. There Mrs Gifford sat, legs crossed, and lit a cigarette from a gold lighter. She was very well preserved for her seventy-plus years.

'Now, what can I do for you? It's been a long time since the coppers came to call.'

'Just information,' said Michelle. 'You've heard about the Graham Marshall case?'

'Yes. Poor lad. What about him?'

'Your husband was in charge of that investigation.'

'I remember.'

'Did he ever talk about it, tell you any of his theories?'

'John made a point of not discussing his cases at home.'

'Do you remember Ben Shaw?'

'Ben? Of course. He worked with John.' She smiled. 'Regan and Carter they used to think of themselves. *The Sweeney*. Quite the lads.'

'His notebooks covering the Graham Marshall case are missing.'

Mrs Gifford raised a finely pencilled eyebrow. 'Well, things do have a habit of disappearing over time.'

'It just seems a bit of a coincidence.'

'Coincidences do happen.'

'I was just wondering if you knew anything about Shaw, that's all.'

'Like what? Are you asking me if Ben Shaw is bent?'

'Is he?'

'I don't know. John certainly never said anything about it.'

'And he would have known?'

'Oh, yes.' She nodded. 'John would have known.'

'I understand your husband was a commando during the war.'

'Yes. A real war hero, John was.'

'Do you know if he owned a Fairbairn-Sykes commando knife?'

'Not that I saw.'

'He didn't have any mementos?'

'He gave everything up when he was demobbed. He never talked about those days much. Look, where is all this leading?'

Michelle didn't know how to come straight out with it and ask her if her ex-husband was bent, but she got the impression that Mrs Gifford was a hard one to deceive. 'You lived with Mr Harris for twenty-three years,' she said. 'Why leave after so long?'

Mrs Gifford raised her eyebrows. 'What an odd question. And a rather rude one, if I may say so.'

'I'm sorry, but—'

Mrs Gifford waved her cigarette in the air. 'Yes, yes, you've got your job to do. I know. It doesn't matter now, anyway. I waited until the children left home. It's amazing how much one will put up with for the sake of the children, and for appearances.'

'Put up with?'

'Marriage to John wasn't a bed of roses.'

'But there must have been some compensations.'

Mrs Gifford laughed. 'Compensations? My dear, we lived in that poky little semi in Peterborough almost all our married life.'

'I don't know how to say this diplomatically,' Michelle went on.

'Then bugger diplomacy. Come on, out with it.'

'There seem to be some anomalies in the original investigation into the Graham Marshall disappearance. Things seem to have been steered in one direction, away from other possibilities, and—'

'And my John was the one doing the steering?'

'Well, he was senior investigating officer.'

'And you want to know if he was being paid off?'

'I'm asking you if you noticed anything that might indicate he was receiving extra money, yes.'

'Well, if he was, I never saw any of it. I can tell you that much.'

'So where did it all go? Wine, women and song?'

Mrs Gifford laughed again and stubbed out her cigarette. 'My dear,' she said, 'John was strictly an ale and whisky man. He also had a tin ear, and you can forget the women. I've not told anyone except my present husband this, but I'll tell you now, John Harris was queer as a three-pound note.'

DAVE GRENFELL GOT UP and accompanied Banks to the bar. For old times' sake, they were in the Wheatsheaf, where the three of them had drunk their very first pints of beer at the age of sixteen.

Over the first pint, they had caught up with one another to the extent that Banks knew Dave worked as a mechanic, as his father had said, and still lived with his first wife, whereas Paul was cheerfully unemployed and gay as the day is long. Coming hot on the heels of hearing Mrs Gifford's revelations about Jet Harris over the phone from Michelle, this last discovery shocked Banks only because he had never spotted any signs of it when they were kids.

Still, back in 1965 people denied, pretended, tried to 'pass' for straight. Even after legalisation, there was so much stigma attached to it. Banks wondered how hard it had been for Paul to come out. Clearly Jet Harris had never been able to do so. And Banks was willing to bet a pound to a penny that *someone* had known about it, and that someone had used the knowledge to their advantage. Jet Harris hadn't been bent; he'd been blackmailed.

Banks's thoughts returned to the photo he had found in Graham's guitar. He hadn't told Mr or Mrs Marshall, hadn't told anyone except Michelle. Graham must have put it there, Banks assumed, and he had done so because he wanted to hide it. But why had he posed for it and where was it taken? The fireplace looked distinctive enough. Adam, Banks guessed, and you didn't find those just anywhere.

They carried the drinks back to the table, where Paul sat glancing around the room. 'Remember the old jukebox?' he said.

Banks nodded. The Wheatsheaf used to have a great jukebox.

'What do you listen to now, Alan?' Dave asked Banks.

'Bit of everything, I suppose,' Banks said. 'You?'

'Nothing much. I lost interest in music in the seventies, when we had the kids. Remember Steve, though, the kind of stuff he used to make us listen to on Sunday afternoons? Dylan and all that.'

Banks laughed. 'He was ahead of his time, was Steve. Where the hell is he, anyway? Surely someone must have been in touch with him.'

'Hadn't you heard?' Paul said.

Banks and Dave both stared at him. 'What?'

'Shit. I thought you must know. I'm sorry. Steve died of cancer. About three years ago. I only know 'cos his mum and dad kept in touch with mine. I hadn't actually seen him for years.'

After a brief silence, they raised their glasses and drank a toast to the memory of Steve, early Dylan fan. Then they toasted Graham.

Banks's mobile rang. 'Sorry,' he said. 'I'd better take it.'

He walked out into the street. 'Alan, it's Annie,' said the voice at the other end.

'Annie? What's happening?'

Annie told Banks about the Liz Palmer interview.

'You think she's telling the truth?'

'Pretty certain. DS Gristhorpe interviewed Ryan Milne at the same time and the details check out. They haven't been allowed to get together and concoct a story since they've been in custody.'

'OK,' said Banks. 'So where did Luke go?'

'We don't know. There's just one thing . . .'

'Yes.'

'The diazepam that Dr Glendenning found in Luke's system.'

'What about it?'

'Well, he didn't get it at Liz and Ryan's flat. Neither of them has a prescription and we didn't find any in our search.'

'They could have got it illegally, along with the cannabis and LSD.'

'They could have,' said Annie. 'But why lie about it?'

'That I can't answer. What's your theory?'

'Well, if Luke was freaking out, then someone might have thought it was a good idea to give him some Valium to calm him down.'

'Or to keep him quiet. What next?'

'We need to find out where he went. I'm going to talk to Luke's parents again tomorrow. I'll also be talking to Gavin Barlow.'

'Why?'

'Maybe there was still something going on between Luke and Rose, and maybe her father didn't approve.'

'Enough to kill him?'

'Enough to make it physical. We still can't say for certain that anyone *murdered* Luke.'

'Fair enough,' said Banks. 'And don't forget that Martin Armitage was out that night, too. What's happened with him by the way?'

'He appeared before the magistrates this afternoon. He's out on bail till the preliminary hearing. You getting anywhere?'

'I'll tell you when I see you.' Banks ended the call and went back into the pub.

'So you're a copper,' said Paul, shaking his head when Banks sat down again. 'I still can't get over it.'

Banks smiled. 'Funny how things turn out. Do either of you remember anything odd happening round the time Graham disappeared?'

'You're not working on the case, are you?' asked Dave.

'No,' said Banks, 'but I'm interested in what happened. I mean, I *am* a copper and Graham was a mate. Naturally, I'm curious.'

'Did you ever tell them about that bloke by the river?' Paul asked.

'It didn't lead anywhere,' Banks said, explaining. 'Besides, I think it's a lot closer to home.'

'What do you mean?' Paul asked.

'Do you remember Donald Bradford?' Banks asked. 'The bloke who ran the newsagent's?'

'Dirty Don?' said Paul. 'Sure. I remember him.'

'Why did you call him Dirty Don?'

'I don't know.' Paul shrugged. 'Maybe he sold dirty magazines. It's just something my dad called him. Don't you remember?'

Banks didn't. But he found it interesting that Paul's dad had known about Bradford's interest in porn. Had anyone told Proctor and Shaw all those years ago when they came to conduct the interviews? Was that why the notebooks and action allocations had to disappear, so that suspicion wouldn't point towards Bradford? Next to the family, Bradford should have come under the most scrutiny, but he had been virtually ignored. 'Did Graham ever tell you where he got those magazines he used to show us?'

'What magazines?' Dave asked.

'Don't you remember?' Paul said. 'I do.'

Banks turned to Paul. 'Did he ever tell you where he got them?'

'Not that I remember. Why? Do you think it was Bradford?'

'It's possible. A newsagent's shop would be a pretty good outlet for things like that. And Graham always seemed to have money to spare. I think Graham had something going with Bradford, most likely something involving porn. And I think that led to his death.'

'You think Bradford killed him?'

'It's a possibility. Maybe he was helping distribute the stuff, or maybe he found out about it and was blackmailing Bradford.'

'Graham? Blackmailing?' said Dave. 'Now, hold on a minute, Alan, this is our mate Graham we're talking about.'

'I don't think things were exactly as we thought they were back then,' said Banks. 'And I don't think we knew a hell of a lot about Graham, either, mate or not.' He looked at Dave. 'For God's sake, Dave, you don't even remember the dirty magazines.'

'I remember lots of things. Just not looking at those magazines.'

'But you did,' said Paul. 'I remember you once saying pictures like that must have been taken at Randy Mandy's.'

'Randy Mandy's?' Banks asked. 'What the hell's that?'

'Don't tell me *you* don't remember, either,' said Paul, exasperated.

'Obviously I don't,' said Banks. 'What does it mean?'

'Randy Mandy's? It was Rupert Mandeville's place, that big house up Market Deeping way. Remember?'

Banks felt a vague recollection at the edge of his consciousness. 'I think I remember.'

'It was just our joke, that's all,' Paul went on. 'We thought they had sex orgies there. Like that place Profumo used to go a couple of years earlier. Remember that? Christine Keeler and Mandy Rice-Davies?'

Banks remembered. The newspapers had been full of salacious 'confessions' around the time of the Profumo scandal in 1963.

'I remember now,' said Dave. 'Rupert Mandeville's house. Bloody great country mansion, more like. We used to think it was some sort of den of iniquity back then, somewhere all sorts of naughty things went on. Whenever we came across something dirty we always said it must have come from Randy Mandy's. You must remember, Alan. God knows where we got the idea from, but there was this high wall and a big swimming pool in the garden, and we used to imagine girls swimming naked there.'

'Vaguely,' said Banks. 'This Mandeville still around?'

'Wasn't he an MP or something?' said Dave.

'I think so,' Paul said. 'I remember reading about him in the papers a few years ago. I think he's in the House of Lords now.'

Conversation meandered on for another hour or so. When Banks said he had to go, Dave took his cue, and Paul said he wasn't going to sit there by himself. They walked back to Banks's parents' door, their first stop, and said good night. They all made vague lies about keeping in touch and then walked back to their own separate lives.

MICHELLE WAS EATING warmed-up chicken casserole and watching a documentary on ocean life when her telephone rang late that evening.

'Hope I didn't disturb you,' Banks said when she answered it. He told her about Bradford's 'Dirty Don' epithet and the rumours they used to hear about the Mandeville house.

'I've heard of that place recently,' Michelle said. 'I don't know if I read about it in an old file, but I'll check up on it tomorrow.'

'Going by the photo I found in Graham's guitar and the information you got from Jet Harris's ex-wife, I think we'd better look into anything even remotely linked with illicit sex around the time of Graham's murder, don't you?'

'That's it!' Michelle said. 'The connection.'

'What connection?'

'The Mandeville house. It was something to do with illicit sex. At least it was illicit then. Homosexuality. There was a complaint about goings-on at the Mandeville house. I read about it in the old logs.'

'Tomorrow might turn into a busy day, then,' said Banks.

'Can you stick around, or do you have to head back up North?'

'One more day won't do any harm.'

'Good. Why don't you come to dinner tomorrow? Believe it or not, I'm quite a good cook if I put my mind to it.'

'I don't doubt it for a moment.'

Michelle hung up. She was tired, but she went into the kitchen and hefted out a box of her china and kitchenware. Looking around at the mostly empty cabinets, she tried to decide the best place for each item.

12

As Annie rang the doorbell of Swainsdale Hall, she felt a surge of anxiety at the thought of seeing Martin Armitage again. It was foolish, she knew; he wasn't going to assault her—not in front of his wife—but she still had an aching jaw, a loose tooth and a forthcoming dentist's appointment by which to remember their last meeting.

Josie opened the door and collared the dog as Annie walked in.

Robin Armitage sat on the large living-room sofa in jeans and a navy-blue top, flipping through a magazine. She stood up when Annie entered, gave her a thin smile and bade her sit down. She asked Josie to bring in some coffee.

'Is your husband not home?' Annie asked.

'He's in his study. I'll ask Josie to send for him when she brings the coffee. Are you making any progress?'

'Some,' said Annie. 'That's why I wanted to talk to you both again, ask you a few questions.'

'Are you all right? Your mouth still looks bruised.'

Annie put her hand up to her jaw. 'I'm fine.'

'I'm really sorry for what happened. I know Martin is absolutely guilt-stricken.'

'No hard feelings,' Annie said, which wasn't exactly the truth.

Josie came in with the coffee and Robin asked her to call Mr Armitage down. When he walked in a minute later, he was contrite and embarrassed. 'Please accept my apologies,' he said. 'I don't know what came over me. I've never laid a finger on a woman before.'

'It's all right,' said Annie, eager to move on. 'Actually, I have a few more questions for both of you.'

'I can't imagine what more we can tell you,' said Robin. 'But please go ahead.'

'First of all, do either you or your husband have a prescription for Valium or any other form of diazepam?'

Robin frowned. 'Martin doesn't, but I do. Nerves.'

'Have you noticed any missing lately?'

'No.'

'Would you?'

'Of course.' Robin reached for her handbag on the sofa beside her and took out a small plastic container. 'Here they are,' she said. 'Look. Almost full. Why do you ask?'

Annie looked. 'It's just that the pathologist found traces in Luke's system. We were wondering where he got it from.'

'Luke? Valium? Certainly not from us.'

'And I assume he didn't have a prescription of his own?'

Martin and Robin looked at one another, frowning. 'Of course not,' said Robin. 'Someone else must have given it to him.'

'Is that what killed him?' Martin Armitage asked.

'No,' said Annie. 'It's just another complication I'd like to get out of the way, that's all.'

Annie struggled to phrase her next question. Talking to these two was like walking on eggs, but it had to be done. 'Mr Armitage, what did you do when you went out the night Luke disappeared?'

'I told you. I just drove around looking for him.'

'Drove where?'

'Eastvale.'

'Any particular areas or streets?'

'I don't remember. I just drove around. Why is it important?'

Annie's chest felt tight, but she forged ahead. 'Did you find him?'

'Of course I didn't. What are you talking about? If I'd found him, he'd be here safe and sound right now, wouldn't he?'

'I've seen a demonstration of your temper, Mr Armitage.' There, it was out. 'I also know that you and your stepson didn't always get on.'

'What are you suggesting?'

Armitage's tone chilled Annie, but it was too late to stop now. 'If anything happened that evening. Some sort of . . . accident . . . then it's better to tell me now than have me find out by other means.'

'Accident? Let me get this straight. Are you asking me if I found Luke, picked him up in my car, then lost my temper and killed him?'

'I'm asking you if you did see him that night, yes, and if anything happened between you that I should know about.'

Armitage shook his head. 'You really are a piece of work, DI Cabbot. First you act rashly and probably cause my son's death, then you accuse *me* of killing him. For your information, I did exactly what I told you. I drove around Eastvale looking for Luke. It was probably pointless, I know, but I had to do something. I needed to act. I couldn't just sit around and wait. I didn't find him. All right?'

'Fine,' said Annie.

'And I resent your accusation.'

'I haven't accused you of anything.'

Martin Armitage stood up. 'It shows how little progress you've made, scraping the bottom of the barrel like this.' He left the room.

'That was cruel,' said Robin. 'Martin loved Luke like his own son, did his best for the boy, even if they didn't always agree.'

'I'm sorry I had to ask those questions,' Annie said. 'But the solution often lies close to home, and we'd be derelict in our duty if we didn't pursue such lines of enquiry. Did you know that Luke had a girlfriend?'

'Certainly not.'

'He never said anything to you?'

'I don't even believe he had a girlfriend.'

'Everyone says he was mature for his age, and he was a good-looking boy, too. Why shouldn't he?'

'He just never . . . look, I don't understand all your questions. Don't you think he just wandered off and someone kidnapped him?'

'No,' said Annie. 'I don't think that's what happened at all.'

'Then what?'

Annie stood up to leave. 'Give me a little more time,' she said. 'I'm getting there.'

MICHELLE HAD MADE three important discoveries before lunch that day. First, she had gone back to the logbook for the summer of 1965 and found the reference to the Mandeville house. On August 1 that year, an anonymous informant had telephoned the station with allegations of underage sex, homosexuality and drug-taking. A young DC called Geoff Talbot had gone out to make enquiries and arrested two men he found naked together in a bedroom there. After that, nothing more appeared on the case except a note that all charges were dropped and an official apology issued to Rupert Mandeville, who, she discovered from an Internet search, had served as a Conservative Member of Parliament from 1979 to 1990 and was granted a life peerage in 1994.

It took Michelle a bit longer to track Geoff Talbot down, as he had left the police force in 1970 to work as a consultant with a TV company. Eventually, she managed to find his address in Barnet, north London. She had rung him and he had agreed to talk to her.

After that, Michelle had enlisted DC Collins's aid and discovered through Land Registry records that Donald Bradford's shop had been owned by a company linked to Carlo Fiorino, the late but unlamented local crime kingpin. The company had also owned Le Phonographe disco and several other newsagents' shops in the area.

What it all meant, Michelle wasn't sure, but it looked as if Fiorino had set up the perfect retail distribution chain for his wholesale porn business, and who knew what else besides? All this she told to Banks as she drove down the A1 to Barnet.

'Bradford must have got Graham involved somehow, through the magazines,' said Banks. 'But it didn't stop there. He must have come to the attention of Fiorino and Mandeville, too. It helps to explain where all that extra money came from.'

'I know he was your friend, Alan, but you have to admit it looks as if he was up to some unsavoury stuff, as if he got greedy.'

'I admit it. The photo must have been Graham's insurance. Evidence. He could use it to blackmail Bradford into paying him more money, only he didn't know what he'd got himself into. Word got back to Fiorino and he signed Graham's death warrant.'

'And who carried it out?'

'Bradford, most likely. He didn't have an alibi. Or Harris. I mean, we can't rule him out completely. Despite what his ex-wife told you, he could have kept the commando knife, and if he was being threatened with exposure as a homosexual, he might have been driven to kill. Remember, it wouldn't only have meant his career back then, but jail, and you know how long coppers survive behind bars.'

'Jet Harris searched Graham Marshall's house personally just after the boy disappeared,' said Michelle.

'Harris did that? Searched the house? How do you know?'

'Mrs Marshall mentioned it the first time I went to talk to her. I didn't think anything of it at the time, but now . . . a superintendent conducting a routine search?'

'He must have been after the photo.'

'Then why didn't he find it?'

'If that photo had been Sellotaped to the inside of Graham's guitar, nobody could know it was there without taking the guitar apart. It was only because the adhesive had dried out and the tape had stiffened over the years that the photo broke free and I found it.'

'I suppose so. But does that make Harris a murderer?'

'I don't know. It's not proof. But he was in it. Deep.'

'I also rang Ray Scholes this morning,' Michelle said. 'Remember, the detective who investigated Bradford's murder? It turns out there was a Fairbairn-Sykes knife among Bradford's possessions.'

'What happened to it?'

'Forget it. It's long gone. Sold to a dealer. Who knows how many times it's changed hands since then?'

'Pity. But at least we know it was in his possession when he died.'

'You said the photo was evidence. But what of? How?'

'Well, there might have been fingerprints on it, but I think it was more dangerous because people would have known where it was taken. I doubt there are that many Adam fireplaces around, and probably none quite as distinctive as that one. The rug, too.'

'You're thinking of the Mandeville house?'

'Sounds a likely place to me. I think this is where we turn off.' Banks picked up the street guide and directed Michelle to the pleasant suburban semi where ex-DC Geoff Talbot enjoyed his retirement.

Talbot answered the door and asked them in. Michelle introduced herself and Banks.

Michelle and Banks followed Talbot into the kitchen, which had a central island surrounded by tall stools.

'You didn't give me much of an idea what you wanted to talk about over the telephone,' Talbot said.

'That's because it's still a bit vague,' Michelle said. 'How's your memory?'

'Not so bad for an old man.'

Talbot didn't look that old, Michelle thought. He was carrying a few pounds too many and his hair was almost white, but other than that his face was unlined and his movements smooth and fluid. 'Remember when you served on the Cambridge Constabulary?' she asked.

'Of course. Mid-sixties, that'd be. Peterborough. It was called the Mid-Anglia Constabulary back then. Why?'

'Do you remember a case involving Rupert Mandeville?'

'Do I? That's the reason I left Cambridgeshire. If it comes right down to it, it's the reason I left the force not long after, too.'

'Could you tell us what happened?'

The kettle boiled and Talbot filled the teapot, then carried it on a tray along with three cups and saucers to the island. 'Nothing happened,' he said. 'That was the problem. I was told to lay off.'

'By whom?'

'The super.'

'Detective Superintendent Harris?'

'Jet Harris. That's the one. Oh, it was all above-board. Not enough evidence, my word against theirs, anonymous informant, that sort of thing. You couldn't fault his arguments.'

'Then what?'

'There'd been rumours for some time about things going on at the Mandeville house. Procurement, underage boys, that sort of thing. Ever heard of Carlo Fiorino?'

'We have,' said Michelle.

Talbot poured the tea. 'Rumour has it he was the supplier. Anyway, the problem was that Rupert Mandeville was too well connected, and some of the people who attended his parties were in the government, or other high-level positions. Of course, I was the naive young copper fresh from probation, proud to be in CID, thinking he could take on the world. Well, I soon learned the error of my ways. When the super found out I'd been out there and caused a fuss, he had me in his office and told me in no uncertain terms that Mandeville was off limits.'

'An operation like that, and one like Fiorino's, would need police protection,' Banks said. 'And Harris was it. Or part of it.'

'Exactly,' said Talbot. 'He got me transferred out of the county before my feet even touched the ground. Cumbria. Well, I ran into one or two nice little gentlemen's agreements between local villains and constabulary up there too, so I called it a day, resigned from the force. Best move I ever made.'

'What happened that day you went to the Mandevilles?' Michelle asked.

'It was a Sunday morning. I was by myself when the switchboard patched the phone call through to the office. A woman said there'd been a party going on since the previous night, and she was convinced some of the girls and boys were underage and people were taking drugs. She sounded frightened. She hung up very abruptly, too.'

'So you went?'

'Yes. I logged the details and drove out there.'

'Did you meet the woman who'd phoned?'

'Not that I know of. I mean, if she was there she never came forward and admitted she was the one who phoned.'

'What did you find inside?'

'It was more like the aftermath of a party, really. Some people were sleeping on the sofa, a couple on the floor . . .'

'What kind of people?'

'A mix. Young and old. Businessmen. Mods. One or two of the girls looked like swinging London types, miniskirts and what have you. There was a funny smell, too, I remember. At the time I didn't know what it was, but I smelt it again later. Marijuana.'

'What did you do?'

'To be honest, I felt a bit out of my depth. I wasn't even sure if any of it was illegal. I mean, the girls and the men didn't *look* underage to me, but what did I know? I talked to a few people, took names. A couple of the girls I'd seen before at Le Phonographe. I think they also worked for Fiorino's escort agency.'

'You used your notebook?'

'Yes.'

'What happened to it?'

'Same as usual, I suppose.'

'You also found two men together?'

'Yes, in one bedroom I saw two men in bed together. Naked.'

'Did either of them look underage?'

'No. One I pegged at early twenties, the other older, maybe forty. But it didn't matter how old you were back then.'

'So what did you do?'

'I . . . er . . . I arrested them.'

'Did they resist?'

'No. They just laughed, put their clothes on and went back to the station with me.'

'What happened then?'

'Jet Harris was waiting for me. He was furious.'

'He was at the station waiting for you? On a Sunday morning?'

'Yes. I suppose someone must have phoned him from Mandeville's.'

'What did he do?' Michelle asked.

'He had a private talk with the two men, let them go and had his little chat with me. That was the end of it. No further action.'

'How old was Rupert Mandeville at the time?' Michelle asked.

'Quite young. In his thirties. His parents had been killed in a plane crash not too long before, I remember, and he'd inherited a fortune.'

'Thank you, Mr Talbot.'

'You're welcome. Look, I can't see as I've been any help, but . . .'

Banks placed the photograph of Graham Marshall in front of him. 'Do you recognise that boy?'

Talbot paled. 'My God, isn't that the boy who— His photograph was in the papers only a few weeks ago.'

'Did you see him at the Mandeville house?'

'No, but that's Mandeville's living room. I remember the sheepskin rug and the fireplace. Does that mean what I think it means? That the boy's death is connected with Mandeville and Harris?'

'Somehow,' said Michelle. 'We're just not quite sure how yet.'

They stood up and Talbot showed them to the door. 'You know,' he said, 'I felt that there was more going on than met the eye. I've always wondered what would have happened if I'd pushed it a bit harder.'

'You'd have probably ended up under a field with Graham Marshall,' said Banks. 'Bye, Mr Talbot. And thank you.'

GAVIN BARLOW was in his study when Annie called, and he invited her to sit with him there while they talked.

'I won't take up much of your time,' Annie said. 'It's about your daughter. She came to the station and made some pretty serious allegations about Lauren Anderson and Luke Armitage. Why would Rose want to make trouble for Ms Anderson?'

'I don't know.'

'Was she jealous?'

'Of what?'

'Of the attention Luke got from Lauren Anderson?'

'Why don't you ask Lauren?'

'I will. But I'm asking you first.'

'And I'm telling you I don't know.'

They stared at one another, and Annie tried to weigh up whether he was telling the truth or not. She decided he was holding something back. 'What is it, Mr Barlow?' she asked. 'If it's nothing to do with Luke's death, it will go no further than these walls, I promise.'

Barlow sighed and stared out of the window.

'Mr Barlow?'

He turned back to face her, and his façade of benevolent authority had disappeared. In its place was the look of a man with a burden. 'Ms Anderson. Lauren. If you've seen her, you must have noticed she's an attractive woman, quite the Pre-Raphaelite beauty,' Barlow said.

'What happened? Did you have an affair? Did Rose find out?'

'Oh, good Lord, no. Nothing like that. I might have flirted a bit, but Lauren wasn't interested in me. She made that quite clear.'

Annie frowned. 'Then I don't understand.'

'Lauren came to see me in my office shortly after Christmas. Her father had been diagnosed with Alzheimer's and she was upset. I put an arm round her, just to comfort her, you understand, and Rose chose that moment to come barging in with some family matter . . . Well, Rose misread the situation and went running off.'

'I see,' said Annie. 'Did she tell your wife?'

'No. No, thank God. I managed to talk to her. I'm not sure she quite believed in my innocence, but she agreed not to say anything.'

'And that's the root of her animosity towards Lauren Anderson?'

'I should imagine so.'

'You *were* attracted to Lauren, though, weren't you? What did you call her? A Pre-Raphaelite beauty?'

'Yes. As I said, I'm only human. And she *is* a very attractive woman. You can't arrest a man for his thoughts. At least not yet. The damn thing is, I'd done nothing wrong, but because I wanted to I felt as guilty as if I had, anyway.' He gave a bitter laugh. 'Funny, isn't it?'

'Yes,' said Annie. 'Very funny.' But her thoughts were elsewhere. Barlow might not have given her the answers she was hoping for, but he had certainly given her plenty to think about.

'WELL, IF IT isn't our two lovebirds,' said Ben Shaw, opening the door to Banks and Michelle. 'What do you two want?'

'A few words,' said Banks.

'And why should I want a few words with you?'

'Des Wayman,' said Michelle.

Shaw shut the door, slid off the chain and opened it, walking away from them, leaving Banks to shut the door behind them and follow. The house was far neater than Banks had expected. The only booze in sight was a half-empty bottle of Bell's on the living-room table, a full glass beside it. Shaw sat down and took a slug, without offering his guests anything.

'So what porkies has Mr Wayman been telling today?'

'Stop pissing around,' said Banks. 'You told Wayman and a mate to work me over and get me out of the picture. It backfired.'

'If he told you that, he's lying.'

'He told me, sir,' said Michelle, 'and, with all due respect, I think he was telling the truth.'

'Wayman's nothing but criminal scum,' Shaw said. 'And you'd take his word over mine?'

'That's neither here nor there,' Banks went on. 'DI Hart has done a bit of digging into your days with Jet Harris, and we were just wondering how much the two of you took in from Carlo Fiorino.'

'You bastard!' Shaw lurched forward to grab Banks's lapel but he was already a bit unsteady with drink, and Banks pushed him back into his chair. He paled, and a grimace of pain passed over his face.

'What is it?' asked Banks.

'Fuck you.' Shaw coughed and reached for more whisky. 'John Harris was worth ten of you.'

'Come off it, Shaw, the two of you were as bent as the day is long. He might have had a good excuse for it, but you . . .? You couldn't remove every scrap of evidence from the archives. All your arrests were for burglary, assault, fraud and the occasional domestic murder. Doesn't that tell you something?'

'What, smartarse?'

'That all the time Carlo Fiorino was running prostitution, illegal gambling, protection, porn and drugs with absolute impunity. Sure, you had him or one of his henchmen brought in once or twice for questioning, just for the sake of appearances, but guess what—either the evidence disappeared or witnesses changed their statements.'

Shaw said nothing, just sipped more whisky.

'Carlo Fiorino fed you his opposition,' Banks went on. 'He had eyes and ears out on the street. He knew what jobs were going down. It made you look good and deflected attention from his own operations, which included supplying Rupert Mandeville with as many bodies as he wanted for his "parties", male and female.'

Shaw slammed the tumbler down on the table. 'All right,' he said. 'You want the truth? I'll tell you. I'm not stupid. I worked with John for too many years not to have my suspicions, but I never took a penny in my life. And maybe I blinkered myself, maybe I even protected him, but we did our jobs. We brought down the bad guys. I loved the man. He taught me everything. He had charisma, did John. He was the kind of bloke everybody noticed when he walked in the room. He's a bloody hero around these parts, or hadn't you noticed?'

'And that's why you've been doing everything in your power to scupper DI Hart's investigation into Graham Marshall's murder? To protect your old pal's reputation. To do that you get someone to break into her flat, try to run her down, have me beaten up.'

'What are you talking about?'

'You know what I'm talking about.'

He looked at Michelle, then back at Banks, a puzzled expression on his face. 'I certainly never had anyone intimidate DI Hart in any way. I wasn't worried about her. It was you I was worried about.'

'Why's that?'

'You're the loose cannon. It was you I needed to keep an eye on. It was different for you. Personal. You knew the victim. I could tell the first time I saw you that you weren't going to let go.' He shook his head and looked at Michelle again. 'No,' he said. 'If anyone had a go at you, DI Hart, it wasn't down to me.'

Banks moved on. 'What about Graham Marshall?'

Shaw looked surprised. 'What about him?'

'Did you know what really happened to him? Have you been covering that up all these years, too?'

'I don't know what you're talking about.' Shaw's voice was little more than a whisper now.

'Well, let me tell you what we believe happened,' said Banks. 'Donald Bradford most likely killed Graham. He owned the kind of knife that was used and Graham trusted him. All Bradford had to do was drive down Wilmer Road and tell him something else had come up, to get in the car. That's why he took his bag of newspapers with him. He thought he would be going back to finish his round later.'

'What possible motive could Bradford have?'

'That's where it gets complicated, and that's where your boss comes in. Donald Bradford distributed pornographic magazines and blue films for Carlo Fiorino. Fiorino had quite a network of newsagents working for him. I'm surprised you didn't know about it, you being a vigilant copper and all.'

'Sod you, Banks.' Shaw scowled and topped up his glass.

'Somehow or other,' Banks went on, 'Graham Marshall became

involved. Maybe he found some of Bradford's stock by accident. I don't know. But Graham was a street-smart kid and he had an eye for the main chance. Maybe he worked for Bradford to earn extra money, or maybe he blackmailed him for it. Either way, he was involved.'

'You can't prove any of this.'

'Graham came to the attention of one of Fiorino's most influential customers, Rupert Mandeville,' Banks went on. 'I know he posed for some nude photos because I found one at his house. Whether it went any further than that, I don't know, but we can tie him to the Mandeville house, and we know what went on there. Mandeville couldn't afford to come under scrutiny. He was an important person with political goals to pursue. Graham probably asked for more money or he'd tell the police. Mandeville panicked, especially as this came hot on the heels of Geoff Talbot's visit. He got Fiorino to fix it, and Jet Harris scuppered the murder investigation. You knew that, knew there was something wrong, so you've been trying to erase the traces to protect Harris's reputation. How am I doing?'

'What would it matter if he told the police, if we were all as corrupt as you make out? Why go so far as to kill the kid if Bradford thought we could control the outcome anyway?'

'That puzzled me for a while, too,' Banks said. 'I can only conclude that he knew which police officer *not* to tell.'

'How do you mean?'

'Graham had definitely been to the Mandeville house. What if he saw someone there? Someone who shouldn't have been there, like a certain detective superintendent?'

'That's absurd. John wasn't like that.'

'According to his wife, John Harris was homosexual. We don't know if Mandeville or Fiorino found out and blackmailed him or if they set him up. Maybe that's how he took his pay-offs from Fiorino and Mandeville, in young boys. I think Graham saw him there and made it clear to Bradford that he'd go elsewhere with his story.'

Shaw turned pale. 'John? *Homosexual?* I don't believe that.'

'One of my old schoolfriends has turned out to be gay,' said Banks. 'And I didn't know that, either. John Harris had two damn good reasons for keeping it a secret. It was illegal until 1967 and he was a copper. Even today you know how tough it is for coppers to come out. But back to Graham. He threatened to tell. I don't know why. It could have been greed, but it could also have been because Mandeville wanted him to do more than pose for photos. Anyway, Graham had the photo as evidence, a photo that could incriminate

Rupert Mandeville. He compromised the whole operation. Mandeville's *and* Fiorino's. That was why he had to die.'

'So what happened?'

'The order went down to Donald Bradford to get rid of him. Bradford had to be at the shop by eight o'clock, as usual, that morning. That gave him an hour and a half to abduct Graham, kill him and dispose of the body. It takes a while to dig a hole that deep, so my guess is that he planned it in advance. Either that or he had help and another of Fiorino's henchmen buried the body. Either way, with Harris on the payroll, Bradford could at least be certain that no one was looking too closely at his lack of an alibi.'

'Are you saying that John Harris ordered the boy's death—'

'I don't know. I don't think so. I'd say it was Fiorino, or Mandeville, but Harris had to know about it in order to misdirect the investigation. And that makes him just as guilty in my book.'

Shaw closed his eyes and shook his head. 'Not John. No. Maybe he did turn a blind eye to one or two things, but not a murdered kid.'

'It's the only thing that makes sense of later events,' Banks went on. 'The botched investigation and the missing notebooks and actions. I don't know who got rid of them—you, Harris or Reg Proctor, but one of you did.'

'It wasn't me. All I've done was discourage DI Hart here from digging too deeply into the past.'

'So Harris took them himself when he left,' said Banks. 'That makes sense. He wouldn't want the evidence hanging around for anyone to see if Graham's body ever did turn up. Insurance. Cast your mind back. You were there in the summer of 1965. You and Reg Proctor covered the estate. What did you find out?'

'Nobody knew anything.'

'I'll bet that's not true,' said Banks. 'I'll bet there were one or two references to "Dirty Don" in your notebooks. One of my old mates remembered referring to him that way. And I'll bet there was a rumour or two about porn.'

'Rumours, maybe,' said Shaw, 'but that's all they were.'

'How do you know?'

Shaw scowled at him.

'Exactly,' said Banks. 'You only know because Harris told you so. You were just a young DC back then. You didn't question your superior officers. If anything showed up in your interviews that pointed in the right direction—Bradford, Fiorino, Mandeville— then Harris ignored it, dismissed it as rumour, a dead end. You just skimmed the surface, exactly as he wanted. That's why the action allocations are missing, too. Harris was in charge of the investigation. He'd have issued the actions. And we'd have found out what direction they all pointed in—the passing paedophile theory, later made more credible by Brady and Hindley's arrest—and, what's more important, what they pointed *away* from. The truth.'

'It's still all theory,' said Shaw.

'Yes,' Banks admitted. 'But you know it's true. We've got the photo of Graham, taken at Mandeville's house, Bradford's connection with the porn business and the possible murder weapon, and the missing notebooks. Go ahead, see if it adds up any other way.'

Shaw sighed. 'I just can't believe John would do something like that. I know he gave Fiorino a lot of leeway, but I thought at the time that he got his reward in information. A bit of tit for tat.' He looked at Michelle. 'What next?' he asked.

'There'll have to be a report. I'm not going to bury this. I'll report my findings and any conclusions that can be drawn to the assistant chief constable. After that, it's up to him. There might be media interest.'

'And me?'

'Maybe it's time to retire,' Banks said. 'You must be long past due.'

Shaw snorted, then coughed. He lit a cigarette and reached for his drink. 'Maybe you're right. I've got cancer,' he said, glancing towards Michelle. 'That's why I've been taking so much time off. Stomach.' He grimaced. 'There's not much they can do. Anyway, maybe retirement isn't such a bad idea.' He laughed. 'Enjoy my last few months gardening or stamp collecting or something peaceful like that.'

Banks didn't know what to say. Michelle said, 'I'm sorry.'

Shaw scowled. 'Now, if you're not going to charge me or beat me up, why don't the two of you just bugger off and leave me alone?'

Banks and Michelle left. Back in the car, Banks turned to Michelle and said, 'Do you believe him?'

'About not being responsible for the burglary and the van?'

'Yes.'

'I think so. What reason has he to lie about it now?'

'It's a serious crime. That's reason enough. But I think you're right. He was just doing his best to protect Harris's reputation.'

'Then are you thinking who I'm thinking?'

Banks nodded. 'Rupert Mandeville.'

'Shall we pay him a visit?'

'You want me along?'

Michelle looked at Banks and said, 'Yes. I feel we're getting near the end. Graham Marshall was your friend. You deserve to be there. I'd just like to stop off at the station and check a few things out first.'

'Mandeville won't tell us anything, you know.'

Michelle smiled. 'We'll see about that. It certainly won't do any harm to yank his chain a bit.'

13

It didn't take Annie long to drive to Harrogate and find the small terraced house. Vernon Anderson answered the door and, looking puzzled, invited her into his spartan living room. She admired the Vermeer print over the fireplace and settled in one of two armchairs.

'I see you have an eye for a good painting,' Annie said.

'Art appreciation must run in the family,' said Vernon. 'Though I confess I'm not as much of a reader as our Lauren is.'

On the table under the window was a newspaper open at the racing page, some of the horses with red rings round their names.

'Any luck today?' Annie asked.

'You know what it's like,' Vernon said with an impish grin. 'You win a little, then you lose a little.' He sat on the sofa.

Vernon Anderson didn't look much like his sister, Annie noted. He had dark hair, short tight curls receding a little at the temples, and he was thickset, with a muscular upper body and short legs. If there was any resemblance, it was in the eyes; Vernon's were the same pale blue as Lauren's. He wore jeans and a T-shirt, and sandals over white socks.

'What's all this about?'

'I'm looking into the kidnapping and murder of Luke Armitage,' Annie said. 'Your sister was his teacher.'

'Yes, I know. She's very upset about it.'

'Did you ever meet Luke?'

'Me? No. I'd heard of him, of course; of his father, anyway.'

'Martin Armitage?'

'That's right. I've won a few bob on teams he played for over the years.' Vernon grinned.

'Lauren said she was visiting you the day Luke disappeared. That'd be a week ago last Monday. Is that true?'

'Yes. Look, I've already been through all this with the other detective, the one who came by a few days ago.'

'I know,' said Annie. 'That was one of the locals helping us out. It's not always possible to get away. I'm sorry to bother you with it, but do you think you could bear to go through it again with me?'

'It's just as I told the chap the other day. Lauren came here for dinner and we had rather too much to drink, so she stayed over.' He patted the sofa. 'It's comfortable enough. Safer than trying to drive.'

'Admirable,' said Annie. 'Does your sister visit you often?'

'Fairly often. Though I can't see what that's got to do with anything.'

'I just want to make sure I've got all the times right, for the record. You'd be amazed if you knew how much of our job is just paperwork.'

Vernon smiled. 'Well, as I remember, she arrived at about six o'clock, and that was it. We ate at around half past seven.'

'What did you cook?'

'Venison in white wine. From Nigella Lawson.'

'And no doubt there was a fair bit of wine to wash it down with?'

'A couple of bottles. That and the Grand Marnier.'

'So you went to bed around what time?'

'Me? I'm not sure. It's a bit of a blur. Probably around midnight.'

'And your sister stayed all night?'

'Of course.'

'How do you know?'

'I remember going to the toilet once. You have to go through the living room. She was asleep on the sofa then.'

'What time did she leave?'

'About eleven o'clock the following morning.'

'It must have been a bit of a rough morning for you at work, after all that drink. Or did you take the day off?'

'I'm presently unemployed, if it's any of your business.'

'Did you ever get any hints that Lauren's relationship with Luke might have been a bit more than the normal teacher–pupil one?'

'I certainly did not.'

'She never talked about him in an affectionate way?'

'I've had quite enough of this,' Vernon said. 'It's one thing checking up on times, but quite another to suggest that my sister had some sort of affair with this boy.' He stood up. 'Look, I've told you what you want to know. Now why don't you just go and leave me alone.'

'All right, then. Just one more thing before I leave you in peace.'

'What?'

'I understand you have a criminal record.'

Vernon reddened. 'I wondered when that would come out. Look, it was a long time ago. I forged my boss's signature on a cheque. It was a stupid thing to do, OK, but I was desperate. I paid the price.'

'Well, that's all right, then, isn't it,' said Annie, who was thinking it was amazing what people would do when they were desperate. 'Thanks for your time, Mr Anderson.'

Vernon said nothing, just slammed the door behind her. Annie had noticed a bookie's on the main road, just round the corner from Vernon's street. She glanced at her watch. Just time for a quick visit.

IF THIS WAS the face of evil, then it was remarkably bland, Banks thought as he and Michelle were ushered into Rupert Mandeville's presence by a young man who looked more like a clerk than a butler. Mandeville reminded Banks of the old prime minister, Edward Heath. Casually dressed in white cricket trousers, a cream shirt open at the collar, and a mauve V-neck pullover, he had the same slightly befuddled look about him as Heath.

The sheepskin rug was gone, replaced by a carpet, but the fireplace was the same one as in Graham's photograph.

At least they now had some idea how Mandeville knew about the progress of Michelle's investigation. According to a local reporter Michelle had rung from the station, Mandeville had spies everywhere; it was how he had managed to survive so long in politics. It was also rumoured he had close contacts within the police force. That must have been how he knew so much about the investigation into Graham's death, and the threat it was beginning to pose for him.

Mandeville was courtesy personified, pulling out a chair for Michelle and offering refreshments, which they refused. 'It's been years since I had a visit from the police,' he said. 'How can I help you?'

'Would Geoff Talbot's visit have been the one you're thinking about?' Michelle asked.

'I can't say I remember the young man's name.'

'You ought at least to remember the reason for the visit.'

'It was a mistake. Look, I sense a little hostility in your tone. Can you please either tell me why you're here or leave?'

'We're here to ask you some questions relating to the Graham Marshall investigation.'

'Oh, yes. That poor boy whose skeleton was uncovered some days ago. Tragic. But I don't see how that has anything to do with me.'

Banks took the photo from his briefcase and showed it to Mandeville, who looked at it without expression.

'Interesting,' he said. 'But, again . . .'

'Do you recognise the boy?' Michelle asked.

'I'm afraid I don't.'

'Do you recognise the fireplace?'

Mandeville glanced towards his own Adam fireplace and smiled at her. 'I'd be a liar if I said I don't,' he said. 'Though I hardly imagine it's the only one of its kind in existence.'

'I think it's unique enough for our purposes,' Michelle said.

'Photographs can be faked, you know.'

Michelle tapped the photo. 'Are you saying this is a forgery.'

'Of course. Unless someone has been using my house for illicit purposes in my absence.'

'Let's get back to 1965, when this photo was taken, in this room,' Michelle said. 'You were quite famous for your parties, weren't you?'

Mandeville shrugged.

'Parties that catered for every taste, including drugs, prostitutes and underage sex partners, male and female.'

'Don't be absurd.'

'This boy was fourteen when that photo was taken.'

'And he was a friend of mine,' said Banks.

'Then I'm sorry for your loss,' said Mandeville, 'but I still don't see what it has to do with me.'

'You had him killed,' said Michelle.

'I'd be careful, young lady, making accusations like that.'

'Or what? You'll have your chauffeur break into my flat again, or try to run me over?'

'I was actually going to warn you about the possibility of slander.'

'I did a bit of homework before I came out here,' Michelle said. 'Checked into the background of your employees. Derek Janson, your chauffeur, served a prison sentence for burglary fifteen years ago. He came to be regarded as somewhat of an expert at picking locks.'

'I know about Derek's background,' Mandeville said. 'I happen to trust him completely.'

'I'm sure you do. When the investigation into Graham Marshall's disappearance was reopened, you did everything in your power to put me off.'

'Why would I want to do that?'

'Because he was using the photo to blackmail you, so you asked Carlo Fiorino to take care of him, and he obliged.'

'Well,' Mandeville said, 'that's quite a story the two of you have concocted. It's a pity that none of it will stand up in court.'

'Maybe you're right,' Michelle said. 'But you still have to admit that it doesn't look good. Some mud's bound to stick.'

'What do you intend to do now?'

'Whatever I can to make sure you pay for what you did. For a start, we'll have a nice chat with Mr Janson.'

Mandeville smiled. 'Derek won't tell you anything.'

'You never know. We're not without influence with ex-cons. Then there's Geoff Talbot's notebook. Jet Harris didn't bother to remove that from the archives. No reason to. There was no investigation.'

'I don't know what you're talking about.'

'Names,' said Banks. 'Talbot made a note of the names of the people he talked to when he came up here. I'm sure if we dig around a bit, we'll find one or two people who remember the old days.'

Mandeville's face darkened. 'I'm warning you,' he said, 'if you attempt to spread these vicious lies about me, I'll have your jobs.'

But Michelle was already striding towards the front door.

Banks took the opportunity of a few seconds alone with Mandeville to lean in close, smile and lower his voice. 'And if DI Hart so much as trips on a banana skin, I'll be right back here to rip out your spine and shove it down your throat. Your Lordship.'

He couldn't swear to it, but judging by the change in Mandeville's expression, he thought he had got his point across.

IT WAS EVENING when Lauren Anderson led Annie into the book-lined living room. Lauren was barefoot, wearing ice-blue jeans and a white sleeveless top. Her shoulders were pale and freckled, like her face. Her mane of auburn hair was fastened behind her head by a leather hair-slide. 'What do you want?' she asked. 'Have you caught them?'

'I think so. But first sit down and listen to what I have to say. You can correct me if I'm wrong about anything.'

'I don't know what you mean.'

'You will in a minute. Sit down, Lauren.' Annie crossed her legs and leaned back in the armchair. She had worked out how to approach Lauren on the drive back from Harrogate, then made a couple of phone calls and picked up DC Winsome Jackman, whom she had instructed to stay outside in the car for the time being. 'We know where Luke was shortly before he was killed,' she began. 'Did he ever mention a girl called Liz Palmer to you?'

'No. Why?'

'Are you sure? She meant a lot to Luke.'

Lauren shook her head. 'That can't be true. I don't believe you.'

'Why not, Lauren? Why can't it be true?'

'Luke . . . he didn't . . . he wasn't like that. He was devoted to art.'

'Oh, come off it, Lauren. He was just a randy adolescent, like any other. This Liz was a bit older than him and she—'

'No! Stop it. I won't have you tarnishing Luke's memory.'

'Tarnishing? What's so wrong about a fifteen-year-old boy losing his virginity to an older woman? It's a time-honoured tradition, even if it is technically sex with a minor. Who cares about a few petty laws? Especially if it's the boy who's underage, and not the woman. At least we know now Luke got to enjoy the pleasures of sex before he died.'

'I don't know why, but you're lying to me. There is no "Liz".'

'Yes, there is. I can introduce you.'

'No.'

'What is it, Lauren? Jealous?'

'Luke meant a lot to me. You know he did. He was so talented.'

'You were lovers, weren't you?'

'What if we were? Are you going to arrest me for that?'

'No. I'm going to arrest you for murder.'

Lauren jerked upright. 'You can't be serious.'

'I'm serious all right. You see, Liz and her boyfriend live about five minutes' walk from here, and Luke was distraught when he left their flat. I asked myself, where would he go? Maybe it took me too long to come up with the right answer, the *only* possible answer, but that was due to the clever smoke screen you put up. The kidnapping. We thought we were looking for a man or someone closer to home. But Luke couldn't have gone home because the last bus had gone and we checked all the taxis. That leaves you. You're the one he talked to about his emotional problems. How long had you been lovers, Lauren?'

Lauren sighed. 'Near the end of term. It just happened. We were looking at some pictures. Pre-Raphaelites. He remarked on my resemblance to one of the models.'

'Elizabeth Siddal, Dante Gabriel Rossetti's first wife. You do look a lot like the paintings of her, Lauren. A typical Pre-Raphaelite beauty, as someone said.'

'You know?'

'We found Luke's shoulder bag at the other flat, too. I read over his recent writings and found a lot of classical references that were of a sexual nature and stressed a kind of Pre-Raphaelite look. There were also references to Ophelia, but I don't think it was Shakespeare Luke had in mind. It was John Everett Millais. He painted Ophelia and used Elizabeth Siddal as a model. But what I don't understand is why. Why did you kill him, Lauren? Was he going to leave you?'

'You don't understand anything. I didn't kill him. You've got no proof. I've got an alibi. Talk to Vernon.'

'I've already talked to Vernon,' said Annie, 'and I'd trust him about as far as I could throw him. Your brother lied for you, Lauren. Only natural. But I'm willing to bet that he helped you get rid of the body. You couldn't have done it all by yourself. And he's the one who hatched the kidnapping scheme. That had all the hallmarks of an afterthought. It wasn't the reason for Luke's disappearance and death. Your brother thought he'd try and cash in on it and he's small-time enough to ask for only ten thousand. He's a gambler, Lauren. And a loser. I talked to his bookie. Your brother's in debt up to his eyeballs. Did you even know what he'd done after he'd helped you?'

Lauren shook her head. 'I don't believe he'd do anything like that.'

'The thing is,' Annie went on, 'that our scene-of-crime officers found minute traces of blood on the wall where Luke was shoved over into Hallam Tarn. Minute, but enough to provide a DNA profile. I think that profile would match you or your brother. I'm also certain that when our men come in here and go over your place, they'll find traces of Luke's blood. Now that might not be conclusive in itself, but it's all starting to add up now.'

Lauren looked at Annie, her eyes red-rimmed and almost unbearably sad. 'I didn't kill him,' she said, in a small, distant voice. 'I would never have harmed Luke. I loved him.'

'What happened, Lauren?'

Lauren eyed Annie sadly and began her story.

'DO YOU THINK I might have a word alone with your husband?' Banks asked Mrs Marshall at her house that evening.

'Bill?' she said. 'You know he can't talk.'

Banks looked at the invalid who, judging by the hard expression in his eyes, knew he was being talked about. 'Can he write?'

'Yes,' said Mrs Marshall. 'He can scribble a few letters.'

'That'll do,' said Banks. 'Can you get me a pad and pencil?'

Mrs Marshall brought Banks a pad and pencil from a drawer.

'Come on,' said Michelle, taking her by the arm. 'Let's make some tea. I've things to tell you.' Banks and Michelle had agreed on a sanitised version of events to tell Mrs Marshall. If the media dug too deeply and the story hit the news, then she might find out more than she wanted about her son's life, but that was for the future.

When they had gone into the kitchen, Banks put the pad and pencil on Bill Marshall's knee and settled in front of him, gazing into the expressionless eyes. 'I think you know why I want to talk to you.'

Bill Marshall made no sign that he understood.

'You used to spar with the Krays,' he said. 'Then, when you came up here, you fell in with Carlo Fiorino and did a few strong-arm jobs for him. Am I right? Can you nod or write something down?'

Bill Marshall did nothing.

'OK, so that's how you want to play it,' Banks said. 'Fine. I'm not saying you had anything to do with Graham's death. But you knew who did it, didn't you?'

Bill Marshall just stared at Banks.

'See, the trouble with people like you, Bill, is they insist on working outside the law. You've no use for coppers, have you? Want to know what I think happened? Well, I think Donald Bradford wasn't cut out to be a killer of young boys. I don't think he had much choice though. Fiorino pushed him into it. After all, Graham was *his* responsibility, and Graham was in a position to do a lot of damage. Shortly after the killing, Bradford sold up and moved out. Fiorino didn't like people escaping his control, being out of his line of sight. Especially if they knew as much as Bradford did and were fast becoming unstable and unreliable. Bradford was guilt-ridden by what he had done.'

Marshall still showed no reaction. 'So what does he do? Well, he could pay for a hit. But he knows you. He knows that whatever you do, you'll do it yourself, you won't go running to the police. So he tells you that Bradford killed your son, though not on *his* orders. He convinces you Bradford was a pervert. He also gives you Bradford's address.'

Banks could tell by the anger and hatred in Bill Marshall's eyes that he was right. 'You went up to Carlisle, didn't you? Then you broke into Donald Bradford's flat and waited for him to come home. You knew Bradford was a tough customer, so you attacked him from behind with a cosh. I don't blame you, Bill. The man murdered your son. But you let your wife suffer all those years. Maybe you didn't know where the body was, but I bet you could have found out. Instead, you said nothing to your wife or daughter. All these years they've lived not knowing what happened to Graham. That's unforgivable, Bill.'

Marshall held his gaze for a while, then grasped the pencil and scrawled on the pad. When he had done, he handed it to Banks. There were three words in capital letters: FUCK OFF COPPER.

'HE CAME TO ME, like you said,' Lauren Anderson began. 'He was in a terrible state. I held him and just tried to calm him down. I'd already realised I had to end it. I just hadn't been able to find the courage. I thought I'd got him calm enough, so I started talking about it, you know, how we should probably cool things for a while.'

'How did he react when you told him you wanted to end the affair?'

'He didn't want to accept it. He said he couldn't bear to lose me.' Lauren started crying. 'He said he'd kill himself.'

'What happened next?'

'He stormed off to the bathroom. I gave him a couple of minutes, then I heard all the things falling out of the cupboard into the sink, glass breaking, so I went after him.'

'He was after the Valium?'

'You know?'

'We know he took some Valium shortly before he died, yes.'

'I have a prescription. But I suppose you know that, too?'

Annie nodded. 'I checked.'

'He had the bottle open, and he poured some tablets into his hand and swallowed them. I struggled with him over the bottle. We fought, pulling and pushing each other, and then he went down. He was in his socks, and the floor tiles can be slippery. His feet just went from under him and he hit his head on the side of the bath. I tried to revive him, mouth to mouth. But it was no use. He was dead.'

'What did you do then?'

'I panicked. I knew if any of it came out I'd be finished. I didn't know where to turn, so I called Vernon. He said he'd come right away and not to do anything until he got here. The rest you know.'

'What happened to Luke's mobile?'

'It fell out of his pocket in the car. Vernon took it.'

'*Did* you know about the ransom demand?'

Lauren shook her head. 'No. I'm so sorry for what happened.' She grasped Annie's wrist. 'I'd never have harmed Luke. I loved him. Maybe if I hadn't been so insensitive, tried to end it when he was so upset, it might not have happened. I've relived that moment over and over again ever since it happened. I can't sleep. Nothing seems to matter any more. What's going to happen to me?'

'I don't know, Lauren,' Annie said. Lauren would probably get off lightly, she told herself. If Luke had died during a struggle, the object of which was to stop him taking an overdose of Valium, and if Lauren had not known of her brother's botched ransom demand, then she wouldn't get a very stiff sentence.

Lauren would lose her job, though, and, like Norman Wells, she would become a pariah for some; the seductress and corrupter of youth. And the family would suffer—Robin and Martin—as it was all dragged into the open. This would be a high-profile trial, no doubt about it. Neil Byrd's son, a famous model and a sports star. Not a chance of escaping the media circus.

BANKS LAY IN BED late that night listening to Neil Byrd's CD on his Walkman after dinner with Michelle and a phone call from Annie. 'The Summer That Never Was' was the first song on the CD, though the liner notes said it was the last song Byrd had recorded, just weeks before his suicide. As Banks listened to the subtle interplay of words and music, in his mind, Luke Armitage and Graham Marshall became one. They might have died in different ways for different reasons—not to mention in different times—but they were just two kids lost in a grown-up world, where needs and emotions were bigger than theirs, stronger and more complex than they could comprehend. Graham had tried to play the big leagues at their own game and lost, while Luke had tried to find love and acceptance in all the wrong places. He had lost, too. Accident though his death was, it was a tragic accident made up of many acts, each of which was like a door closing behind him as he moved towards his fate.

Banks tried to go to sleep. But the song had left him with such a feeling of desolation and loneliness that he ached with need for someone to hold and found himself wishing he had stayed at Michelle's. He almost took out his mobile and rang her, but it was past two in the morning. Besides, how would she react if he showed such neediness so early in their relationship? She'd probably run a mile, like Annie.

He could hear his father snoring in the next room. Though Arthur Banks would never actually admit anything, Banks could tell that his father had been proud of him for his success in solving Graham's murder—though he insisted Michelle had done most of the work— and for not trying to cover up Jet Harris's role.

How strange it was to be at home in his old bed. As he drifted towards sleep, he imagined his mother calling him for school: 'Hurry up, Alan, you'll be late!' In his dream, he fastened his tie as he dashed downstairs for a quick bowl of cornflakes and a glass of milk before picking up his satchel and meeting the others in the street. But when he walked out of the door, Dave and Paul and Steve and Graham stood there waiting for him with the bat, the ball and the wickets. The sun shone in a bright blue sky and the air was warm and fragrant. There was no school. They were on holiday. They were going to play cricket on the rec. 'It's summer, you fool,' Graham said, and they all laughed. *The summer that never was.*

PETER ROBINSON

Readers of any of the thirteen detective
novels featuring the very English Inspector
Banks may be surprised to learn that their
author has lived in North America since
1974. Peter Robinson was born in
Castleford, Yorkshire, but in his twenties
went to Canada to study at the University
of Windsor in Ontario—and stayed on.

Alan Banks's adventures are firmly based
in and around the fictional English town of
Eastvale, a setting that Peter Robinson developed partly out of nostalgia and
partly so that his characters could exist in an entirely separate world to his
own. 'I'd become interested in [Ruth] Rendell and similar writers who were
able to view a particular area of England through their detectives' eyes. I
wanted to re-create England in my writing, so I invented a large market town
in Yorkshire. And then came Banks.'

A good deal of *The Summer That Never Was* takes place in 1965, a
year when both Peter Robinson and Inspector Banks were in their mid-
teens. How much does the author think he has in common with his creation?
'A fair bit. We share an interest in music and other tastes. And since I've
been looking more into Banks's past lately, I've come to think that we may
well have been the same person till about the age of eighteen or nineteen.
But after that we went in completely different directions. Now he's doing a
job that I don't think I could do. Plus, he's more physical than I am. He's
not afraid of getting down and dirty, whereas I don't like violence at all. I'd
probably faint at the sight of blood!'

Despite winning numerous awards for his work, Peter still has some
unfulfilled literary ambitions. 'I'd love to have written Hammett's *The
Maltese Falcon,* or almost any of Chandler's, like *The Big Sleep.* I'd love
to write a really great American private-eye novel in the American style.
But it's a voice that is alien to me. If I try to write in it, it sounds false, like
my trying to speak with an American accent. But I'd still, some day, like to
write the sort of dialogue that Bogey could read with a straight face.'

THE CHRISTMAS

TRAIN

David Baldacci

Tom Langdon would never choose to take a train—
but this winter he's been left with no alternative. Just a
few days before Christmas, he must travel almost 3,000
miles by train from Washington, DC, to Los Angeles.

Making the best of a bad situation, Tom decides to use the
time to write, reflect and get his life back into shape.

But the reality, with a film crew, a boys' choir, a
clairvoyant, a couple of newlyweds and a singing
conductress on board, will be quite, quite different.

CHAPTER ONE

Tom Langdon was a journalist, a globetrotting one because it was in his blood to roam widely. He'd spent the bulk of his career in foreign lands covering wars, insurrections, famines, virtually every earthly despair. His goal had been simple: he had wanted to change the world by calling attention to its wrongs. But, after chronicling all these horrific events and seeing the conditions of humanity steadily worsen, he'd returned to America filled with disappointment. Seeking an antidote to his melancholy he'd started writing light stories for ladies' magazines, home-decorating journals, garden digests and the like. Now, after memorialising the wonders of compost and do-it-yourself wood flooring, he wasn't exactly fulfilled.

It was nearing Christmas, and Tom's most pressing dilemma was getting from the East Coast to Los Angeles for the holidays, to see his movie-actress girlfriend, Lelia Gibson. After years of appearing in third-rate horror films she'd begun doing voice-over work and now supplied the character voices for a variety of enormously popular Saturday-morning cartoons. No one belted out the voices of goofy woodland creatures with greater flair than golden-piped Lelia Gibson. As proof, she had a shelf full of awards, an outrageously large income, and a healthy share of syndication rights.

Tom and Lelia had hit it off on an overnight flight from Southeast Asia to the States. At first he thought it might have been all the liquor they drank, but when that buzz burned off a couple of hours out of LA, she was still beautiful and interesting—if a little ditzy and eccentric—and she still seemed attracted to him. He stayed over in California, she visited him on the East Coast, and they'd been a comfortable, if informal, bi-coastal item ever since.

The fact that they didn't live together year-round was a decided advantage, Tom believed, over the complex hurdles facing couples who cohabitated. He'd been briefly married but had never had kids. Today his ex-wife wouldn't accept a collect call from him if he were haemorrhaging to death on the street. He'd had an opportunity for a wonderful life with another woman, Eleanor Carter, but the relationship had fallen apart. He now fully understood that not marrying her would forever stand as the major mistake of his life. He was forty-one and had just lost his mother to a stroke; his father had been dead for several years. Being an only child, he was truly alone now. Half his time on earth was gone, and all he had to show for it was a failed marriage, an informal alliance with a California voice-over queen, a truckload of newsprint and some awards. It was a miserable excuse for an existence.

Yet, ever the man of action, and with wanderlust upon him once more, Tom was taking the train to LA for Christmas. Why the train, one might ask, when there were perfectly good flights that would get him there in a fraction of the time? Well, a guy can only take so many of those airport security search wands venturing into sacrosanct places, or ransacking of carry-on bags, before blowing a big one. The fact was, he'd blown a big one at La Guardia Airport.

He'd just flown in from Italy after researching yet another bit of fluff, this time on wine-making. Now, he was tired, cranky and hung over. He'd slept for three hours at a friend's apartment in New York before heading to the airport to catch a flight to Texas. He'd been given an assignment to write about teen beauty pageants there.

At the security gate at La Guardia, the search wand had smacked delicate things of Tom's person that it really had no business engaging. Meanwhile, another security person managed to dump every single thing from Tom's bag onto the conveyor belt. He watched helplessly as very personal possessions rolled by in front of interested strangers.

To put a fine finish on this very special moment, he was then informed that a major warning flag had been raised regarding his ID. Thus, instead of flying to Dallas he'd be enjoying the company of a host of FBI, DEA, CIA and NYPD personnel for an unspecified period of time. That was his absolute limit. So, the lava poured forth. Using language he ordinarily wouldn't use within four miles of any church, he'd launched himself at the security team, grabbed their search wand and snapped it in half. He wasn't proud of his violent act, although the rousing cheers from some of the other passengers did lift his spirits a bit.

Thankfully, Tom received only a stern warning from the magistrate he appeared before and instructions to enrol in anger-management classes, which he planned to do as soon as his uncontrollable urge to maim the fellow with the search wand subsided. However, the other consequence of the blowup was that he'd been banned from flying anywhere within the United States for the next two years.

And that's what brought on his epiphany. Being unable to fly was a divine omen. He was going to take the train to LA and he was going to write a story about it. He had a grand motivation, beyond spending the Christmas holiday with Lelia. Tom Langdon was distantly related to Olivia Langdon, a lovely, but ultimately tragic person who gained lasting fame by marrying the prolific scribe known to his friends as Samuel Clemens, but known to the world as Mark Twain.

Tom had long known of this connection and it had inspired him to earn his living with words. Twain had also been a journalist, starting at the *Territorial Enterprise* in Virginia City, Nevada, before going on to fame, fortune, bankruptcy, and then fame and fortune again.

Though he'd won many awards, Tom didn't believe he was a writer with the ability to create memorable prose that would stand tall and strong over the aeons. Not like Mark Twain. Yet to have even a marginal connection to the creator of *Huckleberry Finn* made him feel wonderfully special.

Just before he died, Tom's father had told him that, according to legend, during the latter part of his life Mark Twain had taken a transcontinental railroad trip over the Christmas season. He'd supposedly taken extensive notes about the trip but for some reason had never distilled them into a story. That's what Tom's father had asked Tom to do: take the train ride, write the story, finish what Twain never had, and do the Langdon side of the family proud.

When Tom heard his father's mumbled request, he was struck dumb. Travel across the country on a train during Christmas, to finish something Mark Twain *allegedly* hadn't? He had thought his father delirious from his final suffering, and so the wish went unfulfilled. Yet now, because he could no longer fly unless he was fingerprinted and shackled, he was finally going to take that trip for his old man, and maybe for himself too. Across almost 3,000 miles of America, he was going to see if he could find himself, clean up the mess he'd made of his life.

However, had he known what life-altering event would happen to him barely two hours after he boarded the train, he might have opted to walk to California instead.

CHAPTER TWO

Tom got out of the cab in front of Union Station in Washington, DC, where his train trip would begin. He had reserved a sleeping-car compartment on the Capitol Limited train to Chicago for the first leg of his journey to the West Coast. The venerable Southwest Chief would handle the second, much longer jaunt.

In preparation for his trip, Tom had immersed himself in Mark Twain's life, work and wit. He'd reread *The Innocents Abroad*, Twain's account of a five-month journey on a steamship to Europe and the Holy Land, and thought it one of the funniest, most irreverent travel books ever written. Tom wasn't going abroad, but in many ways, like Sam Clemens fresh from the Wild West, he felt like a pilgrim traveller in his own country, because, ironically, he'd seen far more of the rest of the world than he had of America.

The 'Cap', as the Limited was affectionately known, would leave DC at precisely 4.05pm, making twelve stops before arriving in the Windy City punctually the following morning at 9.19am. Tom picked up his tickets, checked his ski equipment with the baggage agent—Lelia and he were going to the elegantly chic slopes of Tahoe for Christmas—and observed the grandeur of Washington's Union Station.

The train would be boarding shortly, so he headed to the departure area. Even though some train stations had recently implemented baggage screening, a person could still literally arrive at the last minute and make their journey. There were no security checkpoints, no nosy wands, no inane questions about whether you'd let a stranger load a small thermonuclear device in your carry-on bag while you were in the men's room. You just jumped on and went. In the modern world of endless rules, the simplicity of it was very refreshing.

Tom sat down and began studying his fellow passengers. An attractive young couple sitting next to Tom were holding hands, looking very nervous. Next to them was an elderly man of the cloth taking a little siesta, his feet up on his duffle bag. Sitting across from the priest was a slender woman with angular features. Tom couldn't really tell her age because she was wearing a long, multicoloured scarf round her head, almost like a turban. She also wore wooden shoes the size of thirty-pound dumbbells. Spread on the chair next to her were tarot cards, which she was poring over. When anyone passed she'd glance up with a look that seemed to say 'I know all about you'. It was a little unnerving. Tom had had his palm read by an old fellow in the Virgin Islands once. He'd promised Tom a long life filled with kids, a loving wife and nothing but good times. Tom had often thought about hunting the liar down and getting his money back.

A few minutes later Tom grabbed his bags and headed to the platform. The mighty Capitol Limited was calling his name.

THE AIR WAS VERY COLD, fat clouds holding the promise of snow or at least sleet. In such weather airplane passengers worried about flight delays and icy wings, but such inclemency meant nothing to the stalwart Cap bound for Chicago. Tom's spirits started to soar; the beginning of any journey always drove his adrenaline level high and he was desperately ready for an adventure.

He walked to the front of the train and gazed at the twin diesel electric engines. He'd read about these monsters. Each weighed a staggering 268,000 pounds, cranking sixteen cylinders and packing 42,000 horsepower.

Today the Cap's configuration of cars, called the 'consist' in trainspeak, was two engines, one baggage car, three coaches, two sleeper cars, one dining car and one dormitory transition car. The transition car was where most of the service crew was quartered. It had high and low doors that allowed the double-decker cars to have access to the single-level cars, hence the term 'transition' car.

Tom found a sleeping-car attendant and showed him his ticket.

'Next sleeper car down, sir. Regina will take care of you,' the fellow told him.

Regina was standing in front of an impressive sixteen-foot-tall double-decker train car that was called a Superliner, the heaviest passenger-train car in the world. She possessed flawless, dark brown skin and seemed to Tom to be too young to be working anywhere. She was wearing a red and white Christmas hat, and she had just finished assisting the nervous young couple. Tom stepped forward and showed her his ticket, and she marked him off her list.

'OK, Mr Langdon, you're on the upper level. Compartment D. Stairs are to your right and then left down the hall.'

Tom thanked her and gingerly placed a foot on the august Capitol Limited. His experience with sleeper cars was limited solely to having seen the movie *North by Northwest*, directed by Alfred Hitchcock and starring the impeccably elegant Cary Grant and a very sinister James Mason. From that film, he knew that his sleeper compartment would be elegantly appointed and spacious, with room for a couple of beds, a nice study area, a small foyer in which to formally receive visitors, and a full bathroom with whirlpool tub.

He started to climb the stairs as instructed by Regina. With luggage the going was a little tough, the stairs turning at tight ninety-degree angles. When he looked up, he realised he faced a considerable obstacle.

She was old, dressed in what looked to be a nightgown although it was not yet four o'clock, and was teetering on the top step, coming down. Tom was on the second to top step. 'Excuse me,' he said.

'Coming through,' the woman announced in a thunderous baritone.

'If you'll just let me squeeze past,' he replied. But that was out of the question. She wasn't nearly as tall as Tom, but she was, to put it delicately, considerably wider in frame.

'Hi there, Regina,' the woman called down.

'Hi there, Agnes Joe,' said Regina.

Neither of them backing down, Tom and Agnes Joe engaged in an awkward tango, one foot forward, one foot back.

Finally Tom said, 'Agnes Joe, I'm Tom Langdon and I'm in Compartment D. If you can just step back for a sec—'

He never finished the sentence, because instead of stepping back, she gave him a little nudge with a meaty forearm which sent him stumbling down the stairs, to hit bottom flat on his back.

Agnes Joe followed his plummet and was polite enough to gingerly step over his prostrate carcass before handing Regina some cash. 'Here you go, honeypie. Thanks for taking my bags.'

Tom seriously doubted this was how Mark Twain had begun his cross-country railroad journey. He picked himself up and headed over to Regina after glaring at the old woman as he passed her.

'I'll get your bags, Mr Langdon, just put them over there while I get everybody checked in.'

'Thank you. And it's Tom,' he said, handing Regina a few dollars. 'So have you been working on this train long?' he asked.

'Four years.'

'That's a long time.'

'Shoot, we have people been on this train twenty years.'

Tom glanced back at Agnes Joe, who was slowly making her way back up the stairs.

'So you know Agnes Joe?' he asked.

'Oh, sure, she's been riding this train for 'bout, oh, ten years, or so I hear.'

'Ten years! She must really like the ride.'

Regina laughed. 'I think she has family she goes to see. She's nice.'

Tom rubbed the spot where 'nice' Agnes Joe had walloped him. 'Is she on this sleeper car?'

'Yep, right next to you.'

Oh, joy, joy, he thought.

He went back to the stairway where Agnes Joe was, inexplicably, still on the exact same step.

'Agnes Joe, do you need some help?'

'I'm fine, honeypie. Just give me a little time.'

'Maybe if I get in front of you and pull?'

Tom's plan was to get in front of her, run like hell, and lock himself in his magnificent suite while Cary Grant kept guard outside.

'Just give me some space, sonny!'

She finished this last retort with a heavy elbow that somehow found Tom's left kidney. By the time the pain had ceased and he was able to straighten his torso, Agnes Joe was gone. Damn if he didn't feel like a war correspondent again.

CHAPTER THREE

After taking two strides from the doorway of Compartment D, Tom had bumped into the opposite wall. There was a sink, a tiny closet, a chair by a fold-down table and a large mirror on the wall across from the bed. The picture window was huge and gave an inviting view of the outdoors, where snow was starting to fall, getting him into the Christmas spirit. OK, it wasn't bad, he decided. In truth, space-wise, it easily beat first class on an airplane.

This impression lasted until he opened the door to his private bathroom. Actually, according to the sign posted inside, this was the bathroom *and* the shower. He looked at his girth and then eyed the chamber some more. He was reasonably certain that he could wedge himself inside. Of course, once in, it would take three or four strong men with heavy machinery to free him.

He turned back and was about to sit down, when he saw something flash past the wall opposite the bed. At first it didn't register, it was so fast. But then it happened again. It was Agnes Joe. How could that be? This was *private* accommodation. Then he saw the problem. The walls between compartments must open, perhaps for maintenance or something, and the result was that he could see into the woman's room. In his reporting days he'd bivouacked with dirty, spitting camels, desert nomads and other unwashed persons. But he really didn't want to sleep with Agnes Joe.

As he went over to the wall to push it back into place, he peered through the crevice between their rooms and found himself cornea to cornea with the woman.

'You best not be peeping at me, sonny boy,' she said. 'Besides, you don't want to look at my old stuff, honeypie. Find yourself some girl closer to your own age.'

OK, Tom thought, the lady is the town eccentric. He decided to play along. 'Your stuff looks pretty good to me.'

'Don't you try to sweet-talk me—it won't work because I'm not that sort of girl. But we could have a drink together in the lounge car after supper and get to know each other.' She batted her eyelashes.

'Now that's an offer I'd be a fool to refuse.'

She gave him a playful smile. 'I'm sorry about knocking you down the stairs, Tom. My hand must have slipped.'

'If it had to happen, I'm glad it was you.'

He turned and saw Regina standing there, his bags in her hand. She glanced over at the wall and shook her head. 'Did that wall pop out again? I told maintenance to check it.'

'Hi, Regina,' said Agnes Joe through the opening. She pointed to Tom. 'You watch that fellow, he's slick.'

'OK.'

Regina brought his bags in and pushed the wall back into place. 'Sorry about that.'

'That's OK. She seems pretty harmless.'

'I wouldn't be too sure about that.' She sat down on the edge of the bed and pulled out a notepad. 'Dining car opens at five thirty. Or if you don't want a reservation in the dining car, you can get some food from the café. It's in the lounge car, the one past the dining car, lower level. Just show your ticket to Tyrone—he's the lounge-car attendant. It's all free for sleeping-car passengers.'

'I'll eat in the dining car. How about seven?'

She wrote this down. 'While you're eating, I'll come in and get your bed made up.'

'Is there a dress code or anything in the dining car?'

Regina looked amused. 'Well, I've seen people wear just about anything a person can wear on this train. What you're wearing is fine.'

He questioned her about the small size of his shower/bath, and she told him that larger facilities were available on the lower level on a first-come, first-served basis. 'Most of the physically enhanced people opt for that,' she added diplomatically.

As she rose to leave, Tom said, 'I'm a journalist, writing a story about my train trip across the country.'

She looked very interested. 'Are you taking the California Zephyr to San Fran, or the Southwest Chief to LA?'

'Southwest Chief to LA.'

'That's a great train. The Chief has a cool history. And they're wonderful people on board; you'll have fun. Most people who work the Chief never want to leave.'

Tom pulled out his notepad and started jotting things down. 'The way you describe it, the trains almost seem like people.'

'Well, they sort of are. I mean, you spend so much time on them, you learn their quirks. It's like having a relationship. I know it sounds strange, but that's the way it is.'

'Hmmm, with some of the relationships I've had, dating a hundred-ton diesel might be a welcome change.'

Regina laughed. 'My mother, Roxanne, works on the Southwest Chief, as the chief of on-board services. I'm going to see her when we get into Chicago. I'll let her know you'll be on. Now *she* can tell you some stories.'

'Is that common? I mean, do lots of family members work for Amtrak?'

'Well, I've got my mom, and I don't know how many uncles and aunts and cousins and such spread all over. That's how I found out about working on the trains. And my son works for Amtrak too. He's a coach cleaner.'

Tom stared at her. 'Your son? You look like you just got out of high school.'

'Agnes Joe was right: you *are* slick.' She smiled. 'But thanks for the compliment.' Her expression grew serious. 'Where I come from, working on the train is special. People look up to you, you know?'

Tom nodded. This element really intrigued him. He'd have to work it into his story. 'You think people on the train will talk to me?'

'I bet they do.'

As she left, Tom felt the train start to move. He checked his watch. It was 4.05pm exactly. The legendary Capitol Limited was on its way.

CLEARED FOR TAKEOFF by rail-traffic control, the train soared down the metal- and wood-ribbed runway, heading west, just as the young Mark Twain had when he'd made the trek from Missouri to Nevada on a bouncy stagecoach, sleeping on mailbags at night and riding on top by day. While he encountered much that was beautiful and rare, he also fought desperadoes, ornery Mexican pugs, bad food and boredom. Tom Langdon, in contrast, was pulled along by 1,000 tons of raging horsepower and enjoyed a comfy bed, a toilet, and Agnes Joe in the next room. Tom wasn't yet certain whether he or Mark Twain had got the better deal.

He called Lelia on his cellphone. He hadn't told her about the train trip because he wanted to surprise her. She was certainly surprised, but not in exactly the way he had intended.

'You're taking a train all the way across the United States of America?' she yelled. 'Are you insane?'

'Folks used to do this all the time, Lelia.'

'Right, during the Stone Age.'

'It's for a story, about Christmas.' He didn't want to share with her the other reason he was doing it, because he wasn't really sure how she figured in his future—the one he hoped to discover on this trip.

'I've chartered a private jet that leaves at six o'clock sharp on Christmas Eve.'

'I've got my skis, I'll be there. The train gets into LA that morning.'

'What if it's late?'

'Come on, it's a train. We make our station stops, we pick up passengers, we roll along, and we get into LA in plenty of time.'

He heard her let out a long sigh. Lately she'd been letting out many long sighs. They had a seemingly ideal relationship. They ate out a lot, took romantic walks along the beach in Santa Monica, shopped on Fifth Avenue, slept until noon, and then didn't see each other for a couple of months. If more marriages were put together like that, Tom firmly believed, the divorce rate would plummet. So, he wondered, why all the sighing of late?

'Just get here. I don't want to mess up everybody's plans.'

'Everybody? Who's everybody?'

'The people going with us to Tahoe.'

This was news to him. 'What people?'

'Friends from the industry—my agent, my manager, and some others. We talked about this.'

'No, we didn't talk about this. I thought this was just going to be you and me. We've done this the last two years.'

'That's right, and I thought a change would be nice.'

'Meaning what? That you're getting bored being with just me?'

'I didn't say that!'

'You didn't have to. The army of people you invited into our Christmas says it loud and clear.'

'I don't want to argue about this. I just thought that a nice group of people together for Christmas at Tahoe would be fun. It's not like we won't be spending time alone, we will. I only booked us one bedroom, honey. And I bought a new teddy, just for you. It has a Christmas theme, a naughty one,' she added breathlessly.

It had always bothered him that women thought they could win an argument with a man simply by appealing to his baser instincts. And yet he heard himself saying, 'Look, baby doll, I don't want to argue either. I'll be there on time, I swear.' He clicked off and for a few moments had visions of naughty teddies dancing in his head. Sometimes I'm such a guy, he thought ruefully.

THE FIRST STOP, Rockville, Maryland, came barely twenty-five minutes after leaving Washington. Near Rockville was a modest white church where F. Scott Fitzgerald was buried in fulfilment of his request to be planted for eternity in the country. Tom made a mental note to write out very specific instructions concerning his own interment, then pulled out his laptop and entered some observations for his story, though thus far he hadn't really seen all that much.

He got up to see whom he could find to talk to. The train started up again, and he placed one hand against the wall in the corridor to steady himself. As he passed Compartment A, the elderly priest he'd seen in the waiting area earlier came out and bumped into him.

'Hello, Father,' Tom said.

'Retired now,' the holy man said amiably. 'Though I still dress like a priest because I own no other clothes besides a chocolate-brown polyester leisure suit from the 1970s that I still ask forgiveness for. I'm Father Paul Kelly.'

'Tom Langdon. You spending Christmas in Chicago?'

'No, I'm going on to Los Angeles. My sister and her offspring live there. I'm spending the holidays with them.'

'Taking the Southwest Chief, I guess.'

'The very one.'

'Me too. Maybe I'll catch you in the lounge car after dinner. We can whittle down some cigars I brought.' Tom had noticed the stem of a pipe sticking out of the priest's coat pocket.

Father Kelly placed a gentle hand on his sleeve. 'Bless you, my son. Trains are the civilised way to travel, are they not? And perhaps we'll see those film people around too.'

'What film people?'

Father Kelly drew closer. 'They came in a grand car, pulled up almost to the train. I discreetly enquired as to who they might be, being a curious person by nature. From what I could gather, one of them is a famous film director or producer or some such, the other is a star or maybe a writer. They're taking the train across the country in preparation for a film about such a trip.'

'That's pretty coincidental,' Tom said, and he explained that he was writing a story about the train journey. The priest seemed pleased to hear it. 'Well, you picked the right subject. I've taken many a train in my time, and they're always full of surprises.'

AFTER HE LEFT Father Kelly, Tom passed through the next section of sleeping accommodation, the standard compartments, without bath or shower facilities. Here, the smaller compartments ran down both sides of the car, with an aisle in the middle. Tom noticed that across this corridor were stretched a pair of hands, holding one to the other, and as he drew closer he saw that it was the nervous young couple.

'OK, do I have to pay a toll to pass through?' he said jokingly.

They both returned his smile.

'Sorry,' the guy said, while the girl looked away shyly. They were about twenty and with their blond hair and fair skin, looked like brother and sister.

'So, on your way to Chicago for the holidays?'

'Actually . . .' began the young man a little sheepishly.

'Steve,' interrupted the girl, 'we don't even know him.'

'Well,' Tom said, 'it's different on a train. Being on this long journey together opens people up. I'll go first. I'm a writer, doing a piece about a trip across the country. There's my story, so what's yours?'

The two looked at each other, and Steve said, 'Well, actually, we're getting married.'

Tom extended his hand to them both. 'Congratulations. That's great. I'm Tom, by the way.'

'Steve. My fiancée is Julie.'

'So are you tying the knot in Chicago?'

'Uh, no, we're getting married on the train,' Steve said.

'The train? This train?'

'No,' said Julie. 'On the Southwest Chief, on the way to LA. It leaves tomorrow afternoon.' Her accent sounded Southern to Tom, while Steve's suggested New England origins.

'That's great. I'm going to be on that train too. So is your family already on board, or are they meeting you in Chicago?'

'Our families don't know and don't approve of us getting married,' said Julie dabbing at her eyes with the back of her hand.

Steve looked at Tom and tried to affect a carefree attitude. 'So we're doing it on our own. Because we love each other.'

Julie said, 'His family doesn't approve of me. They think because I'm from some little podunk Virginia town in the Appalachian Mountains, that I'm some sort of white trash. Well, my father might have worked in the mines since he was sixteen, and my mother never finished high school either, and'—she looked at Steve—'his parents are high society in Connecticut, but my family is not trash. They're every bit as good as his.'

'So, does *your* family approve of the marriage?' Tom asked Julie, trying to defuse the tension a little.

'They like Steve a lot, but they think I'm too young. I'm in college. We both are, at George Washington University in Washington. That's where we met. They want me to finish school before I get married.'

'Well, that's understandable, especially if they never had a chance to go to college. I'm sure they just want the best for you.'

'The best thing for me is Steve.' She smiled at him, and Tom could tell the young man's heart was breaking at what she was going through. These two might be young, but they were old enough to be absolutely head-over-heels in love.

Julie continued, 'I'm going to finish college, and then I'm going on to law school, at the University of Virginia. I'm going to do my parents proud. But I'm going to do all of that as Steve's wife.'

'Well,' Tom said, 'it's your life, and I think you should follow your heart.'

'Thanks,' Julie said, and she gave his hand a pat.

If only he'd followed that advice with Eleanor Carter, things might have been different. Ironically, they too had met in college. Both journalism majors, they'd decided to be a team after graduation. They'd done some investigative reporting in the States and scored a couple of big stories, before taking the leap and signing on as the entire overseas bureau for a fledgling news service. They had collected the experiences of a lifetime—several lifetimes, in fact. They'd fallen in love, like Steve and Julie. They should have been engaged and married, yet it had ended so abruptly that Tom still found it intensely painful to think about their last moments together.

'So, is the minister on board?' For a second Tom thought Father Kelly might be officiating, but he'd said he was retired and surely he would have mentioned a wedding.

Steve said, 'He gets on in Chicago. And so do our maid of honour and best man.'

'Well, good luck to both of you. I take it everybody on the train is invited?' he added.

'We sure hope *somebody* will come,' said Steve.

'Right,' added Julie, 'otherwise it will be a pretty lonely wedding.'

'No bride should have to settle for that. I'll be there, and I'll bring all my train friends with me.' Tom didn't yet have any train friends, but how hard could it be to make friends on the Cap?

'Lounge car at nine in the morning,' said Steve. 'The station stop is La Junta.'

'That means "junction" in Spanish,' said Julie. 'Seemed appropriate for a marriage.'

'I'm curious: why the train in the first place?'

Julie laughed. 'I guess it'll sound silly, but after my grandfather came back from World War Two, my grandmother met him in New York City. They'd been engaged before the war started but postponed their wedding because Gramps refused to leave her a widow. He said that if he made it through the war, then it was God's way of telling them they were meant to be together. Well, he made it back of course, and Grandma, who'd been waiting four long years, went to New York City with plans to get married up there, but so many other soldiers were doing the same thing that it would have taken them weeks. So they paid a preacher to get on the train with them, and once they crossed into Virginia, they were married.'

'And I assume things worked out?'

'Fifty-five years of marriage together. They died within a week of each other two years ago.'

'Well, I wish you both the same,' Tom offered, then he headed for the lounge-car café.

As he went through the dining-room car, he nodded to the attendants who seemed to be working hard to get dinner together, so he decided not to hit them with a lot of questions. He ventured on to the lounge car, where a few people were sitting around watching the TV and others were idly gazing at the passing countryside.

He made his way down the spiral staircase and found Tyrone, the lounge-car attendant, working in a small, but neatly organised space. There were refrigerated cabinets loaded with sandwiches, ice cream, assorted goodies and hot and cold drinks.

Tyrone was about thirty, Tom's height, and looked like Elvis, only he was black. Tom like the effect a lot.

'I'll be open in about twenty minutes, sir,' said Tyrone. 'My delivery was in late. I'm usually up and running by now. I'll make an announcement on the PA.'

'No problem, Tyrone.'

Tyrone looked Tom over with interest as he methodically laid out his wares. 'Hey, you the writer guy Regina told me about?'

'I'm the writer guy, yes.'

'Cool. What do you want to know?'

'For starters, whether you're an Elvis fan.'

He laughed. 'It was the hair, right, man? It's always the hair.'

'OK, it *was* the hair.'

'Thankyou, thankyouverymuch.' Tyrone did a little bump and grind. 'I know all the songs, all the hip moves. The man could cut it pretty good for a white dude.'

'You been on this train long?'

'About seven years. I've been with Amtrak since '93.'

'I bet you've seen a lot.'

'Oh, let me tell you, I've seen some stuff. People come on a train, man, it's like they lose some inhibition gene or something. Hey, you want a soda or something?'

'Unless you got something stronger, and I'm really hoping you do.'

Tyrone opened a beer for him and Tom settled against the wall.

'So I take it you like working here?'

'Hey, it's a job, but it's fun too. I got me a little entertainment routine that I'm always working on. I have fun with the passengers, and the kids, especially. Man, there's something about trains and kids, they just go together, you know what I mean?' He kept talking as he worked. 'I like it here. The crew is a team, we all pitch in, cover each other's back, like a family.'

'Think you'll stay on the Cap?'

'Don't know. What I'm really thinking about is moving up the ladder to where the real money is.'

'Where's that? In management?'

Tyrone laughed. 'Management? Get serious. The cash is in being a redcap. Them dudes make tip money like they're printing it.'

'I want a drink and I want it now!'

They both turned and stared at the speaker, an unhappy-looking man dressed in a three-piece pinstripe suit.

Tyrone rolled his eyes. 'How you doing, Mr Merryweather?'

'I'm not doing good at all, and I want that drink. Scotch and soda on the rocks. Right now.'

'I'm not open yet, sir, if you could come back—'

Merryweather stepped forward. 'This gentleman has a beer that I'm assuming came from you. Now, if you refuse to open the bar for me, then'—he glanced at Tyrone's name tag—'then, *Tyrone*, I suggest you start looking for other work because once I get off this train you'll be unemployed.' He checked his watch. 'I'm waiting, Tyrone.'

'Sure, coming right up, no problem.'

Tyrone mixed the drink and handed it to the man. Merryweather sipped it. 'More Scotch—you people never put enough of the liquor in. Are you stealing it for yourself?'

'Hey,' said Tom, 'why don't you lighten up?'

Merryweather turned. 'Do you happen to know who I am?'

'Yeah, you're a jerk and obviously very proud of it.'

Merryweather smiled so tightly it looked as though his cheek balls might pop through his skin. 'Tell him who I am, Tyrone.'

'Look, I'm putting a bunch of Scotch in your drink. Why don't we just call it a truce?'

'I'm Gordon Merryweather. And I'm the king of the class-action lawsuit. Piss me off, and I'll see you in court, and I'll walk away with everything you have—although, from the looks of you, you clearly don't have much.'

Tom stepped forward, his fists balled.

'Oh, I hope you do,' said Merryweather. 'Then I get to put you in jail too.'

Tyrone stepped between them. 'Hey, everything is so cool, it's like it's snowing right inside the train. Let's all walk away now. It's Christmas, right. You going home for Christmas, Mr Merryweather, to see the wife and kids? Bet you're bringing them lots of presents.'

'I'm divorced. My children are spoilt brats unworthy of either my affection or my largesse.'

With that, Gordon Merryweather walked off, sipping his Scotch. About halfway down the corridor they heard him laughing.

Tom looked at Tyrone. 'I'm surprised he didn't say, "Bah, humbug."'

Tyrone shook his head. 'You don't want to mess with that man. He'll tie you up in court for years. His picture is right in the dictionary, beside the word *nightmare*.'

'No offence, but why is the "king of the class-action lawsuit" taking the train? He probably can afford his own jet.'

'From what I've heard, the oh-so-tough Mr Merryweather is afraid to fly. I wish he'd just buy his own train and stay off mine.'

'Well, thanks for stopping me from knocking that Scotch down his throat. I actually have plans for my life that don't include prison. And thanks for the info and the beer.'

Tyrone smiled. 'No problem. Any time. Come on back after dinner. I serve some hard stuff.'

CHAPTER FOUR

Tom went back to his compartment and looked out of the window; it was already dark at five fifteen. They'd just cleared Harpers Ferry, West Virginia, a place immortalised when John Brown made his famous raid on the federal armoury there prior to the start of the Civil War, and was sent to the gallows.

Deciding it was finally time to hunt down the film people, Tom passed along the cars in the opposite direction from the dining room and found himself in the other sleeping-room section. He was sure that Hollywood types would only travel first class, so he drifted towards this section, hoping the movie folks would come out of hiding.

The curtain of the first compartment was pulled tightly across the opening and he could see nothing, although he heard someone moving around inside. At the next compartment he could see that the curtain was pulled back a bit. He stopped and took a quick peek. Pacing the small space was a tall young man with a flat-top haircut wearing a dark turtleneck. As he turned, Tom could see that he was wearing a phone headset with his cellphone riding in a belt clip.

This couldn't be the famous director, could it? This guy didn't seem like the director type. He had to be either a star or a writer. Tom's money was on his being a writer. He seemed like the young, hip scriveners much in demand out in LA.

Tom went to the next compartment. He was about to take a look when a man slid the door open and almost collided with him.

'Sorry,' the stranger said. 'I was just told I can't smoke in my compartment.'

Tom glanced at the unlit cigarette in the man's hand, then quickly ran his gaze over the fellow. He was of medium height, early sixties, with thick silver hair and a healthy California tan. And he was dressed very expensively in black slacks, white silk shirt, tweed jacket and Bruno Magli shoes. He just reeked of casual millions.

'They have a smoking lounge on the lower level,' Tom advised.

'Well, I guess that's where I'm headed then. Tried a hundred times to kick this habit. Did the patch, even hypnosis. Nothing.'

'I was a two-packer a day, but now I limit myself to the occasional cigar.'

He looked interested. 'How'd you manage it?'

'Well, my life sort of depended on it.'

'I hear you. Who wants to die of lung cancer?'

'No, that's not what I mean. I used to be a news correspondent overseas. I was in a convoy of journalists that was attacked by guerrillas and when we ran for the mountains, a guy from Reuters, about fifty and a heavy smoker, didn't make it. He dropped to the ground, probably due to a heart attack. My own heart and lungs were near to bursting; it seemed like every smoke I'd ever had was coming back to haunt me. I haven't touched a cigarette since.'

'Wow, what a story. War correspondent, huh?'

'Not any more. The most dangerous things I report on these days are how to construct his-and-hers closets in a way that allows the husband actually to live, and the harrowing pitfalls of home barbecuing.'

The man laughed and put out his hand. 'That's funny. I'm Max Powers, by the way.'

Tom thought he had recognised him, and when the man said his name it all clicked. He *was* a very famous director, regularly in the top ten of the most powerful people in Hollywood. He was known for his enormous box-office successes, but he'd also been nominated several times for Academy Awards, and had taken the grand prize home a few years ago.

'Tom Langdon. I've seen a lot of your movies, Mr Powers. You really know how to tell a story.'

'Thanks. That's all I try to do. And it's Max.' He slipped the unlit cigarette into his shirt pocket and looked around. 'We're trying to cobble together a story about this mode of transportation.'

'Because there's something about a train?'

'You got that right. My old man was a conductor on the Santa Fe passenger line back in the days when trains were really the classy way to travel. He'd arrange it so I could ride up with the engineer and, let me tell you, there's no greater feeling in the world. Ever since, I've known there's a story to be told about riding the rails, and now I'm finally doing something about it.'

Tom told him about the story he was writing and some of his impressions of train travel. 'It's not getting from A to B, it's the ride in between that counts. That's the whole show,' he said. 'This train is alive with things that should be seen and heard . . .'

Max gripped Tom's arm excitedly. 'You understand exactly what I'm trying to get at here.' He suddenly smacked his forehead. 'I just had an unbelievable brainwave. Look, you're a writer, seen stuff all over the world . . . You and my writer should team up—I mean, for this trip, for the research part. Swap notes, stories you've heard. And I'm not talking for free. I'll pay you. You write your story, fine. But the same stuff you're doing for your story can help my writer put the film plot together. It's perfect. Two bangs for one. Get it?'

Tom nodded. However, he wasn't really looking forward to working with the ten-year-old with the headset. But to Tom's surprise, Max led him right past the compartment of the headset-wearing hipster and went to the next compartment and rapped on the glass.

'You decent? It's Max.'

The door slid open and Tom felt every bit of breath leave his body. Eleanor Carter stared back at him.

Max said, 'Eleanor Carter, Tom Langdon. Tom, Eleanor.'

Tom and Eleanor just exchanged stares for so long that Max finally said, 'Um, do you two know each other?'

'It was years ago,' Eleanor said quickly.

She was even more lovely now than the last time Tom had seen her, and that bar had been set pretty high. She was tall and slender, her auburn hair still shoulder-length and sexy. Her face, well, there were a few more lines, but the big green eyes still packed a wallop and made Tom want to find a chair to sit in before he fell over. She was wearing grey wool slacks, stylish black, low-heeled shoes, and a white sweater with a blue shirt collar sticking out.

'How have you been?' Eleanor asked coolly.

'I've been working. Mostly here in the States for the last year,' Tom managed to say.

'I know. I read the piece on Duncan Phyfe furniture you did for *Architectural Journal*. It's the first article on antique furniture that made me laugh. It was good.'

Tom's gut tightened, and his throat dried up as those big emerald eyes bored into him. The sensation of imminent doom was somehow of solace to him, as though the end would be quick and relatively painless. He found his voice. 'So you're a screenwriter?'

Max said, 'She's one of Hollywood's best-kept secrets. She specialises in script doctoring. You know, where a script has real problems and you need a miracle? Eleanor whips it into shape, like magic. I finally talked her into doing her own original screenplay.'

'I'm not surprised—she was always a terrific writer.' There was no response to this compliment. Tom felt cement shoes forming round his ankles.

'So what's up, Max?' Eleanor said. She obviously didn't want a trip down memory lane; she wanted to bring this all—meaning Tom—to a hasty close.

Max explained his 'brilliant idea' to Eleanor, while Tom stood there wondering whether he should throw himself under the wheels of the Cap. It couldn't be clearer that Eleanor wasn't at all pleased with the percolations of the director's genius.

Yet she said, 'Let me think about it, Max.'

'Absolutely. Hey, I tell you what, later, we can have a drink. Somebody told me they drink on this train.'

'They do,' Tom said. Then he added jokingly, 'In fact, the whole train is a bar.' He looked at Eleanor, but she was simply staring into the distance.

'Done, then. Drinks around, what, eight?' said Max.

'OK. They serve dinner here too. I have a dinner reservation at seven?' Tom looked at Eleanor, trying to will her to say she'd join him.

'I had a late lunch in DC,' she said. 'I'm skipping dinner.'

Max said, 'Yeah, dinner's not good for me either, Tom. I've got a few calls to make.'

'Well, don't starve yourself.'

'Not to worry: Kristobal brought some of my favourite stuff on board. I'm more of a snacker, really.'

'Kristobal?'

'My assistant. He's in the compartment right there.' Max pointed to the compartment where Tom had seen the headset kid.

At the mention of his name, Kristobal emerged from his room.

'Do you need anything, Mr Powers?'

'No, I'm fine. This is Tom Langdon. He might be helping us on our project.'

Kristobal was young, handsome and well-built. He probably made more in a week than Tom made in a year. He also seemed efficient and intelligent, and Tom instantly disliked him for all those reasons.

'Excellent, sir,' said Kristobal.

Tom reached out and they shook hands.

Max said, 'OK, that's settled. Eleanor will think about it and we'll have drinks at eight, and now I have got to go smoke before I start hyperventilating.' He looked around, puzzled.

Tom pointed, 'That way, two cars down, through the dining room, into the lounge car, down the stairs, to the right and you'll see the door marked "smoking lounge".'

'Thanks, Tom, you're a gem. I know this is going to work out; it's an omen. "A chance meeting", my palmist said, and look what happened.' He stuck the cigarette in his mouth and hustled off.

Kristobal retreated to his compartment. And then it was just Eleanor and Tom. For a few moments they stood there, each refusing to make eye contact.

'I cannot believe this is actually happening,' Eleanor finally said. 'Of all the people to see on this train.' She slowly shook her head.

'Well, it kind of took me by surprise too.' He added, 'You look great, Ellie.'

Eleanor's eyes focused on him. 'I'm not going to beat around the bush: Max is a wonderfully gifted film-maker, but sometimes he comes up with off-the-wall ideas that just won't work. I really believe this is one of them.'

'Hey, I don't want you to do something you don't want to.'

'So I can tell Max you're not interested?'

'If that's what you want, Ellie, that's fine.'

'That's exactly what I want.' She went back inside her room and slid the door closed.

Standing there, he wondered if it was too late to get a refund on his train ticket based on the recent occurrence of his living death.

TOM STAGGERED BACK to his compartment and collapsed on the bed. Eleanor on this train? It couldn't be possible. He'd never envisioned sharing his journey of self-discovery with the one person whose absence from his life may well have led him to take the damn trip in the first place! And yet whose fault was her absence? He'd never asked her to stay, had he?

As he sat up and stared out of the window into the blackness, he suddenly wasn't on a train heading to Chicago; he was in Tel Aviv. They'd chosen the city because of its proximity to Ben-Gurion

Airport, which meant they were never more than two hours' flight time from the sort of stories Eleanor and Tom were there to cover. The Middle East was nothing if not unpredictable in its predictability. You knew something would happen; you just didn't know where, or what form it would take.

During the years they'd lived in Israel, they'd travelled the country in search of stories. They'd visited Jerusalem and had swum in the Jordan River. They had also ventured to Bethlehem because Eleanor had wanted to see the place where the Son of God had been delivered into a sinful world. Though he was not a particularly religious person, it was still a humbling event for Tom, too.

The two American journalists had been among the very few in Israel who celebrated the holiest of Christian holidays. Every Christmas they had put up a small Christmas tree in their apartment, cooked their holiday meal and opened presents. Then they looked out on the darkness of the Mediterranean and took in the sights and smells of the desert climate before falling asleep in each other's arms. Those Christmases in Tel Aviv were some of the most wonderful of Tom's life. Except for the last one.

Eleanor had left the apartment to do some last-minute shopping. Forty minutes later she came back and said that she wanted to go home, that she was tired of covering the perils of this strange world. At first Tom thought she was joking. But she started packing, then called El Al to get a flight home. She tried to book Tom one too, but he said no, he wasn't leaving. Everything had seemed wonderful barely an hour before. Now his whole life had collapsed.

He questioned her as to what had caused her to make this major, life-altering decision, without bothering to consult him first. The only answer she gave was that it was time to go home. They talked, and then the talk snowballed into an argument, and it was downhill from there. By the time she had her bags packed they were screaming at each other, and Tom had become so confused and distraught that to this day he couldn't remember half of what he'd said.

She took a cab to the airport, and Tom followed her. Finally, it was time to get on the shuttle bus. That was when Eleanor, her voice calm, asked Tom once more to come with her. If he really loved her, he'd come with her. He remembered standing there, tears in his eyes, feeling only a deep stubbornness fuelled by anger. He told her no, he wasn't coming.

He watched her ride up the escalator. She turned back once. Her expression was so sad, so miserable, that he almost called out to her, to tell her to wait, that he was coming, but the words never came. Instead, he turned and left her, as she was leaving him.

That was the last time he'd seen Eleanor, until five minutes ago. He still had no idea what had happened to make her leave. And he still had no rational explanation as to why he hadn't gone with her.

The warm compartment, the hum-hush, siss-boom-bah of the wheels, his overwrought mind and the darkness outside combined to push him into a troubled doze.

WHATEVER IT WAS must have hit Tom's sleeper car directly. The sound was very loud, like a cannonball clanging off the side. He almost fell off the bed. He checked his watch. Six thirty. They were slowing down fast. Then the mighty Capitol Limited came to a complete stop and, looking out of his window, Tom saw that they were nowhere close to civilisation. He smelt something burning.

In the darkness outside he saw lights here and there, as train personnel checked what damage had been done.

He went out into the hallway and saw Father Kelly.

'Did you hear that?' the priest said.

'I think we hit something,' Tom replied. 'Maybe there was something on the track and we ran over it.'

Regina walked by with a worried look, carrying a huge cluster of newspapers all balled up.

Tom said, 'Hey, Regina, what's up?'

'We hit something, that's for sure. But we'll be heading on shortly.'

He looked at what she was carrying. 'I take it you're really into newspapers.'

'Somebody stuffed them in the trash can. I don't even know where they came from. Only newspaper on this train is the *Toledo Blade*, and we don't pick that up until early tomorrow morning.'

She walked off. Tom was starting to feel very smart for building extra time into his travel schedule. It looked like he was going to need it. In Twain's day, the trip of nineteen hundred miles from St Joseph, Missouri, to California by stagecoach took about twenty days. While Tom had to go over a thousand miles further than Twain, he was being pulled by something a little more potent than equine power. And yet Tom was starting to think of small islands where he could hide out from Lelia when he didn't show for Christmas.

Agnes Joe joined them. She was still wearing the nightgown, but she had a robe on over it. 'We hit something,' she said.

'Appears that way,' Tom replied, as he tried to get past her.

However, he found that when Agnes Joe faced him head-on, the woman's body actually spanned the entire width of the corridor. Amtrak needed to build its trains larger to accommodate the widening of Americans.

She pulled an apple from her pocket and started chomping. 'I remember once three—no, four years ago—we were heading up right about here in fact, when, bam, we stopped dead.'

'Really? What happened?' asked Tom.

'Why don't you come in my compartment, set yourself down, get comfortable, and I'll tell you.'

Father Kelly and Tom exchanged glances, and then the priest scooted into the safety of his rabbit hole, leaving the journalist all alone. So much for the support of the Church in times of crisis, thought Tom.

'Well, I'd like to but I have to get ready for dinner. My reservation is at seven.'

'Mine too.'

With the look she gave him, Tom began to think she really had a thing for him. All he could do was give her a weak smile as he finally managed to squeeze past and into the safety of his compartment. He locked his door, drew his curtain, and would have slid the bed against the door had it not been bolted to the wall.

LATER, AS TOM surveyed the dining room, his mind once again drifted to thoughts of *North by Northwest*. In the film Cary Grant, on the run from the police and the train conductor—as a poor fugitive from justice, Cary had no ticket—comes into the elegant dining car. The splendidly attired maître d' escorts him to the table of the ravishingly sexy Eva Marie Saint. Turns out she'd tipped the waiter to seat Cary with her. Beautiful women were always doing that to poor Cary Grant. Eva Marie conducted a sort of sophisticated verbal foreplay right there at the table, in one of the most subtly erotic movie scenes ever. Right now, in the role of Eva Marie, Tom could only see Eleanor. And wasn't that pathetic, he told himself—pathetic that there was no possibility of it coming true.

He was seated across from two people, a middle-aged man in a suit and tie and a woman who, unfortunately, looked nothing like Eleanor, or Eva Marie. Across the aisle from them were Steve and Julie, talking in low voices and still looking very nervous.

The subject of the stalled train was dominating the conversation.

'This is the second train I've been on this week where something has happened,' said the woman across from Tom. She introduced herself as Sue Bunt from Wisconsin. She was about fifty or so, tall and on the heavy side, and her hair was cut very short.

'How about that,' the man in the suit said. He didn't offer his name.

'I usually don't take the train, but the flights aren't as convenient on my circuit any more,' she explained.

'What do you do?' Tom asked.

'I'm a sales rep for a health-food company,' she said as she slathered her roll in butter.

'Happy holidays,' said the waitress as she came over and presented them with complimentary glasses of eggnog, a Cap holiday tradition, they were told.

'Happy holidays,' they all replied, and then Sue asked the waitress about the condition of the train.

'Conductor said we'll be up and running in no time. We just ran over something on the track.'

They placed their orders. Tom ordered the prime rib and asked for a screwdriver as his appetiser. He was just putting the cocktail to his lips when he felt himself being propelled to the side of the dining car. He turned and there was Agnes Joe wedging in next to him, leaving him about six inches in which to eat his dinner.

'Hi, Agnes Joe,' the man and Sue said in unison.

When Tom looked her over he was stunned. Agnes Joe's hair was done, she had on some make-up, and she didn't look nearly as old as before. It was such a stark transformation that he could only stare.

'Hello, Agnes Joe,' said the waitress. 'You want the usual?'

'That'll be fine, with extra onions.'

'I take it you ride the train a lot,' Tom said as the waitress walked off.

'Oh, I love the train and the people on it. I tried flying for a while. I'm a licensed pilot in fact, general aviation, but I prefer the trains.'

For Tom the vision of Agnes Joe crammed inside the cockpit of a two-seater Cessna, her hammy fingers curled around the yoke, her enormous feet on the rudder pedals, wavered right on hallucinatory. He ordered a glass of merlot as a chaser, ate his meal, which was wonderful, and looked around the car. At one table an attractive African-American woman was having the moves put on her by a young, handsome Korean. At another some corporate suits were supping with the tarot card lady, who had her cards spread out in front of the remains of her Shenandoah Valley baked chicken. The easy coupling of commercial power and whimsical tarot cards over a hearty feast: maybe there really was something about a train, Tom marvelled.

CHAPTER FIVE

As soon as dinner was over, Tom fled to the lounge car, which, he soon discovered, was known by all seasoned train travellers as the *bar* car. Tyrone fixed him up libation-wise, then he went and sat in the car's upper level. The train still wasn't moving, but at least he'd stopped smelling smoke.

The TV was on and showing the movie *The Grinch Who Stole Christmas* and a gaggle of kids and their parents were gathered around watching it. In other corners of the car there were little groups of people chatting and drinking, and a few solitary types who just stared out of the darkened windows at their own reflections. Tom sipped his gin and focused on a group of adults sitting nearby. One was reading, one was knitting, another was listening to music through headphones.

'Are you all heading somewhere for Christmas?' he asked with what he hoped was a friendly expression. He found that gin always made one appear relaxed and happy, if a bit fuzzy in the head.

The knitting lady looked up and smiled. 'South Bend, Indiana. I'm spending the holidays with my grandson. I'll probably end up cooking and cleaning and doing his laundry for him, but that's OK. That's grandma stuff. And it's Christmas. Who wants to be alone?'

'You got my vote there,' Tom said as he introduced himself.

She reached out and shook his hand. 'Pauline Beacon. You live in the DC area?'

'Yes, right in DC.'

'I don't know how you take the traffic.' This came from the guy who'd been reading a book. He was mid-forties, balding and soft in the middle. 'I'm heading back to Toledo. I was in Washington on business and had to rent a car and drive around that Beltway thing you folks have. I don't know how you people do it. It's like the Wild, Wild West on wheels. Crazy.' He shook his head. 'I'm Rick,' he said and smiled. 'Just call me Toledo Rick.'

'So I take it you folks like trains,' Tom said.

'I don't like to fly,' said Pauline. 'And trains are a connection to my childhood. How about you?'

Tom said, 'I fly a lot, but it got to be a little old. I thought I'd try a more civilised way of getting around.'

'Well,' said Rick, 'I normally fly too, but I got this great deal on a train ticket.' He frowned. 'Only right now it doesn't seem like such a great deal. At least I'll be home for Christmas.'

'You have a family?'

'A wife and six children. Four are teenagers, three of them girls. I don't even come close to understanding anything about them.'

At that moment Agnes Joe came in with a beer and settled down with them. She didn't introduce herself. As in the dining car, everyone seemed to know her already.

'How about you, Tom?' asked Rick. 'Where you heading? Family?'

Tom shook his head. 'I don't really have any.'

'Well, everyone has family somewhere,' said Pauline.

'Not everybody,' said Agnes Joe. 'I'm a loner too.'

'I didn't say I was a loner. I'm a reporter. Been all over the world. Probably have friends in sixty or seventy different countries.'

'Friends are friends, but family is family,' stated Pauline, and maybe she was right.

'Divorced or never married?' asked Agnes Joe. She glanced at his naked ring finger in response to his surprised look.

'Divorced. Although my marriage was so brief I never really felt married.'

'Well, you obviously didn't marry the right woman,' said Pauline.

'How can you know for sure?' asked Toledo Rick.

'Lots of ways,' ventured Agnes Joe. 'Mostly it just feels right. Like you don't care if you eat, drink, sleep, or even breathe so long as you're with that person.' She glanced at Tom. 'You ever feel that way about anybody?'

They all looked at Tom awaiting his answer.

'Hey, that's getting a bit personal,' he said.

'Well, there's just something about a train,' quipped Pauline with a smile as she effortlessly knitted one, pearled two.

Tom stared out of the window for a moment.

'What was her name?' asked Agnes Joe quietly.

'Eleanor,' he finally said.

'Been a long time since you've seen her?'

'Actually, not that long ago. But what's past is past. I'm going out to LA. To spend Christmas with my girlfriend, Lelia.'

'Is she an actress?' Pauline asked excitedly.

'In a way, yes. You ever catch Cuppy the Magic Beaver on Saturday-morning TV?'

Pauline stared at him blankly and dropped a stitch or two of her knitting. Tom decided to drop the whole line of conversation.

They all watched as one of the attendants, dressed as Santa Claus, came into the lounge car. In a flash all the kids, even the older ones, deserted the Grinch and gathered around the man in red.

'That's nice,' Tom said, as Santa handed out goodies to everyone.

'They do it every year,' said Agnes Joe.

Tom looked at her. It had just occurred to him that Regina had said Agnes Joe rode the trains a lot, to visit her family, she thought. Yet Agnes Joe had just confessed she was a loner. So where was she going on all these trains?

'Are you going all the way to Chicago?' he asked.

'That's right.'

'Spending the holidays there?'

'No. I'm heading on to LA on the Southwest Chief. Like you.'

Agnes Joe for about two days on the Chief. He wondered what would happen if he jumped off the train right now while it wasn't moving. Just as he was about to speak, the Cap gave a lurch and started on its way again. A cheer went up and a voice came over the PA system. 'Sorry for the delay, folks, but we've got everything patched up. We have a technical team standing by at the next station. We'll be there a little while to make sure everything's OK, and then we'll push on. We've called ahead and nobody will miss train connections. Thank you for understanding.'

Toledo Rick and Pauline excused themselves and left.

Agnes Joe leaned close and said, 'The Southwest Chief is a great train with wonderful views of the mountains and the plains. Goes through eight states on its way to the coast.'

'That's interesting.' Tom was convinced that she'd searched his compartment and found his ticket for the Chief. He resolved to booby-trap his room using the heaviest object he could find.

'Yep, it's a nice trip. Good way to get to LA.'

'I bet it is.' Tom put down his drink. 'So, what are you heading to LA for?'

'I have friends out there. We visit each other at Christmas. This year it's my turn to go west.'

'Sounds like a nice tradition. Regina said you travel by train a lot. And it seems like people know you.'

'Oh, I'm just a friendly sort. Always have been. Just because a gal's petite and naturally shy doesn't mean she has to be a meek little wall-flower all the time.'

At first Tom thought she was serious, but then she smiled at her own joke, and he reluctantly concluded that Agnes Joe wasn't so bad. If she'd just stay away from his kidneys and personal belongings everything would be fine.

'So this gal you're seeing, you serious about her?'

'Depends on what you call serious,' Tom said. 'We've been seeing each other off and on for about three years.'

'Off and on? What, is that a California thing?'

'It's *our* thing.'

'Well, I wouldn't advise you to get married. I've tried it twice and neither worked out.'

'Do you have any kids?'

'A girl, all grown now, of course. That was from my first marriage. I met husband number one when we worked together at Ringling Brothers. I was one of the performers. Horsewoman, gymnast, even did the high-wire in my younger days.'

'The trapeze!'

She stared at him. 'I was a little lighter then. My daughter still works for the circus.'

'Do you see her often?'

'No.' With that, she picked up her beer and left. He should have been relieved, but he wasn't. The woman was growing on him, like a wart maybe, but still growing. And there were inconsistencies in her background that intrigued the investigative reporter in him.

As he sat there, the train flashed through the Graham Tunnel and soon after slowed as it approached Cumberland, Maryland. The Cap jauntily made its way down the middle of the town's main street.

They would be crossing into Pennsylvania soon. The state lines were oddly configured here, so that at certain times the engine and the tail of the train could be in Maryland while the middle of the Cap was in West Virginia.

As he sat there staring at the snow falling, Eleanor and Max walked in, trailed by the faithful Kristobal. Tom took a deep breath, finished his drink, and contemplated ordering up cocktails in bulk from his friend Tyrone. He figured he'd need every ounce of alcohol possible to survive this.

Eleanor had changed into a long turquoise skirt and white denim shirt with a chain belt around her slim waist. Her hair was tucked up. Perhaps, Tom thought, she'd showered, the steamy, soapy liquid pouring down over her long, curvy . . . No, he absolutely could not go there and expect to retain his sanity. Yet the fact that she had freshened up and was here to see him was wonderfully reassuring, until he noted her expression. Homicidal was the word that drifted through his mind.

'Tom!' boomed out Max, in that enthusiastic voice that said 'I'm both filthy rich and fun to be around'. 'Sorry we're late. Eleanor and I had a few things to clear up. Boy, what a ride so far, huh?'

Kristobal stared out into the darkness. 'Well, at least we're moving.'

'Your first train ride, Kristobal?' Tom asked.

'And hopefully my last.'

'He's from another generation,' said Max, as he playfully slapped his assistant's arm. 'He's not train folk; not like you and me.'

'Well, Ellie and I took quite a few trains when we were overseas,' said Tom. 'Remember that, Ellie?'

'I go by Eleanor now. And, no, I don't really remember.'

The gin had now warmed Tom from his toes to his mouth, which had become an 80mm howitzer. 'Right. Ellie, that's clearly in the past. Out with the old, in with the new and improved.' He looked at Max. 'So, you said you and *Eleanor* had talked.'

'Yes, we discussed things. And if you want, you two can get started right now.'

Tom glanced at her in confusion. 'I thought—'

'When Max gets excited about something, his enthusiasm spreads rapidly and overwhelmingly,' she explained in a tight voice without meeting his gaze.

'Well, how should we begin?' Tom offered pleasantly.

Max said, 'What have you discovered so far?'

Tom sat back and cradled his glass. 'Well, there's a crazy woman named Agnes Joe on board who outweighs me and yet once performed on the trapeze for Ringling Brothers.' He pointed to Steve and Julie. 'Those two are getting married on board the Southwest Chief. Oh, and Elvis Presley has been resurrected as a black man named Tyrone who serves a concoction called a "Boiler Room" in the lounge car. And there's a priest on board, who might have to give me the Last Rites if we don't get to LA on time because my girlfriend will murder me.'

As he said this, Tom stared right at Eleanor. She'd walked out on *him*, after all. She blinked. The lady actually blinked. He had no idea whether it was a reaction to his statement, but it sobered him up a bit.

'Wow,' said Max, 'you've really got around already.'

'Once a world-class reporter, always a world-class reporter. Just like Ellie—I mean, Eleanor.'

'She never really talked about that part of her life.'

Eleanor said quickly, 'Maybe Tom and I should get to work, Max. We don't have all that much time. I might have to get off in Chicago and fly to LA. It's personal business, Max. It just came up.'

Tom put down his drink. *I bet it did, in the form of me.*

Max didn't look pleased at Eleanor's change of plan, but then he eyed Steve and Julie. 'You say they're getting married on the Chief?'

Tom explained the situation with their respective families.

'That poor girl,' said Eleanor with genuine sympathy. 'That's not how weddings are supposed to be.'

With all the discussions of weddings Tom took a quick peek at Eleanor's hand. There was no wedding band, or engagement ring. It was hard to believe she hadn't found someone else.

'So what's the angle of your screenplay?' he asked Eleanor. Tom knew nothing about movie-making, but he now attempted to take on the air of a seasoned celluloid impresario.

'Depends on what we see on board. Max wants a romantic comedy. I'm leaning towards a mystery with a high body count.'

'Why not both? Done properly, there's nothing funnier than a pile of stiffs on rails.'

Max pointed at Tom and looked at Eleanor. 'See? I love this guy. He goes outside the box. You ever think about writing for movies, Tom?'

Tom's gaze went to Eleanor. 'Not until about two hours ago.'

'It's not as easy as it looks,' she said.

'Hell, what is?' he shot back.

Max excused himself and walked over to Steve and Julie, followed by Kristobal. Max started talking animatedly to them, but Tom couldn't hear any of it. It must have been exciting, however, because Steve and Julie looked stunned at whatever the director was saying.

'Max plotting something?'

'He usually is,' replied Eleanor.

'I never would have figured you'd end up in LA.'

'We all have to end up somewhere.' She glanced up. 'Look at you. From Beirut to Duncan Phyfe?'

'Covering wars is a young man's game. I'm not that young any more,' Tom said. 'Besides, how many ways can you write about people wiping each other out? I ran out of adjectives five years ago.'

'Did you ever end up changing the world?' Though the statement itself appeared sarcastic, the way she asked it was not.

'Look around,' he said, 'and there's your answer.'

'You lasted longer than most.' *Longer than you*, thought Tom. She paused before asking, 'How are your parents?'

'I've lost them both. My mom just recently.'

'I'm sorry, Tom. They were good people.'

He thought about telling Eleanor why he was on the train but finally chose not to. The intimacy just wasn't there any more.

They watched as Max and Kristobal rushed off, leaving the stunned couple beached in their wake.

'Where should we start?' asked Eleanor finally.

Tom pointed at Julie and Steve. 'That looks like a good place.'

After Tom had introduced Eleanor, Steve and Julie took turns explaining, in awed tones, what Max Powers had proposed.

'He's going to cater the whole event, with decorations, and even have some sort of music too,' said Julie.

'And he's paying for everything,' added a relieved-sounding Steve. 'He said he'd work it out with Amtrak.'

'Is he really the famous movie director?' asked Julie.

'He is,' answered Eleanor. 'And his heart is almost as big as his ego,' she added.

'I feel like we just won the lottery,' said Steve, as he gripped his bride-to-be's hand.

'Where in Virginia are you from?' Eleanor asked Julie.

'You probably never heard of it, Dickenson County.'

'My dad went to Clintwood High. Two of my aunts live in Grundy, Virginia.'

'Oh my gosh!' said Julie. 'I've never met anybody who even knew where it was.'

'I grew up on a little farm in eastern Kentucky that would make Clintwood seem like a metropolis.' Eleanor looked at them both. 'I think it's very brave what you're doing.'

'We don't feel very brave,' said Steve, laughing nervously.

'If you really love each other, you'd be surprised what you can accomplish.'

Julie gripped Eleanor's hand. 'You came from where I did, and look how you turned out. It drives me crazy that his parents can't see that it doesn't matter where you're from, it's where you're going.'

Eleanor said, 'You're not marrying Steve's parents. And it may be that they think no one is good enough for their son. But give them time, and you may see them come round. If they don't it's their loss.'

At that moment Father Kelly walked in and asked if they would like to join him in the lounge downstairs, where a high-stakes poker game was taking place. They adjourned from further talk of nuptials and repaired to the adult section of the bar car.

TOM HAD WALKED into many poker war zones in his life; such places were usually inhabited by cagey, stone-faced, underpaid journalists looking to supplement their income. On the surface, the group in the lounge car looked fairly innocent, but these were the types one had to watch out for, he knew.

Since the 'chips' being used in the game were actually potato chips, they bought several bags, and on a dare from Tom, Eleanor even purchased one of Tyrone's Boiler Room concoctions. She downed it in one swig and sat down to play some cards.

'That just ain't human. You telling me you know that lady?' Tyrone whispered.

'I'm not sure,' Tom replied.

They raced through poker, blackjack and gin rummy, and finished with about as many potato chips as they'd started with, plus lots of material for both Tom's story and Eleanor's movie. There was one gent with six fingers who won far more than he lost—Tom was guessing it had something to do with that extra digit, though he couldn't prove it—and there was also an obnoxious type who belittled his neighbours' card-playing errors. Eleanor leaned over and whispered into Tom's ear, 'That guy gets butchered in the film's first act.'

As they rose to leave, Tom pulled out his Havanas and pointed at Father Kelly, who had proved himself a nimble card-player. 'The smoking lounge beckons, Father.'

Eleanor followed them, though Tom knew she didn't smoke, at least she hadn't when he'd known her. He glanced at her with a questioning expression.

She shrugged. 'Max is the boss. In for a dime, in for a dollar.'

Most of the seats in the lounge were taken, but they found three near the back. Father Kelly and Tom coaxed their cigars to life while Eleanor sat back and closed her eyes.

'Tired?' Tom asked between puffs. 'You must still be on West Coast time.'

'Actually, I spent a week in DC before we started.'

'What's in Washington?'

She never opened her eyes. 'Somebody.'

Tom lowered his Havana and let his gaze wander. *Somebody*. Eleanor had somebody. Well, why shouldn't she have somebody? She was still young and smart and beautiful. And he had somebody, sort of.

Tom's pursuit of Eleanor had commenced the moment he saw her on campus. As she'd walked by it seemed everything slowed, and that it was just the two of them in the whole world. It wasn't just her beauty, it was how she carried herself, how she spoke, how she looked you in the eye and really listened to what you had to say. Yet it was more than that even. As Agnes Joe had said, Tom didn't care if he ate, slept, or even breathed so long as Eleanor was around. Her temper exerted its own attraction. Her opinions were uniquely her own, and she would fire them off with deadly accuracy. Almost always an eruption was followed by the gentle touch of her hand and her lips against his, for at last he'd won her heart over several rivals.

Tom's musings were interrupted by a man appearing at the doorway. He was six foot four, and slender, about twenty-five or so, and appraised them all with a very smug look. He had chic stubble and faded jeans, yet his silk shirt was an expensive designer production. A fake slob, Tom deduced.

Under one arm the man was carrying a chessboard and box of chess pieces. Tom watched as he methodically set up shop and, over the next hour, vanquished all comers. The guy was good, really good. The average match time was only ten minutes. With each defeat, as his foe stalked off in disgrace, he'd laugh and then call out in a loud, condescending voice, 'Next victim!' If Tom had had any chance of beating the guy, he'd have gone for it, but even checkers taxed him too much.

After a while Father Kelly left. Tom didn't expect to see him back because the priest had imbibed quite a bit. 'If I had to conduct Mass right now, I'm not sure I could. I'm not even sure I could tell you how many components there are to the Holy Trinity.'

Tom bade him good night and then watched as Eleanor rose and challenged the chess king, whose name, they'd learned, was Slade. All eyes turned towards her as she sat down across from the hated one and made the first move. Tom hadn't even known that Eleanor played chess, and then it came back to him. When they'd lived in Israel, they'd become friends with a rabbi who was an exceptional chess player. He'd taught Eleanor a strategy that was almost foolproof.

Three moves later, Tom saw just the tiniest hint of a smile from Eleanor and he found himself smiling conspiratorially in return. Four moves after that the mighty Slade was staring in disbelief. Eleanor had his king in check with nowhere to flee. The smokers gave her a standing ovation. Spurred on by drink and emotion, Tom clapped until his hands were red. Slade grabbed his chessboard and pieces and stalked out, muttering something about beginner's luck. If Eleanor hadn't had *somebody* in Washington, Tom probably would have kissed her.

CHAPTER SIX

The figure who entered Tom's sleeper was dressed in black and intent on plucking an expensive-looking pen; then Father Kelly's silver cross was swiped. After that the thief flitted to the other first-class sleeper suites, pinching Max's gold-plated money clip, Eleanor's silver brush, and Kristobal's designer sunglasses. The last target was Gordon Merryweather's suite, where the thief stole the lawyer's watch, cash and Palm Pilot. The crimes took all of ten minutes and, by the time Regina walked down the corridor, the thief was gone.

TOM AND ELEANOR stood outside the smoking car talking.

'You nailed that guy. The look on his face was beautiful.' He gave her a hug that she only partially returned. 'Thank God for a chess-playing rabbi in Tel Aviv. What was his name?'

'I don't remember,' she said quietly.

He looked at her and all his fine spirits melted away. *Rabbi Somebody, Tel Aviv, the scene of the final meeting—final bloody battle was more like it.*

He shouldn't do it, he knew he shouldn't do it, but he was going to anyway; he asked, 'Can you tell me now, since you've had all these years to think about it, why you walked out on me?'

'You're saying you don't know why?'

'How could I? Not one thing you said made any sense.'

'Because you weren't listening, as usual.'

'That's a crock and you know it.'

'I don't have to stand here and listen to you raving.'

'You're right. Sit down on the floor and I'll keep going. I've had years to prepare. In fact, I can keep raving until the good old Southwest Chief runs into the Pacific Ocean three days from now!'

'I knew this would happen—as soon as I saw you. You haven't changed a bit.'

'Why did you walk out on me?'

She shook her head wearily. 'Tom, if you don't understand why by now, there's nothing I can say that would clear it up for you.'

He stared at her. 'I'm sorry, I'm sort of rusty on female-encrypted speech. Can you help me out here? What the hell did you just say?'

'Even after all these years you still haven't accomplished it.'

'Accomplished what?'

'Growing up!' she snapped.

Before he could answer, they heard singing. The next minute a group of Christmas carollers, composed of both train crew and passengers, gathered around them, Tyrone leading the pack in a hearty rendition of 'I'll Be Home for Christmas'.

'You two want to join in?' asked Tyrone. 'A lady who can slam back a Boiler Room like that is a lady I need to get to know.'

Eleanor stalked off, arms folded across her chest.

Tyrone looked at Tom. 'Hey, man, was it something I said?'

'No, Tyrone, it was something *I* said.' And Tom walked off too.

On the way back to his compartment he heard laughter drifting up from the lower level of his sleeper car. Laughs—he could use some right now. He hurried down the stairs and headed right, to the less expensive sleeping accommodation. At the end of the corridor, he saw Regina and the tarot card lady talking outside a compartment.

Regina waved him over.

The tarot card lady still wore her multicoloured headdress, but was now in slippers. She turned out to be rather petite, with intensely luminous blue eyes filled with mischief and charm. He thought he smelt incense coming from her compartment across the corridor.

'I'm assuming those are your digs,' he said to her.

'Why, Mr Langdon, you have psychic powers of your own,' she said with a throaty laugh.

'How did you—' He stopped and looked at Regina. 'OK, no aliens need apply. You told her.'

Regina said, 'Meet Drusella Pardoe, Tom, and you don't have to tell Drusella anything, she already knows it.'

Drusella put out a dainty hand. 'My good friends call me Misty. And I already know that we're going to be good friends, so you just go ahead and call me that.' Misty had a Southern accent augmented by something a little spicier.

'New Orleans?' he said.

'By way of Baltimore. Very good, Tom.'

'I hear you're working with those film people, Tom,' said Regina.

'Is that really Max Powers?' asked Misty. 'I love his pictures.'

'That woman with them,' said Regina, 'on the passenger list it said Eleanor Carter, but I think she's really a movie star or something, travelling, you know, incognito. That lady has class. And she's drop-dead gorgeous. Is she a movie star, Tom?'

'Actually, I know her, and she's a writer, not an actress. Although

I wouldn't disagree with you about the drop-dead-gorgeous part. We did some reporting together years ago.'

'I heard it was a little more than that,' said Misty.

Tom stared at her. 'What do you know about it?'

'Word travels faster on a train than anywhere else except maybe church. People overhear things.'

'I have to go now, ladies,' he said.

'Me too,' said Regina.

As they walked off, Misty called out, 'Oh, Tom?'

He turned back, and she fanned out her tarot cards. 'I just have this little premonition that we are connected somehow.'

'Misty, he has a girlfriend in LA he's going to visit for Christmas,' said Regina. 'She does the voice for Cuppy the Magic Beaver on TV.'

Tom stared at her, stunned. 'How do you know *that*?'

'Agnes Joe told me.'

Tom looked at the women, exasperated. 'With you two, what do we need the CIA for?'

'Now, Tom,' drawled Misty, 'a grown man needs a grown woman. Cartoons can't keep you warm at night, sweetie.'

'That Misty is a piece of work,' Tom said to Regina after they had climbed the stairs.

Regina smiled. 'Oh, she's just Southern friendly, is all.'

'I take it she rides the trains a lot.'

'Oh yeah. She tells people their fortune, reads their palms, does the card thing, all for free. She has a little shop in the French Quarter just off Jackson Square. I've been there; it's cool.'

'You really seem to get to know your passengers.'

'They mean a lot to me. Actually—'

'You little thief!'

They looked up, and there was Gordon Merryweather stomping towards them. 'I've been robbed, and I'm betting you did it. In fact, you're the only one who could have done it. I'll have your job, and you'll be spending Christmas in prison,' he roared.

'Hold on,' said Regina, 'I don't appreciate your tone, or your accusation. If you're missing something, I'll file a report.'

'Don't read me the little speech,' snapped Merryweather. 'I want my things back and I want them back right now.'

'Well, since I don't know what those things are, or who took them, that would be a little difficult, sir.'

Tom stepped between them. 'Look, Gord, I'm not a big-time lawyer like you, but I do know that unless you have direct evidence of who took your stuff, then you're slandering this woman in front of a witness, and that can be a costly thing.'

Merryweather eyed him. 'What do you know about slander?'

'Name's Tom Langdon. I'm an investigative reporter. Won a Pulitzer, in fact. I wrote one story about an American lawyer in Russia who was doing some really bad things. He's currently writing his own appellate briefs in prison. And if I've found one thing that's even mightier than legal papers filed in court, it's a story in the newspaper that the whole world can dig their teeth into.'

Merryweather snapped at Regina: 'My Palm Pilot, two hundred in cash, and my Tag Heuer watch. I want them back before I get off this train in Chicago, or heads will roll.' He stalked off.

'My mother taught me to love everybody, but she never met Gordon Merryweather,' muttered Regina.

ELEANOR WENT to her compartment, closed and locked the door. She sat down on the bed, which Regina had made up, flicked the light off and sat there in the dark, watching the snow coming down even harder. It didn't bother the Cap much; the train seemed to be going at full tilt. Her fingers moved across the cold glass, marking intricate symbols on the smooth surface.

In her mind's eye she was transported to Tel Aviv. Over Christmas she'd been so happy, and yet so miserable there, that the schizophrenic quality of her existence had come close to driving her insane. And maybe it had on that Christmas morning when her future with a man she loved had disappeared. She still remembered looking back at him as she was heading up the escalator at the airport, and how he'd turned away and left her. At that memory, the tears started to spill, and the tight control with which she'd come to lead her life eroded. She'd thought him incapable of doing this to her ever again, and yet he had, with no more than a look and a word or two. She was helpless.

There was a knock on her door and she tensed, holding her breath. She wasn't ready to see him again, not right now, possibly not ever.

'Eleanor? You're not sleeping, are you?'

She let the breath out in relief. It was Max, not Tom.

'Just a minute.'

She put on the lights, wiped her face with a wet towel, ran her fingers through her hair and opened the door.

Max quickly stepped in and closed the door behind him. 'You OK? You don't look very good.'

'Probably just tired.'

'Well, it's all set up, the wedding stuff. I talked with the Amtrak folks, they had no problem with it.'

'That's wonderful,' Eleanor said quietly.

'So how's it going with Tom? You guys getting some good stuff?'

'Great material. I'll be putting some notes together soon.'

He looked at her tenderly. 'You want to tell me about this Langdon fellow? If you ask me, it seems you two were a lot more than reporting colleagues.'

'Do you remember when we first started working together, you asked me what made me want to write, what drove me?'

'Sure I remember. I ask all my writers that.'

'Well, Tom Langdon is the answer to that question. I loved him, Max. Loved him with everything I had to give. When it ended there was this void, this hole in me as large as a dead star. The only outlet I had was the written word.'

'Lucky for me, not so good for you,' Max said quietly. 'So you loved him, he clearly still cares for you, what happened?'

She stood up and paced in the small area. 'Two people can care for each other but not want the same things. Then it doesn't work, no matter how much they love each other.'

'So what does Tom want?'

'I'm not sure he even knows. I know what he doesn't want: to be tied down anywhere, or by anyone.'

'And do you know what you want?'

'Who knows, Max? Who really knows what they want?'

'Well, I'm not the best person to ask—my interests keep changing. But I guess that's part of life. Maybe to be happy, maybe that's what we're all looking for.'

'Many people never find it, and maybe I'm one of them.'

'Eleanor, you're a smart, talented, successful, beautiful woman in the prime of your life.'

'And maybe that woman doesn't need a man in her life to be complete,' she said.

'I'm not saying everybody has to be married to be happy. But don't assume you *don't* need someone in your life to be happy either.'

MAX LEFT AND WENT to Kristobal's compartment, where he observed his assistant tearing his room apart.

'What are you doing?' asked Max.

'Looking for my sunglasses.'

'Sunglasses! Look out of the window, it's night-time.'
'I mean they're missing.'
'So buy another pair.'
'These cost four hundred dollars.'
'Uh-huh. Look, the wedding is a go.'
'Terrific, sir. You're a genius.'
'So you keep telling me. Now I don't want any screw-ups.'
'When have I ever let you down, Mr Powers?'
'I know, but see, nobody's that good, and I just don't want the first time you do fail to be this time. OK?'
'I understand, sir.'
'You're a good kid, but when we get to LA I'm cutting your pay.'
'Why, sir?' asked an astonished Kristobal.
'Because even I don't spend four hundred bucks on sunglasses.'

TOM HAD FALLEN ASLEEP for a while but was now wide awake. He got up and took out his notebook, but couldn't find his pen. Eleanor had given it to him when they'd first gone overseas together. He searched everywhere, finally gave up and, hearing music, stepped into the corridor. The song was coming from Agnes Joe's compartment. He moved to the threshold and cautiously peeked in. Agnes Joe was sitting down, fully dressed, and on the fold-down table next to her was an old phonograph. He recognised the song. It was 'Silent Night'.

Agnes Joe looked up, saw him, and seemed a little embarrassed at being discovered. 'I hope the music isn't disturbing you.'

'Hey, what better than Christmas carols during Christmas week?'

'I bring this little phonograph with me everywhere I go. It belonged to my mother. Come on in and listen.'

He sat down on the couch and she eyed him keenly. 'Regina told me how you helped her out with the nasty lawyer. You did a good deed tonight, Tom. Played guardian angel.'

'Well, they say there are more guardian angels during the Christmas season than at any other time.'

'I've never heard that. Did you just make that up?'

'Actually, I did, I think.'

They sat and listened to several more uplifting carols. The compartment smelt of lilac soap and was very neat. Tom noted a very full duffle bag wedged in between the chair and the wall, with a blanket partially covering it. When he looked up, Agnes Joe was staring at him, a look of sadness on her face. Just then a family of four—mom, dad and two children—passed down the corridor, laughing.

'Trains are nice over Christmas. It's really a great way for families to travel together,' said Agnes Joe.

'So how come you're not spending Christmas with your family?'

'A girl has to be asked to the party, doesn't she?'

'So you and your daughter don't get along?'

'I get along fine with her. She seems to have a problem with me.'

'I'm sorry, Agnes Joe. I really am.'

'I've got lots of friends on the train though. I say that your family is where you find it. You just have to look. Like you.'

'What do you mean, like me?'

'That film lady, Eleanor. She's the Eleanor from your past, isn't she? The one love of your life?'

'We're not even friends now.'

'But you could be. And a lot more.'

He shook his head. 'No. Too late.'

'You're wrong there. I've seen enough in this world to know that two people who can make each other that miserable must love each other a lot.'

Tom didn't intend to waste his time on something that clearly would never happen. He'd lost Ellie once and it had devastated him; he was never going to chance being that hurt again. He thanked her for the musical interlude and went back to his compartment.

Father Kelly popped his head in. 'You haven't seen a silver cross lying around, have you? I can't seem to find it.'

'That's strange. I'm missing a pen.'

The priest shrugged and walked off as Tom's cellphone rang. He checked his watch and saw it was after midnight. He clicked the phone's answer button. 'Hello?'

It was Lelia calling from LA. 'I've been tracking you on the Internet. According to the schedule you're in Pittsburgh. Right?'

Tom looked out of the window. The train was slowing and he saw a station sign: Connellsville, PA. They were far from Pittsburgh. They must have stopped again while he'd been asleep. 'Yep, you can see the stadium from here,' he said. 'Do you realise it's after midnight my time?'

'You can't possibly be sleeping on the train—isn't it far too noisy and bumpy?'

'Actually it's a very nice ride, and I *was* sleeping,' he lied.

'You can set up right over there, Erik,' Lelia said to someone.

'Erik, who's Erik?' asked Tom.

'He's my FBTT.'

'FBTT? Sounds like a disease.'

'Full-body therapeutic technician. It's all the rage out here. Erik is going to do my lower back, hamstrings, and give me a pedicure.'

'Lower back and hamstrings. Anything in between those points?'

'What?'

'Are you clothed during this process?'

'Don't be silly. I have a towel on.'

'Oh, gee, that's a relief. Look, why do you need this guy to come to your house to do all this? I thought you belonged to that fancy spa.'

'My back was hurting, and my toenails really needed some emergency work: I'm wearing open-toed high heels tomorrow.'

'Yeah, I guess that does qualify as a crisis. How do you know this Erik?'

'He's my kickboxing instructor. He's an FBTT on the side.'

When Tom had gone to one of her kickboxing sessions in LA he had found it inhabited mostly by accountants, lawyers, actors and chefs who paraded around in designer spandex, flailing at rubber bad guys with their feet and fists. Two or three modestly rowdy kindergarteners could have vanquished the whole lot of them.

'The six-foot-four blue-eyed Adonis guy from Sweden, that's Erik? That guy is in your house right now while you're in a tiny towel?'

'Jealousy: I like that, it's healthy for a relationship. And Erik is Norwegian.'

'Fine, could you put Norway Erik on, please? I'd like to make an appointment with him for when I'm out there. I think my back is going to need some work after this train ride.'

'You have to promise you won't be mean. I know how you can get sometimes. Promise?'

'Absolutely. Hey, my back is hurting and I like a little FBTT as much as the next person.' He heard her passing the phone over with some words of explanation.

'*Ja*, this is Erik, may I help you?'

'Erik? Tom Langdon. Before I make an appointment I was just wondering if you have an infectious disease disclosure policy.'

'Excuse me? This thing I do not know.'

'It's all the rage everywhere, except possibly where you are. Let me explain it in simple terms. Since you work with people's bodies and you come in contact with human skin, you run the risk of being infected with some serious contagious diseases, which you could then potentially pass on to other clients, like me. So I wanted to know what safety precautions you take. For example, I'm sure Lelia has informed you about her hepatitis Z condition and the serious risks associated with it.'

'Hepatitis!'

'Although there are, of course, no cures, the new drug therapies work wonders, and the side effects are fairly limited: nausea, loss of hair, impotency, that sort of thing. In fact, death only occurs about half the time, if it's caught early enough.'

Tom heard the phone drop and then feet running away on Lelia's highly polished hardwood floors. Then he listened as she frantically called out, 'Erik, Erik, come back!'

After a door had slammed, Tom heard the phone being picked up.

'What exactly did you say to him? And I mean *exactly*! I distinctly heard him say hepatitis!'

'Hepatitis? Lelia, I said *gingivitis*. I asked him if he had gingivitis, because my old masseuse did, and I have to tell you, it was really not enjoyable, breathing really bad breath for an hour. I guess Erik's English isn't that good.'

'I don't believe you, Tom Langdon. Do you realise what you've done? My back is killing me, and what about my toenails?'

'Perhaps Tylenol and an emery board?'

'This is not funny,' she yelled.

'Look, I'll call you when we get into Pittsburgh.'

'What? I thought you *were* in Pittsburgh.'

Tom slapped his forehead at this gaffe. Under enormous pressure, he struck on what seemed a brilliant plan. 'Uh, Lelia?' He tapped the phone. 'Lelia, you're breaking up. I can't hear you.'

'Tom, don't you dare try to pull that—'

He spoke loudly as though to a hearing-impaired idiot: 'IF . . . YOU . . . CAN . . . HEAR . . . ME . . . I'LL . . . CALL . . . YOU . . . WHEN . . . WE . . . GET . . . INTO . . . CHICAGO.' He clicked the off button and sat back. The phone rang again, but he didn't answer it. It went to voicemail and then he turned it off.

The train slowed and as he squinted into the darkness, he could make out the tombstones of a small cemetery.

Unnerved by the proximity of so many lost souls, Tom rose and went strolling once more. He had never done so much walking as he had since setting foot on this train.

MOST COMPARTMENTS were dark at this late hour, and he saw no one in the corridors. In the lounge area the lights had been turned down, and it was empty as far as he could tell. The train started up again and he balanced himself against one of the seat backs. He recoiled when his hand touched skin.

Eleanor looked up at him, as startled as he. She was holding a cup of coffee. 'God,' she said, 'I didn't even hear you come in.'

He eyed the coffee. 'Still have insomnia too?' They'd both suffered from it, perhaps because of too many time zones and too many horrors that came back to torture them in their sleep.

She rubbed her temples. 'Funny, I thought I was over it. It seems to have come back recently.'

'OK, I get the hint. I can find another place to mull my truly limitless future.'

'No, I can leave,' she said.

'Look,' said Tom, 'we're both adults. I think we can coexist on something as big as a train, at least for a little while.'

'That's actually very mature of you.'

'I have my moments.'

They were both silent as the Cap picked up speed again, beating the tracks at nearly eighty miles an hour.

'I've been wondering why you're really on this train,' Eleanor said. 'You were always into getting there the fastest way possible.'

'I told you, I'm doing a story about a train trip, which is a little difficult to accomplish unless you actually ride one.'

'Is that all?'

'Why shouldn't it be?'

'Because I know you too well, I suppose. You don't have to tell me.'

He told her anyway about his father's wish and what he was doing about it. Then he added, 'OK, now, being the suspicious, paranoid, conspiracy-theorist investigative-reporter type, I have to tell you, your being on this train seems like one heck of a coincidence.'

'We were supposed to be taking the Capitol Limited yesterday.' She looked at her watch. 'Well, since it's already tomorrow, I mean the day before yesterday. But then apparently Max's plans changed, he got into DC a day later and we had to take the train you were on. Trust me, if I'd known you'd be on this train, I wouldn't have been.'

'So it was really that bad, huh?'

'Look, we didn't work out, it happens to millions of people. Some folks just aren't the marrying kind.'

'I was married once.'

Eleanor was clearly stunned by this. 'What?'

'Well, it was over so fast—the marriage, I mean—that I barely remember it.'

Eleanor rose, her fury barely contained. 'Well, I'm glad you loved a woman enough to actually ask her, however long it lasted.'

'Ellie, it wasn't like that, it was the worst decision of my life—'

She turned and walked out. He watched her leave as the Cap came to a stop, and said quietly, to himself, *Actually it was the second-worst decision of my life.* Then he said out loud, 'What the hell is going on? I could've walked to Chicago faster.'

'What is going on,' said a voice from the corner, 'is that a freight train is on the tracks up ahead blocking the Cap's way.'

In the darkness, a figure rose and seemed to float towards him. Tom thought he was about to encounter the Ghost of Christmas Past.

But when the fellow came into the small wash of ambient light from the window, Tom let out his breath. He was tall and lean, salt-and-pepper haired, about sixty or so, with handsome, chiselled features. He was dressed in a white button-down shirt, tie and dress slacks. He was also wearing what looked to be a conductor's cap.

'Do you work on the train?' asked Tom.

'No,' he said, taking off his cap and shaking Tom's hand. 'Although I used to. Retired now. Name's Herrick Higgins.'

Tom introduced himself and they sat down.

'How long were you with Amtrak?'

'Sometimes it seems like my whole life. I was actually around when it started up in '71. Been a railroad man since I took my first breath, just like my father was. He worked the UP, the Union Pacific.'

Higgins looked out of the window. 'This route is laid over what used to be a turnpike. George Washington owned stock in the turnpike company. I often wonder what he would say, seeing the old Cap running up and down that same path. But maybe not for much longer. Future doesn't look too good for long-distance passenger trains. Government's talking about busting Amtrak up, privatising, spinning off the Northeast Corridor.'

'Well, America is such a large country, train travel just doesn't make a lot of sense.'

'Oh, sure, if you're into the destination only as opposed to the trip itself. It's been my experience that for most folk who ride trains it's the journey itself and the people they meet along the way that matter. You see, at every stop, a little bit of America, a little bit of *your* country, gets on and says hello. That's why trains are so popular at Christmas. People get on for some friendship. How do you put a dollar value on that?' Higgins rubbed his chin and looked at the floor. 'I'm not saying that riding the train will change your life, or that passenger rail will be a big moneymaker one day. But no matter how fast we feel we have to go, shouldn't there be room for a train, where you can just sit back and be human for a little while? Just for a little while? Is that so bad?'

As Tom LEFT Herrick Higgins and walked slowly back to the sleeper cars, the Cap started up again. Over the sounds of the rolling train he heard something else, something that made him race down the corridor and clamber down the stairs.

Sitting against one of the bulkheads with Eleanor's arms around her was Julie, sobbing.

'What's going on?' asked Tom.

In a voice often halted by sobs, Julie explained that Steve's parents had called. They'd found out what the couple were planning and had threatened to disown and disinherit Steve if he married Julie. Steve, apparently, hadn't been very decisive in telling them he was going ahead with it. In fact, he'd started to waffle so much that Julie and he had had a serious argument and she'd fled.

'Where is he?' asked Tom.

She told him that Steve was back at his compartment.

'I'm going to see him.'

Tom stalked off and soon found young Steve staring forlornly out of the window. For the next ten minutes, he read the younger man the riot act, and voices and tempers flared on both sides, until Tom finally asked, 'Do you love her? Do you? It's really that simple.'

'Yes,' Steve said without hesitation.

'Then you take her without reservation or disclaimer. You take her without qualification, with no strings attached by anyone else, because that's what loving someone means. If you let that woman out of your life, you're a fool. She may be the one woman in the entire world who will make you happy. If you blow it, there's no going back, Steve, trust me.'

'I love her, Tom, I really love her.'

'Then that's all you need, that's *all* you need.'

Steve looked past him. Tom turned, and there were Eleanor and a red-faced Julie. They'd apparently heard pretty much everything. Julie flew to Steve's embrace.

Tom stepped out and closed the privacy curtain. As he and Eleanor walked away, she said, 'That was a good thing you did. I'm impressed.'

'Why sit around and watch someone mess up his life?'

At that moment a depressed-looking Kristobal came by.

'God, Eleanor, I've been looking everywhere for you. Max is going to cut my salary. Can you talk to him?'

'Why is he cutting your salary?'

'Oh, because of a little misunderstanding about a pair of sunglasses I lost.'

Tom looked over at Kristobal. 'And my pen is missing, and so is Father Kelly's cross.'

'My silver brush has disappeared too,' said Eleanor.

'And Mr Powers said his gold-plated money clip is gone,' added Kristobal.

'That creep, Merryweather, is missing some stuff too,' said Tom. 'I think we have a thief on board. I'll tell Regina and she can file a report with the Amtrak police when we get into Chicago.'

THE CAP FINALLY ARRIVED in Chicago at eleven thirty the next morning. Tom came down with his bags, thanked Regina, and gave her a generous tip.

'I believe I should be paying you,' she said, and they shared a hug. 'I'll introduce you to my mom in the station lounge later.'

'I'm looking forward to meeting her.'

Tom saw Herrick Higgins getting off further down and pointed him out to Regina. 'He's a really interesting guy. Too bad he had to retire. He really loves trains.'

Regina said, 'Herrick didn't retire, he was laid off. Budget cuts, him and two hundred other managers. It's a shame. That man knows more about trains than anybody. He rides the train at his own expense. If we have room, we let him bunk in the dormitory car with us. It's sad, real sad.'

Tom saw Max and Kristobal up ahead, and he joined them.

'Where's Eleanor?' he asked.

'Already inside.' Max looked upset. 'I think she's trying to get a flight to L.A. I'm not happy about that. Can't you talk to her, Tom?'

Tom laughed. 'If you *really* want her to take a plane, I'll talk to her, sure. Otherwise I think I should just stay out of it.'

With the snow coming down ever harder, they headed toward the warmth of bustling Union Station. Ahead lay a journey of almost twenty-three hundred more miles—almost three times the distance they'd just ridden—together with twenty-six train stops. Curiously, though, Tom felt ready for anything.

As it would turn out, he'd need to be.

They headed to the Metropolitan Lounge, found an empty area, and spread out. Tom sat comatose while Kristobal made numerous phone calls, and Max met up with Steve and Julie and various other people to go over arrangements for the wedding.

Amtrak police came, led by Regina, and they all filed their theft reports. They were told that a search for the thief or thieves was ongoing, and that it was likely that more than one person was involved because of the number of items taken. In all probability, the gang had got off the train before Chicago. Tom held out little hope that he'd ever see his pen—or Eleanor—again.

He was therefore very surprised to see her walk into the lounge with Kristobal about an hour later. She slumped next to Max.

'When's your flight leave?' he asked.

'It doesn't. Everything's booked solid. Ironically, the fastest way to LA right now is by train.'

Max sat back and winked at Tom. 'Sorry to hear that. Guess you'll just have to slum it with us rail bums.'

Regina returned a few minutes later with a woman who had to be her mother, although the two didn't look at all alike, except in the eyes. If it was possible, the woman made Agnes Joe look petite.

'This is my mother, Roxanne,' said Regina, before Roxanne took over the show in a booming voice.

'I understand you babies are cold, tired, depressed and ROBBED! Umm-umm. We can't have that. The good Lord won't hold sway for long over that sorry state of affairs.' A few minutes later, blankets, pillows, snacks and other items appeared. It was much appreciated by them all; even Eleanor appeared to be in better spirits.

Roxanne settled down in their midst and looked at her daughter. 'Now, Regina, don't you have a train to look after? You think the little old Cap is gonna take care of itself without your sweet touch?'

'I'm going, I'm going,' Regina said, smiling.

Roxanne turned back to them. 'Regina tells me we got us a couple getting hitched, and that old fortune-telling lady named Misty riding with us. Hey, thought you'd be on the New Orleans train headed home, baby.'

They all turned to see who she was talking to, and there was Misty in full prognosticator regalia, her arms lifted to the ceiling.

'I just had a premonition that my destiny this holiday season lay west instead of south, isn't that right, sweetie?' She batted her eyelashes at Max.

The obviously smitten director smiled and said, 'I've never had my fortune told so well nor so energetically as last night.'

'How you doing, Misty?' said Roxanne. 'Hey, you know that fortune you told me last time, girl?'

'The number 153 special, about the huge following of young males you'd encounter in your life?'

'That very one. Well, honey, it came true. Although, to tell you the truth, sweetie, I was hoping for something a little closer to my own age.' She pointed to a stream of young African-American boys in uniform pouring into the lounge. 'That's the LA Boys' Center Choir. They performed at Carnegie Hall and now they're heading home for Christmas, and it's up to yours truly to make sure they get there intact. Y'all excuse me for a bit.'

They all watched as Roxanne went over to the group of youngsters and tried to get their attention. They looked tired, bored and ready to do anything except listen to yet another adult.

An enormous bellow poured forth from Roxanne. The young men instantly formed two tight columns, their eyes wide and full of fear. Roxanne marched them over to one corner of the room and talked to them in a low voice.

A minute later she turned to the crowd in the lounge and asked, 'You folks want to hear some singing while you wait for your train?'

They all said that they would love to.

Roxanne turned to her young consignees, did some vocal warm-ups, and then led them in a series of Christmas classics.

Max said, 'They're terrific.'

Misty sat down beside him. 'She leads the choir at one of the biggest Baptist churches in Chicago, and she's also a lay minister there. Roxanne Jordan can sing gospel and the blues like no one I've ever heard, and I live in New Orleans! And any passenger who's ridden on a train with her comes out of it a better person.'

As the singing wound down, Roxanne led the choir out in a conga line, singing and making train noises while the audience applauded loudly. Amtrak management, who'd come from their offices to watch, just smiled, and clapped along with everyone else.

Everyone except Steve and Julie, who looked as if they were in a state of panic. The minister had arrived but the best man and maid of honour, married friends of theirs from college, had just called. They'd been in a traffic accident on a snowy road in Michigan. The best man had a broken leg and was lying in a hospital bed, and his wife, of course, wasn't going to leave him.

'I knew this was not going to work,' moaned Julie. She shook her head, then stopped and stared at Eleanor. 'Would you be my maid of honour? Please? I know I can count on you.'

Eleanor was taken aback, but then agreed, for what else could she do? Then Steve looked at Tom and said, 'Well, if it weren't for what you said to me on the train maybe there wouldn't be a wedding at all. How about being my best man?'

Tom looked at Eleanor and finally agreed as well. At that, Eleanor rose and walked away.

THE SOUTHWEST CHIEF was a very long train with many Superliner cars and a shining snowplough on its front engine. Tom found, to his surprise, that his deluxe accommodation had shrunk to an economy sleeper through some error that couldn't be corrected because the train was full. He'd not only have to use the communal shower but also the communal toilet for the next 2,000-odd miles. This would never have happened to Cary Grant and Eva Marie Saint.

His sleeping-car attendant, Barry, came by. He was in his late thirties, with an impressive physique. He was polite and professional, but after Regina and Roxanne, Barry seemed sort of a letdown.

Tom decided to call Lelia. There was no answer, for which he was very grateful. He left a message, saying he was sorry about Erik and the misunderstanding about the gingivitis, and then hung up.

To get his mind off his troubles he started thinking about the thefts. Pretty much all the first-class compartments had been hit, with one exception: Agnes Joe's. She hadn't come forward when the police had taken their report, so presumably the thief had skipped her. But why—unless Agnes Joe was the thief? Pretty stupid, though, to steal from everyone except yourself. Or perhaps not stupid but brilliant? Because most people would come to the conclusion he just did. And he'd seen the duffle bag in her room that was stuffed to the gills . . .

As he was thinking this, the Chief pulled away from the station. He looked at his watch: 3.15pm, right on time.

Just then Kristobal came by with a camcorder. 'Mr Powers asked me to take some shots of the train and people and such. He said we can look at it later, and maybe it'll give us some story angles. Oh, Eleanor asked me to ask you what you were wearing to the wedding.'

'Asked you to ask me? OK, great, tell her I'm wearing Armani. I always wear Armani to train weddings. She knows that.'

Kristobal brightened. 'Cool. I'm wearing Armani too.' He swung his camera around and walked off.

The Chief roared along in a leisurely southwest direction, making four quick stops in Illinois before passing over the mighty Mississippi. They were now in Iowa. The only stop in that state was at Fort Madison, which they made at about half past seven. As they headed on towards Missouri, Tom made his way to the dining car, where he shared a meal with Father Kelly, Misty, Steve and Julie.

Tom glanced at Misty. 'You and Max seem to be hitting it off. Although he seems like a guy who has lots of lady friends.'

'Oh, honey, I know it's just temporary. Trains have a way of bringing very different people together, but once the trip is over, so is the attraction. And I'm way past getting my heart broken over a man, if that's what you're thinking.'

'It is, and I'm glad to hear it.'

'I have to tell you,' the priest confessed to Steve and Julie, 'I've never attended a wedding on a train before. I think it must be a first.'

'Actually, it's not.'

They all looked across the aisle to where Herrick Higgins was eating his dinner.

'It's happened before, back in 1987, on the Texas Eagle. They called it the Love Train, because there was a legendary conductor on board the Eagle by the name of Zeb Love. He had a heart of gold and the showmanship of a world-class entertainer. Well, on July 4, 1987, on the Texas Eagle, a couple got married and Zeb Love was right there. He even went celebrating with the wedding party when they got to Forth Worth.'

'Well,' said Julie, 'I hope our wedding is half as nice.'

'Oh, it will be,' said Higgins. 'Roxanne Jordan, I understand, is taking charge of the musical entertainment. With that woman involved, good things will happen. Trust me.'

UP IN THE PACIFIC NORTHWEST a significant meteorological event was taking place. Competing highs and lows, butting cold and warm fronts, and upper-level winds that were increasing to enormous speeds were mixing and beginning to move in an easterly direction. A similar confluence of weather elements had formed in nearly the same place during one of Mark Twain's trips across the Nevada Territory over 140 years before. The result had been a blizzard the likes of which most folks had never encountered even in those wild frontier climates. If the story was to be believed—and, in that regard, one was always on dangerous ground with Mr Twain—the episode very nearly cost the esteemed author his life.

Largely undetected by the national weather forecasters, the ferocious storm turned in a southern direction when it slammed into the hard wall of the northern Rockies and slid down the spine of the mountain range. Its destination seemed to lie right along the path of the Southwest Chief.

LATER THAT NIGHT the thief was once more making the rounds of the sleeper cars, even more cautiously this time because of the heightened state of alertness. The thief's efforts were aided by the fact that many people were either eating dinner or attending a very special event in the lounge car where Roxanne stood belting out song after song. The LA Boys' Center Choir, too, had stayed up a little late and was listening with rapt attention.

Tom was in a far corner of the packed lounge, humming along. After the show was over, the passengers gave her a standing ovation, and then people hung around discussing in noisy detail all that they'd just seen and heard.

Meanwhile, back in her compartment, Eleanor was making some notes about potential plots, but struggling to concentrate. She kept doodling on her pad, until she realised she was spelling 'Tom Langdon' in fat, three-dimensional letters. She ripped up the paper and threw it away, then lay back with her hand over her face.

'Troubles?'

Eleanor looked at the doorway, where Roxanne was standing and dabbing the sweat from her face with a facecloth.

Eleanor sat up. 'Just a little frustrated, I guess.'

'Well, you missed a fine show in the lounge car.'

'Actually I heard it. They piped it in over the PA. You were terrific.'

Roxanne glanced at the floor, which was littered with paper. 'How's the story coming? We could use a blockbuster Max Powers movie about trains to get the government excited about us again.'

Eleanor gave an embarrassed smile. 'Well, I have to admit, I don't know all that much about trains. I haven't taken one since I was in college, at least not in this country.'

Roxanne perched on the edge of the bed.

'Well, I've been working these trains longer than most, and I still don't know it all. I guess that's why I like my job so much: something new every day. Sometimes it's good, and sometimes it's not so good, but it keeps me hopping and using my head, and that's a good thing.'

'How long have you worked this train?'

'Oh, me and the Chief have been courting now going on twenty-one years. Know every bit of sagebrush in New Mexico, every wheatfield in Kansas, even know some of the farmers by their first name. Wave to 'em when we go by.'

Eleanor pulled out a fresh piece of paper and made some notes. 'I bet the farmers wave back.'

'Girl, I've got three marriage proposals in the last two years. One gent tied a banner to his John Deere and raced the train. It said, "Will You Marry Me, Roxanne?"'

'That's pretty creative. It's nice to be popular.'

'Oh yeah, farmers like their women with some meat on 'em, and I fit that bill.' She stood up. 'If you're having trouble coming up with ideas, why don't you come with me to make my rounds? I guarantee it'll stimulate your creative juices.'

AFTER ROXANNE'S SHOW Tom went for a stroll. The lounge car was still full and the dining car was serving its last meal of the day, thus many of the sleeper compartments were empty. It was a perfect time for a thief to strike again, and Tom wanted to see if the crook on the Capitol Limited had managed to hook a ride on the Southwest Chief. He also wanted to check out one sleeper in particular.

He knocked, and when he received no answer he poked his head inside Agnes Joe's compartment. It was empty. The phonograph was set up on the fold-down desk, but few other personal possessions were laid out. Two suitcases were against one wall. Tom didn't bother with those. He was more interested in the duffle bag that was wedged between the wall and chair, and covered with a blanket.

He drew the privacy curtain closed and unzipped the bag. Inside were newspapers balled up, just like the bunch that Regina had been carrying on the Cap. He looked at some of them. They were from various editions on the East Coast. Unable to make sense of this, he kept looking through the bag until he found a photograph of Agnes Joe and someone whom Tom took to be her daughter. They seemed happy or at least cordial. He wondered what had gone wrong since the picture had been taken, why the mother wasn't spending Christmas with her only child.

He put the photo back in the bag and slipped out of the compartment. He went to the other section of sleepers, stopped dead, ducked inside a vacant unit and peered out cautiously. Agnes Joe was emerging from one of the others. She looked around to see that no one was watching, then she headed off in the opposite direction. Tom slipped out, moved down the corridor, and peered into the compartment she'd been in. He was about to go in to determine who was staying there, but he heard people coming and walked away. However, he got the letter of the unit, and he figured it would be easy to find out whose it was.

As he came through the lounge car he saw Herrick Higgins peering anxiously out of the window.

'What's up?' asked Tom. 'You look a little uptight.'

Higgins smiled, but Tom noted there wasn't much sincerity behind it. 'Oh, nothing much. Just watching the snow coming down.'

'Well, snow can't hurt a train.'

Higgins didn't smile or nod in agreement. 'We'll be hitching on a third engine at La Junta before we cross the Raton Pass,' he said.

'Is that normal practice, or because of the snow?'

'Oh, it's normal. See, it's quite a climb, and a third engine just adds a nice little comfort zone.' His gaze returned to the snow falling outside, and his expression grew serious again.

Tom walked on, but he glanced nervously back at the old railroad man, trying without success to read his thoughts.

As ROXANNE AND ELEANOR entered the coach car housing the boys' choir, Roxanne pulled out a can of Lysol and started spraying everywhere. 'OK,' she said, 'now, do not try to deceive Ms Roxanne about this for she has five sons of her own and lots of grandsons, and thus she has a PhD in what she likes to call "stinky young men syndrome", and that just won't cut it on Ms Roxanne's train. Do we all understand this?' All the young men nodded. 'Good, now I have two showers reserved for you for the next hour, and we will make good use of that time, won't we?' They all nodded again. 'Three minutes per boy per shower, for this train does many wonderful things but it does not make water out of air. And we will come out with not one dirty digit because there will be an inspection—oh yes there will. And the good Lord will look down upon all of you squeaky clean young men and He will bless you this Christmas like no other.'

As the lads marched out, Eleanor asked, 'How did you end up being the choir's caretaker?'

'They're good boys, with a lot of potential, but also lots of things in their way too, especially where they're going back to. Every single one of them is going to make it. I'm taking a month-long vacation this summer, and we're going to go on the road, me and those boys, and we're going to play some places, and they're going to see some things that will make their bellies burn to do the right thing in life. They'll find dreams they never thought they even had, and old Roxanne will be right there holding their hands till they don't need me being Momma any more.'

'That's quite an ambitious undertaking,' said Eleanor.

'But they're worth it, don't you think?'

Eleanor smiled. 'I think they're more than worth it. You sure you're not an angel dropped from heaven onto the Southwest Chief? You sound almost too good to be true, and I mean that with mountains of respect.'

'Well, honey, I'm a sixty-three-year-old fat woman with sore feet, high blood pressure, and the beginnings of diabetes. I don't have all that much time left, and I can either spend it complaining about the things I never got in life, or I can do something I love and help people along the way. I decided to keep plugging till I drop.'

They stopped at one seat and Roxanne put her hands on her hips. 'Excuse me, what we got here, shug?'

The young man, about twenty-five, was reclining in his seat without any clothes on. Luckily, the space next to him was unoccupied, the car was darkened for sleeping, and no one else had noticed.

'Hey, it's cool,' said the young man.

'I bet you're cool, you ain't got no stitch of anything on.'

'Well, I'm from Arizona, this is how everybody sleeps in Arizona.'

'Is that right?' Eleanor had averted her gaze, but Roxanne sat right next to the man. 'Now let me get something straight, slick. We're not in Arizona, we're in Missouri, and if you don't get all your clothes on right now, you're getting off this train before we get to Kansas City.'

The young man chuckled. 'I gotcha there. La Plata was the last stop, and there's not another one until KC.'

'That's right, there's not, is there?' Roxanne stared at him pointedly until it started to dawn on the guy.

'You wouldn't put me off in the middle of nowhere? You can't do that?' he sputtered.

'I wouldn't call the middle of Missouri the middle of nowhere. I mean, folks live there. So it has to be *somewhere*. I know that the farms are quite a ways apart, and it's December and cold as I don't know what, but it's not *nowhere*. In fact, the place we'll let you off, all you got to do is walk about thirty miles southwest and there's a

motel or something like that if memory serves me correctly.'
'Thirty miles! I'll freeze.'
'Well, not if you have your pants on. And be optimistic about life.
I don't tolerate whiners. You're young, you can probably make it.'
The man's eyes bulged. 'Probably?'
Roxanne pulled out her walkie-talkie. She didn't depress the
button, something Eleanor noticed but the young man didn't.
'Service boss to the conductor and engineer. We got us a red alert,
situation one-four-two, repeat one-four-two. We'll need to stop and
discharge a passenger. Over.'
'Wait!' said the panicked man. 'What's a one-four-two?'
'Oh, honey, that's just train talk for an uncooperative passenger.
On big fancy planes, they just tie you up and sit on you, because they
can't open their doors six miles up.' She smiled sweetly. 'But on
Amtrak we just kick your little disruptive butt off wherever we want.
Now, we do provide a flashlight and a compass to help guide you.
That's Amtrak policy, and a good one I think.' She looked out of the
window. 'Mercy, the snow's picked up again, looks like a regular
blizzard.' She spoke into her walkie-talkie. 'Service boss here again.
On that one-four-two, bring a shovel and a first-aid kit with frostbite
applications for the passenger. Over.'
'I'm dressing, I'm putting my clothes on,' yelled the young man.
'You can cancel the one-four-two thing.'
Roxanne looked at him solemnly and shook her head. 'I'm afraid
it's a long trip and for all I know you might try this nonsense again.'
'I swear to you,' said the young man as he frantically dressed,
'I will not take any clothes off again. I will sleep in my clothes.
I promise.'
'I don't know. You feel that? The train's already slowing down, and
the engineer might get mad if I tell him it's a no-go.'
'Please, please. I promise. No more nudity.'
Roxanne sighed heavily and then said into her walkie-talkie, 'OK,
service boss here again, let's cancel that, repeat, cancel the one-four-
two.' She stared at the young man. 'Now look here, baby, I see one
inch of something I shouldn't, then you going off this train. I don't
care where we are. No more reprieves, we understand each other?'
He nodded meekly and then pulled the blanket over his head.
'Night-night, Arizona,' said Roxanne as she and Eleanor walked off.
The two women went down to the lower level and sat at a table.
'You've had a busy night,' Eleanor remarked.
'Oh, honey, this was pretty tame. The things I could tell you.'

'I wish you would.'

'Well, maybe we can spend some time together off the train.'

Eleanor was beginning to think that she could get Max to make Roxanne a paid consultant on the film project.

'How many kids do you have besides Regina?'

'Nine, all grown of course. And twenty-three grandchildren.' Roxanne shot Eleanor a glance. 'You have any kids?'

Eleanor shook her head. 'Never even been married.'

'Now, you want to tell me how a beautiful, smart, successful sort like yourself never landed a good man who loved her?'

'Maybe I'm really not that beautiful, smart or successful.'

'Baby, take one look in the mirror. And I doubt you'd be working with a man like Max Powers if you weren't pretty well endowed in the brain and talent department.'

'Well, it happens, you know. All sorts of people end up alone.'

'Yes, and there's always a reason for it too. Care to tell me yours?'

Eleanor looked away and fiddled with her fingers while Roxanne studied her closely. 'Wait a minute, let me guess. You found you a good man who loved you, only it didn't work out, maybe he never asked that all-important question, and you finally went your separate ways.' She added quietly, 'Until you saw him again on this train.'

Eleanor glanced at her sharply.

'The way you and Tom Langdon act around each other it's pretty clear. Plus the train gossip grapevine is alive and well.'

Eleanor's face flushed. 'Well, my goodness, if I'd only known how transparent I was.' She took a deep breath. 'Tom Langdon is a wanderer, always has been, always will be. He craves change like other people need food. He's the sort who couldn't make a commitment if his life depended on it. And, no, he never asked me to marry him.'

'But I hear you haven't seen him in years. Maybe he's changed.'

Eleanor shook her head. 'Men like him don't change. He's travelling the States writing fluff instead of covering wars, but that won't last. Six months from now he'll be off doing something else. I lived with him for years. I know how he thinks.' She paused and added, 'And he has a girlfriend in LA.'

'You think he's made a commitment to her?'

'I doubt it.'

'You mean you hope not.'

Eleanor just looked away.

Roxanne said, 'Let your heart be your guide, girl. If you truly love him, I say give him another chance.'

CHAPTER EIGHT

Kansas City was a major stop where many people got on and off and the train was refuelled and restocked. Tom took the opportunity to step out for some fresh air before the bachelor party started. The snow was falling hard, and he sought shelter under one of the over-hangs. He glanced over in surprise as Eleanor climbed off the train and headed towards him.

'Little stuffy on the train,' she explained.

'Yeah.'

They both stood there awkwardly, until she said, 'I can't tell you what a shock it's been seeing you.'

'I thought a million times about contacting you over the years. But I never did. Call it pride, stubbornness, stupidity. Take your pick, they're all there.'

'Well, I guess with the way things ended I can't blame you.'

He drew closer. 'Do you believe in second chances?'

She pulled back a bit. 'Tom, I can't take that hurt again. I can't.'

'You left me, remember?'

'After all those years of being together, it was time to put up or shut up,' she said bluntly. 'I needed a commitment, and I didn't get it. I assumed your career took priority over everything else.'

'People can change, Ellie.'

'So I've heard. You have a girlfriend you're going to see for Christmas. Are you ready to commit to her?'

'It's not that sort of relationship.'

'Of course not, you're not that sort of man.' She shook her head and looked away.

Tom gripped her shoulder and turned her towards him. 'It's not that sort of relationship because I don't love her. There's only one woman I've ever loved, Ellie, you know that. Nothing in my life has been as good as what we had. Nothing! I've been searching all these years for something.'

'Tom, don't do this to me, please.'

'So why did you come out here? It's freezing.'

'I . . . I don't know.'

'I don't believe that. I think you know exactly why.'

'Maybe I do. I've been looking too,' she said, 'and not finding.'

'It can't be just a coincidence that we're both on this train. It's an omen, don't you see? It was meant to be.'

'You sound like Misty. Love doesn't work that way. It's not some magic fairy dust. It's something you work at every day.'

As the full force of those emerald eyes fell on him, Eleanor's gaze became as hypnotic and intoxicating a thing as Tom had ever experienced. He moved closer to her, sliding an errant strand of auburn hair out of her face with his hand. Then his fingers moved to her cheek and gently rubbed it. She didn't move to stop him.

'Well, maybe it's time I started to work at it.' He took a deep breath, glanced up for a second, and his gaze held on a figure walking his way. He shook his head in disbelief. This was the second shock that he'd received in a little over twenty-four hours. How many more thunderbolts could he survive?

It was Lelia Gibson striding towards the train, a caravan of red-caps tugging along her prodigious baggage in her wake.

Tom took a step back from Eleanor, who'd closed her eyes, her lips searching for Tom's but not finding them.

'Ellie.'

She opened her eyes. 'What's wrong?'

'Think of the worst bit of timing you've ever had in your life.'

'What?' she asked in a bewildered tone.

He glanced once more at Lelia. She was closing in. He wasn't sure if she'd seen him yet, but it was only a matter of time. He pointed towards Lelia. 'My sort of girlfriend in LA? That's her. Lelia Gibson.'

Eleanor swung round and stared at the approaching group.

'Did you know she was boarding the train?'

'No, that qualifies in the total shock-of-a-lifetime category.'

Eleanor folded her arms across her chest and moved away from Tom. It was then that Lelia barrelled down on her target.

'What are you doing here, Lelia?'

'Is that all I get after travelling all this way to surprise you? Do you know you can't get a direct flight from LA to Kansas City? I mean, what is that about? I had to fly through Denver. It was a nightmare. And all I get is "What are you doing here, Lelia?"' She gave him a hug and a kiss, and he felt extreme guilt, for they were dating after all. Rediscovering Eleanor had caused him to nearly forget all that.

'I'm sorry, it's just a shock seeing you.'

'Why don't we get on the train and I'll fill you in on everything.'

'Everything, what everything?'

'Later, after I unpack.' She gave her ticket to one of the redcaps and told them to get her bags on board, tipping them generously with both money and a dazzling smile. She was dressed in classic Hollywood, meaning expensive and eye-catching. The poor Kansas City redcap battalion would never be the same, Tom felt certain.

As they walked towards the Chief, Lelia slipped her arm round Tom's. 'You know, I've never been on a train before. And for the holidays too, it's kind of nice. Do they have massage services on board?'

'Uh, no.'

'Well, maybe you can give me one—a massage, I mean. Oh, I brought the naughty teddy,' she added coyly, leaning up against him.

As they were boarding, Tom saw Eleanor out of the corner of his eye. She was watching them both closely, and for one of the few times in his life he felt completely helpless.

Lelia set up in her sleeper compartment, but not without some complaints as to its lack of spaciousness and queries as to whether there were any rental units with access to a private valet. A hopelessly smitten Barry, the sleeping-car attendant, went off, determined to accomplish all that she had asked.

Tom came by her compartment after she'd settled in. 'I like what you've done with the place,' he said, smiling.

'Where are you staying?'

'In the poor person's sleeper down the road a piece.'

'Well, you can sleep in here tonight.'

He sat down on the edge of the turned-down bed. 'Look, I have something to tell you.'

She put her hand over his. 'I think I know what you're going to say. That's the reason I flew all this way.'

'It is?' *How could she have known about Eleanor?*

'After all, we've been together for a while now, and decisions have to be made.'

'I couldn't agree with you more.'

'I didn't want to tell you over the phone and I couldn't wait until Christmas, because this might change our plans for the holidays.'

Tom sighed in relief. 'I really think we're on the same page here.'

She put both hands on his shoulders. 'Tom, I want to get married.'

All he could say was, 'To whom?'

'To you, silly.'

'You want to marry me? You flew all this way to tell me you want to get married? To me?' He rose in his agitation. 'Lelia, this is a long way from seeing each other a few times a year for fun and games.'

'Don't you think I know that?' She stood up. 'I'm not getting any younger. My biological clock isn't just ticking, its alarm is ringing, and I've hit the snooze button so often it doesn't work any more.'

'You're saying you want to have children?'

'Yes, don't you?'

'How do I know if I want kids? I didn't know you were going to come and propose tonight. Let a guy catch his breath, will you.'

She put her arms round him. 'I know it's all of a sudden. But we're good together, Tom, really good. I've got plenty of money and we can do whatever we want. We'll travel, play, enjoy good times, and then settle down and have a huge family.'

'Huge? Huge family? How huge?'

'Well, I'm one of eight.'

He looked at her petite frame. 'You work out six hours a day. Are you saying you're going to let your body bloat up eight times? Even if we space it out a kid every two years, you'll be sixty by the time the last bundle of joy pops out, Lelia.' He put a hand through his hair with an impulse to tear most of it out. 'I can't believe this.'

'I know this is a lot to throw at you. It's two days to LA. Take your time and think about it. Then let me know.'

'You want me to let you know if I want to get married and have eight kids, in two days?'

'Well, depending on your answer, we'll have a lot to do, so, yes, promptness would be appreciated.' She kissed him on the cheek and took his hands in hers. 'Now, what were you going to tell me?'

He just stared at her open-mouthed, then turned to leave.

'Where are you going?'

He found his voice. 'To the bar.'

As TOM STAGGERED to the lounge car to find support at the bottom of as many tequila shots as he could fire into his body, the Chief hurtled on to Lawrence, Kansas. They'd reach that stop at about one thirty in the morning, followed by Topeka, Newton, Hutchinson, Dodge City and Garden City, their last stop in Kansas before entering Colorado. La Junta, the site of the marriage, was the second stop in Colorado, and about two hours from the Raton Pass.

The storm was now ploughing south, knocking against the immovable frame of the Rocky Mountains. The area had seen above-normal snowfall, and the mountaintops were heavily wreathed in white, but no serious damage was reported, and while forecasters had their eye on the moving mass of wind and moisture, they had no reason to believe it was any different from countless other storms.

Tom was intercepted by Max and Misty before he could reach the lounge car. 'I need a drink,' he told Max. 'I need a drink so unbelievably badly. If I don't get one I'm not responsible for my actions.'

Max said, 'I've got every drink you can think of plus a case of chilled wine in my compartment. Let's start the bachelor's party right now. And I decided, why limit it to the guys?'

'Actually,' said Misty, 'I think that was my idea.'

'How'd you manage all the booze?'

'I just phoned ahead to Kansas City and said "Charge it". This isn't exactly rocket science, kids.'

'I love it when he calls me kid,' said Misty. 'Makes me feel young.'

'We have a wedding tomorrow, and you, Eleanor and the others are playing pivotal roles. So we have to rehearse too.'

'I don't think that's such a good idea right now, Max,' said Tom.

'Don't be silly. Take it from me, I know what I'm talking about. I do this for a living. You have to rehearse or else you'll screw up. Now come on, kiddies, Uncle Max always gets his way.'

The man literally skipped down the corridor, obviously enjoying himself immensely. Misty followed, and that left Tom to trudge miserably after them.

Max sent Kristobal to round up Steve, Julie, Eleanor, Roxanne and the minister who'd be conducting the service. The latter was tall and trim, with short grey hair, a wise look and kindly eyes.

Max's compartment consisted of a suite of two rooms.

Tom looked around at the spaciousness. 'How'd he manage this?'

'He's Max Powers,' said Misty.

The director passed out pieces of paper stapled together. 'OK, here's the script for tomorrow including each scene—I mean, each part of the wedding.'

Tom slid over to Kristobal, who was manning the bar that had been set up in one corner. 'Got any Scotch?' he said.

'I'm afraid all we have is twenty-five-year-old single-malt Macallan's. It's Mr Powers's personal favourite.'

'Well, I guess that'll have to do, won't it?'

Tom sipped his Scotch and looked over at Eleanor, who was studiously going over the script and trying mightily not to make eye contact with anyone, particularly him. He had just worked up the courage to go over to her when Lelia flounced in.

'I understand there's a bachelor's party going on.' Then Lelia's gaze fell upon Max Powers. Tom noted that as soon as the director saw Lelia, he tried to hide behind Misty.

'Max? Max Powers?' said Lelia. 'My God, it *is* you.'

Max turned back, acted surprised, and said, 'Lelia!'

Tom said, 'You know each other?'

'Oh, it was years ago,' said Max quietly.

'But it feels like yesterday, Max,' said Lelia. 'I auditioned for one of his films, a minor role. It was years ago, but he was already a legend,' she added in an awe-struck tone.

'Now, Lelia,' said Max nervously, 'my ego is big enough . . .'

She didn't appear to hear him. 'I didn't get the role. You remember the film, Max?'

'No, sweetie, I really don't. I've lost so many brain cells since then.'

'It was *Fall of Summer*, about a young couple falling in and out of love during a summer holiday. I never really knew why I didn't get the part of the girl's best friend, Bambi Moore.'

'Obviously one of my biggest mistakes, Lelia. I made lots of them early on in my career.'

'Well, you had the decency to take me to dinner one night. Do you remember that?'

'Of course, dinner. It was lovely.'

'And dinner stretched to breakfast. I trust you remember that part of the audition.' Lelia hiked her eyebrows and puckered her lips.

'Let's break out the booze,' shouted Max, 'and get this rehearsal really rolling.'

AGAIN AND AGAIN Max put them through their paces.

Finally Tom called for a break, over Max's protests, which were quickly shouted down by all hands.

Lelia walked over to Eleanor while Tom looked on in horror at this imminent clash.

'I understand you're the maid of honour and Tom is the best man. How fun and convenient for you.'

'You really think so?' said Eleanor. 'Those weren't the adjectives jumping to my mind.'

'Tom and I are going to Tahoe for Christmas,' said Lelia.

'You went from LA to Kansas City and got on a train headed back to LA so you can go to Tahoe for Christmas? That's quite a circuitous route to take.'

'Well, I had something very important to ask Tom.'

'Oh, what was that?'

'To marry me.'

Eleanor looked over at Tom furiously, and then Lelia said,

'Somebody told me you and Tom once dated. You know, it's funny, Eleanor . . . it *is* Eleanor, isn't it? Tom never mentioned your name. I guess it wasn't a memorable relationship.'

'Sure he mentioned my name,' said Eleanor. 'Probably when you two were in bed together.' Lelia's mouth dropped so far Tom could see the woman still had her tonsils.

'So, how's everyone doing on drinks?' was all he could think to say.

With one more fierce glance at Tom, Eleanor said to Lelia, 'Don't worry, honey, you can have him.'

As Eleanor stormed out Tom raced over, but Lelia grabbed him. 'Did you hear what she said to me?'

Tom watched as Eleanor disappeared down the corridor.

'Tom, did you hear me?'

He finally looked at her. 'Lelia. Shut up.'

Lelia spun round on her heels and left.

As people started to trickle away, Tom looked so miserable that Max finally came over to him. 'You look like you could use another drink.' Max mixed two cocktails and the men sat down. Max slapped Tom on the thigh. 'Sorry there wasn't a girl popping out of a cake at the bachelor party. I didn't think it would be appropriate with the ladies present.'

Tom finally focused on the director. 'So, you—what—*dated* Lelia?'

'Well, I wouldn't call it dating, actually. It was just the one time, as far as I can remember. My memory is not what it was. Hey, did *I* hear right? Lelia asked you to marry her?'

Tom nodded.

'Man, I guess women do that these days. So does that mean if you divorce she has to pay *you* alimony?'

'She won't have to pay me anything. We're not getting married.'

'Look, Tom, I'm not trying to butt in or anything, but Lelia *is* beautiful. Don't rush your decision, you might not get another chance. No offence, but you're not exactly a spring chicken.'

'You're right, she's rich, she's beautiful—and I don't love her.'

Max let out a long sigh. 'I've done the deed four times now. Who knows—maybe there's a fifth in the works for me.' The director's expression grew sombre. 'Patty was my first wife, married right out of high school. We had four kids. We were dirt poor but she never complained, not once. She could stretch a buck further than anyone I've ever met. I was just starting to make it in the movie business when she died.' Max grew quiet, looked out of the window at the passing countryside. 'Yeah, I loved Patty with everything I had. I'll always love Patty. My three ex-wives?' He shrugged. 'I loved them, in a way. But not like Patty. I guess there's something special about your first love. Now I just play the field and I have fun. You know?'

Tom nodded. 'I know.'

Max drew closer to Tom and said in a low voice, 'Why aren't you and Eleanor together?'

'You saw what happened. She just stormed out of here.'

'Well, you can't blame her. Your girlfriend flies in from LA to propose. Now, God knows I'm no expert in affairs of the heart, but that's not exactly the ideal way to win back the love of your life.'

'I've tried, Max, I've really tried.'

'Well, you know what? If she's really *your* Patty, I'd try harder.'

ELEANOR WAS BACK in her compartment about to swallow a sleeping pill of enormous diameter when someone knocked on her door.

'Eleanor? It's me.'

She tried to identify the voice through the dulled filters of her overwrought mind. 'Julie?' She went to the door and opened it, and there stood the young bride-to-be, tears in her eyes, holding a long garment bag. 'What's the matter? Steve's parents called again?'

Julie shook her head. 'And neither did mine.'

'Can I come in for a few minutes?'

'What? Oh, um, sure.' Eleanor slipped the pill in her pocket.

The two women sat on the edge of the bed.

'So your parents didn't call and you're sad because . . .' she coaxed.

'Well,' Julie began, 'I suppose a girl envisions her parents being at her wedding. You imagine your father giving his little girl away and your mom telling you everything's going to be OK. And, well, I don't have any of that.' She burst into tears and sobbed for some time while Eleanor held her tightly. When she finally stopped, she wiped her eyes and looked embarrassed. 'I'm sorry. I'm a grown woman and I should be able to handle this, but I just feel so alone.'

'You have every right to feel that way, and I guess I've been a pretty lousy maid of honour.'

'Well, you don't even really know me.'

'It shouldn't matter. We're both women. You're going to be a bride tomorrow. That's all I should need to know.'

'Have you ever been married?'

'No,' said Eleanor quietly, 'but I've thought about it a lot. Imagined every detail of it, down to the finger foods and flower displays. I don't dream about it as much as I used to, though. As years go by, the chances of it happening steadily diminish.'

'All you need is someone who loves you and who you love back.'

Eleanor smiled though she actually felt like bawling harder than Julie just had. 'Yep, that's all you need.' She touched the garment bag Julie had set on the bed. 'What's this?'

'It's my wedding gown. I haven't tried it on since I bought it. I thought maybe, you know . . .'

'What a wonderful idea,' said Eleanor.

'You sure you don't mind? It's late and I'm sure you're tired.'

'Actually, I *was* tired, but now I'm not.'

Eleanor helped Julie into her dress, a simple, elegant outfit of creamy white that fitted perfectly. As she was about to place the veil on Julie's head, Julie took it and put it on Eleanor. The two women stood side by side in front of the full-length mirror.

'You look beautiful, Julie.'

'So do you.'

They started laughing hysterically.

Later, while Julie was in the bathroom, Eleanor was about to pack up the gown when she held it up to her and looked in the mirror.

'Ellie?'

She looked over to where the door to her compartment had slid open with the curves of the track and the acceleration of the Chief. It was Tom, staring at her as she stood there, covered by another woman's wedding dress.

At that moment Julie came out of the bathroom and looked at each of them. 'Sorry if I interrupted something.'

Eleanor lowered the gown and carefully packed it away while Tom watched. She handed the garment bag to Julie, gave her a hug, and said with a smile, 'Sleep well, your whole life changes tomorrow morning. For the better.'

Julie kissed her on the cheek, turned, and walked out past Tom, who still stood there, looking as awkward as he did confused.

'What do you want, Tom?'

'You looked really beautiful in the dress, Ellie.'

'It's late, shouldn't you be with Lelia?'

'I don't love Lelia!'

'Well, she seems to love you. I assume you must have shown some affection, or made some promise to her, because I find it hard to believe the woman would have flown all this way to ask you to marry her out of friendship or kindness. What did make her come all this way?' She folded her arms across her chest and waited expectantly.

'How do I know? She's nuts.'

'You've been seeing each other how long?'

Tom sputtered, 'About three years. But off and on.'

'Off and on? And you expected her to be content with that?'

He just looked at her blankly as she continued. 'So she wanted to make a commitment but you didn't. You were perfectly happy with popping in, popping out, sharing the good times not the bad, and going your solo way when you felt like it?'

'It's not like that, Ellie. I'm not like that any more.'

'Sure you're not. You haven't changed. Not a bit.'

'It would be different. With the right woman.'

Eleanor rubbed her temples. 'Listen, we have a wedding to do tomorrow. Someone *else's* wedding. I need some sleep.'

'We can't leave it like this.'

'Oh yes we can, and we are. We'll do our duty tomorrow, we'll get to LA, and we'll go our separate ways. This time for good.'

'Ellie!'

'Goodbye, Tom.' She slid the door closed.

DAWN BROKE over the high plains of Colorado near the New Mexico border, but the sun was completely hidden by a vast sky of threatening clouds. The snow lay thickly over the ground, covering the ubiquitous sagebrush. Most folks assembled for an early breakfast, because word had spread rapidly about the approaching nuptials. As the train neared La Junta, the excitement grew and virtually all the passengers and crew crowded into the lounge car to watch the wedding. A group of musicians Max had hired and who'd come on board early that morning played the traditional 'Wedding March' and other tunes. Kristobal filmed the entire event, and Max directed, with most people on the train not even knowing this was a Max Powers production of sorts. Tom and Eleanor played their respective parts, though Tom, for one awkward moment, couldn't find the ring and then for one even more awkward moment seemed to be trying to place it on Eleanor's finger instead of handing it to Steve.

The bride and groom kissed as the train stopped at La Junta, and everyone on board threw rice. A third diesel engine was attached to the Chief to help the train over the pass. The crowd lining the track roared in appreciation at the 'Just Married' sign that had been hung on the last car of the Chief with strung tin cans below it.

Then the party on the train really started, highlighted by the enormous feast that Max had paid for. As the official wedding photographer took photos, Roxanne came sweeping out in a flamboyant costume that was definitely not Amtrak standard issue. She was trailed by the LA Boys' Center Choir, also dressed in their finest. The crowd grew quiet and Roxanne and the choir began to sing. They sang classical songs, then the blues, and a string of tunes from Nat King Cole to Sinatra. Roxanne did her best Aretha Franklin impersonation, belting out the queen of soul's signature piece, 'Respect'. The crowd was so into it by this time that people were standing and shouting out each letter with her: 'R-E-S-P-E-C-T!'

Max could only sit back and smile. Roxanne looked over at him, and then she pulled him up and they danced together, at which point everyone else joined in.

Lelia pulled Tom over, but he managed to promptly pull himself away, citing nausea, which wasn't altogether a falsehood. Poor, deserted Lelia looked around and spotted Kristobal, who was packing away the video equipment.

'Care to dance?' she asked him. Kristobal looked up and his eyes perceptibly widened at her glamorous figure and attire. 'You work for Mr Powers, don't you?' Kristobal nodded. 'I'm Lelia Gibson.'

His eyes widened further and he blurted out, 'Lelia Gibson, the voice of Cuppy the Magic Beaver? It was my favourite show when I was a kid. My little brother still watches it. You're terrific.'

Lelia looked flustered. 'You watched it as a child? My, I have been doing the show a long time, haven't I?'

Overwhelmed, Kristobal dropped all pretence of professional dignity. 'And Sassy Squirrel and Freddy the Futon and Petey the Orange Pickle, they're all classics. Look, I don't mean to gush, but I just can't believe you're on this train. Would it be asking too much to ask for your autograph? My little brother is going to freak.'

'Why, certainly you can have my autograph, um . . .'

'Oh, where are my manners? I'm Kristobal Goldman.' He gave her hand an enthusiastic shake that almost lifted petite Lelia right out of her outrageously expensive, open-toed three-inch heels.

'I tell you what, Kristobal, I'll autograph anything you want if you'll dance with me.'

An astonished Kristobal bowed deeply, and off they went.

WHILE EVERYONE was at the wedding party, about twenty more compartments were robbed of various items, from watches and rings to bracelets and even Max's pair of Bruno Maglis. Once more the thief made a clean getaway, quickly melting into the crowd of partygoers.

DURING THE NIGHT BEFORE the wedding the storm had settled over the border between Colorado and New Mexico. Locked in place by a high-pressure system, the clouds were now so heavy with moisture that something had to give; and it did at about three o'clock in the morning, with the Chief still over eight hours away. The snowfall gauges were filled within an hour; the strong instruments erected to quantify wind-speed were toppled in thirty minutes. All commercial flights were instructed to give the area a wide berth and all nearby ski resorts were closed. By seven o'clock conditions were near white-out. Then at nine thirty there was a sudden lull in the storm and the forecasters predicted that it would rapidly dissipate.

Someone once said to Mark Twain, upon the occasion of a sudden rain shower, that he hoped the storm would stop, where-upon Twain had replied that the odds were good because it always had. Twain had never put much stock in weather predicting, no doubt sensibly concluding that the science of foretelling what Mother Nature intended was a fool's gamble.

Well, some things hadn't changed, because even with satellites, super Doppler radar and other state-of-the-art devices to help them, the meteorologists following the current storm got it wrong. The blizzard had been merely resting. Now millions of tons of Pacific moisture and galelike winds were perfectly poised to add one to the history books.

CHAPTER NINE

Most of the wedding partygoers had dispersed, but Max and Misty, Kristobal and Lelia, and Herrick Higgins were still sitting in the lounge car watching as the train started its ascent of the Raton Pass. As the gradient grew steeper, and the deep whine of the three engines grew louder, there was a creeping uneasiness among the passengers. The vast amounts of snow being pushed off the track by the lead engine's plough could be seen at every curve. It was a wonder that the engineer could see at all with all that white flying around.

Kristobal said, 'Uh, what happens if one of the cars comes loose? Do we just go barrelling down into the abyss?'

Higgins replied, 'No, the automatic braking system comes on and the car stops. Train technology has come a long way.' He pointed out of the window. 'We'll climb to 7,580 feet at the highest point.'

'That's pretty high,' said Kristobal.

'Well, it's not the highest track elevation in this country. That's on the California Zephyr past Denver at a little over 9,200 feet. We go through a half-mile-long tunnel that runs under the Raton Pass, and once we get out of that we're in New Mexico. We'll descend down the eastern side of the Sangre de Cristo Mountains and into Raton, which is at an elevation of 6,666 feet.'

Misty looked stricken, and she grabbed Max's arm. 'Did you say 6,666 feet? Are you sure that's the elevation? Exactly?'

Higgins looked at her over the rim of his coffee cup. 'Yes, ma'am.'

'Oh my God!'

'What's wrong, honey?' asked Max.

'Don't you see, 6-6-6-6? It's the worst possible combination of numbers, it's even worse than a triple 6.'

Max turned pale. 'You're right, the mark of the Devil, plus another 6. Totally bad karma.'

'Is this really a problem?' asked a nervous-looking Kristobal.

'In my line of business, it doesn't get much worse,' said Misty emphatically. 'Can we stop the train?'

'Isn't there a brake rope to pull, like in the movies?' asked Lelia. She was seated next to Kristobal and anxiously clutching his arm.

'Uh, no, not any more,' said Higgins. 'Now just calm down, it'll be OK. The Chief runs this route twice a day, east and west.' He checked his watch. 'We'll be entering the tunnel soon. But we won't be in it long. In and out in a blink and then on to New Mexico.'

Tom eyed the diamond ring in his hand. It had belonged to his mother, and ever since her death he'd carried it with him. He pocketed it, adjusted the tie that Kristobal had loaned him for the wedding ceremony, took a long breath and knocked on Eleanor's compartment door.

She slid the curtain back, stared at him, then drew it across again and he heard the door lock click into place. He rapped on the glass again. 'Ellie, I really need to talk to you, right now.'

'Go away!'

'I need to ask you something, and I'm going to ask you right now.'

She flung the door open so hard that metal plunked hard on metal. 'I thought I'd made myself *more* than perfectly clear!'

Tom reached into his pocket for the ring and started to shakily descend to his knees.

THE EVENTS THAT FOLLOWED happened with terrifying suddenness. The interior of the train was thrown into darkness as the Chief entered the tunnel. All of the snow covering the southern crest of the mountain closest to the train tracks broke loose under pressure from relentless wind gusts and tons of new-fallen snow. The avalanche raced down the mountainside at tremendous speed, hitting the steel fence located between the mountain slope and the train tracks with such force that it not only flattened the fence but also ripped it off its supports.

This collision sent an automatic red alert to Amtrak Central Dispatch who, in turn, instantly communicated to the engineer of the Southwest Chief that he should stop the train dead in its tracks.

The Chief had just emerged from the tunnel under the Raton Pass when the signal was given, and in fact the engineer didn't need the warning by Amtrak because he could see the awesome spectacle through his windshield. So powerful was the tidal wave of snow and rock that he whispered a quick goodbye to his wife and kids.

As the train lurched to a halt, everyone sensed that this wasn't a normal stop. Thankfully, they couldn't see what the engineer could, but they all heard a growing rumble that was immediately identifiable to several people on board.

'It's an avalanche,' shouted Tom, as he looked out of the window. Eleanor paled. 'My God.'

He grabbed Eleanor, threw her on the floor, ripped a mattress off the bed, and put it on top of her, and then covered the mattress with his body as the train continued to shake and the sounds of the mountain's snowy skin sliding off became deafening.

Back in the lounge car everyone was under the tables. Max and Misty clung to each other, and Lelia and Kristobal did the same.

Miraculously, the enormous sideways thrust of the hurtling snow stopped before it knocked the train off the track. However, when the engineer finally opened his eyes, the only thing he saw was an impenetrable wall of snow. He managed to report in to Amtrak and was told that a second avalanche on the other side of the tunnel had taken another slide fence with it. Had it arrived a minute or two earlier, the Chief would be at the bottom of a ravine. The Chief was now sandwiched in, unable to go either forward or back, and the storm, apparently, was just getting started.

The meteorologists weighed in with an updated forecast. The region was being blasted by a winter storm the likes of which hadn't been seen in thirty years.

Higgins, who had also crawled under a table, looked to the sky as high winds began to sweep off the mountain and buffet the Chief with such power that the enormously heavy train was rocking back and forth unsettlingly. Looking out of the left-side window, no one could fail to see that it was a long way down. With the snow continuing to fall, another avalanche couldn't be ruled out. And the next one just might take the Southwest Chief with it.

AN HOUR LATER Roxanne issued an announcement over the train's PA system, telling people what had happened and what was being done to help the trapped train. With twin mountains of snow blocking both the way to LA and the rails back to Chicago, and a blizzard hammering the region with high winds and snow, it would be best if people could remain calm and in their compartments.

Herrick Higgins had gone up to speak to the engineer and had come back looking worried. Tom and Eleanor had joined Misty and Max in the lounge car, where they alternated between staring out of the right-hand window at a sheet of white snow, tensing with each slam of wind against the wall of the train, and peering out at the 200-foot drop off the left side of the train.

'I knew this was going to happen,' said Misty. 'Four sixes, how could it not happen?'

'Well, I've been doing this a long time,' said Higgins, 'and it's never happened before. Train travel is the safest way there is to get around.'

'Could there be another avalanche?' asked Misty.

'It's Mother Nature,' he replied, 'so anything's possible, but I think with two avalanches already, most of the snow that's going to come down already did.'

Tom looked at the old railroader. 'So what now? How do they get to us? We can't exactly wait for the spring thaw.'

'No, we can't. With the track blocked by all that snow and the weather the way it is, there's not much the freight company can do. And there's really no place for a small plane or helicopter to land, even if the weather settled down.'

Roxanne came up looking exhausted. In the last hour or so, she'd been calming passengers, consoling the boys' choir, making people more comfortable. She sat down and caught her breath. 'Well, on top of all this, it seems that the crook that hit the Cap got on board the Chief—a bunch of people have reported items missing.'

Max shook his head. 'This is truly amazing.' He and Misty exchanged glances.

'The good thing,' said Higgins, 'is that we added the third engine at La Junta, so we have an extra power plant to help us through.'

'What do you mean?' asked Max.

'The electrical power that keeps the lights, heat, et cetera going comes from electrical generators in the engines—generators powered by the diesel-fuel engines. Head-end power, it's called.'

'So when we run out of fuel, we run out of electricity,' said Tom.

'Basically that's right. But an extra engine gives us more time.'

'How much more time?' asked Max.

'Hard to say. We took on extra fuel in Kansas, but the Chief refuels at Albuquerque, about two hundred and fifty miles from here.'

'And it took a lot of fuel to climb the pass, so the diesel tanks aren't exactly full,' said Tom. Higgins nodded. 'So we could be talking hours here, couldn't we, before the power goes?'

'Well, the engineer is doing all he can to conserve fuel.'

'Can't we put all the passengers in a few cars and cut off power to the others?' suggested Max.

'No, the system doesn't work that way. Whether the engines are heating three cars or ten, it's the same fuel consumption.'

'Why not just turn some of the engines off?' asked Eleanor.

'Burns too much fuel to get them started again,' said Roxanne.

Higgins nodded. 'And you have to keep the engines idling to prevent the pipes from freezing. In weather this cold, once you turn off the head-end power and the heat fails, you have less than an hour before the pipes start freezing. Then you have no water for drinking or sanitary requirements.'

'I'm glad we put on extra food in KC,' said Roxanne. 'We'll start rationing right now, because we have no idea how long we'll be here.' She rose to go back to work. 'If I need help, I'm sure I can count on all of you, right?'

They all nodded back. She smiled bravely and trudged off.

Four hours later it grew dark. Most people returned to their compartments and covered themselves with blankets.

Tom stopped in on Father Kelly, who was reading his Bible. 'You know, you might want to lead a service on the train, Father, to lift people's spirits.'

'I'm a little rusty, I'm afraid.'

'It's like riding a bike, you never really forget how to do it.'

Tom found Max and Misty cuddled together in the double deluxe. Misty was still depressed, but Max had regained his jocularity even with his missing pair of Bruno Maglis. 'Figure the person who took them needs them more than me. I got way too much stuff as it is. But I have to tell you, with everything that's happened, this will make a great movie—if I just live through it to actually film it.'

'Thanks, Max, that's very encouraging,' scolded Misty.

'Aw, come on, Misty, it's all written in the stars. Tell me, what's your prediction? What do the cards tell you?'

Misty sighed, pulled out her tarot cards, shuffled them, and then began laying them out, one at a time. As she did so a deep frown creased her forehead. Finally, she said, 'That's funny. Apparently we're going to be rescued.'

'That's good news,' said Max. 'How?'

'Well, by something with six legs.'

'Six legs?' said an incredulous Tom.

Max rose and went to the bar in the corner. 'Well, until the six legs come, I need another bourbon. You drinking with us, Tom?'

'Maybe later, I've got things to do.'

'Like what?'

'Like finding something with six legs, that's what.'

THE STORY of the trapped train hit all the national and international news wires and the world awaited further developments. Back at Amtrak HQ, rescue preparations were at full throttle. Communications had been set up with the freight company that owned the track the Chief was sitting on, and the two organisations were mapping out a strategy that would be executed when the weather abated. For now, though, it seemed to just keep getting worse. Since the train still had fuel, heat and provisions, the situation, while serious, was not life-threatening. Sit tight, they were told, and help would eventually get to them.

MOST PEOPLE CHOSE not to eat dinner in the dining car, preferring to stay in their rooms and either snack or not eat at all, which helped with the food-supply burn rate. The Chief only had food for about another day or so.

And the fuel problem was even worse. Higgins explained to Tom and Eleanor, 'Once the fuel runs out, we have lots of problems that will rapidly get worse. No water, pipes bursting, no heat.'

'And if we do run out of fuel, even if they reach us, how can the train move? It's not like the air force where they can refuel in the air,' said Tom.

'Well, they'll attach engines with full tanks to the Chief and pull her along. But, like you said, they have to get to us first.'

'So maybe instead of waiting for help to get to us, we need to get to help.'

'Where?' asked Eleanor. 'We're in the middle of nowhere.'

'Any ideas, Herrick?' asked Tom. 'You probably know the Amtrak route as well as anyone.'

Higgins thought about this for a bit then finally shook his head. 'No, that wouldn't work.'

'What? Say it.'

'It wouldn't work,' he insisted.

'Herrick, right now, I'd take the craziest idea you have. Maybe we can make it work.'

Higgins shrugged. 'There's a resort near here called the Dingo. It's a big place, very well equipped and with lots of manpower. Problem is, you have to travel over some pretty rough terrain to get there, maybe a four-hour hike. It can be done by people in good physical shape in fair weather, but it would be impossible in this storm.'

Tom stared at him. 'But not on skis.'

'You have skis?' asked Higgins.

'I was going to Tahoe for Christmas. I've also got boots, gloves, flares, compass, helmet light, you name it.'

'It's really rough terrain, Tom.'

'I've skied just about everything there is, Herrick, in all sorts of conditions. All I need from you is a direction.'

'Do you really think you can manage it?'

'I can promise you my best shot. And what do we have to lose?'

'How about your life?' Eleanor said.

'Well, it's my life, isn't it? It's not like I've got anyone to mourn me.'

At that, Eleanor got up and left.

Higgins quickly gathered together the conductor, Roxanne and the train engineer to discuss it with Tom further. The conductor didn't like the plan at all.

'He's a passenger. And while I appreciate the offer, Tom, if anything happens to you it'll be my responsibility. I can't let you go. We just need to sit tight and help will come.'

'Maybe we can contact the owners at the Dingo and they can send someone here,' Higgins said to the engineer.

The man shook his head. 'The storms disrupted the signals. My last call in to Central was hours ago. Haven't been able to get them on the horn since.'

Roxanne added, 'We've even tried all the cellphones on the train, and nobody's got a signal. We can't reach Amtrak Central Dispatch or the resort. Might as well be in the Stone Age.'

'Look,' said Tom, 'I'm not going to just sit here and let this storm devour us. I'll sign any waiver you want, absolving you of all liability.' He gazed at each of them. 'Just let me try. That's all I ask. If I can't get through, I'll come back, simple as that.'

They all looked at each other, and finally the conductor and the engineer slowly nodded. 'OK.'

Tom went to the baggage car with Roxanne and retrieved his ski equipment. Back at his compartment he was readying things when he felt someone behind him. It was Eleanor.

'I don't want you to go.'

'OK, stop right there. I'm going.'

'I guess you think you're going to save the train and everyone on it.'

He looked up sharply. 'Yeah, that's the general plan.'

'Don't you think you might be running away instead?'

'I'm going out in a blizzard and risking my life to get help and you're calling me a coward. Thanks a hell of a lot.'

Eleanor didn't shrink from this verbal attack. 'Do you really want to know why I left you in Tel Aviv? Maybe you should hear it, since you might not be coming back.'

He looked at her for a long moment and then said, 'Well, I have to say your timing is as bad as mine but, sure, lay it on me.'

'You're a loner, Tom, and that's how you like it. You're responsible for yourself only, no one else.' He started to erupt, but she froze him with a look. 'I've been waiting years to say this, and I'm going to say it and you're going to listen.' She paused. 'I loved you, Tom, with everything I had. I loved you. You had me totally and completely.'

'*Had* you, past tense.'

'Don't you realise that while we were together you were kidnapped, imprisoned, and almost killed three times? You kept taking those crazy risks and you never thought about what that was doing to me. Every time you went out of the door I didn't know if you were coming back. I just wanted to go home. I didn't want to watch you go on another assignment wondering if I'd ever see you again. I wanted a white picket fence, a back-yard garden, and a husband who left at nine and came home at five. Only you never asked. I guess the wandering was more important to you than I was.'

'You gave me an ultimatum, Ellie. You gave me a few minutes to make a life-altering decision.'

'No, I didn't. I'd been asking you for years, you just didn't want to hear it. When I told you I wanted to leave that morning, it wasn't spontaneous. It took me weeks to work up the nerve. Well, I got my answer.' She prepared to leave. 'Now, you can go and try and rescue the train. Off on another adventure, all by yourself. I hope you'll be safe and I hope you write a great story based on it. But don't think that you're doing it for anyone other than yourself.'

She left. Tom sat there, staring after her, his hand in his pocket, idly fingering the ring.

THE DINING CAR was full for breakfast and Roxanne watched worriedly as the supplies in the kitchen dwindled. The food in the lounge car had been exhausted the night before and tempers were starting to flare. There were a number of infants on board, and as diapers and milk started running low their cries put everyone further on edge.

Father Kelly finally found the courage to hold a prayer service in the lounge car, and it was well attended by all denominations. The priest stumbled at times, but his effort was sincere and people came up to him afterwards and thanked him for lifting their spirits.

When Higgins wasn't consulting with the train crew on how best to conserve fuel and power, he went out into the storm and personally checked under the cars for freezing pipes. When he came back in it was lunchtime, and over several cups of coffee he regaled the dining-car patrons with stories of the Wild West. Children and adults alike listened with wide-eyed awe.

Agnes Joe had been staring out of the window of the dining car for quite some time. When Roxanne asked her what she was looking at, the woman pointed at something that Roxanne had to squint to see through the falling snow.

'It's Christmas Eve, you know,' said Agnes Joe.

Roxanne nodded. 'You're right, honey.'

A bit later Eleanor came into the car and joined Agnes Joe and Roxanne. They were looking out of the window, and Eleanor followed their gaze. Two men, heavily clothed, were struggling to bring something covered in a tarpaulin into the train.

The first man was Barry, the sleeping-car attendant. As he came on board, hefting his end of the load, the tarp fell off the object he was carrying, and Eleanor saw that it was a pine tree. As the second man climbed aboard, his hood fell away and she gasped—it was Tom.

'Christmas deserves a Christmas tree,' he explained. 'Actually, it was Agnes Joe's idea.'

They set it up in the lounge car on a hastily fashioned base, and children came and decorated it with everything from fake jewellery to plastic action figures to a long strand of tinsel that a woman had brought with her for a family Christmas in Albuquerque. Several of the children made a big star from paper and glue, coloured it a shiny silver, and hoisted it on top of the tree.

Tom had sat with a cup of coffee and watched as the tree overcame its modest origins. 'It's beautiful.'

Eleanor was gazing at the tree and then glancing at him. 'Mind if I sit down?'

He motioned to the empty seat.

'I thought you'd be gone by now,' she said.

'Yeah, well, sometimes plans change. I decided not to go. I decided to stick it out here. One for all and all for one.'

She sat back. 'I have to say, I'm surprised. I didn't think anything I could possibly say . . .' Her voice tapered off.

He finished for her: 'Could get through my thick head? Look, Ellie, I just decided that it would be better to stay here and help. By the time I got to the ski resort, *if* I got to it, the storm would probably be over and the cavalry would have arrived.' He paused. 'And if not, well, then better to be here too.' Their eyes locked for a long moment, and then he abruptly stood up.

'Where are you going?' she asked.

'I've got some things to take care of. Long overdue.'

A few minutes later Tom stopped by Lelia's compartment to tell her his decision on marriage was no. 'I really care about you, but I'm not going to marry you and have eight kids. I hope you understand.'

She didn't look like she understood at all. Tears streamed down her face, and she clutched at his arm. 'Isn't there anything I can say or do to change your mind?'

He shook his head. 'I don't love you, Lelia. And I'm pretty sure if you think about it enough, you'll see that you don't love me either.'

'It's just that we've been together for so long.'

'Complacency doesn't equal love.'

She sniffed into her handkerchief and said in a trembling voice, 'I don't know, maybe you're right.'

At that moment Kristobal emerged from her bathroom and looked at them both.

'Kristobal?' Tom said, clearly surprised.

'Am I interrupting something?' the young man asked.

'No,' said Tom, 'but apparently I am.'

Lelia looked at him innocently. 'Kristobal's been helping me

through these trying times. And he gives a wonderful back massage.'
'I'm sure he does.'

Tom left and walked down the corridor more relieved than he'd been in a long time, now that Cuppy the Magic Beaver was no longer bearing down on him. He felt sorry for Kristobal, but he was a big boy.

One positive, if surprising, event had occurred. All the items that had been stolen on the Chief—and many that had been taken during the trip on the Capitol Limited—had been returned to their owners. No one had seen anything, and no one could explain why the thief had experienced such a dramatic change of heart. Roxanne and Father Kelly simply put it down to a Christmas miracle.

After dinner, everyone was asked to gather in the lounge car where a mock stage had been set up at one end. Max served as the master of ceremonies, whipping the crowd into a frenzy of expectation by calling out, 'Do I hear something? Do I hear a special something coming?'

All attention was riveted on the stage and a child screamed out excitedly, 'It's Cuppy the Magic Beaver!' And then another little boy called out, 'And there's Petey the Orange Pickle!' And then Sassy Squirrel and Freddy the Futon joined their famous puppet friends onstage, and the good times began.

Working the hand puppets from behind the stage were Lelia and Kristobal. Lelia always carried the puppet characters with her in case she ran into any children; she often gave them as gifts.

Santa arrived precisely on schedule, played by Barry, and gifts were dutifully handed out by Santa's elves—Tom, Eleanor, Max and Misty. The passengers contributed gift-wrapped presents they'd brought with them. Everyone participated with good grace and humour, and the children were happy and laughing, which relieved the adults' tension immensely.

The boys' choir sang Christmas carols with Roxanne, and everyone joined them, giving it their best. As the night deepened and little mouths started yawning with increasing frequency, folks said their good nights and strangers slapped each other on the back, declaring it a very fine Christmas Eve. Then they went off to sleep.

Eleanor and Tom went with Roxanne to settle the choir down. They were about to leave when one of the boys called out to Roxanne. She sat next to the little boy, whose name was Oliver. 'What's up?'

Oliver was usually a happy-go-lucky sort, but now he looked worried. 'Patrick said there's no God.'

Roxanne gasped. 'What? Patrick, you get yourself over here, boy.'

Patrick came up in his striped pyjamas and glasses. He was one of the older boys, tall and lean, with a very confident manner.

Roxanne towered over him and put her hands on her substantial hips. 'Explain yourself. Why'd you tell him that?'

All the other boys poked their heads over their seats to watch and listen. Tom and Eleanor exchanged glances.

He adjusted his glasses. 'It's a simple process of elimination, an evolutionary cycle, really.'

'Come again?'

'Well, first there was the Tooth Fairy. You lose a tooth, you put it under your pillow, and the next morning the tooth is gone and there's money in its place. Most kids discover that's a myth when they're five or so, although I learned it much earlier.'

'You're ten now, Patrick,' said his brother Tony, 'and you still put your teeth under the pillow.'

'That's because I want the money, Tony, not because I still believe.' Patrick turned back to Roxanne. 'And then you had the Easter Bunny, another falsehood. Next up is Santa Claus. That fellow who played him tonight, for example: wasn't that one of the train—'

Roxanne eyed the younger children, who looked ready to cry at what Patrick was about to say. 'Let's move on, Patrick,' she interrupted, 'and let's get right to God.'

'Very well. If there was a god of good, then why would he let something like this happen? We're supposed to be home right now, spending Christmas with our families. Instead, here we are in the middle of a snowstorm running low on fuel and food.'

Roxanne sensed that, despite his confident presentation, Patrick was as scared as the rest of them. She sat him down next to her and cradled Oliver on her lap. 'Now, the problem with your reasoning is that you're assuming our being stuck here is a bad thing. Let's look at the facts. What happened tonight?'

'The snow fell harder, and the kitchen ran out of food.'

'Besides that.'

Oliver spoke up: 'We celebrated Christmas Eve and opened presents. That's a good thing.'

'We could have done that with our families,' countered Patrick.

'True,' said Roxanne, 'but would your families be scared and hungry, in a strange place with people they don't know?'

The boy thought about this. 'Well, no.'

'See, I'm questioning whether it's a bad thing to have a bunch of people who're scared and hungry and wanting to be anyplace but here for Christmas, spend the evening together and have so much fun that they're laughing and singing along and giving away presents to people they don't even know.' She looked at Tom and Eleanor. 'You two had a good time tonight, didn't you?'

Eleanor smiled at the children. 'It was one of the best Christmas Eves of my life.'

'Well, I guess you have a point there,' conceded Patrick.

Tom added, 'Maybe God made sure you'd be on this train so that you could sing and make scared people forget about their troubles for a while by listening to some beautiful music.'

'That's another good point,' agreed Patrick.

'You see,' said Roxanne, as she tucked Oliver in and then led Patrick back to his bed, 'it's often said that God works in mysterious ways. You have to really think about what He's trying to do. You can't be lazy and believe in God. It takes spirit and faith and passion to really believe. Like most things worthwhile in life, you get back what you put into it. Only with faith, you get back a lot more.'

She covered him up. 'Any other questions?'

Oliver raised his hand. 'Just one, Miss Roxanne. Can you take me to the bathroom?'

LATER THAT NIGHT, Tom and Eleanor stood side by side staring out of the window at the snow.

'Well,' said Tom, 'it's almost Christmas, and I don't hear anything stirring, not even a mouse.'

'Right now I'll take a rescue team over old Saint Nick and his reindeer pitter-pattering on the roof.'

'Where's your adventurous spirit, your romanticism?'

'I used it all up, with you,' she shot back. She touched him on the arm. 'Why didn't you go? The truth now.'

'I forgot to oil my skis.'

'I'm serious, Tom.'

He looked at her. 'Ellie, I told myself that I came on this trip to fulfil my dad's wishes. But I really did it because there's a huge hole in my life and I had no idea how to fill it. It's been there for a long time. And writing for *Ladies' Home Journal* wasn't plugging it.' He struggled. 'But the reason I didn't go out there,' he continued, pointing out of the window, 'is because of what you said. You know, all these years I believed you'd walked out on me, that you had abandoned me. I never really saw that it was actually the other way round.' He paused. 'I'm sorry, Ellie, I really am.'

She slowly reached out and took his hand in hers.

He looked around puzzled. 'You know, I wasn't kidding. It really is quiet. Too quiet.'

They couldn't have known, but earlier the last drop of fuel on the last diesel engine had been used up. And while they were standing there the back-up battery-powered lights ran out of juice too. The Southwest Chief finally fell silent and dark.

And then the quiet was shattered by a rumbling sound, the Chief started to shake and screams erupted from the coaches. Tom and Eleanor looked at each other.

'My God,' she said, 'it's another avalanche!'

CHAPTER TEN

The plunging snow had hit the right side of the train and piled so high that one couldn't see out of the windows any more. The crushing weight of the snow against the Chief was actually starting to tilt it. The plan in response to this crisis was simple: total evacuation of the train, which, under the circumstances, was far easier said than done. Yet 341 passengers made their way from car to car, until they reached the last coach, while Amtrak personnel counted heads and searched every nook and cranny so no one would be left behind.

Covered by blankets and guided by flashlights, the long line of people trekked the short distance to the tunnel. Elderly and disabled passengers and the very young were carried or otherwise assisted. No one complained or fretted about his or her place in line.

Water, blankets, pillows, first-aid kits, whatever food was left, and any article that could conceivably come in handy were carried off the train. The engineer, whose name was Ralph Perkins, and who blamed himself for not backing the train into the tunnel while he still had fuel, now didn't want to leave his post. After Roxanne and Higgins had spoken to him, the latter explaining that the snow build-up to the rear of the train might have prohibited that manoeuvre anyway, he finally agreed to leave the helm.

Tom, Eleanor, Max, Misty, Kristobal, Father Kelly and Agnes Joe worked as hard as the crew in carrying, assisting, cajoling and hauling until all were safely ensconced in the tunnel.

Tom got out his skis and gear, and Eleanor borrowed a pair from a female passenger who had also planned to holiday at Tahoe. Together the two ferried a large quantity of supplies over the packed snow with relative speed.

Camp was set up in the tunnel. Tom surveyed the situation. The lighting was poor, the food levels low, the blankets too few. The worst problem, though, was the cold. With the burden of less oxygen at that elevation, and the tunnel acting as a funnel for the wind, it was clear that neither the elderly nor the very young passengers could survive there long. The conclusion was inevitable. Tom went over to the engineer and Roxanne and spoke with them quietly.

Eleanor, who was helping folks settle down, glanced up and saw the meeting taking place. She joined them in time to hear Roxanne say, 'You don't have to do this, Tom, but I love you for it.'

'I'm going with you.'

They all turned and looked at Eleanor.

'No, you're not,' said Tom.

Eleanor looked at the others. 'I taught him everything he knows about skiing.'

'Eleanor, I can't let you go with me.'

'I'm not asking for your permission. If you want to travel solo, fine; I'll have some coffee waiting at the resort for you when you finally show up.'

Roxanne hiked her eyebrows. 'I think you'd be a lot smarter teaming up with this woman than trying to go it alone.'

Tom looked at each of them and finally his gaze settled on Eleanor. 'One more job together?'

'Let's go.'

AFTER SAYING their goodbyes, Tom and Eleanor, loaded with gear, headed northeast back through the tunnel. From memory, Higgins had put together for them a rough map of the area and directions to the Dingo, which Tom carried wrapped in plastic in his pocket.

The air was frigid and very thin and soon they were both breathing hard. The tunnel was completely dark, so they had snapped on their battery-powered helmet lights. They had to carry their skis because there wasn't any snow inside the tunnel.

'At least we don't have to worry about a train coming,' said Tom.

'And here I was thinking our luck was all bad.'

As they walked the half-mile to the other end of the tunnel, their hands reached out and gripped firmly. At the end of the tunnel they strapped on their skis.

'You ready?' Tom asked. Eleanor nodded.

They stepped out into the near whiteout conditions, and headed up a crevice in the mountain, each thrust of the ski poles arduous. In a very few minutes, they'd completely disappeared into the storm, their bodies caked with ice, their limbs growing increasingly numb.

OFTEN THEY HAD to wedge their limbs and ski poles against the rocky sides of an ascent to lever themselves on. In some cases they had to take off their skis and, roped together, simply climb. After clearing all these obstacles, they reached flat land and made good time on their skis, despite heading directly into a wind that seemed to increase with each push of their poles.

The first disaster occurred when Tom fell through a thin patch of ice and about ten feet into a hole. With Eleanor tugging on a rope she tossed down to him, he was able to climb out, but he'd lost his cellphone and the compass was damaged.

They contemplated going back, but decided to keep going. Tom had a good idea, he thought, of the direction, and had picked out some landmarks to help him maintain the correct course.

Every step was difficult and they kept having to stop and turn away from the wind to catch their breath. Their chests burned, and their state-of-the-art clothing was barely holding its own against the numbing conditions.

When it started to grow dark, Eleanor said, 'Maybe we should make camp around here.'

'Good idea. We can't be that far from the resort.' At least he hoped they weren't.

They pitched their tent and Tom got a small fire going. They used it to cook a quick dinner and also to thaw their water. They ate and then settled back, close together under blankets, to watch the snow pile up around the tent. The storm seemed to weaken and it grew quiet. They could now talk without having to shout.

'Just so you know, I told Lelia no. She took it very well.'

'I'm surprised.'

'So was I, until I learned why. Lelia has a new beau.'

'What? Who?'

'Kristobal.'

'Kristobal! You've got to be joking.'

'I'm sure they'll be very happy together.'

They grew quiet and snuggled closer.

'Have to conserve body heat,' explained Tom.

'Absolutely.' She sighed. 'Look, if we don't make it back—'

He put a hand to her mouth. 'Let's try to think positively. Misty would probably call it a purple aura of power or something.'

She gripped his hand. 'If we don't make it back, I want you to know I never stopped loving you. Not even after all these years.'

He put his arm round her. 'We'll make it back.'

As Eleanor shivered, Tom wrapped his arms round her, trying to transfer his body heat.

'Who would have thought we'd find each other after all this time and end up on a mountain in the middle of a blizzard?' she said.

He dug something out of a zippered pocket in his tunic. 'Like I said before, I am the king of bad timing.' He rose, then went down on one knee and carefully put the ring on her finger.

She looked at him, her eyes wide in amazement.

'I realise it's been a long time in coming—way too long, in fact. But you're the only woman I've ever loved and I'll do all I can to make you happy. Will you take me with all my faults, weaknesses, idiosyncrasies, pig-headedness and outright stupidity?' He paused, drew a long, even breath, and said, 'Will you marry me, Eleanor?'

She began to cry, right after she said yes.

As SOON AS THEY had finished sharing an official engagement kiss, the tent blew away and a load of snow fell on them, nearly burying them alive. Tom fought through the layers and pulled Eleanor out. 'We have to find shelter,' he shouted over the wind.

They struggled on, Eleanor growing so weak that Tom had to half carry her for a quarter of a mile or so until his strength gave out too. He laid her down, took off his outer jacket, and covered her with it. Then he said one final prayer and lay down on top of Eleanor, using his big body to block the snow. He sought out her gloved hand and held it tightly.

They seemed to be lying there for hours, the wind howling. Then, in Tom's mind, he could see a little boy reaching out to him. It was Tom as a small child, reaching out to his adult self, pulling him back to the relative safety of childhood. This was, he concluded, after the numerous near misses in his chequered career, probably his time to go. He looked at Eleanor and kissed her lips. She didn't respond and the tears finally started to trickle down Tom's frozen cheeks.

The little boy's image grew more and more vivid. Tom could now actually feel the fingers on his cheek, rubbing his hair. The little boy was speaking to him, asking if he was OK. The vision was more real, more potent than any dream he'd ever had. He kept his grip on Eleanor's hand, even as he reached out to the young Tom.

The child poked him again and Tom's eyes fluttered open, closed, and then opened again. The glare of sunlight was painful.

'Are you OK, mister?' asked the little boy, squatting next to him.

Tom managed to sit up, look around. The sky was a vast, azure blue, the sun warming, the air chilly and pure. He stared at the boy, unsure if this was what heaven looked like or not, and finally managed to ask, 'What are you doing all the way out here?'

'I live here,' replied the little boy pointing behind Tom. 'The Dingo.'

The enormous redwood buildings of the mighty Dingo resort, in all their beauty, stared back at him. Eleanor and he had almost perished five feet from warm fires, hot chocolate and hot tubs.

Tom stood on shaky legs, gently woke Eleanor.

'Are we dead?' she asked, her eyes still closed.

'No,' said Tom, 'but just so you know, you're engaged to an idiot.'

He carried her toward the main lodge as a number of adults spotted them and came running to help.

BOTH ENDS of the tunnel were filled with sunlight. The storm had passed, and Higgins, Roxanne, the conductor, Max, Misty, Lelia, Kristobal, Father Kelly and Agnes Joe sat on the ground and discussed what to do next.

'I think,' said Father Kelly with great sadness, 'that a memorial service might be in order. For Tom and Eleanor, I mean.'

Max said testily, 'It's a little early for that, Padre.'

'If they'd made it to the Dingo, we would have heard by now,' said the conductor. 'Nobody could have survived all that time out there. I never should have let them go. It's my fault.'

Roxanne said, 'They were two of the bravest people I ever met.' She pulled out a handkerchief and wiped at her eyes.

Barry, the sleeping-car attendant, burst into their circle and shouted, 'Quick, you've got to see this!'

They followed him through the tunnel until they reached the far end. 'Look!' he said.

They stared at the horses, riders and large sleighs coming their way in a long, impressive procession. It was as if they'd been transported back in time and this was a wagon train of pioneers on their way to new lives in the West. One of the riders in front lifted his hat to them.

'That's Tom!' said Roxanne.

The rider next to him waved.

'And that's Eleanor,' shouted Max. He raced forward to meet them, slipping and sliding in the snow.

Misty said to herself: 'Six legs.'

'What?' said Kristobal.

'We were saved by six legs. Four from the horse and two from the rider. Six legs.' She whooped and ran after Max, her long scarf dazzling in the beautiful sunlight.

The timely arrival of food from the good folks at the Dingo lifted everyone's spirits. As the passengers ate and drank, people crowded around Tom and Eleanor and heard their amazing story of survival.

'The guys from the resort knew of this route to the train tracks that the horses and wagons could navigate. A lot easier than the path we took, but you couldn't even see it with the storm going on.' Tom shook his head. 'Five feet from the front door and didn't even know it. It's the luckiest I've ever been.'

'It wasn't luck, Tom,' said Father Kelly. 'It was a miracle. I ordered one up special for you.'

The conductor's walkie-talkie barked and he held it up and pressed the button. 'Go ahead,' he said.

'Amtrak Central Dispatch to Southwest Chief, come in.'

The conductor nearly screamed. 'This is the Southwest Chief.'

'Where is everybody?' asked the voice.

'We evacuated the train. We're in the tunnel. What's the status of the rescue crew?'

'Just look out of the tunnel,' said the voice.

The conductor raced to the end of the tunnel, where there came a deafening roar as twin helicopters appeared over the ridge.

'We've got a replacement train on the western side of the landslide with three fully fuelled engines,' said the voice on the walkie-talkie.

'But how do we get to you?' said the conductor. 'There's a mountain of snow between us.'

'Not for long. We've been working on this for a while now. Stand by.'

'Roger that.'

After ten minutes he heard a series of loud pops, and watched as the twenty-foot-high wall of snow in front of the Chief collapsed and slid harmlessly down the mountain. Small explosive charges carefully laid at key load-bearing points had worked their magic. Revealed beyond the now missing wall was the replacement train, its powerful engines running. Hundreds of volunteers swarmed off the replacement train and began clearing the rest of the track while the passengers slowly reboarded the Chief.

Early the next morning the track was ready, the fresh engines attached, and for the first time in a long time the wheels of the Southwest Chief began to turn. Special arrangements had been made permitting the Chief to make only a few of its scheduled stops, including a long layover in Albuquerque. As the train made its way down the mountain on its way through New Mexico and then into Arizona, the people on board rested peacefully at last.

They stopped in Albuquerque for about three hours to refuel and take on more supplies, and to let passengers take a walk and enjoy the sunshine.

Tom and Eleanor told the others of their engagement; Max was especially pleased. Lelia even gave Tom a hug and wished him the best. From the way she was clinging to Kristobal, and the young man's smitten expression, Tom figured it would only be a matter of time before their own nuptials were formally announced.

There was a marketplace near the station, where Native American women were selling jewellery and other wares, and Tom and Eleanor strolled there in the sunshine and talked about their future.

'By the way, you never told me who you were seeing in Washington,' Tom said. 'Do you have a Lelia in your life?'

'Not exactly. It was my grandmother.'

They stopped at a little café and had a drink and something to eat. Agnes Joe joined them, extended her congratulations, and sipped a cool lemonade in the sunshine.

'I sometimes think about retiring here,' she said.

Tom glanced sharply at her. 'Retiring? I thought you were retired.'

'Soon enough,' she answered cryptically.

'What is it that you do?'

'Oh, a little bit of this, and a little bit of that.'

'It's a funny thief that returns stolen items as gifts on Christmas Eve,' he said.

'Craziest thing I've ever heard of,' agreed Agnes Joe.

'Pretty generous of the crook,' commented Eleanor.

'Not too generous, since he was only giving people back their own property,' countered Agnes Joe.

'Or she,' said Tom under his breath.

AFTER DINNER that evening many people, including Steve and Julie, went to the lounge car to watch a video of the wedding ceremony that Kristobal and Max had prepared. To Tom, Steve looked exhausted, and he noted with a smile that as soon as the film was over, Julie grabbed his hand and pulled him back to their suite.

It was late at night when they entered Arizona, and Tom found he couldn't sleep. He looked in on Eleanor but she was sleeping soundly and he didn't want to waken her so he walked the corridors.

While he was rambling, the train slowed and then stopped. He peered out the window. There was a station here, but he'd thought there'd be no more stops until Los Angeles. He shrugged and kept walking until he arrived outside Agnes Joe's compartment. The woman's phonograph was still playing its Christmas tunes. Her unit was dark, and he assumed she must have fallen asleep while the music played. Then the phonograph started skipping, repeating the same lyrics over and over. He tapped on the glass of the door and called her name. There was no response so he slid open the door. 'Agnes Joe?' His eyes adjusted to the darkness, and he saw that the compartment was empty. He tapped lightly on the bathroom door, receiving no answer. He eyed the duffle bag in the corner and was tempted to look inside again. He unzipped it and put his hand in. The newspaper was gone, but out came several items, including a watch, a pair of earrings, and a very expensive pair of sunglasses. He stood there trying to decide what to do, when he heard footsteps. He put the items back, zipped the bag closed, shut the compartment door, and then slipped inside the bathroom.

The compartment door slid open. The light came on. He'd left the bathroom door open a crack, and he peered out through the sliver.

It was Agnes Joe. She held a piece of paper in her hand, and her expression was serious. How was he to escape? Wait until she was asleep? He was about to sit on the toilet when the train started up again. The rocking caused him to lose his balance and he knocked against the wall and shot his hand out to steady himself, accidentally gripping the shower control and turning it on. The water hit him with a chilly blast, causing him to scream out a few choice words.

He managed to turn the water off in time to stare out at Agnes Joe, who'd opened the door and was studying him as though he were a curious breed of animal at the zoo.

'Would you care to tell me what you're doing in my shower?'

He emerged, wiped himself down with a towel, and explained about the phonograph, his coming in, and getting rattled when he heard footsteps. The story might have worked, if he'd zippered the duffle bag up all the way. But in the darkness he hadn't quite managed it. Agnes Joe looked over at the bag and then back at him.

He decided on a full-frontal assault. He opened the bag and pulled out the items. 'You care to explain what you're doing with these things? I'm willing to listen.'

She reached in her pocket. What she pulled out made Tom take a step back, his expression one of total shock.

A FEW MINUTES LATER, an ashen-faced Tom rapped on Max's door. It took a few moments for the director to answer, and another minute or two before he opened the door.

'I need your help,' said Tom. 'We'll need Kristobal too.'

Max glanced behind Tom and saw Agnes Joe.

'It's important,' said Tom.

They collected Kristobal from Lelia's suite, woke up Roxanne and brought along Father Kelly too. Converging in the lounge car, they sat at a table, where Tom pulled out Kristobal's designer sunglasses, Max's Bruno Maglis and Father Kelly's cross, and placed each in front of its respective owner.

One man looked totally bewildered at what was in front of him, so confused that he never noticed Agnes Joe leaning towards him.

Father Kelly gave out a yell as the handcuffs closed around his wrists. He tried to get up but was wedged in by Max and Kristobal.

Agnes Joe flipped out her credentials, repeating the action that had stunned Tom earlier in her compartment. 'I'm Amtrak police. Undercover Division. And you're our thief, John.'

Tom looked at her. 'John?'

She nodded. 'I was suspicious of him and got his fingerprints on a beer glass before we were stuck at the Raton Pass. At one of the station stops I sent in an ID request. At the station we just left I got a notice back. His real name is John Conroy, and he's no priest.'

'And all the stuff I found in your bag?' asked Tom.

'Roxanne had got those items for me from some of the passengers, as evidence we might need later. I got you, Max and Kristobal involved so we could take Conroy without anyone getting hurt or him suspicious. I swiped his cross out of his compartment. When I laid it down in front of him, I thought it would confuse him enough for me to get the handcuffs on with no scuffle. You're no spring chicken, Conroy, but it's been my experience that you never know.'

'I hate to admit this, but I looked through your duffle bag before and just found newspapers,' said Tom.

'I know, I could tell someone had searched it. The newspapers that Regina found in the trash were from Conroy's duffle bag. He had stuffed it full of them to make it look like it was packed as far as it could go. But once he got on the train, he ditched the papers and had a relatively empty bag to fill up with his loot.'

They called Barry to stand guard and trooped to Conroy's compartment, where a number of the stolen items were in his duffle bag.

'What I don't get is why he returned so many things,' said Tom.

'Something is funny about that,' said Roxanne, 'but at least we have our thief. Now let's all get some sleep.'

Tom did just that until about six in the morning, when there was a tap on his door and he woke and answered it.

Agnes Joe was standing there with two hot cups of coffee. 'I thought I'd better bring this as a peace offering for waking you up so early.' She was dressed in blue slacks and a sweater and she had a crisp and efficient air about her.

'You'd make a great actress,' said Tom. 'I had no clue that you were anything other than, well, I mean . . .'

'An eccentric old woman with nowhere to go during the holidays? Yeah, it's a good cover. I've busted drug dealers, swindlers, theft rings and others with my bewildered look and my stupid dresses.'

'Well, I suppose your cover is sort of blown now.'

'That's OK, I wasn't joking about retiring. It's time to move on.'

'So was any of the rest of your story true?'

'I worked for Ringling Brothers, not as a trapeze artist but as a horsewoman. I've been married twice, and I do have a grown daughter.' She paused and added, 'And we are estranged.'

'Sorry to hear that.'

'Well, she read about the Chief being trapped, and she called last night, to make sure I was OK. First time I'd heard from her in a while. We're going to see each other when I get into LA and take another shot at it.'

'I'm happy for you, a late Christmas present. So what did you want to see me about?'

'Well, I've got a bit of a dilemma and I wanted your advice. I obtained more info on our fake priest. He was busted years ago for petty thefts—I mean, almost thirty-four years ago. He's been straight since, real job and everything.'

'Why the return to crime after all that time?'

'His wife of over thirty-three years just died. With her gone, he didn't know what to do. He was lonely. They had two kids, but one died in an accident and another from cancer.'

'Boy, that's tough. And it seems like his life of crime stopped when he married her.'

'Exactly. Now, I've dealt with lots of criminal types and I've heard all the sob stories and I'm not swayed by that stuff. But the other thing he told me, that's why I have the dilemma.'

'What is it?'

'He returned the stolen items on Christmas Eve as presents. The only ones he didn't return, the ones we found in his bags, were nothing much, and he left cash, more than enough to pay for them. I've confirmed that with the passengers they belonged to. He didn't mean to hurt anyone. All he talked about was his wife. And he really helped when the train was stuck.'

Tom let out a long breath. 'I see your dilemma.'

'What would you do?'

He thought about it. 'Well, I got a second chance on this trip, and maybe Conroy deserves one too. Have you called the police yet?'

'Yes, but I gave them no particulars.'

'Is the train making any more stops?'

'It can, at Fullerton, a couple of hours before we get into LA.'

'Well, maybe the Chief should stop at Fullerton.'

'Maybe it should. I don't think Conroy is going to jump into a life of crime. In fact, I know some people near Fullerton who can help him.' She rose. 'Thanks, Tom. I think we made the right decision.'

He smiled at her. 'So what's your real name?'

'If I told you that, it wouldn't be a secret, now would it, honeypie?'

AT FULLERTON the train stopped and an elderly, tired-looking gentleman got off, no longer wearing priest's clothes. Some friends of Agnes Joe were waiting for him, and they drove off, hopefully taking John Conroy to a better life.

Tom went to the communal showers to get washed before they arrived in LA. As he was going in, Steve the honeymooner was coming out. Tom went inside the dressing area and as he started to disrobe, he saw a wallet on the floor under the counter. He stooped to pick it up, thinking it must be Steve's, and some of the contents fell out. He got down on his knees to retrieve them and glanced at one of the cards he picked up. It was a SAG card, a Screen Actors Guild membership card, with the name Steve Samuels on it. Tom quickly looked through the rest of the wallet. He found Steve's driver's licence—his *California* driver's licence—and the picture confirmed that it was Steve, of Steve and Julie, only he wasn't a student at George Washington; he was a dues-paying member of the Actors Guild.

THE SOUTHWEST CHIEF pulled into the beautiful Art Deco Los Angeles Union Passenger Train Terminal a few minutes ahead of its revised schedule.

Herrick Higgins was met by several senior Amtrak executives, who congratulated him and thanked him for his help. Then he was offered his old position back, riding the rails and trouble-shooting; an offer he accepted on the spot.

Max Powers got off the train and answered lots of reporters' questions. He looked over to where Roxanne and the boys' choir were doing the same. 'Hey,' he called. 'I'll be in touch, count on it.'

She smiled. 'I am, baby, I am.'

Then he and a group of passengers, including Kristobal, Lelia and Misty, left the station and got into a stretch limousine waiting for them outside.

Inside the limo Max took out three envelopes and handed them one by one to Steve, Julie and the minister. Then he popped a bottle of champagne and poured out glasses of the bubbly.

'Good job, guys,' said Max. 'You'll all be in my next picture. Who knows, maybe it'll be about the train.'

Misty said, 'Max, when you told me what you'd done I couldn't believe it.'

'Well, sweetie, though I'd known you only a short time, I knew you could keep a secret.'

'*You* couldn't believe it,' said Lelia. 'How do you think I felt? Max Powers calls me after all these years and asks for a favour. Some favour, to fly out to Kansas City and pretend to propose. I don't know what I would have done if he'd accepted.'

'I knew my man, Lelia. I was pretty sure he wouldn't,' said Max.

'Pretty sure!'

'I had to make certain he really didn't love you and you didn't love him.' Max beamed. 'But you're a fine actress. And see what you gained from my little plan.'

She patted Kristobal on the arm.

'You never told me you had contacted Lelia and included her in the plan,' said Kristobal. 'I had no idea who she was until she told me her name.'

'I'm a man who has this insatiable need to surprise people.'

'And you did all this for Eleanor?' asked Misty. 'And she doesn't know about any of it?'

Max nodded. 'Not a thing. Eleanor is the daughter I never had. I'd do anything for her. As long as I've known her, she hasn't been truly happy. I knew there was something in her past. I did some snooping and found out that Tom Langdon was the big loose end in her life. She couldn't go forward. So I've been tracking the guy for about six months. When he booked this trip it was a perfect opportunity for me, because I really wanted to do a train film.'

'And the wedding?' asked Misty.

'What better way to make people who should have got married rethink what might have been, than to put them at a wedding together? So Julie is from the same sort of place Eleanor is from, and Tom reads Steve the riot act after he starts to waver on his decision. That was a good twist, because it may as well have been Tom saying all the things he was feeling. Of course, that was all planned. Every time Tom and Eleanor had a blowup, we had a plan ready.'

Kristobal said wearily, 'And they had lots of blowups. It was draining, keeping up with them the whole trip.'

'You did good, Kristobal. And I'm *not* cutting your pay.'

'That's a lot of details you covered, Max,' said Misty.

'I'm a director, sweetie. My whole life is details.'

'Uh, sir, you didn't somehow order up the avalanche, did you?' Kristobal wanted to know.

'Hey, even I'm not that good.'

There was a rap on the window.

'Must be the luggage,' said Max. He rolled the window down. Tom leaned in and looked at them all.

Max said nervously, 'Hey there, Tom. Just giving the newlyweds a ride to their honeymoon palace.'

'I'm sure,' said Tom. He handed Steve his wallet. 'You dropped it in the shower. Your driver's licence and SAG card are in there. Figured you'd need them.'

'Tom,' said Max, 'I can explain.'

Tom held up a hand. 'I have only one thing to say to you. Thank you.' Tom shook hands with Max and then looked around at everyone. 'Merry Christmas and Happy Holidays,' he said. He walked away from the limo and found Eleanor, who was watching him curiously.

'Who was in the limo?' she asked when he reached her.

Tom glanced back at the car which was pulling away. 'Santa Claus,' he answered.

'Santa Claus? Right. We're a little old to believe in Santa Claus.'

He put his arm round her as they walked off. 'Well, around Christmas, it can be a good thing to believe in magic. You never know, your wish just might come true.'

DAVID BALDACCI

David Baldacci, born and brought up in the state of Virginia, where to this day he lives with his wife and young family, has been consumed by a desire to write since he was a boy. From high school to university, and even during a busy law career in Washington, DC, he devoted every spare moment he could find to writing stories.

It should have come as no surprise, therefore, that Baldacci's first published novel, *Absolute Power*, shot to the top of the American best-seller lists (in Britain it won W.H. Smith's 'Thumping Good Read' award for fiction) and was subsequently made into a film starring Clint Eastwood and Gene Hackman. Since then Baldacci has become a full-time writer with seven more best sellers to his name, *The Christmas Train* being the most recent. This novel is filled with so many colourful characters and incidents that one can imagine it might have been written for the big screen. Does Baldacci think in terms of a film script when he writes? 'I've written screenplays and I do think my novels are very visual, but I'm in the book business. Thinking of a book as a movie is tempting, but you'll find yourself twisting plot and creating characters to fulfil some cinematic goal rather than writing a good book.'

With more than thirty-three million copies of his books in print worldwide, David Baldacci is frequently away from home on book-signing tours or making guest appearances on television and radio. So how does he find the time to write? 'I can write anywhere. On a plane or a train or a boat. In a corner, with a screaming child in my lap! I've done all those things. If you wait for the perfect place to write, you'll never write anything.'

Somehow, in this fast-paced life, Baldacci also manages to run workshops for youngsters who are interested in creative writing, and he and his wife have founded scholarships to help deserving students to pursue careers in the creative arts. 'With two young children of my own, I'm intensely interested in education, equal opportunity and just helping to raise good kids. And it's vast and wonderful, the power of the written word.'

RAIN FALL. Original full-length edition © 2002 by Barry Eisler. British condensed edition © The Reader's Digest Association Limited, 2003.

THE SHADOW CATCHER. Original full-length edition © 2002 by Michelle Paver. British condensed edition © The Reader's Digest Association Limited, 2003.

THE SUMMER THAT NEVER WAS. Original full-length edition © 2003 by Peter Robinson. British condensed edition © The Reader's Digest Association Limited, 2003.

THE CHRISTMAS TRAIN. Original full-length edition © 2002 by Columbus Rose Ltd. British condensed edition © The Reader's Digest Association Limited, 2003.

The right to be identified as authors has been asserted by the following in accordance with sections 77 and 78 of the Copyright, Designs and Patents Act, 1988: Barry Eisler, Michelle Paver, Peter Robinson and David Baldacci.

ACKNOWLEDGMENTS AND PICTURE CREDITS: *Rain Fall*: pages 6–8 Getty Images; photomontage: Curtis Cozier; page 145: Janelle McCuen. *The Shadow Catcher*: pages 146–148: Corbis; page 293: Robin Matthews. *The Summer That Never Was*: pages 294–296: photomontage: Rick Lecoat @ Shark Attack; page 441: Clifford Robinson. *The Christmas Train*: pages 442–444: illustration by Dave Lynx @ The Organisation; page 539: René Durand (Lubbe).

DUSTJACKET CREDITS: Spine from top: Getty Images; photomontage: Curtis Cozier; Corbis; photomontage: Rick Lecoat @ Shark Attack; illustration by Dave Lynx @ The Organisation.

Printed by Maury Imprimeur SA, Malesherbes, France
Bound by Reliures Brun SA, Malesherbes, France

223AS